This Royal Breed

This Royal Breed

Judith Saxton

HEINEMANN : LONDON

First published in the United Kingdom in 1991
by Grafton Books
This edition published by Heinemann 1997

1 3 5 7 9 10 8 6 4 2

William Heinemann
Random House UK Limited
20 Vauxhall Bridge Road, London, SW1V 2SA

Random House Australia (Pty) Limited
20 Alfred Street, Milsons Point, Sydney,
New South Wales 2061, Australia

Random House New Zealand Limited
18 Poland Road, Glenfield
Auckland 10, New Zealand

Random House South Africa (Pty) Limited
Endulini, 5a Jubilee Road, Parktown, 2193, South Africa

Random House UK Limited Reg. No. 954009

A CIP catalogue record for this book
is available from the British Library

Papers used by Random House UK Limited
are natural, recyclable products made from wood grown in
sustainable forests. The manufacturing processes conform to
the environmental regulations of the country of origin

ISBN 0434 00296 8

Printed and bound in the United Kingdom by
Mackays of Chatham PLC

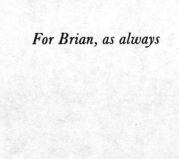

For Brian, as always

Acknowledgements

I should like to thank, first and foremost, Alan Hague of the Norfolk & Suffolk Aviation Museum, Flixton, Suffolk, for taking me round the museum and showing me their large collection of aircraft and memorabilia, a good deal of it relevant to the men of the 2nd Airborne Division of the US Army Air Force during the Second World War. I am also indebted to the staff of the American Memorial Room in the Norwich Central Library, who found the books which would help me most in endeavouring to build up a picture of American servicemen in Norfolk during the war.

Further information was given me by the International Library, Liverpool, and thanks as usual go to Marina Thomas and all the other members of staff in Wrexham Branch Library for unfailing help and support.

The marvellous books on the island of Jersey and on the cultivation of orchids are too numerous to mention, but if you get the chance to visit the Eric Young Orchid Foundation on Jersey you will see where my idea for the Pure Madonna came from, and will learn a great deal about those strange and beautiful plants. One book which breathes the spirit of wartime Jersey better than any other, though, is *A Doctor's Occupation*, by John Lewis, not only an excellent work of reference, but an easy read into the bargain – thank you, Dr Lewis!

Prologue
1922

Charles Laurient sat in the window of Le Chat Gris and looked out at the rain as it fell on the tables and upturned chairs outside. It was a cold day, though spring had officially arrived and the chestnut trees lining the roadway were beginning to unclench their green fists and thrust forth tentative, curled leaves, and the rain had cleared the street of passersby. Only the pigeons investigating the paving stones and waddling out of the way when passing vehicles threw bow-waves of water over the kerb were able to appreciate this definite sign that winter was over.

God knew it was a depressing outlook, yet Charles could not prevent a half-smile from tugging at his lips. He was in Paris in April; even the rain, tinkling through down-pipes and along gutters, seemed merely to be cleaning the streets and houses in anticipation of fine days to come. Charles had looked forward to this Paris trip for months, and now that it had arrived he was not going to let a few hours of persistent rain damp his spirits.

The waiter, an elderly man whose feet must have been hurting, judging by the snail's pace at which he shuffled, put Charles's order down in front of him: *café au lait*, croissants still warm from the oven and a dish of that white, creamy butter which is somehow so peculiarly French.

Charles nodded his thanks, his mouth watering as he pulled the cup towards him. He breathed in the fragrant steam, the smell warming him as much as the coffee itself would presently do. He was twenty-five years old and in Paris – what more could he ask? He had enough money to last a month if he was careful, and leave of absence for the same period. He had a cheap room on the top floor of a very small hotel, absolutely no commitments and an enormous zest for living which so far had never been allowed full rein. Now, just for a month, he would become a part of the Paris scene, enjoying the freedom of the Left Bank, living the Bohemian life to the full. He could sketch competently and his water-colours had been admired, so if he ran out of money he could either paint for his living or sell his gold wrist-watch and cuff-links. He could scarcely apply to Edouard Laurient for money after his father had agreed to allow his younger son a month's freedom from the ties of work and home.

The Laurients were a rich and ancient Jersey family, with a large estate on the island and business interests in several countries. In accordance with tradition Charles, the younger son, had gone to university to read languages and then to law school, finally being articled to the family firm in St Helier. He had worked hard because it was his nature to accept a challenge, but his heart was in neither languages nor the law. He appreciated that Maurice, as the elder son, had the right to do things which were denied to him, but he still watched his brother's career with a certain envy. Maurice's allowance had been double what Charles had received, though Maurice had read English only in such time as he could spare from playing rugby, squash and cricket, drinking vast quantities of alcohol, leading his peers in any form of jollification which might present itself and womanising to an extent which caused his mother, Bernice, to shake her head at her beautiful but wicked son.

Maurice only managed to scrape a pass degree, but the delight with which the news had been received far outweighed the temperate reception of Charles's own first-class honours. The second son, Charles remembered ruefully, was supposed to be the brainy one. The heir would employ others

10

to use their brains on his behalf; a younger son had to make his own way in the world.

Charles, however, was as much under Maurice's spell as anyone. Who could fail to love the tall, slim young man with his thatch of fair hair, laughing blue eyes and easy, friendly manner? Charles himself was stocky, dark-haired and olive-skinned, more like his father than his blonde, easy-going mother, but he did not think this mattered in the least. After all, a lawyer is as good or as bad as his last case. His clients cared little if he had curly hair but a great deal whether he was familiar with the case of *Rex v. Patterson*! The head of the family, on the other hand, would find his looks and charm extremely useful. Maurice would need to socialise a good deal, and personal magnetism can do much to smooth the path of a man with wide business interests such as Maurice would one day inherit.

Except that things had not worked out the way the Laurients had intended. When Charles had just finished at law school and was about to become articled, Maurice had been killed in a flying accident.

It had dealt Bernice a blow from which, Charles thought, she had never fully recovered. Maurice had been the apple of her eye, the handsome and charming son for whom a beautiful and maternal woman longs. She loved Edouard, she loved Charles, but there had been a depth of understanding between her and Maurice with which the others simply could not compete.

So Charles's sudden elevation to the position of heir to Augeuil Manor and the Laurient fortune had been an unwilling and gloomy affair. Bernice and Edouard did not make matters easier, giving him conflicting instructions as to how he was to conduct himself, and frequently leaving him to his own devices and then blaming him for his subsequent actions.

But somehow they had soldiered through. Charles had been despatched to London for a session with the firm that

11

dealt with the Laurient stocks and shares, and had had a year working with René Dubois, the estate manager. Charles and René had been friends from their schooldays, so this was in fact one of the pleasanter chores which came the new heir's way. He had also, at his own insistence, continued to study law and, to help his father and try to mend the older man's injured heart, he took up orchiculture, Edouard Laurient's greatest passion.

This last had brought father and son together in a way that nothing else could have done; sometimes, Charles even suspected that Bernice was jealous of their mutual passion for the Royal family, as Edouard called his orchids. So Charles felt that he was doing all he possibly could to prepare himself for the day when he would take over at Augeuil Manor when, after two years, he suggested the Paris trip.

'Is it that damned sketching?' his father enquired suspiciously, glaring at his son from under thick, still-black brows. 'You aren't hopin' to make your fortune from those daubs of yours, are you, hey?'

Charles, who had a natural aptitude for drawing, tightened his lips for a moment, then smiled and shook his head. His father distrusted men who painted, wrote books or designed clothes, dubbing them 'queer'. What was more, Edouard had shown pretty plainly that he worried over having a son who did not constantly chase women. Better not let him think the worst!

'No, of course not, Father. But I'd like a complete change; a rest, really. The last couple of years have been a strain on us all, I think.'

And Edouard Laurient had suddenly clapped his son's shoulder and said, gruffly, that Charles was a good fellow, and deserved a break.

'Get it off your chest, whatever it is,' he advised. 'You don't meet many gals . . . I want you to marry locally, of

12

course, but you'll want to . . . well, to . . . to meet gals, and there's no better place than Paris for *that*!'

So Charles had boarded the ferry, and then the train, and had come to Paris. He had booked into his cheap hotel the previous week and had spent a glorious few days exploring the city and settling in.

Now, however, his croissants were getting cold. He broke one in two and dabbed butter on to it. His hotel did not serve meals and his small room was unheated, so a good deal of his money went on food and on fuel for his fire. The egg-shaped *boulets*, made of compressed coal-dust, burned well and gave off a good heat; better than wood which, though cheaper, tended to flare up and die into ash before the room was even warm.

Already, though, he had spent quite a lot of money on theatre trips. He had been to four theatres in five evenings, to the Moulin Rouge and the Folies Bergère as well as the Opéra and more conventional entertainments. Having discovered the delights of the live stage, he intended to go at least four times a week until he could no longer afford it, and then he would go to the cinema and enjoy great acting from the screen idols of the day.

He tried to push away from his mind the recollection that, in four weeks' time, he would be at home once more, struggling to learn to do what Maurice had done so naturally – to be an heir his parents could be proud of. Even thinking of the estate office, the study where his father kept track of his stocks and shares, his interests in a big firm of soap manufacturers and two coal-mines, his directorship of a small bank, made Charles decide to try to spin the one month into two. Life at Augeuil Manor was so cramping compared with this! He had seen Ezra Pound, the great American poet, and Gertrude Stein yesterday, just sitting in a cafe chatting and drinking coffee. He had felt quite dizzy at his own proximity to such greatness . . . he would start to sketch as well once the rain stopped.

13

Sitting in the warmth of the little cafe, gazing unseeingly out at the rain pattering on the green-painted tables and chairs, he tried to plan the rest of his morning. He was not too far from the Musée du Luxembourg. On a wet day like this it would be sensible to study the techniques of the many great painters whose work was on view there. Since his coffee was finished and his croissants no more than a memory, therefore, he stood up, reaching for his damp jacket which hung on the back of his chair. He was halfway to the counter, intent on paying the waiter, when there was a commotion at the door. Charles turned to look and saw two girls, shaking umbrellas, talking, smiling. One was blonde, her hair darkened to gold by the rain, the other . . . Charles stared. Hair cut into a fashionable bob with the colour and sheen of a blackbird's wing fell across her face, and a pair of slightly slanting, sloe-black eyes met his, whilst in her cheek a dimple appeared for a moment as she smiled ruefully – a three-cornered, altogether delightful smile – at her own soaked and sodden state.

Charles dragged his eyes from her and ordered another cup of coffee. Then he walked back across the room, but this time he took a chair which faced into the cafe instead of out towards the pavement. From this position he took in the girl's general appearance. She was tall and slender with a haughty little nose which had just the suspicion of a hook to it, and a mouth whose lower lip was poutingly soft and full, the upper a delicate pink bow. Her skin was white as milk and she wore a thin green sweater which clung to her beautifully shaped breasts and was moulded to her waist by a narrow leather belt. Her skirt was dark green and black, a tartan, with pleats, and like the jumper it clung to her rounded hips and the long, lithe line of her thighs.

She must have been aware of him looking for suddenly she raised her eyes and for a moment they both stared, gazes locked. Then she turned away, a slight flush warming

14

her cheeks, and Charles took out his diary and studied it, watching the girls covertly now as they settled themselves at a nearby table, ordered, and put their heads together to chat.

The other girl, the blonde, was also fashionably cropped, her hair teased into tiny curls. She had big, baby-blue eyes and a rounded figure, and was wearing something pink and fluffy which made her look soft and vulnerable, though girls who danced on the stage in Paris were scarcely likely to be that.

The thought surprised Charles, made him look at the blonde girl with more attention. What had made him think of dancers? A second glance, however, and he knew. She *was* a dancer; he had admired her performance only the previous evening, at the Folies Bergère. She had come on and off the stage a score of times, he supposed, in a dozen different costumes, performing routines which looked exhausting but did not cause her to lose her bright smile for one moment.

But the other? He knew with absolute certainty that he had never set eyes on her before . . . could she be a show-girl too?

They were sitting at the next table to his and speaking in English; now he concentrated on their voices. Soon his ear could pick out the differences; the blonde had a sharp accent, the other a soft, country intonation. Devonshire, Charles decided, or possibly Cornwall. Coming from Jersey, where the locals spoke in patois and most of the children were bilingual in French and English, he knew that his ear for accents was not as keen as that of a native Englishman, but he was fairly familiar with west country speech and thought he was not far out.

Having sorted out who owned which voice, he listened to what they were saying.

'. . . we can make ourselves a substantial snack before

15

the show, and then eat out after,' the blonde was suggesting. 'Someone might even offer to buy us dinner . . . did you meet Alfred, Helen?'

Helen! And her face would have launched a thousand ships . . . a thousand thousand, Charles told himself fervently.

'Alfred? No-oo, I don't think so. Unless you mean that scraggy young man with the red-spotted tie?'

Her voice was low, musical, with an undertone of amusement.

'No, that's not Alfred, silly, that's Jean-Pierre. Alfred's English and most awfully rich. He often treats two or three of us to a meal after the show. He's . . . gracious, how can I describe him? He's tall, and sort of willowy, and he wears a monocle.'

'A what? Oh, you mean an eyeglass – why didn't you say so at first?'

'An eyeglass, then. Do you know him?'

'Of course I do, Mavis! There aren't many young men who can stand in the stalls and touch the circle!' Helen's giggle, Charles thought, was the most beautiful little purr of amusement. 'Does he like dark girls, though? I'm quite willing to put up with a little eccentricity for the sake of a good meal – dancing makes me so *hungry!*'

'He likes all girls,' Mavis said with commendable frankness. 'He isn't at all sexy, you understand, he just likes the company of pretty females. If he's in tonight, I'll introduce you.'

'It's kind of you,' Helen said. To the waiter, hovering, she added, 'Two coffees, please, and two of your small cakes.'

The waiter shambled off and Charles resumed his study of the two young women. Both dancers, eh? Well, if they had not been in Paris very long, which sounded quite likely since neither seemed to have a regular boyfriend to take them out after the show, then it should surely be possible

16

for him to scrape an acquaintance? He thought about going boldly over to their table here and now and introducing himself, but decided against it. One did not 'pick up' respectable girls, and, despite their calling, he was sure that they were both very respectable indeed. However, there was nothing to stop him attending the show that evening and sending them a message in the interval, suggesting a meal later. Helen and Mavis, he repeated to himself, calling the waiter over and ordering a third *café au lait*. Helen and Mavis. For he guessed that he would not be allowed merely to call for Helen, not the first time anyway. There were some very odd young men in Paris, and until he was better known, how was the management to judge whether he was the sort of fellow to try to take advantage of a young woman in the chorus?

Charles drank his coffee slowly and listened to the quick English chatter at the next table. It appeared that both girls had been working their way across Europe with various dance groups and had been in Paris no longer than he. Their talk ranged from their dancing schools to other girls in the chorus, the general tendency of the nudes in the various tableaux to be either witless or too spiteful for words, and their shared dislike of a prudish comic at the theatre who nevertheless pursued the chorus with either lewd suggestions or threats to get them dismissed. Charles was sure they had forgotten him, but even so when they decided to leave they jumped up so quickly, donning their long, shabby black coats and seizing their umbrellas so unexpectedly, that Charles actually had to break into a run when he emerged from the cafe to keep them in sight.

For at the last moment he was seized with doubt that they really were dancers from the Folies. He thought he remembered the blonde one – Mavis – from there, and they were certainly dancers, but he would feel happier if he knew where they were lodging. He was on fire with desire to actually meet Helen, to touch her hand, smile into her eyes.

It was still raining, which complicated Charles's pursuit. He sloshed through puddles, dived across roads, skirted abandoned stalls and ignored itinerant beggars. He managed to get no more than half a dozen yards in their rear and would undoubtedly have followed them to their destination had it not been for the children. As they passed a tall building the double doors opened and a rabble of infants poured out. They were met by a gaggle of mothers, and though Charles did his best to get by without trampling the young underfoot it still took time. When he reached the opposite pavement and looked around him once more, neither a black head nor a golden one was to be seen. Helen and Mavis had disappeared.

Despite his honourable intentions, meeting the two girls out of the theatre did not prove as simple as Charles had supposed. For one thing, he had no experience as a stage door johnny, and for another he was never the only young man hanging about waiting for the girls to emerge. Indeed, the crowd on several occasions was three deep. Thus it was that when Helen and Mavis – always together – came lightly out of the shadowed doorway, there was always someone who knew them well enough to call out, identify himself, whilst Charles simply stood there, hungry eyes fixed but tongue, alas, cleaving to the roof of his mouth with shyness. If only he could find out where they lived, so that he might approach them there instead of outside the crowded stage door!

In the end, he resorted to guile and subterfuge. He did not go to the show but went and chatted to the stage doorkeeper instead. He mentioned all the girls, encouraging Dagbauld to talk about them too, and presently these tactics paid off.

'They're a nice bunch, this lot,' the man said in his rough, idiomatic French, graciously accepting the bottle of beer Charles offered. 'They're off to Versailles tomorrow –

18

that's their day off. My, but the tall, dark one's got culture like a redhead gets freckles; always on at me to find out opening times at the museums, art galleries and such. Knows more about Versailles without even going there than I do . . . and me a Frenchman born and bred! Told me this morning that the king who built it made it the seat of government to house six thousand souls . . . said there's fountains there that ran with wine in the olden days . . . she's a card, that one. Nice girl, though. Good dancer, too, they say – not that I ever see a show right through.'

'It's interesting that she likes museums and so on. Somehow I hadn't thought a pretty young thing like the blonde girl would go much on ancient monuments,' Charles said rather disingenuously. He could almost see Dagbauld's ears prick up.

'The blonde one – Mavis, she's called. If that one turns up at Versailles tomorrow I'll be surprised,' Dagbauld said dismissively. 'Why, the dark girl wants them to catch the nine o'clock train. Can you credit it? Those girls are on stage till near midnight. They don't usually get out of bed until noon, but Helen . . . that's her name, Helen . . . says there's a lot to see and anyone who's going with her has to be on the station by ten to nine. Which means, if you ask me, that around noon tomorrow the other girls will be buying yards of bread and cheap wine to take in the Tuileries for their lunch.' He chuckled, then took a long drink of beer, breaking off to wipe his mouth and chuckle again. 'Always short of money, they are, so Helen told them to bring a picnic, all five of them.' He shook his head, and finished off the beer. 'Oh, I can read them like a book, I can! Mavis'll stay in bed till noon, then wander down to the San Raphael to see if Claude will buy her lunch. He has a crush on her – he's the son of the owner, working as a waiter for a few weeks – and if he's on duty he'll buy her lunch just to be able to smile at her a few times, poor fool. Then she and one or other of the girls will walk along the river and talk to the fishermen, and then they'll go round the shops and pick out what they'll buy when they next have some money. And if she's on tomorrow night she'll rush in here five minutes before her first call, shedding her clothes down the corridor as she runs for the dressing-room ...' He laughed squeakily, shaking his head indulgently. 'I'm an old man; it means nothing to me. I've seen it all, I have.'

Charles returned some suitable answer, tipped Dagbauld as lavishly as he could afford and strolled back to his hotel room. At least, he strolled whilst he was in sight of the theatre, but once round the corner he ran, just for pleasure, and laughed aloud. Trains for Versailles left from La Gare des Invalides, and she would be on the nine o'clock! Of course it was always possible that the other girls would make the effort and turn up to keep Helen company, but he even felt equal to that. Dagbauld had said that Helen was keen on culture, which undoubtedly meant that she would want to see the palace and not merely sit in the grounds and admire the fountains and the long lawns. So he would offer to accompany her round the State chambers ... he would fall into conversation with her, offer to loan her his copy of the guide book ... he would find some way of getting to know her.

He had deliberately gone to the stage door whilst the show was in progress so that he would not have to compete for the doorkeeper's attention, and now it was nine o'clock, dark and rather chilly. In his room the fire had long gone out and the bread rolls and pink, thinly sliced ham which had looked so appetising earlier seemed stale and unattractive now. Still, they would do for breakfast.

It did not take him long to clear the grate and lay a fresh fire, but he did not put a match to it. Instead, he washed his hands in the cold water left in his jug, dried them on his old piece of towel and picked up his coat. He would walk down to Le Chat Gris, which was quite near and a good place to eat, and order oysters, bread and white wine. He would have his meal as near to their log fire as he could get, and when he had finished he would walk along the banks of the river until he was truly worn out. Only then would he be able to sleep, for the excitement engendered by knowing Helen's whereabouts next day would otherwise render him wakeful all night and in no shape to dazzle her next morning.

On the way down the stairs he met his neighbour, the girl in the next room. She was clattering up the stairs, leading a young French soldier by the hand. She greeted Charles with unabashed cheerfulness and Charles smiled back. So she was clearly on the game – so what? It was a free country and she was a pretty girl with a liking for expensive finery and few talents other than the one she was about to exercise. He reflected that he had suspected she was a street-walker and not a respectable girl as soon as he had clapped eyes on her. With Helen, it had been just the opposite. He had seen the chorus girls in their flimsy feathers and lace, but had not doubted for an instant that Helen and Mavis were pillars of respectability both. He rather suspected that his mother would be shocked merely by the fact that Helen danced in public; his father, he feared, would simply assume that she was a part of Charles's growing up. But I, Charles told himself, stepping out into the mild darkness, know better.

He strolled through the dark streets, breathing in the night-scents as he turned first left and then right. Facing the Seine he smelt the soft, stagnant river-scent; when he turned away from it he caught the fragrance of early spring flowers in the gardens; when he entered the rue Bonaparte he could smell coffee, and knew he was nearing Le Chat Gris.

Inside, he took off his coat, settled himself at a table near the fire, and beckoned the waiter. He ordered, then leaned back in his chair, basking in the warmth. Now he was free to think about the morrow, plan his arrival at La Gare des Invalides. Instead, he thought about his father, and Edouard's delicately hinted remarks concerning Paris, and women. The older man had clearly hoped that Charles might take a leaf from Maurice's book and become, if not a womaniser, at least a bit of a gay dog. Charles, who was nowhere near the innocent his father thought him, did not choose to make his affairs public knowledge. He had had a brief and difficult liaison with a hard-faced young woman in St Malo, and an even briefer though much more enjoyable affair with the wife of a business acquaintance of his father's. He was quite a different person from his elder brother. Maurice, who enjoyed living dangerously, nevertheless bowed to his father's expressed wish that he would, eventually, settle down and marry a local girl with useful connections. That, Charles knew, was why Maurice had lived at such a hectic pace: because he had no desire to find Annabel Choiville in his bed. He had agreed to marry her when he was ready to settle down, and only Maurice and Charles had known that Maurice was determined not to marry until he was forty.

Charles did not intend to become his brother's deputy in marriage. He would choose his wife for something other than her father's business connections and the fact that the family owned land which abutted on the Laurient estate. Edouard, on the other hand, persisted in regarding any woman but Annabel as a mere diversion, and said openly that looks, sex appeal and character were delightful in a mistress but unnecessary in a wife. Bernice, when appealed to, always cast her eyes to the ceiling and sighed. Hers had been a marriage of convenience which had become a love-match, Charles knew, but not everyone was so fortunate.

So it seemed best to Charles to keep his private life a secret so far as his parents were concerned, and his closest friend, René Dubois, agreed with him.

'You must stand up to your father over this, the way

Maurice never did,' René said seriously. 'A cold woman does not become a cuddly armful just because she is rich. Don't let anyone push you into marriage, Charles.'

It was all very well for René. He had recently married his childhood sweetheart, Elise, and was idyllically happy. Charles was not one of Elise's admirers, but he could see that the young couple were very much in love and he envied them that. René had no father in the background encouraging his son to find girlfriends, as though by sleeping with several pretty young things he would lose the desire to do so and would settle down happily with boring and self-opinionated Annabel Choiville.

But now that Charles had seen Helen, love at first sight had suddenly become a reality and not merely something which happened to other people. He dreamed about her, imagined every dark head in a crowd to be hers, planned his days around the desire to meet her in person at last. He did not think of her in connection with marriage – she seemed too light and lovely a creature to immure at Augeuil Manor – but he could not look beyond his time in Paris to an era when she would not be for ever in his thoughts. Charles Laurient was rapidly drowning in love – for a girl who did not know he existed!

The sun woke him. He lay for a moment, wondering whether he should get up and draw the curtains across, for he had been too eager to get to sleep the previous night to bother with such things then. But with the very act of opening his eyes the day had begun for him, so he jumped out of bed and hurried to the window. The sweetness of early morning stole into the warm, sleep-enriched air, and Charles took a deep breath of it before looking out over the patchwork roofs towards the river. It was going to be a fine day, if the scarves of mist which he knew must lie above the water were anything to go by.

Charles glanced at his watch. Six o'clock. Far too early

23

to get up yet; he might as well go back to bed. But even as the thought crossed his mind he was pouring water into the blue bowl with the red poppies round the rim and fishing the soap out of the cupboard. Better wash, now he was up, and then dress; no point in pretending the day was not already well into its swing.

Ten minutes later – it had not been a very thorough wash – Charles was making his way down the stairs, across the empty foyer with its smell of dusty carpet, furniture polish and cigarettes, and into the cool, empty street. The sun had not yet risen; only an air of expectancy, and a pinkish gold line on the eastern horizon, showed that it was about to do so. Charles decided to walk down to the Seine, but as he crossed the rue des Fosses he heard a soft clunking sound and saw, coming towards him, a herd of black goats. They were wearing collars, some with flattened bronze bells, and an old woman was driving them. A thin black and white collie darted at their heels.

Intrigued, Charles turned towards them; the woman smiled, revealing gapped and broken teeth. She had the seamed brown skin of one who has spent most of her life out of doors, thin grey hair pulled back into a tiny, tight bun, and the black and voluminous clothing favoured by most peasant women. But her eyes were bright and lively, her smile sweet.

'Good morning, monsieur,' she said as soon as they were near enough to exchange words. 'Spring has come this morning, I believe, for I'm warm as toast and the sun is not yet up. Would you like some milk?'

'I have no jug,' Charles said regretfully. 'They look very fine goats.'

'Yes, they're good goats,' the old woman agreed. She held out a battered tin cup, fastened to her skirt by a length of string. 'I can sell you some to drink right now, if you like. The milk of black goats is very rich, very strong – you won't need any breakfast when you've drunk it.'

24

Charles laughed and capitulated. The old woman squatted on the kerb, selected the nearest goat and pulled it towards her. She milked it very neatly into the tin cup, which she then untied from her person and handed to Charles.

'There . . . best milk in Paris, that. Drink it down!'

Charles handed her a small coin and sipped at the rich, creamy liquid. It tasted of the goats, hairy and strong, but it was good, none the less. Whilst he drank, standing by the kerb, the sun came up; long fingers of gold crept across the street, touching the goats' sturdy shapes and lighting wicked sparkles in their slanted, devilish eyes. In his mind's eye Charles saw the river – the ripples, touched with gold, the water sparkling under the new rays, the trees which bent over it stirring and whispering as the sun rose.

Another customer approached, enamel jug at the ready. She was young and plump with red hair and a small child at her knee. The old woman began milking at once, the threads of milk sizzling on to the enamel with a high whine. Charles finished his own drink and handed the cup back to the goat-woman, who thanked him with a nod and stopped work for a moment to tie it back on to its string. Then she began to hiss milk into the jug once more, her gnarled fingers quick and deft on the nanny's long, pink teats. The dog sat and panted, watching her, and presently, the jug filled, she directed the jet of milk towards her dog. To the child's delight the collie promptly got into line and began drinking the milk without letting a drop of it touch the ground.

'Bravo,' the redhead said, and the child cheered too, and the goat-woman smiled at them, squirted a last jet into her dog's mouth, and got up from the kerb. The whole cavalcade moved off and Charles continued on his way, dodging the goats who took absolutely no notice of him as he threaded a path between them to gain the opposite pavement. Clearly they were well used to their saunter through

25

the streets of Paris each morning. And I might have missed it all, never known about it, marvelled Charles, heading now for his favourite cafe, were it not for wanting to arrive at La Gare des Invalides in time for the nine o'clock train to Versailles.

He reached the cafe to find the waiter already busy standing the chairs and tables in their usual positions on the pavement. Charles strolled over; there was a marvellous smell of hot bread and good, strong coffee. The goat's milk was still sweet in his mouth but despite the old woman's prediction he found he was very hungry; if they were open for business he might as well eat now as later.

They were quite willing to serve him. He sat down on a green painted chair before a round wrought-iron table, and watched white doves pecking between the paving stones. A cat, thin and quick, came and wound round his ankles, purring so loudly that it sounded like a small but lively engine. It was a young cat, its eyes wide and green, innocent of the wicked ways of the world. It knew only kindness, the taste of fresh milk, the plateful of chopped scraps, and the quick flutter of the doves as they clattered up from the paving at its approach. When it had made love to Charles's ankles it suddenly set off in pursuit of a piece of paper which the breeze had swirled out from beneath a table and sent skittering into the roadway. It captured the paper and came back to leap on to Charles's table and be shooed off by the waiter, bringing *café au lait* and croissants.

Charles thanked him and sipped coffee; he was aware of a great happiness, a contentment which encompassed the cafe, the coffee, the cat. He savoured the feeling as he savoured the fragrance of the coffee, the melt-in-the-mouth croissants with the blandness of butter and the sharp sweetness of raspberry jam. Somewhere, somehow, he would meet Helen today. He knew it at that moment as surely and safely as though someone had just whispered reassurance in his ear. He would meet her and they would

26

have a good time together, because it was his fate to be happy in Paris on this particular day.

On the other side of the street a woman in a print overall and a black headscarf was cleaning the pavement in front of her shop, swishing buckets of hot, soap-sudded water across the grey stones. Steam arose from the wet paving and the woman was singing softly. Her voice rose in a folk song, old as time, which she had probably learned at her mother's knee.

For Charles, it completed the perfection of the morning.

A couple of hours later, Charles was surrounded by people, his ears dinned by noise, as he watched the train for Versailles draw in to its appointed platform and kept an eye open for Helen. Even so, he nearly missed her. He expected her to be running to the train, but instead she, like him, was waiting for someone. She stood at what must be a previously arranged spot, under the clock, staring out towards the entrance as though it was the doorway to heaven. It was not until a voice announced the imminent departure of the train for Versailles that she turned reluctantly away from her vigil and climbed aboard, with many a backward glance over her shoulder as she did so.

Charles was right behind her. She was wearing a skirt and jacket in pale blue cloth with a dark fur collar. Her shoes were highly polished black courts, her gloves matched her jacket, and on one shoulder was pinned a bronze-red rose. Her head was bare, the sun making her hair shine like dark water, and she had a bag over one shoulder which looked as though it contained something very heavy – she was weighed down by it, heeling to one side as she walked like a ship in a gale.

She collapsed into the first vacant seat and Charles took the one opposite. It was not an empty carriage, unfortunately; a stout Frenchman with an attaché case occupied the seat next to Helen and the rest of the compartment was

27

taken up by a family of four, a fat baby in a pink and white wrapper and an immense picnic hamper which clinked whenever one of the children touched it.

The journey to Versailles took about thirty minutes, and Charles put every one of them to good use. He studied Helen's profile as she sat watching the countryside flash past, and by the time they arrived he could have drawn her from memory – the small, hooky nose, the high forehead, the wing of bright hair which fell forward and was impatiently tossed back. But though Charles could – and did – watch her, it proved impossible to enter into a natural conversation with her whilst the garrulous family squabbled and shouted and laughed and the man with the attaché case tried to tell everyone that he was not a-pleasuring like them but on a business trip. Even when the train reached Versailles and they climbed down and set off for the palace, Charles did not feel he could approach her. Instead he allowed her to walk a little in front of him with a guide book, at which she stared intently, held in one hand. The two of them, half a dozen feet apart but separated by miles as far as the unconscious Helen was concerned, crossed the wide *place* and approached their destination. But once actually outside the great rambling pile of buildings, Helen hesitated, glancing doubtfully from guide book to palace and back again. Clearly, she was as lost as he despite her book and Charles approached her at long last, determined to take this opportunity of asking her if she needed help. After all, it was no crime for one sightseer to speak to another!

'Er . . . excuse me. I see you've got a guide book and I'm afraid I left mine in my hotel. I wonder . . . could you tell me if that's the Cour de la Chapelle . . . or is it the Pavilion Gabriel? I seem to remember someone telling me I should start with the Cour de la Chapelle . . . it's awfully *big*, isn't it!'

The girl turned; for a disconcerting moment huge dark

eyes regarded him narrowly, and then her mouth curved into the enchanting smile that Charles felt he knew quite well and the eyes warmed into friendship.

'I'm not too sure; I was hoping someone would tell me which was which, actually,' she said. She held out the guide book so that he, too, could read the page. 'Are you English? You speak it awfully well, if not. As for what *that* building is . . .' She pointed with a blue-gloved finger. '. . . I think it must be the Cour d'Honneur, because of the railings in front of it, and those statues. Perhaps one shouldn't try to identify things, but should just enjoy them?'

'I am English, more or less,' Charles said easily. 'Let me look at your guide book for a moment . . . ah, yes, I see it all!' He smiled down at her and offered his arm. 'Shall we go together? I'm Charles Laurient, by the way, on a month's holiday in Paris. And you are . . .?'

'I'm Helen Salling,' the girl said cheerfully. 'I'll be glad of your company, Mr Laurient, and I'm . . . but why should we pretend? You know very well what I do for a living, I'm sure, Mr Laurient!'

Charles felt his face grow hot. How could she possibly know that he had haunted her, dreamed about her? But he was straightforward by nature and had no intention of trying to deceive her.

'You're a dancer at the Folies,' he admitted. 'How did you know I knew?'

'I've a good memory for faces,' Helen said. 'You were in Le Chat Gris when Mavis and I came in from the rain. Then you were outside the stage door a couple of times . . . you were watching me at the station in Paris . . . you've been hanging about hoping to scrape an acquaintance with Mavis or me, haven't you?'

'Well . . . yes. With you,' Charles said.

'It's sensible of you to say it straight out.' Helen's face was sparkling with amusement, Charles decided thankfully. She was clearly more intrigued than annoyed. 'Well, now that we know each other shall we take a look at this place? I believe it takes three days to see everything, but I just can't spare the time, so it'll have to be today or nothing. Are you game to gallop round Versailles with me?'

'Rather!' Charles said eagerly. 'Can I have a go with the book?'

She handed it over quite readily and Charles, after a short scrutiny, led her into a vestibule with white marble walls and pointed out the figures of Glory and Magnanimity depicted thereon.

'And next we see the chapel, and the royal pew,' Charles told his companion. 'We'll save the gardens until last, I think . . . I hope those shoes are comfier than they look!'

'They aren't too bad,' Helen said. 'I wish I hadn't brought such a huge picnic, but I thought the others were coming. Mean beasts – I suppose they're all curled up in bed still!'

'Is that what's in the bag?' Charles said, highly amused. 'Look, you won't be needing that . . . what is it, anyway? Not sandwiches, surely?'

'Wine, oranges and sultana cake,' Helen said ruefully. 'They're all cheap and filling, you see.'

Gently but firmly, Charles took the bag from her. He walked over to one of the officials, spoke to him for a moment, and then returned to Helen, leaving the bag behind.

'What have you done with it? How on earth did you manage to make him understand? And what did you tell him?' Questions tumbled eagerly from Helen's lips. 'Oh, I wish I could speak French properly, though I do try!'

'I asked him if he would keep it for us until we reclaim it this evening,' Charles told her. 'You won't need it today, for I intend to buy us a splendid luncheon. We'll need it,

30

you know, after tramping round Versailles for hours together.'

He half feared she might refuse this tacit invitation but instead she clung on to his arm, beaming up at him.

'How wonderful! Right you are then ... lead on, Macduff!'

They had a perfect day. The weather continued clear and sunny, and the palace showed them its best face. They toured the royal apartments until they both had stiff necks from gazing up at the ornate ceilings, they examined every fountain, every statue, every courtyard, lake and carefully contrived view. At lunchtime they had a huge meal at the first-class restaurant in the palace grounds. Charles of course insisted on paying, though Helen put up a token resistance. As she told him, a young lady of the chorus is not generously paid and usually curbs her appetite until the evening meal.

'During the day we eat lots of bread and cheese and fruit,' she confessed. 'My mother would have been shocked, but it doesn't seem to do me much harm.'

Charles, eyeing her delicious figure, agreed, and gained considerable enjoyment from watching her tackle her meal with zest.

Later still they hired a boat and rowed down the Grand Canal, Charles taking the oars whilst Helen lay back and watched. Then they changed places and Helen rowed for a while with an expertise which made Charles open his eyes a little.

'You're not a city girl?' he asked, and Helen admitted, in the attractive country accent that Charles still couldn't quite put his finger on, that she had had a rural childhood and sometimes felt very homesick for poultry pecking round the yard and ponies tethered to the rail.

Charles, in his turn, told her about the four-hundred-

31

year-old manor house, and of his father's hobby and his own interest in it.

'My father says that one day the family will make more money from orchids than from early potatoes,' he said, grinning down at her. 'They certainly are fascinating things – more like animals in many ways than plants. You should hear him talking about them . . .' Highly daring, he added, 'Maybe one day you will.'

Helen shot a quick glance at him and he saw the colour invade her cheeks. Then she adroitly changed the subject and splashed water at him.

They caught the last train back to Paris and had dinner together, for she was not on stage that night. In a peaceful little restaurant down by the Seine, with a glassed-in canopy overhead but the frontage open to the river, they ate onion soup with crusty bread, scarlet lobster with salad and crêpes flamed in brandy and doused with cream.

That night, Charles accompanied Helen to the little *pâtisserie* in the rue St Médard above which her room was situated. They kissed at first lightly, then with more fervour. He left her reluctantly.

The following night he kissed her more passionately yet, on the stairs which led to her room, and parted from her more unwillingly than ever.

On the third night they did not part.

Charles had been sketching in the Tuileries when René found him. He had spent the morning there, making the most of the strong, clear light, but when his hand grew tired he decided to call it a day and turned for home.

Home was no longer the small hotel; he and Helen shared a couple of attic rooms above a greengrocer's shop in a little alley leading down to the river. Not that Helen lived there all the time; it was rather too far when she was doing a late show and 'doubling' in a restaurant cabaret to earn extra money. Then, she and Mavis simply trundled to

32

their old room and collapsed on to their pillows in the none-too-early hours, sleeping the better for not having to make allowances for anyone else in the bed.

'Flat on my face, elbows out, and snoring,' Helen had said ruefully, when Charles had asked her just why she wanted to sleep alone sometimes. 'When you're dancing until getting on for midnight at the Folies and then go on to do a late-night cabaret you're fit for nothing else, dear Charles.'

He would have liked to tell her to give up the cabaret, but despite the fact that he was earning money fairly steadily from selling his sketches they were still hard up. Charles's month was long gone and so was the money he had brought with him to Paris. His father had written a couple of times, not exactly demanding that Charles should return but definitely suggesting that enough was enough, and saying that whilst all work might make Jack a dull boy, all play was liable to do something very much worse.

The last letter, though, had come from his mother.

'*Try and get back home fairly soon, Charles,*' she had written. '*Your father's in a ferment of excitement because he's bred a hybrid which he can't wait to show you. It's something special. He's had some quite famous horticulturalists over to see it, but he won't tell anyone how he bred it . . . only you, because he says you'll understand. He's called it "Pure Madonna", and I must say I can see why – the way the petals are formed and the colours make it look just like the head of the Virgin Mary; it's quite uncanny. The trouble is, dear Charles, it doesn't have a very long flowering; it's nearly finished and he would so like you to see it before it's over.*'

The letter had gone on to discuss other things, but it had stirred Charles's sleeping conscience. A little, but not enough. He was in love, in Paris, and happy. He toyed with the idea of marrying Helen and taking her back with him, but he did not think she would want to come. She was revelling in her dancing, her newfound freedom, the friends she had made. She would not willingly leave them all behind to be the wife of a glorified farmer!

He had sounded her out on the subject, though, and she had cuddled up to him and said, very sweetly, that it was 'a bit soon' to talk about marriage and settling down.

'I've only just made a life of my own,' she said plaintively. 'I can't just give it up like that . . . in a year, perhaps . . .'

So now Charles made his way across the gardens, a smear of charcoal on his cheek, the sketch book under his arm and a bag slung over his shoulder with various impedimenta crammed into it. And saw René Dubois, coming towards him.

'René!' Charles ran the few yards that separated them and grabbed René's shoulders. 'My dear chap . . . whatever are you doing here?'

'I've come to take you home,' René said, returning the rough embrace. 'Your father needs you.'

'Well, yes . . . I'll be coming quite soon. I've met the most wonderful girl . . .' Charles began, hitching the bag back on to his shoulder, for it had slid off when René hugged him. 'I'm selling my drawings; I'm quite solvent. Give me a week or two . . .'

'Charles, your father's *dying*,' René said fiercely. 'Your mother's at her wits' end; you must come home.'

Charles, who had turned René in the direction of his rooms, stopped short in his tracks. He swung round so that he and René were face to face.

'Dying? My father? Nonsense, man, he's the healthiest chap I know! Or . . . has there been an accident? What on earth's happened?'

'M. Laurient was fine a few days ago; then he had some sort of a seizure. He was in the hothouse . . . the doctor says the trouble is he fainted or something and just lay there getting hotter and hotter. Your mother found him eventually, when he hadn't come in for lunch, and was nowhere to be found at dinner-time. She called the doctor, of course, and they got him up to bed. She telegraphed you . . . but I remembered your father saying you weren't at the hotel any more, and when M. Laurient had another attack first thing yesterday . . . I got the ferry and came over. I telephoned the house early this morning, hoping for good news, but instead your mother told me to tell you that if you didn't hurry . . .'

He left the rest of the sentence unsaid. Charles stared, shock rendering him almost speechless. His father, dying? Old Edouard was such an indomitable fellow, short and sturdy, strong as an ox, with a marked liking for getting his own way and no patience whatsoever with illness, particularly his own.

'He . . . he's in *bed*?'

It was incredible; he had never known his father have so much as half a day in bed. It was totally out of character!

René cast his eyes to the sky.

'Yes, Charles, he's in bed. He's had a – a stroke. His speech is affected. Are you coming, or am I going to have to drag you?'

'Drag . . . of course I'm coming!' Charles set off at the fastest walk he could manage. 'I'll have to pack . . . leave a note for the . . . the friend I share my rooms with . . . what time's the next ferry? Can we get home today?'

He loved his father; he had not known how much until now. Oh, the old man had been unfair to him sometimes, but that had all happened long ago. Of late years the two of them had got to know one another better, and had become friends. How could I have stayed away so long? Charles wondered, as he and René strode along the crowded pavements, for it was lunchtime and people were making their way home or to bars and cafes for the midday meal. But then he had never realised how badly his father needed him, had believed him to be immortal, capable of managing the estate and his own life with ease, merely wanting Charles at Augeuil Manor because he was the heir.

They reached the greengrocer's shop and Charles ran up the stairs two at a time. There was no one in the flat. Helen was at a rehearsal, though she would be back in time for tea. Charles put René in the picture about the girl he loved – her photograph, in stage makeup and very little else, adorned the mantelpiece – as he was cramming clothing into a bag. He had few enough clothes and fewer possessions, but what he had he had better take with him; heaven knew how long it would be before his father was well enough to let him return to Paris. Edouard was clearly gravely ill, that much René had made plain, but he could not possibly be *dying*; he was not yet seventy and the Laurients were a long-lived race.

'Wish I could see Helen, but I'll leave her a note,' Charles muttered. 'Oh, and some money – she'd better have what I've got left – and I'll leave the sketches, tell her to sell them.'

He sat down at the table and rapidly filled one of the pages of his sketch book with an account of what had happened. Then he put the money into an envelope, scrawled her name on it, and stuck it on the mantelpiece, with the note folded beside it.

'There! I've said I'll write later . . . I want to marry her, René, *mon vieux*, so I'll have to come back here as soon as I possibly can . . . now let's go!'

Helen refused Charles's formal offer of marriage the week after his father's funeral. She thought that he was lonely, that perhaps he felt sorry for her, but most of all she refused because she could not bear to lose this marvellous life of hers which she had so recently acquired. She had worked hard at her dancing, but it had been luck, really, which had got her the job in the Folies – someone falling ill, a friend with an entrée to the company – and she had no intention of relinquishing it to become some farmer's son's wife.

She had grown very fond of Charles, but she was, when all was said and done, only seventeen, though she had told him she was twenty-one. At seventeen, she told herself, her life was in front of her. She could meet a prince and fall in love with him, or a film star or, better still, a film producer who would take her to Hollywood and make her famous.

She had stayed in their rooms for a couple of weeks, paying the rent first with the money Charles had left, then with the proceeds from his pictures, and finally with her own hard-won francs garnered from dancing in the late-night cabaret. But now she had moved back in with Mavis, and she was not sorry. She had got so fiercely lonely for Charles in their rooms that there was no bearing it, and she knew she would feel better in a trice if she had someone in the room with her at night so that she wouldn't lie awake in the dark, too tired to sleep half the time, with her legs hurting and her feet throbbing with pain. And anyway, once she had turned down his offer of marriage, she seemed to see Charles in every bit of the rooms they had shared, sitting in the armchair opposite her own, shaving over the tiny sink, lying in bed, naked, with that sweet, lazy, cat-with-cream smile on his mouth which came after lovemaking.

So she told him she was very sorry but she did not love him enough to give up her career, and she moved back in with Mavis. And the pain in her feet got less because she no longer needed the money quite so badly now she was only paying for half a small and grubby attic. But the pain in her heart got worse, because she missed . . . she missed . . .

So she took a lover, a short, square Frenchman who had a butcher's shop quite near the theatre. He was handsome and it turned out he was also quite rich, and he was an energetic and demanding lover and she told herself half a dozen times a day that soon she would stop even thinking about Charles and certainly those stupid, pointless things, regrets, would cease troubling her.

Alain Chantenay might really have been the man for her, but she was destined never to know for sure. No more than three weeks after she had tossed love aside and taken her career to her bosom, she discovered she was pregnant. Other members of the chorus had commented that she was heavier on her feet, often out of step, and then she realised she was having a job getting into some of the tighter costumes. She went to the doctor, who confirmed her worst fears.

'The young man . . . he will marry you? A pretty girl like you need have no fears on that score, I am persuaded,' he said with heavy jocularity. 'However, should you need that the baby does not come, should you wish an abortion . . .'

Helen was well aware what he meant by an abortion, but she was frightened, and very young, and, suddenly, desperate. So she ran away. She left her share of the room, she left the Folies, she left Alain Chantenay, the butcher from the rue Richer . . . but she could not leave her condition. She remained pregnant, and frightened.

She knew, of course, that Charles Laurient was the father, but in her flight she had forgotten his address and anyway, having refused his offer of marriage so decisively, she could scarcely go running to him now, expecting him to help just because she was having a baby! However, she knew that though he sounded very French, and spoke the language like a native, he was in fact English, because he had told her so. She knew his name, and that he had a four-hundred-year-old manor house. She supposed, doubtfully, that she could go to England and search for him. She could even send a forwarding address to Mavis.

In the event, she did none of these sensible things. She simply packed all her possessions into two limp cloth bags, which promptly became two bulging cloth bags, and boarded a train for Boulogne. There she took a berth on a ship sailing for England, and when they docked she did not find it difficult to get another job . . . this time on a ship heading home.

For Helen Salling had come not from the English west country but from the New World when she had run away from home to become a dancer, and now she was running back, this time to become a mother. She worked her passage as a waitress in the dining saloon of a large liner, and when she was sick in the mornings the other girls thought it was the motion of the ship and Helen never disabused them.

New York was as foreign to her as Paris had been – she scarcely understood a word spoken to her for three or four days – but she got another job as a waitress, this time on dry land, at a rather smart restaurant on 56th Street. It was in theatreland, which caused her some pangs, but with her figure daily getting larger it was pretty clear that she would not be dancing on Broadway – or anywhere else for that matter – for some time to come.

She gave birth to her baby in a Home for Destitute Girls where they bullied her, tried to take her baby away from her to give it out for adoption and finally drove her into running away for the third time.

Helen was now just eighteen years old, and calling herself Mrs Helen Laurient. She did not want the sort of trouble she had seen come to girls who were known to be 'easy', so she invented a husband for herself, a husband who had died in Europe.

She called the baby Daniel Sheridan Laurient. But mostly, she called him Laurie.

1

1936

Rochelle Dubois came cautiously out of the kitchen door, both hands gripping her breakfast, a slice of bread with a thin spreading of jam and a thicker one of yellow clotted cream. She trod softly, because she was not supposed to take her breakfast out of doors, but she was well aware that in all the fuss and bustle of her parents' leaving for a day out in France she would probably be overlooked.

The Dubois family lived in what had once been the coachman's cottage at the end of the stable block. It was a pretty place, for René was good with his hands and Elise was a natural gardener, so that the creamy stone was covered with roses, wisteria and other climbing plants. They raced up the walls and tapped on the bedroom windows, and small though Rochelle was she still loved to lean on her window-sill and smell the blossom so close and feel tendrils of the creeper touching her face.

Rochelle paused a moment in the doorway to listen; behind her she could hear her mother commanding her father to look for her handbag. No, not the black one, that was her everyday one, but the dark blue one with the white trimming.

'But I can't find my pipe,' René shouted. 'I always take my pipe when I'm buying stock. I need it . . . have you seen it anywhere, *chérie?*'

They seemed to be occupied enough not to notice her defection, so Rochelle began to cross the stableyard. She did so with care, for even the daintiest Jersey cow is not particular where she raises her tail and deposits a cow-pat. Rochelle skirted the still-steaming piles and padded determinedly out of the yard and into the formal gardens.

Having managed to avoid getting cow-muck on her white strap shoes she was able to concentrate once more on her bread and cream, eating it carefully so as not to dribble food on to her gingham dress or over her white pinafore. Although her mother would be out all day, there was still Mme Barfleur, the housekeeper up at the manor, to contend with. Mme Barfleur always gave an eye to Rochelle when her parents were away on estate business, and she would not be pleased if her charge turned up at lunchtime looking like a ragamuffin. Therefore it behoved Rochelle to eat up, wipe her hands on the nearest patch of grass and continue on her way.

On a normal day, of course, Elise would never have let her small daughter slip away so early, for Rochelle was being conscientiously raised to be useful about the house. Because she was only eight she was not expected to do much actual cleaning, but her tasks befitted her small size and equally small experience – she dusted the lower halves of chairs, tables and sideboards, she brushed round the legs of the furniture, leaving the great bare spaces of floor to her mother's superior bristle-power, she shook out the linen and folded it ready for ironing and popped peas out of their pods and scrubbed new potatoes ready for the pot.

In the garden she planted seeds, under Elise's supervision, and weeded. She had tried to rake the paths, but it always ended in tears, so that task would remain her mother's until Rochelle was a good deal taller. She had her own little watering can, though, and on summer evenings she was quite useful, watering away at the borders and occasionally nipping off a dead-head.

Of course, this was only in holiday time. When she was at school she could not do nearly so much, for she had to go in to the village each day, either on foot or in the trap if someone was going that way, and when she came home at night she had reading to practise and writing and sums and was generally too busy to be much help.

But now it was holiday time, for the schools had three whole weeks off for Easter and only one of them had been used up so far. Rochelle, who quite liked school but infinitely preferred the holidays, gave a little bounce and crammed the last piece of bread and cream into her mouth. Then, with care, she licked each finger until it was clean and pink. She meant to go to the greenhouses and help M. Laurient, and he would not appreciate sticky doorhandles. Looking round her as she went, Rochelle reflected that the greenhouses were a really good idea; not only did she love them but she would – of course! – shut the door once she was inside and be quite unable to hear should her mother or father call her. She felt a tiny bit guilty because they might want to say goodbye to her, but then they could have taken her with them had they wanted her company. Not that they would. Rochelle knew, without resentment, that her parents loved her but not as much as they loved each other. They were a perfect pair; she always felt, just a little, that she was tolerated rather than welcomed when they were together. They were a lot older than the parents of most of the children in her class, she knew that . . . but she did not understand why this should mean she some-times felt an outsider when she was with them.

Just now, however, Rochelle was escaping from her parents as they were escaping from her. She would go to the hothouses, they would go to France. Poor them, with only pigs and cows to look at, Rochelle thought now, as one small hand closed firmly round the door of the first greenhouse; I have my orchids!

She thought that she had always loved the orchids; certainly one of her earliest memories was of being held up to look at the Royal breed through the glass. She had cried, trying to say she wanted to go in, to touch the fine, delicate blossoms, but no one had understood her.

Later she had toddled here, in her stiff petticoats and little dresses with soft shoes on her small feet. But someone

43

had always pursued her, and anyway she had not been tall enough to reach even the lowest of the door handles, far less to turn it and admit herself.

M. Laurient had told her that the orchids were called the Royal family and she had understood at once why this should be so. They were so rare, so stately, that it was the only title for them. Once, he had told her, his father had made a wonderful hybrid called Pure Madonna which people had come for miles to see. But the secret of the breeding had been lost, for old Edouard Laurient had been taken very ill with some dreadful ailment which meant he could not speak. M. Laurient had not told her this, but Rochelle had heard others mention it.

And now M. Laurient was trying to recapture the secret, to breed Pure Madonna again. Or rather he had been trying for years, since long before Rochelle was even born, but had recently begun to think that he might be nearing success at last.

'He still feels it was his fault that the secret was lost all those years ago,' René sometimes said. 'Old M. Laurient knew very well what he needed to tell – he could have written it down. But Charles and I took a few hours too long, and in that time the old man staggered downstairs and out to his beloved glasshouses, presumably to try at least to mark the hybrid, for the last flowers had faded and died. He must have had another stroke in the garden, for they found him within a couple of feet of the greenhouses, dead on the gravel path.'

At this point, Elise usually said, 'He wasn't that old, René,' and René would reply, 'Ah, but the first stroke had aged him ten years; madame told me so when we got back from France.'

The rest of the story Rochelle knew by heart. How young M. Laurient, her own M. Laurient, had come rushing back from Paris to find his father already dead, and had hurried to the glasshouses to see the hybrid, only to find hundreds

44

of plants, any of which could have borne the flowers of the Pure Madonna.

The following year he had waited confidently for the plants to bloom again and most of them did so . . . but none bore the strange and beautiful flower which his mother's letter had led him to expect.

In those days, René told his small daughter, M. Laurient's knowledge and expertise amongst the Royal family was in its infancy. He had done his best to keep the orchids alive, but somewhere along the line he had failed, and in the nature of things the one hybrid which he most longed to see in bloom had been one of the ones to die.

If he had had his father's breeding notes, if he had even known the stud plants involved in the mating, young M. Laurient could have reproduced his father's experiment and seen the Pure Madonna for himself. But because he had lingered in Paris for a few minutes longer than he should have done they had missed a train, and in consequence had missed a ferry. Thus they had come into the harbour at St Helier many hours later than René had intended.

So now, Rochelle thought, as she slipped into the first glasshouse and closed the door gently behind her, M. Laurient is determined to breed the Pure Madonna in his father's memory. René said so, and René must be right for he was the nearest thing to a friend M. Laurient had. Rochelle knew this was true because Maman said so sometimes, and also because she had seen with her own eyes that only René joked with M. Laurient, only her father dared to contradict him when they were discussing estate business. Everyone else, even her rather fiery maman, deferred to him, gave him best.

I wonder if it's good for him to get his own way so much? Rochelle wondered, as she paused in the first aisle, breathing in the smell of the sphagnum moss, the diluted plant-feed and the plants themselves with total enjoyment. She

45

was not yet nine, but she had been brought up in a completely adult environment and often, rather to Maman's disapproval, sounded more like a little old woman than a child.

But whether it was good for him or not it was what happened, and privately Rochelle thought it was probably good for everyone, including herself, to have their own way. And just now she was doing exactly what she most liked, so she pushed M. Laurient out of her mind and concentrated on the plants which crowded the greenhouse staging on either side of her.

They were in good health; she knew that at once just by touching a leaf here, the potting compost there. They had been soft-watered the previous evening and were still enjoying that delicious draught, but presently, because it was such a brilliantly sunny day, they would begin to suffer from the heat. There were blinds which could be rolled down and windows which could be propped open with the help of a long pole which stood at the end of each greenhouse. Rochelle adored opening the windows, but hesitated, nevertheless. She never did anything in here which might annoy M. Laurient, and though she had no doubt that when he came in he would immediately start opening windows and pulling down blinds, he might not be pleased to find that Rochelle had forestalled him. She always studied, not to please M. Laurient, exactly, but to keep on the right side of him. She had been told over and over, not only by her parents but also by all the staff at the manor, that M. Laurient did not like children and merely tolerated her for her parents' sake and because she showed such a lively interest in his pet plants. Her maman, in particular, stressed that she should be careful never to put a foot wrong in case he realised she was just a nuisance and forbade her admittance to his glasshouses.

He was, she knew, a quick-tempered man. Once, René told her, M. Laurient had been very different, but after his father's death, quickly followed by that of his mother, he had grown taciturn, difficult.

'There was a young lady, too. M. Laurient wanted to marry her but she said no,' René explained. 'These things can turn a man into a recluse, make him bitter. We are fortunate, I sometimes think, that M. Laurient has his orchids.'

With that sentiment Rochelle heartily agreed. What would I do, she wondered now, without the Royal breed? She had spent so much of her early childhood with them that she often thought she knew what they were feeling – thinking, too. She could sense when a particular plant was about to flower or when it was in need of something such as a stronger mineral content in its feed or a sunnier – or shadier – position.

Moving slowly between the serried ranks of orchids, she talked to them softly as she moved; small talk, really, nothing important, just a few words pointing out that presently, when M. Laurient arrived, they would have the windows open and the blinds down, so they should drink in the warmth and the sunshine whilst they had the chance. She found one plant whose thick, fleshy leaves had a flaccid feel; she touched the potting compost and thought it was too dry.

'Were you missed last night at soft-water time?' Rochelle murmured. At the end of the greenhouse was a large rainwater tank with a dipper leaning against it. She had to climb up on to the staging to reach, but she filled the dipper and carried it cautiously back to the dry plant. She tipped it on to the moss with great caution – it would not do for the stem or leaves to get wet – and trickled water into the compost drop by drop.

When moisture began to seep out of the bottom of the pot she knew she had watered enough and tipped the remaining contents of the dipper back into the tank. She loved watering; the plants drank thirstily and little sounds came from them, though M. Laurient had told her long ago that it was from the compost and the clay of the pot that the little squeaks and murmurs derived. Maybe, she thought sceptically now; but if so the orchid was merely using the compost and the clay pot to say what it had no other means of expressing – thank you, that was a delicious drink.

She was about to jump down from the staging again when the door at the end of the greenhouse opened to admit M. Laurient. He was in his shirtsleeves, his jacket over his arm, so he would clearly not have to be prompted about opening the upper windows. She stood, poised, on the staging, not wanting to jump down and startle him, waiting for him to catch her eye.

He was a tall man, or he seemed so to Rochelle, though he was of a height with her father. He was dark, too, but the sides of his head were streaked with white, which made him seem older than René. When he caught her eye, as he presently did as he moved down the greenhouse, he did not smile. He was not a very smiling man, Rochelle knew. But he gave a little nod, a curt movement of his head, and she was sure his dark eyes softened as they fell on her.

'Good morning, monsieur. I've watered one who thirsted.'

'Thank you, Rochelle.' He was always polite to her despite her few years. 'I watered them last night, though. They should have been all right for another six hours or so.'

'It was only one,' Rochelle said hastily. 'You must have missed him, monsieur; he's . . . that one.' She indicated the plant just watered with one pointing finger.

'I don't see how I could have missed that one, right in the middle,' M. Laurient objected. 'Wait now . . . I know! Your father came into the greenhouse to talk to me. I believe I walked back along the staging with him and then

48

came back and started . . . yes, I'll have started one further along. Good thing you picked it out.'

It was the longest speech Rochelle had heard M. Laurient give for some weeks and she glowed with the praise, skipping along beside him as he examined each plant. Presently, as they arrived back at the greenhouse door, he addressed her again.

'Have you been to the nursery house yet?'

Rochelle shook her head. 'Not yet. I was a little early because Maman and Papa are off to France and did not need me for anything.'

'Ah, yes, of course.' He looked down at her and actually smiled. 'You didn't want to go with them?'

'They don't want me with them,' Rochelle said matter-of-factly. 'They never do.'

Charles Laurient grunted. 'More fools them. I think we should open the windows in here before we go, don't you?'

She smiled eagerly up at him, the strange ways of parents forgotten in her pleasure at what was to come.

'I'll do it . . . I may, mayn't I? I can reach, you know. You go and check the nursery!'

Charles Laurient watched her for a moment as she staggered up and down with the long pole, dexterously opening the windows, then moved away, smiling to himself. It had been the only gift he could offer her, the only consolation with which to make up for her parents' strange lack. Opening windows might seem a small enough thing, but he had known it would give her pleasure. Odd little creature that she was, he thought she was on the whole fairly oblivious of her parents' strange lack of affection for her. It was not even a lack of affection, really, for René was very fond of his funny little daughter and Elise loved her with a rather impatient emotion which Charles hoped would turn to something warmer as the child grew. It was more an afterthought, their love for their daughter, and it

49

glowed with a very small light compared with the brilliance of their feeling for each other.

That, of course, was why he always felt sorry for Rochelle. René and Elise had been deeply in love for fifteen years, and for seven of those years they had been content simply to have each other. They had not regretted their childless state, they had revelled in it, and with the sudden eruption of Rochelle into their lives they had drawn closer than ever, almost in collusion against a common enemy – their baby.

Charles had seen it right from the start, he told himself now, entering his nursery and pausing to check the temperature, the moisture of the air and the general feel of the house. All seemed well – which was more than could have been said for the Dubois' nursery, eight years ago. It was as though Elise did not want to handle her baby. She fed her in her cot with a bottle which she held to the child's mouth. No cuddling, no closeness, no skin-to-skin mothering for Elise and little Rochelle.

Charles, who had often felt that he himself was very much an afterthought to his own parents, realised for the first time that he had been truly loved, though not indulged as Maurice had been. He had mentioned the matter to René once or twice, but René was an orphan, brought up by strangers who had valued him merely for his ability to plough and sow, reap and bind. You could not expect René to understand much about parental love. And Elise, Charles finally concluded, was that strange thing, a totally unmaternal woman. She had given birth to her child, had fed her and was bringing her up, but she could not give what she simply did not have. All her love, every last scrap of it, was showered upon René, the man she had chosen, and there was none left over for the little girl who had been, so to speak, thrust upon her. Elise did what she did purely from duty. Hence the small light.

It's a good thing I'm not a father, Charles told himself

50

as he entered the nursery house. Perhaps I'd be even worse at it than René – although at least I do know what love is, and how unfair it is to shut a little girl out. But he had gone about loving all the wrong way. First he had virtually run away from Paris, merely leaving a note for Helen, and then, once his father's funeral was over and he had begun to come out of his morass of self-blame, what had he done? He had *written* to her – written, when he should have dashed across to France and overwhelmed her with flowers, gifts, and his singleminded love.

Because his love *had* been singleminded. Within a month of receiving her refusal he had told himself that he had behaved like an insensitive fool and had gone back to Paris to propose in person, to explain, to woo her into returning with him. To find her gone, her room empty, not even Mavis around, though he had run her to earth in the end, at the Comédie Française, where she had been a bit abrupt, merely telling him that Helen had decamped one night, never to return.

He had come home to Jersey, heartsore. For months he had advertised in all the English national newspapers without getting a single reply. Then he had decided she had gone and he must make the best of it, and had begun, tentatively, to socialise once more.

But his heart had not been in it. He simply was not interested in any other woman as his wife. He did take a mistress, in a half-hearted way, visiting her when he went to market or had some other reason for going into town, until one day he realised he was impatient to get the visit over so he could return to the manor to try something new in his hybridising experiments.

He had never visited her again and had never regretted it. I'm a loner, he told himself now, turning his trays of tiny pots a fraction as he did each day so that the plants would grow upright and not be tempted to lean towards the source of light.

He still went back to Paris from time to time. Half expecting to see her there? Yes, he confessed it, though it would never happen, not now. Fourteen years had passed since they had loved – she was no doubt a plump matron now, married to a rich man who could give her everything she wanted. She had probably forgotten Charles's name, his face, his very existence. But the trips to Paris had a sort of bitter-sweet fascination. He went to their rooms, he walked round Versailles, he haunted the theatre where she had danced and the streets where they had walked, arms round each other. But he never found her and he never expected to do so. He was beginning to let time dull the ache for her, replace her face in his mind with other faces – the flower-faces of his orchids.

He had started to try to breed Pure Madonna out of guilt, because the secret had been lost through his thoughtlessness, but it soon became an obsession with him for its own sake. The flowers were not only beautiful, they were weird, clever, more like animals, as he told Rochelle, than plants. They were brilliant mimics, they often throve more or less on air, and the sheer difficulty of hybridising them was a challenge to anyone who called himself a gardener. He knew, now, that it was not just for his father's sake that he was trying to recreate Pure Madonna; it was for his own. He had produced some lovely hybrids, but the best was yet to come and he waited for these seedlings to reach maturity, to flower, with scarcely controlled impatience.

The hybrids which might turn out to be Pure Madonna were on his left. They had been reared with every care, the tiny, dust-like seeds given to compatible foster-parents so that they would not be inadvertently destroyed by a breath too much of breeze, or a too-zealous watering. That had been three years ago; now they were sturdy, in their own pots, their leaves strong and deep green, their roots not penetrating the rich compost at all but a-tiptoe above it, only touching it through the thick layer of sphagnum. In

52

two years, Charles dreamed, turning the pots, in two years, who knew? Any one of them might be a beautiful new hybrid, any one of them might make his name.

Through the glass, as he turned the corner to walk up the other side of the house, he saw Rochelle approaching. Bob-bobbing along, so full of a sense of achievement and happiness because she had opened the windows in the first glasshouse that he found a smile tugging at his lips. She was small, even for her age, yet by dint of leaping up and stretching she had managed them all.

He did not like children, everyone knew that. He had no patience with them, no urge to hold small bodies in his arms or on his knee. But Rochelle was different, she had a certain something . . . she was not like a child, he told himself defensively, she was as sensitive to the plants as a fully grown gardener would be, and she never prattled, or tried to amuse him or got under his feet. She must play sometimes, he supposed doubtfully, but if she did it was not in his greenhouses. There she was mature, serious, with a mind which drank in all the information he cared to give her much as the orchids drank in their soft water.

Sometimes he wondered whether he was right to allow her to do so much for the plants, but he was intrigued by her affinity with them. She referred to them as 'he' or 'she', talked to them constantly whilst she was in their company, and could undoubtedly diagnose incipient sickness in a plant. She could often suggest a cure, too – a cure which, if questioned, she would maintain the plant itself had asked for, though she did not pretend the plants actually talked to her. Indeed, the few times he had pressed her he had seen by her expression of baffled distress that she had no idea how she knew what she did. And although he did not believe she could communicate with the plants, he accepted that she had an awareness of their needs which he himself lacked. As unicorns are said to trust virgins, so he had begun to believe his orchids trusted Rochelle. At any rate, they were the better for her loving care, and he thought that in an odd sort of way Rochelle was the better for giving it. That the orchids needed her and she needed them filled some small, starved corner in her, a corner which her parents' cool good sense had left high and dry.

The door, opening quietly, brought him round to face her as she slid inside. She came across to him.

'Did you manage?'

'Yes, monsieur. I opened all the windows, and later I could bring the blinds down if you wish. Well, I'm almost sure I could,' she amended, obviously realising that this might be a tough task for one so small. 'I could try . . . I'd like to try.'

'We'll see.' He picked up a plant, turning it this way and that. It was looking good . . . he handed it to his small companion. 'What about that one? It's a hybrid, of course, but I'd imagined that the offspring of phaius and cymbidium would be a little larger, more substantial somehow.' He held it out to Rochelle. 'What do you think?'

Rochelle took the pot and held it close to her cheek. She had very large, dark blue eyes which looked larger than they perhaps were in her small, pale face. He watched her as she closed her lids, bent her head . . . then straightened and looked up at him.

'She's fine, but we should weaken her feed a little, so that'll mean the food of all that batch, won't it? She's growing a bit too fast, that's the trouble. If we keep on feeding her so richly she'll just shoot up and get leggy; you won't want that, I don't suppose.'

'You're right. The feed *is* a little . . .' He broke off to take down the list of instructions on the wall and amend it with a stout black pencil. 'Well done, Rochelle.'

Was it just acute observation? Was her eye so much keener than his that she could see already that the plants were growing too fast? But conjecture was useless; he had been wondering how she did it for two years now and had never found a satisfactory answer.

'Monsieur, can I help you bed them down this evening? I know I can't as a rule, but Maman and Papa will be back very late, Mme Barfleur says, so I don't have to be in bed as early as usual.'

'I don't see why not. I'm repotting some Cattleyas later, and tomorrow young Joseph's coming in to paint the glass roofs with summer cloud. It's more effective than the blinds, and we don't want any losses through sunburn.'

'Oh, thank you,' Rochelle chirruped. 'How are the tiny babies? Have you been up to them yet?'

The 'tiny babies' were the 'fostered' seedlings in the parental pots. Now they were big enough for Charles to count the tiny leaves. In a month or two they could be put out two or three to a pot. Rochelle loved doing that.

'I have, but . . . we'll just walk up again.'

She was an odd little thing, but he enjoyed seeing that sweet smile light up her face, the big eyes sparkle. He glanced at his wristwatch, for he usually gave the second half of the morning and most of the afternoon to the estate, only returning here in the early evening. He really should go straight to the tropical house . . . but they would just take another look at the seedlings.

Presently, their inspection finished once he had opened the windows and at Rochelle's suggestion stood a tray of young odontoglossums down below the staging to give them a break from the sunshine, they made their way to the tropical house. It was the pride of Charles's collection and he paused, as he always did, in the entrance to take a deep breath of the exotic scent of rotting tree stumps, stagnant water and the orchids themselves.

'Shall I get our sprays?' Rochelle called, darting ahead of him. She did not wait for a reply but went straight to the rainwater tank and began filling first the large spray and then her own small one. She handed the large one to

Charles and watched for a moment as he pumped the fine mist into the atmosphere, then followed suit. Charles, walking slowly, spraying steadily, could almost see the fleshy tropicals relishing the treatment; no wonder Rochelle believed that orchids could communicate! Even he, so much more earthbound, could sense the pleasure the orchids seemed to feel as the fine mist beaded leaf and stem.

They worked in companionable silence until lunchtime. Then Charles made his way back to the house, saw Rochelle dance off into the kitchen to be fed by Mme Barfleur, and went on into the dining room.

He sat down to a light meal of clear soup, grilled sea bream and leeks in a cream sauce, followed by Mme Barfleur's home-made ice cream. She was an excellent cook, in the island tradition, and never grumbled that her talents were wasted because she so often cooked for one. She fed the staff equally well, he was sure, and all his food was beautifully prepared and presented.

Charles finished his meal, declined coffee, and went for a slow walk round the garden before starting work in the estate office. As he stared ruminatively at some rose bushes in heavy bud he felt the wind freshen on his cheek. All Jersey men are seamen, so he noted the change of wind direction without even having to think about it. René and Elise might have a livelier sea than they had anticipated on their voyage home. He would make sure a taxi met the ferry, even if it was later than expected.

Charles opened the door into the estate office and crossed to the desk. René was an efficient and careful manager, and knowing that he would be away all day himself had made sure that the books were to hand, book-marks of dark yellow paper in the pages which Charles would most want to see. The maps on the walls were up to date, showing where the fields had been planted and what still remained

56

to be done, so all Charles had to do was sit down behind the desk and draw the ledgers towards him.

He started with the milk yields and was soon absorbed. Outside the sun shone as though it were midsummer instead of spring and the wind freshened, gusted, died.

Charles worked on.

2

In the manor kitchen Rochelle, the housekeeper's grand-daughter Olivia and Mme Barfleur herself sat down to a very different repast with the maids Lucrèce and Emilie. They had leek and potato soup, apple pie and glasses of milk, but it was every bit as delicious, Rochelle thought, as the elaborate meal she had seen Emilie carry through to M. Laurient in the manor dining room.

As they ate, Rochelle glanced round her at the kitchen, almost as familiar to her as the much smaller one at the cottage. It was a huge room, for the scrubbed wooden table which was used for staff meals and the equally large one on which Mme Barfleur did her pastry cooking were almost dwarfed in the cavernous space. It was full of furniture, too. Welsh dressers which held both the kitchen crockery and the fine china used in the dining room, cupboards for every imaginable cooking utensil, hooks crowded with copper-bottomed pans, enormous spoons, huge ladles, sieves, forks, whisks and the like.

It was a cosy place, though, despite its size. The front of the range was usually left open and not only did it warm the room, the orange and yellow flames cheered the eye. The red floor tiles were always well scrubbed, and Mme Barfleur had scatter-rugs here and there, all brightly coloured and very clean. Even the window, which looked out over the stable-yard, had a sill crammed with brightly blooming pot-plants, for Mme Barfleur liked flowers and saw to it that the garden supplied her with what she termed 'something bright' for every month of the year.

Now, in April, she had a good display of short, sturdy tulips and sweet-smelling hyacinths jostling for space, and the colours – scarlet for the tulips and brilliant blue and white for the hyacinths – were not only eye-catching but patriotic as well. Rochelle approved of them, wished her own mother had a bit of colour in their kitchen, regretted that Elise favoured pots of herbs. They smelt delicious, Rochelle admitted, but they were pretty dull to look at whilst you struggled with the washing or wiping up.

The meal over, Mme Barfleur set Lucrèce to washing up and bade the children dry the dishes. Rochelle was as careful as could be, though it was only the kitchen crockery and not the fine, gold-leafed dinner service, but she knew that she could never be as neat and efficient as her friend Olivia.

Olivia was two years older than Rochelle, and they were great friends. She was a typical Jersey beauty, with thickly curling golden-brown hair, large blue eyes, and creamy skin. Rochelle was not a self-conscious child, but she knew that beside her friend she looked very small, thin and plain. She could see no merit in her own hair, which was short, black and silky, nor in her pale skin which was so fine that the veins showed through like blue threads; and her eyes, which were so dark a blue that people often thought them brown, were nothing beside Olivia's big, baby-blue orbs. However, she had managed to convince herself that when she grew up she would look just like Olivia and this satisfied her, for now.

'Grandmère,' Olivia said presently, when their work was finished and they were putting the dried crockery and cutlery away in its respective drawers and cupboards, 'can we go down to the beach in a minute and dig some cockles for our tea? If you'd let us, I could take some home to Maman and you could keep the rest,' she added craftily, for Mme Barfleur frequently grumbled that her daughter, Olivia's mother, did not supply her family with good, home-made food but preferred shop-bought cakes and pies.

Rochelle watched the housekeeper's face hopefully; she

knew as well as Olivia that there was nothing Mme Barfleur relished more than fresh cockles with her home-baked bread and butter, washed down by a cup of hot, strong tea.

Mme Barfleur had been pressing cooked vegetables through a sieve to make a *potage*; now she stopped for a moment, the sieve in one hand, a metal spoon poised above it, whilst she considered the request. She was a large, heavy woman, fond of her own cooking and equally fond of a little nap after a meal. She was also – rather oddly, to Rochelle's mind – a worrier. She doted on Olivia and took the responsibility for the two children very seriously indeed, but on the other hand if she did not let them go off to the beach she would feel it her duty to keep them occupied somehow all through the long, warm afternoon.

'Cockling? Well . . . which beach?' she asked at last. 'I won't have you going all the way to the big one by yourselves and there's no one free to take you, not with René and Elise away. But if you mean the little one . . . can you dig cockles there? . . . then I dare say that would be all right.'

'Thank you, Grandmère,' Olivia said quickly, before Mme Barfleur could change her mind. 'We'll go to the little beach, of course. It's too far to walk to the big one, and anyway the cockles are huge from the other. Aren't they, Chelle?'

'Yes . . . and when we've got the cockles we can hunt for shells,' Rochelle cried eagerly. She had a collection of oyster shells, mostly found on the beach, though one or two had been begged from Mme Barfleur when M. Laurient had had oysters for lunch. She thought that nothing exceeded the thrill of finding one on the sand, its soft, pearly lining like a fairy's bath, so smooth and silky it felt to the touch, whilst the outside was so rough and pitted that the contrast was almost unbelievable.

'Very well then, you can go to the beach this afternoon,'

60

Mme Barfleur said. 'But although it's the holidays, you'll have to give me a hand tomorrow afternoon. I'll be making butter, and curd cheese. I could do with some help from the pair of you.'

Olivia and Rochelle knew that shaking cream into butter could be exhausting work, but any job done together was more fun than one done apart so they agreed quite happily to help. Besides, working in the dairy brought its own reward: there would be a pat of butter and probably a little jug of cream to carry home to their parents, and the Augeuil clotted cream or Mme Barfleur's delicious butter was a welcome addition to anyone's diet.

'Have you finished? Come on then, Chelle,' Olivia commanded, wanting to get away before her grandmother changed her mind. 'We'll go and get our buckets and the cockling rakes.'

The two children hurried out of the kitchen and across to the tack-room. Old Albert, who had worked at Augeuil Manor for sixty years and kept all the harness and saddles in first-class order, was also custodian of such things as hoofpicks, ice-skates, cricket bats and cockling impedimenta, for when the Laurient brothers were young all their gear for outdoor sports had been kept with the riding things in the tack-room. The children fetched the buckets and rakes, then went back to the kitchen. Mme Barfleur insisted on their donning the sensible jerseys which both possessed, and handed Olivia a bag full of food to be consumed down on the beach.

'Come on, Chelle,' Olivia said, ready first as always, whilst Rochelle was still struggling to pull her jersey down round her skinny little body. 'We're going to get enough cockles for *everyone* . . . we'll load the buckets to the brim!'

'All right, I'm ready,' Rochelle panted, hurrying across the stable-yard after her friend. 'Will we get enough cockles for M. Laurient?'

'Of course not, Chelle; what an idea! He's gentry, and gentry eat oysters and lobsters, not cockles and winkles.'

'That's silly. Oysters and lobsters come from the sea, the same as the cockles,' Rochelle objected. 'I bet he eats cockles!'

'No he won't; cockles take too long,' Olivia said, skipping ahead as they came to the gate which led into the meadows they would have to cross to get to the beach. 'The gentry like to eat at once. They don't want to have to fiddle with teeny things like cockles.'

'Then why did he dig cockles when he was a little boy, with this very rake?' Rochelle demanded, feeling sure she was about to be proved right for a change. 'Answer me that, Miss Clever!'

Her father had once said that to Rochelle and she had been very taken with the expression, though she had not found an opportunity to use it before. Olivia, however, had an answer for most things and this was no exception.

'Why, when he was a little boy he wasn't gentry, you duffer,' she said calmly. 'Don't you ever *think*, Chelle? I say, the cows are coming over this way . . . what shall we do?'

Rochelle, born and bred on the estate, knew very well that the animals were merely curious and would not harm them, but she did not intend to let Olivia have things all her own way.

'You walk slowly on, towards the stile,' she commanded. 'They know me, so I can run over there and haroosh them back where they belong. You'll be quite safe once you're in the lane.'

She suited the action to the words, running across the grass towards the cows, who immediately backed away, expressions of mild alarm crossing their pretty fawn faces. Rochelle made vague noises and whirled her arms a bit and then trotted back to her friend, who had gained the

62

further side of the meadow and was now perched on top of the stile.

'There you are,' Rochelle said, climbing the stile in her turn as Olivia dropped down into the leafy, meandering little lane which led to the shore. 'Nothing to worry about; they just wanted to see who we were. I say, I wonder if there are tadpoles in the pond still, or whether they've all turned into little frogs?'

There was a deep and fascinating pond beside the lane which, weeks before, had been swarming with tadpoles. Rochelle liked most creatures but Olivia did not, so the older girl seized back the initiative by forbidding her friend to push her way through the hawthorn hedge which separated the lane from the pond.

'It won't do, Chelle,' she said. 'Either we want to dig lots of cockles or we don't . . . and it's no good saying you'd rather find the frogs, because Grandmère wouldn't be too pleased if we went back empty-handed.'

'Oh, all right,' Rochelle said. The two girls wandered down the lane, the buckets clanking against their legs, the jerseys very soon feeling much too hot despite the sea breeze which lifted the hair from their foreheads. 'Can I take my jersey off, Livia?'

'Not until we're on the beach,' Olivia decided. 'Oh, look, there's the gap – race you!'

As a challenge it was rather foolhardy, for though Olivia was unquestionably the larger and stronger Rochelle was a good deal faster on her feet. Now she flew along the lane, the bucket bumping against her knees and her feet stirring the dust, whilst Olivia thundered behind her, complaining now and again that she had ricked her ankle, that it wasn't fair, and that she had a stitch in her side and must rest.

But Rochelle had reached the gap and was content, now, to wait. She stood in the gap, which was framed with scratchy marram grass, and simply gazed out to sea.

The bay was small, a half-moon of sand with arms of

63

dark rock stretching out into the sea and lots of enticing rock-pools. There was anchorage for boats to one side, seaweed-draped. The sea was right out, and on the horizon the waves danced as if they longed to come in, over the rich, oozing mud, over the shell-dimpled strand, over the wave-ribbed beach itself.

Without taking her eyes off the scene before her, Rochelle kicked off her sandals and began to heave her jersey over her head. Olivia, arriving beside her, tried rather breathlessly to remind her that jerseys were not to be removed until they reached the sand, but Rochelle had had enough of being bossed for one afternoon and tore it off, then tied its arms round her waist so it would not impede her progress as she climbed down to the beach, for the narrow path was steep and she was already burdened with bucket, rake, and a share of the bulging paper bag with their tea in it.

'It's just right for cockles,' she said as she knotted the arms securely about her. 'You can almost see them bubbling in the mud from here. Come on, Livia!'

She did not wait for Olivia's response but charged down the path, sure-footed as a goat, arriving on the sand long before Olivia, who came at a more respectable speed. Once on the flat, Rochelle raced for the rowing boat which was drawn high up the beach, beyond reach of the hungriest tide. It belonged to the estate but the children were not yet allowed to take it out; they usually left their outer clothing on its sandy wooden bottom and pushed their food under the thwarts out of the sun. Today, Rochelle's sandals and jersey quickly followed the food, and then she tucked her skirt into her voluminous knickers and turned to survey Olivia, who was following suit, her face a little flushed as she struggled with a skirt both longer and fuller than Rochelle's brief skimpy one.

'Are you ready, Livia? Shall we go down to the mud? The fattest cockles live there.'

'I *know*,' Olivia said, not throwing her clothes in a higgledy-piggledy heap on the bottom boards as Rochelle had done but folding her jumper neatly and placing her shoes carefully side by side. 'We'll go down now, but don't let's run. The bucket's made a pink mark on my leg.'

'All right,' Rochelle said submissively. She felt she had done quite well for one day. The two of them, now suitably attired for cockling, set off for the tideline.

Once there they scanned the mud with experienced eyes and began to drag the cockling rakes through the ditches and up the ridges, bringing the cockles, some still bubbling, to the surface. The fatly ridged white shells clattered into the buckets, while Rochelle's narrow feet sank into the mud right up to the ankles, and Olivia, balancing carefully on the ridges, pointed out to her young friend that if the tide suddenly turned she would be caught, sure as sure. Rochelle, raking and harvesting, only smiled. Much she cared! Everyone got muddy when they were cockling. She raked until her bucket was piled high and nearly impossible to carry, then she flung her implement down.

'Mine's full now, Livvy,' she said happily. 'I can't get it any fuller – it's fuller than the brim, it's in a pointed cone! Can we paddle for a bit to wash the mud off?'

Olivia, who had also filled her bucket, pushed damp curls off her forehead and nodded wearily.

'Yes, I suppose we might as well . . . you'll have to get clean before we can go back up the beach.'

'Had we better carry the buckets back to the boat first, though?' Rochelle said as she stood hers down. 'Look how it's sinking in! It'll probably have disappeared by the time we get back.'

Olivia heaved an exaggerated sigh.

'Oh, all right, I suppose we'd better. We could have a look in the bag, see what Grandmère's packed for us!'

Mme Barfleur belonged to the school of thought which believes that a child deprived of food for more than a couple of hours will probably die of inanition, so both girls had high expectations of the bag, and they were not disappointed. When they opened it it was to find two of Mme Barfleur's delicious beef patties, two eating apples and a large slice each of rich fruit cake. Rochelle regretted that there was no lemonade, but appreciated that the bottle would have made the bag too heavy for them to carry. She seized her apple and bit into it, grateful for the sharp juice, then jammed the cake and the patty into the pocket of her apron. She would eat them as she paddled and searched for shells.

It was delightful in the water, and the tide was sufficiently far out for the children to reach the island in the bay without once getting wet above the knees. They clambered inside the little reef of rocks and began to search the pools, which were deep and shaggy with seaweed, rich with life.

Rochelle crouched by a shelf on which anemones waved; the snake ones with their sinister, trunk-like appendages and the fat scarlet ones like living chrysanthemums. She put an exploratory finger into the centre of one above the waterline and it closed tight like a shiny red button. It felt like a strawberry jelly but it would not be teased into opening, the mouth in the centre tightening in disapproval at her touch, so she put her hand into the water, where the anemones were in full flower and snatched at her fingers with their light, intense embrace.

Rochelle teased each of the living blooms in the same way, until her finger had been clutched and spat out in disgust by all the denizens of the shelf, and then she chased a tiny green crab-baby underwater until it buried itself in the soft sand. Only then did she uncurl herself from her absorbed crouch and wander over to where Olivia was poking in a forest of dark seaweed with a piece of salt-soaked stick.

'What've you found?' she asked curiously. 'A big crab, or a fish?'

Olivia straightened, showing her friend a face flushed from long bending.

'It doesn't want me to know what it is,' she said disgustedly. 'It keeps well under the weed, and it's so thick here there's no dislodging it. I can't even wade; the water's too deep.'

'If I stand where you are and poke with your stick, and you come over here and put your face near the surface and stare, you're bound to see something,' Rochelle said. 'I always hope for water babies myself, or a very small mermaid, but it's usually only a crab or a lobster.'

'Yes, all right. I mean, I know fairies don't exist, but lots of sensible people believe in mermaids and water babies,' Olivia said, revealing that she, too, lived in such hope. 'Come on, then. You climb up and I'll climb down.'

But they were barely settled in their new positions when the calm of the pool was disturbed by a small crested wave racing across its surface. Both girls straightened, albeit reluctantly.

'Oh dear, the tide's turned,' Olivia said. 'Now we'll *never* know, and it probably was something really rare and special. Come on.'

With one accord the children turned for the shore. Though neither of them possessed a wristwatch they had learned to tell the time accurately enough by the position of the sun and the state of the tide. Now they knew without having to think about it that in order to be home in time for tea they must return to the stranded boat. Once there, there were still legs and feet to be dried, socks and sandals to be put on once more, and the heavy buckets of cockles to be carried all the way back to the kitchen at Augeuil Manor.

Whilst they shook out their skirts and hitched their knickers, dragged low by the weight of material stuffed into them, back to waist-level, they chatted in the inconsequential way children will when they are tired but happy, with comfortably full tummies but the prospect of a good tea still ahead.

'We could have got some winkles whilst we were on the island,' Olivia said, vigorously shaking her jersey to free it from sand. 'Not that I like picking them – they're too like snails.'

'Oh, snails . . . 'member what your maman and mine told us about snails in the market at St Malo?'

Both girls giggled. A year ago, their parents had gone off on a shopping trip just before Christmas. In the market at St Malo, whilst buying Christmas fruit from one of the stalls, Elise had noticed a string bag bulging with snails hanging from one of the struts of the stall. What had intrigued her, though, had been that a good score of the erstwhile occupants of the bag had made off and were feasting on the nearest vegetables. When they had pointed this out to the stallholder, however, he had shown no surprise or annoyance at all.

'What does it matter?' he had said, yawning and scratching the side of his huge stomach. 'If there are any left unsold they'll come home with me on the cabbages or in the nets. Either way I'll make my profit, whether from fatter snails or from selling my vegetables.'

This had particularly amused Rochelle as she had heard old M. La Sorgue, the gardener at the manor, grumbling mightily over the depredations snails made in his kitchen garden. But this fat peasant could not have cared less. As he said, a ravaged cabbage meant fatter snails. She had told M. La Sorgue the story, but he had merely remarked that those who ate snails were savages anyway.

'Yes, I remember. It's funny when you think about it that the thought of eating snails is horrid, yet we both love cockles and winkles and they're only sea-snails really, when all's said and done.'

'Ye-es, but cockles don't have little faces, like snails,' Rochelle said. 'Mind, if I saw a snail in the glasshouses I'd stamp on it quick as quick. I wouldn't let it feast on my dear ones!'

They were now dressed and ready to move on. Heavily laden, heeling sideways, they began to trudge up the cliff path.

'Oh, you and those plants!' Olivia said indulgently. 'Anyone would think they were alive to hear you talk!'

'They are alive. More alive than some people . . . and a lot more alive than snails or cockles!'

But though she said the words she kept her voice low, and Olivia gave no sign of having heard. Olivia didn't like orchids, Rochelle knew. She thought there was something nasty about them, even whilst agreeing that some had wonderful scents and others brilliant colours.

'The leaves are too fat and sleek, and the flowers look as if they're sneering at you,' she had once said. Rochelle had forgiven but she could not forget.

Head down, feet splayed inside her sandals to get a good purchase on the path, she slogged up towards the lane, looking forward to the end of the climb – the bucket was heavy and had to be kept level, or some of the harvested shells would undoubtedly fall out. What was more, when they reached the pond beside the lane they would also reach the little stream which fed it. The water was cool and clear; it would be good to quench the thirst which the apple had done little to allay.

They reached the top and paused for breath; Olivia was deep pink, her chest heaving up and down, and even Rochelle's slight form was showing a certain amount of strain. But they set off again, both knowing that this time they would stop by the stream and slake their thirst.

They were actually kneeling and drinking water thirstily from cupped hands when Rochelle gasped. Water cascaded down her front as she stared, wide-eyed, at her friend,

69

drops running down her pointed chin and plopping on to her dress.

'What was that, Livvy?'

'What was what?'

'Didn't you hear it? You must have! A sound like brakes screeching and then the most awful scream.'

'I didn't hear anything. Only a blackbird telling all the others that we're here,' Olivia said. 'Oh, dear, now my bucket's fallen over.' She righted it and began picking up spilt shells. 'Was it my bucket clattering, perhaps? Don't tell me you heard the cockles scream when they fell!'

'No . . . but they do scream,' Rochelle said, wiping a hand across her wet face and picking up her own bucket. 'I've heard them, often. When your gran'mère and my maman cook them they scream when the water gets hot, really they do.'

'They don't do anything of the sort, silly,' Olivia said impatiently. 'When they get put on the stove and the water boils they die, but their shells squeak. Now!'

'Well . . . I don't go into the kitchen any more when Maman's cooking cockles,' Rochelle admitted. 'Nor into the yard when they're killing chickens or pigs. And once the grey cat had too many kittens and Papa put them in water . . . but I try never to think of that.'

Olivia shuddered sympathetically; she agreed that grown-ups could be very heartless, and then she suggested they play 'I spy' and a game was promptly started. But Rochelle knew that Olivia did not truly understand the kittens' agony. She herself had known the terrified flutter of the heart as the water closed over them, the dreadful finality of hope as it invaded small lungs, closed small eyes, the sudden limpness of the innocent, day-young bodies . . . for a moment she had hated her father and his indifference over the miracle that was those kittens. It had been such a pointless execution, for the grey cat's offspring were always excellent mousers and lived off the farm save for a saucer

70

of milk morning and evening. Who would have been worse off had those kittens been allowed to live?

Olivia had forgotten the game and was talking again, and Rochelle was glad to turn from her own thoughts and listen. Olivia liked animals, but she did not have the fellow-feeling for them which Rochelle thought she herself had been born with. Sometimes she felt she knew just what it meant to be one kitten too many, and then she chided herself, for she had no brothers or sisters and her parents looked after her well and were very fond of her. But they did not have feelings like hers for animals. Indeed, the only person who came anywhere near her in that respect was M. Laurient. When he lifted an orchid from its pot he held it as though he valued each thread-like rootlet and did not want to break any of them. When he held a day-old chick in his hand he attended to the pitter of its tiny heart, never holding with fierce indifference. Only he allowed Rochelle the free expression of her feelings, knowing that he would never jeer, though he might smile from time to time. He encouraged her to give an opinion and did not only pretend to listen, as Maman and Papa did, whilst really attending to something else. M. Laurient really listened; even took her advice, sometimes. I wish M. Laurient was my papa, Rochelle found herself thinking, and was shocked at her own wickedness. Good girls loved their parents and never wanted them to be any different – why can't I be like that, Rochelle thought guiltily. It isn't that I don't love them, because I really do; it's just that sometimes I wonder if they wouldn't be equally happy without me.

'. . . so I thought I might wear my hair in bunches, just for school, you know, only Maman says it's plaits that keep one's hair curly and I do think it's nice to have curls so I suppose I'll have to put bunches off until I'm older and my hair is different.' Olivia stroked a thick ringleted curl. 'Why don't you plait yours? It's getting quite long, and it might curl if you did.'

71

Rochelle jerked back to the present, to the lane, the high, grassy banks where violets and primroses grew amidst the grasses and where, in the summer, she and Olivia would find wild strawberries. She sighed at the thought of her hair. It would never curl, no matter what Maman might do. Occasionally Elise got fed up with her daughter's rain-straight locks and Rochelle was forced to spend anxious and fretful hours sitting with wire curlers in her hair, forbidden to move her head because as soon as she did a curler would slip out and leave her with one lank lock.

'Maman has tried to plait my hair,' she said apologetically now, 'but the plaits won't stay. They come undone when the ribbon slips off . . . I've got very slippery hair, I'm afraid.'

'Yes, it isn't a bit like mine,' Olivia agreed. She bounced her curls in the palm of one hand, a curiously mature and coquettish gesture. 'But your hair feels awfully nice, Chelle, even if it is rather ordinary looking.'

'Does it?' Rochelle, who brushed her hair morning and evening and never gave it a thought in between, tried to look gratified by this crumb of praise, but she could not help reflecting that people rarely feel each other's hair, whereas they look at it all the time. And Maman, as she brushed and combed and tutted, was apt to complain that no kirby-grip or tortoiseshell slide or ribbon made would stay put longer than a few seconds in her daughter's straight and shiny locks. She made it sound as though Rochelle deliberately polished her hair into a state of civil disobedience each morning, Rochelle thought sadly.

The children came up the last stretch of lane but did not attempt the stile with their full buckets. Instead, they went the longer way round, skirting the house itself, going through the little pear orchard which a long-ago lady of the manor had planted so that she might have a loft full of the delicious fruit, and so to the yard. And there was Mme Barfleur standing in the doorway, clearly waiting for them.

72

'Grandmère, we've got heaps!' Olivia shouted as soon as they were within earshot. 'Shall we bring them straight in, or do you want to wash them out first?'

'Bring them in, dears,' Mme Barfleur said. She stood aside to let them pass, and as Rochelle came level with her she put out a hand and smoothed the soft, shining black hair off the child's forehead. With her touch, Rochelle felt a thrill of foreknowledge spear through her, so strong and frightening that she thumped the bucket down on the kitchen floor and turned to stare up at the older woman.

'What is it, madame? What's happened?'

'There's been a . . . a sorry accident. I'm afraid, dearest, that your maman and papa are . . . are . . .'

Her voice faltered to a halt. Rochelle felt her own small face grow pinched and white as the words Mme Barfleur feared to say said themselves in her mind.

'They're dead, aren't they?' she said, her voice flat and toneless. 'My maman and papa are dead.'

'They took a taxi – it was involved in a fatal crash only minutes out of the port. My dear, the shock has been dreadful . . . come and sit down. Emilie will make you a cup of tea . . . Emilie!'

Rochelle stood where she was, trying to take in what had happened. A car accident had killed them both – both? Olivia timidly put an arm round her shoulders; she knew what Olivia had done, had seen the movement out of the corner of her eye, but she could feel no touch, no warmth. It was as if her body remained in the kitchen but the rest of her was far away, curled down inside herself trying to make sense of what she had heard.

'Poor Chelle . . . sit down, do.'

Olivia murmured the words, her voice faint, a little frightened. Rochelle continued to stand. Maman and Papa were dead. Dead? But they could not possibly be dead. She had seen them only that morning – Maman looking very pretty, her beautiful dark hair curled around her head, in a smart brown suit with a cream blouse and little cream shoes, Papa handsome and glowing with bustle and importance; he loved a day in France. They had been going to buy some pigs for fattening, to investigate a new type of tractor recommended for hill ploughing, to talk to a man who was interested in processing seaweed for use on the land. She had heard the talk over the past few days ... they had so looked forward to their outing, what God could have been cruel enough to snatch it from them?

'Rochelle, my dear ... come to me.' Mme Barfleur pulled Rochelle close to her big, comfortable bosom and Rochelle did not resist, but she did not go willingly, either. She simply let herself be pulled about, like a rag doll. 'Petite, you can't take it in yet. I understand. A terrible thing has happened to you, a terrible thing, and it's more than your mind can accept. But Maman and Papa are happy with Jesus; their sufferings are over.'

Firmly, though politely, Rochelle pulled free. She walked to the back door and opened it. Standing there looking out, she saw that the sky was as blue as it had been earlier, the sunshine as golden. Mme Barfleur had said that Maman and Papa were with Jesus. Somehow, that made the whole thing seem final, a reality which she must accept. Somewhere within her there was pain, waiting for the release of tears. But even deeper was another conviction: once again, Maman and Papa had gone off somewhere together, leaving her behind.

Alone.

3

Four days passed. Rochelle ate meagrely, spoke less, seemed to be enmeshed in a nightmare from which she could not wake. Her whole way of life had been changed overnight; she had no certainties any more, no normal, foreseeable future. She felt lost, and terribly alone.

She attended the funeral wearing a hastily cobbled-up grey dress which made her look so thin and pathetic that people seemed shy of speaking to her. Not that it mattered; seeing the world as though from behind a pane of thick and insulating glass, nothing seemed to affect her.

She had been told she could not go back to the cottage in the stable-yard and in her present dazed state she did not think to ask why. She merely lay down each night on a camp bed in Mme Barfleur's room and slept and woke, sometimes roused by the dawn light, at other times by Mme Barfleur's astonishing snores. She had not seen M. Laurient, who had been sucked into a whirl of activity, arranging for the bodies to be transported back to the island, seeing to the funeral, doing René's work as well as his own. She had not even visited the orchids, save on the first day of her bereavement when she had gone briefly to the glasshouses in search of M. Laurient, only to be told that he had gone to France.

It had seemed like the final straw; was she to lose him, too? Had her wicked thought in wishing him her father lost René his life? Would it now lose M. Laurient his life in turn? Until she heard that he had arrived back safely she was frozen with fear, and only when she glimpsed him crossing the long lawn did the fear melt and a more natural sorrow make itself felt.

75

But now, on the fifth day, she woke as dawn greyed the sky in the east and slid out of bed, padding across the cold lino to the chair on which her clothes had been placed the previous evening. She put on the grey dress since it was there, and her long black lisle stockings and the black button shoes, but even though she was only just awake she was aware of a change in herself. She had wept at the funeral, released by the sorrow about her and by the words of the service. She had wept into her pillow at night, before sleeping, and it was as if tears needed to be shed before she could pick up her life once more. Now, dressing stealthily so as not to disturb Mme Barfleur, she decided to go straight to the cottage and take off the grey dress. She had other clothes, all of which fitted her better, and she had a sudden vision of Elise at that moment which greatly comforted her.

May the Good God have mercy on me, the child looks a perfect fright, Elise would have said. *It's a fine summery day . . . she should be in her old blue gingham with the calico apron. Run along, Chelle, and dress yourself properly.*

Maman wanted what was best for me; she couldn't help loving Papa so much that I seemed a bit of a nuisance sometimes, Rochelle told herself now, astonished that it could, in the end, be so simple. There had been no lack in herself, but perhaps too much good in her father.

Creeping down the stairs, crossing the carpeted landing with an astonished look about her – for she could not remember actually seeing this part of the manor on the other occasions she had passed through it – Rochelle felt as though she had been ill for days and had only just recovered. Down in the kitchen, with the range warming the room and the smell of yesterday's meals comfortingly familiar, she paused for a moment to look around her before struggling with the bolts on the big back door. The kitchen cat, in her basket before the range, was nursing four kittens; they all looked up at her, ever hopeful, but she only smiled at them. Mme Barfleur always drew the curtains back before she went to bed at night so the room was gently grey, the plants on the windowsill beginning to claim back their natural colours from the night's uniform blacks and whites. Will I live here for always, now, Rochelle wondered, in the kitchen with Mme Barfleur, Emilie and Lucrèce? What would happen to their cottage, to her own small room, to the box of toys and the battered belongings which her mother had owned as a child?

But a child has no voice in its destiny; Rochelle was well aware of that. She drew back the bolts and slipped out, ran across the dew-wet paving and tried the kitchen door. It was unlocked. She opened it, slipped inside, then shut it. She turned to face inwards . . . and felt her heart give a great leap of shock.

The room was empty. Oh, the chairs, table and dresser were there, but all the comforting normality of food hanging from the beams, a clutter of coats and sticks and boots in one corner, herbs on the windowsill, the cat in her basket . . . they were gone. The room had an air of cleanliness which Rochelle found positively offensive. Who had done this? How could they take, not only her parents, but her home, too? She ran across the kitchen, no longer bothered that she might make too much noise, and clattered up the stairs. She ignored the main bedroom and threw open the sloping door of her own room.

It was horribly tidy and the bedding had been taken from the narrow bed, but it was still discernibly her room. Rochelle let a huge sigh of relief escape her, then went to the cupboard. She opened it and there were her clothes, complete even to a sunbonnet she had not worn for ages and the big rubber boots she would grow into in another year or so.

Carefully, but as quickly as she could, Rochelle took off the grey dress, the stockings and the button shoes and slipped into her blue gingham and calico, her old jersey for warmth, and her sandals. Then she looked curiously round her room. Odd, how it seemed different, even a little unwelcoming, the place which had once been her own particular retreat.

She headed for the stairs, then hesitated. She put her head round the door of the main bedroom, staring yet shy, feeling very much an intruder here.

The bed had been stripped in this room, and by the general look of it most other things had gone too. Certainly the clothes cupboard was empty, the door gaping open, and all the dressing-table ornaments, the silver-framed pictures, the hairbrushes and combs, her mother's scent-bottles, had disappeared. Slowly, Rochelle began to descend the stairs. She did not mind that the bedroom had been emptied, because her parents would not mind either, now they were with Jesus, but she was a little curious as to why. Who would take the things and where would they put them? Her own clothing and toys had been left but her bedding had gone. Why? And why remove the comfortable jumble of a lived-in home which had once adorned the kitchen? It did not make sense. She would have to ask Mme Barfleur what was going on.

Properly dressed now, to her way of thinking, Rochelle left the cottage and crossed the yard once more. She went through the walled kitchen garden, bypassed the herb garden, and plunged on to the long lawn. The lawn sloped and was dotted with great trees which made it look very beautiful, though M. La Sorgue cursed them when he was trying to mow, as he cursed the rocks which suddenly erupted from the turf at the far end. He would have liked to pull them out like rotten teeth from a healthy mouth, but M. Laurient told him they were rooted in the bones of the earth itself and could not be moved. Rochelle was glad; she thought the rocks delightful, especially since they were good to climb, and would have been upset had M. La Sorgue ever had his way.

She ran down the long lawn now, her feet soon soaked, for the turf was grey with dew, only her footsteps, as she looked back, brilliant green to show where she had been. First one out, Rochelle thought exultantly; no one else is even up yet, in all of Augeuil Manor!

The ducks were about, though. As she ran she heard the beat of their wings, *whish, whish,* overhead and saw a pair of mallards making their way down the lawn, as she was, towards the lake at the bottom. She stopped for a moment and heard the long *whoosh* as they landed on the water, saw the glass of the surface become troubled, and then she veered to her left, hurried through an arm of the orchard and plunged into the woods.

It was beautiful here, even in the early light, but Rochelle did not linger, despite seeing as she ran various enticing things . . . a big bunch of fleshy brown flowers growing on the trunk of a tree, a thickening in a thorn bush which could be a bird's nest, a blur of colour which might mean that the early purple orchids which grew at that particular spot were in flower. She had an appointment to keep, a promise to herself.

Through the woodland and out of it, on to a narrow, steep-dropping lane. A water lane, with a stream running beside it, and a pond, a deep and sinister affair where no children, however foolhardy, played. It was called the Devil's Dip and had a fearsome reputation, but Rochelle valued it mainly for the family of water-rats who lived in the bank and could regularly be seen, by the quiet and slow-moving, swimming on their various errands across its dark depths.

Now, however, she scarcely gave it a glance. She hurried on, and the lane dipped and fell again before emerging from the trees which had shrouded her going and she was on an open, gorsy clifftop, with the track looping casually down towards the sea thundering on the rocks below.

The lane would have taken Rochelle right down to the

shore – though very soon it stopped being a lane and became a narrow and treacherous footpath – but about fifty feet above the sea there was a wide ledge, well fenced, from which you could look down on to the boiling cauldron of waves and rocks beneath. Rochelle stopped here, a trifle breathless, and looked expectantly out to sea. Her father had once told her that to watch the sunrise here was one of the best experiences one could have, and she had never watched a summer sunrise. She had been forbidden to come here alone, promised that one day, when she was older, René would bring her to see the sunrise and then take her down to where she could see for herself how the violence of the waves had formed tunnels and channels in the primeval rock, but now this would – could – never happen. She felt that in one blow all her promises of good behaviour, never to come here alone, had been lifted from her. She was disobeying no one by watching the sunrise from this ledge and then continuing on down to the shore. If she waited until the adults had sorted themselves out there would be other rules, more prohibitions. She would make this one gesture of defiance, and then she would settle down under whatever yoke they placed on her.

There was a long line of gold on the horizon now, which was beginning to flame blood-red against the silver-blue of the sea.

Rochelle settled down to watch.

Charles Laurient had been stunned by the death of his old friend and his wife, and then he had been dragged into such a welter of duties that his thoughts for Rochelle had all been of the variety which promises to do something tomorrow. He had no idea what to do with the child, his first impulse – to let things continue as they were – being out of the question since she could scarcely live alone in the cottage. A second idea, that she must have relatives who would care for her, had been proved equally impracticable at the funeral yesterday. The child's aunt, who lived in St Helier in a small terraced house with no garden and a view of the other side of the street, had made it clear that she considered herself in every way unsuitable to take charge of a young girl. Indeed, she was not, in fact, Rochelle's aunt but her great-aunt, and had been retired from school-teaching some three years. Besides, Laurient could not bear to think of the youngster in a situation so alien. And Mme Barfleur, though sympathetic, had made it clear that she, too, considered herself to be no suitable person to have charge of Rochelle.

However, on the estate there was a childless couple, the Mendes, who ran their smallholding efficiently but always seemed to have time to spare for any youngster who needed a bit of mothering. During harvest-time the couple would take in a boy who wanted summer work and treat him like a son, giving him not merely work but attention and affection too. If they would agree to have Rochelle it might well be the best solution. She would not be on the spot, but it would be a simple matter for her to come over to the manor two or three times a week to see Mme Barfleur, her friend Olivia and, of course, the orchids.

Laurient had been awake since the birds first started to murmur in the eaves, but now he decided to get up and do his morning round of the orchid houses. Then he would be free, after breakfast, to go and see the Mendes and make his suggestion. It was only fair to the child, who must be pretty unhappy and beginning to worry, too, about what her future might hold.

As soon as he was dressed he made his way downstairs through the silent house. He was outside and about to cross the kitchen garden to start work in the glasshouses when he spotted Rochelle. She was in her old blue dress and apron and she was running.

He did not know why this should make him uneasy, but it did. It was early, yet if ever there was purpose in a child's attitude it was in Rochelle's now. He remembered with a horrid sense of foreboding what a terrible shock she had had, what tragedy had suddenly robbed her short life of its meaning and purpose. So what was she doing, out so early and alone? She must have given Mme Barfleur the slip . . . he had better call out to her, fetch her back.

Yet he knew he would not do so even as the thought crossed his mind. She had been stunned, subdued, at the funeral yesterday, but now her step was light, her head up. No, he would follow her; perhaps her expedition was innocent and lighthearted enough. Children were odd little creatures; he had never pretended to understand them. Perhaps she needed this time alone, instead of being perpetually surrounded, as she had been over the past four days.

He set off after her, across the long lawn, past the rocks rearing out of the turf. His legs were longer than hers, and his stride, a countryman's pace, ate up the miles, but she was moving fast. He caught a glimpse of her in the orchard and saw that she was crossing into the woodland, and then she disappeared amongst the trees.

Reaching the trees, he was at a loss for a moment which way to go. She had trodden softly; there was no sound ahead of him . . . and then he remembered the Devil's Dip. Surely she had not gone there? Local rumours abounded, but he did remember that ten years ago a girl had drowned herself there. She had been pregnant and the boy had found himself another woman and left the island with her. He broke into a trot, finding that his heart was thudding and anxiety had brought sweat out on his forehead. Surely . . . she was such a happy child . . .

He came out on to the lane and hurried towards the Devil's Dip. It lay quiet in the steadily strengthening light. No child stood above it, nothing disturbed its dark calm. With a lighter heart Laurient went on, and then he remembered the dangers of the path down to the shore at this point, the fearful height of the cliffs, and the ferocity of the sea against the rocks far below. Once more, he began to hurry.

He came out of the trees and saw her ahead of him, sauntering along now, no longer hurrying. He saw her reach the ledge and settle herself against the fence, elbows spread, chin on hands. From behind he saw her silhouetted as the sun edged up and up and the sea was flooded with red and gold, so beautiful that his eyes watered – or he told himself they watered – and he had to blink to clear them.

He had kept well back, so that he could dodge behind a rock if she turned suddenly to make her way home, but even so he could hear her small, clear voice though he could not hear what she said. She raised her arms and shouted something, then turned away. The sun had risen fully now, and the light was almost blinding across the polished surface of the sea.

Laurient dodged back out of sight. Not for worlds would he have let her think herself spied on. But he heard no sound of her coming up the steep lane after him and risked another peep.

She was gone. The ledge was empty; the sun rose with no spectator standing there to see its splendour.

For a moment, horror gripped him; then he ran as fast as he could down the remainder of the lane and on to the ledge. He did not know quite what he expected to see – a tiny figure, crushed on the rocks? – but what he actually saw was Rochelle's back view as she hurried down the narrow, twisting path towards the shore.

This time he followed her at once, not troubling to keep out of sight. What on earth was the crazy child doing? He knew very well that her parents had forbidden her to come here – had it not always been forbidden to children, probably time out of mind? He could remember his own parents telling their boys that they would have the hide off them if they came down the Devil's Dip path – when they were older, perhaps, but until then they must be content with safer playgrounds, and the island abounded with those.

Of course, that was it! Little devil that she was, she would naturally take the first opportunity to see what all the fuss was about. She had no papa, now, to take her to see the sunrise as he and Maurice had been taken by a father who realised that to forbid a six-year-old was one thing, but to forbid boys of twelve and fourteen was tantamount to daring them to come.

But still, even merely looking was dangerous. The path was liable to cliff-falls, and there were several places where you had to jump a sizeable gap in order to continue down without a sudden death-plunge. What was more, she would never get up the path again. She might be able to jump downwards but she would never manage the same leap on the upward climb.

The wind was very fierce and strong now. He could not run for fear of frightening her into a fall, nor call for the same reason. All he could do was follow, heart in mouth, and pray that she would see reason, turn back. She was concentrating totally on her progress, so what with the sound of the wind and the thunder of the sea she was very unlikely to hear him following.

She reached the first big gap in the path and stood stock still for a second, forefinger in mouth, gazing down. She'll realise she can't make it – she's an intelligent kid, Laurient told himself, but he was relaxing too soon. Decisively she did what he had never even considered – she swung herself over the edge of the path on to the rocks and began to climb down them, surefooted as a goat, not appearing to hesitate at all, though she tested each foothold before letting it take her weight. You could tell she was island born and bred, Laurient thought with more than a trace of pride; she was as at home on the rocks as she was in his glasshouses, with never a trace of fear of the treacherous drop.

He dared not follow lest he kick loose rock on to her head, so he kept to the path, jumping the gap with only a momentary coldness in the pit of his stomach. And presently, was glad he had. She was stuck. From above she had been unable to see that one particular stretch of rock was an overhang; she was not tall enough to hang from her hands and drop safely to the next hold, which was a good eight feet lower. She crouched on the edge, her silky black hair falling forward, trying to find a way down which would not end in a bad fall.

Now was his chance to get her out of this without either of them losing face. He hurried down the path and round another bend, then forsook the tiny ledge and set off sideways across the rock, climbing in a way he had not done for twenty years.

He reached the ledge below her and was glad he had done so, for just as he came round the corner, thankful that his shoes were rope-soled and sensible, Rochelle apparently decided that she could manage the drop, backwards. She was on the very edge, her legs already waving in the air, the rest of her inching over. Had she dropped and not kept her balance – and he did not see how she could have kept it – she would have bounced backwards off the ledge and straight into the sea snarling and worrying at the rocks below. As it was, she nearly knocked him over, which would have been the end for both of them, because he was not prepared for her sudden take-off, nor for her shout as she came, and only just managed to grab her and keep his balance himself.

The shock, he reflected, must have been just as great for her; she twisted in his arms, giving a muttered gasp and exclaiming, 'Merde!' before adding, 'Oh, I'm so sorry, I didn't mean . . . are you all right?'

'Yes, I'm all right; you?' Laurient stood her down and

turned her deftly on the narrow ledge so that they were facing one another. 'Do you know, Rochelle, what would have happened had I not been here?'

She glanced sideways and a brief shudder rippled through her, then she smiled up at him with perfect confidence.

'Oh, I'd have been all right. I'd already had a word . . . you see, Papa was to have brought me here, so I just reminded him that he should take care of me and jumped.'

So that was what she had shouted! But he would have to rid her mind of that particular misconception; it could prove far too dangerous.

'Rochelle . . . how old are you?'

He had to shout; the wind was not only tearing at them, as though anxious to see them plummet into the sea below, it was also whipping words from their mouths as soon as they were spoken. He should have started to consider how to get back to the path, but he thought he ought to clear up the matter of René's abilities as a guardian angel first.

'I'm eight . . . why?'

'Because you're old enough to know that your father's in heaven, not involved in mortal affairs any more. My dear child, he can't help you if you do something foolish, and it isn't fair to expect him to try.'

She frowned, then gnawed the side of her finger. Clearly, this must be given some thought.

'He can't? Not even so soon, before he's – he's had a chance to settle in?'

His mouth twitched but he hung on to sobriety, albeit with an effort.

'No, not even now. So you see, you might have been killed.'

'Mm hmm . . . but he sent you, didn't he!'

'Me?' He was taken aback and thought it probably showed. 'No, of course he didn't send me. I was up early and thought I'd come down to the point and see the sunrise . . . it was just luck.'

'Was it, monsieur? Do you often come down here to see the sunrise, then?'

'Well, not often . . .' He saw the trap and smiled reluctantly. 'I see what you mean, Rochelle, but you mustn't think that your papa will be able to save you from the consequences of your actions because it just won't happen.'

'No, I suppose not. But you were here, monsieur. You catched me.'

'Caught,' he corrected automatically.

'So you see,' Rochelle continued, oblivious, 'in a way, I was right. You did catch . . . caught me.'

'All right, I get your drift. Now, how are we to get up again from here?'

'We haven't got down yet,' Rochelle pointed out. 'I *do* want to see the tunnels and things, monsieur. Now that you're here, couldn't we go right down and take a look? You'll take care of me, won't you?'

Laurient wavered; it had been years since he had done the climb and she was a spunky little kid. It wouldn't take long, might even be safer to go right down and see if there was an easier way up.

'Well, all right; it might be better, anyway. But you'll do exactly as I say, is that understood?'

She smiled up at him, small, peaky face pink with reflected sunrise.

'Of *course*, monsieur. If you're going to look after me instead of Papa, I'll do just what you say. Always.'

It complicated matters even further, of course. He had never for one moment considered taking her into the manor and keeping her there himself, yet suddenly it was a *fait accompli* because she trusted him and he found he could not let her down.

He had to apply to the great-aunt, of course, but no one could have been more pleased to be painlessly rid of the child than she. She even found him a respectable young woman to move into the manor and look after the child. Her name was Georgina Harris and she was from England, a young schoolteacher in her twenties who had worked in tough London schools until it was found that she had a weakness in her lungs. Nothing serious – yet, they said. Get out of the city, work in the country somewhere, find clean air and a quiet existence and you'll live to be a hundred.

She had come to the island and had been sent to the great-aunt because Mlle Bourge had said she would take her as a lodger for a few weeks, just until Miss Harris found a permanent place. To be offered a home at Augeuil Manor, with the trifling proviso that she took care of one small girl, must have seemed a wonderful opportunity, for Charles Laurient had no intention of taking in paying guests and made it clear to Miss Harris that she was free to come and go as she pleased. He wanted no money from her towards her keep, but Rochelle must be her main concern.

Georgina Harris was a plain little person with mousy hair, pale eyes and a freckled complexion, but she had a kind heart and a good deal of common sense. Within minutes of meeting her Charles Laurient knew he had found the very person to take care of Rochelle – she was sweet-tempered, without personal vanity and intensely interested in children. He saw her with Rochelle – who was inclined to be suspicious and a little stiff – and realised, as Rochelle's careful barriers crumbled before the older girl's transparent friendliness, that he could not have found anyone better for the job had he searched for years.

The only one not perfectly delighted with the arrangement was Mme Barfleur. She had stated positively to her cronies that whatever fate befell the little Dubois girl she could guarantee that M. Laurient would take no interest in her whatsoever, would not raise a hand to help. Did he not thoroughly dislike children, and had he not spent all his time since his father's death fiddling about with them nasty orchid-flowers as though they was the most important thing in the world, with not a thought for more gainful employment? Charles Laurient listened to the gossip and smiled to himself when others chuckled over Mme Barfleur's total failure, in this instance, to correctly forecast what would happen to young Rochelle Dubois.

Sometimes, however, he reflected that but for his chancing to be in the garden at an extraordinarily early hour of the morning, but for his having spotted Rochelle nipping off . . . who could tell that Mme Barfleur's predictions would not have been exactly right? He knew that he had not intended for one moment to become personally embroiled in a small girl's fate – a small girl with no claim on him whatsoever, save that he had been her father's employer and closest friend – so Mme Barfleur was wrong not by a mile but by a whisker.

But then he would catch sight of Rochelle in the glasshouse or pattering across the hall first thing in the morning, on her way to school, and wonder whether he would really have washed his hands of her completely, sent her off into the wide world. He had grown accustomed to having her about, in the glasshouses, avidly learning how best to treat the orchids, pollinating, sowing seed, feeding, watering . . . could he simply have pushed her out of his mind, done without her restful companionship?

On mature reflection, he did not think he could. If she was troublesome, difficult, he could always farm her out with the Mendes; that particular option was still open.

Once or twice, when she turned her head in a certain way, or when the silky hair fell forward, screening her face, he was troubled by an elusive likeness to Helen Salling, who had once been his mistress and still, sometimes,

89

invaded his thoughts. But he knew that this was just a type of wishful thinking, the type that makes you recognise the back of a head in a crowd as that of the beloved – only it never is. Besides, Helen had been a very beautiful woman, and Rochelle was a plain little thing. All they had in common was night-black hair, the sort of skin which goes with it, and an economy of movement which most dancers have as a matter of course, though few children share the gift.

He often wondered about Helen; where she had fled, and why, with whom. Sometimes he tried to imagine her as she must be now – fatter, calmer, less intense. She would have children . . . perhaps she had a daughter and that daughter might be very like Rochelle.

It was fascinating to imagine her bringing up a little girl with black hair and slanting eyes whilst he brought up such a little girl as well. He wished he could find some way of getting in touch with Helen. Even if they could never again be lovers it would comfort him to be her friend.

But there was no way. She had disappeared long ago, and he supposed she never thought of him at all now.

And it was pointless – pointless! – for him to think of her. But every spring, when he went off to Paris on a business trip, he dreamed again under the chestnut trees in the Little Luxembourg, and searched the crowds in the Latin Quarter for a certain face.

4

Laurie was sitting on the stoop eating an apple when he saw his mother coming wearily along the sidewalk. He stopped chewing and smiled at her. He thought her the prettiest woman in the world, but even his biased eyes could see that she looked both tired and discouraged this evening, so it behoved him to find something cheerful to say.

'Hey, Mom,' he shouted as soon as she was near enough to hear his voice, 'I got three apples today, helpin' Miz Ella Andrews to chop wood.'

It made her smile, just a little one, and that was good, but the smile got switched off pretty soon and somehow that made it worse, because there was such a contrast in her face between smile and after-smile. Laurie ate the last bit of his apple, the core, then got to his feet and ran to meet her, telling her to lean on his shoulder because she looked tired, adding that she'd soon buck up when she got outside of the ground beef and taters that were simmering on the fire.

His mother smiled again, but did not lean on his shoulder; instead, she kissed the side of his face and rumpled his thick dark hair until it stood up all over his head.

'You're getting to be a good cook, hon. I'm tired because things aren't . . . well, I'm afraid we may find ourselves moving on in a day or so.'

He nearly stopped walking at the words, but forced himself on just in time, so she didn't notice. If there was one thing he dreaded it was moving on, because it seemed you were never any better off, and sometimes things even got worse. It just seemed as though it was important for Mom to move on whenever she lost a job. In fact, he realised, looking back on his much-travelled life, moving on was a symptom of this Depression. It wasn't just Mom. Everyone thought they would be better off somewhere else . . . but what had made her suggest it? The usual?

'They pay you off, Mom?'

She was a good waitress, nice-mannered, neat, quick with a smile and light on her feet. She'd do anything, too, they soon found that out. She'd cook and wash up, scrub floors and clean vegetables, hump heavy sacks of refuse out the back, so long as she was paid. And this rooming house, he thought, as they turned into their own home, could have been a lot worse. Their room was small but it was cheerful, and easier to heat in winter than a larger place. The people were real neighbourly, too. He heaved a sigh, but inside himself. Still, if they'd paid her off . . .

'Well, Mom? Did the place close?'

She shook her head wearily and opened the door of their room. The beef smelt good, rich and tasty. It's all trainin' for later, he told himself with some pride. If I can cook this good at twelve, by the time I'm, say, fifteen I'll be first rate. Mom was taking off her thin, patched jacket and throwing it over a chair, pulling the pink checkered handkerchief off her head so's he could see the shine on her black hair.

'No, Laurie, the place didn't close and I've not been paid off, either. Not yet. It's a family business, though, so I reckon tomorrow or the day after, when they start to work things out, they'll ask me to go. You can't blame 'em. They've been good to us.'

'Family? What d'you mean, Mom?'

'Well, the Chavezes have kids, right? And a half-dozen brothers, coupla sisters. One of the sisters married a share cropper and he's lost his farm . . . killed himself a month back. So she turned up this morning at the restaurant with

92

three little kids and all her stuff in paper parcels . . . they'd ridden the freight trains all the way from Memphis . . . poor girl, with little kids an' all. Mr Chavez, he's so nice, so kind . . . but the place isn't doing so good, they don't have no electric light any more, just kerosene lamps, and the prices have had to go awful cheap, else we wouldn't get folk in. The sister's a pretty little thing; she could wait on as well as I can. I'm the only person employed there now who isn't family.'

'Yeah,' Laurie said slowly. He glanced regretfully round their small room, suddenly cosier and more welcoming than ever. 'But where'll we go, Mom? Can't you get another place here, waitressing?'

His mother shrugged; clearly she was in no mood to try to plan for disasters ahead. Perhaps later one of them would think of a way to earn themselves some money which wouldn't mean moving on. Mom must be as tired and disillusioned by it as he was – maybe more. He could only faintly remember the earlier times when they had worked, moved, nearly starved, worked, moved, gone on relief, moved, worked, and so on and so on. She tried so hard to do right by him. She even saved a little each week, and rarely ate a proper meal, saying that they fed her at the restaurant, or in the bar, or even in the kitchen if she was working for private people.

'Waitressing? I doubt it. It's family who come first, hon, and that's the truth. But there must be something else . . . I'll try to think something up.'

'OK; I'll think too,' Laurie said. He got their plates and spoons out of the cupboard and put them down on the rickety wooden table. 'Shall I dish up?'

'Sure, hon. Did you put salt in?'

They both giggled. One time, Laurie had sugared a mutton stew and salted apple pie. It had spoilt their meal but given them a good laugh. Sometimes, Laurie thought now, a good laugh was better for you than a meal, even if you were hungry. Look at Mom! Laughing took years off her – years!

'Sure I put salt in,' he said now, pretending indignation as he spooned out the ground beef and the taters all soft and fawny brown through being cooked in the same pan as the beef. 'If we do have to move on, Mom, couldn't we do farm work? Then I can earn too.'

They had worked as fruit pickers one year, on the West Coast. Laurie had eaten peaches until his face had shone with juice, and he had bathed in the sea and learned to swim just like a fish, but they had saved nothing and lived in squalor. Mom had enjoyed seeing him becoming brown and fit but she had hated the shack made of old cardboard boxes in which they had lived that summer. As soon as they could they had appealed for Traveler's Aid to get back to the East Coast, where Mom was convinced she would find work. She had done so, as well . . . for a while. Everything, it seemed to Laurie, was for a while.

'Fruit picking, you mean? Oh, no, Laurie. I know you'd as soon miss school as not but it isn't what I want for you, hon, nor what your father would want. I want you to go through college – you can start at sixteen if you go for a teacher – and the Depression can't last for ever. One day you'll go to college and get yourself a good degree . . . law, perhaps, like your daddy, or even medicine . . . and then you'll be set up for life.'

'Sure; one day,' Laurie said soothingly. He did not think the Depression would ever end, he thought it was too established now. He had known no other life, and everyone he knew was either struggling or scraping a living. He did not know one single person who was on easy street.

His mother talked, sometimes, of her own childhood, of beautiful clothes, enormous meals, the regular allowance received by each child. He knew she was telling the truth, for she was a very truthful person, but he could not believe that such times would ever come again. How could they?

94

Those children had had a bedroom *each*. Now people lived all in one room, and no one had a whole house to themselves. And everyone worked, because otherwise you just didn't eat. There were bad things, too. Once he had seen a man thrown off a train by a feller in uniform and then shot; right in the face, the feller had shot the other man. He'd seen guys not a lot older than himself thrown in the pen because they were what was termed vagrants. Even teachers were sometimes unpaid, because the city itself had gone bust – even the *police* were not always paid . . . yet they were the ones who leaned the hardest on the vagrants, the beggars, the people who couldn't make it no matter how hard they tried.

In his twelve years he had watched protest marches, strikes, parades, on all of which people told other people they had no jobs, no food, no hope. Yet no one did anything. There *were* rich people; the banks were rich and some of the people who came into Mom's various restaurants were rich . . . why didn't they *do* something, for Chrissake? But his mother was talking as she spooned in the thin stew; he listened.

'. . . go back to my parents,' she was saying. 'I don't want to have to hang on anyone's sleeve, Laurie, but I'm getting so tired! And it's been so long . . . I don't know how they're fixed themselves. But if things get too bad . . .'

It was a conversation she held with herself often. There was a reason for not going home to their own family, she had explained. She had run away to be a dancer and her father, a stern and righteous man, had not approved, had thought it sinful. She had loved Laurie's daddy dearly, had been wrested from him by circumstances beyond her control, but her parents would merely condemn her for having brought a child into the world without first marrying the father.

She had not told him he was a bastard until he was ten, and she only told him then because she was ashamed of

95

the way he and some of his schoolfellows were treating a half-caste boy in their grade. Laurie had joined in the derision – *black bastard, your mom goes with white trash* – and had been first slapped and shaken and then stunned with the truth by his own outraged parent. 'You'd better learn, hon, that you're a bastard yourself,' she had hissed at him, her beautiful face pink with temper. 'That little guy's no better and no worse than you . . . you're a bastard yourself!'

Later, she had been calmer, had explained better. She should not have said it, she told him, because it was not strictly true. Sure, she had never actually married his daddy, but it had not been because he did not want her to do so, and they had lived together for quite a long time in Paris.

It had not taken away the stigma in his mind, though. He knew Mom was a real lady and he would never tell her secret to anyone – but he did wish she was married, that he did not have a secret to keep. And now when he heard someone use the word bastard it hurt him; he felt an actual stab of pain at the sound, and at the same time a little cold shiver of fear . . . if they knew about me, what would they say then?

'. . . but as summer's coming on, we could try a small town, perhaps. See if we can both get some work. You'll need all the money I can earn and anything you can scrape together if we're to get you through college.'

'Mm hmm.' Laurie scraped his spoon round his plate, then reached for a slice of bread and wiped up the last delicious smear of gravy. 'Mom . . . what about those cousins? The ones you went to sometimes when the summers were hot and your parents needed to be away on business?'

'Aunt Edie and Uncle Bud? And Tom, Cissie, Rupe, Albie . . .'

'That's right. They had a farm in Iowa; you've told me

what fun you had there. Wouldn't they let us work there, give us a roof?'

'Well, I don't know.' Mom pulled a face, scowled down at her untasted bread. 'Here, want this slice too? More'n I can possibly eat – I had spaghetti today. Now, where was I? Oh, Aunt Edie and Uncle Bud. Well, I guess I don't want to put it to the test, hon. That's durn cowardly, but it's the way I am.'

''Tain't cowardly,' Laurie said stoutly. 'That's just pride, Mom, and there's nothing wrong with pride, you've said so often.'

'True. And anyway, no point in meeting trouble; it may never happen.' Mom stood up and went over to the sink, poured water into the kettle, stood the kettle on the fire. 'We'll have some coffee, shall we? And there was a jelly roll they didn't need . . . Mr Chavez said I might as well have it as throw it out.'

Laurie took the cake, smiling as he did so. As if Mr Chavez would have thrown out food! Whilst Mom washed up the plates he tipped a few beans into the coffee grinder and turned the handle, enjoying the delicious smell of the coffee as the beans were ground down to usable size. By the time he had done the kettle had boiled, so he put the coffee into a small pan, tipped the boiling water on top and then put the pan over the fire, to give it a bit of extra heat. Coffee was quite a treat.

Presently they sat down again, and sipped coffee and ate the jelly roll very slowly, savouring every bite. Then Mom said it had been a long day, and had Laurie finished all his school work, and Laurie said he had, which was true, and they both got ready for bed. Mom took off her black skirt and blouse but left on her long thin petticoat and got into bed like that and Laurie took off his sweater and pants and got into bed in shirt and shorts, because it was a warm evening. If it had been cold, he would have kept his sweater on. Neither bed was a bed, of course, in the accepted sense

97

of the word. They each had a thick pile of newspapers in one corner of the room with whatever bedding they had managed to acquire on top.

If we leave, we'll leave everything in this room, Laurie reminded himself. We don't have the money to take things with us, just enough to take ourselves.

It made the bed seem warmer, more comfortable. Laurie cuddled down and even the noise of the newspapers, creaking and settling under him, seemed a good sort of noise. Homely instead of irritating.

He sighed. Oh, well. Perhaps it would never happen.

Two days later Mom came in, shoulders sagging, and plonked a paper sack of groceries on the rickety table. Laurie, boiling eggs in a small pan, turned and would have cheered at the sight of such a quantity of food but for the look on his mother's face.

'Paid off,' she said as their eyes met. 'Poor Mr Chavez couldn't give me no bonus, but he got a pile of keeping food – dried stuff, tinned stuff – and said good luck. Mrs Chavez cried.'

Laurie tried not to let his own shoulders sag, but it was hard. He had come in from school happy; his teacher was good, the other kids friendly, he was making out all right. Now it'd be a long train ride with more nothing at the end.

Mom looked at him, and maybe the set of shoulders determined not to sag says as much as a cry of pain. She crossed the room and put her arms round him, hugging him to her slight bosom.

'Laurie, hon . . . we'll try the country, then, if you'd like that. A little place I know . . . just a hick town, but the people were friendly last time I was by there. Will that make it easier to leave?' She let go of him to rummage in the sack, producing two candy bars. 'Here, one each. Then we'll decide what to take and what to sell.'

* * *

They sold most of their stuff, in the end, and didn't have to go to Traveler's Aid for their tickets. They caught the train the respectable way and got out on a tiny country platform where the benches were painted grey. Nelsonville, the sign over the stationmaster's office said.

They walked into the little town . . . a one-horse town, Laurie thought happily; dust was thick on the sidewalks, and the roads weren't made up, but somehow he sensed that this place might be right for them.

Mom seemed to know where she was going. She walked along the road past the store, a run-down little rooming house – you couldn't call it a hotel – a drug store, and a gas station. Laurie could see she was looking for something or someone, half hoping, half dreading that she'd find it. They reached the end of the street and there was a taxicab, a very old one, drawn up under the shade of some trees. Mom walked over to it. There was a man asleep behind the wheel; Mom tapped on the glass, only the window was open and her hand fell on the man's shoulder.

'Excuse me! Oh, gee, I'm sorry. I thought . . .'

The man rubbed his eyes and munched with his mouth. He had a long, droopy white moustache.

'Yes'm? You want a ride someplace?'

'Umm . . . can you tell me whether there's anyone out at the Colliers' place? Any of them still there . . . the Colliers, I mean?'

The man shook his head as if to wake himself and then looked up at Mom, half frowning, half smiling.

'Sure is. Young Sheridan Collier farms there now; the old people died a year or so back so he's on his own.'

Mom smiled, and it was a smile of pure relief.

'I see. In that case, would you drive us there, please? My son and I.'

Sheridan Collier? Laurie had never heard the name before but it set up an uneasy feeling in the back of his mind. And why did Mom look so pleased . . . she hadn't said she knew anyone in Nelsonville. But she was climbing into the taxicab, so he followed suit.

They drove quite a ways, Laurie noted. It was good country, with woods, water, and fields and fields of crops. A great deal of corn, some cereals, and other more interesting stuff. Salad crops, a field of long lettuce, another of tomatoes – though they were still green – another of squash. Orchards, too: pears, apples, plums. There were beasts grazing in meadowland; cows, horses, even oxen. It was, he thought, well maintained.

They came to a small house presently, and the cab driver stopped outside the picket fence.

'There y'are, sister.' He named a sum and Mom paid, and then the two of them, with their blanket rolls and one small suitcase between them, got out and stood in the warm sunshine, blinking towards the house. Laurie looked at Mom and she was nodding to herself, then suddenly she straightened her shoulders and pushed the small gate open. She marched up to the front door and banged on the knocker.

Laurie followed her and stood behind her, feeling extremely awkward. Mom knew why they were here, who would answer the door, but he had no idea and dreaded facing a stranger who he might suddenly be told was his uncle – cousin – grandfather! But instead a young, brown-faced man came to the door, looking uncertainly from one to the other.

'Yes, ma'am?'

Mom looked rather taken aback; whom had she expected? Certainly not a guy of sixteen, seventeen!

'Oh! Is Mr Sheridan Collier at home, please?'

The sun was lengthening into evening; the young guy glanced up at the sky and then behind him.

'No, ma'am, not yet, but he ain't gonna be long. Would you keer to wait in th' kitchen?'

'Um . . . thank you.' Mom caught hold of Laurie's sleeve

100

and towed him in with her when he would have hung back. They went down a short passage and into a pleasant kitchen, low-ceilinged with small windows overlooking a stable-yard. The young guy cleared his throat.

'Kin I get you a drink, ma'am? Miz Potter made us some lemonade a day or so back . . . it's good.'

Mom accepted the lemonade on behalf of both of them, and the guy was right: it was good. But Laurie could see that neither party was exactly happy; both wondered who the heck the other was and neither wanted to ask. Laurie decided he had no such inhibitions.

'Are you a Collier, then?' he asked as he finished his lemonade. 'I'm Daniel Laurient and this is my mom, Helen Laurient.'

Mom blushed; she must have known she should have told the guy at least her name before walking into the house the way she'd done, Laurie thought.

'How d'you do, Miz Laurient . . . Daniel,' the young guy said, his voice husky with embarrassment. 'I'm Lindsey Collier; Sheridan's my daddy.'

Laurie could feel a drop in temperature as clear as clear. He frowned, puzzled.

'Nice to know you, Lindsey,' he said politely, however. 'Where's your mom?'

It was the question hovering on Mom's lips, he realised, but he had not known that when he asked.

'She's dead; died jest a month or so after I was born. An' I'm fourteen now, so it's been a whiles.'

Laurie looked startled; fourteen, and the guy looked at least sixteen!

'Jeez, you're sure big for your age,' he remarked. Lindsey looked gratified.

'I take after my pa,' he said proudly. 'He's a big guy. Would you like more lemonade, Miz Laurient?'

'No thank you, Lindsey,' Mom said faintly. 'Um . . . when did you say your . . . Mr Collier would be home?'

'I think that's him comin' across the yard now,' Lindsey said. 'I'll just . . .'

He slid out of the back door on the words and was gone.

'To warn his pa,' Laurie hissed at his mother, expecting a smile, but got none. She was looking worried, anxious almost. Just what is she up to, Laurie wondered again. Was this guy a long-lost relative? Someone she had known as a child?

The mystery was soon solved. The back door opened and a tall, thickset man strode into the room, stared hard at Mom, opened and shut his mouth a couple of times, and then shouted: 'Nell!' and crossed the room in two strides to take her by the shoulders and gaze earnestly into her face.

'Nell, it really *is* you! It must be a dozen years! How are you? You're married, then? And the boy . . . yours, of course.'

Mom nodded, then shook her head.

'I *was* married,' she said, her voice very low. 'He died long ago. My son . . . let me introduce you. I call him Laurie, but his name's actually Daniel Sheridan Laurient.'

There was a long silence. Sheridan Collier looked from Laurie to Mom and back again several times, and then at his own son, hovering by the back door, too shy, it appeared, to come back inside.

'Daniel Sheridan?' he repeated at last. He sounded dazed. 'Is that what you said, Nell?'

Mom nodded. She looked frightened; Laurie couldn't understand it at all.

'Here, boy.' Sheridan Collier beckoned Laurie to stand over by the back door and pulled his own son to stand in line. Laurie tried not to scowl but it was hard work, because the guy was undoubtedly comparing him with his own great overgrown lad . . . and Lindsey had probably had good food and fresh air all his life, not the sort of things that he, Laurie, had been forced to eat nor the cramped

conditions he had been brought up in. But Mr Collier was
nodding slowly, as though he had just realised something.

'Yes . . . I can see it. He'll be . . . gettin' on for twelve,
then?'

'More or less,' Mom said. She sounded surer of herself
now, not so uncertain. 'We've had a struggle, Sherry. The
boy and I.'

He nodded again. Slowly. It occurred to Laurie that he
was not a man who ever acted hastily. He would take his
time and think things out and not act until he was
absolutely sure he knew what he was doing.

But in this he wronged the older man, for Sheridan
suddenly seized Mom by both hands, drew her close – and
kissed her on the mouth.

'You'll stay?'

He spoke the words against her face; they were muffled
but clear enough. Laurie wondered whether Mom was
being offered a job as a kitchen maid or a farm worker or
what . . . but why had Mr Collier kissed her? They were
clearly old friends . . . Laurie felt so confused that he could
have screamed. What was going on? Why all the mystery?
Why had Mom not told him she knew a guy in Nelsonville
who might give them a job?

'Yes, Sherry, I'll stay. If you're sure you want me to.'

The man nodded vigorously and put a heavy arm round
Mom's shoulders.

'Sure I want you! I'll do the right thing by you, never
fear. And the boy'll be a strong 'un – he'll be worth his
keep. He and Lin can work together . . . we'll do just fine.'

It was not a big house, but it seemed like a palace to
Laurie. He was to sleep with Lindsey; Mom whispered to
him that he was a big boy now and it was better that he
take the opportunity of sharing what would be almost a
room of his own. She would sleep elsewhere. When he was
taken into the outhouse to wash up for tea, Mr Collier and
Mom had a long, muttered discussion in the front room

103

which Laurie was not privileged to hear. When they came back into the kitchen they were composed but bright-eyed, Mom especially, and she bustled round helping to get the meal. It appeared that someone called Enie Warbell usually prepared the food, though she did not stay to eat it, having a man of her own to feed.

As they sat round the scrubbed wooden table, a generous meal laid out, Laurie reflected that it was a far cry from the room they had recently quit. Outside was the farm, birds called from the woods, a cow lowed. Inside was the food, wood burned in the stove – there seemed to be no shortage of fuel – and upstairs he had a tiny bed of his own because Collier had always intended to have two boys.

At tea they drank milk and ate home-made bread spread with farm butter and honey from the Colliers' own bees. There was a raised pie and potatoes baked in the embers of the fire, well salted and with melted butter inside. Laurie ate until his stomach felt like a tight little drum. He had never eaten so much in his whole life – and he had never felt so full, either.

That night he suffered from awful pains in the stomach and determined never to be so greedy again . . . but at the same time he knew you should never turn food away, because you could never tell where the next meal was coming from, or whether it would arrive at all. As he lay there suffering, clutching his stomach, he heard sounds from the room next door. Grunts and cries and mutters and the creaking and pinging of bedsprings.

Undoubtedly Mom was also suffering from too much rich food. Laurie wondered whether to go through and commiserate with her, but decided against it. Neither of them had been sick, so they had much to be thankful for. The food was still doing them good, no matter how little their underworked stomachs might appreciate it.

Mr Collier had told him that he might lie in a little next morning, though Lindsey would be up at five as usual to

104

milk. Laurie wanted to get up at five too, but because of the pains he did not sleep at all until the early hours and then of course he overslept, waking at seven with the sure knowledge that Lindsey had been gone for hours.

He got out of bed and felt Lindsey's covers; they were cold. He wondered whether to go down now and see if he could help . . . but he was still pretty tired and the bed was enticing.

Next time he woke it was full day; sunshine streamed in through his window and there were sounds to indicate that other people were going about their daily business. He got out of bed – how strange to have a real bed and not just a slippery pile of old newspapers – and pulled on his jersey and pants, slid his feet into his old sneakers. He went down to the kitchen but no one was there, so he washed at the sink and then looked round for something to eat. He had a couple of slices of bread and butter, feeling guilty since no one had said he could eat, and then drank some milk out of a tall white jug with a gold rim which stood under the stone sink, on the cool floor. Then he made for the back door. He would go and see if he could help Lindsey to milk those cows!

It was a strange sort of day, but Laurie thoroughly enjoyed it. He found Lindsey easily enough, though the cows had been milked long since, it appeared. However, the older boy found him plenty to do and the two of them worked side by side in perfect amity for a couple of hours. Then Lindsey looked up at the sun overhead, remarked that it was time they ate, and headed back to the house.

They had been hoeing cabbages and Laurie was not sorry to leave off; his back was not used to the continual stooping and ached like mad, but he was proud to have kept pace with Lindsey, who was a good deal taller and heavier than he. He liked the other boy very much. Lindsey was calm and capable, not talkative and probably not particularly bright, but good-natured and willing to show Laurie how to tackle each job until he thoroughly understood what he was doing.

'We grow 'spargus there; that takes some weedin',' he remarked as they made their way back to the house. 'Have you seen the hogs yet?'

Laurie said that he had not.

'Show you, after we've et.'

In the house once more, Laurie looked round the kitchen for his mother or Mr Collier, but the room was empty. Lindsey saw him looking.

'Pa's taken your ma into town, shoppin',' he disclosed. 'There's a pile of stuff Pa's wantin', now you and your ma's here.'

'Oh? What sort of things?'

'Well, tools, I guess. You was usin' Pa's hoe out there. With four of us . . . an' then there's vittles. Mostly we eat off the land, but some things we buy in, like coffee, grits, flour.'

'Mm hmm. So . . . you think we're stayin', Mom and me?'

'Guess so,' Lindsey said slowly. He went and peered inside the wood-burning stove, then threw in some more logs from the basket nearby. 'Guess you ain't movin' on for a whiles, Laurie.'

'Do you mind me being here, Lindsey? And Mom?'

Lindsey turned from a dreamy contemplation of the stove to the pantry, from which he brought out a loaf of bread and a sizeable chunk of cheese. Then he produced a jar of cider and two glasses, and dived under the sink for a couple of apples. He arranged the food and poured the drink, then beckoned Laurie.

'C'mon, siddown. It'll be good havin' you here. And your mom. Less work all round for me and Pa.'

'Yeah. And come the autumn we can go to school

together,' Laurie contributed, cutting himself a hunk of cheese and taking an apple. 'Where is school, Lindsey?'

'School? I quit.'

'Oh. Well, you're older'n me. Mom won't let me quit.'

Lindsey smiled tolerantly, chewing bread and cheese.

'Pa'll talk her round.'

Helen sat in Sheridan's room and examined herself closely in the round, fly-spotted mirror above the chest of drawers. It was better placed than most, since the light from the narrow window fell full on her face as she crouched on the threadbare strip of coconut matting.

'Helen Anna Collier,' she said slowly to her reflection. 'Helen, what in hell did you do that for?'

Her own face looked back at her; thin, big-eyed, the slant of them somehow more obvious now that the lines were so much in evidence. Her nose, which she hated but thought aristocratic, was already freckling up after only a couple of days in the sun. Still, lots of people liked freckles, and hers always faded when winter came.

She did not intend to tell Laurie what she had done in town, whilst he thought she was shopping. She was, in a way, ashamed of herself, because she had turned Sherry down years ago when she first came back from France and met him, a young widower looking for a woman to console his loneliness in the great city of New York. But in those days, despite knowing she was pregnant, she still believed life had something better in store for her than a country hick and a few acres shared with his father.

Now, with all her hopes long dead, she looked at Sheridan's round, open face and saw that he was the sort of man who would never compromise. In New York City he had slept with her every night for a week and made vigorous love to her, hoping to wheedle her into returning to his farm with him. But here, in his own place, it would be marry or go.

It was extraordinary how he had changed in the dozen years since she had seen him last, because although they had shared a bed last night she had had, in the end, to seduce him. She had known he would not touch her otherwise. And once seduced he would take marriage for granted, she knew; no decent girl, in his eyes, would behave so with a guy unless she wanted him to make an honest woman of her.

And she had led him to believe Laurie was of his getting. Why not? she asked herself miserably now, seeing the guilt in her reflection's dark almond eyes. Why not? Charles Laurient was undoubtedly married and happy. She would never see him again in this world, so why not make the most of the time she'd got left? She was strong enough, healthy enough, but she could not take much more. Trekking round the country, living on air half the time so that Laurie shouldn't go short . . . it would sap her strength in the end.

She did not intend to tell Laurie what she had done. He would find out she was married to Sheridan, she supposed, but if she was careful he need never discover that Sheridan thought himself Laurie's father. Only . . . perhaps she had better tell him and swear him to secrecy, because if the boy came out with his real birthday Sheridan might well start doing sums in his head . . . might even come up with the right answer. And then she and Laurie would be out on their asses, and lucky to escape without a beating.

It was a real dilemma, because Laurie valued her memories of his father, hugged to himself the secret that he *was* a Laurient, with an English daddy who lived in a manor house four hundred years old and spoke French better than a native.

She could admit to him that she had lied to Sheridan . . . but how could she expect Laurie to grow up straight and honest if he knew his mother had lied? The face in the mirror stared back at her and suddenly she saw it, not as the girl's face she had known for so long, but as the face of a worried woman heading fast for middle age. She saw the threads of pure silver at her temples, the blurring of the clean line of her jaw, the thinness of her, where she had once been slender and supple with a dancer's strength and poise.

And Sheridan had married her. He had not harked back to the perfection of the young Helen, nor to her cruelty in taking his money and love all those years ago but throwing his proposal of marriage back in his face, sending him away from New York with his tail between his legs because she thought she could do better. All he had thought was that she must have wanted him as he had wanted her; he had clung to her and wept against her breast because she had come to him after all, had wanted him, after all.

You are thirty years old and you could be taken for forty, Helen told her reflection, and saw it wince and was almost glad. You've married Sheridan Collier now, for better for worse, and you must start thinking about him as well as about Laurie . . . and you can just forget yourself and your stupid urge to be thought well of by your son. You can tell him he probably is a Collier and if he thinks you're a tramp then who's to say he's not right?

After all, the boy couldn't be hurt by the lie as much as Sheridan had been hurt already. She would not deepen the wound, increase the pain, by letting him discover the truth. In a day or so she would take Laurie to one side and tell him that he was half-brother to Lindsey Collier.

When they had been at the Collier place a week, Helen told Laurie she was very sorry, he was not Charles Laurient's son but Sheridan Collier's. He was half-brother to Lindsey and she did hope he would forgive her for pretending that Charles had been his father . . . the truth was she had been with both men and had not been entirely sure, but now she was sure, so she had married Sheridan, and

109

would Laurie kindly remember that his birthday was no longer to be celebrated in January but would be in May.

'You've told Sheridan lies,' Laurie said at once, his eyes very bright and angry. 'That wasn't right, Mom.'

Helen had decided that if by some evil chance Laurie outfaced her she would get angry and scold him; instead, she burst into tears and told him she could not take any more and she was truly sorry and she wished she were dead.

He was very good, very adult. He patted her shoulder and said he would remember that his birthday was now in May, and then he said he would probably have done the same in her place and he was happier here than he had been anywhere else for a long time.

For a whole year, in fact until he was thirteen and a half, he worked hard on the farm and lived the lie that he was really Laurie Collier, but never for one moment did he begin to believe it or stop telling himself every night that Mom couldn't help it, that the lie had hurt no one and he was still his father's son.

Then his mom, who had grown very fat and rather slow, though she was looking younger and fitter and better in every other way, told him that she was expecting a baby. And the baby was born and it was a boy, and they called him Robin.

Robin was a nice baby and Laurie rather liked him, but he was working so hard on the farm and so hard in school that he had scarcely any time to play with his new brother. And ten months after Robin was born Mom had another baby, and it was another boy. They called him Arnold and he cried all night and most of the day and Mom got thin and cross, and then one day, when he was working away at his schoolwork all hunched up in a corner of the kitchen, she told him he might as well quit, because there was no way, with the two little boys, that she would be able to help him through college. Just to keep food in all their mouths meant that any spare money had to go to try to buy a bit more land in order to work even harder.

'No more school, then?' Laurie asked.

'You'll do as well at home,' Sheridan said, a little guiltily perhaps because Laurie was clever and they all knew it. 'Perhaps, one day . . .'

But Laurie put his books away and came back into the kitchen and sat and thought. The house was bursting at the seams with babies and Mom seemed to think she owed it to Sheridan to keep having them . . . he looked at her sideways and saw the swell of her belly and knew that a third small Collier was on the way.

That night, Lindsey heard him putting his things into bags. He propped himself up in bed on one elbow and stared at Laurie through the stripy moonlight.

'Laurie? What you doin', feller?'

'Leavin' home. Don't make no rumpus, Lin.'

Lindsey lay down again, but turned his head to whisper straight into Laurie's ear, for Robin was in a truckle bed in one corner of the small room.

'Wish I could come as well. But 'twouldn't be fair.'

'No. I'll come back one day, Lin.'

'Sure you will.' Lindsey leaned up on his elbow again as Laurie tiptoed across the floor towards the door. 'Take care now, feller.'

'You too,' Laurie whispered. He got the door open, then paused in the doorway.

'Lin?'

'Yeah?'

'Take care of my mom, hey?'

'Sure will. 'Bye, now.'

''Bye, Lin.'

Down the creaking stairs – only no one would hear him because the only thing that woke them was Arnold's mutterings – and across the moonlit kitchen, pausing to

111

take a last look round as he began to close the back door behind him.

Nappies hung on strings across the room, little night-gowns and romper suits and bibs and things on every available surface. Bottles waiting for the formula, an old baby carriage pushed up against the pantry door.

Regrets? Very few. This was the Collier home now. There was no room in it for a Laurient.

Laurie slipped out into the moonlight and pulled the door shut behind him. Its click sounded loud in the night silence but nothing stirred, no voice exclaimed, no footfall sounded on the floors overhead.

He was halfway to the road when, behind him, he heard Arnold start to bawl.

It was a good sound to get away from.

Laurie began to run.

5

'Harry . . . oh, Harry, wait for me!'

Rochelle came flying down the front drive, later than she had meant to be because she had just dashed down to the glasshouses to visit the orchids before beginning her school day.

Long before, Miss Harris had agreed to become Harry, because living full-time at the manor meant that she and Rochelle were constantly in one another's company, and M. Laurient did not approve of his ward's using Miss Harris's first name. However, he had no objection to the nickname and even used it himself when they were in casual conversation. Now Miss Harris stopped and turned to shake her head sadly at her young charge.

'Chelle, Chelle, will you never learn? When I say I shall leave the house at eight-thirty that's precisely what I mean. Where have you been? Except I don't know why I ask, because I know the answer: to the glasshouses, of course.'

'Yes, that's right. M. Laurient promised me that if I had time this morning I might plant out the seedlings that I mated last autumn, so I made time . . . well, I'm not going to be late for school, am I? You're never late, Harry.'

'I can't be late; I'm supposed to set a good example,' Harry reminded her. 'Come along, then – let's put our best foot forward. It's a lovely day again, isn't it? What will you do after school?'

The summer term was nearing its end; soon the holidays would be upon them and Harry would make a tearful departure and go back to Norfolk, to her parents' fine house in Norwich where she had been brought up. They had wanted her to get a job at home, at one of the big girls' schools in the city – the High School, or Thorpe House School, or the Mackie Academy – but she had always wanted to help the less privileged and had opted for London, living quite cheerfully in slum conditions herself until the day they discovered a patch on her lung.

When she had first come to the island she had found the hills difficult. They made her wheeze, and she had to slow down every two or three paces. A strong wind exhausted her, she never swam, and her nature walks were confined to the arduous trek down to the village school from the manor.

Now, after three years of island living, good eating and clean air, she never wheezed, could climb the steepest hill step for step with Rochelle and rarely felt tired. Her sense of humour, which had almost deserted her during her illness, came back twofold, and so did her ability to love. And here on the island she loved everything – everyone! Rochelle was her darling, of course, but she was fond of Olivia, friendly with Mme Barfleur, and on good terms with all the staff, both at school and at Augeuil Manor.

But she nursed a deep passion for M. Laurient which she was wryly aware was hopeless. She and Rochelle often speculated on why such an extremely attractive man had never married, but no one knew the answer, though the guesses were many and wild. He was certainly never likely to look to a plain and skinny schoolteacher for anything other than faithful service.

But loving him enriches me and doesn't hurt him, Miss Harris thought now, as Rochelle tucked a small brown paw into the crook of her arm and danced along beside her. Sometimes she dreamed of going home to Norwich and meeting the man of her dreams – he always closely resembled M. Laurient and was usually called Charles – but by and large she was content with her life as it was. She lived in the same house as her hero all year round save for three weeks at Christmas, three at Easter and eight in the summer, and was at liberty to talk to him, amuse him and listen to him when he felt like holding forth. What more could she ask? A physical relationship would probably be frightening and rather horrid, Miss Harris told herself, and took to sea-bathing and long walks.

'Harry . . . you know Henri Napoule had one of Pod's puppies?'

Miss Harris nodded; she did not approve of her charge's choice of names for her two dogs – the bitch was Pod and the sire Senna – but she remembered the litter of adorable, chocolate-brown labrador puppies well. There had been six of them and Rochelle and M. Laurient had taken as much care over who should be allowed to take a pup as most people take over fostering a child.

'Well, he had the little bitch M. Laurient called Runt, only Henri calls her Copper.'

'Yes, I know. She's grown up very nicely, I believe. Henri was boasting about her ability as a gun-dog last autumn, wasn't he?'

'Yes, he was. Well, guess what? She's had puppies!'

'Really? Well, that is nice. What sort of puppies?'

'That's the odd part. They aren't all brown, like she is – some of them are a sort of yellowy gold. I don't know how she's done it, but I'd love to see them, and Henri did say that if you and me went round to his farm after school his daddy would show us the litter. Do you think he's telling the truth when he says they aren't all brown?'

Oh dear, Miss Harris thought. The child lives on a farm, she sees animals behaving in a . . . a very animal-like way all around her, but I don't believe she has the slightest idea that offspring are created by the antics of a male and female of the species! But the walk to school was a mile or more; she could start telling Rochelle a bit about the birds and the bees as they walked . . . and come to think of it, she suddenly reminded herself, Rochelle does know quite a lot even if she isn't aware of it, because she and M. Laurient

115

spend hours selecting stud plants – parents – for their new hybrids. Rochelle often clamours to be allowed to use the wand to transfer the pollen from one flower to another to create the seeds.

Emboldened by this recollection, Miss Harris began to explain to Rochelle that, as with a hybrid, the father of the puppies also had a hand in their colouring, the shape of them, even whether they would become good gun dogs like their mother or merely pets, if that was what their father was.

Rochelle listened and nodded, seeming to take it all in, and then remarked that she would ask Henri whether the father-dog had been a yellow labrador, which would seem likely in view of the colour of the litter.

'There you are, then,' Miss Harris said heartily, very relieved to have got over what was undoubtedly a difficult hurdle so lightly. 'It's the same for all living creatures, Rochelle . . . every child is a mixture of its mother and father. Sometimes a tiny baby can look the very image of one or other of its parents, though as its own character begins to develop the likeness usually becomes less marked.'

Rochelle said she quite understood, that indeed it made a lot of things clear to her which had been a mystery before; and Miss Harris, smiling and discussing Jersey cows and their small, dainty-footed beauty, told Rochelle about the big, lumbering cows of the mainland and how the Jersey was kept a pure breed because of the high quality of its milk, cream and butter and because it was ideally suited to conditions on the islands, its small size and neatness making it a far better proposition where grazing was limited than some of its great lumbering sisters.

By now they were fast approaching school, and the conversation turned to other subjects. Rochelle began to talk about orchids and how careful one must be, when

116

selecting one's stud plants for a particular breeding, that one did not choose a species which had a strong dislike for conditions or plant food to which the other parent plant would need constant access. This led to discussion of 'living' plants such as the sundew and the Venus fly-trap, and Rochelle, in discoursing happily on how M. Laurient had promised, one day, to buy such specimens purely for her interest, soon forgot all about the puppies, or at least all about their conception.

'Well, here we go,' Miss Harris said, as they entered the school gates. 'What lesson do you have first, Chelle?'

Rochelle, pulling a face, said that it was current affairs. It was a new subject in school and at first everyone had thought how interesting it would be to learn about the great world beyond the island, but very soon Rochelle, at least, was extremely bored. Her teacher, an earnest, bespectacled man in his forties, felt it incumbent upon him to teach about the Nazis in Germany, the Maginot Line, Mr Chamberlain and his 'peace at any price', and a number of other things which, to tell the truth, were double Dutch to most of his pupils. She said as much to Miss Harris, who smiled sympathetically but said that she, too, felt ashamed at how divorced from affairs on the mainland they were here in Jersey.

'We ought to talk about it more at home, I suppose,' she said vaguely, pausing in the corridor outside Rochelle's classroom. 'M. Laurient has several excellent wireless sets ... why don't we listen to the news with him in the evenings?'

But Rochelle gave it as her opinion that this would be very poor sport, particularly as M. Laurient often started to listen in the best of humour and came out of the library afterwards grim and silent.

'Nevertheless, it would be educational,' Miss Harris said firmly, trying to ignore the fact that it would also give her valuable moments longer in M. Laurient's company, as well as the chance for some serious conversation.

'Ye-es. Tell you what, Ha ... I mean Miss Harris,' Rochelle said. The nickname was strictly barred in school. 'If I listen to the news with you and M. Laurient tonight and do my very best to understand, would you come with me to see Henri's puppies after school?'

'Very well; only you won't ask any more about the puppies whilst we are at Henri's, will you, Chelle?' Miss Harris said warily. She could just picture herself being asked some embarrassingly intimate question concerning the means by which two dogs produced a delightful basketful of puppies whilst the cynical Henri and perhaps even his father looked on.

'No, I won't,' Rochelle said, looking rather surprised. It was clear that she had no idea what her teacher had in mind. 'I expect I'll see you at dinner-time.'

'Yes, all right. Off you go.'

Miss Harris watched indulgently whilst her charge sauntered into her classroom and immediately became embroiled in a deep discussion with Flora de Chenot, a child who already, at barely eleven, was beginning to blossom into a pretty young woman. Miss Harris was extremely glad that her own charge was still so much a child ... but then Flora was half French and so, Miss Harris thought tolerantly, would naturally mature rather earlier than a child of the islands like Rochelle.

Rochelle, for her part, got through her school day all the more easily because she knew that at the end of it she and Miss Harris would go to the Napoule place to see the puppies, and to Rochelle dogs ranked above most human beings as her preferred companions. Cats were very popular as well, on a par with orchids in her personal preference list, though cats were capable of far more emotional responses than even the most intelligent of her flower-friends.

As soon as the bell rang for the end of afternoon school Rochelle rushed over to Henri, assuring him that Miss Harris and herself would gladly accompany him home even without the added attraction of his mother's cooking, for Henri had another draw besides the puppies – his mother made the best treacle cakes on the island and was very generous to her son's friends.

The three of them set off, walking quite fast because Mme Barfleur served meals promptly to time and could be very cross if one was late. Rochelle only ate in the kitchen now at holiday times and when Olivia was visiting her grandmother, but even so she knew better than to be late for meals. M. Laurient was punctual as well, and told Rochelle that she had best follow suit, for he did not intend to get into Mme Barfleur's bad books for her sake. So Rochelle, heedless in most other matters, did make a real attempt to be on time for meals.

And when they arrived at the Napoule smallholding they were glad they had hurried, for it gave them longer with the puppies. Rochelle and Henri knelt on the floor of the stable, their knees cushioned by the thick straw, and adored, and even Miss Harris was enchanted with the five fat and cuddly puppies, three yellow and two brown, which played and mock-fought amongst themselves.

'I suppose we should be going, now,' Miss Harris said at last, eyeing her wristwatch. 'We'll have to hurry if we're to be in good time for dinner.'

'Oh . . . five more minutes,' Rochelle pleaded, but just then their hostess came hurrying out with the lure of a cup of tea and some freshly baked treacle cakes spread with lovely butter, and the three of them went into the kitchen.

'Henri would like to keep a pup,' Mme Napoule told them as they sat on comfortable chairs and ate the hot cakes. 'But we've got good homes for them, and Copper will be having other litters, I dare say.'

Rochelle opened her mouth to speak, glanced at Miss Harris, and asked for another treacle cake. Miss Harris had the feeling that she had just escaped an awkward question and stood up decisively, brushing crumbs off her lap.

'That was delicious, Mme Napoule,' she said warmly. 'But we have to run now – Mme Barfleur insists that we are on time for her meals and I'm sure that even though we've eaten far too much here she'll expect us to clear our plates. Thank you, Henri, for showing us the puppies,' she added. 'Rochelle loved them, didn't you, Chelle?'

Rochelle assured the Napoules that she had indeed loved the puppies, and then teacher and pupil hurried off along the gentle summer lanes, reaching the manor just in time to rush upstairs and change out of their day-clothes.

'It's silly,' Rochelle often grumbled, 'to dress up just to sit and eat a meal, when we need our oldest clothes on straight afterwards to work in the glasshouses.'

'But M. Laurient dresses up,' Miss Harris explained. 'If a gentleman goes to so much trouble, surely his ladies should do the same?'

'His ladies!' Rochelle said, much impressed. 'Are we his ladies, Harry?'

'Indeed we are; that's why we always leave the table and drink our coffee by ourselves, in the garden room,' Miss Harris said. 'That's so that the gentlemen can drink their port.'

'Yes, but . . .'

'I know. There's only one gentleman and he usually comes and joins us after about two minutes and drinks coffee as well. But in the old days . . .'

'They did things better, then,' Rochelle riposted, with a twinkle. Mme Barfleur was always reminiscing about the old days, when there had seldom been fewer than ten people sitting down at the long table in the dining-room and often a score or more. 'I like being alive now, though. Don't you, Harry?'

And Harry admitted that she did. She did not add that she much preferred to have M. Laurient to herself at dinner each night, was glad not to have to share his precious company with a great many other people, but that was what she meant. She sometimes suspected that Rochelle knew it, knew how warmly and uselessly she loved.

Not that it mattered; Rochelle was a good girl. Miss Harris knew she would no more give away her secret than she would snap the heads off her favourite orchids.

Now, Rochelle came into Harry's room through the adjoining door to have the buttons on the back of her dress done up. There were a great many, but eventually Rochelle, looking very sweet and demure in white broderie anglaise, would be a sight to delight the most critical guardian, and M. Laurient was scarcely that. Harry, used to the task, buttoned with the speed of light and then swung her charge round to look critically at her.

'Very nice. It's a pity ribbons won't stay in your hair, but you still look beautiful,' she said, giving Rochelle a hug. 'White stockings . . . hmm, you'll need a new pair quite soon . . . white strap-shoes . . . yes, you'll do.'

'I look like a snowflake,' Rochelle moaned, examining herself in Miss Harris's full-length mirror. 'This skirt is too short . . . my legs look like poor old celery stalks.'

'No, more like asparagus,' Miss Harris said, laughing at the child's scowl. 'You look very nice, really you do, but I agree it won't fit you for long. Never mind. And if you don't care for white I'll get you something darker next time. Now let's go down.'

Downstairs, M. Laurient waited in the hall. They walked into the dining-room together and sat down whilst Emilie hovered with a large silver tureen which would be barely half full.

121

'Thank you, Emilie,' M. Laurient said as his bowl was filled with cream of celery soup. He turned courteously to his dinner companions. 'And how did your day go, Harry . . . Rochelle? How was school?'

Miss Harris answered quietly as she always did that her day had gone very well indeed and that 4B were in grave danger of learning something unless they mended their ways. M. Laurient smiled and Miss Harris, whose natural tendency to blend in with any background had been offset, this evening, by rose-coloured velvet, wished that he would comment on her new dress and knew, sadly, that he would not. Had she walked in clad only in a petticoat he would not have commented because he was not the sort of man to notice a woman's dress. But he noticed Rochelle's.

'That child's dress will be indecent in another month,' he remarked to Miss Harris presently, when the soup dishes had been cleared and they were awaiting the advent of Lucrèce with *Poulet au gratin à la crème landaise*. The menu for each evening's dinner was seldom a secret, since Rochelle usually entered the house through the kitchen door, and also because of the mouth-watering smells which tended to pervade every corner of the manor by the time the meal was ready.

'Yes, it is a little tight,' Miss Harris conceded. Rochelle was busily buttering a crusty bread roll and ignored the trend of the adult conversation. 'Perhaps I could get her something in St Helier at the weekend; something darker would be more practical, possibly.'

M. Laurient's brows went up; Miss Harris swallowed and felt her cheeks warm. He looked incredibly handsome when he gave her that particular look!

'Practical, Miss Harris? For an evening dress which is worn only perhaps for an hour each night? No, let's not court practicality for such a garment. Besides, the white sets off Rochelle's black hair.' He chuckled. He was clearly in a good humour, though for what reason Miss Harris could not fathom. 'What do you think, Chelle? Would you like a dark dress for a change?'

Rochelle was about to reply when Lucrèce and Emilie came in with the main course, and conversation was suspended while M. Laurient served the succulent chicken with its crispy cheese topping and the rich, creamy mushroom sauce. Miss Harris, for her part, served tiny new potatoes and *mange tout* and thought what a blessing it was that she seemed to be able to eat any amount of rich food but never put on weight.

'Well?' M. Laurient said presently, when the maids had gone out again and everyone had been served. 'Would you like a dark dress, Rochelle? As Miss Harris and I agreed, the one you're wearing won't last you much longer.'

'A dark one? I don't mind at all; I wish I could wear something looser, though,' Rochelle said, tugging irritably at the tight, high neck. 'Monsieur, may I ask a question?'

M. Laurient laughed. 'Of course! When did I ever stop you from asking questions, petite?'

'Well, never. Anyway, we went to see Copper's puppies today, me and Harry. Do you remember Copper, monsieur? You called her Runt because she was the smallest of Pod's litter, but Henri Napoule calls her Copper. She's had five of the dearest little puppies, and we went to see them and Harry explained to me about father and mother dogs . . . she said it was like orchids.'

M. Laurient cast a somewhat hunted look at Miss Harris, who kept her eyes firmly on her plate. She hoped for all their sakes that the difficult question she had dreaded earlier in the day was not about to be asked, but if it had to come she was glad it was being directed at M. Laurient and not herself.

'Yes, you could say it was like orchids, Rochelle. Now tell me about the puppies. How many were dogs and how many were bitches? Was there a particularly fine one? I have two excellent gun dogs but I suppose there's always

123

room for another . . . what would you say to having another puppy, Chelle?'

Miss Harris could see that this was a transparent attempt to take the child's mind off questions which perhaps should not be aired at the dining-table, but she could also see that it was going to fail. Rochelle had an obstinate look about her mouth; she was going to ask her question now come hell or high water!

'Oh, that would be lovely, monsieur. But the puppies are not all brown, like Copper; there are three yellow ones as well. And what I want to know, monsieur, is – when they decided that Copper should make some puppies, who used the wand?'

There was an astounded silence. Miss Harris did not understand the question and was about to ask for an explanation when she caught sight of M. Laurient's face. It was grave enough but she could see a muscle jumping in his cheek and his eyes were lit with suppressed laughter. Yet when he spoke his voice was admirably steady.

'What makes you ask, Chelle?'

'Well, when you and I decide that two stud plants should make seed together, one of us uses the mating wand to transfer pollen from one flower to another. And in the wild it's the bees, moths, things like that, isn't it? So with puppies . . .?'

Light dawned on Miss Harris and after one startled glance at M. Laurient her eyes returned to her plate and stayed there, though she could not entirely control the tiny movements in her shoulders as she fought an urge to laugh. The innocent darling . . . but what would he say?

'Um . . . who uses the wand. Yes, that's a good question, Chelle. In the wild, of course . . .'

'In the wild there are bees and moths and so on,' Rochelle repeated with a touch of impatience. 'But with the Napoules . . .'

124

'And what about with us, chérie? When Senna and Pod made those puppies . . .?'

'Oh, I know it must have been you who used the wand, monsieur,' Rochelle said readily. 'I was much younger then . . . so was it M. Napoule or was it Henri?'

'M. Napoule is the head of the household,' M. Laurient replied, after only the slightest hesitation. 'But when you are older, petite, you will learn that some things can be done without . . .' his voice wobbled a little, but corrected itself '. . . without the help of a wand. Let us say in this instance that it was M. Napoule who decided that Copper should have a litter and made arrangements accordingly. Does that answer your question?'

'Yes, thank you,' Rochelle said politely. 'It's very fortunate, isn't it, monsieur, that there were three yellow puppies and two brown ones and that they were not born half and half?'

'Very fortunate. But nature does not let such accidents happen within the same species. Copper and the father of the puppies were both labradors, you see. Had Copper been mated with a different sort of dog, their progeny might have been very odd . . . you've seen the spotted dogs some people own down in the town, have you not?'

'Mongrels,' supplied Rochelle, nodding vigorously. 'Yes, I've seen them. That, then, would be bad hybridisation?'

'More or less. Now eat up or Emilie will be hovering outside the door with the *Gouère aux pommes* going cold.'

'Ooh, is it really *Gouère aux pommes*?' Rochelle said, diverted by the thought of one of her favourite puddings. She began to eat her chicken as fast as she could. 'As to the puppy, monsieur, I would rather we kept one of Pod's babies, the next time she has a litter.'

'It shall be so, then,' M. Laurient said comfortably. He looked across at Miss Harris and, untypically, winked at her. Probably he had been as aware as she what thin ice

125

had just been skated over, she thought. She smiled back, a small, prim smile.

'That's grand. And monsieur, when we go down to the glasshouses to put the orchids to bed for the night . . .'

The talk lapsed into horticulture and Miss Harris contentedly stopped listening to them and turned to her own thoughts. During the long summer vacation this year she had intended to go to Europe, but she had been advised by her parents that this would not be sensible. Not this year.

'War has been avoided by Mr Chamberlain's policies, to be sure,' her father had written. 'But that does not mean we shall never have a use for the trenches which have been dug in the parks, nor for the air-raid shelters which some people are erecting. Europe, just now, is neither a good nor a safe place to be, with Hitler's fascists marching and our allies on tiptoe to defend themselves should he strike at them next.'

He seemed to be of the opinion, however, that things would right themselves in some mysterious manner in the next year or two and that, if she came home this year, she might easily get her European tour next summer. But France is in no danger, she reminded herself, sitting at the table as Emilie placed the golden-topped *Gouère aux pommes* before them. M. Laurient dug the spoon in and helped Miss Harris and Rochelle, finally giving himself a small portion, and then the jug of yellow Jersey cream was passed around.

'It's a bit like pancakes and a bit like baked apples and a bit like brandy sauce,' Rochelle observed, having ecstatically tasted her first spoonful. 'I think Mme Barfleur is the best cook in the world!'

And Miss Harris, eating her own pudding, could only agree.

'Will you be gone long?'

Rochelle stood at the foot of Miss Harris's bed and

126

swung one foot backwards and forwards, watching, large-eyed, as her friend packed. It was a ritual which happened every Christmas, every Easter and at the start of every summer holiday, but Rochelle had never got used to it. She always felt uneasy, as if this time Miss Harris might simply not bother to return, even though past experience should have comforted her. The two of them had lived at the manor now for over three years, which meant that Miss Harris had gone back to England . . . well, not quite as often as she might have, but at least seven times, and she had returned just as she had promised on each previous occasion. Rochelle wondered if her uneasiness stemmed from the fact that her parents had gone to France and not returned, but decided that she was just being silly. Miss Harris would go, Miss Harris would return, and she herself would have a marvellous summer because she always did.

Olivia, who came up to the manor most weekends, actually moved in during the summer. Not for all the holiday, of course, but for quite long periods at a time. Though she had never lost her ascendency over the younger girl, Olivia was easier to deal with now that Rochelle was the one actually living at the manor, acknowledged as M. Laurient's ward and able to go down to the kitchen with messages for Mme Barfleur. Olivia still bossed, but she no longer bullied and the girls were close friends.

Now Miss Harris closed the lid of her case and began to struggle with the straps which ensured that it stayed closed on its long journey by sea and rail, to say nothing of the pony-cart from the manor to the port.

'Long? No, of course I shan't be gone long. I have to be back before school starts again at the end of September. And I'm taking M. Laurient's orchid articles up to London first, remember, along with the photographs of the improvements in the glasshouses. The Royal Horticultural Society is extremely interested. They're going to publish his experiments with the hybrids for everyone to read.'

127

'They were my experiments too,' Rochelle chirruped, sitting on the suitcase so that her small weight might make it easier for Miss Harris to close the lid. 'That man took my picture as well, only I don't suppose they'll put that into a paper, do you?'

'I'll send it to you if they do,' Miss Harris promised. 'Oh, Chelle, I always miss you – and the manor – but I'll miss you more than ever this year. Things seem so . . . so uncertain.'

'I know, everyone says so. Just think, in only a bit more than six months' time it will be 1940! Can you imagine that? Doesn't it sound *old*? Forty seems old whether it's a person or a year, don't you think?'

'Oh, forty isn't *old*,' Miss Harris said at once. 'Why, M. Laurient must be past forty, I should think . . . you don't think of him as old, do you?'

She herself was thirty-six and had for some time regarded forty with trepidation. If one reached forty and was still a spinster one might as well not bother even to hope.

'M. Laurient isn't old. He's just right,' Rochelle said at once. She was very partisan towards her guardian; Miss Harris had noticed it in a thousand different ways. 'Why, when I'm sixteen M. Laurient will be forty-seven and I'm going to marry him. You can't think he's old . . . it's different for men.'

'I think that the difference between sixteen and forty-seven is rather too much for happiness,' Miss Harris said, rather amused at Rochelle's forthrightness. 'Does the gentleman himself have no say in the matter? I've heard him say several times that he isn't the marrying kind.'

'I know, but he knows me so well he's bound to want to marry me, especially as I want to marry him ever so badly,' Rochelle pointed out. 'I could be even more useful to him if we were married. He could take me to France when he goes, and to London to that horticultural place . . . oh, I could be ever so useful to him.'

'Well, that's for the future,' Miss Harris said, suddenly aware that Rochelle's feelings on the matter and her own were rather distressingly similar. She, too, had thought wistfully how very useful she could have been to M. Laurient had things been different. 'Can you help me down with my things, Chelle? The pony-cart will take me down to the port in less than an hour and I do like to be ready in plenty of time.'

An hour later, Rochelle waved Miss Harris off and then rushed further along the lane to a point where the ground was high enough to enable her to see the pony-trap again as it rattled on to the main road. Her violent waves were answered, but she stayed there long after the trap was no more than a dot, and only when it rounded a bend and disappeared did she return to the manor. She walked slowly, scuffing a pebble ahead of her with her toe, and when she got back home went straight to the kitchen.

'She's gone,' she announced unnecessarily to the assembled company. Mme Barfleur, Emilie and Lucrèce were sitting round the kitchen table drinking tea and eating what Rochelle recognised as honey and almond cake; her mouth watered hopefully and when Mme Barfleur looked up and smiled she knew her hopes were about to be realised.

'Come in, petite, and have some cake and a glass of milk,' Mme Barfleur said hospitably, waving to a chair and pulling the cake towards her in order that she might cut a hefty slice. 'Has the good Miss Harris gone, then?'

'Yes,' Rochelle said gloomily, casting herself into the chair and accepting the slice of cake with gratitude. 'I love the summer holidays so much, and I love having Olivia to stay, but I do miss Harry.'

Mme Barfleur clicked her tongue reproachfully; to her way of thinking a lady should always be given her title and 'Miss' went with Harris just as 'Madame' went with

129

Barfleur. Had Rochelle chosen to call Miss Harris 'Tante', that would have been acceptable too – but Harry! Ah no, it was not right.

'She has her own family to think of,' she said, sipping hot tea whilst Rochelle poured herself a glass of milk. 'You would not have her neglect her old mother and father, surely? And one day, you know, she'll take you back with her to Norwich, so that you can see the place where she was born and brought up.'

'Yes . . . only I don't particularly want to go to England,' Rochelle explained. 'Nowhere could possibly be as nice as here. Even Harry never pretended that it was.'

'Well, well, everyone loves their own place best,' Mme Barfleur said indulgently. 'Just one more small piece, then, Emilie, before we start the dinner.'

'What is it tonight?' Rochelle asked, her voice thickened by the cake. 'Something special?'

'All my cooking is special,' Mme Barfleur said portentously whilst Emilie and Lucrèce ate cake fast, chattering to each other in the singing island patois. 'But tonight, because old Jean has delivered some fresh sea bass, we shall have *Grillade au fenouil* for a main course with a brandy and chocolate mousse for dessert.'

'Delicious,' Rochelle said. 'You set light to the bass for that, don't you? Can I come and hold the taper for you?'

'We flambé the fennel,' Mme Barfleur admitted. 'Aren't you going to ask which soup will be served with this marvellous dish?'

'Which soup?' Rochelle asked obediently, but with real interest. One day, when she was M. Laurient's wife, she might have to cook herself – or at least employ someone to do it for her – and she wanted to know how it was done. Besides, all Islanders were interested in good food.

'A clear chicken broth, with croûtons,' Mme Barfleur said, jerking her head at the stove on which a large blackened pan simmered. 'It goes down well before fish.'

130

Rochelle nodded seriously. She made a mental note that a clear soup with croûtons complemented a fish dish. Then she finished up her milk, wiped her moustache away with the back of her hand, and got down from the table.

'Thank you for my *goûter*,' she said. 'Is M. Laurient in the glasshouses, do you know?'

'Very probably,' Mme Barfleur said. She heaved her bulk out of the chair and came across to the back door as Rochelle went out into the yard. 'Don't be lonely for Miss Harris,' she called as the girl turned to wave to her. 'After all, it is the end of June and she'll be back in mid-September; that's only about ten weeks away. Just you wait – it will go like lightning, and then there she'll be, getting off the ferry, happy to be home with us all again.'

Rochelle was about to make some lighthearted retort when she felt an icy hand grip the back of her neck. Just for a moment it was as strong as a physical sensation, so that she almost turned round to see who had caught hold of her, and then she realised that it was fear and horrid apprehension and nothing more.

'I – don't – know,' she said, so slowly that Mme Barfleur, who had turned to go into the kitchen again, glanced round. 'I've got a horrible feeling that she won't be back this September.'

She said it with enough conviction to make Mme Barfleur blink before she began to scoff gently. Nonsense, she said; in effect, why should not your teacher return? But Rochelle could only shake her head and wonder why she was suddenly so sure that Miss Harris would not be stepping off the ferry when September came along that year.

'Run along to monsieur,' Mme Barfleur advised, seeing that Rochelle was still standing in the stable-yard. 'What a foolish little thing you are. Monsieur will tell you – she will be back. She's too fond of us all to stay away, and what's more she likes her work.'

'Yes, of course, you must be right,' Rochelle said as the cold feeling on her neck slowly receded. 'She'll come back – she always has before.'

She began to walk, at first slowly and then with increasing speed, towards the glasshouses and M. Laurient.

It was the end of June, as Mme Barfleur had said. The year was 1939.

6

'You mean she won't come back? Just because there's a war on? But wouldn't she be safer here? They say the Germans will bomb Britain, but they won't bother with us, will they? We don't have armies and things. I'm sure she'd be safer here.'

Olivia stopped speaking and Rochelle was glad; what was the use of denying something when it was patently a fact? Today was Sunday, 3 September 1939, and war had been declared between Germany and Great Britain. M. Laurient had immediately tried to telephone Harry at her Norwich home, only to be told there was a long delay and all the lines were jammed, but he was as certain as Rochelle that Harry would not return to them. So she and Olivia had headed for the little bay and sat in the sand with the sunshine warm upon them and talked . . . or rather, Olivia talked. But now she was looking expectantly at Rochelle, so the younger girl took a deep breath and tried to explain.

'If she came back, Livia, some people would say she was running away. And if she had come back already it might have meant that she had no choice but to stay here for as long as the war lasted – you can't just cross the sea and change countries when you're at war with someone, though I'm not quite sure why. For the time being, we'll just have to write letters and telephone. When the lines are open again, of course.'

'It'll all be over by Christmas,' Olivia said. 'We'll have beaten them by then . . . or do you think they'll make peace with us when they realise we aren't just going to give up like the others?'

Rochelle shrugged.

'Don't know; let's not keep on about it. It's bad enough up at the house, with everyone either silly and excited, like Emilie and Lucrèce, or grave and unhappy like M. Laurient and Mme Barfleur.'

'All right. What shall we do then?'

Rochelle looked around her. The scene, idyllically beautiful, no longer seemed quite real. It was as though a sheet of totally transparent but very strong glass had been inserted between herself and her surroundings. She remembered, vaguely, that at the time of her parents' death something very similar had happened. M. Laurient had broken through the glass then, though, and until this moment it had not happened again. What was it? Shock? But, awful though it seemed this war would be, it did not affect her at all, nor any of her school friends. Oh, some children would go away, that had all been talked about a year ago, but the hard core of the Islanders themselves would remain. There could be no fear, this time, that M. Laurient would pack her off to relatives or children's homes or even boarding schools. He had asked her, quite casually, many months ago, whether she would like him to send her to the mainland when war broke out – not if, when – and she had looked around her – they had been in the tropical house at the time – and said, incredulously, 'Send me away? From *these*?' and he had shrugged and smiled and said that it was how he felt, too.

'Let's paddle,' she suggested at last. 'The tide's nearly low enough to reach the island.'

They always wanted to reach the island, but it was a destination rarely arrived at because it was only possible at low tide. But today, as Rochelle had said, it should be easy enough to wade out. Then they could poke around in the pools and tiny caves, climb on to the cap of grass and seapinks, and pretend to be the first settlers on a foreign shore.

'Yes, all right,' Olivia agreed. She jumped to her feet,

scattering sand. 'Shall we leave our food here or take it with us?'

It would have been sensible to leave it, probably, but it would be much more exciting, Rochelle considered, to eat it actually on the island, queens of all they surveyed. She said as much, so she and Olivia took a handle each and set out for the island.

It was marvellous to wade through the crystal water, watching the reflection of the ripples dancing on the sand below, to see the flicker of tiny fish, the quick sideways scuttle of a crab, the slow surge of a bed of kelp. At first the water deepened as they waded; then, as they neared the island, it began to grow shallower, and at last they were there, the ring of rock which protected the island all that lay between them and their destination.

'We'll have to walk round, until we find a gap,' said Olivia. 'I'm sure there's one on the other side.'

There was; they walked carefully along the ridge of higher sand, getting wet to their knickers at a point where it dipped near the rocks, but reached the island in good order and climbed up the miniature cliff to slump, happily tired, in the green grass at the top.

They ate their food in dreamy contentment, leaving the fruit until last so that it would quench their thirst. Big purple plums went down well, even their sourness welcome to the girls, and then Olivia sat up and dusted her hands on her skirt.

'The water's gone down; we can play now,' she announced. 'If there were more of us, what a good place for "Rescue" this would be! I suppose we can't do it with only two, though?'

'No . . . but we could take it in turns to attack the island whilst the other defended,' Rochelle said, jumping to her feet. 'I'll defend first . . . you be the attacker, trying to get up.'

'We-ell . . . you mustn't actually push me back on to the

rocks. You could easily break my back,' Olivia cautioned, getting to her feet as well. 'Tell you what, say we count a foot on the island as a win . . . or a hand on the grass? We could try both.'

Both proved far more difficult than either girl had anticipated. Olivia circled, bent double, but provided Rochelle stood on the topmost ridge she could see Olivia no matter how her friend crouched, and that meant that the moment Olivia attacked, Rochelle was there to defend, with a quick shove, the other's attempts at invasion.

'Tell you what,' Rochelle said as, flushed and breathing hard, the two met to confer. 'I'll attack this time . . . but we'll make a rule that you aren't allowed to stay on watch all the time, you have to come down every time you count fifty, and patrol the beachy bit for another count of fifty. That'll give me more of a chance.'

This proved a great success. It was more exciting for both parties and meant that they changed places frequently, the score mounting up rapidly on both sides. They grew so excited that they nearly missed the tide, but at last Olivia realised that the water was growing deeper as she skulked round watching for her chance to attack, and she called Rochelle down off the ridge.

'Tide's turned,' she shouted. 'We'd better get back, Chelle.'

They waded through the glinting channel and began to trudge across the flat expanse of hard, wet sand.

'That was fun,' Rochelle observed, turning to watch the island as the waves encroached on their erstwhile playground. 'It quite took my mind off this war business.'

'And mine. Tell you what, though, Chelle, that game we were playing . . . that could easily be a war game. The one on the island would be the good one, the Jerseyman, and the one attacking and trying to get aboard could be the Jerry.'

Rochelle frowned, biting her lower lip.

136

'Yes . . . but that isn't how they fight wars, is it? I mean, they whoosh over frontiers – that's why we're in a war, because they went into Poland – but they don't ever attack islands do they?'

'Of course they do; England's an island, Chelle, and they're frightened of being attacked. Why, the German navy's quite big enough to carry soldiers over the Channel, I suppose.'

They had reached the shore by now and were trudging up the beach; tiredness was making Rochelle's limbs feel heavy, yet there was a pleasant languor in the way she walked, the feel of salt drying on her legs and feet, the tug of the breeze in her hair. On such a day she could not imagine that the game she and Olivia had played could ever become real, earnest, with the prize the island which was her home.

'England wouldn't let it happen to us,' she said confidently. They reached the stranded boat and she leaned inside for her sandshoes and jersey. 'It's a good game, though.'

'Yes, it is. Better than "Rescue" when there are only the two of us.'

'We'll play it again,' Rochelle said, sliding her feet into her sandshoes. 'Let's hurry back, though; I'm starving in spite of all the food Mme Barfleur packed for us.'

'Me too. As it's the weekend I'm staying for dinner, but I can't stay the night. Maman needs me tomorrow.'

Rochelle nodded. Mme Barfleur's son-in-law Cyril Buchet had gone to England by air to join one of the forces. Young Mme Buchet had shed a good many tears and Olivia had looked mournful for a day or two, but in fact she was extremely proud of her papa and wanted to tell everyone that, since he was a fisherman, he would probably join the Royal Navy and speedily rise to captain his own vessel.

'Yes, I expect she'll need you more than ever with this

war. I wonder if M. Laurient will go? I suppose he'll have to, do you think?'

Olivia gave her the indulgent glance more usually bestowed on the sweet but decidedly simple. Rochelle ruffled, but then subsided. She was, after all, two years younger than her friend.

'No, Chelle, he won't go, he's far too old! They want young men, like my papa, and Jacques, who's seventeen. When you are past forty you are quite safe, I believe.'

'Then how old is M. Buchet?' Rochelle asked, torn between relief that she would be allowed to keep her guardian and annoyance that he should, by implication, be so old as to be past it. 'I shouldn't have thought he was so very young.'

'My papa is thirty-one, which is a good age to learn to be a sailor. Besides, he'll tell them he's only twenty-five and they'll believe him. He has such black curls and such laughing eyes that he doesn't look any older.'

'M. Laurient is awfully strong, and I think he's young-looking as well,' Rochelle pointed out. 'He was in the Great War. He was something important in the army – a captain, I believe. They may ask him to help them this time as well.'

Back at the manor, Rochelle had high tea with the staff, though Mme Barfleur laughed at her and said it was a wonder she wasn't fatter than Hugo-pig in his sty, the amount she put away. Since she would presently have dinner with her guardian, and would, Rochelle admitted, eat every morsel, there was a certain amount of truth in what she said, but as soon as high tea was over Rochelle left Olivia and the maids clearing and washing up and hurried through the garden to the glasshouses.

M. Laurient was in the nursery, lovingly examining the young and tender plants which enjoyed the mild, damp atmosphere he had created here. He smiled as Rochelle came in but she could see at once that he was preoccupied.

'Hello; have a nice afternoon?' He did not wait for her reply but continued at once: 'I'm wondering whether I shall manage to get a flower from Pure Madonna before the war really hits us, or whether I'll have to wait until it's all over to see whether we've done it this time.'

'Why shouldn't we have flowers whilst it's going on?' Rochelle asked curiously. She lifted a pot, tapped it, then reached for the dipper of rainwater. She stood the pot in a shallow dish and poured water carefully round the base, standing back when her task was completed and the water was gradually being drawn up by the thirsty seedling.

'Because in time of war you aren't able to have fires whenever you want them, let alone fires which heat a greenhouse.'

Why not seemed silly, but Rochelle said it anyway, her smooth brow puzzling into a frown.

'Why not? Because ships and aircraft can't get through to bring you things you can't grow yourself; wood will be short, coal and coke almost non-existent. Men will risk their lives getting even a cake of soap across the sea to us, so we won't have much and what we do have will be rationed.'

'Oh. And the orchids won't flower without heat.' It was a simple statement; she knew as well as he how hard they had to work to recreate the sort of environment in which the orchids could thrive. 'Will they die, then? All our little ones?'

M. Laurient had been pottering amongst the plants, setting them to rights for the night, but at her words he swung round, one brow climbing, his expression half amused, half thoughtful.

'All our little ones? That's a quotation . . . wait a minute.' He put a hand over his eyes, his lips moving, then lowered

139

his hand again. 'Got it! "All my pretty ones? Did you say all?" It comes from a play by Shakespeare, *Macbeth*.'

'Does it? Was the man in that play talking about orchids, then?'

M. Laurient moved back amongst his plants, dribbling water into pots, turning them so that they would grow up straight. He answered without looking at her.

'No, not orchids. Children. Macbeth had killed his children.'

'That's worse,' Rochelle said decidedly, and was relieved to see him smile. 'Why did Macbeth do that?'

'It's too complicated to tell you now. But what I was starting to say, Rochelle, was that if war comes to the island we shall be lucky to get any of the plants through it. I'll do my best, of course, to keep Pure Madonna alive, even if it doesn't flower . . . indeed, as you know, we may still not have bred Pure Madonna; we shan't be sure until it does flower . . . but for the rest, we may have to let them lie until the war's over. And that isn't all. I'm going to take certain basic steps which may be necessary or may not be, but I want them to be a secret, just between you and me. Can you keep a secret, Chelle?'

'You know I can,' Rochelle said. 'I never chatter about things; I haven't told *anyone* how close you think you've got to Pure Madonna, just in case we're wrong.'

'That's true. Very well, then. I'm going to stow some things away safely so that after the war there'll be something left. I'll take you with me when I choose my spot, show you how to get to it, but I'll not say a word to anyone else.' Still with his back to her and speaking as though to himself, he added, 'You're just a child; they won't suspect a child of knowing more than she ought. But . . . not a word to anyone, Chelle; understand? Never tell anyone until after the war, and then if I'm still around we'll bring the stuff out. If . . . but that's enough for now, I think.'

'Will you put away orchid seed?' Rochelle asked presently, as the two of them continued to water the plants. 'It'll live for years, won't it?'

M. Laurient shrugged, then smiled.

'Possibly; it wouldn't hurt. But I had more tangible assets in mind. Money, silver and so on. In a small island like this food shortages could mean . . . well, I don't want to think about it, but I'm going to take what precautions I can.'

And presently it was time for dinner, or rather time to change for dinner, and Rochelle ran indoors to her own room and put on the blue cotton dress which dear Harry had had made quite two sizes too big, for expansion, she said.

Washing and dressing, she thought about M. Laurient's words and was intrigued by the prospect of what she thought of as a squirrel's hoard. Food, he had said. It would have to be tinned food, unless things like onions and dried herbs counted? Things like the long Italian spaghetti which Mme Barfleur had sent over from the Continent, and pulses like haricot beans, might well keep for quite a while, but it depended where M. Laurient intended to hide them. If he meant to dig a hole in the garden they would not last long!

Rochelle donned the blue frock, struggled into a pair of cotton stockings and fastened them to her liberty bodice, wondering whether it would really matter if she missed out her stockings in future, for the weather was still warm and there was no Harry, now, to remind her that she was a budding lady and ladies had to get used to irksome things like stockings. It seemed a bit mean, though, to take advantage of Harry's involuntary absence, so she put on her strap-shoes, banged her head three times with the brush, and set off for the dining-room.

It seemed strange to sit down to dinner just the two of them, for since Harry had been away M. Laurient's estate manager, John Pilling, had eaten with them, sometimes

141

with his wife Joan, with her mannish haircut, tweed suits and brisk, no-nonsense voice. But John and Joan were English and had gone back to the mainland to join the armed forces. John hoped to be accepted into the Royal Air Force so of course Joan wanted the WRAF; they had promised to write, had been desolate to leave and would come back as soon as the war was over.

'We'll probably see you in time for the spring planting,' John had said, as he had shaken M. Laurient's hand. 'Thanks for everything, Charles . . . you know I wouldn't leave if I could reconcile my conscience with staying.'

M. Laurient had shaken his hand and gripped his shoulder very hard.

'Give 'em one for me, John,' he said. But later, to Rochelle, he had added, 'John was too young for the last lot. Everyone said that'd be over by Christmas, too.'

'It lasted longer than that, though, didn't it?' Rochelle said, and was appalled to be told that in fact it had lasted four whole years and had ended, not in an outright victory for the Allies, but in an armistice, whatever that might mean.

Now, sitting close together at the big table, because it would have been absurd to sit at opposite ends, Rochelle put her thoughts into words.

'Will you get someone to replace John, monsieur? Only so many of the young men have gone to the mainland . . . though the older ones are left.'

A shadow for which Rochelle could see no reason crossed his face, and then he smiled and picked up his soup spoon.

'Yes, it'll have to be someone older, someone who can't go off to fight. I'm going to do the job myself.'

Rochelle picked up her own soup spoon, feeling her face grow hot. How could she have been so insensitive? M. Laurient must hate to feel that he could not go and fight, although she, personally, thought it a very good thing. But to act as estate manager would mean that monsieur would be far too busy to fret because no one wanted him to be a soldier, and that was a good thing. But he was speaking, carrying on as though she had not said anything untoward.

'. . . so you'll have to work even harder than you do already on the orchids,' he was saying, 'because I'll be doing not only the manager's job but quite a lot of the physical work as well. Someone has to milk the cows and plant the wheat and do all the other things which we take for granted, and with all the young men gone – and most of them will go, I'm sure of it – it's going to be left to those who remain to see that we don't starve.'

'I'll help,' Rochelle said eagerly. 'Olivia will as well, I'm sure.'

'Good. After tonight, I'm going to tell Mme Barfleur that we'll all eat in the kitchen. Bringing meals up to the dining-room just for the two of us is ridiculous; a waste of time, energy and fuel.'

'What about school?' Rochelle said hopefully. 'I know you've always let me and Livia do a bit of apple and pear picking, but this year surely you'll want us much more than just in the evenings and at weekends?'

'Yes, but I won't have your education interrupted. We'll work something out. Incidentally, the article on our glass-houses and the breeding we're doing came this morning – want to read it?'

'Oh . . . yes, *please!*'

The article was produced. Rochelle was thrilled to see the manor pictured and a good few of the orchid species as well, and to read M. Laurient's name several times over and always in glowing terms when it came to his hybridi-sation achievements.

'Who will read it?' M. Laurient said in answer to Rochelle's query. 'Why, it'll be read all over the world by people who care about orchids. Even in Germany they'll read it and be interested in what we've been doing.'

143

'Gosh,' Rochelle said reverently. 'And you haven't even bred Pure Madonna yet – not to flowering, I mean.'

M. Laurient smiled at her. It occurred to Rochelle for the first time that he smiled much more than he used to; he was altogether easier and more approachable now that they were, so to speak, a family.

The thought delighted her. She and monsieur were a family! She smiled to herself, spooning in the rich and fragrant chicken soup.

'Ah, Mme Barfleur. It's a dreadful day, but I have business in St Helier, so I thought you might take the opportunity of spending a day or so with your daughter. Rochelle will be staying with her aunt and I shall put up at an hotel. The house won't be left empty, of course, since the dogs will be here and I shall be coming in early and late to see to them, but there's little point in your not seizing an opportunity which may not come too often, with manpower so low.'

M. Laurient had made good his threat to eat in the kitchen, and poor Mme Barfleur was most ill at ease sharing a table with her employer. In fact she had not yet done so, making excuses and doing bits and pieces of cooking so that she usually sat down, with a bob of her head in his direction, just as he was rising from his chair.

Now Mme Barfleur, carrying her plate across the kitchen as he was halfway to the door, stopped in her tracks like a shot rabbit.

'Go into St Helier, sir? Why . . . for the *day*?'

'For two days,' M. Laurient said patiently. 'I'll run you in today – when you're ready, of course – and you can stay there all day tomorrow. Tomorrow night too, if you like. I'll pick you up first thing Thursday morning, if that would suit you.'

'And . . . and you won't be here yourself?' Mme Barfleur put her meal down on the table and began to ruffle herself

144

up, just like an angry turkey cock, or a cat who sees a dog. 'That would be most imprudent, sir . . . most imprudent! You and Chelle go off by all means, and you needn't worry yourself that I'll waste my time or idle whilst you're gone, but keep an eye on the place I will and must. Why, suppose something happened . . . someone broke in? And not a soul bar Senna and Pod to say them nay . . . and those creatures, if you don't mind my saying so, sir, would likely show the burglars where to lay their hands on the decent silver if only they would also cut them a chunk off the ham in the pantry.'

Rochelle, still seated and eating toast, smiled at this unkind but realistic picture. She adored both Senna and Pod, but was honest enough to admit that Mme Barfleur had got the dogs taped; neither Senna nor Pod would show a tooth to an intruder who came armed with good things to eat – or not until they had devoured the offerings, anyway.

Emilie and Lucrèce had left, to work in a munitions factory on the mainland. They had been good, hardworking girls, but because M. Laurient had closed up a good part of the rambling old manor house they were not too badly missed. A couple of women came up from the village two or three times a week to do the rough work and to help out if they were needed, but otherwise Mme Barfleur and Rochelle did what was necessary. Rochelle, indeed, was becoming a useful cook and enjoying it very much, though it still came a long way behind orchiculture in her favour.

'My dear madame,' M. Laurient said patiently now. 'I understand your feelings, and I would undertake to stay here myself for the two nights in question, if I could. But there are things which must be done . . . I must close the house down, just for those two days.'

Rochelle, knowing full well that she was not going to her aunt's for two minutes, let alone two days, watched with some interest to see how M. Laurient would carry this off.

She did not think that Mme Barfleur would simply let herself be hustled off to St Helier without some sort of explanation, but she underestimated the older woman. Mme Barfleur stared from face to face, and then, suddenly, a big, broad smile broke out on her troubled countenance.

'Oh! Oh, I *see*, sir. Why on earth didn't you say? What the eye doesn't see the heart doesn't grieve over, eh? Not that I think there's the slightest necessity . . . the Maginot Line will hold 'em, and unless they take France they've no chance of taking the islands. But . . . you're very right. Yes, yes, I'll go to St Helier to see my daughter, and if it helps I'll take Rochelle with me.'

'It's very good of you, madame, but our arrangements, in that area, have already been made. So would you like to pack a bag with a few necessities and we'll be off at ten o'clock, if that would suit you? It's a pity it's raining – this sea-mist is likely to hang about for a couple of days, I'm told – but beggars can't be choosers.'

Mme Barfleur smiled; she all but winked, Rochelle was much amused to see. Clearly, the older woman was well aware of what would go on in her absence and thoroughly approved.

'Yes, of course, sir. I'll pack a bag right away. And if there's things missing when we get back I won't raise a dust because I'll know . . . if you see what I mean, sir . . . that they're in a safe place.'

M. Laurient nodded curtly but Rochelle could see his mouth twitching; then he beckoned Rochelle out of the room.

'You've packing of your own to do,' he reminded her whilst they were still in earshot of the kitchen. 'Go and get your bag, there's a good girl.'

'Do we still have to pretend?' Rochelle whispered as soon as they were alone. 'Can't I stay here whilst you run Mme Barfleur into St Helier?'

'No; we have to play out the entire charade,' M. Laurient

assured her. 'You see, we don't want anyone to be suspicious and to wonder what we're doing, so I shall indeed stay at an hotel each night and you must really stay with your aunt.'

'Have you *asked* her?' Rochelle said incredulously. 'When you explained what you were going to do I thought it was all a pretend.'

'Well, most of it is,' M. Laurient admitted. 'What we have to do, my child, is muddy the waters. Your aunt will know that you are spending one night with her, because that is exactly what you will do . . . no, I've not asked her yet, we'll do that when we take Mme Barfleur to stay with her daughter . . . and during the day she will assume you are with Olivia or one of your other friends, they will assume you are with your aunt . . . and you'll be with me, at the manor.'

'But how will I spend the other night? And where will my aunt think I am then?' Rochelle asked. 'And why is it necessary, monsieur? Especially as Mme Barfleur seems to know that it's all a pretend.'

'I would trust Mme Barfleur where I would trust few others,' M. Laurient said drily. 'But what does she actually *know*, Chelle? Only that I am going to hide away some family silver and so on. She has no idea that there is any more to it than that.'

'She doesn't know about the tins of food, then.' Rochelle put a foot on the stair. 'Shall I go and pack?'

'What tins of . . . oh, never mind. Yes, you go and put some things into your bag. Your aunt will be glad to have you for a night, I feel sure, when I tell her I'm going to be away on business and don't want to leave you at the manor alone.'

They drove to St Helier in the Sunbeam, snugly out of the rain behind the perspex windows. The sea-mist swirled about them as they neared the shore. It was a stinker of a day, Rochelle told herself, and hugged within her bosom the thought that this was the most exciting day of her life. M. Laurient was going to show her and her alone where he intended to hide his treasures for after the war. She would keep his secret no matter what, she thought dramatically, and lost herself in a daydream in which booted Nazis pursued her through just such a sea-mist as enveloped the island today, screaming threats and curses, begging, imploring . . . but she ran ahead of them all, laughing back at them, the secret safe with her.

Mlle Edith Bourge was not pleased to see them, but she agreed, grudgingly, that the child might spend one night in her small spare room.

'But I can't do with a child under my feet all day,' she continued, for all the world as though Rochelle was two instead of twelve. 'I know it's raining, but surely she can find someone to visit in the town? Bring her back at bedtime and I'm sure I'll do my best to see she has a good night's rest.'

With suitable expressions of gratitude, M. Laurient and Rochelle left her suitcase with her aunt and disappeared once more into the sea-mist.

'Are you sure you can manage that bag? It's not too heavy for you? If it is don't for heaven's sake just drop it. Put it carefully down somewhere safe and I'll come back for it.'

M. Laurient and Rochelle had carried their stout canvas bags down the winding path and past the Devil's Dip. They had gone to the little ledge above the fierce rocks and had turned to their left and continued on down. Now, standing at the edge of the latest rock-fall, M. Laurient addressed Rochelle, who smiled back at him, eyes burning with excitement though her hair clung wetly to her head and her face was beaded with moisture. They could just about see each other; should one of them have moved five or six feet away they would have been out of sight entirely.

'Of course it isn't too heavy, monsieur! But when we go down shall I need both my hands? Because if so, shouldn't I tie the bag to my wrist?'

'Hmm . . . better still, I'll fasten it between your shoulders, like a knapsack. And mine, as well.'

They stood on the path, Rochelle trying not to shiver with cold and excitement mixed, and M. Laurient tied the bag round her shoulders with a length of rope which he cut with a pocket knife. After that he secured his own and then, prepared, he stepped off the path and began to swing himself round and down, out of sight.

Rochelle waited several minutes and then followed him. She was an old hand at rock climbing; she and Olivia sometimes came out after seabirds' eggs, though never at this particular spot, which was far too dangerous. But she knew that one must not follow another closely lest a trifling crumbling of the rock land in the eyes of the one below and cause a really bad accident.

With her hands free and the weight on her back not enough to unbalance her at all, she went down the rocks like a monkey and was soon at the overhang which had baffled her once before. On that occasion, M. Laurient had climbed across lower down, but since then a further fall had made an unbridgeable gap in the path he had taken. She crouched above the bulge and tried to peer down.

'M. Laurient . . . what shall I do? Will you catch me if I jump?'

'No . . . stay there. When I've got rid of my bags I'll come back, and you can lower your bag down to me and ease yourself very slowly over the edge.'

His voice echoed up to her though he spoke quietly. Neither of them thought that anyone would be about on such a day, but even so it behoved them to speak quietly after all the trouble they had gone to in order to be unobserved.

'All right.'

She lay on her stomach on the ledge and looked down, over the bulge. At first she could see nothing, but then he appeared dimly through the mist; she could just make out his dark head and the shoulders of the thick fisherman's jersey he was wearing. She, too, had such a jersey on; it reached halfway to her knees and was an excellent disguise against the grey of the rocks. Not that they were likely to be spotted in the mist and the rain, but they could not tell when the mist might suddenly begin to clear. Should a wind get up it could happen in seconds, almost.

Even as she watched, however, the mist claimed him. She tried to tell herself that a patch of deeper grey was M. Laurient as he climbed downwards, but it was soon clear that he must, by now, be far too low for her eyes to pick him out. She drew back with a little sigh and glanced around her instead.

The ledge had fat cushions of sea-pinks in the crevices and thyme grew against the solid cliff itself, its tiny purple florets beaded with even tinier drops of moisture. Up above her, sand martins, or perhaps even swifts, had nested in holes in the sandstone. She could see half a dozen holes, but only three had the telltale white streaks of guano which denoted occupancy. It was odd to lie there and hear the sea thundering on the rocks below yet be unable to see anything but the swirling mist. There was no breath of wind and in the silence quite tiny sounds came clearly to her ears. The soft tap-tappeting of moisture drops pattering off the shaggy clump of grass close to her right ear, the tiny whispering sound of moving blades as a snail-let not much bigger than a pinhead brought its transparent body and cream and brown striped shell out of a clump of grass and on to the thyme.

'Rochelle!'

M. Laurient's voice sounded like a peal of thunder to one whose ears had become attuned to a snail's slow progress, and Rochelle jumped. She leaned forward across the overhang once more, and there, only feet below her, was M. Laurient's dark, upturned face, a lock of hair hanging across his forehead.

'Yes, monsieur? I'm ready!'

'Good. Then lower your bag . . . carefully, now.'

Rochelle unslung her bag and lowered it, swinging, from the overhang. M. Laurient stood on tiptoe and just managed to grasp the material as it dangled above him.

'All right . . . drop it!'

Rochelle let go of the rope and saw the bag safely held, then turned to crouch on the edge. It was foolish, she knew, but even knowing that M. Laurient was below and ready to catch her, she still found herself most reluctant to let go of the cliff and simply fall into space.

But it would never have done to say so, or to show the slightest reluctance, especially after she had been so adamant that she would not worry at all about the climb down. So she closed her eyes, gritted her teeth, and dropped.

And it was all right, as she should have known it would be. She fell less than a foot before she was caught securely, then placed on the rock. M. Laurient patted her shoulder and picked up her bag, which he had put down whilst he fielded her.

'Well done. Now, can you follow me? I know you don't like to get too close, but you've got to see where I go, and from now on it's none too straightforward. Just remember, if you're not sure you're safe, stay exactly where you are and tell me. Don't let me go on, assuming you're following. Right?'

'Yes, but I dare say I climb better than you,' Rochelle said with no humbleness whatsoever. 'If I knew where you were heading I could probably beat you to it.'

'It's possible,' M. Laurient said, instead of telling her not to be so cocky as he would have done in other circumstances, Rochelle felt sure. 'Now, I'm off.'

He turned to his right and set off, spread out over the surface of the wet, gleaming rock, clinging with fingers and toes, even his hard, flat stomach seeming to have some sort of adhesive contact with the rock. Rochelle, following, was ashamed of her earlier remark. She climbed well for a girl of her age, but she could not compare with M. Laurient. However, this was no time to tell him so; right now she needed all her breath and wits and courage simply to follow him and keep him in sight so that she could copy each movement he made.

It was all right, though. Perhaps because of the mist M. Laurient never got further than a couple of feet ahead of her, and because she was watching him and never considering the possibility of falling or even thinking about the drop to the rocks below it seemed no time at all before he had stopped and was guiding her on to the tiny ledge on which he himself was balanced.

'There you are,' he said breathlessly, still holding on to the rock but turning to smile at her. 'No bones broken. Can you see where we're going?'

Rochelle looked all round; great pinnacles and towers of rock surrounded them, and below, only a matter of feet away now, the sea raged and sucked and crashed on the rocks. Near at hand two mighty rocks leaned close, with a narrow, dark crevice between them, but there could not possibly be room in there for a man of M. Laurient's size; it was even doubtful, Rochelle thought, whether she herself could squeeze in. And anyway, when − if − she did, she would only come up against the cliff.

She pointed to the crevice, however, since it was the only thing remotely resembling a hiding place that she could see.

'Not in there? It isn't big enough, surely? Besides, when the spring tides come that crack'll get wet, won't it?'

'It will. Follow me, though.'

He turned sideways, with her bag in one hand, and slid,

like a lizard, into the crevice. Rochelle followed him . . . too closely, as it turned out. A muffled voice bade her keep off his heels, and then she could tell by the feel of the rock around her that he had moved on, leaving her squeezed in the crevice like a living fossil.

Galvanised by this horrid thought she put on a spurt and burst out of the crevice into a sizeable cave – and one, moreover, which sloped up. Which meant that anything stored in here should be out of reach of even the highest spring tide.

'Over here, Rochelle.'

M. Laurient's voice echoed eerily round the cave. Rochelle groped her way towards him. She could see the shine of his eyes and teeth and very little else, but once she reached him she could also see, against the far wall, the three canvas bags. They were not on the floor of the cave but up on a rocky ledge which might, she reflected, have been made for the purpose of keeping the bags above floor-level.

'There! We can keep a lot of stuff here and no one any the wiser. But the actual money . . .'

'You're putting money here? Oh, but monsieur, what good could that possibly do us? I thought, when you said silver, you meant knives and forks.'

He gave a snort of laughter, shaking his head at her.

'Not knives and forks, precisely, but that type of thing. And when I say money I mean . . .' he took one of the canvas bags off the ledge '. . . I mean this, Chelle.'

He opened the neck of the bag, not without difficulty, for it was securely closed by a wide leather strap with metal fastenings.

'See?'

M. Laurient had carried that bag and now Rochelle saw why. It was full of what she would have loosely described as 'treasure': gold chains, bracelets, lockets, necklaces, even some rings and brooches. She saw the hard glitter of

153

diamonds and the softer glow of amethysts, sapphires, the winking eyes of opals and moonstones.

'Monsieur, whatever is all this? It's treasure, isn't it – a pirate's hoard!'

He laughed again, but indulgently now.

'It's what they call negotiable assets. We can't live on bracelets, I know that, but we can sell them, bit by bit, if we have to do so, and buy food with the proceeds. But actually I'm hoping we won't have to touch anything here. I hope we'll be able to leave the stuff in safety and bring it out again after the war.'

'Except for the tins,' Rochelle chirruped. 'We could need to eat them, couldn't we?'

'What's all this about? You mentioned tins before. Did you think I was going to start hoarding food down here, petite? I'm afraid it's far too perilous a climb to risk bringing sacks of tinned food down here, far less popping down a couple of times a week for fresh supplies. No, I'm afraid tinned food will just have to stay in the larder or the still-room and take its chance.'

'Or . . . if I can think of somewhere safe, could we put some things in it?' Rochelle suggested eagerly. She was loth to see her squirrel's hoard vanish into the mists of fantasy. 'Only think, monsieur, how useful it would be to have plenty of tins tucked away. If you really think that food will grow short, of course,' she added dutifully.

'Well, you think hard, and in the meantime we'll spend the next couple of days doing our best to get the stuff I don't want to see commandeered tucked away down here,' M. Laurient said. 'I'm afraid I want all sorts brought down as it is – one or two of the better paintings, which I intend to wrap in thick layers of oiled paper, all the household silver, and of course all the gold and jewellery which I've bought over the past few weeks.'

'Oh . . . this isn't family jewels, then?' Rochelle said, rather disappointed.

154

'Some of them are indeed family jewels, but others I've bought. I sold the big car and converted the money into precious metal, and I've done the same with most of the money in the bank. I shall keep on doing it, bit by bit, until I see which way the land lies. Gold will lie quiet anywhere and get more and more valuable, you see, petite. The paintings are not perhaps terribly valuable yet, but I think they will be one day, when the Impressionists come into their own, and there are one or two studies of the manor and the island itself which I'll keep down here. Now, are you rested? Ready for the next trip?'

'I'm fine,' Rochelle said truthfully. 'Monsieur, is there any way anyone else can reach here, except for the way we came?'

'That's a good point; we'll have a look when we get out of the crevice.'

They squiggled their way through the crevice and stood, once more, on the ledge of rock. Carefully, they both surveyed the scene. You could look right or left and see only the piled up rocks; behind you was the cliff and the cleft; in front, the boiling sea, the waves crashing on to rocks which could only just be seen yet would crunch up any boat which ventured near as teeth crunch the titbit which is slipped between them.

Above, the overhang, then the slippery and difficult climb which no one would undertake unless they had a reason for so doing. It was, Rochelle thought, the safest place in the world.

'There's no other way, is there, monsieur,' she said finally, having stared with all her might. 'How did you find the cave in the first place?'

'By chance. So far as I'm aware, I'm the only person alive who knows it's there. My brother Maurice knew, of course, since it was he and I who discovered it . . .'

'How? I mean, a grown man wouldn't squiggle into that crevice, would he, monsieur?'

155

M. Laurient smiled and shook his head at Rochelle.

'Alas, petite, I was as foolish as you when I was a lad; Maurice and I had been forbidden to come here, of course, as our father had been forbidden as a boy, but to forbid is to tempt, so we came. One bright summer's day, very early, as the sun came up, we climbed down the cliff to the sea and crouched on the slippery, salt-washed rocks and saw the tunnels and blow-holes and great pillared entrances which the sea had made for itself, and we marvelled.

'Later, we climbed up again. But we lost our way . . . the path is not marked at all down there, as you can imagine, with so few going that way . . . and we climbed too far to the left. When we came out on this ledge we looked up, saw the overhang, and realised we should have the greatest difficulty in continuing on upward.

'You can guess that we were worried . . . just a little! . . . at the thought of what our papa would do to us. We had been forbidden even to come to this spot; how much more wicked would our father consider it that we had actually descended the cliffs! So we saw the crevice and entered it, hoping that it would become a chimney further in, up which we might make our way . . . have you ever climbed a rock chimney?'

'I think so; you rest your shoulders on one side and your feet on the other and go up like that; is that a chimney?'

M. Laurient regarded Rochelle with some awe.

'Yes, that's right. And *you*'ve climbed . . . but that's beside the point at the moment. The point is that we wriggled and pushed our way in, discovered the cave, found there was no way through and came out again. But this time we did not attempt to go up. We could see that there were just too many overhangs, so we went sideways. After some tricky foot- and hand-work we reached the path which, in those days, was not broken by rock-falls, and made our way home.'

'I see.' Rochelle smiled and hugged herself. 'I knew you were quite a bad little boy, monsieur, but I did not know how bad!'

'Hmm. Well, now that you do know, don't let it go to your head, because I can promise you a beating and no food for a week if you do anything so foolish.'

'But I'm doing it right now,' Rochelle said, heading for the rock wall. 'And since I'm following you . . .'

'You know very well what I mean. Stop, now, and let me go first. As you keep telling me how good you are, you may try to go ahead of me on our third or fourth journey, but not yet.'

The sea-mist and occasional periods of rain continued all that day. Rochelle was returned to her aunt's house, dried out and dressed in neat, sensible clothing, went to bed, slept like a log, and was awoken well before the sun was up or dawn was even lightening the sky in the east by a discreet cough beneath her window.

She rushed out of bed and appeared like a jack-in-the-box, pushing her head out into St Michel Street, heedless of the soft, smoky touch of the rain on her cheeks.

'Yes, monsieur? Is it time?'

'It is. You're sure you want to come? There's no need, now that you know everything.'

His voice was pitched low, almost lower than the sound of the sea, but Rochelle could hear every word. When he had said he would come under her window and cough she knew she would wake at once. He was the most important person in her life. She would have known his cough amongst a million others; his step was as familiar to her as her own voice. Now she did not bother to reply, knowing that he had little hope of her backing out; she simply turned and left the window, reappearing seconds later beside him on the cobbled street.

'Did you bring the car? Where is it?'

He shook his head, taking her elbow and steering her along the sleeping street.

'No; too noisy. I brought an old friend of yours and mine.'

It was Cobble, the stout bay who pulled the pony-trap. But he had no vehicle behind him today, just a saddle and bridle.

'I rode in,' M. Laurient said, his voice still low. 'He's a sturdy beast; he'll carry us both. Sit on his rump.'

He gave Rochelle a leg up, then mounted, bringing his foot forward across the animal's withers instead of throwing it backwards over the rump. Rochelle giggled.

'I didn't know you could ride sidesaddle, monsieur! Have you slept?'

'A little. Don't worry yourself about me. I could climb those cliffs blindfold. Did you sleep?'

'Like Pod does, only I don't think I snored,' Rochelle said. 'What shall we tell my aunt?'

'Oh, merely that you came out for a walk before breakfast and met me. I've already pushed a note to that effect through her letter-box.'

They had gone quietly, at a walk, through the streets of the town but now, on the outskirts, M. Laurient clearly decided they could risk a little more noise. He clicked his tongue and dug in his heels and Cobble broke into a fast, rather bucketing trot.

'And what shall we be taking to the cave today?' Rochelle asked rather breathlessly, clinging to M. Laurient's waist with both hands and to Cobble's round and slippery rump with both legs. 'It must be the paintings, I suppose.'

'That's right. I took your advice and bought a heap of tins, by the way, and some dried food which I'm packing in oiled paper and bottling jars. Have you thought of anywhere yet?'

Rochelle chuckled.

'Yes, I have. I'll show you later.'

* * *

By noon they had stocked the little cave with more than a dozen stout canvas bags and a great many parcels wrapped in oiled paper, string and sacking. They ate a hearty meal of cassoulet which Mme Barfleur had left out for them, followed it up with an apple pie smothered in yellow cream, and then, girding up their loins as M. Laurient put it, set off once more, this time with casual indifference, for they were merely going to take a look at Rochelle's hiding place.

She led the way, down the road to where the Devil's Dip lay, deep in woodland; here she stopped, triumphant.

'See that thickening in the copse over there, monsieur? Once it was a little cottage, just one room and a stable, but ever since the murder no one will go inside it, except me and Livvy. We've been in often. It's very tumbledown, the roof's caved in and the windows aren't there so all sorts of rubbish has blown in, but . . . follow me!'

Laurient followed, half amused and half exasperated by the sort of childish rumour-mongering which could turn a suicide into a murder in one generation. But once in the ruin he had to respect Rochelle's spirit, for it had a brooding air which made the hairs on the back of his neck prickle erect. After some trouble she lugged up a section of boards, showing him, with pride, the dark hole beneath.

'It was their cellar,' she said, getting on to a rickety wooden stair and disappearing. 'It's smelly and dark down here, but no one knows about it but me and Livvy, and I'm sure she's forgotten it.'

Laurient could see that she was right, though he decided they would have to make it more difficult to raise the section of boards. Accordingly, he reinforced them with heavy timber from the old rafters and removed the rusty old hinges so that the section was not identifiable as movable. He could lift it with the greatest difficulty but needed Rochelle's help to drag it away so that they could descend, and this, he was sure, would deter a solitary thief from investigating further.

159

Then the long treks began, only this time they loaded Cobble with panniers, and by nightfall, though the two of them – probably the three of them – ached in every limb, they had done the job. The cellar was stocked to the rafters and the trapdoor soon scuffed into complete invisibility with dust and broken twigs from the wood. It would have taken a genius, Rochelle happily proclaimed, to discover their hoard.

'Or possibly a bloodhound,' M. Laurient said gloomily. 'I'm sure all that food has a very distinct aroma to a dog.'

'In tins? Pooh!' Rochelle declared robustly. 'And all the rest of the stuff is either wrapped in oiled paper or it's in jars. Don't worry, it'll be there when we need it, I feel it in my bones.'

'I hope so, since what I feel in my bones is very probably chronic arthritis from being out in the rain,' M. Laurient said sourly, clutching at Cobble's bridle.

'Arthritis? What's that?'

'It's something the very old get from damp and hard work,' M. Laurient said wryly. 'I hadn't realised I was very old until today.'

'You aren't! You're as young as anything!' Rochelle cried at once. 'My bones ache too, and so do Cobble's. You aren't old, truly you aren't.'

Her voice was so impassioned that M. Laurient laughed and put his arm round her shoulders, giving her an affectionate shake.

'Little goose! We're all young and fit then, and you can come with me in the Sunbeam and fetch Mme Barfleur back home.'

7

Laurie sat in the bath and scrubbed his back with the long-handled brush and sang a little; he was happy.

Oh, not ecstatic or anything like that, but today was his seventeenth birthday, he was having a party, of sorts, and his best friend, Goldie Bawsan, and he were lighting out for the flicks as soon as they were free to do so.

Indeed, lying there thinking over the past few months, Laurie knew that he was more than happy, he was damned lucky. He had run away from home a scrawny lad, with no real idea of how he was going to get work or make ends meet. He had stuck his head into every sort of trouble going, had been cheated and taken advantage of, and had been in the pen twice through no fault of his own. And then he had met up with Goldie, who was also on the loose, having left his family years ago and miles away after his father had split his head open with a fence-post upon Goldie's refusing to hand over the tiny amount of money his mother had hidden away before she died.

'We're on our beam ends,' Goldie had said one night, as the two of them crouched under a railway embankment and ate some scraps of bread which a dog would have refused. 'Ever heard of the CCC?'

'Nope; what is it? What's it stand for?'

'Civilian Conservation Corps. It's a bit like the army, only you get paid, you get fed, and you get to do kinda interestin' work. A guy was tellin' me you plant trees, dig ditches, look after forestry, that kinda thing. They want strong guys like us. What say we go along?'

'We-ell . . . would they take us?'

'Guess so. Roosevelt wants guys like us let to be useful, I

heard someone say. And then there's the war in Europe. You're nearly seventeen, I'm somewhere round the same age, and if we join the CCC we'll be half trained by the time they need us to fight.'

If Laurie had been doubtful it was because he dared not hope. This CCC sounded too good to be true. He could not believe that they would take him in, let him work for his living – and feed him as well!

But Goldie insisted, so the two of them went along. And contrary to Laurie's expectation, they had no trouble. They enlisted, underwent what they assumed must be a medical inspection, were passed fit, and were sent along to the store to draw suitable clothing and to be told where they would sleep that night.

To a couple of guys who had had nothing, all of a sudden it seemed they had everything. Three excellent meals each day, companions who had once been in the same desperate straits that they themselves had just emerged from, and work which tired their bodies but gave them back their self-respect.

So now, on his birthday, Laurie lay in the bath and sang. They were camping at present, in large tents, planting a forest. A truck brought them young trees, they dug trenches, planted, firmed down, moved on. They were outside all the time, except when they slept under canvas at nights, and they were better fed than most of them had been for many a year. It was what they most wanted from life – work, dignity, friendship and a sense of achievement.

That morning they had been told that the job here was nearly finished, which in any other circumstances would have sent a thrill of real fear through them. But not now, not with the CCC on their side. They would be needed someplace, they would go there, do the work, see that they had done a good job, and move on to tackle another problem someplace else.

One of the lads who worked with them was a German;

162

Fritz, they called him. Of course the war had nothing to do with America, Laurie knew, but he disliked Fritz because his own real father was in the war – bound to be. No Laurient would allow himself to be passed over, Laurie was sure of that. He had dreamed sometimes, of making his way down to the coast somehow and of getting on a ship bound for Britain. Once there, he would find his father and offer his services . . . or alternatively he would offer his services and then find his father . . . perhaps they would be in the same regiment, or flying the same sort of aircraft, or aboard the same battleship. Laurie's dreams were not yet practical in any sense.

But until then, Laurie was building himself up, ready for whatever might happen. He was tall and strong and becoming self-confident. He knew that he was far brighter than most of his fellow-members of the Corps and now he was beginning to realise that he was also taller, more muscular, with a greater capacity for sticking to the job in hand, no matter how hard, until it was finished. Even Goldie found it tough to keep up with Laurie, yet when they had first joined Laurie had been struggling just to finish each day so that he could collapse on to his bunk.

At first, he had spent all the money he earned – which was little enough, merely a few cents pocket money – on extra food, but now he had begun to save it up and plan what he would do with it. Clothing was provided, but he bought himself a checkered shirt and some proper shoes, then a pair of trousers instead of the jeans they worked in. He could not spare money to buy newspapers or books, but he found it was easy enough to bum a paper off someone who had finished with it, or to borrow a book provided he always returned it.

On his seventeenth birthday, though, it was beginning to snow, the first few tentative flakes of the winter. They knew that if it snowed up here they would be sent down to the south where the weather was more clement; there they

163

could work all winter through with no fear of the frost clamping down on them and freezing the ground so's the little trees couldn't stretch their roots and flourish. Or they would find them something else to do – he had been in the CCC more than a year now and they never lacked work. Once, he and Goldie had fought forest fires for months. They had gotten the smell of burning wood into their pores, just about, but it had taught them a lot. If the Depression ever ends, if they ever need guys like us, we could take on firefighting, no problem, Goldie had said when it was over at last and they were on their way to another assignment.

So, just in case they were sent off soon, to some spot where there was no cinema, no Cindy-Jean to cuddle up to him in the back row, Laurie jumped out of the bath, towelled himself hard, and then began to dress. Presently, ready for the outing with his wet hair slicked into a cowlick on his forehead, he went through to the mess-hall, where Goldie sprawled in a chair, waiting for him. He was reading a magazine, his forehead corrugated with pain over the small print. He looked up and sketched a mock salute as Laurie entered, then threw the magazine down on the chair opposite.

'Hi, bo! Ready?'

'Sure am. C'mon.'

They thought nothing of jog trotting the five miles to town, arriving in Main Street without so much as a heaving chest. That's what the CCC has done for the both of us, Laurie told himself, as they approached the cinema. And there was Cindy-Jean with her yellow hair in a pony-tail and her friend Louisa-May beside her.

They were actually in the cinema and preparing to share the biggest bag of popcorn you ever did see when Goldie dropped his bombshell. Not that he knew it was a bombshell, of course, since Laurie had never talked about himself much.

'Hey, bo, I was readin' 'bout one of your milord cousins

or some such thing in that theyer magazine,' he said suddenly, leaning across Cindy-Jean to punch Laurie lightly in the shoulder. 'Feller's gone and got hisself a big ole place and he's rearin' rare orchids . . . seems he bids fair to beat all of Europe in that line.'

Laurie sat very still; he tried to tell himself that Goldie didn't read too good – which was true – and that he had probably made a mistake, that the name was spelled different, that the whole thing was a hoax. But he knew in his bones that what Goldie had said was the gospel truth. He remembered Mom, long, long ago, telling him that his father's father had been crazy about some old flowers, and, when pressed, she had said they were orchids. The old man had discovered a rare one, it seemed . . . no, that was wrong; he had *bred* a new one, just as if flowers were animals and could be cross-bred to produce a new species . . . and it had had something to do with his death, and with the sudden disappearance of Laurie's daddy, though he could not, at this distance in time, remember where the connection lay.

One of the girls piped up with a comment about being proud to sit by someone who was related to a Britisher right now, with the war and all, and the subject passed off, but Laurie sat through the rest of the film in a daze; all he wanted was for the performance to be over, not so that he could walk Cindy-Jean home and try to put his hand up her skirt, previously the sum of his desire, but so that he could get back to camp and read that magazine.

'It's your birthday . . . I gotta buy you a birthday drink . . . I gotta give you a birthday kiss . . .'

Laurie was a gentleman, though he would probably have denied it as a deadly insult had anyone said it in so many words. As it was he sat through the film and the meal which followed, he walked Cindy-Jean home and kissed her absently but fairly thoroughly, he hung around whilst Goldie did his best to make it with a far from reluctant

Louisa-May, and then he hightailed it for the camp, with Goldie well behind him and complaining bitterly that his feet wanted a slower walk, apparently, than Laurie's great clod-crushers did.

'Where's that magazine?' Laurie said breathlessly as soon as they re-entered the camp. 'Go get it, Goldie. I'll put the kettle on.'

Coffee was brewed and poured by the time Goldie returned waving the magazine triumphantly in one hand.

'Here it is. I ain't *half* had to scrat around to find it,' he said, spreading the magazine out on the kitchen table. 'Here . . . that's the bit you're after.'

And there it was; Laurie took a great deep breath and then held it as his eyes ran down the page. Charles Laurient . . . blah, blah, blah . . . Augeuil Manor, on Jersey, the largest of the Channel Islands . . . blah, blah, blah . . . best collection of orchids in Europe . . . more delicate hybridisation taking place now at the manor than anywhere else in Europe. Yes, there could be no doubt whatsoever: the dark, slightly saturnine man at the head of the page must be his father. And Goldie, reading slowly and stumblingly over his shoulder, inadvertently confirmed it.

'He sure is one of your kin,' he remarked presently, placing a stubby finger on the photograph. 'My, he's the spittin' image of you, Laurie! Why, he could be your daddy!'

Laurie tore out the pages concerning Charles Laurient and the orchids from the magazine and put them at the bottom of his battered old gladstone bag and brought them out from time to time to gloat over them. For if the CCC had given him a reason to hold his head up again, the article in the *Horticulture Times* gave him a purpose in life from which, he decided, he would never swerve. He would go to this island, this Jersey, and find his father. And he would bring

166

him the sort of present a man like Charles Laurient would most appreciate.

He would take him an orchid.

Working in the forests and country places, Laurie was familiar with most of the common orchids, but because of his suddenly devouring interest in the plants he began to discover all sorts of other things about them. The most interesting, from his point of view, was that the best and rarest orchids grew in South America . . . and though he had shrunk from taking ship to go to Britain, there to search for a father who, he suspected, did not even know he existed, he had no qualms whatsoever about going deep into the jungles of South America in search of rare orchids which he would then carry across half the world – and a world at war, furthermore – to place at Charles Laurient's feet.

It was strange how, once he had made up his mind where his future lay, things fell into place for him. He had been unable to find employment until he and Goldie had enlisted with the Corps, but now he could go to a big horticultural institute and almost demand to work in their orchid house, because he knew so much about the plants.

He did know a lot, too. He studied frenziedly, and discovered, as one does, that others were as caught up in the life-cycles of these remarkable plants as he was himself. He got his job at the Institute because he had first spent many hours of his own free time collecting and cataloguing as many species of orchid as he could find in the forests during his time with the Corps.

Once in the Institute, he settled down happily to work twenty hours out of the twenty-four, to eat as well as he could afford and to sleep when he could no longer keep awake. The head gardener of his particular section of the Institute immediately recognised a fellow-enthusiast, someone who was not merely earning a living but was caught up in his work. He lent Laurie books, taught him more

167

about orchiculture than Laurie had dreamed of, and eventually, and as usual by accident, discussed the experimentation taking place at Augeuil Manor with this amazing protégé.

'Dot on the map, that's what that theyer Jersey is,' he announced, inaccurately but forcefully. 'And one guy's got a stranglehold on hybridisation. He's runnin' short on specimens, mind, because no one's going out collectin' these days. But does that deter him? No siree, no way does it deter him! He jest keeps on a-breedin' an' experimentin' an' one of these days, when that durn fool war's over, he's gonna come up with the orchid to end it all . . . some fancy name, can't remember it offhand . . .'

'The Pure Madonna,' Laurie said, but his friend just laughed and said very probably and trust a Brit to think up a name like that, and the talk moved on to the rights and wrongs of horse muck in a greenhouse and whether misting should be suspended at flowering time.

Laurie had his whole future planned out. He knew where he was going and what he wanted to do when he got there, and when he had managed to scrape enough money together he'd go into the jungles and find something so rare, so beautiful . . .

He was in his room, studying the merits and demerits of pest control with nicotine spray, when he heard, with only half his attention, the name of the island which meant more to him than anything else. Quickly, he put down his book and leaned over to the little wireless, turning the sound up.

It was thus he learned that the Germans had invaded the Channel Islands, after Great Britain had declared them a demilitarised zone.

Rochelle sat on the staging in the tropical house and talked solidly to the orchids whilst the Germans invaded the island. She could not think what else to do. There was a curfew in operation, all the adults looked drawn and

168

worried, women were weeping in the streets and everyone expected the worst. Many had fled to the mainland after France had fallen, and in the past three days more had followed, by air, by sea . . . one felt they would have swum had it been practicable.

Now, those who were left were the hard core, the people who were Jerseymen through and through and could not even contemplate leaving their homes and responsibilities. M. Laurient had never thought of going; they had never even discussed it. Indeed, he had got very cross with M. Le Clerc when that gentleman had come round one evening to offer to send Rochelle away with his own young daughter.

'*No*, Robert,' M. Laurient had said with quiet forcefulness. 'I wouldn't dream of sending the child away from everything she holds dear; besides, who can tell? She might be very much worse off if the Nazis then invaded the mainland, and no one can say for certain that it won't happen. Once more, dear Robert, we are ill prepared for war.'

So Rochelle had not gone, and neither had M. Laurient, and now they were waiting, as patiently as they could, to see what the future held in store.

Yesterday M. Laurient had hidden two wireless sets. He said that as soon as the Germans landed they would commandeer all the cars and wireless sets so that Jersey people could no longer travel freely nor hear what was going on in the outside world.

He had several wirelesses, so he took one of the best ones and built it as unobtrusively as possible into the tropical house. It was underneath the soft water tank and could not be seen unless one lay flat on one's back with one's head under the tank and peered upwards . . . and managed to spot it in the tangle of other things up there such as pipes and cobwebs.

Another was in a hayrack in the stable; it was permanently covered with dusty old hay which had been sewn on to the casing with coarse string. It was very convincing but also rather difficult to turn on. Still, no doubt they would manage when the time came.

For her part, Rochelle took her own little set and shoved it up the chimney in the stable-yard cottage. She and M. Laurient had discussed how long they would be able to remain in the manor. If, as M. Laurient seemed to believe, they would speedily be turned out so that the German High Command might inhabit the house, then they might as well have a wireless on hand in the only other habitable dwelling on the estate which was not already occupied.

Olivia had come to stay, because school was closed until they knew just what was going to happen; she said that there had been an enormous white cross on the town square but M. Laurient said that it had since been removed, presumably because the invasion had now been accomplished. Rumour had it that the hated swastika flew over Fort Regent, but Rochelle had not seen it herself; M. Laurient had been firm with her on that particular point. She was to stay on the estate until he gave her permission to leave it, he had said the previous day when setting out in his car. Don't go to the beach, don't walk on the roads, don't talk to anyone on the telephone except me or Mme Barfleur.

Rochelle hated the Germans, of course, because M. Laurient did, although he had never put such feelings into words. But she knew him so well that she could, by now, read his thoughts, or at least the hatred which simmered within him. She resented the curfew, but then it had been in force before the Germans arrived, and she appreciated the shutting of the schools. Her fear was that once the enemy settled in schools would open again, and perhaps the Nazis might even expect the pupils to learn the German language.

'So you see,' Rochelle said earnestly to the orchids

nearest her, 'we must be prepared for *anything* – the Boche could walk in here tomorrow and take over the manor and just tell us to root you out and throw you on the rubbish heap – not that we *would*,' she added hastily, almost feeling, in her own slender bones, the shudder that ran through the flowers. 'We shall do our best to keep you safe – and then you're terribly valuable, so even the dirty Boche won't let you be harmed. They might even take you back to Germany to flourish in the glasshouses over there – if they have such things.'

Rochelle was about to launch into a further diatribe when the door at the far end of the greenhouse opened and Olivia appeared, saw her friend and came down the aisle towards her.

'There you are, Chelle! Grandmère is about to cook tea and M. Laurient is back. He's got the car full of bicycles . . . one for you, one for me, one for him, and a spare. Can you ride a bicycle?'

'Yes, I think so,' Rochelle said, with vague memories of once trying at school and managing to wobble for several yards before the machine had crashed to the ground. 'Can you?'

'No, but I'll soon learn. Are you coming up to the stable-yard? We can practise there for a bit until tea's ready.'

The first days of the Occupation passed. Rochelle learned to ride her bicycle, and when the schools reopened she and Olivia cycled off each day and came home by the same means each evening. Once or twice they saw German soldiers who sometimes ignored them, sometimes waved, and occasionally even spoke in their harsh, guttural language, but for the most part life, it seemed, jogged by on an even keel.

Commandeering motor vehicles meant that first the Sunbeam and then the Morris were regretfully driven into St Helier for the last time and handed over to the authorities. Rationing began to sidle, unobtrusively at first, into their lives and Mme Barfleur wrung her hands and bemoaned the lack of ingredients. Even so, the manor was better off than most, because with their large herd of milkers they still managed to make butter, cheese and cream and to use far more of it than the Germans suspected.

Because it was summer the orchids did not need extra heat and they flourished; but Pure Madonna had not yet put in an appearance. One of the hybrids which M. Laurient had high hopes of did flower, but the bloom was not the one they wanted. Old M. Laurient had taken some photographs of his orchid, and later M. Laurient himself had sketched the flower from the photographs and coloured it according to his mother's recollection of the original, so they did have something to go by. Rochelle often hung over the framed picture, which was kept in the estate office, and was sure she would recognise the real thing even when it was only in bud, but as yet the perfect bloom eluded them.

Summer gave way to autumn and Rochelle and M. Laurient coddled the orchids as best they could, though it was beginning to seem unlikely that they would be able to heat the houses during the winter. They collected seed and moved all their most valuable specimens into one glass-house, and Rochelle and Olivia spent a weekend carrying blankets down there, because the occupation forces were commandeering quantities of bedding from everyone and M. Laurient said that if they could keep some of the warmer blankets at least they might save the orchids from the worst of the cold, when it came.

Then, of course, the inevitable happened. One of the German High Command came visiting, ostensibly to discuss with M. Laurient details of his agricultural programme for the coming year but really, they all thought, to cast an eye over the house. And what he saw he liked, for three days later they received a peremptory order telling them that Augeuil Manor was to be used to house the German High Command. M. Laurient and his dependants would be allocated rooms in the attics, and would of course have the use of the kitchen.

'Reading between the lines, that could mean that they intend Mme Barfleur to cook for them,' M. Laurient said grimly to Rochelle and Olivia, as they sat in the kitchen by the stove. 'Our best course is to move out, all of us. We'll go into the Dubois' old cottage; Rochelle can share a room with Mme Barfleur, and Olivia when she stays, and I'll have the other one. There's a decent sized kitchen and a good living room, as well as all the usual offices. We'll manage for the duration of the war.'

'The troops say it'll all be over by Christmas and they'll be in England,' Olivia said. 'They're very confident, very sure of themselves.'

Mme Barfleur had been ironing; now she turned and fixed her granddaughter with a steely stare.

'And what might you know about the troops, miss?' she enquired. 'Do you talk to them young fellers, Livia?'

'No ... everyone knows that's what the troops are saying,' Olivia said. But Rochelle saw the flush mount her friend's cheeks and for the first time it occurred to her that Livia was growing up. There were breasts pushing against her school uniform, and now that it had been mentioned she realised that Olivia *did* look at soldiers as they cycled along the road – never two abreast, since that was a punishable offence now – and that soldiers looked back at her.

'Hmm,' Mme Barfleur muttered. 'Well, see that you don't, my girl.'

'Of course not, Grandmère,' Olivia said. 'But ... they're only boys, you know. Most of 'em hate being here as much as we hate having them. Maman says ...'

'I thought as much.' Mme Barfleur nodded grimly, her

cheeks even more flushed than Olivia's. 'I'll have a word with your mother, my girl. If she's encouraging you . . .'

She left the sentence unfinished, and Rochelle knew that there was little anyone could do. Either Olivia would see for herself that there were few better ways of making enemies of the Islanders than fraternising with the occupying forces, or she wouldn't. Time would have to tell. It was hard on Olivia, because she lived in town during the week, though she was out at the manor all the weekend. Olivia's mother had no husband at home to take care of her and already it was being said that Germans billeted on her were luckier than most. It was not a remark made with approval, either.

So, next day, the girls helped to move the family out of the manor and into the cottage in the stable-yard. Contrary to Rochelle's expectations it proved to be rather fun to live in a small house with a limited amount of space, but it was not so exciting to realise that Germans were everywhere; they could not go down to the greenhouses without an officer asking whither they were bound.

'We could move to the dower house,' M. Laurient said thoughtfully, when he and Rochelle, in the confines of the nursery house, were discussing their position. 'It hasn't been used by the family for generations, but the people who leased it, the Ansleys, were one of the first families to evacuate themselves to the mainland. It hasn't been used by the troops at all because it's not a very convenient little house – it's deep in the woods and you can't get a car up to it easily. We're too near them here. I've a feeling that they aren't going to be the best of neighbours in the next few weeks.'

'Why not?' Rochelle asked. She and M. Laurient had been trying to listen to the news on the wireless in the tropical house, but it was impossible; there were just too many Germans roaming around.

'Why not? Haven't you gathered, petite, that there's an

174

air battle raging in the skies above Britain which will make or break the Luftwaffe? You've seen the waves of planes going over . . . and you must have heard the numbers of planes brought down by the RAF. Didn't you put two and two together?'

'Ye-es . . . but, as you say, there are so many German planes! Can the British really win?'

M. Laurient grinned at her. All of a sudden he looked very young.

'Can they? Of course they're going to win, petite. And when they do the Boche will turn even nastier than they are already, so it behoves us to be tucked up in the dower house by then.'

'Listen to that wind!'

Winter must be officially with us now, Rochelle thought, as she and Olivia gathered close to the wood fire in the parlour of the dower house. Already she was very happy here, far happier than she had been when they had lived in the stable-yard cottage with the enemy lording it in the manor only yards away. What was more, they had managed to get the wireless out of the stable and into the dower house without being spotted, which was just as well, since a couple of weeks before the Germans had confiscated all the wireless sets in civilian hands on the island – or thought they had. So now, in their little house out in the woods, Rochelle, Olivia, Mme Barfleur and M. Laurient could sit with the curtains drawn and the door locked and barred and listen to the news . . . and then to light music or whatever else they could hear coming over the air from the BBC.

'It's a gale,' M. Laurient said, from his seat on the big old fireside sofa. 'I wish we weren't quite so surrounded by trees, but still, it's November, which means that the trees are bare and offer less resistance to the wind.'

'Good,' Mme Barfleur said sarcastically as a roaring

crash nearby indicated that at least one giant of the forest had bitten the dust. 'I just hope that was a fair way from the outbuildings.'

'Oh . . . the glasshouses!' Rochelle was on her feet in a moment, halfway to the door. 'We'd best go and see . . . we could move some of the frailer specimens . . . suppose a tree crashes through the glass . . .'

'Sit down and possess your soul in patience,' M. Laurient advised, though not unkindly. Rochelle had no doubt that he was as eager as she to see that the orchids did not suffer. 'If we bring a frail plant out in this wind, what do you think will happen to it? Eh?'

'Oh!' Rochelle retraced her steps and collapsed on the rug once more. 'But soon, if the wind drops for a moment . . .'

'The heart of the hurricane, is that what you're hoping for? Well, fair enough. If the wind really does drop we'll make a mercy dash and see . . .' Another frightening roar and a scream rent the air as another tree fell. 'Just sit still, Rochelle; think of the danger. What good would it do the orchids – or me, for that matter – if we were both killed? Then there would be no one to take care of them.'

Rochelle had considered arguing but at those words she smiled sheepishly and heaved a great sigh.

'Oh, all right, monsieur, we'll wait until it eases off a bit. But have you ever heard a storm like it? Don't you wish you were out at Wilderness Point, beyond Devil's Dip, watching the sea?'

'No, because the wind would snatch you over the cliff in a moment and hurl you down to watch the sea at closer quarters than even you would like,' M. Laurient assured her. 'It's a good thing we aren't on the telephone here, because I'm very sure the lines must be down all over the island, especially where there are trees . . . now just sit *still*, you girls!'

The injunction was unnecessary for both girls sat like stones in the sudden and complete darkness.

'Electricity lines down,' M. Laurient's voice said. 'Mme Barfleur, who is most familiar with the layout of the kitchen?'

'The candles is in the dresser drawer, right hand side, and there's an oil lamp, the one you take when you go out at night, by the sink,' Mme Barfleur said calmly out of the blackness. 'You'd best go, sir. Like as not I'd rick my ankle and be laid up for days.'

'I'll go!' Rochelle squeaked, only to be promptly squashed.

'You will *not* – didn't I tell you to sit still?'

Rochelle sighed, but vouchsafed no reply, and presently there were sounds of muffled cursing from the direction of the kitchen, a crash and a short, sharp swearword – 'that was monsieur trying to get a light,' Olivia interjected – and then M. Laurient came back, a lit candle in one hand.

'Here we are! I'll stand this one on the mantelpiece and light the other from it . . .' he suited action to words '. . . and presto, we're in business!'

He sat down again. Mme Barfleur, who had been knitting, picked up her work but put it aside after only a few stitches.

'It's no use trying, what with the noise of the wind and the poor light,' she said, raising her voice to be heard above the tempest. 'There'll be no need to search for wood tomorrow, sir; there'll be whole trees to be cut up and carted away. Mind, the wind's making the fire draw a mite too hot for comfort.'

'It's nice to be warm,' Olivia said, holding out her hands to the blazing stove. 'It was bitterly cold in school today, wasn't it, Chelle?'

'Yes, it was nippy,' Rochelle admitted. 'The wind seemed to get in every crack, but it wasn't half as wild as it is now. When does a gale become a hurricane, monsieur?'

'Right now, I think,' M. Laurient said placidly. 'As soon as it drops I'm going up to the house. There's the old walnut near the dining-room window – if that goes it'll make a nice mess of the dining-room. The oak by the barn could do quite a lot of damage as well. Then there's the pitched roof of the manor itself . . . we usually lose a tile or two in rough weather. This lot could be responsible for the place needing a whole re-tiling job, I imagine. And of course, as Rochelle will presently remind me, there are the orchids . . . even with the two larger greenhouses more or less empty tremendous damage could be caused to the remaining ones in a gale like this.'

'I'll come. Please, monsieur, don't try to say I can't,' Rochelle begged as soon as M. Laurient stopped speaking. 'I must see what's happened out there. Don't you want to take a look, Olivia?'

Mme Barfleur was adamant that the last thing she wanted was to see the results of such a gale a moment before she had to, but Olivia admitted that she, too, was curious.

'Very well. All three of us will go when the wind drops, and Mme Barfleur may remain to prepare hot drinks and a bite of food for when we get back,' M. Laurient said. 'Now, you two have done your homework, I assume?'

Rochelle assured him that she had, though she added that it seemed unlikely that anyone would be in school on the morrow to take it in.

'If there are trees across the road we won't be going in ourselves,' she said with relish. 'I wouldn't mind a holiday. Think how much work we could do in the greenhouse if they shut the school for a week or two!'

'Then, if you've done your homework, shall we play cards? Or if the light's not good enough for that you two can entertain us with a song, or a poem, or something.'

There was an outcry at the last suggestion, but Rochelle jumped up to fetch some Snap cards, and in the excitement engendered by the simple game the gale raging outside was almost forgotten. Indeed, when the last hand was played and the cards laid down, it was realised that the wind had dropped considerably. Though it still howled round the house it did not have the ferocity which had impressed the girls earlier.

'I'm off to bed,' Mme Barfleur said, getting ponderously to her feet. 'I'll set the kettle on the stove and put out some bread and jam, so you'll have something to line your stomachs when you get back indoors again. Don't let the girls be too late, now,' she admonished M. Laurient as she headed for the kitchen.

'We'll just take a quick look at the damage,' M. Laurient assured her. 'We shan't be more than twenty or thirty minutes, I don't suppose, but if one of those crashes was the greenhouse going I'd like to rescue at least some of my specimens.'

He pulled on a heavy old coat and watched as the girls, too, donned coats, scarves and boots.

'Ready?' he said when at last they were all well muffled. 'All right, then. Hang on to my arm, Chelle – and you can hang on to the other one, Olivia. Now.'

He flung open the back door and both girls flinched as the wind threw itself at them, flattening their eyelashes into their eyes and making breathing suddenly difficult.

'All right? Still want to come with me?'

Neither girl bothered to reply. They simply heaved on his arms and brought him, chuckling, out into the night.

It was rough still, the wind tearing at them, torn cloud fragments racing across the face of the moon riding high in the dark sky. Above them the limbs of the trees were still storm-lashed, and the ground was littered with debris – branches, fencing, what looked like half a haystack – whilst to Rochelle's distress a dove, meek and smooth even in death, was caught up in a fallen branch nearby.

'Hold tight!' M. Laurient shouted, and set off into the

woodland which separated the dower house from the manor itself. The three of them slogged along, heads down, until they reached the wall which divided the cultivated garden from the woods. Here, to their astonishment, they found that the wall itself had been knocked down for some considerable distance – at least twelve feet – so that provided they were careful as they stepped over the loose bricks they could simply enter the garden without going round by the wrought-iron gate.

'Have to rebuild that,' M. Laurient shouted. 'My God, look at the orchard!'

Trees had gone down in a path, as though a giant scythe had cut a swathe through them. Apple, pear, plum, they had all suffered the same fate and lay tangled and broken in the long grass.

'It's bad, but it's not nearly as bad as it might have been,' Rochelle shouted as they went over to study the fallen trees. 'They are all the middle ones . . . I'm so glad the ones near the glasshouses seem to have escaped.'

'It's as though the tail of a tornado caught them,' M. Laurient said incredulously. 'Come on, let's see what else has gone.'

They emerged from the orchard to discover that one at least of the glasshouses had been hit by flying debris, for glass lay thickly scattered and sparkling in the moonlight, but the orchids seemed to have been spared; certainly no tree or other large structure had fallen just there. But the great old walnut tree was leaning at a drunken angle, its upper branches wedged into the old roof tiles of the manor.

'They'll have to mend it,' M. Laurient said, with a sort of sour satisfaction which Rochelle could well understand. 'They won't be able to ignore it and simply go on living there. That roof will have to be completely re-tiled and re-guttered. And some of the stonework's gone.'

'I suppose it's because it isn't really their own house, but it looks as though they're all in bed,' Olivia remarked as

180

they neared the manor itself. 'Oh no, I forgot. I suppose their electricity has gone as well.'

'Yes, of course. I was wondering why we couldn't see any lights,' M. Laurient said. 'We'll just walk round the house and check on the stable-yard cottage and the stables themselves . . . though no doubt the Huns have checked that the horses are all right.'

They crossed the familiar, much-loved ground, inhabited by alien forces now. Rochelle would have known when they crossed the herb garden even if the night had been pitch black, because of the scent of the crushed and battered plants . . . the glorious lemony smells, the rich herby ones, all of them, as though an army of pickers had been at work.

They entered the stable-yard. The stables appeared to be intact, but a chimney had gone on the cottage; a huge, shattered chimney pot lay on the paving and sizeable chunks of the actual brickwork surrounded it.

'If anyone had been out here . . .' Rochelle breathed, and did not finish the sentence. She was remembering her own loudly expressed wish to leave the house and run through the woods . . . what a silly idiot she had been!

'It looks as though everything's all right here . . .' M. Laurient was beginning when Olivia stiffened. She tugged on his arm, then leaned round him to speak to Rochelle.

'Look, Chelle . . . there *is* a light, in the kitchen, I think. They aren't all in bed. Someone's probably in there with a candle.'

'Oh, yes, but it isn't a candle. They must have got hold of a lantern,' Rochelle was beginning, when she suddenly stopped and shook M. Laurient's arm. 'It *isn't* a light . . . it's on fire!'

8

For one long, shocking moment the three of them just stood there, staring. M. Laurient's hand had been holding Rochelle's elbow; now his fingers slid down until he was grasping her hand, but she was sure he was unaware that he had moved at all. He was staring at the house, his face lit now by the glow rather than by the cold moonlight, and Rochelle knew, suddenly, that he was torn, aching with a terrible decision.

The house was crowded with Germans, all of them upstairs and asleep. If they were to turn round now and leave as quietly as they had come the chances were that this nest of the enemy would perish in the flames, for she did not think the roar of the fire would reach the sleepers whilst the wind continued to howl about the house, and by the time the smell of scorching timbers warned them it would be too late.

They were the enemies of Britain and they had to be beaten at almost any cost. M. Laurient had been told pretty bluntly that he was too old to join any of the armed forces and, though he was doing his best on the island to keep at least a semblance of normal life going for all those dependent on him, she knew that he would dearly have loved to be able to fight.

If he said nothing, now, he would know that he had been responsible for the deaths of not only a great many Germans but also a considerable number of the enemy's top command. Some people would consider it his duty to say nothing; others would consider it equally his duty to raise the alarm.

And then there was the manor. For four hundred years

it had given shelter to the Laurient family. It had seen countless brides enter the wide front door for the first time, it had seen births and deaths. It was a beautiful, gracious home and though M. Laurient seldom spoke of it she knew he loved the house as he might have loved a wife: deeply, passionately.

Could he stand by and see the manor perish along with the enemy?

Rochelle thought afterwards that she would never know what made him move – towards the house, not away from it – but she was immediately aware that his mind was made up, his purpose fixed.

'Olivia, go round to the front door and hammer and ring. Rochelle, the french windows leading into the rose garden. I'll see whether I can get across the kitchen and into the rest of the house. Make all the noise you can; scream and yell and shout as you go . . . we've got to wake them.'

Rochelle was glad to scamper round the stable-yard, back through the herb garden and over to the french windows. On the other side of them was the library; the thick velvet curtains were drawn but no light chinked out. Clearly she could not wake anyone within, but she could surely gain admittance?

'Wake up . . . fire, fire, fire!' She shrieked at the top of her voice as she ran, but the small sound was simply carried away by the wind, and even when she threw herself at the french windows and began to try to turn the handle she did so without a murmur coming to her ears above the noise of the elements.

There was no help for it – it would have to be violence. As she looked round wildly in the moonlight she could see nothing handy to throw through the glass . . . but there was a terrace only feet away and she was fairly certain that the swingseat which stood there, denuded of cushions and canopy at this time of year, might well offer a weapon of some description.

It did. She wrenched off one of the long metal poles which controlled the swing and ran at the window with it. She swung it crazily at the glass but must have checked at the last minute; it bounced off at a tangent, hurting the palms of her hands but doing no other damage.

Rochelle gritted her teeth and swung again, harder this time, more deliberately. The metal rod connected with the glass and was through it at once, splashing her with fragments. She cheered thinly against the wind and bashed again. This time the hole enlarged considerably. Long wicked shards of glass crashed on to the broken paving and Rochelle, seeing victory ahead, plunged both hands through to turn the key in the lock so that she might get in.

The key was not in the lock. Whether it had been removed in order to make access more difficult or whether it had fallen to the floor under her onslaught she had no idea, but it meant she must do quite a lot more glass-bashing. Rochelle swung her metal rod again and again, until the entire pane was gone save for a fringe of wicked glass teeth round the frame, and then she stepped cautiously through the aperture. She was in!

She had swished the curtains apart as soon as she had a hole in the glass so now she was able to see the room in the dim light. She crossed it quickly, opened the heavy oak door, and stared out at the well remembered hall. It looked so peaceful, so normal, in the half-light that she nearly stopped, aghast at her own violent invasion. Had she dreamed the whole thing? Was she really on an errand of mercy or would she be shot for illegal entry?

She began to cross the hall with lagging steps . . . and as she drew level with the baize door which separated the kitchen regions from the rest of the house she heard an odd sort of thump and the door opened and for a second only, before the door swung shut again, she caught a glimpse

184

into hell. Red, yellow, orange, the flames glared at her, reached for her, and smoke, thick and white, rolled across the hall, bringing with it an evil smell of burning.

As the door swung, she thought she saw someone . . . just a glimpse of something moving . . . and she ran towards the door. She put out her hand to open it, but the handle was so hot that she cried out, and then she realised that she could not open it without letting the fire through. It was clearly only held back, even now, by the baize door.

So instead she put her mouth as close to the door as she could and shrieked, 'I'm in, monsieur! I'll wake them up!' and forsook the hall and belted up the stairs, screaming her warning as she went.

'Fire, fire, fire!'

She was actually on the upper landing and hesitating outside the first door when she remembered the gong. Long ago, when there was a full staff at the manor, the gong had been rung at mealtimes, and even in her time Mme Barfleur had occasionally struck it to call everyone in for dinner. Rochelle turned and ran back downstairs. The gong was still there, praise be, with its round, brazen face and the little gong stick with its chamois-leather head.

But she did not bother with the stick; she simply threw herself at the gong, kicking and beating at it with her fists, frenziedly clouting, until the noise ringing in her head was far louder than either the roar of the fire or the howling of the wind.

She knew it was the right thing to do not only for the Germans, who were erupting out of their doors like bullets from so many guns, probably cursing her in their horrid language but certainly decisively woken, but also for M. Laurient and Olivia. They would guess that someone had got in, would realise that not even the piglike Boche could sleep through such a racket, and would stop risking their own lives and start fire-fighting.

'Fire, fire, fire!'

185

She stopped beating the gong for long enough to sound her alarm, then beat again; she was, if the truth be told, enjoying herself now. She had often longed to crash a booted foot against the gong. Now she was hitting it with everything she'd got, and it was good; a release of tension, and enormous fun besides.

She might have continued to pummel the gong for another hour had she not been caught firmly round the waist and lifted off her feet. A voice said in her ear, 'Cease the racket, *Liebling*. Only the dead are not awake, and they may slumber for all I care until the day of Judgement! What is it?'

'Fire!' Rochelle squeaked. She wriggled, and her captor put her down and turned her to face him. It was the tall, fair-haired man she sometimes saw curiously peering through the glass of the greenhouse at the orchids, and at herself and M. Laurient as they moved amongst the plants. Hauptmann Kussak, the German commandant on the island.

'Fire? Where? Did you see who started it?'

'In the kitchen . . . don't touch the baize door!' She gabbled the words, not really taking in his last question. 'Please . . . get the men down. They must help to fight it. M. Laurient's out there now with buckets of water.'

She had no idea what M. Laurient was doing, but she guessed that it would be something practical. Fetching buckets of water, in the circumstances, seemed likeliest.

The German turned towards the baize door and put his hand on it, then snatched it back and bent his head. He was listening to the roar of the fire in the kitchen quarters beyond. He nodded, then moved back to the bottom of the stairs and bawled what sounded like orders up to the men still hovering on the landing in various stages of undress. Then he returned to Rochelle. For the first time she realised that he was wearing a pair of long, dark-coloured trousers or pants which came in tightly at the ankles, and a khaki

186

vest – nothing else. She could see pale curly hairs on his upper chest and shoulders and, looking down in some embarrassment, saw that his feet were bare and very pale and clean, the toe-nails half-moons of white, the toes themselves straight and separated, not a bit like Rochelle's own toes which tended to cuddle up together as though they could not bear to be far apart.

'The men will clothe themselves, as I will. It's very cold outside, and they'll work better if they're warm. How did you get in?'

'I bashed a hole in the library window,' Rochelle said. 'You'd locked the windows and taken the key away.'

'Not me, but . . .' He said something in German, under his breath, then frowned and reached down, taking hold of her hands. 'What's all this? Let me see!'

Rochelle looked down at her hands beneath the cuffs of her coat and nearly screamed. They were streaked and mottled with blood. Yet she had felt nothing, had been totally unaware that she had so much as cut herself, let alone suffered the severe lacerations she could just see as her coat fell back from her wrists. The long slashes opened up like mouths as she moved and gushed more blood on to the floor-tiles.

'That's bad. Here!' The Hauptmann tore off her coat and jersey, and pushed her sleeves back to reveal the damage. Then he ripped off his vest and without hesitation began to tear it into strips which he used to bandage her arms extremely tightly from wrist to elbow, working swiftly and efficiently so that it was barely five minutes later that he stood back, pulled her jersey down over her head again and helped her into her coat.

'There!' He patted her shoulder, then turned away towards the stairs. 'You are a brave girl, and when morning comes you must see the doctor to make sure there's no glass in the cuts. Go back to your father now and tell him we shall be with him as soon as we can.'

187

Father? But he was halfway up the stairs and already German troops were thundering down; she kept them away from the baize door, and then she turned to go out the way she had come in.

No one hindered her; they were going out of the front door themselves, calmer now, talking loudly rather than shouting, clearly bent on fighting the fire.

Rochelle got halfway across the library and discovered that she was very tired . . . very tired indeed. In fact she doubted whether she would be much help in the fire-fighting, for she felt very odd. The room seemed to be wavering about her, the curtains looked as though they were under water and the mantelpiece, the books and the chairs were all undulating gently.

Should she sit down in a chair, just for a minute? But that was no way to repay M. Laurient . . . he would worry if she did not reappear now. She got across the room somehow and stepped out through the window with exaggerated caution, like a drunk. She stumbled and lurched her way across the paving stones, through the herb garden, back to the stable-yard. There were men everywhere . . . the buckets of water she had prophesied were a fact and someone had a fat hosepipe connected up. Water was arcing up out of the end-piece and hissing and sizzling as it fell on the flames licking, now, around the back door.

Rochelle went over to a bucket and tried to pick it up. It was full, of course, and so extremely heavy . . . but *that* heavy? So heavy that she could not even budge it from the ground? She thought that perhaps she ought to move away from it for a moment, possibly even stand upright, and she made valiant efforts to do both these things, but instead, very slowly, she tipped forward, just managing to avoid a head-first plunge into the bucket and its contents, and fell with remarkably little noise or fuss on to the paving stones. Sounds faded, the fire seemed very far away, people came and went, but Rochelle did not care for any of them. She was tired and now she would sleep.

Rochelle woke. She was in a bed in a room that was unfamiliar to her but it was clean and white, and she could hear someone talking a little distance away. Something was holding down her right arm, though . . . she tried to move it and it was heavy, immobilised by something.

She had not yet done more than glance about her briefly, but now she opened her eyes and deliberately looked all around. She was lying in a bed, propped up by pillows, and there was a tube leading into the back of her wrist. The wrist and her hand lay on a board and she appeared to be wearing a sort of white linen garment which was a good deal too large and gave the impression of crackling when she moved.

The room was small, square, and white. It held two beds; one was empty and she was in the other. Her bed had a sort of table beside it with a glass and a jug of water on it. She discovered that she was very thirsty and almost certainly in hospital, and tried to think back to the excitements of the night before. But she could only remember standing in the hall and being told to leave by the Hauptmann.

The large linen garment had long sleeves; one had been pushed back to fasten her wrist to the board. She looked curiously at her arm and saw that it was criss-crossed by red lines with black marks at intervals. She looked harder and suddenly everything clicked into place. She had cut herself quite badly getting into Augeuil Manor and the German officer had bandaged her up. She had fallen down in the yard and now she was in hospital. The black marks were stitches, and . . . ugh! There was a large glass container full of what looked like raspberry vinegar to one side of the bed and the raspberry vinegar was trickling through a tube which led, eventually, into her wrist.

189

It's blood, they're giving me blood, Rochelle told herself with some surprise. Why on earth? Is that what they do if you bleed an awful lot – give you someone else's blood? And then the door in the wall opposite opened and someone's head appeared in the aperture; a German head in a peaked cap.

Rochelle had been lying very still; now she closed her eyes all but a slit. She did not want anyone to know she was awake before she had worked out what was happening to her. But through the slit she watched until the man had gone, closing the door softly behind him, and then she opened her eyes again.

A German soldier had just looked in on her. Did this mean that the Hauptmann had brought her here? And did it mean . . . oh, my God, was this German blood trickling into her veins? She did not want German blood. She would not have it. It would make her partly German, and besides, she did not want to have to be grateful to them for *anything*, because they were M. Laurient's enemies. They had taken away his house and forced him to move into the dower house in the woods; they had set fire to his beautiful home and not taken care of it at all; they were the enemy, the enemy!

She was struggling to get the tube out of her arm and causing herself a lot of pain, tears pouring down her cheeks, when the door opened again. One moment she was tugging desperately at the tube, the next there was an arm round her shoulders and a familiar face close to her own. A hand firmly took hold of both of hers, preventing her from doing any more damage to the tube or to herself.

'My dear child, my poor petite, you mustn't tug at the tube. You need that blood or you won't be able to come home and take care of us all.' Mr. Laurient's smile was gentle, his dark eyes understanding. 'You don't despise my blood, do you? I felt so guilty for having told you to get inside by the french windows that I had my blood specially

190

taken so that it could make you strong again. I sat by your
bed last night and held your hand and blood trickled
straight from my arm to your wrist, from my veins to yours.
Now lie still and I'll tell you all about the fire and how
quickly it was put out, thanks to you.'

'I thought . . .' Rochelle began dreamily, but was swiftly
hushed, the hands holding hers gripping tightly, warningly,
for one instant.

'I know what you thought, you foolish child, but remember where you are! No good can come of saying what you
thought – and anyway, you were wrong, weren't you? The
blood is mine – or are you going to say you don't want my
blood either, and hurt my feelings dreadfully?'

Rochelle giggled. It wasn't much of a laugh but it was a
start.

'As if I would! Am I a part of you now, monsieur? Is a
bit of me true Laurient?'

She had loved him for so long, wanting him for a father
right from earliest childhood because she had found, in
him, the interest and affection lacking in her relationship
with her own parents. She had never let him see it, though,
despite the fact that they had shared the same house, the
same interests, and in all that time he had seldom touched
her, never kissed or caressed her. She had not known how
she had longed for some sign of affection until this moment,
when she was weak and totally dependent. Now, she gently
freed her hands from his and reached up to touch his face,
just a light touch but nevertheless an overt sign of her love.

'Yes, you are now a true Laurient,' he said firmly,
catching her hand in his own fingers. 'And a true Laurient
never refuses good red blood from another one, so don't
you forget it!'

Rochelle smiled and smiled, her hand in his, feeling that
it had all been worthwhile, even her suffering, if it meant
that she would be accepted as a true Laurient, as almost a
daughter of the house.

'I won't forget, monsieur. Thank you very much. I am honoured to have your blood.'

'What was it like, in that hospital? Were the Germans kind to you? I did ask M. Laurient but he just said you were getting better and that you seemed bright and cheerful, and Grandmère wouldn't let me visit you, not at all, not even once.'

Olivia had been delighted to welcome Rochelle home once more and had lost no time in bustling her out of the dower house and into a quiet spot on the cliffs where gorse and blackberry abounded and where heather formed such a thick cushion that in the summer the children threw themselves on to it as on to a comfortable air-bed. But now, in late November, they had simply walked until they found a spot where they could couch down on the dried-out undergrowth, in the shelter of a furze patch, and talk in private out of the biting wind.

'It was all right,' Rochelle said indifferently. 'They were very polite and the food was quite good. And one of them, Hauptmann Kussak, brought me books and jigsaws and sometimes sat on the end of my bed and talked and played games. He's very old, of course, but quite nice, for a German.'

'He isn't very old at all,' Olivia said, widening her eyes. 'He's far younger than M. Laurient, for example. Probably only twenty-three or four – about ten years older than me.'

'He's old compared to you and me, then,' Rochelle said. 'When I went into hospital, though, I hated them all, but now I do know that some of them aren't bad. M. Laurient said the same; he hates what they are doing to our country and to the rest of the world, but he says you have to remember that certain of them, such as Hauptmann Kussak, are career soldiers and good men who don't, in fact, like what they are forced to do.'

'Well, there you are.' Olivia sat triumphantly back on

her heels and pulled a dried grass stem with which she began to stab at the back of her hand as she spoke. 'They aren't all beasts and brutes. Some of them are nice, honestly they are.'

Rochelle nodded idly, then rolled over on her stomach and peered through the thick gorse stems which surrounded them towards where the cliff-edge dropped away to the beach below.

'Ye-es. But that shouldn't make any difference, you see, Livia. M. Laurient explained it to me. It's a bit like playing some game or other, tennis perhaps, for your country. You need not hate every tennis player opposed to you, but you must realise that your only course is to beat them. You should never allow yourself to fraternise with them or the will to win might not be as strong.'

Truth to tell, though, the affair of the fire at Augeuil Manor had, in some way, tested not only M. Laurient and Rochelle herself, but also the Germans, or so Rochelle had come to believe. The gratitude of the Germans, most of whom were well aware that they owed their lives to the prompt action of the Laurients, as they collectively called all those who lived at the dower house, was a burden to M. Laurient and Rochelle and possibly even to themselves. In a way, Hauptmann Kussak had told them, it would have been easier had they been able to tell themselves that M. Laurient's concern had been solely for his property. But had that been the case he could have relied on his own ability to douse the flames before they had devoured more than the kitchen wing, knowing that in all probability the smoke and fumes would have killed at least some of the men sleeping directly above.

In addition, the Germans did not see themselves quite as the Islanders saw them, as a temporary unpleasantness. They were confident that they would be here for years, conquerors who would gradually make the islands their own, so it did not seem logical to them that M. Laurient would have saved the manor house simply because he had once owned it.

So, despite themselves, both parties began to be, if not friendly, at least less stiff-necked and suspicious about the motives of the others, although Rochelle thought that, given the opportunity, she would make life as nasty as possible for the people who had taken the manor away from M. Laurient and robbed him of his car, his boat and the easy assumption of authority which had been his before the invasion. She was jealous of these things for him; whether he felt the same she had no means of knowing for sure, but told herself that he was biding his time. He knew that, in the end, the British would win and he would take his old place once more.

But how to explain all these complicated thoughts to Olivia, who simply thought of the German youths as young men to be impressed? Rochelle, two years younger, thought that this was madness and hoped that her friend would soon see sense; she supposed, vaguely, that it was the uniform which attracted the older girl, plus a certain glamour because the Boche had power.

But now Olivia, in her lazy, good-natured way, was putting her own point of view.

'You say it's like a game of tennis which we won't win if we fraternise, Chelle, but to me it's all a game! I suppose I want us to win, but I'm not really thinking of winning or losing very much. I want to have a proper boyfriend who'll look after me and take me to the cinema shows and put his arm round me . . . kiss me, even. Lots of boys want to go with me, but the German dances are more fun. If things were different I'd be after a young man with a car who might even marry me and put me in charge of a lovely big house with lots of servants and all the clothes I wanted. But as it is the only people who can give me things like that are the soldiers, so I'd like to go with them . . . only no one will let me and it's so unfair!'

'You shouldn't think of them as young men,' Rochelle said, but even to herself it did not sound a very convincing argument. 'They're just the enemy. There are other young men, after all.'

'No, there aren't . . . that's the whole point! There are boys, I grant you that, and old men, but all the young ones have gone off to fight, like my papa. And I want a young man *now*, can't you see that, Chelle?'

'No, I can't.' Rochelle admitted. 'So it's no use arguing – you'll never see what I mean and I can't understand how you can even *think* about going with a beastly Boche, so we'll never agree. But one thing has come out of all this – Hauptmann Kussak is absolutely fascinated by orchiculture. He's been quite decent about it, really – actually asking if he may come and watch whilst we work on the plants, when I suppose he could just have barged in and shouted orders.'

'And did M. Laurient agree? To let him watch, I mean?'

'Yes, of course he did. For one thing he could scarcely refuse, and for another, he knows very well that if Kussak is interested in the orchids then we may get some help with rearing them. So tomorrow morning early, M. Laurient and I will be in the glasshouse, waiting to show off our favourites.'

'I'll come down as well,' Olivia said offhandedly. 'I like them too, though I don't pretend to understand them the way you and monsieur do.'

'All right – but don't expect lots of handsome young soldiers to be there, because it'll just be the captain, unless he brings someone else, which I don't suppose he will.'

Olivia laughed and stretched.

'You can never tell . . . I've seen him around with that adorable young fellow with the blue eyes and yellow curls. Shall we be getting back now? It must be teatime. Do you realise, Chelle, that you've *still* not told me much about hospital!'

'That's because there isn't much to tell.' Rochelle got to her feet and dusted fragments of dried heather and bracken off her short grey skirt. 'Come on, then, race you to the dower house!'

Next morning, early, four people assembled in the glass-house to examine the plants. M. Laurient had explained to the captain that they did not look their best at this time of year, but even so – because they had managed, so far, to keep the big house slightly heated by burning a wood fire in the stove for at least a part of each day and night – they still had blooms on some of the later-flowering species.

Hauptmann Kussak was keenly interested in everything. When M. Laurient began to talk of the strangenesses of various species and of the lengths to which, in the wild, the plants had to go to get themselves fertilised so that they might make seed, he was absorbed and fascinated.

In fact it was a very successful visit right up to the last minute, when Hauptmann Kussak made his unfortunate remark. They had gone right through the life-cycle of various species and M. Laurient had quoted a lovely passage from a very old book on Coryanthes macrantha, a plant which depends for its very existence upon the presence of a large humble bee which the flowers trick into the bucket-like hypochile, half full of fluid. The bee flounders out of the liquid and crawls along the inner surface of the bucket until it finds a passage which only just fits a smaller insect and has to be considerably stretched to enable the humble bee to pass. As the bee squeezes its bulk into the narrow passage large amounts of pollen attach to its wet body, and thus laden the bee escapes, to start greedily eating on the labellum of another Coryanthes macrantha flower. Soon the bee will find itself inexorably sliding into the second hypochile, and after its immersion will once more push and shove its way down the passage. This time

196

the pollen on its back is scraped off on to the stigma, and fertilisation has taken place.

'And do you have a specimen of this particular plant?' the captain said, looking around him. 'It must be difficult indeed to grow in captivity.'

Rochelle saw M. Laurient's mouth twitch at the captain's choice of word, but he merely said that he had no specimens at present, though they had been brought to Britain from their South American habitat several times over the past fifty or so years.

'Ah! Then perhaps I shall be fortunate enough to see this plant at Kew, in the not too distant future,' Hauptmann Kussak said hopefully. 'They will surely have a specimen.'

There was a short, frosty silence before Olivia said innocently, 'But isn't Kew in London? Are you going to London, Hauptmann?'

Rochelle was watching the German's face and saw the colour flood up under the thin, fair skin. Since the air battle which had raged over the mainland, and had clearly not been one of Germany's successes, there had been far less talk of an immediate invasion. It was clear to the Islanders at least that the Fatherland was no longer confident of an early end to hostilities.

'Well ... perhaps,' was all Hauptmann Kussak said now. He turned the subject rather cleverly by suddenly slapping his pocket and saying to M. Laurient: 'Talking of London reminds me; a letter has been delivered for you. It's not from London, of course, but from a neutral country – the United States of America.'

M. Laurient took it from him, turned it over a couple of times, and then said, with an indifference which might or might not have been assumed, that it was from an elderly cousin who lived somewhere in Texas.

'Well, thank you for showing me around,' the German said, sketching a salute in their general direction. 'I will do what I can to see that your wonderful plants are not allowed to die.'

'He could have opened that letter, you know,' Olivia said to Rochelle as they made their way back to the dower house for breakfast. 'I think it was nice of him to simply hand it over.'

'Yes, I suppose now one must thank a man for not behaving badly,' M. Laurient said bitingly over his shoulder. 'Come along, girls, look lively. Mme Barfleur may only be able to give us porridge but it's still best eaten hot!'

When breakfast had been eaten and the children despatched to school on their bicycles, M. Laurient took his letter to the small back room in the dower house which he used to store his books and those papers pertaining to the estate which he had been allowed to remove from the estate office. He still ran the place, of course, but was supposed to do the bookwork on the premises rather than here.

He sat at the desk, staring at the envelope. Helen? Could it possibly be Helen, after all these years? The name was correct, the address too . . . but why would she write after so long a silence? He had always assumed she had lost his address or had simply lost interest. Why open old wounds after so long?

He slit the letter open with his old ivory paperknife which was carved to look like a crocodile, and spread out the thin sheets – there were two of them. He frowned at the greeting, *Dear Charles Laurient*, and then turned to the last page and the signature.

Yours sincerely, Daniel Laurient, it said.

M. Laurient frowned. He could not recall a cousin named Daniel, but in fact it was an old family name. His father's youngest brother had been Daniel, but Maurice and Charles had not known their uncle at all well because he had gone abroad, first to Britain and then to America, to seek his fortune before his nephews were even in school. Possibly this could be a son or grandson of that Daniel . . . but there was only one way to find out.

He put the letter down before him, flattened it with a hand on either side, and began to read.

Dear Charles Laurient, You don't know me, perhaps you don't even know of my existence, but I hope you won't mind my getting in touch like this. I'm almost eighteen years old and my mother's name is Helen; her maiden name was Salling. I am at present an air cadet in the Army Air Corps in Texas and happened to see your name and address in a magazine devoted to orchid cultivation. I am a considerable enthusiast for these flowers and worked at the Institute in Louisiana, in the Orchid Houses, so I thought I'd drop you a line. Had things been different I should have hoped to visit you; perhaps when peace comes this will be possible.

I know you and my mother were good friends once; you met in Paris, she told me, the year before I was born. I am able to tell you that she is in good health and would no doubt send you her best wishes but I have not been in touch with her for some weeks and so she does not know I am writing this letter. She is married now and has several children, my half-brothers and sisters. She thinks a lot of you still and regrets that she lost touch. I think it would give her pleasure to know that I had written to you.

Well, sir, I must close now but here's hoping that you and I will meet up sometime. I think of you most days and also of your work with the orchids.

Yours sincerely,
Daniel Laurient.

Charles Laurient sat a long time, just staring down at the letter. But he was not seeing it; he was seeing a face that, of late, had grown misty and difficult to recall. Now it was as clear as though he had last set eyes on it yesterday – the shining wing of black hair, the clear pale skin, the blue of the eyes, the curve of the lips, the dimple which came and went in her cheek.

After a while he folded the letter into a small square and put it into the bottom drawer of his desk. Then he locked the drawer. And then he leaned back in his chair again and gazed at the blotter before him.

He had a son. The boy had not said it in so many words but he was as certain of it as though he had always known, in his heart, that he was not childless. A son. And Helen was married, but still thought a lot of him. Inexplicably, he realised that he was happy, that there was a quiet area of calm and certainty in his mind where there had once been turmoil and discontent. She had not thought him unworthy. And she had told the boy about him, by the sound of it had boasted about him, made him sound the sort of fellow a boy would be proud to own as his father.

It was strange how good it made him feel, to know that the lad existed and wanted to meet him. Once, he was sure, he would have been horrified to find he had an unknown son, even frightened at the possible call on his emotions. But not now; now he knew he could be a decent father if he was given a chance, just as he could be a good husband if he ever met anyone who mattered enough.

And it was largely due to Rochelle. She had broken down the barriers of his hurt pride, erected because a woman had rejected him and because of his inward conviction that he was not capable of any sort of strong emotion or real love. She had come to mean more and more to him; she had stolen into his life until he could not imagine his world without her. When he had seen her lying, blood-stained and unconscious, on the stable-yard paving, he had known that love comes in many different guises and for many strange reasons. He loved Rochelle not because she was his responsibility or because she was the child of the only man he had ever felt strong friendship for, but because she needed him, and because she had trusted him with the gift of her own love.

She was adorable, too. He knew that now, though he

would once have denied it emphatically. She was not a pretty, cuddly child, but she had character and sweetness and she had put him on a pedestal and believed him to be the sort of man he wished he was.

Does love beget love, then? He had seen love shining out of the child's eyes for three years and had told himself that it was just gratitude and a shared affection for the orchids. When she had lain in that hospital bed he had known that it was much more than that. She was the daughter he had never had, he was the father she had never been close to, and suddenly he had not been afraid of the waves of emotion that her brush with death had engendered in him, but had embraced his love gladly, had cuddled Rochelle as she needed to be cuddled and had seen her blossom as a result.

He had blossomed too, but quietly, internally. He might never have realised it had the boy not written.

And he discovered that he was glad, too, from the bottom of his heart, that he had woken the German soldiers and saved the manor. He wanted the house to be handed down to another Laurient; he intended to acknowledge his son right away, before another hour had passed. And he was glad because, one day, a German might show compassion to his son Daniel . . . an eye for an eye and a tooth for a tooth, a life – or lives – for a life. Some day, perhaps, Daniel might be embroiled in this wicked, wasteful war and some day it might be his life which hung in the balance. If so, Charles could only hope that the god of battle would remember that the Germans owed the Laurients many lives and would save his son.

Charles leaned down and opened a drawer halfway down his desk. He withdrew from it a parchment; a will form. Mostly it was already filled in, but there was one space, because he had no obvious heir to whom to bequeath the manor. He was only forty-three, and had thought that, when the war was over, he might marry simply to beget children. But now he had a child. It did not worry him that he had not married Helen. The boy was his, bore his name, and that was all that mattered.

He got out a pen and poised it over the inkwell whilst he rehearsed the words he must write. And then, steadily, he filled in the space.

My children must not be cheated out of their inheritance just because there's a war on, he told himself as he wrote. My daughter Rochelle is as dear to me, probably dearer, than my son Daniel; they must both have a share in the manor after I'm gone, the son of my body and the daughter of my love. Perhaps, he mused, filling in the names and the details, the ties of love between himself and Rochelle would always be stronger than the tie of blood between him and Daniel. But it did not matter; they would share the manor and all the good things – and the bad – which would come with the bequest.

He finished writing, blotted his words, then read them over carefully. His legal training came in useful here; he had committed no solecisms, made no errors, left no unfortunate loopholes. The codicil was sound and would hold water when witnessed.

He slipped the will into the drawer from which he had taken it, locked the drawer and stood up. He was unaccountably tired and found that he was also extremely hungry. He glanced at his watch; in the kitchen just across the corridor Mme Barfleur would be making tea. The children would be coming in at any moment, hungry and thirsty, to make short work of whatever was offered.

I must tell Rochelle about Daniel, he said to himself, turning the door handle and letting himself out of the study. It's only fair that she should know. But not now, not yet. It's too soon. Her own recently won status as his dearly loved child was too precarious, too recent, to stand the knock.

But later, I'll tell her, he promised himself, pushing open the kitchen door. Later. I owe her the truth.

9

It had taken three months for Laurie's letter to reach Jersey and it took an equally long time for Charles's reply to make its way back to the United States. And by then, with the best will in the world, Laurie was not watching the post expectantly.

His life was very full. He had no particular girlfriend but he knew a lot of girls; he had three good friends in the AAC, all of them passing steadily up through the ranks to win their wings; and although at first they had all denied that America would ever enter the war, it was pretty clear now that they had been wrong. The only thing in doubt, Laurie often thought, was the exact date at which his country would decide that enough was enough.

Laurie and his friends had bought an old Dodge and used it to get off the base and into the nearest town. Because it was such a big car they could get themselves and their girls into it and go off on expeditions which usually ended in kissing sessions, with couples entwined on all the cracked leather seats. Sometimes Laurie thought he had met a special girl but somehow she was never quite special enough to stop him from wanting to meet the next one, and, anyway, he told himself that with entry into the war imminent it would not do to get involved.

His friends felt the same. There was Russ, a skinny blond lad of nineteen, who charmed all the women. Then Stu Hoff, the oldest of them at twenty-four, a serious young man with horn-rimmed eyeglasses which he wore for reading and a long, gangling body which looked as though it would have to be folded to get into the BT-13 cockpit. The third member of the little crowd was José Santander,

203

a South American with large brown eyes, olive skin and a droopy black moustache. The four of them did well with the girls and enjoyed driving their old car as fast as it could go, which wasn't very fast, around the shanty towns and cattle ranches and sheep farms. José was a farmer's son himself and enjoyed chatting to the slow-thinking, long-striding cowboys and the drawling, self-confident ranchers. But none of them even considered settling down with any of the pretty, pert girls who came into town for the dances and parties which the cadets frequented.

When Russia entered the war in the summer of '41, there was an expectant buzz round the air base. But somehow, even when American shipping was intercepted and American nationals insulted, it was never quite bad enough to bring about a confrontation.

Laurie and his friends were preparing for a really memorable Christmas when the news came through that the Japanese had bombed the American fleet in Pearl Harbor. At last, was Laurie's initial thought; at last we'll be in it too!

They were. And within a few days of the confirmation of war between America and the Axis powers, Laurie had his letter.

December had not been particularly cold, but nevertheless there was a bright fire burning in the recreation room at the base. Laurie was sitting in front of it, scanning a handful of papers. He and the rest of his group wanted to leave together when they were posted, and were wondering whether it would make a difference if they showed an intelligent interest in, say, the same sort of aircraft. Everyone wanted to fly fighters, of course, but it had struck them that there would probably be more call for bombers at this stage of the war. The Flying Fortress was about as big as you could get and there was a course in Florida for training on it. 'If we all put in together,' Stu said, 'there's a chance we might all get sent there together as well.'

So Laurie was filling in forms, after a good deal of heavy thought, when Ricky Seltatz, a scruffy little cadet but a very good flier, came whistling into the room. He stopped whistling when he saw Laurie, however.

'Hi, bo! There's mail for you, on the board.'

Laurie laid his papers down with the pen on top of them and stood up. He stretched and yawned, then addressed the younger man severely.

'Ricky, if you've just said that to get me out of my chair I'll make you sorry!'

'It's for you. Blue envelope, black ink writing. Go on, I won't take your chair.'

'You better not,' Laurie grumbled, but set off at once for the board in the foyer of the cadets' quarters. It was a large plywood edifice criss-crossed with lengths of elastic which held the letters until their owners came along and claimed them.

The letter was there all right, and it had foreign stamps on, too. Laurie's mother wrote a couple of times a month, now that she knew where he was, but he had had her latest letter only the previous day. One glance at the envelope and his heart started beating overtime. He knew, as he touched it, that it came from his father.

He went back to the recreation room and tore the envelope open. Ricky was playing pool against himself at one end of the room; no one else had yet got back from town or from flights. By the time Laurie had read three lines his face had warmed with pleasure. Charles Laurient had come straight out with it and called Laurie *son*, said he was delighted with the news and intended to acknowledge Laurie – only he called him Daniel – as his heir. He added that when circumstances allowed he could imagine no greater pleasure than to meet his son and to show him Augeuil Manor, which would belong to him one day.

And of course to my daughter Rochelle, the letter continued, but Laurie had expected his father to have other children so this news did not throw him, especially when the letter went on to explain that Charles had adopted Rochelle after the death of her parents and that she was twelve years old and as devoted to the manor and to the orchid collection as he was himself.

The friendly tone and general air of the letter delighted Laurie, and he noticed that his father did not once grumble about the Occupation nor seem to consider that it would be a permanent bar to their meeting. Wonderful! Of course he had written it many weeks ago and it had been despatched whilst America's precarious peace was still in existence, but Laurie did not doubt that all would be well. Once the United States started to send troops to the Allies' aid, the war would be over in no time!

'Hi, Mom!'

Helen was baking in the kitchen, while her youngest daughter, swathed in a huge pinafore, stood on the kitchen stool and made pies for her dollies with a piece of paste which was already grey and greasy. The little girl stared as the tall, dark-haired young man in the blue Army Air Force uniform ducked his head to get through the kitchen door. Helen stared too, but only for a second. Her dearest child was actually here, at last! She flew across the hard dirt floor and tried to put her arms round him, only he was so large, his shoulders so broad, that she could only seize him by the lapels and smile up into his face.

'Laurie! It's wonderful to see you – wonderful! Fancy you getting in touch with your . . .' She glanced at the little girl and pulled a face. 'Here, Cindy, this is your big brother, Laurie. Just say hello real nice and polite and then go play with Era, out in the yard. Mommy will come fetch you soon's the baking's out of the oven and you shall have a gingerbread boy all to yourself!'

'A whole one?' piped up the rosy-cheeked tot suspiciously. 'A whole one, legs an' arms an' head an' all?'

'Would I lie? A whole one, sure's I'm your mommy.'

The small girl disappeared, leaving the back door swinging, and Laurie, closing it behind her, saw the sturdy legs carrying her at a fast trot across the yard in the direction of the cart-shed. He turned back into the kitchen, smiled at Helen, and then bent over and kissed her smackingly on the cheek.

'Mom, I've missed you! Has anyone ever told you you're a durn terrible letter-writer? I write four to your one, and I'm rushed off of my feet gettin' the big airplanes learned right.'

'Yes, I should be ashamed; but I'm pretty busy myself,' Helen said. She indicated a chair. 'Sit down, you great creature. I can't rick my neck lookin' up at you for hours. Now, tell me 'bout writing to your father – and gettin' a reply, what's more.'

He smiled at her. There was mischief in the smile and some complacence too. For the first time it occurred to her that he was really very like Charles to look at, though his hair and eyes were not so dark and he did not have the indefinable air of smouldering passion which Charles had had. But then he would scarcely exude smouldering passion towards his mother, Helen reminded herself with an inward smile. And then she concentrated on listening as she continued to roll out her pastry and make her apple pies.

'I wrote when I found out his address from a magazine; I'm sure I told you that. Then he wrote back, told me he'd changed his will, named me as his heir . . . never a word about the Occupation, seemed as though everything was jogging on same's before. He was real pleased to find he had a son, though . . . thinks of you 'most every day, he said.'

'That's lovely. He still rearin' them orchids?'

He nodded, beginning to tell her about the flowers, but Helen saw the way he looked at her, quickly, as though checking up, and laughed a little sadly.

'You're thinkin' your mom's got herself a real country burr to her speech, ain't you? I fit in, Laurie, same's you used to do. But they tell me the Army Air Force is the cream – that right?'

'We think so,' her son said. He looked so natural, sitting in the chair, his head leaning back on the cushion, as though he had sat there many a time over the last few years. I treated him badly, Helen thought remorsefully, letting him come second to the other kids just because he was older – and not that much older, either. But whatever's happened it's made a man of him, and a good man, too. She thought of Sheridan's son Lindsey, who had stayed on the farm. No spirit, no fire in his belly, no desire even to think for himself, far less act on it. If he went into the Army it would be as an enlisted man who would simply do as an officer told him. But her boy – her son – was an officer already. He had brains and imagination and, despite his calling, probably twice the muscle of his one-time pal Lindsey.

'And did you have to pass exams, Laurie? Tests an' that?'

'Sure we did. But even in the CCC you could study, if you'd a mind, so I wasn't too far behind everyone else.'

He told her what an officer had said to him only the other day. 'You guys who've come up in the Depression you'll scramble by, you'll do just fine. But your education has huge, gaping holes where you missed school to do work. One day, those holes will have to be filled, else you'll be picked out when all this is over and thought less of.'

Helen shrugged. 'He's right, of course. But if you're sharp, if you listen and think before you speak, you'll get by and no one any the wiser. And most of your generation'll be in the same boat.'

He smiled at her, then lounged to his feet. He was taller than his father, she was almost sure, and when he smiled he had a long crease in one cheek which made him look

208

quizzical, more amused than the smile warranted. He raised one dark eyebrow at her, seeing her staring, and Helen could imagine how a younger heart than hers would have melted. Oh, he was an attractive young animal all right, and knew it – but there was a warmth in his eyes and a sweetness in his smile which told her that he wouldn't break hearts for the joy of it as some guys would.

'Sure, Mom. Can I steal some pie?'

With a sharp cry, Helen rushed to the oven; the pie on the top shelf was perfectly cooked, the crust golden, the apple bubbling. She took it over to the windowsill. Outside, the leaves were blurring the outline of the trees and the birds sang and swooped with joy for the coming of summer and the early sunshine. She stood the pie down and turned back into the room.

'It's impossible to believe we're at war on a day like this,' she said. 'You've done all your training now, have you? Is . . . is that why you've come to see me after so long?'

He nodded; then went over to stand beside her, looking out across the woods and fields which could be seen from the window.

'Yup. They give you furlough before . . .'

'You're going abroad? Oh, but Laurie, you said you could stay here, you could train other guys to be pilots, you said . . .'

'I know, but Mom, I've learned so much and I want to use it. They won't tell you where you're going, but I'm a good pilot. I can fly an airplane just where they want me to. I'd not be happy if I had to stay here and let others do my fighting.'

Helen tried to smile, to let him know that he was right to go, but it was a poor attempt and she knew it. Foolish to care so passionately because he'd been gone . . . oh, years . . . and for all she knew he might have been abroad in any or all of those years. But she felt, now, that he had come back to her, told her his secret desires, his secret yearning. She knew she would never see Charles again and in a way she did not want to. He remembered her as young and beautiful, and she would prefer that he always thought of her like that, never saw the dumpy person she had become with her sagging chin and tired greying hair. But a son expects a mother to grow old; Laurie accepted her as she was, loved her as she was. She did not want to lose this handsome, charming son of hers, before she had done more than spend an afternoon with him.

'Mom? I'll be back, you know that? I'm a *good* pilot; I'll take care.'

Useless to say that his survival would not depend upon his ability as a pilot . . . useless and cruel. She picked up the cooled pie and carried it back to the table, keeping her gaze down, willing herself to blink away the stupid, sudden tears lest they fall and give her away.

'Of course you will, Laurie. It's just foolish of me, but I'll worry about you, so mind you write. I'll write back this time, too. Now there's cream in the pantry . . . d'you like your apple pie with cream?'

Laurie thought about his mother as he flew his Liberator up to Denver; she had put on a little weight, sure, but he thought her slight plumpness attractive, a sure sign that the Depression was over. Her greying hair he scarcely noticed, save that it suited her heart-shaped face. He thought her a beautiful woman and himself a lucky guy to have such a mother. No wonder Charles Laurient had been so crazy about her . . . and he lost himself in a daydream in which the two of them got together again – through his own good offices, naturally – and married and reared orchids together.

The corps were all going up to Denver for the last phase of training for combat. Laurie had already seen the airfield, which was just like the last one so far as he could see, and was now shuttling crews and air-support people, plus baggage, from Texas up to the new base. The four friends were still together, all flying Liberators and all raring to go, though they were now in two pairs. Laurie's co-pilot was José, and the entire crew were men who had been together in training. The navigator was Solly Cohen, a dark, intense young Jew straight from the Bronx with an accent so broad that even Laurie had to listen carefully to catch every word. The bombardier, John South, was a Canadian who had lived in South Dakota for the past five years; the gunners were all fresh-faced boys still in their teens; and Ben Cluda, the top turret engineer, had been with Laurie in the CCC.

With their final arrival in Denver, reality began to break in. They practised emergency landings, using three engines, then two ... sometimes even one. They made 'dead stick' landings, which meant that you pulled your throttles completely off and left them off. It was a hard and a dangerous manoeuvre but one which would possibly save lives one day, if one of the pilots was trying to land a plane with all four engines out.

The Liberators, B-17s, were heavy, lumbering airplanes when compared with the Vultee BT-13s which Laurie had trained on, but they were also rugged and, once you knew their capabilities, reliable. They also flew high – but *high*! Flying on oxygen was new to them, the extreme cold at height was new to them – but somehow, during their final combat training at Denver, they learned to cope with it. And with each other. They flew together constantly, until not only did each feel he knew his individual task in the airplane backwards, but they were like brothers, understanding each other's idiosyncrasies and little ways.

Laurie realised they were winning when their own particular airplane, named *Blue Moon*, developed a small fault and was grounded for a few days whilst the ground-crew worked on it. He and José both agreed that it was like

211

being without a much-loved car . . . they could do things with *Blue Moon* which they would hesitate to do in any other ship because they knew her reaction to every move, every touch. They knew what she would take in her stride, what would make her hesitate a moment, what she would bluntly refuse.

When the day came for their departure from the staging area, they all knew each other too well to worry about what was to become of them. Whilst the ships were checked out they sat around in the officers' club playing gin and talking. Laurie wrote to his mother and also to his father, though he had to send the letter via a neutral country, Spain. He could tell neither of them whither he was bound since he did not know himself, would not know until he and his crew opened their sealed orders an hour out on their flight, but that did not stop him from writing two cheery, optimistic letters.

They left very early one morning, in the grey of dawn. Sealed orders were opened when they should have been, with the ships now up to their cruising height and well out of the way of most sorts of trouble. Solly slit the envelope, examined the contents, and then used the interphone to let Laurie and José, up front, know where they were bound.

'Africa,' he said laconically. 'We're going to Africa!'

In fact, they were in Libya. They reached their new home after a good few days of flying, to find a runway on the desert, a few trucks, some goats and a couple of camels.

'Hey!' Solly shouted, as *Blue Moon* taxied along the runway, raising clouds of yellow-white dust. 'Where's the reception committee?'

The 'reception committee' consisted of a driver and a truck which, they were assured, would take them to the living site. The crew were tired after a long day in the air, but they had no option but to follow their driver back to the truck, and then to sit in the back of it, bumped and thumped, until they reached a pile of tents which had to be erected before they could sleep that night.

'My God!' Laurie said, as he and his men began pitching tents. 'Was that a snake?'

'It was; and there's scorpions,' José said wearily. 'I thought the danger was in the air . . . did you see those other airfields as we came in?'

They had all seen the other airfields; they had recognised their own airplanes in some, German airplanes in others. Earlier in the journey they had experienced flak for the first time, but no harm had come to them since they were high enough to ignore the little white puffs far below.

'Sure we saw 'em,' Solly said bracingly. 'Did you see the beach?'

It cheered them, the recollection that the beach was only a few miles away, and they very soon needed cheering. The accommodation was simply a pup tent, apart from the large tent which was used as a mess hall, and the food was dreadful. It was full of sand and of poor quality, though no one went hungry, or so they were informed by the first people to arrive, who had been here forty-eight hours already.

'We'll bathe first thing in the morning, if we aren't told off for flying duties,' Laurie said cheerfully to his companions as they at last completed the erection of their tents, slung their personal belongings under cover and went off to find the mess hall and try the food for themselves. 'This place can't be as bad as it seems; I've always wanted to see Africa.'

'See Africa . . . see Italy . . . see Crete,' Laurie grumbled as *Blue Moon* took off for her tenth mission in two weeks. 'They never mention that it'll be from a few thousand feet up.'

'Hopefully,' José said, crossing his fingers. 'I got no desire to see 'em close to, fella!'

It made them laugh, which was a good thing. They had

213

flown out to the target and dropped their bombs, with at least one direct hit, and then on the way back they had been buzzed by what seemed like every fighter the Axis powers possessed. Laurie had recognised ME-109s and FW-190s and even one or two Italian Macci 202s. They had inflicted severe damage on the squadron and one at least of the B-24s was unlikely to get back to base, which was always both a worrying and depressing thought.

Laurie knew that *Blue Moon* had been hit, and one of the waist gunners had announced a flesh wound, but the ship was still flying, which was the main thing. Laurie and José took it in turns to get the 'feel' of the airplane, and both agreed that though there was some rudder damage it was not serious enough to interfere with their return flight home.

All the way to the target they had been tense and quiet, knowing that this was a big one. They had been equally tense though not quiet at all during the fighter attack and when Ben Cluda, in the top turret, had shrieked that they'd destroyed an ME-109, they watched the crew descend on lazy parachutes and the shouts and exclamations had been downright rowdy. They had been in oxygen masks whilst they overflew airfields and cities, keeping high to avoid the flak which looked so harmless, indeed so pretty, but could deal such devastating blows if you got too near, but now they were heading home, the masks were off and talk became general.

'We've kept formation pretty good,' someone said, watching the other ships in the squadron as they made their droning way across the blue sky. 'Reckon it's taken us ten missions just to get used to keeping in place at height.'

'If it had been possible to do some practice runs,' someone else contributed, 'we'd have done better. It's durn hard to find yourself doing altitude flying in the masks when it's for real, with guns and flak and enemy aircraft to contend with.'

'Sure; but we've survived this far,' José said. 'Anyone coming for a swim when we get back?'

There was an approving chorus from behind him, everyone using either their lungs or the interphone to indicate approval. It was the best thing about their camp – you could scarcely call it a base – and Laurie, in particular, loved the deep blue sea, the fine white sand and the milky coolness of the water.

It always made him think of his father, perhaps because he had found books about the Channel Islands and read about their wonderful beaches. He was sure his father would be taking advantage of those beaches right now, so long as the Germans hadn't mined them all, and that seemed unlikely since they themselves would need to get on and off the island.

Flying home was always a good time for reminiscence and now Laurie found his mind turning to the orchids and how, when the war was over, he would find a rare specimen and take it to Jersey with him. It was an old dream of his but still a good one, and he let his imagination have free rein. But even whilst he dreamed, reality would keep breaking in. The war must affect the orchids in his father's succession houses, because surely he would not be able to keep them at the right temperature and in the right conditions with the enemy all about him? Laurie had heard dreadful stories of what went on in France and guessed that things would be bad in the Channel Islands as well, though his father's letters, rare to be sure and always many months behind the times, had not indicated anything other than a good few shortages and some irritation over the occupying forces.

Then there was that girl . . . what was her name. Rachel? No, Rochelle, that was it. His father had said she was interested in the orchids, but of course a mere child could

215

not possibly be much help to Charles Laurient over something as complex and difficult as rearing and hybridising. But possibly there was a gardener . . . only was he allowed to spend his time on the orchids now, with a war on and food in short supply?

Below them, the familiar outline of the coast came into view and, a short way beyond, the equally familiar runway. Laurie began to prepare for his landing and around him the crew prepared themselves as well. Even *Blue Moon*, throttling back, seemed to tense herself for the moment of truth, when wheels met solid ground for the first time for several hours.

The ground loomed closer and closer, the wheels kissed, parted, kissed and stayed down. Laurie taxied his ship to an easy halt and cut engines and then they began to scramble out, forgetting the danger through which they had passed, or endeavouring to do so.

As they walked away from the airplane the ground-crew raced forward and Laurie looked back.

Half the tail was shot away; it was remarkable that they had managed to get back from the raid and to land in good order, but by now they were growing used to remarkable happenings. He shook José's arm and jerked a thumb back at the tail; then he and José looked at each other and grinned sheepishly.

Luck, it seemed, was almost as much the name of the game as skill and dedication.

10

'When we've finished here I've got some business to attend to, so why don't you go and find your friend Peter in the village? You could go off somewhere on your bikes . . . though not too far, and keep clear of the troops, won't you?'

Charles Laurient was doling out plant feed in tiny quantities to his remaining orchids. After three years under enemy occupation he knew himself lucky to have any orchids left to rear and hybridise, and it was partly thanks to Hauptmann Kussak. And grateful though he was to Kussak he also knew, though Rochelle did not, that it was because of Kussak that Rochelle no longer had Olivia's companionship, for Olivia had moved in with her German lover some six months previously, and Rochelle missed her sadly. Now, however, she looked up from the delicate task of repotting inchling orchids and smiled at him.

'Can't I come with you? I'm fifteen you know, not five, and whatever business you're attending to, I don't see that I would prove too much of a nuisance if you took me along.'

Charles shook his head at her, but he was smiling too; he couldn't help it. She was a pretty sight for all she was thin as a rake, her eyes huge in her pale little face. Rationing was now almost farcical, since there was very little food to be rationed, and he hated to see her so thin. But he was thin himself; they all were. Even the dogs were beginning to look like greyhounds, with their sunken stomachs and prominent ribs, and though he and Rochelle went to endless pains to keep the animals fed there were days when not even their best endeavours could produce suitable food.

Olivia, of course, was different. Rochelle had been to see her once, in the smart little house which her lover had found for her. Laurient had bicycled round after a couple of hours to accompany Rochelle home and had seen Olivia, very golden-haired and smooth-skinned, very sleek, waving from the doorstep. She had looked, for a moment, oddly wistful as she waved, but then she had sighed and glanced around her at the house and her pretty furniture, and she had patted the fat spaniel at her knee and gone back inside without another backward glance.

'Did you enjoy yourself? Is Olivia well and happy?' Laurient had asked as they cycled home. He saw the scene again, Rochelle's glance at him, quick, almost shy, as she clearly pondered how much to tell.

'Yes, I had a very nice time. She gave me chocolate cake . . . I took a piece for you, too, when she got up to fetch more hot water for the tea . . . and white bread sandwiches with pink fish in. Do you want them now, or later?'

He had glanced quizzically at her, cycling along in her thin blue dress and open sandals.

'And where are these culinary delights hidden?'

'In my knicker-leg. I put a good, stout flour-bag in there just in case I had a chance . . . let's stop by the next bit of wood, then you can have them. They're probably getting a bit mixed up and sticky.'

They stopped and Rochelle produced the spoils. They were indeed mixed up and sticky, but Charles would no more have commented on their state than he would have refused her offer. She watched him as he ate the food – and despite its condition it was delicious – and he knew he was giving her more pleasure than all the rest of her day together.

'That was marvellous,' he said with a sigh, as he finished

218

off the crumbs. 'You're a kind girl to think of me, Chelle. And is Olivia happy?'

She considered, head tilted, dark lashes hiding her eyes. Her hair had not been cut in three years and it spilled, a gleaming black flood, across her neck and over her shoulder. She tied it back for school but had worn it loose today in lieu, she had told him earlier, of a party dress, the blue cotton being too tight, too short and too faded to be considered suitable for a special occasion.

'Is Olivia happy?' she echoed at last. 'I don't know. She's lonely often, but when he's there . . . yes, then she's terribly happy. A little bit afraid, though. She's having a baby.'

He had guessed this was on the cards, though he was a little shocked by Rochelle's calm acceptance of the fact. But after all, Olivia was seventeen and ripely beautiful. If her man loved her, and it seemed likely that this was so, then perhaps all would turn out for the best.

He said as much to Rochelle, who nodded, but doubtfully.

'Ye-es . . . but why won't she tell us who he is, monsieur? Even today, when we were so happy together, she wouldn't let it slip, except his first name, which is Theo.'

'Perhaps he has a bad reputation amongst the Islanders,' Laurient suggested, then wished he had not said it as he saw the shadow flicker across her lively little face.

'You mean like the man who killed the other one with a spade?' There was remembered horror in her dark eyes; Laurient wished he had thought before speaking, but now he must try to undo the harm he had done. Quickly, he shook his head.

'My dear child . . . no, indeed. Olivia would not love a brute like that. Anyway, he was a soldier, and Olivia's lover is an officer. No, I meant perhaps someone nearer the high command who might be disliked because of his office, not because of the way he fills it.'

219

It seemed to satisfy her for she nodded and cycled on, and presently changed the subject herself so that by the time they arrived home they had been chatting amicably enough about the properties of kelp as a fertiliser and the chances of finding gulls' eggs on the cliffs if they went out searching at the weekend.

But now, in the greenhouse, Laurient considered her request to be allowed to accompany him on his 'business'. He would have liked her to go along, and she would probably be very helpful, but . . . he did not want to expose her to any unpleasantness, and there was no doubt that what he was about to do was highly illegal.

'Monsieur? Please?'

'We-ell, it's risky for two of us, but if you'll keep very quiet and just abandon me if there's trouble, I suppose you might be useful.'

She nodded enthusiastically, her eyes sparkling.

'Yes, of course, of course! When do we go? After dark?'

He laughed, giving her a playful cuff on the side of the head. She rode the blow, laughing up at him.

'After dark, in summer? No, we'll leave in about an hour. We'll use our bikes for the first bit.'

'Oh good, good!' She finished putting the last plantlet in its own tiny pot and brushed her hands together. 'Shall we have tea first?'

'Might as well. Though what we'll find . . .'

They made their way to the dower house. When Olivia had finally left her mother's home Mme Barfleur had decided she would move in with her daughter, though she had offered to come in three or four times a week to cook and clean. Charles Laurient had accepted the offer so long as the old woman could manage to get to and from the manor with moderate ease, but six weeks ago Mme Barfleur had explained regretfully that the lift she had relied on had ceased. She did not feel she could walk the distance, had never learned to ride a bike and did not think she could master it at her age, and so their arrangement would have to be suspended for the time being. However, whenever she could manage it she came up to the dower house for a couple of days, during which time she occupied her old bedroom, cleaned through the house like a tornado and made what use she could of any food which Laurient or Rochelle managed to lay their hands on.

In return she was paid a small salary and given any fruit, soap or other commodity they could spare, though she had once said, rather bashfully, that Olivia saw that she did not go short.

Laurient had wondered how he and Rochelle would manage, left to their own devices, but he had underestimated them both. They did better, if anything, than they had done under Mme Barfleur's benevolent but despotic rule. Laurient stole from his own property in order to keep Rochelle fed, for he saw no reason why he should hand over every root crop he grew to the ever-hungry German troops, and he managed, by dint of extreme slyness, to see that every now and then a beast would mysteriously fail to give birth to the calf, piglet or lamb it had been confidently expecting, whilst in the dower house still-room a carcass of meat would put in an appearance, to be preserved, salted down or hastily eaten, depending on circumstance.

'What shall we have?' Rochelle demanded, as they entered the kitchen. 'There's a bit of bread left. And some apples. They're a bit old and wrinkled . . .'

They tended to eat their rations rather early in the week, but Laurient never minded provided there was food available. He looked into the stockpot on the stove and tutted at Rochelle.

'You were out helping me in the glasshouse when you should have been preparing vegetables for the pot. Never mind . . . run over to the kitchen garden and see if you can liberate some peas.'

The peas and beans grew tall and strong in the walled

221

garden; it was quite easy, if you were small and thin, to squeeze between the wall and the rows of vegetables and fill a pan with pods and be off before anyone knew you were there. Laurient was too solid to do it, but Rochelle was a past master at the art.

'OK; shan't be a tick.'

Rochelle grabbed a pan and left the kitchen. While she was gone Charles prepared the bag which he always carried slung round his waist and hidden by his jacket when he went out in the evenings. By the time Rochelle came panting back in, her pan full of pea-pods, he was ready.

'Got them? Well done . . . I've put some water on to boil.'

'Lovely. And now I'll do the turnips and carrots and they can be simmering on the back of the stove whilst the peas cook.'

She was as good as her word, slicing and chopping quickly with the sharp little kitchen knife and then throwing the vegetables into the stockpot and pulling it over the heat. Charles, having cut the dark-coloured bread into two more or less equal pieces – for she would make him eat the larger share if they were noticeably different – went to the pantry and brought out his jar of home-made coffee. It was a weird conglomeration of dried peas, beans, dandelion roots and anything else he considered suitable which he cooked without water and then ground down into a rough sort of powder. With the addition of the ersatz coffee provided by the occupying forces it made, if not an acceptable brew, at least a drinkable one.

'Peas nice and soft? Good, then we'll eat. The coffee's ready.' -

They ate in companionable squalor, sitting close to the open back door, their plates on their knees. Charles looked at her, concentrating on the food, and smiled to himself. A far cry from those long-ago days when they had eaten in the dining-room, enjoying three or more courses, able to be finicky if they disliked something, drinking wine with the food. Of course, they had treats sometimes still, when he went to the food store and extracted tins or packets of rice or macaroni and they feasted, but for the most part they ate merely to keep body and soul together and took little pleasure in the actual act of chewing and swallowing.

He was afraid of using the food store up, because then he would know that there was no reserve, nothing for that rainy day which he had laboured so hard to keep at bay. Only when things were very bad did he make his way down through the woods and past the haunted pond to the abandoned cottage. In winter they were forced to call on it from time to time, but never in summer. The hedgerows would be picked clean, this year as the past three, but, although Jersey people took what they needed, it was the slave workers who tore the green fruit from the trees and crammed it into their mouths, who ate handfuls of barley as they walked beside the ripening crop.

'This is really delicious. There's nothing quite so nice as new peas.'

As he spoke, Charles thought of what he and Rochelle had seen a few months back. One of the Russian workers, almost crazed by starvation and deprivation, had attempted to eat a turnip as he and his fellow slaves carried them from the storage clamp to a lorry. A guard had seen him and come over, knocking the turnip from his hand with a cruel blow from the spade he was carrying. The Russian, skeletally thin, clad in meagre rags, had cringed back – and then appeared to go mad. He had lunged at the guard, snatching at the spade, trying to hit the man whilst at the same time seeking to pick up the turnip, now lying in the mud.

The guard was tall, strong and well fed. Before anyone could do anything he had swung the spade, knocking the Russian prisoner to the ground, and then, with the spade, he had all but decapitated him.

There had been a horrible scream, followed by animal groans, a dreadful bubbling snort . . . and then blood had poured out of the prisoner's mouth, his head had flopped sideways into the mud, and Charles had known he was dead.

It had all happened in a moment. He and Rochelle had been cycling past the field where the tragedy had taken place. They had both wobbled off their machines but Charles had known at once that this was the wrong place to be and had caught hold of Rochelle's handlebars, forcing her to cycle on.

Later, discussing it, he had tried to explain to her that what she had witnessed had been a terrible act and a brutal one, but it was not something that she might one day have to face.

'The Germans respect us; they almost like us,' he had said. 'They fear and despise the Russians and think of them as little better than animals. That terrible, isolated act was something which almost all the troops on the island would condemn, had they seen it.'

But this was not true. He had been discussing the way the Germans treated their slave workers with Cyril Motte, a farming friend who often came over on summer evenings for a drink of the thin beer which was occasionally available, and Cyril had given it as his opinion that even the most civilised of the German troops considered that to treat a Russian as well as he treated a dog would be to unduly honour the Russian.

'They hate them with a personal vindictiveness which I find truly impossible to understand,' he had said, sitting in the dower house kitchen and puffing on an empty pipe. 'When a German fights with an Englishman or a Jersey-man he's fighting an equal, but when he fights with a Russian he feels he's attacking a sewer rat who may give him the plague or some other noisome disease, so he'll use any means to kill the creature and feel no remorse.'

'And the French? There's no doubt the French suffer worse than we do.'

'Ah, that's because the master-race believes that the English are a Teutonic people at heart and will come round, in the end, to see the Hun viewpoint. But the French are Latins. Not as bad as the Russians, of course, but a Teuton despises a Latin and considers him decadent. Not as low as a Russian, but a good deal lower than a Brit. See?'

Charles had seen, but that did not mean he liked what he saw. Which was, he supposed now, as he finished off the last of the tender peas and wiped his dish round with the last bite of bread, why he was off out in a moment, on his bicycle. There was little enough he could do, but he did what he could.

'Are we ready, monsieur?'

Rochelle had cleared her own plate, drunk the last drop of the bitter black coffee and washed up their plates and spoons at the sink. There was no hot water, and soap was saved for personal ablutions, so washing up was, perforce, a sketchy business. She stacked the two plates on the dresser and took her old black coat off the hook on the back of the kitchen door. She slid it on, though it was a mild and pleasant night. But it was better always to dress inconspicuously, though it was a long while to curfew.

'We'll have to shut the dogs in,' Charles said. He was wearing dark trousers and a faded blue shirt; he added a thin black sweater to his outfit, then put on the dark jacket. 'We won't need our coats until later, when the sun is down and it gets cooler.'

'Oh! Curfew's at sunset,' Rochelle said, stopping halfway to the back door. 'Will we be out that late?'

'Probably not. If we are, we'll leave the bikes stacked away in a wood somewhere and come home across country. Don't worry, I've done it before without any repercussions.'

She nodded, but looked troubled. He guessed that she

had heard him coming in late once or twice, but had told herself that he had been in the glasshouse, with the orchids. But as she had said she was a big girl now; better that she should know the truth.

They went openly out to the old stables where their cycles were housed, pushed them along the narrow track through the wood and then, on the road, mounted and began to ride.

It was a delicious evening. As Rochelle and Laurient bowled along Rochelle could smell the purple thyme which starred the short turf and took automatic, loving note of every wild flower which they passed. She also noted chestnut trees, and crab apple trees with their fragile burdens, because later, when autumn came, these trees would mean food to supplement slender rations.

Presently they could smell the sea on the breeze. The evening sun was reddening, but not yet touching the horizon. The light was clear and golden, reflecting brilliance off a pond as they passed and touching each leaf on every tree with its magic.

They had come a good way, but not yet so far that she did not know every stick and stone of the countryside. When M. Laurient dismounted and gestured to her to take a narrow woodland path, though, she realised that she had not been this way for many years and had little or no idea of what they might find. She followed obediently, however, heeding his warning finger to lips. Neither spoke as they pressed deeper into the wood, but Rochelle, trying to see this side of the island in her mind's eye, had a horrid feeling that it led to German-occupied territory. Of course the island was all German-occupied, but what she meant was to detainment centres, or prisons, or simply to barracks where civilians were not allowed.

They crossed the wood, but when she would have continued to push her bicycle M. Laurient shook his head at her. Quietly, he leaned his own machine against a tree, took hers from her and leaned it in the same way. Then he dropped into a crouch and went forward, out of the trees and into the gorse bushes which crowded close to a tall chain-link fence.

It was excellent cover; Rochelle, following cautiously, realised that they would be able to see into the compound beyond the wire with very little chance of being seen in turn. But what would the Germans want to hide which they would keep behind chain-link fencing which could so easily be approached? Not much, she was sure.

But here at least she was to be proved wrong. They reached a spot which someone had obviously used before, since the furze and bramble had been flattened to resemble a dormouse nest in the gorse. Charles Laurient proceeded to lie on his stomach and, following suit, she realised that she could peer straight between the tough stems of the gorse and watch anything happening in the compound.

And it was clear that a good deal was going on. A very large number of filthy, rag-clad men were moving about within, all turning to face a broad gate on the far side of the compound from time to time. Clearly, they were expecting something to happen at any minute.

Rochelle stared, trying to discover just why M. Laurient had come here, for as a rule he avoided places where the slave-workers might be found. To see them so brutally treated and ill-used was painful. Then she heard a tiny, tiny click.

She turned her head. M. Laurient was still lying beside and slightly ahead of her but now he was resting his weight on both elbows and was pointing a small camera towards the compound. Rochelle's movement must have caught his eye for he lowered the camera for a moment and smiled at her.

'Evidence,' he breathed. 'When this is all over . . . we can do so little!'

'I see. Why now, though? The light's not very strong.'

'Wait. You'll see.'

And see she did. Presently a number of the hated Todt troops came and swung open the big gates and then more approached, carrying a big tin bath full of something which steamed. Rochelle swallowed hard as the men in the compound turned and began to press towards the gates, clearly eager for the food which must be in the tin bath. She could see the anticipation in every face, the sudden tension in every figure. This was, she supposed, the big meal of the day.

The men bearing the tin bath were shouting in loud, guttural voices, kicking out with their heavy army-issue boots at anyone who got anywhere near them, and the prisoners, obviously used to such treatment, were hanging back . . . yet they were clearly trying for some reason to edge the men over to the left of the compound, whereas the bath-carriers were using their feet and the weight of the tin bath to win the right-hand side.

Rochelle frowned; German troops who had clearly no part to play in the feeding of the prisoners were lining up now on the far side of the compound, faces pressed to the chain link. They were shouting, laughing . . . it was like people at the zoo watching animals being fed and Rochelle felt her gorge rise. This was hateful . . . why did M. Laurient want to photograph it?

Beside her, the camera clicked, the tiny grating sound inaudible from a few feet away, what with the noise of the prisoners and the noise of the audience. And then, in a short, brutal rush, the men bearing the tin bath broke through to the right-hand side of the compound, and Rochelle saw what they were after.

The entire compound had once been a garden, and on the right was an ancient fish-pond, filthy and mostly mud, but still containing several inches of water. The guards, with a triumphant shout, upended the bath . . . and the

228

entire load of steaming boiled potatoes descended into the fish-pond.

The roar of rage from the prisoners and the delighted shouts and cheers from the watching troops drowned Rochelle's indignant gasp, but she heard, close to her ear, the growl which accompanied the clicking of the camera. M. Laurient must have known what was likely to happen and was determined there should be documentary evidence so that, one day, those who had perpetrated the vile act should be held responsible.

The guards had charged into the meagre water now and were kicking and scuffing the potatoes under their feet, howling with laughter as the prisoners, seeing that it was this or nothing, dived on the food and tried to rescue what they could.

Rochelle put her head down on to her arms. Tears flowed, runnelling down beside her nose, salting her mouth, dripping off on to the smooth skin of her fingers and wrists. The wickedness of it! The needless cruelty . . . and the troops laughing and jeering as they saw men who had laboured hard all day at their behest denied even the poor consolation of a mouthful of food.

But even as she wept, she realised that she had not been brought here to agonise for the men. She was here to tell what she had seen one of these days so she had better keep her eyes skinned. She lifted her head, wiped her nose with the back of one hand, and watched.

And saw more than anyone else. M. Laurient had his camera pointed first at the spectators, then at the perpetrators, then at the Russians scrabbling for the filthy, smashed potatoes. The troops and the prisoners had eyes only for each other and the sun had just sunk below the horizon, so that the grey of evening was creeping across the land.

The gates were still open, just a little. And one of the prisoners had completely ignored the whole episode with the potatoes but had edged round the fracas and was now

229

no more than a foot from the open gate. Even as Rochelle watched, breath held in unbearable suspense, he strolled through the gate and into freedom. And then, instead of running, he turned and walked quite briskly towards the nearest group of huts – and towards the bushes which grew nearby.

He was a young man, fair-haired, and although pitifully thin he looked stronger and huskier than most of his fellow-prisoners. He was moving with confidence too . . . Rochelle dared not shut her eyes but she could pray with them open, fixed.

Please God let him get away; please God let him get away!

There was a shout from the compound and the soldiers picked up their tin bath and headed for the gateway. The prisoners were kneeling in the water and the mud and fishing out handfuls of potato mush, eating it eagerly . . . but the looks they cast at their tormentors boded ill for them should they ever be in a position to retaliate. Rochelle had seen that there were fully armed men, rifles at the ready, near the gate, but when the fair-haired Russian had walked out all eyes had been on the fish-pond. Only one person had been watching the gate and that was Rochelle herself. No one else had noticed anything other than the tragedy – for Rochelle could not think of it as anything else – being enacted in the compound.

Beyond the chain-link fencing the soldiers were dispersing. Night was falling fast now, the dusk growing thicker. M. Laurient had tucked his small camera back into his clothing and now glanced across at her for the first time.

'Are you all right? Never forget what you've seen tonight, petite, and when someone tells you that there are good Germans as well as bad just remember that the good Germans let things like this happen, made no effort to stop it. And they could . . . the men watching could have stopped it, they just didn't choose to do so.'

230

The remark was said so low that only Rochelle could have caught it, but she leaned even closer to reply.

'I'll never forget, monsieur, never. But . . . one of them is out! Did you see?'

He shook his head, clearly puzzled.

'Out? One of the prisoners, d'you mean? No, my dear, you must be mistaken. If you saw anyone go through the gates it must have been one of the troops.'

Obstinately, Rochelle shook her head.

'No, monsieur, I'm certain. I was watching him before. He was in rags . . . he surged forward with the rest when the food came in . . . the other men all crowded between the pond and the food . . .' She gulped, her voice wavering, then steadied herself and went on, 'I wonder if it was arranged, monsieur? The way the prisoners pressed forward, and the one who got away just walking round the outside . . .'

'I don't know; I saw nothing. Rochelle, are you sure?'

Rochelle nodded, but what with the deepening dusk and the gloom in their small, gorse nest she knew he was scarcely likely to have noticed the movement so she spoke as well.

'Truly, monsieur. He is in the patch of bushes by their hut. Is that the hut where they sleep at nights? If so, perhaps he plans to let them out when full darkness falls.'

'They sleep in the compound, winter and summer,' M. Laurient said, but almost absently, as though it was no longer terribly important. 'If you're sure, Rochelle, we must see if we can help him.'

'Yes . . . but what can we do? There are troops all over the place, and they'll leave guards, won't they?'

'I've heard people say that the guards sleep, because where could the Russians go, even if they broke out? We'll wait . . . or do you want to go home now, my poor child, to your own bed? If you can make your way . . .'

Rochelle put a hand out and gently covered his still-moving lips.

'No indeed! I'll stay.'

He did not attempt to dissuade her but merely nodded, and the two of them settled down to wait. After an hour, during which time they had not exchanged a word, Rochelle leaned forward and whispered, 'My stomach's rumbling,' and he turned and nodded, smiling, his teeth a white gleam in the dark.

'Mine, too. It won't be long now, and I've been thinking. He's got no option but to come this way, and if we startle him he might cry out. We'll follow him.'

'All right; both of us?'

'Yes, I think so. If I get ahead, though, can you make your way home alone? Leave the bicycle. We'll get them back tomorrow, unless you feel you can wheel it? You mustn't be caught breaking the curfew, young though you are.'

'All right.'

'And now glue your eyes to that bush and give me a nudge when he moves.'

Rochelle was gratified to hear him say 'when' and not 'if'. Clearly, he now accepted the presence of the Russian prisoner in the bushes by the wooden huts. And very soon his acceptance was justified, for they both saw the movement, quick as a striking adder, and then the man was passing their refuge and making his way quickly between the trees.

Rochelle was already crouching, ready to move. M. Laurient went first, a hand on her arm so that she stopped when he stopped, hurried when he hurried. They emerged from the bushes straight into the wood and they could just make out, ahead of them, a shadow that moved amidst the trees.

'Leave the bicycles,' M. Laurient hissed at her. 'Now . . . carefully!'

But they lost him. One minute he was ahead of them, the next the dappled moonlight and shadow was empty of anyone save themselves. Charles Laurient cursed softly.

'Gone . . . well, we'd best follow suit. Let's make for home.'

They were barely half a dozen yards further on, though, when a man leapt like a tiger out of a tangle of undergrowth and got Laurient round the throat in an armlock. He spat at them, in broken English: 'Oo are you? Vat you vant?'

'It's you! We were trying to catch you up so that we could help you,' Rochelle hissed, since M. Laurient could say nothing with that skinny, sinewy arm around his throat. 'Do let him go. We won't give you away, we're Islanders!'

'I heard you talk,' the man muttered. 'You will help me?' He let go of M. Laurient, who hung his head, breathing deeply and harshly for a moment.

'We'll hide you,' Rochelle said eagerly, still in a voice so low that only someone very near at hand could have heard. 'I watched you escape . . . we'll take him home, shall we, monsieur?'

M. Laurient massaged his throat, then grinned at the other man and held out a hand.

'Charles Laurient. Will you come with us?'

'Radek Pokovski. Yes, if you please.'

Without more ado the three of them started walking once more. They cleared the wood, but on the road M. Laurient would not let them walk down the middle of it, though it appeared to be deserted.

'We'll stick to the hedges,' he ordered. 'Rochelle, you're very quiet and you're used to the terrain. You go first, our friend here can come next, and I'll bring up the rear. And we'll go slowly, if you please, petite. If we have to run I'll give the order, but moving slowly we will attract less attention.'

And go slowly they did. Along the hedges until they reached more woodland, then through the trees like three Red Indian stalkers, then crouching across open moorland, then dodging from one trunk to the next in the orchard.

But they reached the dower house at last. It lay silent, apparently deserted, but M. Laurient was taking no chances.

'Go in, petite,' he ordered Rochelle, in a whisper still. 'Make sure the house is empty, and then come out again with the dogs, as though you were merely letting them out for a breath of air before bed. We will come in then, when we know it's safe.'

Rochelle went towards the darkened house. She pushed open the kitchen door, cringing at the squeak of hinges, and made a fuss of the dogs, who stood up at once and came towards her. Their greeting was always tumultuous, but tonight it seemed more so than usual and Rochelle fancied that the dogs, too, had been worried by their unaccustomed loneliness. Nevertheless, she checked in every room, found them all empty, and then went out with Pod into the moonlight once more, Senna hurrying ahead.

She would have called, but M. Laurient was beside her at once and the other man with him.

'Friend,' M. Laurient said to the dogs, and the hackles which had begun to rise on each back lay flat again and their tails wagged gently in greeting. Any friend of their master's was clearly a friend of theirs, no matter how dirty and unkempt he might be.

And dirty and unkempt he certainly was. They made their way to the dower house kitchen, where M. Laurient lit the lamp – the blackout had been put up before they had left the house earlier – and then bolted the big back door. Only then did the three of them examine each other in the yellow lamplight.

Radek Pokovski was a tall young man with a square-jawed face, pale blue eyes and tanned skin stretched tight over high cheekbones. He was clad in rags so filthy that the smell seemed to hang around him like a physical aura, and his feet were bare, the toes well-spread and seeming to clutch the ground as he moved. His skin was brown from the constant exposure to the sun but it was also filthy – plainly the prisoners were never offered a wash – and Rochelle saw, when she looked at him closely, that there were sores and patches of dry, flaking skin all over his body.

He stood in the middle of the small kitchen for a moment, poised, then moved over so that his back was to the oak dresser. He gave the impression of being at bay and his eyes, flickering over the room, were those of a cornered creature, nervous, suspicious, the terror barely hidden.

Rochelle crossed the room slowly, ignoring him. She opened the pantry door and saw him flinch and start, as shocked by the simple movement as though a storm-trooper had burst in. She selected a bowl of cold potatoes and carried them out into the kitchen together with a frying pan and a knob of fat. She put the pan on the stove, opening the door at the front and stirring the sluggish wood with a poker to make it blaze a little, and then, as the fat heated and began to smoke, dropped sliced potato into the pan.

Out of the corner of her eye she could see their guest. As the smell of the frying potatoes grew stronger he seemed to be drawn, as a pin to a magnet, from the oak dresser, across the kitchen floor, and to her side. She glanced quickly at him but he was not looking at her; his eyes were fixed on the pan and the expression of total longing in them made tears rise to her own eyes. Such a pain of hunger!

As soon as they had browned she tipped the potatoes on to a plate and handed it to the prisoner, who took them – almost snatched them – and then, surprisingly, stopped short, glancing enquiringly at her.

'You some? Your fader some?'

'No, we've eaten. Those are just for you,' Charles Laurient said soothingly. 'Sit down . . . I'll pour you a glass of wine. It isn't the best but it'll help the potatoes down.'

Rochelle doubted if he heard but he smiled and sat down, still staring at the contents of the plate as if he could not believe his eyes. That all these fried potatoes were for him clearly seemed almost more than he could take in.

'Salt,' M. Laurient said, bringing a small silver cellar of that condiment out of the pantry. 'And there's some cold pork.'

The pork was the heel of a joint but somehow, just for a moment, Rochelle saw it through the Russian's eyes as a luxury almost beyond belief. M. Laurient put it on the plate, put the salt cellar down in front of the younger man, and then fetched a bottle of wine and a glass.

'There! Do eat, before Rochelle's cooking goes cold.'

The man needed no second invitation. It would have been embarrassing to watch him eat except that their eyes were scarcely turned away before the plate was clean. He must have swallowed the potatoes whole . . . and then he drank a brimming glass of wine in a gulp . . . and Rochelle knew he was still hungry, endlessly hungry, and with aching pity hurried once more to the pantry. If only she had not been such a careless housekeeper! If only she had saved the bread . . . but there was cheese, and a packet of cream crackers, hoarded for later in the week.

She brought out cheese, biscuits and apples and M. Laurient put the kettle on the stove and the Russian looked at the food and a most beautiful, tender smile passed across his face.

'How good, to a stranger total,' he said blissfully. 'Your own lives you risk, your food you give. I can only thank.'

'That's all right, Radek,' M. Laurient said easily, and Rochelle envied him that ease. 'Just you eat up, and then we'll snug you down for the night somewhere safe. Tomorrow we'll discuss how best to keep you hidden.'

236

The young man squared his shoulders and seized the packet of biscuits and the cheese. He broke the latter into pieces, glanced over his shoulder at Rochelle and gave her another smile.

'You forgive?'

'There's nothing to forgive,' M. Laurient said before she could answer. 'We've seen hungry men before.'

Rochelle remembered the prisoners scrabbling for the fragments of potato in the filthy water and inside her chest a big bubble fought to break out through her throat in a cry of pain and misery, but she forced it back. She would not let her own weakness embarrass this young man who had already been through so much.

And indeed, Radek crunched up the biscuits and cheese and the apples, cores and all, before the kettle had half boiled, and when the coffee came, with all the milk they had left in it, he drank that too, and then he gave a burp of such magnificent proportions that both dogs jumped to their feet. But now he was beginning to know them, Rochelle felt, for he shook his head sadly at himself, then turned to her, bowing in an odd, jerky way from his seat.

'Forgive. I em sorry.'

'You speak very good English,' Rochelle said, speaking for the first time since they had reached the house. 'You are Russian, aren't you?'

'Yes. But English student also, only not for many year. And you? You are of the island? Here you have a language your own but this I cannot know.'

'Oh, patois,' Rochelle said. 'Yes, we speak it, but we speak English too. Both are useful in their own way.'

M. Laurient turned to Rochelle.

'I think just for tonight, petite, we'll put Radek in Mme Barfleur's room. There are clean sheets on the bed and plenty of blankets. But first I think it might be as well if you went up to bed. Our guest will want a wash.'

237

Radek had been following this with a puzzled frown which cleared at the last words.

'Wash? You have soap? Ah . . . vunderful!'

'I'll go up and fetch some clothes, shall I?' Rochelle asked tactfully as M. Laurient took the kettle from the stove and poured water into a basin. 'Radek's taller than you, but he could still fit into a shirt and trousers, I should think. I'll bring them down – and a big towel – in about five minutes.'

'Good girl. Throw the towel down at once, though, would you? Then by the time you're ready with the clothes, our friend here should be all right to put them on.'

Rochelle hurried up the stairs. It was after midnight and she should have been very tired, but in fact she was buoyed up by the sheer thrill of being able to do something. The entire war, so far, had been a frustrating business for M. Laurient and now, she knew, he was in his element. The Islanders had come to the conclusion that they could not form any kind of secret underground movement against the Nazis because the island was too small and reprisals would be too terrible. He did what he could by taking photographs and keeping a detailed diary of events, but although he had assisted in the task of getting a young lad over to France in order that he might endeavour to get back to his home in Spain, he had taken no other active part in helping the war effort. He listened to his wireless set twice a day whenever possible, and when the news was good passed it on to close friends, but other than that all his energies had been channelled into keeping the orchids alive and farming, to the best of his ability, the estate. Since the Germans took about ninety-eight per cent of all crops this was a somewhat thankless task and one which gave him minimum rather than maximum satisfaction. But to whisk a young man from under the very noses of the Nazis would, Rochelle knew, give M. Laurient the sort of pleasure which would do him most good.

Upstairs, she checked that all was prepared in Mme Barfleur's room, pulled the curtains and then hastily drew them back once more. How absurd – she had nearly given the game away. A good few people would know full well that Mme Barfleur was not in residence at the moment and would wonder over drawn curtains in a presumably empty bedroom.

Whilst she went through M. Laurient's clothing to find something suitable for the younger man, she racked her brains to think of some hiding place for him. The derelict cottage in the wood was not a bad place, but if he was there she and M. Laurient would have to keep visiting to take him food and someone would grow suspicious. The glasshouses? The numerous old stables and potting sheds and so on? But with the Germans occupying the manor that would be risky, to say the least. In the end she selected a faded blue shirt and some grey flannel trousers which she remembered M. Laurient once complaining were too long for him, and carried them to the head of the stairs. She had thrown a towel down some ten minutes earlier and now she called softly: 'Shall I come down now?'

'Sure,' said a voice. It was Radek's and it sounded light, pleased with itself.

Rochelle descended the flight, crossed the tiny hall and went into the kitchen. Radek stood in the middle of the room, naked but for the towel wrapped round his waist. He was a pitiful sight, but she tried not to stare at the starting ribs, the sunken frame. His shoulders were broad still, but fleshless, the muscles standing proud. She was pleased to see that he had even washed his hair, which was no longer the colour of dusty hay; it was a clear, primrose blond.

'A blue shirt and grey trousers,' Rochelle said, quickly glancing away when she realised both men were looking at her. 'I'm sorry about the shoes, but all I could find which I thought would fit were sandals ... I could see,' she added, addressing Radek direct, 'that your feet would probably be larger than monsieur's.'

She handed the clothes to M. Laurient who took them with a word of thanks, nodded his approval of each garment, and handed them one by one to Radek. Without removing his towel the Russian tugged on the trousers, buttoned up with his back to Rochelle, and then took the shirt and fastened that as well. Then he pushed his feet into the tan coloured sandals and turned and smiled at them both.

'I thank you. Is all right?'

Assuring him that he looked splendid, Rochelle thought that she had never realised how clothes transform a person. With the shirt and trousers hiding his terrible thinness, and his skin shining from the hard application of soap and water, Radek looked like a different person. Younger, fitter, more . . . more normal.

'You'll be fine,' M. Laurient said. 'Come on, bed!'

Rochelle began to clear away and wash up whilst the two men ascended the stairs and was half finished by the time M. Laurient rejoined her. Without a word he picked up a tea-towel and finished drying the Russian's supper things, and then he spread out the faded old blanket the dogs slept on, closed the front of the stove, banked it up with ash as they did each night and only then turned to Rochelle.

'Well, my child, we must do our best to sleep sound, because we've a score of problems waiting for us tomorrow!'

'Have we? Oh, you mean what to do with Radek.'

'That's right. Because in no circumstances will that young fellow get taken back. He'd rather kill himself and that I won't allow, either. Rochelle, my dear, sit down a moment.'

Wondering, Rochelle sat one side of the stove and saw M. Laurient take the chair opposite.

'Rochelle, in the early days of the war I received a letter from the United States of America. You probably won't remember . . . I said it was news of an old friend, which it was in a way, but I never gave you any other details and now I must do so. Indeed, I would have told you long ago, but the moment never seemed ripe.'

'Yes, monsieur?' Rochelle ventured, when it seemed as though M. Laurient had fallen into a brown study. 'And the moment is ripe now?'

He sighed, then looked at her, rubbing a hand across his cheek.

'Yes. Because of Radek, you see. One of the reasons I'm so glad – so grateful – that I'm to be allowed a chance to help him is that I learned from that letter that I have a son who is probably about Radek's age . . . a boy of twenty or so. His mother left me long ago, never telling me she was pregnant, and then lost my address and had no means of getting in touch with me. The boy read about the orchids and wrote to me . . . I wrote back, acknowledging him as my heir but telling him that his inheritance would be shared on equal terms with you, my adopted daughter.'

'You've got a son. Goodness.' Rochelle's mind was whirling but it did not prevent her from hearing the echo of pride in his voice, nor stop a sick feeling of jealousy from invading her. So he had a son! He wanted to love his son . . . but he loved her, she knew he did, far better than a boy he had never seen who lived in a country so far away that he probably never would see him!

'Yes. My son will be in this war, somewhere. It gives me pleasure to think that maybe a man like myself, far away, can give my boy a helping hand, as I'm giving one to Radek. But most important, Rochelle, if . . . if I should be discovered helping the boy, I want you to get Radek away and into safety no matter what the consequences may be. Only never at risk to yourself . . . understand? I'm old and

241

tough, I can take care of myself, but the boy's weak from what he's undergone and you're only a little girl.'

'A little girl? Only a little girl? Oh, but monsieur, that isn't fair. It wasn't long ago that you said . . .'

He laughed, got to his feet and pulled her to hers, then put a finger across her indignantly open mouth.

'No, no, don't shriek at me. What a dreadful thing to say, to be sure! Rochelle, you are my dear daughter and no one can ever mean more to me than you do, but I want you to know about my boy so that if something does happen to me, and he turns up after the war, you'll know that I didn't try to deceive you and that I accept you both as my children. And now we'd better go to bed.'

'All right,' Rochelle said. 'Monsieur, what's his name . . . your boy?'

'Daniel Laurient, but his friends mostly call him Laurie.'

'Hmm. All right, then. I'll remember what you've said if I ever meet him.'

'If? But I'm sure you will, when the war's over. I want you and Daniel to be friends.'

'All right. I'll go up now, if you don't mind. What time's breakfast?'

They both had alarm clocks in their rooms and usually roused when the sun came up, but Rochelle suspected that she might easily oversleep next day.

'Seven o'clock, I think. You should have seen Radek's face, petite, when he cuddled down in the clean sheets. Oh, I'd like to get them all out of that hellish place, see them all smile like that!'

'Me, too,' Rochelle said fervently, but low; the door to Mme Barfleur's room stood open and she felt she knew how terrified he would be if he was woken by their voices. 'Goodnight, monsieur.'

'Goodnight, Rochelle. Sleep tight.'

Rochelle made her way across her room, tugged the curtains closed and tore off her clothes. She struggled into her skimpy nightie and then jumped into bed, pulling the covers up round her ears. She expected to fall asleep at once, but instead found she was far too excited still, her mind churning impatiently round and round the events of the day and speculating upon those of the morrow. And there was another thought which was not helping her to sleep either, because she knew full well how wicked it was and was trying, unsuccessfully, to suppress it.

If that boy Daniel Laurient was in the war, who could say whether she would ever meet him? He might easily die in battle, easily, and it would be no fault of hers if he did.

It kept her awake for a long time, but she slept at last.

11

Radek remained in hiding with Rochelle and M. Laurient for five days, but it was a nerve-racking time. They were simply too near the manor and the manor was too full of Nazis. What was more, as Radek throve with rest, as much good food as they could scrape together and a soft bed, so he grew careless. Twice Rochelle returned to the dower house unexpectedly in the middle of the day to find him standing bold as brass in the kitchen, once washing dishes, once cooking them a meal for their return.

Remonstrating seemed useless, despite the fact that his half-remembered English was improving daily and at a rate of knots which proved how intelligent he was. In a thoughtless moment M. Laurient had told him about the orchids and he was full of plans to smuggle himself out to the glasshouse by some means, there to help them with their orchiculture. He seemed to believe that once he had escaped he was safe ... so much for his intelligence, Rochelle thought sourly. It clearly did not extend to self-preservation.

On the fifth day, M. Laurient decided that something must be done.

'Mme Barfleur will probably come tomorrow,' he told Radek. 'She is a good woman and would never knowingly betray you, but her granddaughter is mistress to a German officer and you never know when a careless word could slip out. If she knows nothing she will say nothing. Therefore I want you, Radek, to keep well out of sight all day today. I shall go across to the other side of the island, to a friend of mine, and though I must abide by my own rules and say nothing directly to him about you, I shall put out feelers for some safe place where you can stay for the duration of the war.'

'I'll come with you,' Rochelle offered eagerly, but though he smiled M. Laurient shook his head.

'No. I need to talk to Pierre in confidence. It would not be possible with a third person present.'

'Oh, all right. Shall I stay with Radek, then, make sure he doesn't wander off?'

'For a whole day, petite? No, you go down to the village and find a friend to spend the time with. I'm going to chain the dogs.' M. Laurient turned to Radek. 'And Radek, if you unchain them and take them indoors this time, I'll turn you out to fend for yourself.'

The young man grinned, unabashed.

'Sorry, I am most sorry,' he said. 'It was foolish, I see that now. I'll stay upstairs, in my room, and if anyone comes in I'll go under my bed.'

'No one will come in with the dogs chained outside,' M. Laurient said. 'That was why we put them out last time. But it's essential that we do nothing unusual – whilst either Rochelle or myself are nearby we never chain the dogs, so to do so whilst we are merely working in the glasshouse would give rise to comment if not actual suspicion. But with both of us innocently off for the day – I need to see Pierre on estate business, fortunately – it is natural to chain the dogs outside.'

'For fear a Russian prisoner might break loose from the slave-gang in search of food,' Radek said broodingly. 'Yes, I see.'

'And I hope you also see that if you are caught Rochelle and I will either be sent to concentration camps in Germany or simply shot?' Charles Laurient said crisply. 'If you have no thought for yourself, Radek, think of the girl!'

'Shot? Oh, but . . . yes, of course, I am a fool not to have realised . . . I will hide,' Radek said humbly. 'All day I will stay beneath my bed if it will help. All day.'

'There's no need for that,' M. Laurient said, winking at Rochelle as their guest's blond head drooped. 'Just stay up there out of sight, read, eat apples and drink some of that home-made wine ... we'll be back by five or six this evening.'

'I will make a meal,' Radek said, chirping up, then laughing at the expressions on Laurient's and Rochelle's faces. 'No, no, I am not serious ... I will stay upstairs.'

So presently Rochelle chained Senna and Pod to their kennel by the back door, leaving them a big stone basin full of water. It was a brilliant summer's day but there was shade from the trees which surrounded the dower house if the dogs grew tired of the sunshine.

'They'll be fine,' Laurient said as she fussed over them, promising a speedy return for good behaviour. 'What's more, they wouldn't let a snail pass without making enough noise to wake the dead.'

He and Rochelle got their bikes out of the shed and cycled together as far as the village. There they waved goodbye and Rochelle cycled up to the smallholding owned by the de Causis family. Peter, the son, was a lanky, brown-haired boy in Rochelle's class and since Olivia's defection he and Rochelle had spent a good deal of time together. So she called hopefully, thinking that she might spend the day with Peter, helping on the smallholding perhaps or bathing in one of the coves which had not been mined or wired off.

She was disappointed. Mme de Causis came to the door and invited her in, but told her that Peter had gone off with his father to visit cousins on Guernsey.

'A shame you didn't come earlier,' she said, shaking her head and pouring Rochelle a glass of skim milk. 'It's only a day-trip, but good fun for you youngsters. Of course there's a German aboard the boat and their long faces spoil most things, but last time he went Peter trailed a line and caught some sea-bass. And my sister-in-law grows the best tomatoes on Guernsey – they usually bring some back. Still, another time, eh?'

Rochelle agreed that another time would be fun, drained her glass and set off for the village once more. Surely someone would be about who could come out with her?

But everyone seemed to have made their plans. Some of the youngsters were helping in the fields, others had gone off in little groups which Rochelle could have joined had she been earlier. There was a very large seawater pool a short bike-ride away, and a good few of her friends would be there . . .

But they would all have a partner. If Rochelle had been with Peter she would not have missed Olivia's company so much, but Peter was on his way to Guernsey and she did not much fancy making an uncomfortable third with another pair of friends. Her trouble lay, she knew, in being regarded as an ordinary child who had somehow become extraordinary when adopted, to all intents and purposes, by the squire of the local manor. Everyone was friendly – but a good few of her classmates were not entirely sure how to take her, and her obsession with the orchids was generally accepted as being more than a little odd.

Oh, well. Rochelle got back on her bike and decided she would go a really long way, up to the inhospitable north shore of the island, where she had friends she rarely saw.

The L'Oyette family had suffered already from the Occupation; Denise L'Oyette's husband, Claude, had been a fisherman and he had been killed by German bombing on the day before the troops had actually landed. The Germans had clearly believed they must cow the populace before arriving in force.

However, the son had taken over his father's place, running the farm to the best of his ability and taking out his fishing boat whenever it was safe for him to do so. He had got special dispensation from the Nazis to fish from the rocks, since otherwise one was supposed to depart from

247

a specific spot, watched over by troops, and counted both out and back. But Jean-Claude's bit of coastline was too rugged to be a suitable landing point for invading Allied troops, and, since even the Germans knew that he would not leave his mother to face their wrath should he decide to try and take his cockleshell craft through the dangers of the sea right the way across to Britain, he was allowed to fish from his own inhospitable creeks and coves.

If I get there in time, if he's going out today he could take me, Rochelle thought hopefully, as she cycled hard up a steep hill and then coasted joyously down the other side. It was so hot, and she would be able to bathe from Jean-Claude's boat, which was far nicer than merely using the seawater pool.

Before the war, she and M. Laurient had been rather sorry for the L'Oyette family, but now they were generally envied. They lived in far too remote an area for regular German surveillance and as a result they probably lived better than most. Their thin sea-catches were at least all their own, and what food the rock-infested farm-land yielded was also largely left to them. The grazing on the cliffs was by no means lush but they usually managed to have a couple of cows and the odd pig, and when the creatures gave birth there was no one to be surprised by the small size of the pigs' brood, or by the fact that the cows were never – officially – put to a bull. Supervision of a sort there was, but the farm was so far off the beaten track, the yield so small, that they were harried less than most.

So Rochelle cycled over the thin heather and grass on the long, upward-sloping cliff with pleasant anticipation. Her friend Tante Denise would undoubtedly feed her, and sometimes there was cream – a luxury she scarcely ever tasted these days – and occasionally a lobster. She always helped with something during her visits, of course – churning butter, or heaving the big pan of full milk off the

heat so that they could skim off the crusty yellow cream –
but she enjoyed the novelty of working with no Germans
overseeing what she did, and it was pleasant to hear Tante
Denise and Jean-Claude exchanging forthright comments
on the occupying forces which would have been dangerous
for most people to say out loud.

There were informers in the village; everyone knew that.
You might not know who they were but you knew well
enough that if a spiteful person was annoyed with you your
name might be sent to the German headquarters with a list
of your misdemeanours, mostly apocryphal. Fortunately
the German High Command liked these tattlers as little as
the Islanders did, so by and large you would merely be
visited and cautioned. But there was the odd person who
would be sent to Germany as a result of information
received, or imprisoned for long months in the St Helier
gaol where the food was as poor as possible and conditions,
under German rule, appalling.

But it was a sunny day with a blue sky and a brisk
breeze blowing, and Rochelle tried never to wonder who
was secretly tale-bearing because it made you distrust your
dearest friends. Instead, she puffed and blew as the long
climb neared its end, then twisted her wheel to the right
and flew down into the hollow in which the L'Oyettes'
farmhouse was situated.

It wasn't really a farmhouse, she reflected, wheeling her
bicycle across the tiny, sand-strewn yard and leaning it
against the low grey building. It was a fisherman's cottage
which happened to be called a farm. But whatever you
called it, she was happy here and glad to have arrived.

Rochelle knocked on the peeling paint of the back door,
more as a courtesy than anything, because she guessed that
Tante Denise would be in the thin fields or the cow byre,
then opened it. The room, as she expected, was empty, but
a voice from upstairs shouted that the older woman would
be with her in a moment.

She must have seen me as I cycled down the track, Rochelle told herself, and sure enough in a couple of minutes Tante Denise's deeply tanned face appeared in the doorway, wreathed in smiles.

'Chelle, what a lovely surprise! I didn't see Monsieur Laurient with you, so I suppose he's out on business and you've decided to come and see me and Jean-Claude after all these weeks ... when was the last time? But I'm neglecting you, and after such a long ride too! What would you like? There's skim milk, of course, and if you'd like an oatcake we've enough butter to make good eating, and even a smear or two of honey.'

The L'Oyettes had always kept bees, heather being a crop good for little else, and now Rochelle drank skim milk sweetened with honey and ate two oakcakes spread with the sweet, sticky stuff. And all the time Tante Denise chattered away, for she rarely saw her neighbours and her son, like his father, was a quiet, almost taciturn man.

'When you've finished, my dear, I'm going down to the beach to collect kelp. If you'd like to give me a hand ...'

'I'd love to,' Rochelle said happily. Few things were more enjoyable on a hot day than paddling in the shallow pools and padding across wet sand with your kelp rake and the cart standing nearby with the old horse snoozing between the shafts. 'Shall I go and catch Fleur?'

'She's caught; Jean-Claude brought her in earlier. Is that a good dress, Chelle? If so, you'd better borrow some old trousers and a shirt.'

The dress was not a good one, but Rochelle was very short of clothes and a chance to wear trousers and a shirt was rare. She took off her skimpy cotton and put on the clothing which Tante Denise offered, and then, with the trouser legs rolled up in readiness and the shirt sleeves likewise, the two of them set off for the steep path down the cliff which led to what passed for a beach on this side of the island.

250

Fleur was a grey mare at least twenty years old with the long lower lip and dreamy eyes of her kind. She wore an old straw hat to protect her from the sun and a haybag swung by her shoulder for later, for Fleur was a great favourite and would never have been allowed to stand about in the sun with nothing to lip over. The three of them scrambled down the cliff path, Tante Denise in her oldest clothes and Rochelle in her borrowed garments. Rochelle glanced at Tante Denise and thought how wonderful she was – she had been a pretty little thing when her husband had been alive, a natural home-maker – but now she had turned herself into a farmer without losing one jot of her femininity. She was a small woman, with soft fair hair and a pretty, rounded face, though her chin was determined and her mouth, even in repose, was held in a firm line. Her prettiness was still apparent but the soft plumpness had become sturdiness, the pale skin had darkened from being so much out of doors, and her voice had deepened from the constant shouting to the horses and the demands of dealing in a masculine world. Her hair, sun-bleached, seemed to have coarsened, and there were deep lines on her face, but to Rochelle she was still Tante Denise, and a dearly loved companion.

They reached the beach at last, left Fleur and her cart well above the tideline in the partial shade of a tall rock, and began to rake kelp. Whenever the pile was high enough to make it worthwhile, Rochelle and Denise changed their rakes for forks and carried the kelp to the cart. They removed one side for loading and then replaced it as they moved further along the strip of beach.

'Look at my arms. They're bright red,' Rochelle remarked after an hour or so, and Tante Denise told her to roll her sleeves down or she might burn badly.

'I used to burn, once,' she said ruefully, digging her fork into a great mound of kelp and staggering up the beach

251

with it. 'But my skin's accustomed to the sun now. And to the rain and wind, for that matter.'

It was a surprise to them both, therefore, when, just as they had filled the cart, they heard a crack of thunder followed by a low rumble, and saw, coming rapidly towards them from the west, a great mass of black cloud.

'A storm? Oh, confound it, we'll get soaked,' Tante Denise said. 'I wonder, will it last, though? If we crept into that cave and pulled Fleur hard up to the entrance we might ride it out. I wouldn't want to have the cart halfway up the cliff when the rain starts, not after such a long dry spell. It'll make the path like glass for a while.'

'But if we wait here the path will still be slippery,' Rochelle pointed out. 'Wouldn't it be better to run for it?'

They both looked anxiously towards the horizon. The black clouds seemed to be galloping now and the wind had freshened so that they had to shout to hear each other's voices.

'No. Once the rain's taken hold it'll be possible to get up the path if we're careful. I'm afraid of being caught halfway up. Fleur, you see, doesn't like thunder.'

Shouting and heaving, therefore, the two of them hurried Fleur and themselves up the beach and into the cave. Most of Fleur got inside and she had her back to the worst of the storm, but even so, as the lightning got into its stride and crackled across the as yet dry sky, the horse began to shiver and to move her hooves uneasily.

'It's all right, Fleur, it's only nasty noise,' Tante Denise bawled above the now impressive thunderclaps. 'Stay still, my beautiful, hide your head and stay still.'

Rochelle could not help smiling as the great horse dropped her big head into her mistress's embrace and pushed yet further into the small cave, but in fact it was one of the noisiest and most sudden summer storms that she herself could remember. The lightning hurled its lances between the clouds, occasionally arching down to earth, the brilliance transforming the darkness which the storm had brought into vivid, livid light, and the noise was appalling, seeming to reverberate round the little cave until she felt the walls might well crumble under the sound.

When the rain started it was as violent as the thunder and lightning, but of mercifully short duration. It sheeted down, splashing on to the rocks and trickling into the cave itself, but in ten minutes they could hear the thunder receding, grumbling off into the distance, and the lightning, too, faded as the rain gradually ceased.

'Gosh!' Rochelle commented as they emerged cautiously from their small shelter. 'Wasn't that frightening? I mean, I don't mind storms, but I could understand poor Fleur completely. I say, look!'

The beach and the rocks were steaming, for so short had the rainfall been, so sudden the storm, that the land was still baking hot from the recent sunshine and the rain had not cooled it down but had merely soaked everything thoroughly.

Even as Tante Denise was remarking that this was a rare sight, they saw the sea itself. The sun had come out again as the clouds rolled on and it lit a sea dark as ink but relieved by white-tipped breakers which were racing for the shore as though they had a personal rendezvous with the island and did not want to miss a moment. It was a fierce sea, and the wind was catching the spume on the wave-tops and carrying it across the beach in feathery little cloudlets of foam.

'Gosh!' Rochelle said for the second time. 'I don't think we could paddle in that now, Tante Denise.'

'No,' the older woman said. Her voice sounded strange and Rochelle, about to start leading the horse down from the cave to a spot where they could once more climb the cliff path, followed her eyes.

Something was tumbling out there in the waves; something small and dark . . . it looked like a shark's fin, then it disappeared altogether, then reappeared nearer the shore.

'It's a boat! It's a boat, gone down . . . on end,' Rochelle gabbled. 'Oh, what shall we do? Where are the men? Who would be fishing around here on . . .'

The words died in her throat. Only one man fished from this part of the shore, only one man had taken his boat out that day.

Jean-Claude. The beloved son, the only thing, Tante Denise had said soon after her husband's death, that made her life worth living.

But it could not be him! He was an experienced fisherman, would have read the signs, seen the storm approaching, made at once for the shore.

The rocky, tricky, traitorous shore.

'Tante Denise? It can't be Jean-Claude's boat, truly it can't be! You'll see in a minute, because the tide's bringing it inshore. Shall I hold Fleur . . .'

But Tante Denise had loosed her hold on the horse and was running fast down to the water. Like a girl, though without a girl's lightness and abandon. She ran as though she might save a life by so doing. She ran with all her strength and concentration and did not even notice that Rochelle was following her.

They carried him up the beach between them, and he was heavier than in life as though the water still grudged his body to them. They had both risked their lives to get him, wading out in that cruel and violent sea, clutching the rocks to save themselves from being sucked out of their depth, until they could reach the floating jacket, the floating hair. They had got him ashore somehow, and Rochelle had rolled him on to his stomach and tried to bring the water out of him and make him breathe again, and laugh, and speak. She had tried in vain. He was long gone, and his mother knew it. Tante Denise just sat on a rock and now and then smoothed the blond hair back from her boy's quiet brow and let the tears run unchecked down her worn, suddenly old face.

When she had no choice but to acknowledge that they could do nothing, Rochelle fetched the cart down to the sea's edge and began to shovel the kelp, so recently collected, out on to the beach once more. She had done about a third when Tante Denise stopped her.

'No, Chelle. Leave it. There's room enough for him there now, and we need the stuff to use on the land come the autumn. Jean-Claude would agree; he wouldn't mind riding with the kelp.'

He had been a tall, sturdy young man and his mother and Rochelle were neither of them tall, so it was a long and difficult task to get the body into the cart. They managed it at last, and set off once more for the cliff path. They were quiet because there was nothing to say. And because they were both weeping. Weeping for Jean-Claude who had worked so hard and cheerfully to scrape a living for himself and his mother. Weeping for themselves, bereft of him.

There was a parlour in the cottage with a hard horsehair sofa flanked by two rosewood tables. It was the room the L'Oyettes used for weddings, funerals and special occasions. Now, Jean-Claude lay there. Rochelle got roses from the bush by the front window and put them in jam jars and stood them at his head and feet and then Tante Denise took his ragged clothes off and washed him free of sand and salt. Rochelle saw her trying not to wince over the wounds on his body; the rocks had not dealt kindly with this, their child, on his journey back to the shore.

Then Tante Denise fetched the best clothes, which Rochelle had never seen on Jean-Claude in life. A dark suit, a white shirt, black shiny shoes. The shoes were too small because they had been his father's, and his father had been a smaller man. It hurt Rochelle somewhere deep

255

in her throat to see Tante Denise forcing the shoes on to Jean-Claude's white, bruised feet and she turned her head away . . . then looked back, sharply.

With his hair beginning to dry and to curl as it had in life, with his face prison-pale from the water . . . whom did Jean-Claude remind her of? She knew in a moment. He looked like Radek, lying there, only a Radek with peace in his face instead of striving, a Radek who had escaped the Germans once and for all.

But she said nothing. She helped Tante Denise to get the clothes on, and she put a rose in his hands and crossed them on his chest and then she fetched candles, at Tante Denise's insistence, and put them on saucers and lit them, one at his head, one at his feet. And the smell of the candles burning and the wax trickling down mingled with the scent of the roses and Rochelle thought that she now knew what sadness smelt like and she would know for the rest of her life and never see a candle flame flickering on rose petals without thinking of this moment.

Darkness had long fallen when they finished in the front parlour and returned to the kitchen, where the driftwood fire was dead and the ashes cold. Rochelle accepted that she could not leave. Quite apart from the curfew, the brilliant day had been succeeded by a dark, dark night with no moon, only tiny pinprick stars. She could not risk being caught out on such a night.

'Tante Denise, we must eat now,' she said. 'Just some bread and jam and a cup of coffee . . . but you must have something and so must I. We worked hard today.'

'We did,' Tante Denise acknowledged. 'Tomorrow I must work harder.'

Her voice was so quiet, so dreary, that Rochelle's heart bled for her. Now, the work would be hard indeed, with only herself to feed and clothe, only herself to toil. How would she stand it, so far from everyone on this little promontory above the sea which had stolen her son from her?

When the knock sounded on the kitchen door she was almost glad of it, for at least it meant that there would be someone else to help her to comfort Tante Denise . . . though it could equally well be a Nazi trooper come to complain about a chink of light round the kitchen door or to say that someone had reported a person in the house who had no right there.

Rochelle opened the door, since Tante Denise made no attempt to do so, and could have shouted with delight. M. Laurient stood there, his dark face anxious.

'Rochelle, my dear child, I've been desperate with worry! Why ever didn't you come home? You know how dangerous it is to be out after curfew; the soldiers are frightened, trigger-happy . . .' His voice faded as he looked from one face to the other. 'What's the matter? What's gone wrong?'

Rochelle led him to the front parlour. For a moment he stared down at Jean-Claude's pale face in the candlelight and then he put his arms round her and gave her a tight hug.

'Oh, Chelle! He was drowned, of course. The storm?'

'Yes. Monsieur, I *could* not leave Tante Denise, even if I had thought of it, which I did not. It took us a long time to get . . . to get the cart and everything back here.'

'I see. Very well.' He turned her and together they walked back to the kitchen. Tante Denise was still sitting in her old rocking chair by the dead fire. Now she looked across at him, weary beyond belief, old beyond time.

'What must I do now, M. Laurient? There will be forms to fill in, arrangements to make . . . I don't know how I shall face it.'

'Madame, I'll take care of everything. But first I must tell you a story, ask you for the greatest sacrifice you will ever have to make. Rochelle, light the fire again, there's a good girl. We're going to need a bit of warmth before I'm done.'

Rochelle had to go to the woodshed and find kindling to relight the fire, and then she had to hunt for the larger logs, the dried seaweed, the tiny hoard of sea-coal. By the time she got back and was laying and lighting the fire it was clear that M. Laurient had told Tante Denise everything ... all about Radek and how they had helped him to hide from the Nazis, all about the difficulties of keeping him in the dower house, so near the occupying forces.

'And he's like my boy?'

The words came haltingly, the tone almost a whisper.

M. Laurient nodded, patting Tante Denise's bowed shoulders.

'As like as two peas in a pod so far as a passport resemblance is concerned. Both tall, fair-haired, husky. Radek's been starved, of course, but there's a strong frame there; it just needs filling out. And he's a worker, madame, used to the sort of slavery the Nazis put their prisoners through. He would make short work of labouring on your farm ... but it's a lot to ask, I know. It means denying Jean-Claude's death even to your nearest and dearest. It means no funeral service yet, just a quiet interment here, tonight, whilst darkness holds. And then taking in a stranger, who has no claim on you at all, save for the claim of all humanity. We'll understand if I'm asking more of you than you can give.'

'What about the boat? It'll break up, likely, but suppose it does not? Suppose it's cast ashore? There'll be questions asked.'

'I'll give you a boat. We've got one we don't use any more, though it's a sturdy craft enough. I'll bring it over after dark in a few days, whether or not you take Radek in. At least then you can pay someone to do a day's fishing for you, perhaps.'

'And you'll . . . you'll bury him for me? And it shall all be done again, with a church service and the proper words, when they've gone?'

'Yes, of course I will. But you do understand, madame? No one must know, no one at all, save us three. And Radek must know whom he's impersonating. He'll have his papers, his ration book and so on . . . he has to know what you've done for him.'

'Aye. But bring him soon . . . tomorrow.'

'Of course we will. And we'll bury your son tonight, before there can be any talk or suspicion of what we've done. Who knows Jean-Claude well enough to spot the deception?'

Tante Denise shrugged.

'School friends, perhaps, but there's few enough of them left here. If the lad's like . . . he was always a quiet boy, my Jean-Claude; he had no close friends save for lads who've gone from here to fight.'

M. Laurient heaved a deep breath and stood up.

'Good. Will you shake my hand on it?'

Solemnly, Tante Denise shook his hand, then Rochelle's. And then the three of them went out into the tiny yard. M. Laurient looked round him measuringly.

'The soil's thin here . . .' he began, but was interrupted.

'There's a cave down on the shore – Chelle and I sheltered there – it's big enough. The sand's deep . . . you could go down four, five feet and not hit bedrock, I dare say. We'll all dig. I'll show you where.'

They fetched spades from the outhouses. It was still very dark but they dared show no light, especially on the shore. The three of them made their way down the cliffpath, taking extra care, for in the dark a misstep could have been fatal, and finally reached the beach. Tante Denise and Rochelle led the way to the cave and there, without a further word, they all began to dig.

It was easy work, as Tante Denise had implied. It was

259

also an eerie task, digging in the deep, soft darkness of the cave with the sky outside seeming almost light by comparison. When the hole was a full six feet long and several feet deep it began to fill with water, but when M. Laurient remarked on it Tante Denise merely said that it was no matter, all they wanted was sufficient depth for decency.

'And now we'll fetch him,' Tante Denise said as they stood back, chests heaving, but M. Laurient shook his head.

'No. I'll carry him down myself. You two stay here.'

'It's probably safer,' Rochelle murmured as the two of them stood in the entrance to the cave and watched the sky over the sea begin to lighten with the promise of dawn. 'With all of us helping someone might fall, but M. Laurient is very strong. He'll manage better alone.'

'Aye. D'you know, Chelle, now that it's all arranged, I'm not sorry? I'm the only one who could ever truly mourn my boy, because no one else knew him well enough, and this way his death won't seem . . . won't seem real, somehow. It'll simply be something else to trick the Nazis, so I'll be waiting for the end of the war just like the rest of you.'

Just like the rest of you! The words made Rochelle bite her lip, for they said so much. Everyone else would long for the end of the war, but what would it mean to Tante Denise? Life would be a little easier, perhaps, and there would be no curfew to keep her from visiting distant friends, but her life would not noticeably improve. And she would not be waiting for her boy to come back to her, nor for her man to come home.

Victory, when it came, would be hollow for Tante Denise.

It had been a long and exhausting night but once the body had been buried and words read over the grave, at least Tante Denise and Rochelle could do their best to sleep. M.

Laurient, however, had to go back to the dower house so that the troops would assume he had been there all night. There was no harm in Rochelle's having stayed with a friend because she had been helping with farm work and had left it too late to get back before curfew. But a number of people had seen Charles Laurient when he came back from visiting Pierre, and would have wondered at it had they spotted him arriving home again early in the morning.

So the two women waved M. Laurient off just as the first dull grey of dawn crept over the horizon, and then they made for their beds. There they slept like logs, even Tante Denise, for grief can be as exhausting as hard physical effort, and she had seen both that day.

When they woke they realised how hard M. Laurient had worked too, for when they went downstairs there was Radek, sitting in the chair by the fire and feeding it with bits of driftwood. He looked up and smiled anxiously at them as they appeared.

'Hello! Charles brought me . . . he explained. Is all well, am I really welcome here?'

Tante Denise's face had flooded with colour; she clutched Rochelle's hand and Rochelle felt her fingers shake.

'My . . . Radek . . . M. Laurient explained that you must become Jean-Claude? It is true you are very like him . . . I'll try to teach you to talk as he did and . . . yes, you're welcome.'

Now that Radek was actually before her, Rochelle could see the differences as well as the resemblance. The two young men were much of a height and their colouring was similar, but Jean-Claude's face had been thinner, his eyes less bold, his cheekbones less pronounced. But she knew it would not matter; locals were few and far between, and provided Radek was sensible and kept clear of such neighbours as did pop in from time to time he should be able to stay here until the Germans left – and Rochelle had no doubt that they would leave, with their tails between their legs, too. Did not M.

Laurient say so? Had he not prophesied that Pure Madonna would bloom for the first time on an island at peace once more and ruled again by the British?

'Thank you, madame.' Radek turned to the younger girl. 'Good morning, Rochelle. Charles tells me that I am to go fishing when the boat arrives, because Jean-Claude often went fishing. Will you come with me? I am very ignorant; I shall need help.'

'I will come, because I went with Jean-Claude when the fishing was good and the work here could be left,' Tante Denise said firmly. 'But Rochelle shall come with us as well. As soon as the boat arrives.'

'Good. Madame, I cannot express to you my thanks . . .' Radek began to stammer, but was firmly shushed.

'No need, no need. And you will have to call me maman, as my son did, or people may indeed talk. Now I shall get everyone some breakfast and then we must start work.'

Rochelle fetched bread, some precious eggs, even butter, and put on the kettle for coffee or tea, whichever Tante Denise had available. She was delighted to see the change in her old friend who, last night, had looked so aged and careworn. Now she was bustling round with colour in her cheeks, a sparkle in her eyes. She was fooling the Nazis and helping a young man, and some of her former zest for living had been returned to her.

Thank you, God, Rochelle said indiscriminately to the sky. Thank you for helping two people and thank you for M. Laurient's cleverness in seeing that this was possible.

'Would you like an egg, Chelle? Jean-Claude must have one – he needs his food – but you're very welcome; there's enough for one each today.'

Rochelle accepted the proffered egg eagerly, and spread butter luxuriously on slices of Tante Denise's home-made bread. Sadness was still there, in the back of her own mind, behind Tante Denise's eyes, but it was a bearable sadness now.

12

Over the course of the next week, Rochelle had to go about her business as naturally as possible whilst M. Laurient did all the interesting things, like moving the boat, another dead-of-night job.

Radek was useful here, since the boat had to be rowed a good way round the coast, always at night and always in the dark. Once M. Laurient was nearly spotted by a guard, but he slid the boat into a crevice in two large rocks and stayed there for hours, until it was safe to move on again.

And then, when he was finally near enough to the L'Oyettes' place, Radek walked round to meet him and rowed back quite openly in the early hours. He had already put down a couple of crab pots, and had brought the contents to bribe any German soldier who might challenge his right to be about so early.

Mind you, as M. Laurient said, it was a good job that Radek had not been seen because, although it was unlikely that a German would notice his lack of the local accent, another Jerseyman would have spotted it at once. But Radek was sensible and a quick study, with a gift for imitation, so it was not long before he began to be able to burr his speech just as the locals did, and on brief acquaintance it was unlikely that anyone would spot the deception.

And then Olivia came to stay.

Her German lover was busy, it appeared, and she had decided she would like to come and see her grandmère for a few days. There was not much room in the small house in St Helier, and Mme Barfleur took it for granted that M. Laurient would be glad enough to have her cooking his meals for a few days, whilst Olivia and Rochelle spent some time together. Rochelle also thought that this was an excellent scheme, so was doubly taken aback when M. Laurient called her into his study with a grave face.

'Rochelle, I have to talk to you,' he began. 'Sit down, petite.'

Rochelle complied.

'It's about Olivia's visit.'

'Yes, monsieur? I'm really looking forward to it,' Rochelle assured him. 'We shall have such talks . . .'

'Hmm. Now, Chelle, I want to warn you. Olivia is your friend but she is also the mistress of a German officer, and by now her first loyalty may well be to him. So you must be very careful, petite, really you must. Not a word about Radek or Jean-Claude must pass your lips. If I go out you must never be tempted to tell Olivia where I've gone, or indeed that I'm not on the estate. Don't mention Tante Denise at all, and if Olivia suggests going over there, say you can't . . . make up some excuse but don't go whilst she's here in any circumstances. Remember, Olivia did know Jean-Claude vaguely, and even without meaning to do so, she could let slip some remark to her officer which would be a death sentence to Radek.'

'I'll be very careful,' Rochelle agreed. 'I'm careful in front of Mme Barfleur too, monsieur, for the same reason. She would never give us away, but as you said, a secret is stronger the fewer the people who know of it, so I'm always careful. Why, Peter de Causis knows nothing of any of this, and he's my best friend apart from Olivia.'

'That's true. And remember, petite, that Olivia may well be very hurt if she hears you making disparaging remarks about the Germans. She will bear a German baby quite soon, you know. So you must learn discretion, and use it.'

'But monsieur, you said that Olivia was living with an officer, a good man,' Rochelle said, much distressed to think that her friend could have changed so completely.

'She, too, said rude things about the Germans when she was living with her maman. Sometimes she did, anyway.'

'Yes, perhaps. But that was before. Will you promise me to watch your tongue whilst Olivia is with us?'

Rochelle promised. But from the moment Olivia stepped down from the German staff car Rochelle became uncomfortable, no longer natural, and of course Olivia spotted it.

'What on earth's the matter, Chelle?' she said pettishly, when her friend had first agreed to take her round the glasshouse and then abruptly changed her mind and suggested a walk down to the village instead. 'I know you and M. Laurient hid a wireless down there under the rainwater tank, but I never told, did I? Is that why you don't want me in there?'

'N-no, of course n-not,' Rochelle stammered, thoroughly discomposed. 'Don't say it so *loud*, though, Livia. We could be imprisoned or sent to Germany for that, you know.'

'I wouldn't let them,' Olivia said loudly. 'Theo wouldn't let them. I'd tell him and he'd stop it at once. He's very important, Chelle; you don't seem to realise.'

'Yes, I do,' Rochelle said hastily. 'Let's go round the glasshouse then, if you'd like to see the hybrids.'

So they went round the glasshouse and Olivia exclaimed over the poor show compared with the pre-war display and asked if any of the species had been taken to Germany to be 'properly reared'.

This made Rochelle so angry that she could have screamed, but instead she folded her lips tightly and refused to say a word to her friend. Uncomfortably, therefore, they returned to the dower house where Mme Barfleur enfolded a sobbing Olivia in her arms and told her not to worry herself and that Chelle had not meant to upset her poppet.

'I did,' Rochelle said stiffly, when Olivia had trailed upstairs to wash her face and tidy her hair. 'She was

265

horrible, madame, horrible! She said we couldn't look after our orchids properly and they would be better off in hateful Germany!'

'Chelle, I'm sure M. Laurient told you to watch your tongue . . .' Mme Barfleur began, only to have another sobbing female on her hands as Rochelle belatedly remembered her promise. So it was a quiet little group which sat down to supper that evening. Mme Barfleur had not only reminded Rochelle of her promise, but also pointed out that pregnancy does odd things to a woman's temper and makes her sometimes act in a way of which she will later be ashamed.

'So don't worry, petite,' she crooned, drying Rochelle's tear-wet cheeks with the corner of her apron. 'All will be well between you when the child is born, but until then you must be patient and very, very kind to your friend.'

And indeed for ten days it was not too difficult. The weather was fine and sunny, autumn was approaching, fruit ripening and the hedgerows heavy with blackberries, and there was an air almost of relaxation when the small family gathered for their evening meal in the dower house at the end of the working day.

The harvest was always a favourite time and now, with Olivia back where Rochelle felt she belonged, they helped to the best of their ability, knocked rabbits over the head when they fled before the reapers, made corn dollies and drank vast quantities of weak tea out of cans.

In fact they were eating harvest rabbit pie when Olivia's pains started. She quite frightened Rochelle by suddenly grabbing her huge stomach and groaning.

'Aaargh! Oh, that was a *bad* pain . . . Grandmère, it hasn't started yet, has it? The baby, I mean? No, it can't have; it was just a little . . . oh, here it comes again . . . I don't like it, Grandmère, I really don't like it!'

The pains came at intervals until nine o'clock, when they suddenly stopped. M. Laurient had gone out early in the day and was not yet back despite the fact that it was after curfew, but Rochelle hoped that in the circumstances Olivia would not notice. Unfortunately, though, the pains had put Olivia in mind of the fact that she had a bed booked at a small private nursing home nearby, and naturally she looked round for M. Laurient, who should, she stated, be sent up to the manor with a message to send a soldier with a car for her.

'Why can't he go?' she demanded irritably. 'Oh, I know, he's in that wretched glasshouse. You'd better fetch him, Rochelle. He can speak German, I know, so he can explain. I must have a car.'

Rochelle looked helplessly at Mme Barfleur. She was uncomfortably aware that M. Laurient was most certainly not in the orchid house, was probably a good way off and would not be returning until he supposed Olivia to have been long abed. Their precious store of food was being used to supplement Radek's diet until he was in good enough physical shape to do as much on the farm as Jean-Claude had done. Not that he was work-shy, far from it, but it was clearly better that he should regain his full strength as soon as possible. So M. Laurient made a sortie to the abandoned cottage once or twice a week and took the fruits of his labours out to the L'Oyette place. Doubtless he was there now – possibly, under cover of the darkness, he would be taking Radek fishing, showing him some of the tricks which local fishermen had used for years – but wherever he was it was clearly impossible to fetch him back in time to get up to the manor for Olivia's car.

As luck would have it, however, Mme Barfleur insisted that her grandchild should climb into a warm bath, and whether it was the soothing influence of the water or merely that Olivia had imagined herself into a state of panic, the pains subsided and troubled her no more that night.

But she knew, there could be no doubting it, that M. Laurient had broken the curfew.

'I don't mind, you silly little thing,' she said expansively to Rochelle next day, as the two of them scoured the hedges for blackberries so that Mme Barfleur might bottle quantities for use during the winter. 'It's just you not wanting to tell me that hurts ... as if I'd tell anyone about M. Laurient. He's been so good to me and Grandmère.'

Two days later the pains came again, but this time M. Laurient was present and went at once to the manor, fetching both a doctor and a car to whisk Olivia into her nursing home. And next morning, when Rochelle came down for breakfast, M. Laurient was able to tell her that her friend was now the proud mother of a baby boy.

'I'm glad. She's all right, of course?'

'She's fine. Mme Barfleur's gone home, though. She felt she wanted to be nearer the nursing home, and I don't suppose Olivia will come back here.'

'No, I shouldn't think she will,' Rochelle said, scarcely knowing whether to be glad or sorry but conscious that her main feeling was one of relief. It was such a strain having to be polite about the Nazis all the while, pretending that some of them weren't so bad, after all. Though she really did quite like Hauptmann Kussak, who had seen that the small wood-burning stove in the one glasshouse still in use was kept stocked with fuel all winter long. It had been a shocking winter, too, with thick snow in January, and M. Laurient had said that but for the Hauptmann's intervention they would undoubtedly have lost all their little stock, instead of only half. The tropical orchids seemed to have gone into some sort of hibernation, but quite a lot of the others had survived, including the ones which M. Laurient hoped would prove to be Pure Madonna in a year or two.

'With Olivia out of the way, I'll be going over to see Radek once or twice more whilst the fine weather lasts,' M. Laurient said that evening as he and she, alone once more, ate their hard cheese with slices of onion and drank watered wine. 'The lad's doing well, but he still needs a bit of coaching, particularly with the boat.' He laughed, shaking his head. 'He's not a natural with the oars, let alone the sail, and to see him throw a net is enough to make any Jerseyman highly suspicious. I want to get that side of it straightened out before winter so that when spring comes and it's natural for him to resume his fishing trips he doesn't either make a fool of himself or drown.'

'With Olivia out of the way, can I come?' Rochelle asked hopefully, and was overjoyed when, after a short pause for consideration, M. Laurient said she might as well.

'You can keep madame company whilst Radek and I struggle with the boat,' he said cheerfully. 'You'll be glad to see your friend looking so well and cheerful. She really mothers Radek; treats him like a little lad half the time.'

So within three days the two of them, on their bicycles, set off once more for the rocky shores. It was not easy for M. Laurient to get away during the day, since he was working on the estate and overseeing the farming side of a large area, but they left as soon as they had had their evening meal, cycling along at first in warm sunshine and later in the long golden rays of the setting sun.

'We'll work hard tonight. I think I'll leave you with madame and Radek overnight, and then I'll come over on some pretext tomorrow so I can start earlier. You won't be breaking the curfew that way. I can get back easily enough myself, after dark, but two of us would be more difficult.'

They had a good evening. Rochelle went out in the boat with them and tried not to laugh when Radek did things no self-respecting Jerseyman would dream of doing; though as M. Laurient said, his protégé was learning fast.

Later, the two men rowed inshore, deposited Rochelle with Tante Denise, and returned to take advantage of the mild night and the light breeze to cast the net and bring it in a few times. Rochelle, snug in the big double bed with Tante Denise's back pressed against hers, woke for a moment when the men came in, heard the soft sounds of

269

their footsteps as they crossed the yard and the softer sounds of their voices as they exchanged a few words in the kitchen. The next day was a Sunday, when M. Laurient felt he could safely leave the estate to fend for itself for twenty-four hours, but presently he said goodnight to Radek and Rochelle heard him leave, heard the kitchen door swing to, and after a short interval the sound of Radek's footsteps on the stairs.

Now he'll be getting on his bicycle, now he'll be cycling across the moors at the top of the cliffs, Rochelle told herself sleepily, imagining monsieur's dark figure in the pale moonlight. Now he'll be putting his bicycle away very carefully in the little copse . . . now he'll be stealing across the meadow, through the woodland . . . now he'll be at the dower house and climbing the stairs to his bed.

It comforted her to believe him safe and presently she, too, slept.

She awoke in the pre-dawn grey with the nasty feeling that something had just happened to wake her up, but what it had been she could not imagine. She looked round the room, but despite Tante Denise's having pulled back the curtains before they slept she could see very little. She listened next, but there was no sound. She listened harder and could hear, from below, the noisily contented sound of the cat, Jinx, purring as he lay curled up on the rocking chair. There had been no intruder then . . . had she thought there was?

Beside her, Tante Denise's breathing continued even. Was it Radek, then, awake early? But by listening once more she was fairly certain she could hear him faintly snoring through the wall. She smiled to herself; how she would tease him when they went down to breakfast . . . he had woken her with his snorts and grunts, she would tell him.

But it was no use; she could not lie here with the horrid

conviction that she should be elsewhere growing stronger and stronger. She got up, put on her dress and the patched and darned blazer which someone had given her, and made her way down to the kitchen. There, with the fire ticking as it settled and the cat purring as she slept, she decided she would have to go back to the dower house. She would not arrive until after sunrise, so she would be free of the curfew rule by then, and anyway she did not intend to be seen. There were few enough people about at that hour, as she well knew, for the guards tended to stay close to the manor and few bothered to wander down the garden, across the orchard and into the woods just to see what was happening at the dower house.

However, she would have to leave a note for Tante Denise. She wrote a few lines on a sugar bag, propped it against the loaf and slid out into the morning.

It was a typical autumn one, with a ground mist which swirled as she walked through it and a heavy dew, so that when she reached her bicycle it was pearled with moisture and had to be wiped down before she could unchain it and mount.

Oddly enough, once she was outside and in the open her sense of urgency diminished and she cycled leisurely along, sniffing the autumnal smells of the moor and the hedge-rows, even stopping at one point to nip into a meadow and come back with her skirt full of mushrooms. Nice, to go home with a present for M. Laurient, something which he really enjoyed and could eat this morning for his Sunday breakfast.

The sun came up as she cycled and drew a long black shadow on the road in front of her. If she was stopped by a passing German she would show him the mushrooms in the bicycle basket, and even though he would undoubtedly confiscate at least half she would not be suspected of curfew breaking. Children, these days, were constantly reminded of the importance of food and she would be praised by any parent for such a worthy addition to their diet.

She was wondering whether they had any fat left to cook the mushrooms in when she reached the boundary of the manor land. If she had been on illicit business she would have stopped here, heaved her bicycle over the stile and made her way home across country, but since she was on a perfectly respectable errand – mushroom-hunting – she continued along the road and was about to swing into the front drive when she heard a car coming towards her, clearly leaving the manor.

She stopped and got off her bicycle but continued to push it towards the drive. The car slowed between the imposing stone posts, the driver looked left and right, and then the car fairly shot off, with a roar and a screech – the Germans all drove as if the island was seventy miles long and they had entered a road-race – belting past Rochelle so fast that she barely registered who was in the back seat before the vehicle disappeared round the corner of the road, heading for St Helier.

It was M. Laurient. And he had been sitting between two German officers!

'He was breaking the curfew; he lied as to his whereabouts. He had a wireless set concealed in his house. He has been taken to St Helier where he will be imprisoned until he can be tried. He will almost certainly be deported.'

Hauptmann Kussak's face was pale but implacable, his eyes stony. He looked impassively down at Rochelle, standing before him quivering with anxiety and suppressed rage. How *dare* they take M. Laurient off in their beastly staff car like a common criminal? How dare they?

'Deported? Wha-what does that mean?'

She knew, but could not take it in, could not believe. How could they do such a thing to a man who helped everyone . . . had been caught breaking the curfew because

272

he had been helping someone? But they must know nothing about Radek, of course, or everyone would be in trouble. And why on earth had M. Laurient been using his wireless in the early hours of the morning? What did he expect to hear?

'First he will be tried . . . you know what that means, I suppose?' Rochelle nodded dumbly, her eyes still fixed on the older man's face. 'Then he will be sentenced. Either to a period of imprisonment or to be deported – sent away from the island to Germany for a period of so many years.'

'Years? For listening to a wireless? Probably he was only mushrooming. I went mushrooming; why should he not have done so as well?'

'You broke the curfew for a few mushrooms?'

'No, of *course* not. I got up as the sun did and went out for the mushrooms. I never dreamed . . . I did not hear you come; I thought . . . I was coming back from my bicycle ride and met the car in the drive and saw . . . and saw . . .'

She could not go on, could not say what she had seen, but it would haunt her all her life. M. Laurient's pale, set face, the dark hair falling across his brow, his eyes fixed on the back of the man in the front seat. Not a glance for her, not a look! But the familiar frown-line etched on his brow as he tried to reason out what he must do.

'You saw him and it shocked you. I'm sorry, but the fault must lie with M. Laurient. He's been well treated, you know. I've done my best for his plants, tried to keep them alive for him, tried to treat him fairly . . . it was no way to repay me, was it?'

He sounded almost hurt, almost querulous, and Rochelle realised with amazement that he really felt hard done by. He had expected, in exchange for a bit of interest in the orchids, a bit of fuel for the stove, not just gratitude but friendship; compliance. And he had not even been tolerated, if the truth were known. M. Laurient had trodden

273

cautiously around Hauptmann Kussak, but he had never either liked or trusted him.

But instilled in her was that same caution, so when she spoke it was ingratiatingly, because she wanted something still.

'He meant no harm . . . he never harmed anyone, not M. Laurient! Can I see him?'

'No. Later, perhaps.'

Rochelle nodded bleakly and turned to leave the room. In the doorway the Hauptmann called her back.

'I'll do my best for you now you're alone. And at least you know that Laurient will have a fair trial.'

'Thank you,' Rochelle whispered, but inside she was shrieking with angry laughter at the thought of any trial carried out by the Germans being fair. Nothing about them was fair, not their presence here, nor their beastly guttural language which now she would *not* learn, though she had said to M. Laurient that she would try if he thought it wisest. They were all brutes; it was just that some hid the fact more skilfully than others, so she hated them all . . . all! And she would do what she could to embarrass and hurt them, and if they really did send M. Laurient away . . .

She would kill as many of them as she could, starting with Hauptmann Kussak.

'You can't stay here alone, Rochelle. Not now M. Laurient's gone. You must come to us in St Helier.'

Mme Barfleur and Rochelle faced each other across the kitchen at the dower house. Rochelle sighed and shook her head.

'I can't leave, madame – think, how could I? There are the orchids, and there's Pod and Senna – I couldn't just pack up and go. And besides, M. Laurient hasn't been convicted yet. They may well come to their senses and . . . and overlook it. Or he may be sentenced to imprisonment in St Helier. But I can't go . . . the orchids need seeing to every day, and the dogs do as well. And the cat. And our rabbits. And the hens. And . . .'

'All right, petite, I understand what you say. You must realise, though, that a young girl like you cannot stay here alone without talk, possibly even more than talk. And I cannot come back here to live, not when my girl needs me . . . and Olivia likes to know where she can find me when she comes shopping in St Helier.'

'I'll stay. If I have to find someone to stay with me, perhaps I can get a school friend to sleep here at nights, but I won't move. And anyway, we'll know quite soon. M. Laurient has his trial tomorrow, doesn't he?'

'That's right. You'll come into town, of course, though I'm sure you won't be allowed to see him.'

'Yes, I'll come into town. And I'll bring him a bag with some of his bits and pieces packed away in it, just in case they send him to Germany.'

'They've been making enquiries at the bank about his account and any other valuables. One of the girls who works there told Livia that the Germans can't understand why a man with so much property, a shrewd man, has not got a great deal of money stored away. I must say, I was surprised when the whisper went round that M. Laurient has very little money in any of his accounts.'

There was a question hovering but Rochelle, thinking smugly of the sea-cave, soon put a stop to that.

'It'll be in England, I suppose,' she said casually. 'Do you remember he went over not very long before the Occupation? He went to see Mavis, but he might easily have taken money out with him.'

'Yes, that's probably the answer,' Mme Barfleur said easily. 'Then you'll stay for a bit?'

'Yes, I'll stay. Until M. Laurient tells me to go, I'll stay.'

* * *

275

The trial was probably a complete farce. At any rate, Rochelle was told a few hours after it was over that M. Laurient had been sentenced to ten years in a German concentration camp and would be leaving on the next boat, sailing the following day.

Despair is sometimes a numbing emotion. Rochelle did all the right things. She went to the Commander in Chief of the Army in St Helier and asked that a bag of necessaries might be passed to M. Charles Laurient before the boat sailed. She made up a parcel of dried and tinned food and hung about down by the dock so that she could pass it over in person when the boat was due to go. She did not weep; things were too bad for tears.

She saw him once more. He looked thin and gaunt, unshaven. His faded blue shirt was dirty now, his trousers had a hole torn in the knee and the bottoms were caked with mud. They could not speak; he was surrounded, hustled towards the waiting craft, but she saw he carried the bag she had taken in slung over one shoulder and pressed closer, ready to slip the food into his hand if the occasion arose.

It did not. But he looked round desperately and caught sight of her, standing pale and still by the dockside.

He smiled and his dark eyes lit up and she saw him mouth words: 'Take care of yourself – I'll survive!'

And then he was pushed and prodded up the gangplank and aboard the boat and for a moment he turned, to look with hungry yearning over the island which was his home and his heritage.

Then the troops surrounded him and he disappeared into the bowels of the ship.

Rochelle stayed on the dockside until the boat was no more than a dot on the far horizon, and then she went dully back into town. She slung the bag of food on her handlebars and began to pedal back towards the manor, but halfway there she changed her mind and turned off to where she knew she would find a gang of Russian and Spanish prisoners working.

She saw them in the distance and hung about until the guard was looking in the opposite direction. Then she slid into the ditch and made her way round until she was within touching distance of a skinny, desperate man who might have been twenty or sixty, she could not tell, so emaciated and hopeless was he.

'Here . . .' she hissed, and to do him credit he gave her one startled, incredulous look and then walked idly towards the ditch, appearing to be merely moving back from work just finished.

'Que?'

'Food. Take it.'

She handed him the whole bag and the weight of it, which she had found so little bother that she had hung it on her handlebars, made him sit down . . . poor creature, she thought with sudden passionate pity, poor thin, weak creature!

'Gracias,' he whispered, almost lying on the food. 'Muchas, muchas gracias.'

'That's all right,' she said, getting the gist of his meaning. '*Bon appétit!*'

She waited in the ditch until the workers had all moved on, as patient as a cat by a mousehole, and then made her way back to her bicycle and rode home as the sun was sinking.

She had never felt such deep unhappiness. Giving M. Laurient's food to the prisoners had comforted her a little, but she could not truly believe that he had gone, that she might never see him again – or not, at least, until the war was over.

But it did not do to think of that; better to tell herself that it was some ghastly mistake which would be rectified quite soon, and M. Laurient would come happily back and take his place at the dower house as though he had never been away.

She went back to the dower house herself, then. She fussed over the orchids and saw that the windows in the glasshouse were shut and that the pots and plants were cuddled up with blankets to keep any early frost from destroying their tender shoots. She did not light the wood-burning stove. She would save that for later, when the cold days and nights had really arrived. Now there was just a nip in the air, a crispness to the early mornings.

In the house, she fed the dogs, riddled the stove and put on more wood so that it would last the night. Normally she and M. Laurient only lit the fire for an hour or so each day to conserve fuel, but today she was cold and unhappy and very confused, and she would keep the fire in all night, just for once.

She wondered about chaining the dogs up outside but decided she could not bear to be alone in the house. Instead, she took them both up to bed with her, and climbed into her small cot with Pod at her feet and Senna uncomfortably crammed between her and the wall. The dogs were delighted with the treat but slightly wary, too, eyeing the door as though they expected either M. Laurient or Mme Barfleur to come through it to tell them off and send them packing. But presently they both fell asleep and snored loudly. Rochelle, lying squashed and sleepless between them, was comforted by their pleasure and their presence, and did not attempt to kick them aside even when they began gently but firmly to take over more than their fair share of both bed and covers.

At last their snores began to seem faint as sleep claimed her; she knew she was in bed in her own room and yet dreams stalked her . . . nightmares, really. She was on the boat with M. Laurient and they were starving him . . . a Hauptmann with long nails raked them down M. Laurient's much-loved face and she saw the blood run, saw

278

pain in his eyes . . . flew, screaming, at the Hauptmann and scored his face with her nails and saw his blood run and knew a fierce, cruel satisfaction in the inflicting of pain such as she had never felt before.

The dream changed; they were on dry land now, in a little cage with iron bars. She and M. Laurient were crammed together and he was crying . . . she could feel his tears on her bare arm.

The dream changed again. There was food spread out on a big table but they had chained M. Laurient to the wall . . . he was naked except for a tiny loincloth of some rough white material, and his hair was grown long, down to his shoulders, yet it was still he, unmistakable . . . and he could not reach the food. He called to her to help him, said he was starving . . . and she could not move, she was fixed hand and foot to something, could not even raise a hand to assist him.

She struggled, cried out, and woke. It was daylight and Pod was lying heavily across her legs, Senna across her chest. She could scarcely breathe for the dogs' weight, and Senna had dribbled in his sleep so that Rochelle's arm was wet.

Through the small, uncurtained attic window the sun painted golden squares all over the whitewashed ceiling. Rochelle could hear birdsong, smell the rich scent of the autumn woods. Outside the sweet chestnuts would soon lie in their hedgehog shells, waiting for the diligent to turn over the golden piles of leaves and discover their hidden bounty. Fruit was ripening, berries too, and hazelnuts in their little green pixie-hoods hung in clusters in the hedgerows.

But the sunshine could not charm her, nor the thought of the fruits of autumn. She could only lie in her bed and feel the chill of her loss spread over her once more.

M. Laurient had gone.

279

She was alone.

For the first time since the trial, Rochelle wept.

He survived the journey, first by sea, then by train, then marching, in a long column, across Germany. It was pretty country, the hillsides hung with vineyards, little white villages perched between the vines and the broad, placid river.

The camp, when he reached it, was not too bad. It was only a transit camp, though, where he would stay until he was sent on to one of the permanent camps: the concentration camps.

It was here that he heard for the first time what happened to people in the concentration camps. He made up his mind that he would break out of the transit camp if he possibly could, and make his way back into France to see if he could live out the war in hiding. People undoubtedly did; surely he could be one of them? He bitterly regretted so many things, now that it was too late to do anything about them. The sea-cave . . . it had seemed like a good idea, but suppose the child was forced to go there alone, to get something to sell? His stomach turned to ice and his spine crawled at the thought of her going down, let alone climbing back up, with full hands.

Then there was the food cache. He had arranged it specially so that it needed two people to open it, thinking that this would put idle passers-by off the idea of trying to get in. But suppose she and Olivia fell out, or she needed food and had no one to help her?

He worried very little about himself. He had enough to eat, just, and too much to think about. So he channelled all his considerable unused energy into the thought of escape. He could see that it was possible, with a little ingenuity, and he had never lacked that.

The method and route planned, he actually considered trying to get all the way back to Jersey. But it would mean taking one risk too many, he decided at last. From here, though, he could get into France quite easily, using the river, the Mosel. Once he was in France he would work on a farm until the war was over, might even find it possible to get a message over to Augeuil to let them know he was safe.

In his cell with a dozen other men, Charles Laurient was the quiet one, the thoughtful one. He was also the only one who would actually engineer an escape and carry it through successfully. Because he had patience, and could bide his time. And because the urge to go was overmastering, devouring.

13

After Libya and the desert, Norfolk in England was a marvellous place to be.

Laurie had flown in on a beautiful autumn day, but even so when he looked down as he cleared the coast the thing which struck him most forcibly was the greenness of it all. Oh, he had heard from numerous sources that England was so *green*, had sung, in school, of England's green and pleasant land, but he had not expected the rich variety of greens, as though someone had sown the fields and planted the woods and hedgerows with the sole intention of discovering whether they could actually find a hundred or so different greens. If so, they had scored the maximum, whatever that might be, because Laurie, dazzled, could not begin to count them. Even with the yellow and bronze of the grain crops and the rich browns of ploughland, the landscape was primarily green.

And they nearly lost themselves hunting for the airfield, because there were a good few of them down there and most of them were durned well hidden. You could see a bit of runway, sometimes quite a length, in the usual three-cornered shape, but where were the buildings? Every airfield was ringed with buildings, as everyone in the crew knew . . . but when they reached what they were sure must be their destination they could only see one little bitty shed-thing, and a hangar which was camouflaged so well that you really had to peer to make it out.

But the voice speaking over the radio had no doubts. *Blue Moon* was bidden to come in and Laurie throttled back and put her into her approach run.

The runway was short, but the runways in the desert

had been pretty cramped too – only they hadn't had quite so many trees crowding around them. Still, he managed to put the ship down gently and taxi to the spot the tower indicated. And then he leaned back in his seat and smiled blissfully, a smile, he saw when he turned around, which was echoed in the faces of his crew.

It was so quiet and calm out there, with the sunshine streaming down on the trees and the grass! If you listened carefully, you could hear a cow lowing on some nearby farm and birdsong was all around them.

'This is real great,' Solly Cohen breathed, as they climbed down and set off across the grass to the nearest cluster of huts. 'It's something to come back to, eh, Laurie?'

'Sure,' Laurie said easily. 'Something good.'

He was breathing in the clean soft country air and almost feeling his whole body relaxing with a series of tiny clicks and mutters. Behind him a voice said: 'I wonder what the food's like?' and everyone chuckled because Rad Soomas, the tail gunner, was always passionately interested in food.

'And I wonder what the girls are like,' Ben, the engineer, said. 'They tell me English girls have rose-petal complexions . . . all over.'

'We'll find out,' Solly said lazily. 'José, you lika da Eenglish goils?'

More laughter, for though José came from South America his accent was unimpeachable Brooklyn.

'I lika,' José said peaceably. 'I lika all dis!'

'Me, too,' came from more than one throat as they crossed the short green grass and entered the wood which, they could now see, hid the collection of Nissen huts and hastily erected brick buildings which would be their homes whilst the Eighth Air Force was based in Norfolk.

A liberty truck came rattling past with a collection of guys aboard all clearly bound for the nearest liberty town – would that be Norwich City, wondered Laurie hopefully.

283

He had seen it from the air, seen its tall cathedral and lazy river, the castle up on the hill and the patchwork rooftops, and now he would like to see it from ground level. But not immediately, of course. What they mainly wanted right now were hot showers, a good meal and clean beds.

After that, they'd do what they had been brought here to do – carry the war into the heart of Germany. And then, if they survived the bombing raids, they would come back to this particular airfield in this particular quiet corner of green, green England, and climb aboard the liberty trucks and go into that dreaming city and learn – if they had long enough – to love and understand it.

In the ops room, Laurie looked a long time on the big map before he spied Jersey and then he was astonished all over again at how close to France the Channel Islands were, how far from their mother country. He realised, with chagrin, that he must have flown very near the island on his way from Libya, and he very soon realised as well that he was unlikely to overfly it on a mission, since they did not go via France to bomb Germany.

It would have been good to be able to look down on the island from the sky and know that his father was down there somewhere, but now he had a new fantasy to help him get to sleep at night. He would liberate Jersey! When the war ended in the Allies' victory – and he had no doubt that it would so end – he would fly in ahead of all the rest and the populace would cheer and weep and throw flowers, and his father would be there too, cheering and weeping. He would recognise his son from some sort of family likeness, and would stand, amazed, as this younger edition of himself came striding up the road with girls hanging on to his arms and kissing him and promising him anything he liked, just for a smile, a glance.

It was a good fantasy. It helped to exonerate him from his earlier promise – to bring a rare orchid to Jersey when he came, for his father's collection – and often meant that he slept with a smile still touching his lips.

Once the bombing raids began it was not so easy to sleep nights. You lay there and saw again the flak rising up towards you like pretty coloured clouds, and you saw the bombs rain down towards the earth and the tilt of the earth as you turned for home. Then you saw the German fighters . . . the bullets sprayed across your ship, other ships manned by guys you knew blowing up in mid-air, bursting into flame, going into that fatal, endless dive which can only end one way.

No one could ever get clear away, raid after raid. Solly was hit in the thigh and dam' near bled to death before they got home. Louis Ford, the nose gunner, lost two fingers and a thumb from frost-bite; he froze to his chattering, death-spitting gun and by the time they had landed and warmed up a bit his digits were too far gone to be saved.

Blue Moon staggered home after one particular raid to the only airfield she could reach – an RAF fighter station some twenty miles from their own base. The Britishers talked them down and they hit the ground in a belly-flop and tore the ship apart, dam' near. They got out running, all but the tail gunner, who was being part-helped, part-carried, and when the ship suddenly woofed into flames Rad and Max Clarke, one of the waist gunners, were too near. Rad never recovered from his wounds and Max was sent back stateside.

Blue Moon Too was born, and on her maiden flight flew over Bremen and bombed a huge munitions factory which went up like a thousand fireworks. Perhaps it was a fireworks factory, and they had been misinformed or had lost their way.

They got home after that one, but Laurie was warier now, less certain of his future. He was fast, quick-thinking, careful. But so were dozens of other guys – dead guys.

He remembered always now that there could be one with his name on it. As the winter passed, he grew cannier, like an old dog fox who wants to see the spring. He wrote his mom, he fooled with the other guys, he smiled at the pretty English girls and jitterbugged with them and gave them chocolate and nylons, but never asked anything in return.

He just wanted to get to see his father.

That was all.

'Pod, I won't warn you again! Today I'm digging and you're watching, so just sit quiet and watch, will you?'

Rochelle was planting seed potatoes in the bit of cleared ground behind the glasshouses. She had applied to Hauptmann Kussak for permission and it had been granted, which, in view of the fact that the big lawns in front of the manor had recently been ploughed up and used for potatoes, was a good thing. Rochelle would have stolen potatoes if they had refused and they probably guessed as much; at least, permission had come along with a bag of seed potatoes, the very ones she was now tenderly placing in the earth.

Rochelle leaned on her spade and regarded Pod severely. The animal was frisky, presumably because after a shockingly cold and miserable February, March was coming in with winds and some rain but with sunny days too, and this was one of them. Pod raised a muzzle red-brown with earth, opened her mouth in an ingratiating grin and then poked gently at the hole she had just made with one paw, her eyes fixed on Rochelle's face, her tail wagging gently. She was clearly questioning the recent command. Rochelle wanted to laugh but scowled impressively instead.

'*No*, Pod, no more digging. Go and sit with Senna, there's a good girl.'

Pod heaved a sigh and got laboriously to her feet. She was suffering from arthritis as a result of the recent cold weather, and always had trouble walking at first, until her limbs got used to the movement. Rochelle watched the old dog affectionately for a moment before beginning to dig again, feeling more cheerful and optimistic than she had for several months. It really did look as though the long and dreadful winter was over, it even seemed possible that one day she might not be perpetually cold as well as perpetually hungry.

The fuel ration had been cut to almost nothing this winter, and everyone had been forced to search for wood. Usually there were plenty of branches to cut up, but this winter competition had been fierce, and not only from the Islanders. German troops had been scouring the woods as well, and an order had gone out forbidding anyone, on pain of imprisonment, to cut trees or branches. Rochelle was reduced to rising very early in the morning, before the sun was up, and searching whilst frost still crisped the grass and outlined the branches above her head. Often, she was so cold when she got back indoors with her meagre bundle that she could scarcely light the fire she craved. She ate mostly cold food, since it was easier, though she did try to have a cup of hot soup before bed each night.

She had no source of money at first, but this problem had been solved by Hauptmann Kussak, who paid her the money he had previously paid to M. Laurient for the food requisitioned by the troops. Or perhaps he paid her whatever he had paid M. Laurient for managing the estate. Rochelle did not know; she simply accepted the money, if not with gratitude, at least with a semblance of it.

She lived alone, apart from the dogs, though Mme Barfleur, on hearing that M. Laurient had been deported, offered to come back.

'No, thank you,' Rochelle had said stonily. 'I manage very well. I don't need any help.'

Mme Barfleur had been hurt and it had shown, but Rochelle had made up her mind that in future she would trust no one at all. Someone, she was sure, had informed

287

on M. Laurient. It was too much of a coincidence that troops should go to the dower house on the only occasion on which both of them were absent from home all night, and she was very much afraid that it might have been Olivia. So she would keep Mme Barfleur at a distance . . . and never speak to Olivia again as long as she lived, because even if it had not been Olivia who had told tales on M. Laurient, she fraternised with the enemy who had taken him away.

In the depths of the winter, though, she had been so lonely that she had wondered if she might go mad. Cooped up alone in the house, with no heat, very little food, and no company save that of the dogs, she had gone to bed early, night after night, until terrible dreams made sleep impossible. After that, because of the curfew, she simply sat downstairs, wrapped in the blankets off her bed, listened to the night-sounds from outside, and prayed that the war would soon end so that M. Laurient could come back to her.

She did not go to school. She shunned her friends, except for the L'Oyettes, and even there she was afraid to visit often in case she brought the Germans down on Radek.

Besides, there were the orchids. In the coldest weather she had lit the wood-burning stove in the glasshouse and she and the dogs had slept there, curled right up close to the stove, hoping that a combination of their body warmth and the heat from the burning wood might save the plants at least until the spring sun shone once more. She had taken the Hauptmann's advice, too, and put a strong wooden partition up across the glasshouse, so that the small part which still contained orchids could be insulated with old blankets, dusty hay, anything which could hold the heat.

He had visited quite often at first, still intrigued by the flowers, but gradually, as conditions worsened, he had stopped coming, and now she had not seen him for several weeks. Indeed, she believed that he had been recalled and was no longer on Jersey. Peter had come up to see her a week or so ago and had told her that the war was going against the Germans at long last and they were having to recall good young commanders like Kussak to fight, instead of letting them remain in quiet backwaters like Jersey.

'When the warm weather comes I'm going to steal a boat and head for France,' he boasted. 'The Allies will be moving in on France soon, and I want to be there to drive the Huns out when the time comes.'

'You should be here to drive them out,' Rochelle protested. 'How I want to punish the bloody Todt lot! They've killed more people than we'll ever know, I reckon. How many Russians have died? How many more will?'

Peter had shrugged and said he'd leave her to finish off any Germans on Jersey that she particularly disliked. For his part, he wanted to fight before it was all over.

But now the war was far from over and if she wanted to see the end of it she had better get on with planting her potatoes. Rochelle finished the trench she was digging and walked along beside it, dropping the seed potatoes in eyes upwards. Then she piled the earth back on them and began, rather wearily, to dig the last trench.

She was halfway down it when a voice said: 'Rochelle, whatever are you doing?'

Rochelle leaned on her spade and looked up. Olivia was standing by the greenhouse, watching her. She was extremely smart in a leaf-green suit, sheer stockings and a pair of little leather shoes which made even the indifferent Rochelle think it would be nice to own them. Her own feet were clad in the roughly made wooden clogs which most of the island women were reduced to, though she did have some old rubber boots for winter and a pair of ancient sandals for the fine weather, when it came.

She stared at Olivia. Her hair had been set in deep golden waves and fell across one side of her face. The face

289

itself was delicately tinted – the lids blue, the lips deep rose, the skin lightly dusted with face powder. Olivia looked a woman, no longer a girl, and it occurred to Rochelle that her erstwhile friend was a person of some power now on the island. Her lover really must have influence if he could buy her clothes and make-up now, when things were short for everyone.

'Oh, hello, Olivia. What did you say?'

Rochelle's tone was cool and Olivia looked a little taken aback. They had not met, save casually in the street, since her child had been born the previous summer, but she smiled brightly, although Rochelle fancied she could see a shade of anxiety beneath the self-confident outward appearance.

'I asked what on earth you were doing, digging the garden? Surely you could get a man to do it for you?'

'There aren't any,' Rochelle said shortly. She began to dig her trench again.

'Aren't any? My dear child, there are dozens up at the house. Most of them would be glad to oblige, particularly on such a lovely day. Do you want me to ask one of them for you?'

'No,' Rochelle said immediately. 'They aren't men, they're soldiers. Soldiers don't dig people's gardens.'

'Oh, nonsense. They're only human; they'd be glad to help. Most of them are longing for a friendly word – they haven't had many of those these past four years. Do stop digging for a moment, Chelle, when I'm talking to you.'

'Can't,' Rochelle said between clenched teeth. 'Got to get these in before I finish for the day.'

Rochelle hoped that Olivia would go away, but instead her one-time friend sat herself down on the stump of a large tree and clicked her fingers at the dogs.

'Well, if you insist, I'll wait for you. Pod . . . Senna . . . do you remember me?'

Labradors do not bear grudges, particularly other people's. Pod and Senna stared, sniffed, wagged, and then strolled over to let Olivia pull their ears and tickle their chins. Then they sat down, one either side of her, and leaned. Olivia laughed delightedly.

'They do remember me! Well, Chelle, how are you managing? Grandmère told me you were living here alone. I couldn't ask you to live with me, of course, because of Theo and the baby . . . did you know we called him Hans? . . . only now things are different, and I thought maybe if you were lonely . . . and I am . . . we might move in together.'

'No, thanks. I'm not lonely,' Rochelle said. She moved along, dropping the last of her seed potatoes into the trench, and then she back-tracked on herself, kicking in the soil so that the potatoes were covered.

'Not lonely? Oh, I suppose you mean you've got Pod and Senna, but that isn't the same as having a friend, surely? I thought you could come out and live in my little house . . . or I'd come to the dower house if you're still bent on rearing orchids.'

'I'm better alone,' Rochelle said, standing on the trench now to firm her crop in. 'I'm still taking care of the orchids, of course. M. Laurient will expect me to.'

'That's silly . . . how long is he serving?'

'Just until the war's over,' Rochelle said without giving the matter any more thought. 'I can't remember what they said at the trial, but it'll be until then, I suppose.'

She happened to glance up and saw Olivia's face. The older girl was reddening, her eyes filling with tears, her brows drawing down.

'What on earth do you mean? He'll serve whatever sentence he's given, you silly thing; it won't matter when the war ends. Unless you think he'll be released when England falls? Oh, I don't understand you. You should have been nicer to the officers, Chelle, as I was, and then very probably they wouldn't have deported M. Laurient at all.'

Rochelle stepped carefully off the earth and took off her clogs. They were caked with dirt, too heavy to put on again until she had cleaned them. She looked across at Olivia and tried to tell herself again that Olivia was involved with an important and influential man and she had better not antagonise her. But she could feel the colour flooding her face, knew the slow growth of a healthy – and terrible – anger.

'*What* did you say? How dare you insinuate that I'd behave as you did, even for M. Laurient! Get out of my garden, Olivia Buchet, you damned Jerry-bag, or I'll empty my leaf mould all over you!'

'*What*? How dare you! You're just a dirty, ragged little girl! Don't you dare call me . . . that!'

The word, in fact, had never crossed Rochelle's lips before, but now she acknowledged that it described Olivia to a T. The tarts down in St Helier who went with Germans for what they could get were all Jerry-bags, and that was just what Olivia was too, even though her man was so important that Rochelle was not allowed to know his name!

'Get out of my garden then – Jerry-bag!'

Olivia got to her feet, her face sharpened with rage, her whole body shaking with it.

'I'll go straight up to the house and . . .'

'That's right! Go and inform on me, as you did on M. Laurient,' Rochelle screamed, tears beginning to form in her eyes. 'You'd like that, wouldn't you? To see me sent off to Germany, to some horrible camp where I'd die, as he might!'

Olivia had been turning to flounce away but at those words she swung back. She stared, big eyes widening, a finger flying to her mouth.

'Inform . . . on you? On M. Laurient? What on earth are you talking about? As if I would . . . as if I could! Why, the only German I know at all is Theo, and he's seen a good deal more of you and M. Laurient recently than I have. Just calm down, Rochelle, and tell me what you mean!'

'Someone informed on M. Laurient,' Rochelle said, her voice shaking. 'Someone told the troops that he was out after curfew, and that he kept a wireless set in one of the greenhouses. It must have been you. You're the only person besides M. Laurient and me who knew where that set was hidden.'

'I never said a word,' Olivia protested. Her mouth began to tremble. 'No wonder you've been so horrid to me, and won't move into my dear little house. Oh, Chelle, M. Laurient was so kind to me when we were children. I wouldn't betray him for anything . . . nor you! Please don't believe such a thing of me. How can I convince you?'

Rochelle looked at her old friend and knew she was speaking the truth. But she might as well satisfy her own curiosity if she could take advantage of Olivia's present state to learn something.

'Well . . . tell me why you say that Theo saw us – M. Laurient and me – more often than you did.'

'You've not guessed, then? Theo's full name is Theodore Kussak.'

Rochelle stared at her friend for a long time. Things were falling into place now that she knew who Olivia's lover was. Perhaps that was why the Hauptmann had done what he could to help them – because of his friendship with Olivia. And, of course, because of his interest in the orchids, he could easily have found the wireless set whilst poking round the glasshouse in their absence. But what had made him suddenly turn on them, give M. Laurient up to the authorities? She asked Olivia, and got the answer she might have guessed at, had she known more at the time.

'Why, he was as distressed as I was, but the whole matter was out of his hands once a member of the Todt

293

organisation spotted M. Laurient in the woods during curfew. He followed him to the greenhouse and saw him using the set . . . he pounced at once, of course, and poor Theo had no choice but to hand him over. The Todt are hand-in-glove with the Gestapo and no one wants to get on the wrong side of them.'

'I see,' Rochelle said lamely. 'Well, I'm sorry I misjudged you, Olivia. Do you want to come back to the dower house for some tea? There isn't much, but I got an extra ration of macaroni this week and I'm going to open some bottled tomatoes and fry some onions . . . it'll be tasty, and there's plenty for two.'

'Yes, I'd like to come,' Olivia said, still a little stiltedly. 'I would have brought some food . . . I didn't think.'

The two of them, with the dogs bringing up the rear, returned to the dower house. Olivia sat and watched whilst Rochelle cooked the macaroni, added the bottled tomatoes and finally fried some onions and tipped them into the concoction.

'It's very nice,' she said in a rather surprised voice as they ate. 'What will you have for a pudding?'

'Air,' Rochelle said, trying not to sound tart. 'For that's all there is. Tomorrow, if I'm lucky, I'll get my flour ration, though it's hard to know what to do with it with so little sugar, almost no butter, and no hope of margarine or lard to make it go further.'

'What's the ration, then?'

'Two ounces of butter a week, and it doesn't go far, I can tell you. Then I get four ounces of meat a week, and three ounces of sugar. And sometimes there's macaroni, just a bit, and sometimes cheese.'

'And that's *all*?' Olivia's voice was awestruck. 'How can you live?'

'Well, there's potatoes, which I was just planting, and the bread ration, which is two loaves a week. And that's about it. Oh – I get half a pint of skim milk a week, and sometimes a bit more from the dairy up at the manor, if I work there for a few hours.'

'I see. Chelle . . . I'm sorry. I didn't realise. You see, Maman and Grandmère always seem to have enough to eat . . . I just didn't realise.'

'Oh, forget it. The trouble is I'm not very domesticated. Mme Barfleur always used to do the bottling and canning for M. Laurient, so when he went and she stopped coming I just had to use up what there was and hope . . . well, hope I'd last out.'

She hesitated to mention the end of the war again; clearly, so far as Olivia was concerned the war could only have one end, a German victory, whereas every other Jerseyman longed for Allied dominance and freedom from the Nazi yoke.

'And Grandmère doesn't come here any more? I thought, from what she said, that she still came two or three times a week.'

'No. She offered, but I thought she might say something to you and you might say something to . . . to Theo. I thought it was best to manage alone.'

'And . . . you won't use the black market. That's how Maman and Grandmère manage, I suppose. And they've got stuff salted away, I think.'

Rochelle remembered her own food store which she could not use because she was not strong enough to lift the trap door and prop it back. The food just lay there, tantalising her when she was at her hungriest. But she said nothing to Olivia. It would have been downright stupid to have done so, no matter how truthful Olivia had been over informing on M. Laurient.

'I can't afford the black market; very few of us can,' she said. 'I get a little money from the estate, but that's all. I can't earn for myself, not yet. And then there's the dogs. I have to feed them somehow, so any extras which come my way . . . the odd rabbit, or fish if someone's lucky, or stale bread . . . goes straight into Pod and Senna.'

'And . . . and you won't come and live with me? I have plenty of food, and the dogs could come too.'

'No,' Rochelle said, half-regretfully. 'There are the orchids; I've worked terribly hard to keep them alive, to rear those that are left. And then there's M. Laurient. When he comes home I want him to have a home, with me in it. And you never know . . .'

Olivia looked around the kitchen. Rochelle, watching her, wondered what she made of it. If she was remembering it as it had been, when M. Laurient and her grandmother had reigned here, she would probably think it a poor, dirty, cold little place. Rochelle had brought her bedding down during the worst weather and now could not be bothered to take it back upstairs; besides, sleeping down here meant that she could be near whatever fire there was until it died down. The dogs were allowed on the chairs . . . their poor old rheumaticky bones were glad to get above draught-level when the wind was blowing hard under the door . . . and Rochelle did not see the point of putting food away in a pantry when there was so little of it so it stood on the dresser, in small packets and pots, and overflowed, in the case of potatoes, on to the floor.

Her tiny stock of wood was here, too. Easier to keep it by the hearth so that it was always dry and she did not have to leave the shelter of the house to make the fire up. And her entire wardrobe of clothes and shoes was piled none too neatly on the top of the dresser. In fact Rochelle, seeing it through Olivia's eyes, was ashamed to realise that she had turned the kitchen into a sort of one-roomed apartment – or perhaps a one-roomed hovel – just so that she would not have to bother with the rest of the house.

'Don't you ever go upstairs?'

Rochelle stiffened, then relaxed. Her toothbrush was on

the draining board, together with her tiny piece of soap and the thin towel. Olivia was only asking, not criticising.

'Not any more.'

Olivia looked at her. She was struggling with some emotion which Rochelle could not interpret.

'Oh, Chelle . . . will I get like this when my man's gone? Will my dear little house seem cold and frightening? I thought we could be so happy there, you and I, until Theo comes back again.'

'We couldn't,' Rochelle said gently. 'We're different people, aren't we, Livia? We want different things.'

'Yes, I suppose . . . Chelle?'

'What?'

'I'm really *not* a . . . what you called me. I'm really not. I was in a way, at first, but I'm not any more. I love Theo so much, I'd do anything for him, and I love Hans too. So you see . . .'

'Yes, of course I do.' Rochelle stood up. 'Look, Livia, I'll walk you up to the manor. You can get a car from there, I suppose? I don't want to chase you away, but there's curfew, and I like to be snugged down and locked up before dark.'

'Of course.'

The two girls left the house together, walking rapidly through the dusk under the trees. When they reached the house Rochelle turned and would have left with no more than a word of farewell, but she suddenly remembered something.

'Livia . . . why didn't you live at the manor with Theo? I should have thought you'd have liked that. You practically lived there once, after all.'

'Theo wouldn't do a thing like that. It would be bad for discipline,' Olivia said at once. 'He only stayed at my little house when he was on furlough, and at weekends, and sometimes when he felt he could leave someone else in

297

charge. He has a very strong sense of responsibility does Theo.'

'I see. Well, I'd better be getting back.' Rochelle dropped a hand on to Pod's head, fondling the long, chocolate-coloured ears. 'Come and see me again, if you feel like a chat.'

'Of course I will. And if you can tear yourself away from your wretched orchids, come and see me, and little Hans.'

Rochelle said that she would and the two girls parted, Rochelle to tramp home in her wooden clogs to her lonely house in the woods, Olivia to mince in her high-heeled pumps as far as the nearest staff car, which would whisk her back to her 'dear little house'.

Neither, when it came down to it, envied the other.

Laurie woke at one o'clock with an almighty yell, hastily stifled. There was a mission to be flown in a few hours and the men in his hut would not thank him if he disturbed them before time.

He had been dreaming.

Lying there with the dream trying to fade quickly back into his subconscious, he had half a mind to let it, but then curiosity made him start to try to recollect exactly what had caused him to shout out like that, because the dream, at first at any rate, had not been a nightmare. Quite the opposite. It had been the very nicest sort of dream, one which he had all too rarely on the night before a mission.

He had been in an orchard. Sunlight had slanted down through the leaves, dappling shadow and sun on the gnarled silvery-grey trunks, the long, sun-bleached grass, and the fruit which lay on the grass and reddened in the trees.

It had been peaceful there. He was aware the quiet, which was enhanced by birdsong and the chattering of a tiny stream somewhere, but he wanted to explore. He set off through the trees towards what looked like a sunlit lawn further off.

At first, as he walked, he had been aware only of the pleasant things about the orchard, the sunshine and shadow, the birds, the sound of water. But as he continued he realised that there were less pleasant things, too. There was something watchful about the trees, as though they were not quite what they seemed, and all at once, as though at a signal, he snapped into a watchful mood himself. He knew what he was doing here and it was not just wandering, enjoying himself; he was here for a purpose, and that purpose had something to do with the sunlit lawn towards which he was heading. Danger waited for him out there, but it was a danger he had to face. He could not stay lurking amongst the trees; he must go on to the lawn.

And then, walking towards him, came a girl. She was slim, dark-haired, boyish-looking, and her fingers were loosely holding on to the collar of a large dog of some description. He could not bother with the dog; he was too intent on the girl.

She had not seen him. She was singing to herself as she walked, and now and then she bent and picked up an apple, which she put into the basket hanging on her arm. To do so she let go of the dog, which suddenly saw Laurie and stopped short, a growl rumbling in its throat.

The girl looked up – and her eyes met his. A most extraordinary feeling arrowed through Laurie at her glance ... sweetness, tenderness, warmth, they were all there – for on her face, mingling with the shock and incredulity, there was such a depth of pure, selfless love that he could have wept. She loved him – and he had never set eyes on her before.

And then, suddenly, the sun went in and there was movement: a man in a dark uniform pounced from the lawn into the shadow of the orchard ... another joined him and another, another. They fell on the girl, grasping her arms, dragging her back, away from the orchard, back to the lawn.

He went towards them, hot rage engulfing him, meaning to kill them, and he saw the dark green collars, the peaked caps with the eagles, and the jackboots which marked them as Nazis. They had the girl now, were grappling with her, pulling her down, one man forcing her head back by the abundant, gleaming black hair. He hurled himself forward, or tried to do so. He tried to reach her, to shout encouragement, tell her that he was coming, would rescue her.

'I'm coming, petite,' he shouted. 'Pod . . . attack, attack!'

He had woken himself up with his shout, he realised now, lying safe and warm in his own bed in the Nissen hut, with José on his left and Tiger on his right. Dreams were rum things, though! What an imagination he must have, to have called the fat old labrador Pod! And why on earth had he addressed the girl in French? He only knew a few words. He realised he had called her 'little', and felt almost embarrassed, even though he knew very well that it had only been a dream.

But how real it had been – how incredibly real! The bright, sunlit lawn, the peaceful orchard, and the girl. He could still remember her perfectly, every fine-drawn feature of her. The atmosphere, too, seemed still to be something remembered rather than something dreamed. He *must* have been there at some time or other, must have met that girl, grown fond of her. But he knew that he had not. The whole episode had been entirely outside his experience, a figment of his dreaming mind.

Unless it was someone else's dream, of course.

He lay a little longer in the darkened hut, trying to laugh at his own absurdity; as if he could have dreamed someone else's dream! But the conviction nagged him that it was a dream that someone, somewhere, would have understood perfectly, interpreted without effort.

He was still awake when dawn began to bring the hut

300

back to life. He could see the shapes of the men in their cots, the neatly folded blankets at the foot of one whose occupant had died on the last raid. The round coal stove with its big pipe and the uniforms, civvies and work-clothes neatly hung on rails above the ablutions buckets. Someone had slung a leather bag above his head; it looked like a fat, legless pig, moving slightly in the draught which came under the door of the hut and was sometimes strong enough to stir the curls of the man in the next bed.

Go to sleep, Laurie told himself sternly. In a few hours you'll be out of this bed and preparing for your mission and you'll be tired, and that's no way to lead your men.

He closed his eyes and thought about home, and his mother. And was soon asleep.

When Laurie next woke the dream had faded and was insubstantial as . . . as a dream, he told himself, stretching, yawning, climbing out of his cot and going down to the end of the hut for some water. It was cold, but it would wake him up.

Standing there in singlet and shorts Laurie soaped himself, splashed water noisily about, and dried quickly on the rough, khaki towel. Although spring was well advanced it was still chilly at this very early hour of the morning, with darkness still pressing on the windows of the huts.

When they were all dressed the crew ate speedily and with care, except for those who suffered from air sickness, and they merely drank coffee. Then they made their way to the briefing room where Lieutenant Colonel Corpuss, who would lead the group, stood by the curtain which hid the map. When everyone was settled, the navigators with pencils and pads ready, the group leader began to talk, pulling the curtain back as he did so.

The target was in Germany; deeper in Germany than they had so far penetrated. The map showed the target and the routes out and back. Corpuss told them the order and formation in which they would fly, advised on their queries, and reminded them that formation flying was in everyone's interests.

'So if you've any problems with the ship, turn back sooner rather than later,' he cautioned. 'No point in risking everyone for the sake of not turning back. We can close a formation if we know someone has to pull out. The difficulties come when a ship can't keep up, or lags once we're almost on target. Good luck, guys.'

Laurie and his crew made their way next to the equipment hut where clerks handed out the heated suits, the anti-flak garments and the rest of the things they would need. The men shambled out of the hut weighed down with clothing and Laurie sighed as he began to don his flying suit. He was always uneasy in case the suit electrocuted him should he happen to sweat too freely, or wet himself. Still, it was better than freezing to death, and that could happen if you were unlucky enough to get a direct hit at height so that the ship was suddenly invaded by icy air.

'Jeez, this lot weighs,' groaned Tex, who was riding tail gunner in Rad's place. 'You got everything, George?'

George was a waist gunner and a natural comedian. He was a tall, skinny guy who loved to laugh and make others do the same. Right now he had his steel helmet perched on a pile of equipment which he was balancing, rather ingeniously, on top of his shock of pale hair.

'I got every durn thing, cat,' George announced, casting up his eyes to squint at his burden. 'All I need's a big pile of waffles swimmin' in maple syrup, and a mess o' fresh eggs.'

There was a laugh mingled with a groan; the food here was as good as the authorities could produce but it seemed that English hens didn't lay too well in late spring and dried eggs were the order of the day. Furthermore, the Air Force cooks did not seem to have heard of waffles, far less waffles smothered in butter and maple syrup.

'Fresh eggs! All I know is dried,' someone else called out. 'Gawd, them English hens *lay* 'em dried, I declare!'

It was good to laugh, Laurie told himself, as they struggled into their heavy clothing and began to fit the oxygen masks to make sure they were functioning correctly. Now was the time when everyone did their checking. He made sure that the gas was loaded, the guns were swivelling and the ammunition was aboard, to say nothing of the 'eggs' which they would presently offload on to the enemy factories beneath. Each man did a check which was usually double-checked by someone else. When we do go we're as ready as we can possibly make ourselves, Laurie thought.

It was still dark when Laurie began to rev up his engines. He watched the big props begin to turn over, one at a time, as the engines churred, hesitated, and caught fire with a roar. Lieutenant Colonel Corpuss was first off and he taxied his ship to take the place right at the head of the takeoff runway. Laurie came next, *Blue Moon Too* sounding sweet, the night still dark but with that certain something which meant that dawn was not far distant. When they were airborne it would come faster for them, high above the earth, than for mere mortals down below.

Behind him, the crew were joking, talking about a recent liberty ride into Norwich, where they had danced half the night with local girls at the Samson and Hercules ballroom and fought with a redfaced civilian who had called them dirty names and tried to tell the girls all Yankees were diseased.

Someone in another group was getting serious . . . a pretty little WRAF with ginger curls and freckles . . . they rather thought he would make an honest woman of her as soon as his colonel gave him the go-ahead.

The signal from the tower came, and Laurie felt again that familiar sinking feeling; off to battle, boys, whether you will or no. And then *Blue Moon Too* was trundling along the runway, faster, faster . . . will she clear the hedge at the

303

end of the runway, and the trees which cluster beyond . . . she never will, not this time, she's going too slow, there's something wrong, she'll never get up in time . . .

And they were airborne, gaining altitude. He looked about him and saw that they were forming their pattern already. Now he was busy, had no time for nerves, as he checked the place of each ship in the formation, kept his own nose exactly where it should be, watched like a hawk to see that all was going well.

Below him, the wrinkled grey sea, which could never be hidden by the dark, changed; the coast of Holland, he hoped, if they were on course.

'Solly?' The interphone crackled.

'Yeah, Laurie?'

'That's the Dutch coast; we on course still?'

'Sure we are.'

'Great. Keep checking. I'll keep high.'

'Roger,' Solly said. Laurie switched from interphone to radio. 'On course, guys, keeping altitude and heading straight for the target. You-all the same?'

Everyone was.

Presently, with dawn coming up fast, they saw the first flak bursting on their starboard bow. They gained a bit more height at Lieutenant Colonel Corpuss's command, but continued to fly at the same speed, droning above the flat fields of Holland, heading for the target but still too busy to give it much thought.

Other ships were in formation ahead, still more behind; fighter cover was there as well, but out of sight, probably behind and above. It made a guy feel good to think of the fighters up there, watching over the waddling bombers, angels every one.

Time passed. Everyone was cold, scared, fed up. No one would have admitted such a thing for the world, though, oddly, each man knew what the others felt and so there was no need to put it into words. The group leader turned to the northeast and Laurie followed suit, Solly reminding him over the interphone, not that it was necessary, just nice to know that his navigator was wide awake and keeping them in line.

They reached their target at the ETA, and were annoyed but not surprised to find themselves expected; flak was heavy, guns boomed, and streamers of smoke from the smoke pots which the Huns must have lighted to protect their factories hid the target completely from view, though now and then a freak wind-change revealed, for a moment, a cluster of long, low rooftops which looked very like factories.

'John? Got anything in the sight?'

John was the bombardier; he would be doing his best, right now, to pick out a bombable target down on the ground. Useless to drop your eggs into the river, or on farmland. Better to keep flying, hoping for a break in the smoke, or for a change of wind direction so that the factories which must be somewhere below would suddenly be revealed for a moment.

'Hey . . . found one! Hold her steady, Laurie . . . yes, it's a big 'un . . . keep her steady!'

Laurie held her steady, though it was a tricky business. Flak was bursting all around; if they had to stay here much longer he was sure they'd be hit. Then he saw the indicator lights flash on the instrument panel . . . the bombs were falling! John South confirmed it.

'Bombs away . . . let's go, let's go!'

Laurie headed north, trying to get out of the flak, but he could tell by the confusion of sound over his radio that he had been hit. Not too badly, he hoped.

Then black smoke, greasy and thick and shot with flames, licked out of number 3 engine and Laurie felt the plane wallow, as though she were flying, for a moment, through soup and not air. He hauled on the stick and she made a gallant effort to recover, whilst behind him more bombs were released and over the interphone he heard Ben Cluda shout, 'Fighters at eight o'clock!'

There was a staccato burst of firing and then Ben shouted again, 'More fighters! Jeez, there must be forty, fifty of 'em, the big twin-engined jobs, Ju88s. I'm gonn . . .'

His words ended in a gargle. Laurie felt his blood run cold. He shouted into the interphone.

'Ben? Ben, are you all right?'

There was no reply; and *Blue Moon Too* staggered and seemed to gasp as another volley caught her, sending her sideways like a pup kicked by a man ten times her size.

'We're out of formation,' someone called over the interphone. 'Can we get clear?'

'The fighters are on to the Ju88s,' José shouted. 'Keep low, keep clear of the flak . . . we might make it . . . miracles do happen!'

But it was not the time for miracles, not the hour, not the day. *Blue Moon Too*'s card had been marked. They were well off course, having lost too much rudder to have a lot of say in exactly where they went, when Solly suddenly shouted that he could see the Channel ahead.

They hoped, then, that they might make it, though Laurie could have told them that it would be a near thing. Number 3 engine was out and number 2 was coughing, though he had tried every trick in the book to keep it going. And there was an odd sort of smell . . . he thought fuel lines had probably been hit and prayed that there would be no fire to roast them before they could hit the deck.

They were losing height, too.

'I'm going to land her,' Laurie shouted, as the little fields got bigger and the little roads loomed up at him. 'It'll be a field if I can make it . . . we're too low to jump . . . anyone badly hurt?'

'Ben's dead,' someone called out. 'Tex ain't too good . . . flesh wound . . . lost a lotta blood . . .'

'Stick together,' Laurie roared as he brought the plane

306

in and began to cut the remaining engines and do all the things he had practised so often for an emergency landing. 'Hold tight, guys . . . we're down!'

They were. The roaring of the engines and the laboured sounds of flight were abruptly over. Silence descended. They were sitting in what remained of *Blue Moon Too* in a lush water-meadow, with a river not too far distant and a lark singing its head off nearby, apparently regardless of the much larger bird which had just flopped to earth so heavily.

'Everyone alive?'

No answer for a frozen, terrible moment, then moans and swearing came to his ears. They were scared, hurt, battered . . . but alive.

'Right. Out.'

They wasted no time. They bundled out. Nine of them. Ben's body was still in his turret. Laurie had started to say that perhaps someone should go back when there was a tiny crack and they all saw scarlet flame lick down from one engine and across the wing like a hungry little tongue.

'Run for it!' shrieked Tex, his voice cracking with urgency. 'Run for it. The gas tanks . . .'

Everyone tore as far away from the ship as they could, and even in his fear and hurry Laurie was amazed at the turn of speed attained by heavily accoutred men when terror was at their heels.

There was an odd sound, like an old lady burping, Laurie said later, and then a *whump* which was not ladylike at all but outrageously noisy and vulgar. And where *Blue Moon Too* had stood – or rather, lain – there was just a mass of flame with black and oily smoke pouring out of it.

'Do we try to make a run for it?' Tex asked doubtfully. 'Seems we've lighted 'em straight to the spot marked X.'

'We could . . .' Laurie was beginning, when John caught his arm and wordlessly pointed.

At the gateway to the field stood a little old lady all in

307

black, two small children and a figure in uniform wheeling a bicycle. The figure in uniform was without doubt a military figure and even as they watched it produced a pistol from somewhere about its person and waved it in their direction.

'Hands up,' interpreted Laurie, though he could not hear a word the man was saying and would not have understood it even if he could. 'Better safe than sorry.'

He put his hands up to his shoulders and the rest of the crew rather sheepishly followed suit. The military one handed his bicycle to one of the onlookers and clearly, from his gestures, bade another open the gate for him. When that was done he marched through it very stiffly and approached the small group of flyers. It was easy to see that he was absolutely terrified – but he kept the pistol trained on them and Laurie had heard too many stories of the way the Germans treated prisoners to try any funny business.

The military one turned out to be about sixty-five with round eyeglasses perched on his face, a tiny Hitleresque moustache decorating his short upper lip, and a retroussé nose. He knew no English but Solly, it transpired, knew a little German, and after a short though very animated conversation Solly turned to his companions.

'He says we're his prisoners,' he explained laconically. 'He says we're to walk before him, keeping our hands up, or it'll be the worse for us. He's going to take us to the town hall, I think . . . he called it the *Rathaus* and that's the nearest to town hall that I can get.'

'If he says *For you, the war is over* I'll strangle him with my umbilical cord,' José said bitterly, whereupon the military one turned threateningly round upon them and barked a guttural and accusatory sentence which no one had any trouble in translating as 'Don't talk!'

They muttered a bit after that, but kept their voices low, and presently they realised they were being followed – by a little old lady dressed in black, two small children, and a dirty brown and white dog.

By the time they reached the nearby village the small crowd had turned into an admiring throng, most of whom could speak at least a few words of English. 'Hello, Tommy!' was a favourite, and 'Long leeve Mistaire Churchill' another.

'They think we're British,' Laurie said with a chuckle. 'Oh well, I've been called worse things.'

At least it made them smile as they were marched into captivity.

14

'Ah, good morning, Rochelle!' Radek raised his eyes from his work and grinned at her. 'Would you like some potatoes?'

He was digging up main crop potatoes which he had sown, this year, on the sunniest spot on the cliff, working terribly hard to get the soil right, slogging up from the beach with tons of guano, the rich white bird-droppings which could be garnered from below the cliffs where the sea-birds nested, and the rotted kelp which added fibre to the thin, sandy soil.

Rochelle knew all about Radek's potatoes, because she had done quite a lot of the soil preparation. With M. Laurient gone she had been so lonely that as soon as it was safe to do so she had begun to spend more and more time at the L'Oyette farm. She was repaid in food for her toil, which more than suited her, since hard though she laboured on her own small plot it never repaid her as it should have done.

This, she knew, was due to her proximity to the German High Command. Now that it was common knowledge that the Allies had landed in France and were pressing home their advantage and gaining ground on the Axis powers every day, it was becoming more difficult for the Germans to feed their troops here on Jersey. The occupying forces had always had enough to eat, but now, suddenly, they were as short of food as the oppressed and of course they reacted by simply stealing as much food as they could lay their hands on. So Rochelle planted and the hungry soldiers reaped and there was very little she could do about it. She knew from past experience that if she complained it was probable that even more of her crop would disappear, to 'teach' her the unwisdom of admitting that the conquerors had faults.

But the L'Oyette place was remote and difficult to get at, so Rochelle took her seed potatoes and her tiny cabbage plants out to Tante Denise and sowed them there with Radek's help. Then, when they were grown, she could be sure of getting at least as much as she had planted and probably more.

If it had not been for the orchids, and for her hope that M. Laurient might give the Germans the slip and turn up at the dower house, she would have left there months ago. Without him, it was a frightening and dangerous place to be, and the man who had taken Hauptmann Kussak's place was not fond of tropical blooms nor inclined to allow her to use her fuel supply in the greenhouse instead of in the kitchen. He made it plain that if she did not need the wood he would have it for his headquarters, so Rochelle found herself lugging the orchids back to the dower house kitchen and sitting with them by the fire, all of them wrapped in blankets and none of them quite warm enough.

But the orchids she had managed to bring through four years of war were at least still alive. Not flowering, alas – Pure Madonna, if the hybrid they had reared was Pure Madonna, needed more warmth than Rochelle could provide before it would actually bud and blossom – but at least putting forth green leaves in the spring and showing that there was life in the roots and stems.

But now, on this fine September morning, Rochelle could only smile at Radek and say that she would like some potatoes very much and also, if he could spare it, some cabbage and any swede which was fit for eating.

'Sure. Fetch a bucket,' Radek commanded. 'We've done well here . . . good job the Jerries haven't been nosing around. We're well over quota, but as you know Maman takes what they expect in when they expect it, grumbling,

311

of course, that we're unfairly treated because of the poor quality of the land, and they think they're getting all and more than is due to them and they're satisfied.'

'Thanks, Radek,' Rochelle said gratefully. 'I've brought you some runner beans. I know you can't grow them here because of the wind and I've got a bumper crop. The Jerries have as well – it's the walled garden – so they haven't picked mine as thoroughly as usual.'

'Many thanks. Has Maman said anything to you about . . . about my plans?'

'No?' Rochelle sat down, cross-legged, on the grass by the potato patch. 'What's this all about?'

Radek called Tante Denise 'Maman' for obvious reasons, but he had been with her long enough for their relationship to be a very fond one. Mme L'Oyette loved him almost as much as the son she had lost and Rochelle believed that the affection was entirely mutual. However, his relationship with Rochelle was quite different. He thought her a beautiful girl and said so every time they met, talked about after the war as though he would still be on Jersey and Rochelle still a near neighbour, though Rochelle thought that he would probably go away as soon as peace came. Why should he not? He was a victim of this terrible war and would surely want to return to his own country. But now she listened as he spoke, one young person sympathising with the aspirations of another.

'Look, Chelle, Maman is going to find this difficult to accept, but I want to take the boat, and a couple of young fellows like myself, and make my way to France. The boat's up to it, and the Jerries don't watch me the way they watch the others. I could be reported missing, believed drowned . . . and I could get over to France and join the Allies, fight the Nazis instead of having to bow and scrape to them. I've mentioned it a couple of times, but she always says it's out of the question and changes the subject. I wondered if you could tell her?'

'Me? I say, Radek, I suppose I couldn't come with you? I'm pretty strong, and . . . and I could see if I could find M. Laurient.'

Radek grinned. He was tanned from working out of doors all the time, muscular and fit, with the burnish to his skin that only good health can bring. Lately, Rochelle had been aware that she was pretty, that she could interest men and be interested by them, and Radek was very attractive with his blond curls and his even white teeth. He was always squeezing her, teasing her, kissing the side of her face and trying to kiss her mouth . . . why should she feel guilty if she used her obvious attraction for him to persuade him to take her to France?

'You'd come with me? Now that would be rather fun . . .' Radek abandoned his digging and loped over to where Rochelle sat, leaned over and lifted her up as if she weighed no more than a potato. 'We could pose as young lovers to fool the Germans . . . and it needn't be a pose, either!'

'Hmm. But will you take me with you, Radek?'

'I couldn't very well, because I want you to stay with Maman whilst I go,' Radek admitted, standing her down, kissing the tip of her nose, and returning to his potatoes. 'Besides, I can't make off with you yet; you're still just a baby. I'll come back when I've liberated Europe and we can get married.'

'I don't want to get married,' Rochelle objected. 'I just want to come to France so I can search for M. Laurient.'

'I'll search for you,' Radek said. 'Oh, Chelle, I don't believe I could ever meet a girl lovelier or sweeter than you . . . why don't you give me a bit of encouragement? Aren't I good enough for you?'

'It isn't that, you know it isn't. It's just that I can't think of anything besides bringing M. Laurient home. If you do get away to France, Radek, will you really search for him?'

'Yes, when we've smacked the Nazis' heads off their

313

shoulders and made them eat dirt,' Radek said robustly. 'Then you'll speak to Maman?'

'Yes, I suppose I will. But you'll be careful, won't you, Radek? I mean, the Germans don't know you got away at all. If they caught you . . . it doesn't bear thinking about.'

'Thank you, sweetheart,' Radek said buoyantly. His English was so good that Rochelle admitted to herself it was very unlikely he would ever be caught, though he spoke no patois and his French was not even as good as her own. Still, she would make one last plea.

'Radek, before you go off, don't forget that Tante Denise will have to go on supplying her quota and so on. And she might be punished if they found you'd gone in your boat.'

'Just speak to her, Chelle,' Radek urged. 'Don't you see that the German position here is getting harder and harder to maintain? They're fearfully short of food; all they've got is weapons and underground bunkers to hide in. The time's going to come when they're too busy preparing to fight the Allied invasion to count heads.'

'Then you won't go at once?' Rochelle asked, half glad and half sorry that not even the hotheaded young Russian believed things had turned far enough in the Allies' favour for his help to be essential yet. 'That isn't so bad then, Radek. I'm sure we can both talk Tante Denise round for a few months ahead.'

'Good, good. And perhaps, in those few months, I can talk you into seeing that I shall come back for you, sweep you off your feet and make you my bride,' Radek said, and Rochelle laughed and wondered, not for the first time, if he was half teasing and half serious, wholly teasing, or wholly serious. Young men, she decided, were a mystery to her. She had noticed that the young Germans up at the manor, who had been nasty to her three years ago, had gradually become nicer and nicer until now they were making sheep's eyes whenever they chanced to meet. Small presents were offered and scorned, amiable conversations started by them and finished abruptly by Rochelle. That young person, eyeing her reflection in the glass in the neglected bedroom at the dower house, could not see any particular change in herself, but there must be something. She was taller, her hair was longer, her face seemed to have changed in some mysterious fashion and her shape was, she supposed, shapelier. But she was still far too thin, her breasts too tiny to count, and she could not imagine that Radek was serious when he called her beautiful. Improved, perhaps, but beautiful, never! Beauty was golden hair, creamy skin and baby-blue eyes, not night-black tresses, navy-blue eyes and skin so white that blue veins showed through.

'I'll go up to the house now, and see what Tante Denise says,' Rochelle remarked, taking her bucket of potatoes and swinging the handle gaily as she turned for the cottage. 'I'll do my best for you, but I can't make any promises.'

In fact, Tante Denise proved less difficult than she had feared.

'Oh yes, he's crazy to go, as they all are, but he won't just leave me in the lurch,' she said confidently. 'I wouldn't want to stop him, Chelle. I wouldn't have stopped my own son, and Radek has far more reason to hate the Nazis even than Jean-Claude had. But neither will I see him go too soon and walk into a trap. He shall go when the Channel ports are firmly in Allied hands and he's got a good chance of joining men who'll see that he's put to good use.'

Charles Laurient escaped in the gold of late summer, slipping out of the gate when a working party was leaving, mingling with the ordinary German peasants, hard to distinguish in his wooden clogs and faded, patched clothing.

He made his way down to the nearest river, where he stole a boat. He stayed on the river until it became too big, too industrial, and then he took to the countryside, stealing crops for food, staying hidden by day, travelling by night.

315

He was near the border before they caught him, within a stone's throw of succeeding, and that was why they caught him, because near a border post everyone is wary, on edge. He should have waited, bided his time, but he was weak from lack of decent food and a mass of nerves, so he plunged too soon.

He killed a guard. He had not meant to kill him, but they had been wrestling for possession of the machine gun and somehow the gun had been pointing at the soldier when between them they had pulled the trigger. And then it had seemed as if he had to keep hold of the machine gun and turn it, spitting fire, on anyone who tried to approach.

He did not think he had killed anyone else, but he had probably wounded some of them. They overpowered him in the end, and he was beaten and reviled and screamed at before they put him, heavily chained, on a train bound for that concentration camp which he had done so much to avoid.

He arrived there at nightfall; the very air smelt of death, of despair. He heard the gates clang shut behind him and heard the commandant tell him that he had killed a young German soldier and that his own life, from now on, should be without hope, for no mercy would be shown him.

He stared back at the man, eyes dull and indifferent, brain planning how he would escape from here. He could not stay. He would sooner die than stay here.

Weeks passed. Amongst the human skeletons there was another, with a good deal of iron-grey hair and a stubborn, closed face. He was in a cell with twenty others, all filthy, all starved, some in the last stages of terminal illness.

The guards were handpicked for brutality and greed, and Laurient was singled out for any beastliness going because he had escaped once. There was no chance of escape here . . . only one door led out of this place and its name was death. He was 'questioned' twice; the first time

316

he prayed for oblivion and when he was thrown back in the cell he thought he would die, but he was tougher than he had realised. He lived. Sometimes he wished he had not.

On the second questioning his attitude infuriated the torturer – for that was what he was. He demanded to be told details of Allied movements which he knew very well Laurient could have no more idea of than he. He screamed that Laurient had had outside help in his escape, must have had, and could very well have been told the Allies' plans.

Laurient's face was shut again, stubborn. He was deathly afraid of the pain now, though not of death itself, that gentle escape from the hell that was this camp. It was night, and aircraft droned overhead; they took him to a little square room with a barred window which smelt of blood. They tied his wrists with wire and strung him up over a beam, so that his feet were inches off the floor.

Then they left him.

He was nearly finished. He just hung; no point in prayer, promises, certainly no hope, except hope for the end, for merciful darkness. His mouth was dry, gaping, his hands engorged with blood, his body starved of it. He knew he would die soon, and he welcomed it . . . he welcomed it more than he had ever welcomed anything.

He heard the planes drone, but they had no meaning; nothing had meaning but his pain. He was praying now that he would not move, that the wind or whatever it was that occasionally swung him would cease, would let him die without the further excruciating pain that even the tiniest movement caused.

Once the man had come back, had pushed him . . . he had screamed then, thin, high screams, but screaming made him move, and now he just hung and waited.

He heard an almighty roar and then he was swinging

317

. . . not daring to scream, for the pain . . . and he was being hit by something hard, and the lights were so brilliant on him after the lonely dark that he had to shut his eyes tight to exclude the brightness.

He must have passed out. He came round and knew at once that something had changed. He was huddled on a stone floor, vague shapes all about him . . . a hand crept out, touched a concrete block, then wood, and then the hand crept back, hugged itself into his stomach, because poor thing it was hurt so badly, so badly!

He moved; the wire round his wrists dangled. Had they cut him down? But if so, where was his cell? He could see the stars, and now he was aware he could hear screaming, the sound of engines, feet, shouting.

People were here, somewhere.

People had done this to him.

They were coming back! They would string him up again, by his bloodied tortured wrists, and he could not . . . *could* not stand that pain! This time he would beg, weep, crawl, kiss their stinking Nazi feet . . . just to let him alone, to let him die where he was.

I won't do it.

It was a tiny echo, a minuscule fragment of defiance, caught somewhere in the echoing hole that was his skull.

I won't beg them.

I'll beg God.

He lay in the rubble, with the fire engines shrieking and the prisoners screaming and the aircraft overhead emptying their bombs on to this hell-hole, and he prayed directly to God this time, putting all his cards on the table.

I won't beg them. I'm begging You. I'll give You, of my own free will, what I value most, if You'll just help me to get out of it. You can choose – I'll go through the dark door if that's the only way You can see for me, or I'll walk or crawl out of this place here and now. And in return I promise You . . . oh, dear God, You can have my girl and my island.

I'll never go back there, never see her again, live as half a man in some other place . . . but I can't be strung up again. The pain, God, if You knew the pain!

You do know the pain. Of course You do. You suffered, too . . . worse, probably. Take them . . . my girl, my island.

He lay there for a little longer, and then he opened his eyes. He got to his knees and looked around.

The perimeter fence was down; the guard tower from which fat, well-fed guards taunted the prisoners, sometimes fired on them for sport, to see them run and dodge even in their emaciated state, was down. Open country with trees was ahead of him.

He tried to stand but could only manage a sort of Hunchback of Notre Dame crouch. Thus he sidled out across the compound, through the torn and ragged wire and into the trees.

He got quite a long way before he passed out, in a field full of cows, just as dawn was breaking.

Not many people have drunk the water in a cow's hoofprint, but Laurient did when he came round. The misty morning was clearing as the sun grew big in the sky and someone had thrown down fodder for the cows – sugar beet cut into chunks, and sweet hay.

He ate sugar beet until his starved belly was as full as it could hold, and then found the cattle trough and drank water with mosquito larvae swimming in it, tickling his tongue and his tonsils as he swallowed.

The ditch was damp and crowded – little frogs and a water vole lived in it – but it was better than home, because he felt so safe in it. A farmhand came and got the cows in, brought them back. The day brightened, then began to fade.

Laurient slept the clock round, he thought, since he did

not wake the next day until the cows were brought back again after evening milking. Then he looked at his wrists; he could see the tendons and veins, stripped of skin, torn and horribly mutilated.

I should see a doctor, he thought, and managed a watery grin at the absurdity of the thought. He crawled out of the ditch when it was dark and ate more sugar beet before making his way onwards.

He had not been far from a river, and it was by river that his best hope lay. But where would he find a boat? He was weak, and he doubted if he could row far, though the river was a fine, wide one with a gentle current. Give it a few days and he would be able to get along, but just now he needed rest and decent food.

He found both. God was clearly going to keep His side of the bargain; Laurient had not given any further thought to his own promises. Not that he intended to break them. It was just that he could not really remember at the moment exactly what it was he had promised.

A woman found him when he was ten miles or so further on, he estimated. She screamed at the sight of his wrists, and wept, fat tears sliding down fat pink cheeks. She had a husband, a warm-faced, blue-eyed chap who looked at Laurient's wrists and put a hand to his mouth and hurried out of the kitchen. Laurient had dragged himself into the farmyard to steal eggs and the woman had brought him indoors, not knowing he meant to steal, thinking only that he had collapsed in the yard, as indeed he had.

They were Germans, of course, but they were good Christians, they told him later that night. He told them what had happened to him and they were horrified, but could not deny the proof of his mangled wrists.

They kept him a week. He knew it was in reparation for what had been done to him by their fellow-countrymen and was grateful. They fed him well, and the wife bathed his wounds in some stuff which she told him was disinfectant. There were faint signs of sepsis in one wrist, but it cleared.

'You are a very strong man,' the woman said in German. Laurient knew enough of the language to be able to exchange some conversation. He shrugged.

'I am lucky,' he said.

She nodded, delicately pouring the disinfectant, diluted in water, across his wrists.

'Yes. Now you are lucky. But winter will be here soon. What will you do then?'

Their farm was remote, but sooner or later, he supposed, someone would talk. They had children, three boys and a girl. The girl was married and away, the boys in the army. But they would be sure to have leave . . . what would they do if they found him here? His wrists were still raw, using his hands was very painful, but in fairness to his hosts he would have to move on before the winter set in.

'I'll go when healing starts,' he said.

October was golden, the crops good. He left quietly, as he had come, kissing the fat farmer's wife on her fat pink cheek, shaking hands with the old man. They took him down to the river in a hay-waggon, cuddled up amongst the hay, and stole him a boat, which he thought was particularly good of them.

It wasn't much of a boat. It was a tiny, almost circular row-boat made of cracked and peeling wood which needed bailing constantly. But it had belonged to a rich family who lived up-river and who had moved out for the duration of the war, so were very unlikely indeed to miss it. The farmer and his wife clearly did not want a man-hunt to start too near the house that had been harbouring the fugitive, for they saw him off themselves, in the tiny little boat, advising him to keep to one side of the river for a while, when to stop for the night, where the thickest cover was likely to be.

He made good time that first night, lay up the next day, rowed on the following night. He had a big mountain pack of food and a tin cup for water, of which there was plenty whilst he stuck to the river.

It took him a month, but at last he came within sight of what he knew must be the border. He gazed at the border-post longingly, but he had more sense, this time, than to rush it. He prowled back and forth for two days and then decided that it was a long border, with a limited number of posts. France was no longer an enemy country, but occupied territory. He should be able to cross almost anywhere save at a road-block.

He crossed as the first snowflakes fell, on a very cold night when the leaves were turning gold and whirling from the trees, eager to see winter arrive now that the snow had begun.

He had no food left save what he could find, or beg, or steal, but he was in better physical shape than he had any right to be, he told himself. His wrists were beginning to heal and he had accepted a bigger, looser jacket from the farmer which came well down, hiding all but the last joint of his fingers.

He was in the Moselle valley, he realised. Beautiful country, rich in vines and farms, rolling country with hills and vales, good soil, easy living. Could he find himself some safe place here? There were delightful little villages, some nestling on the banks of the river, others crouched at the foot of the hills. If someone would take him in . . . but it was asking a lot. For now, whilst he could, he would continue to live on the land, avoid the Huns and move deeper into occupied France.

Winter came, and with it the worst conditions that the people of the islands had known. There were rumours of a relief ship to be sent by the Red Cross, but none arrived, and what little food Rochelle had been able to store was

322

taken one icy December day by a party of Germans who entered the house on the pretext of searching for illegal radios and left it with Rochelle's tiny store of dried food, root vegetables and flour.

Despite her most frantic endeavours, what was more, orchids either died or simply did not show any signs of life, going into some sort of deep hibernation. She had had a dozen specimens of what might turn out to be Pure Madonna, and of these only two still looked as though they might live until the warmer weather.

So near and yet so far! M. Laurient, in his prison, must know, as she did, that victory was just around the corner, yet what a hollow victory it would be for Rochelle if the war ended and all the specimens of M. Laurient's hybridisation scheme were dead! Another five years' work, uncertainty, regrets, self-blame – they were all waiting for her if she let the two remaining plants die.

Hanging over them in the glasshouse one cold day, examining the parent plant, the seedlings, the whole complex structure of family life which she had tried so hard to maintain, Rochelle came close to shedding tears at the thought of M. Laurient's bitter disappointment should she lose these last remaining orchids. If only she knew more about the plants . . . if only she had paid more heed to M. Laurient's talk of soil composition and air roots and sphagnum moss, of each species' need for light, shade, warmth or coolness, of which orchids store water and which do not, then she would have been in a better position to help them now. But she had relied too heavily on her own instinctive 'feel' for the plants, and that could only help her in conjunction with M. Laurient's expertise. Now, with the plants' well ordered lives topsy-turvy, with their heat expectations flouted most of the time, with even their misting schedule, their repotting and their propagation a matter of chance and luck, what she wanted was knowhow. Instinct availed her nothing.

But it did no good to repine. She had planted them all in the type of fibre M. Laurient had used, she had made sure that the sphagnum moss throve, which should mean that the orchid, too, was getting the right amount of water, she had repotted whenever she could see that a plant was doubling up in its pot – not that this happened often, when most of them were in what could best be described as a state of suspended animation – in short, she had done her best.

Earlier in the war, she and M. Laurient had propagated seed and created some hybrid-seedlings which they had placed tenderly into the pot of a 'foster-parent' who would, by its very existence, see that the seedlings throve. Rochelle had always loved this orchidaceous habit, seeing herself as a seedling put out to grow strong in M. Laurient's pot, and she had helped him to put the tiny hybrids into boxes as they grew large enough to manage without the foster-parent, and then into their own small pots. It had broken her heart when she had lost so many the previous winter, but once again she had done her best. And she did still have quite a collection of different specimens, mainly from the coolhouse to be sure, and if the war ended quite soon, which it must surely do, with the Allies forcing the Germans back all over Europe, she would be able to heat one of the glasshouses again and the five-year-old hybrids she had watched over so carefully would certainly flower – and she would see for herself whether their experiment had succeeded, whether they really had created the Pure Madonna at last.

The snow which had accompanied Laurient's escape across the border soon cleared, but it was a warning. If I am not to be found one night, stiff as a board under some alien hedge, then I must find shelter for the next few months at least, he told himself, but it seemed a terrible imposition. What could he offer anyone, apart from the risk of certain and messy death if they were discovered harbouring an escaped prisoner?

Yet, in the end, he found somewhere.

He had been walking over the hills and through the woods, skirting the vineyards and the river, when he heard the dogs. A hunting pack by the sound of it. It was useless to tell himself that they could not be hunting him, because whether they were or not they could easily latch on to his scent and flush him out. Perhaps they were after someone else, or perhaps they were just being exercised, but the sound of their deep, bloodthirsty baying was too much for him and he left the vineyards and made for the nearest farm.

He hid in the farm-buildings until the dogs had gone, and then a girl came in to milk the cows and he addressed her, mildly, in his excellent French.

She was startled, but friendly enough, though not bright; she had a round, glossy face, tiny eyes and light-coloured hair, unkempt, mostly unbrushed, which went well with a body run to seed and clothing which had seen better days.

But she was sensible; a fellow-Frenchman on the run from the Nazis would always be given help, she assured him, and heard that he wanted to stay somewhere, had no place to go, needed succour which could, he hoped, last until the war was over.

She frowned, biting a fat lower lip.

'Here is too near civilisation,' she said at last. 'But I have a cousin, a woman alone, farming her land with the help of her old grandfather and no one else. You have no papers, of course?'

Regretfully, he shook his head.

'Oh, well . . . but I dare say it can be arranged. If someone has died they can sometimes fool the Boche. Would you go there? You would have to work hard . . . very hard . . . would your hands stand it?'

He noticed for the first time how his hands had turned

325

inwards; it must be the healing. He tried to bring them into a more natural position, but clearly they would not be forced.

'I'll work,' he said. 'I'll do whatever she wants.'

She nodded her big head, chins wobbling.

'Good. My man is fighting for the Free French, but I've plenty of help and the soil is rich. My cousin's land has much clay . . . it is harder to work and less rewarding. But you won't mind that.'

He smiled; he would welcome it, if it meant a degree of safety, an end to this perpetual wandering.

'I'll take you there tomorrow, then. We're harvesting still, so I can take her a load of grapes. It is perfectly possible to do so and rouse no one's suspicion – her grapes need the leaven of ours, which are sweeter and larger. You can hide in the cart until we're on our way, and then you can sit up beside me.'

Her name was Nana and she had long, light-coloured hair and a round, rosy-brown face rather like her cousin's. She was in her mid-forties, stout, good-natured, hardworking. And she accepted Laurient immediately, gladly, because the work, she said, was too much for her, though she started at dawn in the summer and worked until dark.

The old man, Grandpère Rabin, worked too, but mainly in the house whilst his granddaughter toiled outside. They had two cows and he milked them, a pig which he fed assiduously in the knowledge that in the days to come the pig would feed him, and acres of thin mountain land on which the grapes clung, small and gold, ripening in the autumn sun.

'The grapes don't make me much money,' Nana admitted to Laurient, when he had been working out on the hill all day with a big basket, picking as fast as he could. 'Lower down, where the land is flat and not so stony, it's also mostly clay. Vines don't like clay, and not much else does, either. So that's where we keep the pigs . . . only we've just got the one now . . . and the cattle, the hens and so on.'

'And you don't think you'll be asked about me?' Laurient said, amazed at her placid acceptance of his presence, his lack of papers, his thin story of his escape from Germany and the terribly scarred wrists. 'It doesn't worry you that the Gestapo might come?'

She shrugged.

'No one comes here. We have poor grapes and few possessions, and I have always been a plain woman. If the farm had been bigger, the grapes better, I might have been married for my money, but as it is I have none and wouldn't marry now anyway.'

'Then I'll stay,' Laurient said, though the old man, snuffling in the corner by the fire, muttered something about impetuous youth which almost made him smile. Nana did not look her age, it was true, but she certainly gave no impression of impetuous youth.

'Good. We'll work well together. I'll be happy to take your advice, for it's clear to me that you've worked the land before, though not, I imagine, vines?'

'No.' He had not told anyone that he came from Jersey and hesitated now, but decided against it. He was a British citizen, and she would be in greater danger if she was discovered to be harbouring him than if he had been a Frenchman. Perhaps he would tell her one day. But not yet.

Spring came, but Rochelle could not be happy even when the trees began carefully unfolding tiny green leaves. Radek was leaving, Tante Denise, though she hid it well, was deeply unhappy to be losing her foster-son, and food was so short that Rochelle had shudderingly stewed snails for the dogs, and eaten seagull for the first time. She only wished it could be the last, but if the Allies did not come

327

soon she supposed she might as well get used to eating horrible food simply to ensure that life continued.

On a day of flat calm, in mid-March, Radek and two Polish prisoners who had also managed to escape from the Nazis and stay hidden, left the L'Oyette place in their small rowing boat, heading out into the blue, bound for France.

Rochelle and Tante Denise stood, hand in hand, on the clifftop and watched the boat until it was just a speck, then they watched the speck until it met the horizon and disappeared over it. Only then did Tante Denise give a big gulp and mop at her suddenly overflowing eyes.

'He was a good, hardworking boy,' she said. 'I don't suppose I'll ever see him again, but . . . I'll miss him. He was a good boy.'

'You'll see him again,' Rochelle said comfortingly. 'How else is he going to come back to marry *me*?'

She and Tante Denise smiled, but there was a catch in Rochelle's throat which she tried very hard to deny. Men had already died by the thousand in this wretched, miserable war; probably thousands more would die before the end of it. She, who hated the Nazis for what they had done to M. Laurient, was ashamed and shocked now because she felt so sorry for them. There was worry in their once self-confident faces and many of the young boys – for they were little more – who were shipped in from the fighting as they were driven back were starving in real earnest. Rochelle's great-aunt had seen her cat taken and knew where it would end up, and Rochelle herself had seen young recruits eating the snails she had cooked for the dogs . . . worse, they ate rats when they could find them.

Europe was in Allied hands now, and as a result the German forces were falling back on the Channel Islands and, it seemed to the Jersey people, to their island in particular. You could not move a yard without seeing troops – and a poor, ragged, starving lot they were too. But they had guns and underground bunkers and quantities of ammunition and no one doubted that they would make a fight for it and kill half the Islanders in the process.

Electricity and gas were only turned on for a limited period each day, so once again cooked food was a rarity, and to Rochelle's consternation when she planted her seed potatoes German soldiers came in the night and dug them up for food. She cycled over to see Mme L'Oyette, who, remotely though she was situated, admitted that she was not going to plant her potatoes until it was all right to do so . . . until the German troops began to get fed again, she said. After so many years of being more or less safe from the occupying forces she was now seeing large numbers of men being marched down to the rocky shore to pick limpets; they told her they made soup with the aid of any root vegetable obtainable. Naturally, therefore, she could no longer rely on her crops being untouched nor on her livestock remaining untampered with.

Rochelle had the ghastly experience of seeing Pod, fat and jolly as ever, being bundled into a jeep. She ran after it, shouting, shrieking, with tears pouring down her cheeks, but Pod, as it turned out, was far too much of a character for even the hungriest peasant lad to devour. At least, late that night, when Rochelle and Senna had closed up and were drearily making themselves ready for bed, someone knocked loudly on the door.

It was a skinny lad with pockmarked skin, patchy hair and eyes so weary and depressed that once again the familiar feeling of pity rose in Rochelle's throat.

'Yes?' she said warily, however, and then exclaimed with joy as the boy pushed Pod into the room with one knee.

'Dog come in, I bring,' he said in a thick, guttural accent. 'Your dog, yes?'

'Oh, *yes*,' Rochelle said, on her knees on the floor with both arms round Pod's neck and their cheeks pressed close. 'How can I ever thank you?'

'Me peeck some green?' the boy said haltingly. He touched his mouth. 'Hongry . . . hongry.'

Rochelle had been hungry many times, but every two or three months now the Red Cross ship *Vega* brought a cargo of parcels for the Islanders. She got up off the floor and went into the pantry. She had a hard loaf of dark bread, some split pea soup and two large swedes. Recklessly she bundled the food into a bag, saving only a small amount of the pea soup and one slice of bread, and carried it back to the boy. She pointed to Pod, and then to the bag.

'Thank you, thank you,' she said fervently, pushing the bag into the boy's arms. 'I love my dog very much . . . thank you.'

The boy looked into the bag as if he could not believe his eyes and then he made a half gesture towards her, as though to give it back. They could not speak each other's language, but she knew he was saying that she should keep half.

Rochelle put her hand on the labrador's smooth head and felt the movement which meant Pod was wagging her tail. The dog was big and would have made this starving lad a good few meals; God knew what he had risked by returning Pod to her mistress. Firmly, she shook her head.

'No, the food is for you. Thank you again.'

She shooed him out, feeling very adult, and saw him cram bread into his mouth before he was more than a foot from the door.

Rochelle locked up again and went back to her pile of ragged blankets and cushions. It was a windy night and the draught under the back door was considerable but she and the dogs, all curled up together, would keep warm and snug enough until morning. That poor lad . . . he was welcome to what food she could spare, and at least she had some soup and bread for breakfast in the morning.

Just before she went to sleep, however, she remembered that there was to be a distribution of wood in St Helier next day. She would get up, eat her bread and soup – it was too thick with split peas to be drunk – and then make her way down to the harbour. It would be so good to have even the smallest fire, and a hot meal would be a real treat, even if it was only a pan of plain boiled potatoes. The milk ration had been suspended and butter was unobtainable, so mashed potatoes were out of the question.

'Glad to be home, Pod?' Rochelle enquired sleepily as the three of them curled up amongst the bedding. 'You don't know what a lucky girl you are!'

Pod's sleepy tail thumped twice and a warm pink tongue slapped across Rochelle's cheek. Soon, they all slept.

It was a fine day. The sun creeping through the little square window of the attic room in which he slept told Charles that the sky was blue and they would have a good day for ploughing the lower meadow.

It was not really a meadow; it was where Nana had kept the beasts when they had sufficient to make it worthwhile, and he was intent, now, on persuading her to cultivate it. The land was heavy, it was true, but what roses she could grow on it when the war was over! And as he listened to the wireless he knew that it was nearing its end, that soon the Allies would land in Europe and make their way, sweeping the Boche before them, into the heartland of France.

Over the months he had grown truly fond of Nana. She was a sweet, innocent woman, but staunch and true, with courage, humour and the ability to work most men into the ground.

She had stood by him, too, when the Gestapo had come. At her most bovine, she had blinked placidly at them, fed them with the best at her command, and referred to Charles as her poor old fiancé, Charles du Buisse, who had never plucked up the courage to marry her, but bedded her from time to time in the grape-picking season.

331

It made them laugh, though cruelly, scoffingly. They had made rude remarks about her vast behind, sneered at her tumbledown cottage, the thin vines, the gaunt old sow with her litter of piglets. They had taken all but two of the piglets with them, though ... but they had not taken Charles.

When it was over and they were gone she had stood very still, shaking all over. They had been after some American airmen who had parachuted into the region, but they had never questioned the elderly French peasant who had been working in the vineyard when they approached the place. Nana's explanation of his presence had satisfied them.

'Oh, Charles!' she said at last. 'Oh dear, how frightened I was!'

He had admired her tremendously then, capable even of the ultimate gift of deceiving herself, for she admitted that she had not allowed herself to acknowledge that fear until they were gone. He had put his arms round her and pulled her head on to his shoulder.

'Shake all you like now, little Nana,' he said. 'You are the bravest woman I know.'

She had smiled then, and pushed him away, shaking her head at herself.

'No time to waste in shaking for a fear that's past,' she said briskly. 'They've taken six of the piglets, but the calf is safe, and the hens. I hid a great many eggs so we'll have a mushroom omelette tonight, and some fried potato. I've some lard hidden under the house at the back.'

Charles got out of bed and started to dress. He would begin ploughing as soon as he had had his breakfast, try to get the work finished by nightfall, for he knew that as soon as it was safe to do so he must get nearer to Jersey. He could not go back until the war was over, of course, but he wanted to be closer, to feel that the island was within reach. Yet he owed it to Nana to start her off on her post-war career as a rose-grower if he possibly could.

She had green fingers, it was easy to see. No one else could have got the vines to cling to the thin-soiled mountain, no one else could have grown all their own vegetables on the poor ground available. And she loved flowers, always had a few growing round the cottage, though she cared little enough for the house itself. It was Charles, now, who accompanied her into the nearest market town, bought whitewash, kept the place at least tidy, whilst he worked away indoors in the winter, mending, cleaning, and keeping the weather where it belonged – on the far side of the four walls and the roof.

But of course he wanted to go home. He remembered the promise he had made to God that desperate night, though it gave him nightmares to think of it, but God must have known that the vow had been the raving of a mind very near its end. He would not hold Charles to that promise, even though it had been given from the heart.

Would He?

Today, though, he would plough the lower pasture. And tell Nana how to go about setting rose-trees when she could get hold of some. And later he would have to tell her that he would be leaving quite soon now. Any day, in fact. She would take it well; she was that sort of woman. He was very fond of her; he thought that she was good all through, a rare thing. She would wish him well, see him off with her steady smile, and then miss him . . . of course she would miss him. But she would know better than to think he would stay once the war was over. He owed it to his own people to go back, sort out their problems . . . see his orchids.

He did not miss the orchids. It was strange, that, he pondered as he went outside and harnessed the old horse to the plough. Once he had thought of nothing but PM23; now he was indifferent to the Royal family, though his interest would undoubtedly revive once he was back on the island with his glasshouses all round him and his plants waiting for his care.

He missed Rochelle, though. Missed her sorely. He thought about his girl often, in the night, and wondered how she was managing, what she would do when the war was over. She had taken the responsibility for Augeuil Manor for so long . . . how would she take it when he was home again?

She would be delighted, because they loved each other, he and she. No fonder father and daughter could you find, even though there was no blood-tie between them. If he had missed her, she would have missed him . . . they would go to the sea-cave when he got back and he would load her down with all the beautiful things and all the valuable things so that she could buy herself pretty clothes and go to dances and meet decent young men.

But it was a sweet summer day! The plough bit into the heavy clay soil and turned it, pinkish and thick as plum-cake, up towards the sun. By the time he had gone round the field three times he was totally content, the good smell of the earth beneath the blade and the soft summery scents of the tasselled grasses along the low stone wall reminding him of peacetime fields, of the checked tablecloths, the big stone jugs of cider, the pasties and pies for the harvesters.

By evening, he was a happy man, content with his lot. He went in, sweaty and tired, and Nana ran him a bath and helped him to wash his back. He had never been embarrassed to be naked in front of her, partly because she had sloshed water and soap over him and over Grandpère Rabin with equal disinterest, but now, for the first time, he put an arm round her substantial waist as he climbed out of the tin tub and squeezed her.

'Thanks, Nana. You're a good girl.'

To his surprise the colour flooded her face as though she were the girl he had called her. But she just gave him her placid smile and turned to the stove to see to the meal.

Grandpère was sitting in the corner by the warm fire; he was very tiny now, and, with Charles about to do so much work, he scarcely moved save to go to the table at meal-times and to make his way up to bed at night.

'In a few weeks I'll have to be moving on,' Charles continued. 'But not until the Allies have landed, of course. Shall we listen to the news?'

They could get the BBC loud and clear, and presently they heard of the Normandy landings, which had taken place the previous day, and of the Allies' forward march, towards Germany, through the occupied countries, liberating as they went.

'I'll go in a day or so,' Charles said. He looked at Nana. Her face was serene, untroubled. She just gave a little nod and passed him the potatoes. She would never show how she felt, he realised, if to do so would hurt him.

Two days later he left. It would be a long and perhaps a dangerous journey to the coast. It was clear that Jersey would not be liberated for a fair while. The island was heavily defended, full of German troops and prisoners of war, and the Allies were afraid of invading for fear of what would happen to the Islanders.

Nevertheless, he must go, to be nearer his own people. And he knew he owed it to Nana to tell her so.

He would have explained more fully, but she would not let him.

'I understand; of course you must go,' she said. 'Whatever your nationality, your place is at home. I couldn't leave here. If I was taken away by a war I would return. It's my place and I suppose I love it, in my way.'

'I'll come back when the war's over, bring you roses,' he said eagerly. 'You've saved my life, cared for me, shared everything you have with me. I will never forget you, and I must try to repay, just a little.'

She shook her head then. Was her face too impassive,

too blandly lacking in feeling? But it was her one defence, and he would scorn to try to see beyond it.

'No. You've worked very hard, repaid me already. I took no risks, and thanks to you we've kept the place going, which I couldn't have done with only Grandpère to help. Go now, Charles. Don't come back; it would be silly and unnecessary. I won't forget you, either.'

He sensed rather than heard the wistful longing in her tone, but he shut his ears to it because she was right. He must be in his own place, with his own people. Oh, he had been happy here, but only as a stranger.

She got up, when he did, as dawn was touching the vines with grey and the birds were stirring sleepily in the hedges and trees. She went with him, down to the road. He would go on foot, with a back-pack of provisions to keep him fed as long as possible.

In the early light, with a strong wind blowing, they faced one another across the narrow white road. The wind blew her hair out behind her and for a moment she looked like a young girl, and the beauty of her face, which was in its strong bone formation and the perfect, matt cream of her skin, was there for him to see and marvel over.

He stared, like an idiot, and he knew he was trying to imprint her likeness on to his memory so that in the days to come he could see her again, made beautiful by the dawn light and the strong, tugging wind.

'Oh, Charles!' She was laughing at him, teasing. 'Don't look like that. You know you must go – and you're glad to go, too.'

He shook his head, puzzled at himself, then raised a hand and turned away. Towards the coast. Towards Normandy. Towards the island.

'The guy says they're moving us again.'

Solly spoke German and had been of great value when

they wanted to know just what was going on, but now he sighed and spread his hands rather wearily.

The advance of the Allies had been obvious almost from the moment the nine men had been captured, by the way they had been moved around. Laurie said it would have been a good deal simpler just to hand them back to their compatriots as they advanced, but the Germans, it seemed, had other ideas. Every time the various transit camps looked like being liberated the Americans were shoved into a truck and taken somewhere else.

'Again? Does he know where we're going from here?' Laurie leaned on the windowsill and peered to each side. They were in a hastily converted schoolhouse and they could actually see the sea if they looked out of the windows and peered round to the right. 'Unless they intend to put us aboard a ship, I don't see how they can keep us out of Allied hands much longer, do you?'

'Out into the wide blue yonder,' Tom Besnick said wistfully. 'Wouldn't mind a sea voyage – what is that sea, anyway? The Med?'

Howls of derision told him that he was wrong.

'It's the Channel,' Solly said. 'Gee, perhaps they'll take us to England! The guard did say something about an island.'

Laurie stood back from the barred windows and stared incredulously at the dark little navigator, sitting on a school desk and eating a plum. So far as he knew there was only one group of islands near this coast occupied by the Germans . . . could Solly possibly mean them?

'Did he say the Channel Islands, Solly?' he asked. 'Or did he just say islands in the Channel?'

Solly shrugged and copped his plum stone into the empty grate. It was early April, and although they made a fuss and insisted that the fire be lit each evening it was warm enough during the day – they had been moved about so much that they were still in their flying clothes and tended, if anything, to suffer from heat rather than cold.

'Don't recall he said either,' he drawled. 'Just an island.'

'Oh,' Laurie said, his hopes rather dashed. 'Better wait and see then, eh?'

'Or make a break for it when we're being moved,' Louis, the tail-gunner, suggested. Of all of them he was the most anxious to regain their toehold in Britain – he was deeply in love with a Norfolk girl and pined for her more, the others told him, than they pined for a sight of America.

'We'll see,' Laurie told him. 'No point in making a dash for it and getting killed, when if we wait another day we might get liberated.'

'Here comes dinner,' Tex remarked presently, from his station at the second schoolroom window which gave a view over the schoolyard. 'It's hot, that's about all you can say.'

They were not badly fed but the meals were boring and repetitive, with a great deal of bread, potatoes and cereal, no fruit save for the plums they picked during their exercise in the yard outside – the plum trees leaned over the tall fences and must have been a great temptation to the children when the school was used as such – and quantities of bitter ersatz coffee to drink. But Laurie had urged them all to eat whatever was offered, because they had to keep their strength up, and he knew how easy it would be to leave their food and find that, as a result, they were being offered less and less.

They were halfway through an unappetising stew, in which potatoes and swedes predominated, when the door to the schoolroom opened and the round, red face of one of the guards peered round it. He addressed Solly, having already discovered that it was worse than useless trying to speak to any of the others. Laurie wondered whether he recognised the storm of abuse and evil suggestions which

338

came from them as antagonistic, or whether he merely thought they were being friendly.

Solly abandoned his tin plate and went over to the door, presently coming back not only with information, but also with a square, sticky concoction which he proceeded to divide into nine small pieces.

'We're moving in about an hour, and there's another guy they've picked up who'll be coming with us,' he announced. 'We'll be marched a few miles down to a port of some description, and then we'll be put aboard a boat.' He looked at Laurie. 'You were right, fella. We're off to those Channel Islands you talk about . . . Jersey, the guy says. Apparently there's a camp of some sort on Alderney too, but that's for . . .' he shook his head '. . . I couldn't make it out, but some inferior sort of prisoner, evidently. So we're Jersey-bound.'

Two hours later, marching along a winding lane with their boots stirring up the dust, the men discussed, in muted tones, their chances of escape. The new guy, a fighter pilot from a P51 which had been shot down on its way back from a raid over Berlin, told them how he had suffered in a prison hospital as his own pals, supposed to be bombing nearby military installations, frequently missed and hit civilian targets instead, including the hospital, in which many other American and British pilots were being treated.

Since coming out of hospital he had suffered the shunting about which Laurie and his crew found so tiresome. He had crossed Germany in trains, in buses and on foot, sometimes with German troops, sometimes with other prisoners. He said that the whole country was lousy with prisoners, and that the German people were sure they would soon be completely overrun. As far as he could see everyone's main thought was just to move prisoners on, away from their own particular area of responsibility.

'You should see the slave workers, and the rats . . . the

sheer destruction created by the bombing raids,' he told Laurie, as the two of them marched side by side through the misty sunshine. 'It's called saturation bombing, and, Jeez, it's that all right. In fact, that's why I'm here and not in the camp they finally allocated me to.'

'Tell,' Laurie demanded. The new guy, Rocky Tarpallin, was not the sort of person who would simply jump camp for the sake of it. If he'd got out of a camp in Germany and somehow wangled himself this near the coast, he was worth knowing.

'Two of us dug our way out,' Rocky said laconically. 'We were lucky, I guess. We got separated when we were nearly in France, but Frankie's home an' dry by now, I reckon. I got picked up – no papers. They threw me into the local slammer while they decided what to do with me, then fetched me along here.'

'Well, you're getting nearer your base,' Laurie said. 'We're headin' for the Channel Islands . . . for Jersey, in fact.'

'We are? That's great, but if you ask me we'll be home soon. The Huns are on their beam-ends – bumming food off their prisoners half the time. Where's this, d'you reckon, Laurie?'

They had entered a small town and were marching along a sunny street, lined with houses, which led on to a quay where a large motor boat was moored. A crowd of interested locals had joined them, drifting along beside them apparently undeterred by their armed guard. A tanned, white-haired man who had been level with Laurie seemed to want to speak; he was watching the young airmen closely.

'Did you say Jersey, Laurie?' the white-haired man asked.

'Sure,' Laurie said, grinning at the man's use of his name, which he had obviously heard Rocky use moments earlier. He looked curiously at the man, then dropped his eyes and saw that the stranger's hands were severely mutilated, purple with scar-tissue and bent inwards at the wrists.

Embarrassed by the wounds, Laurie did not look towards him again as the long line of prisoners shuffled to a halt, but he felt the man's hand on his, sliding something into his fingers. It was an apple, with a bit of paper wrapped round it, and the stranger was speaking in French now, so fast that Laurie could not possibly follow. Apparently Solly could, though, for he said something back in his drawling but fluent French.

'What was all that about?' Laurie said, as the queue began to move slowly forward, leaving the bystanders behind. 'My French is lousy. Did you see the poor bum's scars, though? He'd sure been in trouble.'

'Yeah. Poor guy. He said he'd written down what he wanted done, after the war . . . to bring villains to justice, he said.' Solly looked round just as they reached the gangplank and stumbled, so that Laurie had to pull him up the first few feet of it. 'Say, we're on board . . . next soil we touch'll be British!'

The boat was pitching a good deal, even in the harbour. Laurie had to grab the rail to keep his footing. He shoved the apple with its wrapping into his pocket, then tried to extract the paper to see what the Frenchman had written. But it was too rough; he needed both hands just to hold himself steady. As the men continued to come aboard he, Solly and Rocky crouched in the stern, clutching anything they could get hold of to stop them being thrown about. And presently, when the boat moved from the comparative calm of the harbour into the open sea, Laurie forgot all about the apple and the Frenchman. He was too busy leaning over the rail and losing every meal he had ever eaten – or at least that was what it felt like.

When he was empty he just lay where he dropped, wondering if he would live to see Jersey. Once he heard

341

someone say they were approaching land and hoisted himself to his knees to peer ahead, but all he saw was the heaving, grey-white water, and just looking at it sent his stomach into convulsions once more.

When the boat docked, Laurie had to be helped on to dry land. He tried very hard to feel emotion as his feet touched the same ground as his father's, but his main thought was overwhelming relief that the voyage was over.

'Put him there for a moment,' a stiff-necked officer in dire need of a shave said to Solly and Rocky, who were supporting their friend. 'You'll be told where to go presently.'

Laurie lolled on a pile of fishboxes and watched indifferently as men marched about, formed into lines and were led away from the quayside. But presently, looking about him with more interest, he realised that there were a great many people hanging about who, when they had seen enough, simply left to return to the town.

Why should not he follow suit? Laurie got rather stiffly off his fishboxes, yawned, stretched, and set off at a saunter in the direction of the town. He fished the apple out of his pocket, crumpling the paper deeper down, and took a bite. He felt better already. If anyone pursued him he would say he was trying to contact his fellow-prisoners. If they did not . . .

They did not.

Half an hour later, weak and still hollow but completely free, Laurie found himself on the outskirts of the town on a hilly road which wandered along between high hedges. The wind was beginning to drop and it would not be long, he realised, before dusk caught him. Better be off the road by then and in some sort of shelter, for all occupied countries had a curfew of some description.

He walked on and presently came to a long, low shape over a hedge which turned out to be a vegetable clamp. He did not much fancy raw swede, but it was better than

342

nothing, he supposed, so he took a couple and walked on till he came to a little shed which had once, judging by the smell, contained chickens. Laurie entered the shed, took some hay from a nearby stack, rolled himself up in it, and soon slept the sleep of the totally exhausted.

He woke when the sun told him it was mid-day and his wristwatch confirmed the fact. Crawling out of the chicken shed, Laurie was conscious of two things. The first was a thirst which would take a river to slake, and the second was a tiny frisson of uncertainty. It was all very well to be free and heading for his father's home, but just where was it? Augeuil Manor was only a name – the tiny village nearby was simply another name. He had no map, and if he asked the way he would be marked at once as a stranger. But provided he chose a local and not a member of the occupying force he should be safe enough. His father was a Jerseyman, after all, and Laurie had heard about the men and women of these islands who were struggling on with a massive German presence yet never collaborating, never giving in.

Which should he ask for, though? The manor or the village? He supposed that it was safest to ask for Rozville, for he might be visiting anyone there. The manor would tie him in at once with his father.

Presently, he saw a village ahead of him, or perhaps a hamlet was nearer the mark. At any rate a cluster of cottages, a shop, and a square, gold-stoned manor house. When he got near enough he saw women queuing outside the shop and a man shoeing a horse in front of what was still a garage.

Laurie approached the smith, who had just replaced the horse's hoof on the ground and was talking gently to the animal as he backed it and changed its position.

'Good morning,' Laurie said a little stiffly, trying to sound a bit English and a bit French. 'A fine day, is it not?'

The man straightened. He was dark-haired, with shrewd hazel eyes which swept up and down Laurie in a remarkably quick and comprehensive survey.

'Yes, it's nice to see the sun,' he said pleasantly. 'Come far?'

'Mm . . . I'm heading for Rozville,' Laurie said, keeping his voice down. 'Can you tell me which way I should go?'

'Got a compass?' The smith grinned at him. 'Flyers sometimes carry them, I believe.'

Laurie moved nearer the man.

'How did you know?'

The smith indicated Laurie's jacket with a jerk of the chin. 'That thing, *mon ami*, is what you might call a dead giveaway, I believe. We have no Huns in flying jackets, nor any Islanders. Wait, I'll send you on your way with a guide for a half mile or so.' He looked intently at Laurie's pale face. 'You are thirsty? You have hunger?'

'Yes to both,' Laurie said. 'But a guide would be more welcome than anything.'

The man nodded, then picked up the horse's hoof and cradled it on his knee.

'Go and sit in the sun for ten minutes. Then I'll be with you.'

The smith gave Laurie a bottle of cold tea to carry away with him and a drink of thin beer. From somewhere he conjured up a thick sandwich packed with tomato. And he produced a skinny boy of ten who, he said, knew the district like the back of his hand – as they all did – and would take Laurie most of the way to Rozville.

The food and drink lessened Laurie's feeling of sickness and the slight dizziness which overtook him if he turned quickly or bent over, and the little boy's chatter and friendly companionship helped to make the four or five miles they travelled together easier to bear. When they entered a wooded valley, however, the boy stopped.

344

'The village is straight down this road. You can't miss it,' he said importantly. 'There is a small harbour and a quay . . . a nice beach, some shops . . . who do you want to see there?'

'A Monsieur Charles,' Laurie said. 'I don't know his other name.'

'Well, ask at the shop, she knows everyone,' his small companion said with complete confidence. 'Only don't go to the back door. She keeps geese and they're very fierce – I'm scared of them.'

Laurie thanked the boy and then said casually, 'These woods . . . are they private property or can anyone walk in them?'

The boy shrugged.

'No one will harm you if you walk in them, I suppose,' he said. 'But if you go through these woods and across some meadows and into a sunken lane you come to the land belonging to Augeuil Manor. You'd best keep away from there – the Germans requisitioned it years ago and they have it still. It wouldn't do to be caught nearby.'

It was a stunning blow. Laurie just stood, staring at the child, who turned away, a hand casually raised.

'Goodbye . . . straight down the road now . . . good luck!'

He was almost out of sight before Laurie managed to get the words out.

'Wait! If the manor's been taken, where are the family?'

The boy paused, his thick brows drawing together in a frown.

'Well, not in the manor . . . somewhere on the estate, I suppose. Goodbye!'

This time Laurie let him go, but did not at once follow the road into the village. Instead he stood stock still, biting his thumbnail and trying to work out what he had best do. Useless to go into the village and ask around – the boy had told him unwittingly what he needed to know. He even knew how to reach the manor, for the lad had pointed out the direction he wanted. But did he want it? How would he find his father now?

As soon as the apple and the paper had changed hands, Charles drifted away from the waterfront. He was in a state of euphoria, scarcely knowing where he was or what he had done.

The young man in the shabby flying jacket . . . he had heard another man call him Laurie, and suddenly, as he looked, it was as though the scales had fallen from his eyes. The dark young face could have been his, thirty years ago. It seemed an impossible coincidence, yet he was sure he had just met his own son. Was that why he had entrusted to him the bit of paper with instructions on it as to where he had hidden the roll of film showing the Russian prisoners? He would be returning to Jersey himself as soon as he could, but he had felt so strongly that he must get a message back so that the guilty should be punished as they deserved. After all, the war was not yet over. He might die, and if he did the secret of the film's hiding place would die with him.

That was why he had painfully printed the note with his poor, crippled fingers clenched round the pencil. Not just because another Charles Laurient, somewhere deep inside him, kept warning him that the film might never be recovered if he did nothing. That other Charles Laurient was trying to tell him something, and it was something he did not wish to hear or understand.

Of course I'll go back, Charles said crossly to himself now, pushing through people and heading for the back streets once more. Of course I will, when the war's over and there are boats for civilians. Why, I could be back in Augeuil Manor in a couple of weeks, hugging the child, seeing the staff, examining the orchids . . .

And in return I promise You . . . oh, dear God, You can have my girl and my island.

346

He had tried to forget the words, but they were burned deep into his memory, deeper than the ghastly scars on his wrists. He remembered the pain, the awfulness of the fear, the terror of making even the tiniest movement.

You do know the pain. Of course You do. You suffered, too . . . worse, probably. Take them . . . my girl, my island.

In his mind's eye, he saw again the wreck of the perimeter fence, the ruined tower, the quiet woodland.

But God was merciful; He would understand that a man would make promises in extremis which he could not possibly be expected to keep.

Take them . . . my girl, my island.

Well, naturally, in unbelievable pain, in desperate fear . . .

He waited until the crowd had dispersed, then returned to the quayside. It looked normal enough; gulls squabbled over a rotten plaice, a cat stalked, tail erect, in the shade of a pile of planking. He looked away from the land, out to sea. Somewhere out there was a tiny dot of an island, his birthplace, the place that was dearest to him on earth. And on the island was a girl who was his daughter in all but blood, and a boy who was his son.

If he turned away now, if he left, he would never see them again . . . his girl, his island – or his son.

But a promise is a promise.

Charles Laurient turned and left the quayside. His face was set and there was pain in his eyes, but there was peace, too.

In the end, Laurie decided to go to the manor and see if he could find a friendly gardener or someone else who could give him the information he needed. He might even spot his father at some point. But it was dusk, the light failing rapidly, by the time he saw the manor through the trees. He recognised it at once from the photographs in the magazine, and gazed longingly at what had once been his

347

promised land. But then he moved away, because he would have to find somewhere to sleep, and he was desperately in need of a drink, as well, the smith's bottle of cold tea being long gone.

He found a stream in a meadow, drank deeply, and filled his bottle, then made his way back into the woods. On the outskirts of the estate was a long-abandoned shed, tumble-down and smelly. But it had part of its roof and would mean that if someone came by he would not be immediately visible as he slept.

Once more he took hay inside with him, rolled it into a bed-shape and lay down on it. So near at last! He had seen the orchard, the wide lawn, even the roofs of the green-houses . . . his father would not be far away. Probably tomorrow they would find one another.

He was almost asleep when it occurred to him that there was one place he would certainly find his father, and probably at a very early hour, before the sun was up. The greenhouses! A good gardener always visited his most precious plants early, particularly if they were greenhouse reared, because, depending on the day, so much might well need to be done. If it looked like being fine, windows must be opened; if a scorcher, blinds drawn down. If it was wet and chilly the heating must be adjusted.

I'll go to the greenhouses as soon as it's light, Laurie vowed sleepily. I'll be there before him. What a surprise, to find the son he had never set eyes on at work on his precious plants! The thought excited him, yet even so, he slept.

Rochelle always visited the orchids as early as she could, and today was no exception. It was going to be hot, for though the sun had not yet put in an appearance there was a fine, white mist curling across the big lawn and swirling between the trees in the orchard. Over the stream it hung

348

thick, cottonwool white, and this almost always meant they were in for a hot and sunny day.

Rochelle was feeling rather pleased with herself. The plants were doing well, better than she had hoped, and though PM23 would not flower this year there was a fair chance that it might do so next, especially if she could find some means of heating the glasshouse through the coming winter.

Rochelle dipped her can into the soft water tank and began vigorously misting. She enjoyed the job; the fine spray falling on leaves and buds was so clearly appreciated by the plants. She felt she could see the grateful leaves stirring, drinking, almost hear the tiny voices she had imagined so clearly when she was six or seven.

It made her feel hungry, though, to see the orchids so plainly being satisfied. Wish I was filled up by water, Rochelle thought wistfully; how lovely it would be never to have that empty, unsatisfied feeling in her middle again. But still, there was breakfast to come. It might only be cold macaroni with a bit of salt sprinkled on it, but she had had worse – only yesterday, in fact, she had done without breakfast altogether because she had run out of food and had no means of procuring any more until she could get into St Helier. But she had bicycled in later and had managed to buy her bread ration and the macaroni she would presently eat, sharing it with Pod and Senna because food for the dogs was getting more and more difficult to come by. Indeed when you saw young lads scarcely out of their teens begging for food and eating it, when it was given, like starving wolves, you felt quite guilty at searching for frogs and beetles and dead seabirds to feed a couple of elderly labradors.

Misting finished, Rochelle half opened windows and drew down the blinds facing the east. Some of the hardier orchids were flowering now, the pollen thickly clustered, and Rochelle thought that later she would come down with her wand and do some fertilising, see if she could have a hybrid or two of her own, war-babies, in five or six years' time. Last year's seedlings were looking pretty sturdy, and though of course none of the tropicals flowered any more – it just not being warm enough to tempt them into bud – some of them were still alive, their greenery smaller than it should have been but lush enough.

Finishing her tasks, Rochelle wandered around checking that all was well, reluctant for some reason to leave, though the cold macaroni called her empty stomach. She thrust a stick into her liquid manure and stirred it briskly. It was mainly guano, and she was a bit frightened of it since she had killed off a whole section of the orchids by using it last year. It must have been too strong, she mused now. But she would know better next time, would water it down . . . and it was good stuff. She had produced gigantic potatoes by watering them with the liquid during a hot, dry spell last summer.

She lifted the stick, twirled it round, and laid it carefully on the tiles. She turned to leave the greenhouse, then stopped short, a hand flying to her mouth. Someone was just the other side of the door. She could see a man's figure through the whitewash . . . he was bending to take the door handle, the door was opening, he was coming in . . .

The man came into the greenhouse and just for one moment Rochelle thought she knew him. Her heart gave an enormous bound and she felt a smile stretch right across her face, knew that her love beamed out of her eyes.

Before she could stop herself she exclaimed: 'Oh, monsieur, you've come back!'

Her euphoria lasted less than ten seconds; then she saw that he was a much younger man and one, furthermore, whom she had never met. He was staring at her almost hungrily. Faint colour stained his pale cheeks, his mouth opened . . .

'It's you! I knew it wasn't a dream, I knew it!'

350

And then, to Rochelle's horror, he pitched forward on his face, crashing into the staging, and slumped on to the tiles.

Can you recognise someone you have never met, Rochelle wondered, as she heaved the young man over on to his back. But she did recognise him . . . it must be M. Laurient's American son. He was so like his father! The same shape of face, the same thick, dark hair, even the same nose. Yet already she could see he was taller than her M. Laurient, huskier, with a breadth of shoulder and a narrowness of hip which was totally unlike the sturdier figure of the older man.

And, having recognised him, Rochelle found that she still resented him. After all her guilty, sublimated hopes, he had come to find his father. But perhaps he would go away again when she told him that his father was no longer here, perhaps he would go back to America and never bother them again. It never occurred to Rochelle to wonder what he was doing or how he had got here. All that mattered was his presence, her only thought how she could get rid of him and ensure that he did not return.

He had fainted, she thought scornfully; what a weak, babyish sort of thing for a grown man to do! And then she looked more closely at him and saw how pale he was and realised that he could only be an escaped prisoner of war and felt, for the first time, a stab of guilt for her hard-heartedness, a pang of pity for him. He must have fainted from lack of food and water. She must get him back to the dower house before someone from the manor began to stir.

He came round when she threw water into his face and sat up, blinking, rubbing his eyes, smoothing the water from his face and then licking the wet palm of his hand.

'I'm sorry,' he mumbled. 'Don't know what happened . . . is there any water?'

Rochelle filled the dipper and held it to his lips. She

knew the water was warm but he gulped it thirstily, then smiled at her. He had a very nice smile. It lit the dark eyes, made him look younger, less ill.

'I'm sorry, I don't know you, but I'm searching for my father, Charles Laurient. My name's Daniel Laurient.'

Rochelle nodded curtly.

'Yes. I'm Rochelle, M. Laurient's adopted daughter.'

He stared at her, his eyes seeming almost to stroke her face so that a little flush burned across her cheeks and she knew her eyes brightened with embarrassment. But he was looking puzzled.

'Rochelle? But ... she's just a child ... twelve? Thirteen?'

'I'm sixteen,' Rochelle said. 'I thought you'd recognised me. When you came in you said something ...'

She could almost see him remembering and being embarrassed. He coughed and looked down.

'Yes. It was just for a minute ...' He looked up at her again, eyes brightening. 'You recognised me, too – you said something about my coming back.'

'I thought you were M. Laurient, just for a moment,' Rochelle explained stiffly. 'He ... he isn't here, you know.'

'Not here?' The young man's face fell. All the happiness seemed to drain out of it in a moment, leaving it bereft. 'Not on the island?'

'No. The Germans deported him nearly two years ago. He was caught after curfew, listening to a wireless. He'd been helping Russian prisoners, slave workers ... they sent him to a camp in Germany.'

'I see.' He shook his head as though to clear it, then looked up at her from his seat on the floor. 'What'll I do now, then?'

Go away, Rochelle longed to shout. Go back to America and forget us, never come here again. But she said nothing of the sort, because she knew very well that he could do no such thing even if he wanted to.

352

'Come back to the dower house with me,' she said as kindly as she could. 'I'll get you something to eat, and a hot drink if I can. And then we'll think what you should do next.'

The young man tried to get to his feet and, with her help, succeeded at the second attempt. Once she had got him upright Rochelle propped him against the staging and went to open the greenhouse door, peering cautiously out. It was still very early, the sun had not yet risen . . . and yet so much had happened! Her whole life had changed in a few short minutes. But the coast was clear, so she put her arm round his waist and they walked together out of the door, across the patch of ground which had once been a garden but was now mainly waist-high weeds and straggly cabbages, and into the woods.

After a meal of hot soup and several slices of bread, followed by some boiled cabbage, the young American looked a good deal better. He sat to one side of the stove in a saggy old armchair and told her something about himself. He had flown the big Liberator aircraft they sometimes saw overhead, and his crew were all in Jersey as well since they had been shot down together.

He had been stationed in England, he told her, in Norfolk, and had waxed quite lyrical over the beauties of that part of the world until she reminded him, sharply, that Jersey was a gem of an island and when he knew it better . . .

She had stopped short then, wanting to bite her tongue out, to take the words back. She was accepting that he would stay, accepting his presence here. But then the dogs came in and Senna wandered across the kitchen to nuzzle against the young American's knee. Pod stared at him, tail gently waving, and he called to her.

'Here, Pod . . . come say hello, like this big fella.'

'How did you know her name?' Rochelle asked curiously,

353

as Pod followed Senna's example. She was watching the young man's face as she spoke and just for a moment read total puzzlement there, before a sort of comprehension dawned.

'Oh . . . guess my father must've mentioned it. It's an odd sort of name for a dog. What's this fella called?'

'Senna,' Rochelle said automatically. 'Did your . . . your father write to you much, Daniel?'

She felt betrayed, as though M. Laurient had deliberately kept a long correspondence hidden from her, but the young man's next words gave the lie to her thoughts.

'I only ever had two letters from him . . . and say, honey, my name's Daniel but all my pals call me Laurie. Even my mom calls me Laurie.'

'Right. Laurie. Look, I have to go out. It would be hard for me to find enough food for us both, but I've a friend in . . . in good circumstances, I suppose you could say. I'll see whether she can get me some extra rations . . . oh!'

She had remembered the cache in the woods; if this young man, this Laurie, would help her, they could start using the food in the store again. And he knew she had thought of something; he looked at her, his eyes questioning.

'What?'

'I'm not sure . . . I'll have to think it over. You stay here. I'll leave Senna indoors and take Pod with me. And I'll see what I can arrange.'

Senna was still leaning against Laurie's leg whilst the young man caressed him, pulling the big, soft ear flaps gently through his fingers. Senna sighed blissfully and closed his eyes, nudging Laurie's hand whenever the caress showed signs of stopping. He had always been a man's dog, Rochelle remembered, quicker to run to M. Laurient than to her, always eager to do his master's bidding. Rochelle was putting on her clogs, and now she snapped her fingers. Pod came at once, eyes bright at the prospect of an outing, but Senna stayed with Laurie.

'Stay indoors, and if Senna barks or growls go upstairs and hide in a cupboard or under one of the beds,' Rochelle ordered as she stood in the doorway preparing to leave. 'I'll be back before evening.'

'Before evening? I sure hope so – I'll be so hungry I'll have eaten the dog if you're much longer!'

He meant it as a joke but Rochelle could not smile. He did not know how some people lived. He sat there with his broad American shoulders and his strongly muscled arms and never knew that some people would eat frogs and beetles just to stay alive.

'I'll be as quick as I can,' she said woodenly, and hurried out into the warm morning, glad to be able to wrestle with her problems without the young American's calm gaze upon her. You could see that despite his years – she thought he was twenty-two or three – he knew nothing of life. He came from one of the richest countries in the world, had never gone short of food, had never been forced to be polite to a race he despised just to keep on living.

But she would not give him away. She would keep him here at the dower house, until the war was over. In a way it would be quite a triumph to be able to present M. Laurient with his son when he came home, as well as with a flowering PM23, if the orchid had matured enough by then. She hugged the thought of his pleasure to her as she headed for the greenhouses. Orchids flourishing, dogs still alive, Radek free to fight for the Allies and Laurie here to welcome him, and all as a result of Rochelle's efforts.

It would not be easy, though, to keep Laurie fed, nor to hide him from the German soldiers who were always around in the grounds of the manor. They took little enough notice of Rochelle herself, but would surely question the presence of a young man, and a sturdy one at that.

355

Unless, somehow, she could trick them, pass him off as someone else?

She had done most of the work with the orchids earlier, but now she simply wanted to think. And finally, after a lot of soul-searching, she decided she could put her plan into action. She left the greenhouse behind, leaving the door open in case passing bees should want to do some pollinating for her, and headed determinedly for the manor.

Left alone in the old house, Laurie went through it room by room, not because he expected to find anything but simply to satisfy his curiosity. The girl Rochelle lived here alone, but why all in one room? And was she really so short of food? First he would examine the pantry.

It was a short examination. The pantry was the walk-in sort with a marble slab to keep things cool, a meat safe, a vegetable rack and a large number of shelves.

There was a bread crock containing one very large, greyish-looking loaf, and there were a handful of potatoes in the vegetable rack together with a swede and three skinny carrots. There was half the cabbage they had eaten that day and a packet of dried peas, almost empty. Other than that there was nothing. Empty shelving, empty hooks in the ceiling which had once held strings of onions and sides of bacon, an empty meat safe.

Laurie bent and looked under the shelves. An empty mousetrap, thick with velvet dust, seemed to indicate that not even mice troubled to enter Rochelle's pantry any more. No wonder the poor kid had looked so worried at the thought of having another mouth to feed!

Then he went into the study. The room had a cold and unused air, and fungus grew on the windowsill. The books on the shelves were mould-spotted, and the account books and papers were so damp that he doubted whether they were usable. He could see, now, why Rochelle had carried all her books, clothing and personal possessions into the

356

kitchen; at least that room had the stove lit now and again and the warmth of human presence.

The parlour was worse than the study, mainly because someone, presumably Rochelle, had chopped up most of the furniture, he assumed for firewood. She had spared a pretty china cabinet with what looked like a full Sèvres tea-service behind the glass, but she had briskly chopped legs and arms off every chair, and little antique occasional tables littered the floor like rather splendid trays with not a leg between them, though for some reason she had left the tops intact. Perhaps she could not bring herself to destroy the careful work, the deep shine, but he thought it likelier that the wood had proved to be a poor burner.

Upstairs, one bedroom, the main one, he suspected, was almost unchanged. The bedstead was brass, the mattress feather, and both were intact. There was a built-in ward-robe, also intact, and a chest of drawers which lacked only one drawer. The marble-topped washstand, however, was legless and the bedroom chair, a spindly thing once, was now just a seat and half the back.

The next room, presumably Rochelle's own, was a sorry sight. The spring and the headboard of the bed were left and nothing else. It had been, needless to say, a wooden bed. The chest of drawers gaped, drawerless, and the top had gone. Splinters all over the floor showed pretty plainly what had happened, and two chair-seats, rather ornate ones with tapestry covers, mutely drew Laurie's attention to the lack of chairs.

There was a built-in cupboard here too, but this one had not been left alone. Someone had tried very hard to chop the broad oak door down; it leaned, but had not given way. Bloody but unbowed, Laurie thought, and had a mental picture of the skinny girl whose name was Rochelle, axe raised, mouth tight, hacking away and nursing bruised fingers and painful wrists every time the axe bounced harmlessly off the hard wood. The cupboard door, he

357

concluded ruefully, was not the only one bloody but unbowed. How many girls of her age would have set about systematically burning their own home down just to stay alive? How many would have succeeded in keeping alive not only themselves but two old dogs and countless frail orchids as well?

Laurie went downstairs again. He sat down and called the dog over to him, then set about thinking. The girl Rochelle resented him, that was clear. Why? Was it because they were joint heirs to the manor? But she should not mind – he did not intend to press any claims save to his father's affection.

She did not know that, of course. Could not know it. Yet she did not seem the sort of girl who would resent sharing material things . . . look at the way she had fed him out of her tiny store. And he had no doubt that she would continue to do so, however much she might dislike it.

The only other reason, then, for her resentment had to be jealousy, and that he really could understand. She clearly adored Charles Laurient, and had done her utmost to keep his orchids alive and his home, if not sacrosanct, at least habitable.

She'll come round, Laurie told himself, tugging the old dog's ears and hearing Senna sigh with ecstasy. She's fierce with me now, and a bit afraid, probably, but she'll come round. He could not remember that odd dream in any detail, but he could remember the look on her face because he had seen it, for a split second, when he had first entered the greenhouse and she had believed him to be Charles Laurient.

He realised, with a small sense of shock, that he would give a great deal to see that look again – directed at himself.

15

When Laurie had been at the dower house for two days, Rochelle decided they had better see if they could open up the food cache. The young American was used to eating large amounts of food, and at this time of year, with potatoes and other vegetables in short supply, quantity was a problem. However, with some of the tinned meat and fish from the cache, Rochelle knew she would be able to swop enough bread and potatoes to at least partially satisfy her guest.

So early one morning, when the weather seemed set fair, Rochelle told Laurie about the food store.

'I'm game,' Laurie said at once. 'But it'll be the first real test, won't it, of whether I'm going to be challenged as an outsider?'

Rochelle had gone up to the manor earlier, and had fallen into conversation with the cook, a man she knew slightly since they sometimes met when Rochelle was working in her part of the vegetable garden and the cook was digging potatoes or cutting cabbage in his part.

'My cousin from L'Etacq is staying with me,' she had told him. 'His mother finds herself hard pressed to feed him, so she said he could come and give me a hand for a few weeks in return for his keep.'

'And you're having difficulty, eh?' the cook said indulgently. 'Well, we mustn't let the lad starve.'

He had given her a bag of potatoes and Rochelle, who had prided herself on never taking food from a German, had put a good face on it and accepted them. But she and Laurie had worked together a couple of times in the greenhouses, quite openly, and he had not been challenged, so perhaps her story had gone the rounds and been believed.

Now, however, Rochelle shook her head.

'No, not really, because I hope we shan't be seen. But it'll be nice to have some proper food for a change.'

The two of them set out into the misty morning, with the sun already strong enough to warm their backs as they walked. Rochelle went a little ahead, wondering how much food was actually left in the store. Except for what they had given to Tante Denise and Radek, she and M. Laurient had only ever used it in winter, and then only when times were really hard. Last winter, the severest yet, when the snow, the cold and the constant high winds had come near to breaking her cheerful spirit, she had longed for the strength to move the trap-door but had had enough sense not to try it. But now, with two of them, it was a different story. To feed M. Laurient's son, she told herself, she would even have robbed the sea-cave, but with a bit of luck that would not be necessary. If they found sufficient food in the cache they would somehow get by until the Allies landed.

Because it was only a matter of time, they kept saying, before Jersey was relieved. The Channel ports were in Allied hands, which was why food was even harder to come by, and the British blockade of the Channel Islands – in the hope, presumably, of starving the Germans out – was successful too. Just let there be enough food there for say three months, Rochelle prayed as they trudged through the woods. If we can feed ourselves for the next twelve weeks, then, what with the finer weather, and the Allies, we shall surely come through.

'Are we nearly there?' Laurie asked presently. He was clad in old clothes of his father's, except for the trousers, because Charles had had nothing which would fit his long-legged son. 'I thought you said it was a fair walk away.'

He asked, Rochelle realised, because they were about to

emerge from the woodland. She grinned at him, sensing a natural disinclination for a dash across open meadows.

'It is quite a way, and we do have to cross the pastures, but we'll keep close to the hedge. You aren't the only one who doesn't much fancy marching across the middle of a field!'

He grinned back at her. Rochelle's heart turned over and she scowled. It was not *him*; he did not have the power to touch her so. It was just his likeness – his damnable likeness – to Charles Laurient.

'I'm glad of that; lead on, then, honey.'

Rochelle led, emerging from the dappled shade of the trees into the full light of a sloping pasture. At the far end of it, cows grazed, their toffee-gold coats gleaming in the sun. No one else was in sight, though they could see the gable end of a cottage surrounded by a thick, freshly leaved hedge.

'When we get to the lane, I'll cross first, then give you a signal when it's clear,' Rochelle said, as they reached the far hedge. She nipped out, enjoying her new role, and presently beckoned Laurie across. Then the two of them plunged into woodland once more.

'There it is,' Rochelle said at last, pausing in her onward rush through briar and bramble. 'Gosh, it's got awfully overgrown since I was here last.'

'Where is it?' Laurie said, peering in the direction she had indicated. 'I can't see a thing.'

'There . . . see that sort of thickening in the copse? That's it. I did tell you it was a bit of a ruin.'

'A bit? It's a total ruin,' Laurie said, as the two of them fought, like a pair of prince charmings, towards the sleeping beauty in the thicket. 'Jeez, honey, you sure hide things good when you hide 'em!'

They fought through, however, and then had to drop to their knees to get inside because a wall and part of the roof had fallen in since Rochelle's last visit. But at last they

361

were there, peering through the gloom across the little room.

'There's the trap-door,' Rochelle said, kicking plaster off the boards with one bare foot. She had shed her clogs outside the crumbling structure, certain that she would have lost them in the struggle anyway. 'You can see why I couldn't lift it alone.'

It was a large section of boards which, to all intents and purposes, simply looked like part of the floor, but when Rochelle got her nails under a certain part the whole lot shifted slightly and Laurie could see that it was, in fact, a trap-door. But because of the way the walls had leaned and the roof had sagged, it would indeed take both their efforts to move it.

'M. Laurient never wanted to make it easy, but I don't think he'd have made it quite so heavy if he'd realised I'd be left on my own,' Rochelle gasped as the two of them strained to get the trap clear. 'Mind you, I doubt whether anyone else would think of trying to move it.'

'Nor me,' Laurie said, heaving. 'Watch out, honey . . . here she comes!'

The trap shifted. Pulling hard, they got it a foot away from the further side, but there it stuck.

'I'd better go down,' Rochelle said rather ruefully, staring at the narrow black gap. 'I just hope there's nothing horrible down there . . . no skeletons, or spiders, or anything like that.'

'I don't think my shoulders would fit,' Laurie said apologetically. 'Otherwise I'd go down real easy. Is it very deep?'

'Not terribly,' Rochelle said briefly. She slid into the gap and promptly disappeared. Her voice floated up, echoing, hollow. 'Gosh . . . pass the bags down. There's still plenty left!'

'There sure is,' Laurie said presently, in an awed tone, as the first bag was handed up bulging at the seams. They

362

were really cushion covers with rope handles, and they held a considerable quantity of tins. 'Gee, go steady, Chelle, they're real heavy!'

Below, Rochelle chuckled hollowly.

'Don't I know it? Here, take this one, then I'll come up.'

She emerged seconds later, dirty, cobwebby, but triumphant.

'That little lot will last for weeks,' she announced, scrambling back on to the cottage floor. 'Do you know, there are two jars of honey in there? Imagine, honey!'

She sounded awestruck and Laurie laughed.

'We'll have some as soon as we get home,' he said. 'It'll sure taste good after plain bread.'

'It'll be heavenly,' Rochelle said blissfully. It was clear she was already, in imagination, wallowing in honey. 'There's porridge oats, too, and tinned milk. Imagine, porridge with honey on top!'

'Sounds good,' Laurie said, his voice reflecting total indifference to porridge, with honey or without. 'Guess we ought to get movin' now, Rochelle, before that durn curfew hits us.'

'You're right,' Rochelle said. She hoisted one of the bags over her shoulder and beckoned. 'Off we go, then! March!'

After a few days, during which she went into St Helier with some of the tins and came back with her 'swops' . . . bread, potatoes and flour . . . Rochelle told Laurie the Germans were in such a state that she thought his presence would be the least of their worries.

'The Allies are winning everywhere,' she said joyfully, dumping her latest rations on the kitchen table and shaking her hair out of her eyes. 'Russian slave workers are walking the streets begging for food . . . don't worry, I gave them some . . . and no one stops them. Mme Barfleur had her radio set confiscated ages ago but she bought a little home-made one from the electrician and she's been listening to

363

the news every night. She says it can't be long before we're liberated.'

'In that case, I'm coming up to see the orchids this evening,' Laurie said firmly. It had rankled that she brushed aside all his offers to help with the flowers, even after he had told her of his work at the Institute. 'After all, there are things I might be able to help with.'

Rochelle sniffed and then admitted, rather ungraciously Laurie considered, that she did have some problems.

'Most of them are grand,' she said defensively. 'But one or two . . . I've tried treating them but I'm afraid of making them worse. I keep them apart from the others, of course, in case they pass their troubles on, but you might be able to think of something.'

'Sure I will,' Laurie said airily, hoping that he was right. 'And I want to get out a bit more, see something of the place. D'you realise I've never even seen the village? And we're surrounded by the sea – why don't we take a picnic down to the beach?'

'We could take fishing lines, I suppose, and try for mackerel,' Rochelle admitted. 'You don't understand, though, Laurie – there are Germans everywhere.'

'Oh, yeah? Hundreds on every beach on the island? Nowhere where two people can be alone?'

Rochelle laughed and admitted that she knew a quiet cove, but would not actually say that they should take a picnic down to it. Laurie could see that she was tempted, that the thought of an outing after so long shut up in the manor grounds beckoned almost irresistibly, but she had been straining every nerve to keep alive for too long to just let go. He saw that it would not be easy to persuade her into doing something for fun and not for reward, but for the time being he was content to have won her agreement to his going with her to the glasshouse.

They were having remarkable weather for the time of year. The temperature had soared into the upper seventies, and this of course had been both good and bad for the orchids, some of them revelling in it, others needing the blinds pulled down so that their delicate leaves did not scorch. Rochelle had spent quite a lot of time down in the glasshouse and had come back once or twice a trifle monosyllabic, which Laurie guessed meant that she was worried about her charges. In a moment of rare confidence she told him that the Cymbidiums, tough as old rope in her opinion, were bearing up, but that the Cattleyas and some of the mottle-leaved Cypripediums did not seem to be appreciating the sudden change of temperature at all and she was a bit worried about them.

But now, in the early evening, with the sky pinking towards the west, Laurie wondered, as he and Rochelle set out for the glasshouse, whether he was about to make a great fool of himself. She was a knowledgeable young woman and had been helping to rear orchids since early childhood. He had worked in the Institute and read a lot of books, but he could not possibly match her for actual experience, and his father, he knew, had been not only an enthusiast but an innovator and an expert.

But he could only do his best, and as they slipped into the glasshouse and closed the door behind them the very smell of the place was enough to bring the memories flooding back. Old Moss Llewellyn, who had been in horticulture for a lifetime and knew more about orchids than most, pottering about the houses, examining, tutting, approving. And himself, seeing in every flower a chance to impress the father he had never known.

Rochelle, however, was talking, and it behoved him to listen.

'. . . sort of dots on the leaves . . . yellow dots,' she was saying. 'And some of the Cypripediums are actually dying, you can see.'

She lifted a plant, its leaves limp and yellow. Laurie took it from her and smiled.

'This one's got red spider. Haven't you suffered from it before? You're lucky, if not – they can go right through a glasshouse and kill the lot if they aren't spotted. See?'

He showed her the minute insect, no larger than a pinhead, which was sucking the sap from the thick, juicy leaves. He showed her, too, the tiny, fine webs which the little creatures wove – a sure way to see if the trouble was actually caused by red spider, he said impressively.

'Oh. How do we get rid of them, then?'

She had said 'we'! Laurie was delighted but knew better than to let it show. Instead, he walked over to the cupboard under the lower shelving and pulled open the door.

'Got any pesticides left? Azobenzene, anything like that?'

'I don't know,' Rochelle said humbly. 'I was never allowed to touch that cupboard. M. Laurient said the stuff was dangerous. I've never even thought about it since he was taken away.'

'Hmm. Yes, there's some Malathion; that'll do just as well. Do you have a spray for pesticides?'

'No . . . but M. Laurient kept one in the back of the cupboard.'

Laurie fumbled in the cupboard and came up with the spray. He took the Malathion over to the rickety table, mixed it and charged the spray, then came back, grinning.

'Bring all the infected plants over here,' he said briskly. 'I'll spray 'em, and then we'll wait and see. Some of 'em may be too far gone, but the others should make it, and we'll get rid of the pests once and for all.'

They set to work at once, Rochelle picking out the plants with yellowing leaves and Laurie dealing with them. When they had finished it was impossible not to notice, Laurie thought, how different was Rochelle's attitude towards him. She did not cut across his every sentence, answer him brusquely, or simply ignore what he said. Instead she gazed solemnly at his face, nodding in agreement, clearly

366

most impressed by his ability to deal the death blow to red spider!

'There are others a little sick,' she said at last, when the quarantined specimens had been dealt with. 'They're more difficult, perhaps, because they're not flowering or doing anything very much . . . they need more heat than I can provide . . . but I know they aren't quite right.'

She had isolated these plants of her own accord and, looking at them, Laurie suffered a surge of self-doubt. They looked all right at first glance, but the aerial roots were thickly covered by white velamen and the plants themselves were poor, the leaves smaller than they should have been, the stems thinner.

'How long have these gone without flowering?' Laurie asked, clutching at straws. 'A year? Two?'

Rochelle looked at him incredulously, a little half-smile appearing; she obviously thought he was joking.

'How long? They've never flowered – they weren't old enough before the war . . . I mean they were immature . . . and since the war we haven't had the heat.'

Laurie nodded, trying not to show the relief which was breaking over him in waves. He found he liked the new admiration in her eyes and had no wish to see it dissipate.

'They're all right, then. It's natural that they shouldn't show any signs of greening up. There's no point, d'you see? The plants have been inactive for so long that they aren't thirsty, don't put out new growth. In fact you've been very lucky to keep them alive the way you have.'

'I've lost a lot, though,' Rochelle admitted. 'Hundreds, if not thousands. Some species have gone altogether; I just couldn't seem to keep them. But . . . I do think M. Laurient will be *quite* pleased with me, because PM23 is still alive and it's a hardy sort of hybrid. I think it will flower when we can give it heat again.'

'Sure it will,' Laurie said comfortingly. 'Well, we've dealt with the invalids, so how about some dinner?'

'Right,' Rochelle said, leading the way out of the glass-house. 'Tomorrow, if it's still this hot, shall we come over really early in the morning? Then it would leave us the whole day to go down to the coast.'

Walking back to the dower house through the trees, Laurie knew that he had won his first small victory. 'We' were going to get the orchids done early so that 'we' could go down to the coast! He smiled at her slim back, moving steadily ahead of him through the trees. She was only a kid, after all. She had had no chance to grow up in the usual way, no dances or boyfriends, nothing to start the normal feminine reactions flowing. She regarded him merely as a young man who might be useful to her orchids, someone she had to feed and talk to, and because of this he had thought of her not as a woman but as a child. But now, watching her as she made her way along the path, he acknowledged to himself that one of these days she was going to wake up to the fact that she was a woman – and he wanted to be around when it happened.

Was she beautiful? Desirable? It was difficult to say. He had known only the jealous, resentful child until this evening. Her hair was stunning. It streamed down to her waist, shining like black water, rippling like a brook in the sunshine, but lovely hair did not make a woman beautiful. He thought of her face, triangular-shaped, with big, dark blue eyes and the pointed and determined chin which was the physical sign of her incredible persistence. She had lovely eyebrows, drawn like the wings of a gull, their fine line black as her hair.

Did those things make her beautiful? He could not say; he only knew he liked to look at her, particularly when she was moving. She had a graceful economy of movement which made one forget her extreme thinness and milk-pale skin and think her healthy, confident.

I'd like to see her tanned to a golden-brown, Laurie found himself thinking. And plumper, more rounded. She spends too much time indoors, fretting over those damn' orchids, and she gives too much food to the dogs . . . and to me. Then, perhaps, I could tell if she was beautiful.

Next day was dull, so Rochelle went into St Helier on her bicycle to listen once more to Mme Barfleur's wireless set.

The whole island was awash with rumour . . . the Allies were pushing into Germany, the Jerries were discussing surrender, the bailiff was about to make an announcement to the Jersey folk telling them the exact date on which they would be freed from the alien presence.

Rochelle listened to the rumours and had an enjoyable half-hour with her friend Peter and his sister Prudence, during which they all gave vent to their feelings about the Germans and what they would do when the enemy was finally crushed.

'But the soldiers themselves . . . most of 'em . . . are only boys,' Prudence pointed out. 'And they aren't even fed as much as we are, now the *Vega* comes in every couple of months with our food parcels from the Red Cross. I wouldn't want to see them hurt . . . it's just the horrible fat officers. And even some of them haven't been too bad lately.'

'No, because it's too risky with the Allies hovering,' Peter said, grinning. 'I wanted to go, you know, to join the forces, but Maman wept and moaned and I stayed in the end.'

'I'm going to see Mme Barfleur and hear the news,' Rochelle said finally, when they had enjoyed a good gossip. 'Want to come?'

Rather to her surprise, Peter looked shifty.

'Better not,' he said briefly. 'Chelle . . . have you been there lately?'

'Yes . . . yesterday. Why?'

'Well, Olivia's there now. Or she was last night. Things are difficult.'

'Difficult? In what way?'

369

But Peter was not prepared to say more, so Rochelle left him, wondering just what Olivia had done.

She was soon to discover.

Mme Barfleur greeted her with open relief.

'Rochelle, ma petite, just the very person I most wanted to see! Olivia's here with the boy . . . she's very unhappy. She needs a friend. Will you go to her?'

Olivia was sitting on the small bed in her old room, brushing her long, curly hair. Hans was doing a jigsaw with big wooden pieces on a tray at her feet and looked up when Rochelle came into the room.

'Chelle!' Olivia said. Her face brightened for a moment, then her eyes filled with tears. 'Oh, Chelle, I'm in such a fix!'

'Tell me,' Rochelle demanded, leaning over to kiss Hans.

'You knew Theo had been recalled, ages ago?' Olivia began. 'Well, he wrote to me at first, lovely long letters, and even later he wrote whenever he could. Then the letters stopped. And . . . and it wasn't only the letters. He'd sent me money, and a friend of his saw that I had enough food . . . as much as they could spare, I suppose.'

'You would have had your rations,' Rochelle pointed out rather reproachfully. She saw no reason to pretend that without German help Olivia and the child would have starved. 'What's more, your mother and your Grandmère would have helped you.'

'Perhaps, but I didn't need help. Not at first. I had my little house, and one of the soldiers dug the garden and planted stuff and there was Theo's money. And then the letters stopped coming and the money stopped as well. Chelle, I went up to headquarters and they just said Theo was missing.' She gulped, mopping at her eyes with a hanky. 'Presumed dead.'

'Oh, Livia, that is hard,' Rochelle said. She sat down on the edge of the bed and put her arm round her friend's shoulders. 'Look, I know you loved him, but it's happening all the time these days, and missing doesn't necessarily mean dead, whatever they may have told you.'

'I know. But do let me finish, Chelle. It's just like you to rush in and start talking before you've heard the full story.'

Olivia was not as upset as she appeared if she could still turn pettish, Rochelle told herself, but was sorry for the thought when she looked again at her friend's tear-ravaged countenance and saw the pain in those big blue eyes. Olivia really was suffering; it was simply a habit to try to keep Rochelle in her place.

'Sorry,' she said remorsefully, therefore. 'Carry on, then.'

'Well, so I didn't have any money coming in and the officer who had brought me food stopped coming . . . he was sent away himself, I believe . . . and this beastly foul young officer started coming to my little house and pretending that he loved Hans. He brought me nice things and paid pretty compliments – it was a comfort, at first. I thought he was charming, and all he seemed to want was – was someone to t-talk to, s-someone to cook him a meal now and then.'

Rochelle was silent, waiting for her friend to continue. Mindful of Olivia's previous strictures, she said nothing, even when the silence stretched and stretched, until finally she had to speak.

'So? I suppose he wanted more than you thought?'

Tears brimmed over as Olivia nodded wretchedly.

'Yes. Oh, Chelle, you don't know what it's like to . . . to want to stay true to your man and to want a cuddle now and then. You're so lucky! I'm only young, and the Oberleutnant – Wolf – is extremely handsome, even if he is a beast . . . and I didn't *know* he was a beast then, I thought he was rather nice.'

The pause stretched. Rochelle cleared her throat.

'So you . . . you gave this Wolf person what he wanted. Is that what you're trying to say?'

'No! That is, not right away. I was very nice to him, and

let him kiss me now and then, but to tell the truth he frightened me a bit, he got so hot and excited . . . and then, one day, when I tried to stop him he just wouldn't.'

'And you gave him what he wanted?' Rochelle said hopefully. She did not find the story boring, exactly, but she did wish that Olivia would come straight out with it instead of going through all this business of pretending that she had done whatever it was against her will when all that mattered, to Rochelle, was the fix Olivia appeared to be in. 'Is that what you're trying to say, Olivia?'

'No it isn't . . . I'm saying he *took* what he wanted!' Olivia snapped. 'You wouldn't know, Rochelle, but when a man's determined a woman doesn't have much choice.'

Another silence, this time so charged with disbelief that Rochelle felt quite ashamed of herself. The truth was, though, that she had very little idea precisely what the Oberleutnant wanted or how he would have gone about getting it. M. Laurient had never allowed her to hang round stables, byres or kennels when animals were making babies, so she had rather less idea than most what went on.

'Sorry!' she said hastily. 'Are you having a baby, then?'

'My God, no! It isn't as bad as that. It was only a few times, and then I discovered he was a Beast and nothing would have persuaded me to let him . . . to let him. No, it's worse than that, in a way.'

'Do you have to . . . do it . . . lots of times before you can make a baby, then?' Rochelle enquired. 'And I don't understand how it is that once you knew he was a Beast you could stop him, but before then you couldn't.'

Olivia burst into angry speech, stopped, sniffled, and then grinned rather waterily at her friend.

'I can't explain, not properly – you'll just have to believe me when I tell you it is so. But now, you see, Wolf says that my only chance of finding Theo is to go back to Germany with him when he leaves the island. And he's told people that . . . that Hans is his baby, not Theo's, though he tries to tell me that this is for my sake, so I'll be sent back to Germany with him . . . then, he says, I can search for Theo.'

'But you needn't go,' Rochelle said sensibly. 'Even if the baby was this fellow's they couldn't make you go, or take Hans away from you. Could they?'

'I don't know,' Olivia admitted, sniffing. 'They have awfully wide powers, though, and anyway, suppose I could find Theo, if I went with him?'

'You couldn't. Germany's ever such a big country,' Rochelle said robustly. 'You stay here with Hans, Livia, and wait and see. If Theo's alive, he'll contact you. If . . . if the worst really has happened, I'm sure Theo would rather you and his son were here, where you can be happy, rather than stuck in Germany with a Beast.'

'That's what Grandmère keeps saying . . . even Maman told me it was foolish to let myself be taken hundreds of miles just on the off-chance. But oh, Chelle, I do love Theo so much, and I miss him frightfully. If he's never coming back, what shall I do?'

'Marry someone else, I expect,' Rochelle said with cruel practicality. 'Lots of the . . . the girls will.'

'Jerry-bags, you mean. Well, I'm not like them . . . I only love Theo!'

'Then stop behaving like one, and pretending you're only considering going to Germany with the Oberleutnant because of Theo, when it must be plain to everyone that you quite *want* to leave with him, which must mean he isn't a Beast at all but merely a handsome young man,' Rochelle said frankly. 'It's quite true, Livia, that I don't know very much about men and what they can and can't do, but you've always been a great one for making excuses to get your own way and I can see it's just what you're doing now.'

'I'm not! You don't understand. It's just that . . .'

'I do understand . . . well, I understand enough to know you quite want to go with Wolf,' Rochelle insisted. 'You're really bored without Theo, I can see that as well, and having Hans to look after isn't enough. If you love this fellow and want to go to Germany with him, say so. Don't make searching for Theo an excuse.'

She waited for another explosion, or more tears, but neither came. Instead, Olivia pushed her hair back and sat up straighter. She also began to look determined rather than merely sulky.

'Yes . . . but people look down on women who go with Germans,' she pointed out. 'They'll think I'm dreadful.'

Rochelle bit back a desire to tell Olivia that she was rather dreadful and patted her friend's back bracingly.

'Nonsense. Besides, what does it matter what people think here, if you're far away in Germany? All that matters, Livia, is whether you really are pining for Theo, or whether in fact you're in love with this Wolf. And whether you'd be happier here with Hans and no one else, or with Wolf in a foreign land.'

Olivia jumped up off the bed. She went over to the dressing-table and peered distractedly at her reflection, then turned once more to Rochelle.

'My eyes are red,' she said inconsequentially. 'I look really piggy with red eyes and yellow lashes. Look . . . I like having a man.'

'Do you?'

'Yes. I don't love Wolf, I don't even like him very much, but I can't bear the thought of spending the rest of my life here by myself whilst the ones who weren't pretty enough to get a German officer marry and have babies and nice homes.'

'Sometimes I wonder why I like you, Olivia Buchet,' Rochelle said indignantly. 'Some people *chose* not to chase the Jerries. Anyway, if you're so extremely beautiful, some poor fool's bound to be taken in by you and ask you to marry him.'

'Do you think so?' Olivia asked hopefully. 'You don't think that when the war's over they'll just snub any girl who's . . . who's been friendly with a German?'

'I doubt it. I mean, all our own men will be coming home, the ones who left before the Occupation and joined the forces in Britain. They won't know or care which girls were good and which were bad.'

'Unless someone tells them,' Olivia said, not bothering, this time, to argue with Rochelle's choice of words. 'There's always some busybody about who tells tales.'

'Well, in that case, leave the island and go to Britain, or America,' Rochelle said patiently. 'It needn't be Germany, girl!'

'Oh, but Germany's the best place to go, surely? I mean, they've got everything. They have a marvellous economy, their schools are the best in the world, their housewives have all the latest gadgets . . .'

'Had, Olivia, had. Don't you see, stupid, that you're talking like a German yourself? When the war's over they'll be the ones at the bottom of the ladder instead of the top. Is that what you want?'

Of all the arguments, it seemed, this was the one that would really count with Olivia. She looked astounded, staring wide-eyed at Rochelle, and then, very slowly, she nodded her head.

'Of course, you're right! I'll stay.'

16

He arrived back at the tumbledown cottage when the grapes on the mountainside were ripening in the late sun as evening was creeping, in purple clouds, over the river plain. He hesitated outside, not knowing where he might find her or what he should say.

There was no one about; she had never kept a dog, though he had tried to persuade her to. She would have had one, but she was afraid to be responsible for another mouth to feed, she had explained. So now, as he approached the cottage, no dog barked, and the fowl in the meadow clucked and murmured and took no notice, probably would have done the same had he been a regiment of militia.

He pushed at the door and it swung inwards; there was no one in the kitchen, no small, wizened figure in the chimney corner, huddled up to the fire.

He knew at once that Grandpère Rabin was dead; gone from here, leaving no trace. Looking round, he thought that his instinct had been right, for the old man's stick, his shabby and disgusting winter hat, were gone.

He looked closer, and saw how neglected, how dirty, the kitchen had grown and for a moment felt a fierce and terrible stab of fear – suppose Nana had gone as well, was as dead as Grandpère Rabin!

He went across to the foot of the stairs, then turned back and plunged into the yard again. She would not be indoors, not now; she would be up on the hillside, tending her vines.

He went up the mountain so fast that the breath began to hurt in his chest and his eyes filled with tears. Where the hell was she? He had come all this way, had faced countless dangers . . . where was she? He had thought of her as the one constant thing in his life, Nana who would never change, would always be true, and now she had gone . . . she was not on the mountainside, not amidst the vines!

He stood at the top on the little narrow pathway which the wild goats used and it occurred to him to look down, godlike, on the landscape laid out below, all details sharp and clear in the cool mountain air.

And he saw her! She was in the field that he had ploughed before he left and she was planting; he could see her bending, straightening, moving on . . .

He ran down the hill and shouted as he ran. He could not bear to see her face indifferent, knew she would have arranged it into pleased surprise by the time he reached her, so long as she had warning. His own face . . . his ugly, old, seamed face . . . would wear the truth on it, he knew.

'Charles!'

She had almost screamed the word and her face . . . ah, her face! That sweet, plain, placid face . . . he had thought it bovine, unemotional! Joy shone like a shout on her brow, her mouth was wreathed in smiles, and tears fell, shining like diamonds, on to the pale cheeks which were flushing as he looked.

'Nana!'

'Oh, Charles, I thought I'd never see you again. I thought . . .'

But he caught her in his arms – a big, firm, satisfying armful she made too – and hugged her with all his strength, until she gave a tiny whimper of protest and he relaxed, but only to kiss her and cuddle her and croon how much he loved her, how he had missed her.

'Why have you come back?' she asked presently, when she had breath to speak once more, and had freed her mouth from his lips. 'The war isn't over!'

'My war is. I've come back, dearest Nana, because I was a fool ever to go. I thought I wanted to go back to my

377

island, but what I really wanted was you . . . and this!' His hand indicated the land around them. 'And I mean want . . . I mean love, Nana. I'm not the man who would marry you for your land. I want you because I've never loved anyone the way I love you.'

And it was true, every word of it. He had thought, for a few minutes on the quayside, that God was asking too much of him in demanding that he give up his girl, his island. But God hadn't grudged him either of them. God had probably known, all along, that Charles Laurient had fallen in love for the first time in more than twenty years and would never be happy away from Nana.

A daughter, he mused as he and Nana, arm in arm, walked back indoors, a daughter is a wonderful, wonderful thing. But a wife, a woman you love with all your heart and with all your body too, is a prize beyond compare.

'And what were you doing, when I came home, that was so important that you never even saw me cross the yard?' Charles demanded presently, as the two of them stood, still clutching each other, in the kitchen.

'Looking after my roses. You said to buy some so I did . . . a great many. Grandpère died a month ago and left me his little savings, so I spent them on . . . oh, on all sorts. Later, when we've had a meal, you must come down and see them.'

'I will,' he said contentedly. 'It's ideal ground for them; they'll thrive for us, Nana.'

She laughed, then kissed him passionately, drawing him towards the stairs. There would be no coyness, no holding back; she would give him her love and her body with the same frankness and generosity she had shown when she gave him his life.

They mounted the stairs together.

All the way home, having listened to the news, exchanged gossip with Mme Barfleur and seen Olivia settled once more, Rochelle thought about what she and the older girl had discussed.

Men. It was true that she knew very little about them, save that she loved M. Laurient and missed him sadly. She had come into contact with very few men, though, now she thought about it. Radek had flirted with her, but she had been far too busy to flirt back or ask herself whether she liked him as anything other than a friend. And now there was Laurie, actually on the premises. He had been with her a week or so and she was getting used to him, to his large appetite, large feet, powerful frame.

She was beginning to think 'we' instead of 'I'. Possibilities reared their heads . . . two of them could do all sorts of things which had been unthinkable for one. He understood orchids, had known at a glance why some specimens had turned yellow, had explained that a plant which takes in nourishment through leaves and aerial roots becomes uncomfortable if fed too richly through the compost in which its roots have so light, so delicate a hold.

He was large, with a big appetite, but he was never greedy; she admired that in him. He was always trying to make her eat her own share and half of his as well, and he agreed completely that they should feed the dogs as well as they possibly could, dividing his own portion more than once with the greedy and importunate Senna, until she had threatened to shut the old dog out at mealtimes.

He was good-looking, too, she told herself now, and was conscious of a stab of pleasure that Olivia had never come his way. Olivia, she knew, would have liked him, might even have taken him away to live in her nice little house with her, for what better insurance could a Jerry-bag have against the liberation than an American lover?

Rochelle frowned, shocked at her own thoughts. If Laurie was fool enough to want a golden-haired beauty who had gone with the occupying forces he could leave — but Rochelle would tell him there had not only been Theo but at least one other man, to her knowledge. If Olivia admits to two, then it may well have been four, she told herself, and was shocked anew that she could feel so spiteful towards her friend just at the thought of Olivia and Laurie together.

She liked him. She had not meant to do so – would have much preferred to remain resentful and jealous – but the fact was she liked him. Liked his appearance, the way his face changed when he smiled, the look of indulgent amusement which crossed it when she said something silly.

Simply liking him, however, did not mean she wanted him to stay on the island. Not once M. Laurient returned. Then, she hoped, life would go back to normal, and normal was just Rochelle and M. Laurient, together, living at the manor, rearing their orchids and hoping that one day Pure Madonna would bloom again.

In other words, she only wanted Laurie's companionship until M. Laurient came home, which seemed rather unfair. And if she was honest, the feeling she had for M. Laurient and the occasional frisson of excitement which shivered up her spine when Laurie, fooling about, caught at her hand or tugged her hair were totally different. She found Laurie exciting, whereas her relationship with M. Laurient was settled, a comfortable thing. Could it be that she was growing up and was more woman, now, than child? That because he had been like a father to her she would always be a child to M. Laurient, whereas this new and exciting relationship with Laurie could become ... something more?

But what mattered, Rochelle reminded herself severely, was getting M. Laurient back and returning to normal. She and Laurie could wait.

'Come on, Rochelle, if we're gonna go we're gonna go. It's overcast, I know, but it'll improve.'

Laurie and Rochelle were standing in the kitchen. They

had got up early, seen to the orchids, hurried back to the house and packed a picnic, and now they were looking out on a sky which was rapidly clouding over and a wind which was definitely freshening.

'It's not a day for the beach,' Rochelle said sadly. 'Are you sure you want to go? We'll leave it till tomorrow, if you like.'

'Nope. We could've gone yesterday, but you thought up some real stupid excuse, so we didn't. Today we go, right?'

Rochelle took a deep beath, picked up the knapsack with their food in it, and slung it on to her shoulder. Then she gave Laurie the benefit of her most stunning smile, and was pleased to see him blink and look taken aback.

'Right, we'll go today. And we'll have fun, won't we? It's a long while since I've had fun.'

She had not meant to sound wistful, and cursed inwardly when she saw Laurie's eyes soften. To distract him, she said: 'What about the dogs? They can be a nuisance, but I hate to leave them behind when they love the beach so much.'

'Bring 'em along; it's OK by me.'

'Good.' Rochelle whistled the dogs, who came galloping up, wheezing. 'Heel, Senna; heel, Pod. Let's go!'

They set off through the wood, then across a meadow and along a deep lane. Birds sang overhead and they could hear a stream chattering somewhere near at hand. Although it was overcast and windy it was not cold, and Rochelle beguiled the time by naming the wild flowers in the hedgerows and on the tall, grassy banks and seeing how many birds she could identify.

'The hot spell's done all sorts of things to the flowers and hedges,' she said gaily as they walked. 'There's lots of blossom out which doesn't usually arrive until May, and some trees are even starting to come into leaf. I got potatoes planted before you arrived, but of course the Germans dug them up again before they could come to anything.'

'Why? Spite?'

'Goodness no, for food. The troops are a great deal worse off than us, now, because they can't have Red Cross parcels and we can, so the young boys are more or less living off the land. It's no use telling them that if they don't let the seed potatoes grow there won't be a crop in the autumn, because all they're interested in is being alive to see the autumn, so I didn't replant. That's why I've only got those leggy old cabbages in the garden.'

'I did wonder. My mom married a farmer, so I know a bit about the land, and I was in the CCC during the Depression – before the war, you know – so I know a bit about estate work, too.'

'I don't even know what the CCC *is*, and I don't have much idea about the Depression either,' Rochelle confessed. 'Tell me, Laurie.'

'It'll bore you,' Laurie warned. How could he tell this suddenly lighthearted Rochelle about the miseries of the Depression, when he wanted so much to make this a splendid and memorable day for her? But there had been good times, after all – he had not starved, and neither had Mom, for all their secret fears.

So as they walked he regaled her with stories of his youth, then told her about the Army Air Corps, which later became the Army Air Force. And then, because she was interested, he told her how M. Laurient had met his mother in Paris, and about their love and what had parted them.

'Golly! I shouldn't be glad it happened, but I have to be, Laurie, because what would have happened to me if M. Laurient had married your mom?'

'Don't know. What did happen to you?'

So Rochelle told him about her parents' death, her great-aunt's unwillingness to take her in, and the solution which had led to her knowing what love was for the first time in her short life.

'That's why I'd do anything for him,' she said earnestly,

when her story was told. 'Anything at all. He's been so good to me and I love him so much.'

'Yeah, I can see that. He's been more of a father to you than to me . . . guess you deserve it and all, because you've been better'n most daughters to him.'

They were crossing a sloping upland pasture which would end, presently, in a strip of woodland. Just under the trees Rochelle stopped short, staring at him.

'What do you mean?'

'Well, that you and he are like father and daughter, I guess. What's wrong with that?'

'Nothing . . . only I've often thought that if M. Laurient wanted to marry me, now I'm fully grown, I'd be the luckiest, happiest person on earth.'

'*Marry* you?' Laurie could not keep the shocked incredulity out of his voice. 'But he's nearly fifty now, and you aren't yet twenty. Anyway, he thinks of you as his daughter – he said so in his letter to me.'

'I don't mind the age difference if he doesn't,' Rochelle said, clearly unperturbed by Laurie's strictures. 'And that letter was written long ago . . . when I was about ten, I suppose. I just think he may feel differently when he sees me again.'

'Sure he may,' Laurie said, trying to sound cheerfully unconcerned. 'Guess he's a great man . . . my mom told me all sorts about him. He treated her well whilst they were together.'

'Yes, he would. He's generous, M. Laurient.'

Laurie muttered an agreement and bit back the words, 'And he's not a dirty old man, honey, so you can forget the marriage bit!' because it would have undone all the good their day out had begun to do. Instead, he changed the subject to the safer one of aircraft, for a rift had appeared in the clouds overhead and in the widening gap they had seen, against the blue, an Allied plane.

'It's too high for ack-ack to start,' Rochelle said, walking

383

along dangerously, her head tilted right back so that she could only see what was high above and not what lay beneath her feet. 'Have you noticed, Laurie, that the guns don't seem to be firing nearly so much these past couple of days? Would you say there was enough blue sky to make a Dutchman a pair of trousers?'

Laurie had not heard the expression before and thought it absurd since one would have to know, first of all, the size of the Dutchman. Wrangling amicably over this, the make and type of the planes which passed over and the reason why the German gunners appeared to be on strike, they made their way down the lane until they reached the gap. Rochelle drew Laurie level with her so that they stood above the cove together.

'Look at that! Isn't it absolutely beautiful? I haven't been here for years and years . . . not since before the war, I don't think. There used to be a boat . . . but it's gone, of course. The Nazis didn't leave boats lying about for people to escape in.'

Laurie looked down on the golden crescent of beach, the sea crashing on the shore, the little island with its cap of grass starred with daisies and cliff-bluebells, the thrift adding its clear pink to the colourful scene from every crevice that was above the tideline.

'Jeez,' he breathed, and as he spoke the sun came out, though the wind continued to tease the sea into a mass of white horses and to whirl the sand into wicked little dancing dervishes which stung the flesh and made the dogs blink and turn their heads away.

'Let's go down,' Rochelle said suddenly. 'We could paddle, you know . . . I wish I'd brought a shrimping net.'

'Never mind. We can see if there's any driftwood and take it back for the stove,' Laurie said. 'Only I wanted you to forget food and things today and just relax.'

'I don't think a shrimping net was for catching shrimps in, really, so much as for messing about with,' Rochelle

384

confessed. 'I hope the sun comes out properly this afternoon, so we can sunbathe.'

But the weather remained fitful and the wind continued
at gale force – not that they minded. The dogs barked at
the waves and ran into the surf, and Rochelle and Laurie
paddled, her skirt kilted round her waist, his trousers rolled
above the knee. Then they collected driftwood and drew
pictures on the hard, wet sand below the tide line. They
ate their meal lounging in a sheltered spot in the rocks, and
afterwards Laurie stretched out, ankles crossed, head on
the bag, and announced that he felt like a nap.

'You go and play if you want to,' he said magnani-
mously. 'But I'm for a snooze.'

'I'll snooze too, then,' Rochelle said. 'Can I share the
bag?'

She was leaning over Laurie and looking down on him,
so that Laurie could see her head outlined against the
bright sky. He smiled sleepily up at her.

'No room, no room. You can lay your head on my manly
bosom if you want.'

He felt her head land with a thump on his chest, then
the giggle that ran through her, making her shake. All at
once he wanted his arms about her, wanted to feel her nice
slim body against him. He flung his arm round her as
though to pull her into a more comfortable position and
managed to get her head into the crook of his shoulder so
that he could squint downwards and see the shine on her
hair, the line of her parting.

'Is that all right? Are you comfy?'

Her voice shook a little, though it tried to sound light,
indifferent, and he could sense her nervousness. He could
sense something else, too, and suddenly felt as old and wise
as a serpent. There was no need to rush things, to grab
her, try to make her aware of her own awakening woman-
hood. Indeed, it might do more harm than good; she might
retreat into the shell of her war-childhood again.

385

No, he could do better than that. Laurie was not experienced with women, but he had known a few, and the girl who lay against him, trembling, betwixt and between, was about to take a step or two on her own account. All he needed to do was to be still and quiet and kind . . . and meet her halfway if need be.

So he lay on the sand, the wily old Laurie-serpent, and felt her turn her soft cheek so that it rested on the bare skin at the nape of his neck. There was a pause whilst she was very still. Then she put her hand on his chest.

'I can feel your heartbeat,' she said.

It was his cue; but dared he take it?

'It beats right through your body; I can hear it through your ribs.'

Gently, with infinite care, keeping it discreetly low, he moved his hand so that it curled round her own ribs.

'I can feel your heartbeat . . . just,' he said lazily. 'But I can't hear it.'

There was another pause.

'If you put your head on my chest, you'd hear it too,' she said.

He rolled sideways, lazily, keeping a firm but gentle hold on her, and pushed his head puppyishly under her arm, to lay his ear to the soft mound of her breast.

'I hear it. It's leaping and jumping . . . but a woman's heartbeat is always faster and less regular than a man's, I believe,' he said. But he knew her heartbeat was skipping because of their closeness.

'Your head's jolly heavy.'

He moved it, lifting it off her, pulling himself up on his elbows so that their earlier positions were reversed: she lay on her back looking up; he leaned over her, looking down.

'Where can I put my head where it won't squash you?' Laurie said plaintively. 'I thought we were going to have a nice sleep.'

She put her hand round his neck and pulled gently. He

saw that she did not quite know what she wanted, except closeness. He lowered his face until it was inches from hers. He would change the game now, take the lead a little.

'I can see right inside your eyes. I can see past the dark, dark blue and into the black pool of your pupil,' he said in deep, thrilling tones. 'I shall rest my nose on your nose and drown myself in your eyes, and then I shall tell your fortune.'

She gurgled with amusement and as his face descended, so hers rose, just a little. And her eyes closed with hypnotic slowness, the faintly azure lids and the dark half-moon of her lashes covering and hiding those brilliant eyes.

It was the signal he had waited for. Slowly, luxuriously, his mouth covered hers. She gave a little sigh, and he felt her lips soften, then gently flutter apart.

He gasped and felt her body accommodate him as he seized her in his arms, crushing her against him. She wanted him as much as he wanted her, and right now that was an awful lot!

He told himself that he must go slowly, be gentle . . . but she grabbed his shoulders, her fingers digging in, her body arching demandingly against his. He could feel his excitement and desire crashing against his self-control like great foaming combers crashing against the shore, but he was not the only one. She was an untried girl roused to a pitch of excitement and curiosity, and would not try to stop him. Her body was shameless. She felt him slide his hands up her bare back, one fingering its way round to take her small, apple-shaped breast, cradling it at first, then touching, titillating . . . she purred with satisfaction, and then, as he ceased to plunder her mouth for a moment, she in her turn explored his, moving against him, an innocent squirming born of pleasure, but enough to make him see that after a little more encouragement she would submit willingly to him, would match his mounting desire with her own.

But he could not do it, not in the present circumstances. Gently, he caressed, cuddled, explored, but would not let it go beyond that. And she, who knew nothing, thought that they had done all that was required of them and lay, sweet and quiet now, gently satisfied, in his hard arms.

'Oh, Laurie!'

'Oh, darling, Chelle . . . was it all right? Are you happy?'

'It was very nice, and I'm very happy. Only . . . will I . . . will we . . .'

'Don't worry, you won't have a baby. Do you know I love you?'

'Well, I love you too, then. You were kind to me, Laurie.'

He smiled down at her. Her long hair was tangled now, and sandy, too. Her face was damp from her exertions but Laurie thought he had never seen her look so placidly content. If lovemaking had that effect on her, he told himself, they should do it every day . . . twice a day!

'You were kind to me as well, Rochelle. You paid me a great compliment, you know; probably the greatest compliment you can pay a guy.'

'Really? What's that, then?'

'You trusted me with your body, Chelle. You trusted me not to betray your trust.'

'Did I?' She smiled up at him, innocent, sleepily content. 'Well, you didn't betray it, did you, so I was right.' She took his hand and carried it to her mouth, biting the knuckles gently. 'Laurie . . . that . . . what we did . . . it wasn't everything, was it?'

'No, honey, it wasn't everything. Everything's for later, for married people. But what we had was good, eh?'

'Sure,' she said lazily, mimicking him, Laurie knew. 'Have you done the other, Laurie? With anyone?'

He remembered a dark, lithe girl of Indian extraction in a bicycle shed in Chicago. A plump blonde college girl who had shrieked like an electric train at the moment of truth and scared him half to death. A skinny, self-righteous

388

clergyman's daughter in Houston who had produced a rubber johnny from her handbag and dam' nearly raped him.

'Sorry, honey, but I'm twenty-two years old. Yeah, I've gone with a woman once or twice.'

'Oh, so you have babies? A wife?'

He laughed, kissing the side of her face, then the soft eyelids, the straight little nose, and lastly, the pink, kiss-swollen mouth.

'No . . . I don't have babies or a wife! Some girls . . . older ones . . . understand these things.'

'Oh. Laurie, can we go to sleep now?'

He cradled her in his arms then, and sang beneath his breath as she fell asleep.

Rochelle awoke and was puzzled at first to find her nose pressed against bare skin, her body close in someone's embrace. But then she remembered, and wriggled free so that she could look down on Laurie, for he had fallen asleep too and slumbered still, looking very young and defenceless with the dark eyes veiled and the firm mouth softened.

Rochelle propped herself up on her elbows and stared at him; it never fails, of course. His head moved, his mouth worked like a baby's when its bottle is removed for a moment, and then she saw the gleam of his eyes between his lashes and he reached for her, sleepily trying to cuddle her back to dreamland.

'No, Laurie,' she said, bending over him and fluttering her lashes against his cheek. A butterfly kiss, her mother had called it once, long, long ago. 'We're losing the afternoon and it's sunny again.'

Laurie sighed, groaned, gave a mammoth yawn and sat up. He knuckled his eyes before rolling over on to his knees and getting slowly to his feet, dusting sand off his trousers – only he always called them pants.

'OK, OK, I'm up,' he said. He turned and gave her his

hand, heaving her to her feet as well. 'What I want to know, lady, is how a decent, God-fearin' girl like you learned to flirt exactly like the bad girls do!'

'I don't flirt; I just behave naturally,' Rochelle said smugly. 'With some people you can love them ever so much – terribly – but you can't show it because they aren't like that. But with others . . . younger ones, I suppose . . . showing it's easy. I say, what's that?'

'Nothing . . . a rock, or a buoy, perhaps,' Laurie said, following the direction of her pointing finger to where something bobbed on the lively, white-topped waves. 'Explain yourself; who's this older person?'

He knew, of course, Rochelle thought, but she indulged him a little, full of the milk of human kindness which had been stifled in her for too long. Her parents had rarely kissed, rarely cuddled her, and M. Laurient had been even more remote. He had shown his love in a thousand ways, but never by clutching her in his arms and giving her a great big hug.

'Why, M. Laurient, of course. He's a quiet man, your father; he doesn't wear his heart on his sleeve. Mme Barfleur said that once, but I never really knew what she meant until now. M. Laurient *couldn't* hug, perhaps, but now – thanks to you, Laurie – I'll be the one to hug first.'

Laurie looked startled, even a little uneasy.

'Ye-es . . . but honey, there are all sorts of different ways of loving someone. My way's the right way for you and me, but maybe M. Laurient . . . my father . . . takes his emotions cooler.'

She considered, head tilted.

'You could be right. But if so, M. Laurient will just have to change, because . . . Laurie, that isn't a rock, because it's moving, and it isn't a buoy. I think it's a boat, broken loose from its moorings somehow.'

Laurie's attention, as she had hoped, was immediately diverted to the object in the water. He stared, then started

390

for the sea at a run, yelling at her over his shoulder as he did so.

'You're right, it is a boat . . . we'd better see if we can get it in. Finders keepers, is it?'

'Yes. Well, otherwise it'd go to the Germans. Can you see if it's painted in any special sort of colours?'

Laurie narrowed his eyes and peered out to sea, then shook his head.

'Nope; could be bright pink for all I can tell. It's well awash. We'd better try and reach it from the rocks; the sea's much too rough for even a short swim.'

On either side of the bay the rocks stretched out, like arms, into really deep water. Rochelle and Laurie ran along the ones on the left-hand side of the bay, for the boat seemed closer to that side, and then had to watch helplessly as it bobbed and tipped only a dozen yards from them but completely out of reach.

'I'll have to go in,' Laurie shouted against the wind, but Rochelle grabbed his arm and held tight, shaking her head.

'No . . . you'll get caught in the undertow. The tide's coming in, so the boat'll get dragged right on to these rocks. Then we'll both climb down and heave her out.'

Laurie, looking at the way the sea boiled below them, had to admit she was probably right. He was, he assured her, a strong swimmer, but not a fool, and was rewarded by her proud and smiling glance. Their relationship had changed dramatically and she was not ashamed to let it show.

'Here she comes,' she announced presently. Laurie joined her on the lowest shelf of all, where already the sea was lapping and sucking at their feet. 'We'll have to stand firm . . . I wish we had a rope!'

'Once we've got the boat, how will we bring it ashore?' Laurie said, as the enormity of their task struck him. It was a sizeable craft, not the little cockleshell he had imagined at first sight. Now that it was coming closer with every wave that reached the shore, he could see that it was not just a row-boat but a small cabin cruiser, though he guessed the engine would be useless, waterlogged by the fierce sea.

'We shan't. We'll just have to work it as far inshore as we can and then hang on to it until the tide turns,' Rochelle said grimly. 'If we can hold on that long, of course.'

'I wish we'd never seen her,' Laurie shouted above the wind. 'We'll be half dead before we've got her safe.'

Rochelle grinned; she looked totally delightful, Laurie thought, with her long hair whipped into sandy rat-tails and her clothing stuck to her beautiful body by the spray and the wind. Her cheeks were pink with excitement, her eyes glowed with it, and he could not imagine why he had ever thought her too thin. She was slim, certainly, but she had curves in all the right places and a whipcord strength that was coming in very useful right now.

For they had the boat at last; two pairs of hands, one strong and square, the other small and thin, gripped the gunwale. And they were lucky. They worked her along as Rochelle had suggested, drawing her nearer the shore, and they came to a cleft in the rocks where the sea surged into a deep pool, high-sided but when the tide was almost at the full not too high to allow the boat to slip in, and whilst the tide remained up it was possible for Rochelle and Laurie to teeter round the edge on the rocks, guiding their find into what was a remarkably safe harbour.

'Wow!' Laurie said wholeheartedly, as they released their hold on the boat for the first time for twenty nerve-racking minutes. 'My fingers are never going to unbend. How are yours, honey?'

'Stiff and sore,' Rochelle admitted with a grimace. 'But they'll mend. She's not so full of water as I thought.'

'No, but she needs bailing.' Laurie heaved her up as far as he could into the shelter of the pool and then gave a triumphant cry: 'A rope – we can tether her here, then.'

The rope was neatly coiled beneath the bows and fastened with a ring to the decking. When uncoiled it was plenty long enough for Laurie to tie it firmly to a high rock. The boat would not get free of that in a hurry, Rochelle thought. Seeing that it was firmly attached, she began to think longingly of the rest of their picnic – and to remember the long walk home – but Laurie was bending over the tiny cabin.

'I'll bail the worst out,' he was saying, his voice muffled by the housing. 'Can't leave her here full of water . . . besides, I want to make sure everyone knows she's . . . oh!'

There was something about the quality of that sharp exclamation, perhaps something about the silence that followed it, which had Rochelle down off the rock and into the watery cabin as quickly as she could go.

'What's the matter, Laurie? Is she badly holed?'

Laurie turned to her. He seemed to spread himself, as if he wanted to hide something from her.

'Go back, honey. There's a body . . . no need for you to see. It looks like a woman.'

But it was too late; Rochelle had already peered round his elbow and seen for herself the body that lay sprawled and awash at the far end of the tiny cabin. It was a woman, smartly dressed, with gold hair darkened and made heavier by the water. Rochelle felt sickness rising in her throat, felt her heart begin to pound.

'Oh, my God! Let me see!'

He heard the urgency in her tone and stood aside, wordless.

Rochelle gazed down on the frozen face, the blue-white skin, the dreadful stillness which killed hope before it was born.

'It's Olivia,' she said huskily. 'My friend . . . Olivia.'

Laurie turned and lifted the head; it rolled helplessly. He said, 'She's been dead a long time, honey. I think

393

rigor's set in and gone again . . . or perhaps that doesn't apply to a drowning.'

'But why should she have drowned?' Rochelle said. All the thrill of finding the boat, the excitement of rescuing it, were as if they had never been. Only this dull shock, this sense of loss, were left. 'She could swim – and anyway, she's in the boat. Why would she have drowned?'

'I don't know, but . . .' Laurie tried to lift the body, to stop the water from lapping at the silk suit, from lipping the white, helpless hands. As he moved it, the heavy hair fell to one side, revealing the white brow . . . white save for a little patch of blue-ringed darkness just above one ear.

'What's that?' Rochelle said, pointing.

Laurie looked, then whistled and looked more closely.

'Shot,' he said briefly. He picked Olivia up in his arms, her golden head lolling against his arm, her legs trailing down, one shoe on, one half off. Automatically, Rochelle reached out and put the shoe properly on. She pulled forward a thick hank of the golden hair and hid the bullet-hole.

'Shot? Who would do a thing like that? And why? Olivia's friend was an officer . . . Oberleutnant something-or-other. No one would have wanted to shoot her!'

'An accident?' Laurie was carrying Olivia out of the boat now. He got ashore rather untidily, but he did not drop his sad burden. He and Rochelle had clambered out along the reef with much laughter and many shouts and squeals. Now they retraced their steps sombrely and in silence. When they regained the sand Rochelle said: 'What are you going to do with her?'

'How far's the nearest house?'

Rochelle shrugged. This was a deserted beach, but on Jersey human habitation was never very far away.

'Perhaps half a mile down the road. Can we carry her that far? And what will the Germans do when we tell them she's dead? We can't say you discovered the body – they're bound to ask questions. Laurie, we must think.'

Laurie laid the body tenderly on the sand and they sat down beside it. The sun was shining again, waterily, and a passer-by might easily have mistaken them for a picnicking party, one member of which had succumbed to the sunshine and fallen asleep.

'Hmm . . . you've sure got a point, honey. If we say we found her that's me up the spout and the boat too, I guess. What'll we do? She's your pal, you said, and someone murdered her, by the looks.'

'If we leave her by the high-tide line, I can go to the cottages and say she was washed ashore. They'll send a party out to fetch her home. Then I'll go to Mme Barfleur's – someone's got to break the news – and find out whatever I can. You must go home, though, Laurie. Straight home.'

'Right,' Laurie said. 'You're the boss on this one, Chelle. Are you sure you wouldn't rather I came with you to the cottages, though? There couldn't be any harm in that.'

But Rochelle shook her head and presently, a little rested from their exertions, they checked their story, and then Rochelle set out in one direction and Laurie in another.

Their perfect afternoon had collapsed around them. Even their discovery of each other was marred by it.

Laurie, trudging home with the food in a bag over his shoulder, cursed the dead girl's sense of timing and then was sorry, ashamed at his own reaction. The poor kid, to die so violently, so young!

But he was glad to reach the dower house, to feed the dogs the rest of the picnic and to put the kettle on the stove, so that they could have some hot coffee when Rochelle returned.

Rochelle told her story first to a fat, smiling woman and then to a thin and cadaverous man. They both expressed horror, went and fetched neighbours, and insisted that she accompany them back to the beach again.

Rochelle went with them, numbed by what had happened. It was only a few days since she and Olivia had sat and talked on Olivia's bed, with Hans doing his jigsaw a few feet away. What could have happened in the short time since then? Poor, shallow little Olivia, who had been no worse than many other girls; all she had wanted was security for herself and her child and a little happiness, a little love. Was it so wrong? Whom could she possibly have hurt so badly that he had killed her for it? Or was it just theft, a snatching of the purse, a shot in the dark, someone so desperate that he had killed for the few small things Olivia had possessed?

The body lay as she and Laurie had left it, save that the tide had come in a little further so that the neatly shod feet rocked in the incoming waves. The cottagers gave warm cries of shock and horror, lifted Olivia on to the door they had brought for the purpose, and carried her back along the road.

'I'll come into St Helier with you,' Rochelle said presently, to the young man despatched to inform the civilian authorities. 'She was my friend. I must see her mother and grandmother.'

The cottagers thought it a good idea; someone had to tell the relatives, better that it should be a person who knew the family already. They plied Rochelle with homemade wine and crab sandwiches – she only took a mouthful of the wine but ate the sandwiches rapidly, hungry all of a sudden now that she was out of the buffeting wind – and then lent her an ancient bicycle. It had a heavy iron frame and solid tyres, but at least it enabled her to keep pace with the young man, who rode a rather more modern machine.

They went to the police first. It was a couple of hours before Rochelle was free to go on to Mme Barfleur's for as soon as the bullet hole had been spotted the authorities realised that this was a case of murder most foul – a young girl shot and thrown in the sea – which they would do their utmost to bring to trial.

But, Rochelle thought as, free at last, she turned her face towards the neat little house Mme Barfleur shared with her daughter, they won't find it easy. Olivia mixed with more Germans than she did Islanders – with officers, what was more – and had probably made enemies. Then there were Russian and Spanish and French prisoners of war, many of them starving, roaming the lanes in search of what they could find to eat. The population was in a state of flux – everyone, even the occupying forces, knew that Germany was on the point of surrender. With the best will in the world, it was most unlikely that they would ever find Olivia's killer.

She approached the house still numbed by the shock of it, knowing that she must tell Mme Barfleur what had happened yet unable to believe that it was true, a real tragedy and not some foolish dream. Olivia would not run to the door when she heard her friend's voice, would not call down the stairs that Rochelle was to come right up because there was something she had to tell her . . . she would face a frightened and bewildered Mme Barfleur, possibly even Olivia's mother, Adrienne Buchet, called home when her daughter did not return from whatever outing she had been engaged on when she was done to death.

She rang the bell; a short wait and Mme Barfleur was opening the door. She looked much as usual, placid, smiling.

'Rochelle . . . come in, come in. I was just doing some knitting, but I baked not an hour since. Do you fancy potato cakes? I even have a little butter . . . Olivia brought me some, and some honey.'

Rochelle followed her indoors, still with the feeling that

it was not true, that Mme Barfleur would presently prove it, produce Olivia from her small bedroom upstairs . . .

In the kitchen, she took a deep breath and put a hand gently on Mme Barfleur's arm.

'Madame, when did you last see Olivia?'

Mme Barfleur was getting out a tray of potato cakes, putting them on a griddle to warm before the fire. She spoke without looking round.

'Yesterday, very early, my dear. She had a letter . . . you won't know about it yet, but such a wonderful letter! She could scarcely eat her breakfast for excitement. Do you remember she was told Theo was missing, presumed dead? Well, she had a letter from him yesterday morning . . . she was in ecstasy, dear little soul . . . saying that he had been injured but was now recovered, and would be coming to the island in a week or two to take her back with him to his home in Germany. She was weeping and laughing and kissing Hans, and then she flew upstairs, put a few things in a bag and left.'

'Oh, madame . . . where did she go? Did she say when she would be back?'

'Why, she went to her little house to make ready for Theo. She took Hans . . . he's been learning to say "Dadda"; he's such a clever boy . . . and meant to clean and polish and cook. I gave her some scallops which came my way, because they were always Theo's favourites. Why do you ask, Rochelle? Do you want to see her urgently?'

Mme Barfleur had warmed the cakes whilst she talked; now she got out butter and honey, put them on the table, and gestured to Rochelle to sit down. Rochelle felt like a murderer herself. She stood stiffly, keeping her eyes down, not wanting to see Mme Barfleur's face when she heard the news.

'Madame, I came to you because Olivia's been found . . . found dead. On the shore. Her body was washed up by the tide. Madame?'

Rochelle had to look up, had to show the pain that was now tugging at her own heart. It was as though she had been in a magic sleep until this moment, when the old woman's agony, disbelief and shock would rouse her to the same feelings.

'Rochelle? My – my girl is *dead*?'

Rochelle strained both arms round Mme Barfleur's considerable shoulders, trying to hug her, but the older woman resisted, not rudely or unkindly, but shrugging her off, struggling to take in what had been said.

'Dead? You don't mean hurt . . . injured, perhaps? Not *dead*, surely? Not when she had so much to live for?'

'Sit down, madame,' Rochelle said gently. 'I'll get you a cup of tea . . . is there tea in the cupboard?'

But Mme Barfleur, though she sat, obedient as a child, did not answer the question. Her lips were moving as though she spoke but not a sound came out.

17

It was fortunate that Adrienne Buchet came home whilst Rochelle was still trying to get the old lady to take in what had happened. She was brisk and sensible with her mother once she, too, had been told of Olivia's death. When they had called a doctor round and Mme Barfleur had been given a sedative and some brandy, she and Rochelle sat down in the kitchen over tea and the cold potato cakes and worked out what must have happened.

'She was so happy she wasn't even afraid of telling Wolf,' Adrienne declared, picking up a potato cake in her rather grubby, nicotine-stained fingers and taking a bite. 'She just rushed off home, and when I said what'll you say to Wolf she just said she'd tell him the truth because she wasn't frightened of anyone with Theo safe and well.'

'So you think she went home, and Wolf turned up,' Rochelle said. 'Was he a violent man? Would he really have killed her?' She remembered with guilt and misgiving her own advice to Olivia to follow her heart and not to let anyone over-persuade her. Olivia had said she was afraid of Wolf, but she said a lot of things she didn't mean and Rochelle had merely thought this was another example.

'I dunno; but she was scared of him all right,' Adrienne insisted. 'Said he could be weird. She had a chat with you a few days ago, didn't she? After that she went and told him she'd maybe stay here and wed an Islander after the war. He said she should remember he wasn't offering her a choice – either he had her or no one did. So I reckon he turned up at her house, she told him Theo was alive and coming back to the island, and he shot her.'

'Oh, my God! And put her into a boat and set it adrift?'

400

'What on earth makes you think he'd do that? I mean, he set a lot of store by that little cruiser of his. He said they'd go off in it if the Germans lost the war, find themselves somewhere to live where no one knew who he was . . . wild talk, silly talk, but that's all it was, after all. Just talk. He came of a good family back in Germany, so I reckon he'll come out of it all right, no matter what. I told Olivia so, but she was that set on Theo . . .' She sighed, running a hand through her harsh, peroxided hair. 'Poor little bugger. Don't make no difference now.'

'So you think he shot her? But will he ever go to trial for it?' When Rochelle thought of poor Olivia's pleasure in her child, her ecstasy over finding that her lover was not dead, she could have killed Wolf with her bare hands . . . how could he do it, and her friend little more than a child herself, barely nineteen years old and too loving and giving for her own good?

Adrienne shook her head doubtfully. She flicked a cigarette packet open and helped herself to one, then held it out to Rochelle.

'Want a fag? Plenty more where these came from . . . oh, you don't, do you? No more did Livia. You're right, of course. I don't reckon anyone'll ever stand trial for shooting my girl, but if Theo gets here before the war ends he'll do his best to see Wolf suffers for what he did. I'll tell him meself, if I have to.'

'I'd better go,' Rochelle said, suddenly realising that the light outside the window was fading into dusk. 'There's been enough trouble today without me finding myself in court for breaking the curfew.'

She went upstairs and took a last look at Mme Barfleur, but that lady was sound asleep and Rochelle knew it was better not to disturb her.

'She loved Olivia so much,' she said as she stood outside the front door grasping her borrowed steed. 'It's going to hit her very hard when she comes to terms with it.'

'It'll hit us both,' Adrienne said sombrely. 'Thank God we'll have Hans; it'll take our mind off things, looking after him.'

Rochelle, agreeing, could only hope that Hans was all right. For herself, as she started to cycle home, she thought that, with the exception of the day M. Laurient had been deported, she had never been so miserable. Olivia dead and Theo, who loved her, coming to find her . . . and the man who did it probably going scot-free. If he had done it. Though who else could have done such a thing?

All the way home on the creaky old bicycle Rochelle tried to tell herself that the tragedy was not her fault, that her advice had been sought and she had given it, never dreaming for one moment that it could come to this.

But there was something else which kept nagging at the back of her mind.

Olivia had loved Theo. But she had let herself be entrapped into making love with another man because Theo had not been around to make love to her. Because of this, she had died.

I love M. Laurient very much indeed, but I let Laurie make love to me, Rochelle thought guiltily. Of course, the cases were in no way similar, and she could not imagine M. Laurient shooting anyone, ever. But the principle was the same. Olivia's unfaithfulness, if you liked to put it so bluntly, had been the death of her. Fidelity was a great virtue, particularly in time of war.

I should never have let Laurie love me, Rochelle finally concluded tiredly as she cycled slowly up the last stretch of road in the gathering darkness. I like him very much and I liked what we did together even better, but that's no excuse, because it's M. Laurient that I love.

The woods surrounding the dower house had never seemed darker or more dangerous. She had been told that an old lady living a little way up the road from Mme Barfleur had been assaulted and badly injured in her own home by a German soldier searching for food. And she must get off the bicycle soon and walk between the dark and somehow threatening trees.

Tremulously, she dismounted and began to push her borrowed bike into the wood.

Laurie heard her coming and went to meet her. He did not want to frighten her so he left the back door open, with light streaming out, and the dogs, of course, came too, leaping and bouncing, delighted to see their mistress after her long absence.

He had not expected Rochelle to be gay and chatty when she returned, but neither had he expected the air of detachment, the chill which hung about her like a physical presence.

'Here, what's up?' he said bluntly, leading her indoors, where he sat himself in a chair and tried to pull her on to his knee. Her resistance was immediate and emphatic. She tugged herself free and scrambled away from him, her cheeks flushing.

'Don't!' she said abruptly, when he put a hand out to detain her. 'Don't!'

'Honey . . . you've had a dreadful day. Tell me about it.'

She told him, her voice small and somehow dead-sounding.

'They didn't know; she'd gone home. Her maman thinks it was Wolf who killed her. She says Olivia was frightened of him, thought him dangerous and violent.'

'Yes, but . . .'

'Theo, Hans's father, had written to say he was all right and was coming back to the island to take Olivia away with him. She was delighted, of course – she really did love Theo, Laurie – and decided to go home to her little house to get things ready for when Theo came. She said she'd tell Wolf that Theo was alive . . . I expect she was so thrilled herself that she couldn't imagine anyone else being upset, not even Wolf who had so much to lose by Theo's return. So she died.'

'Poor kid,' Laurie said. He meant it from the bottom of his heart, but he saw that Rochelle was still ill at ease with him. Surely not as a result of the tragedy? He must be gentle with her, show his love but not pounce on her as he frankly longed to do. It had been such a wonderful day until they had found Olivia, and Laurie longed to hold Rochelle, comfort her and be comforted in his turn. He got up after a few moments and went to the stove, made them each a cup of ersatz coffee, and went to perch on the arm of Rochelle's chair.

'All right, honey?'

She looked at him, then tried a smile. It was a poor effort, but he found it wonderfully cheering after her previous behaviour.

'I'm sorry, Laurie. Olivia and I were very close as children, and I can't help seeing a – a sort of parallel with you and me. You see, in a way, Olivia did wrong to let Wolf believe she would go away with him. She – she let him think she loved him, because she was afraid she might end up with – with no one. So he thought she was *his*, because they'd made love and lived together and things. Laurie, I like you very much, but . . .'

Laurie laughed, then leaned his head against her hair. He put his arm, very gently, round her shoulders. He felt her stiffen but she did not pull away this time.

'Honey, I'm not pushing a claim. We'll take each day as it comes, hey? And now, we've had one hell of a day; let's go to bed.'

They did. But Rochelle lay in her bedding on one side of the stove and Laurie lay on the other and neither tried to get closer, though Rochelle was chilly and miserable, unable to sleep.

'It's snowing,' she said in a small voice after an hour or

so had passed. 'Isn't that awful? Snow, and tomorrow's the first of May.'

'The world's gone crazy,' Laurie said sleepily. 'We had a heatwave a fortnight ago; now you tell me we've got snow.'

He wondered whether to take advantage of the cold and her unhappiness to try to mend the breach Olivia's death seemed to have caused, but then he reflected that it would probably be a stupid sort of thing to do. She would wake up tomorrow hating him – and hating herself more. No, he should take his own advice and push no claims, take each day as it came. That way, perhaps they could regain the delightful relationship they had enjoyed earlier in the day.

So Laurie snuggled down in his blankets and tried to forget that a warm and loving girl lay only feet away from him – a girl who meant more to him than he would have believed possible a week before. He had never been in love, but suspected that he was on the verge of that happy state and, naturally, wanted Rochelle to love him back. But native caution warned him that this was a prey which must be stalked with infinite care and stealth or it would take fright and run. It was hard, when he longed to catch her up in his arms and smother her in kisses, to sweep her off her feet, to take her to the States and give her . . . oh, all the things he had never cared much about, never thought worth having, like washing machines, wall to wall carpeting, and all the food she could eat or even dream of eating. Instead, he must show her friendship and nothing more, until she could share his deeper emotions.

Once during the night, however, he nearly jumped out of his bedding and went to her, because he could hear her quietly weeping. He shook with frustration, and with pity for her grief, but he forced himself to do nothing. Eventually the sobs slowed and ceased, her breathing deepened, and he knew she slept.

Only then could Laurie relax. And presently, slept also.

* * *

405

It took days for Rochelle and Laurie to find out what was happening. The authorities in St Helier did their best to get the occupying forces to bring Wolf before them, but this was complicated by the fact that no one knew Wolf's second name. The man who should have been able to tell them, Hauptmann Klein, was quite positive that he had no Oberleutnant on the island called Wolf.

'It must have been a nickname, I suppose,' Rochelle said to Laurie when she came home with the news. 'They're in a bad state, the Jerries – they literally don't know what to do next. Their forces are surrendering all over Europe, their people are going missing . . . they've always tried to cover up the failings of the master-race, and they're not likely to change now. Someone will probably be executed for Olivia's murder, possibly even the right person, but we shan't be told.'

'And the baby? How's little Hans?'

Hans had been found with an indignant friend who had taken him for an hour and found herself landed with him for two days. He had been dirty, hungry and rather frightened, but a couple of hours with Mme Barfleur, cooed over, fed and spoilt, had brought him, so far as Rochelle could judge, back to his normal happy self.

'He's too young, I hope, for it to scar him,' Rochelle said now. 'He's a happy child, not like . . .'

Her silence spoke, perhaps, louder than words would have done. Laurie let a moment pass and then said lightly, 'Not like you? You were much older, of course. Did it scar you, losing your parents?'

There was a pause whilst she considered her answer, but when she spoke it was coolly enough.

'In a way. You see, I'd always known that I wasn't . . . wasn't essential to my parents' happiness. They were complete as a couple; I always felt outside the charmed circle. But when they died I realised that no one really wanted me, not even M. Laurient at first. He took me in

406

from a sense of duty, I thought. Only as time passed I think I realised that it wasn't as I'd believed; he really liked me very much, he just wasn't a demonstrative man. And then, you see, I was happy.'

Laurie nodded, but he knew he couldn't really understand. His own mother had been a source of constant love to him, even after she'd given birth to the other children. And he found it impossible to see how Rochelle could possibly twist the daughterly love she clearly felt for his father into something so different. It was probably the war, he reasoned, and his father's going away. She had romanticised their relationship; all that would be necessary to set her straight would be his father's return.

It was a happy thought and one he clung to in the days which followed.

'It's over! I can't believe it . . . Laurie, it's over!'

They were crushed in the crowd which surged and shouted around the harbour as the first British naval pinnace came through the pierheads and landed two officers.

They were with an oddly assorted crew, were Rochelle and Laurie; the American prisoners of war milled around them, José with his arm firmly round Rochelle's waist, and half a dozen of the Russian prisoners, who had been in hiding with island families for years in some cases, had come out into the open at last, searching out their friends and fellow-sufferers, trying to find out what would happen to them, all grinning, all on fire with excitement to see the once-proud conquerors humbled, lined up, driven out, as low today as they had once been high.

'The cinemas have reopened,' Solly bawled as the good-humoured crowd parted to let the car with the naval officers aboard make its way to the harbour office. When the Union Jack was hung from one of the windows and the National Anthem sung, Rochelle was not the only one who shed tears; all around her Islanders were blinking and surreptitiously rubbing their eyes, some so full of emotion that they could not get out the words of the song which had been forbidden for five years.

'We could go see a flick,' Solly persisted, to be good-humouredly squashed by his companions, who were all on a high which could only be calmed by action. 'All right already, what'll we do, then?'

'Tour of inspection,' Laurie shouted. 'Let's see what's happening all over.'

They did. In a glorious, noisy gaggle they reeled from one end of St Helier to the other, and then into the surrounding countryside. They saw German soldiers flinging down their arms; every time they met a Tommy they mobbed him, cheering, exclaiming, wanting to know what was happening in the rest of the world, how the surrender was going.

The men asked numerous questions, but Rochelle only had one and she fired it at every soldier and sailor they met.

'What about Islanders deported to Germany? Will they be free soon? How long before they're home too?'

No one knew. At first, letters had been received from those taken away. Later, the letters had stopped coming. M. Laurient had never written; was this a good sign or a bad? But the message of good cheer which Rochelle heard most often was that the concentration camps were being taken over and the occupants would undoubtedly be home soon, though some would need medical treatment before being repatriated.

Rochelle nodded wisely at that. Of course they would have been underfed; that stood to reason. She herself had been hungry, on and off, for at least three of the last five years. Mme Barfleur had started the Occupation fat and was ending it, if not thin, then certainly not a pound over-weight. M. Laurient had been sturdy, square-shouldered.

She would rather he was properly fed and fit before he returned, she informed Laurie seriously. But oh, how she wanted him home again!

She was not the only one. Laurie longed to see his father, as he had ever since he had first read the magazine article about him, but now he had an even stronger reason than a natural desire to know a parent. When Rochelle saw M. Laurient again she would come to terms with her love, he was sure of it. She would see that it was right and proper for a girl to love her father *and* her lover. Giving love did not drain one's supply; indeed from his experience he would say it enhanced it.

He would have liked to tell Rochelle this newly acquired bit of wisdom, but he saw that she was in no mood to discuss such an irrelevancy. At the moment the liberation and her guardian's possible return were all that concerned her – and she was happy. Olivia's death was not forgotten, but she had put it out of her mind as something terrible which had happened in the past.

Now, she looked to the future. As he must.

'Give us another armful, then . . . go on, pile it up. I can manage it.'

Rochelle, thus adjured by Laurie, put an untidy mound of clothing on top of the stack of books in his arms and laughed as he staggered blindly to the back door. They were emptying the dower house and moving back into the manor, though as yet only the kitchen and the library at the big house had been cleaned and made fit for their occupancy.

'You are a fool, Laurie – how can you see over that lot? You'll drop everything as you cross the orchard, and we still don't have enough soap to wash clothes every time they get a bit of mud on them.'

'You could be right,' Laurie agreed ruefully, trying to

squint over the tottering pile in his arms. 'Take 'em off again, then.'

Rochelle took the clothes in her own arms, kicked the back door open and told the dogs, sternly, to stop milling around her and to stay where they were. Neither dog took the slightest notice of this last injunction but followed her happily, keeping far enough back, however, to give at least an illusion of obedience.

Rochelle set off at a brisk pace behind Laurie, who was striding out despite the weight of the books. He had applied to his chief for permission to stay on the island, explaining the situation, and had been told that he might remain until things were back to normal, by which time, it was hoped, his father would have returned.

It was good having him here. Rochelle knew that without him despair would speedily have engulfed her. Mme Barfleur had said she would come back to the manor as soon as they had sorted things out, but for now it was taking her and Laurie most of their time just to clean up, find enough furniture to put something in each room, and make lists of what had been taken so that perhaps, one day, the Germans might make good their depredations.

And in between cleaning the manor, carting their belongings from one house to the other, and cherishing the orchids, they were managing to enjoy the fine summer weather. They had brought the small cruiser out of its rocky fastness, but neither of them had the heart to use it, so they swopped it for a sail-boat with an outboard engine which they could run from the bay nearest the house and had already used several times for fishing. Peter had come out with them to show Laurie how to handle the boat, cast the nets and bait a line, and Laurie had taken to it like . . . like a duck to water, Rochelle thought now, with a grin. They had spent a happy, quarrelsome evening mending some crab pots which they had found cast up on the shore, and had already reaped a small harvest, sailing out after their pots whenever they could spare the time and the sea was calm enough.

'So do I put this lot on the shelves in the library?' Laurie said somewhat breathlessly as they entered the kitchen. 'I must say the Jerries kept the place quite well . . . I mean, nowhere stank, and they didn't write rude things on the walls . . . it could easily have been a lot worse.'

'It stank of Jerries,' Rochelle said. 'Beastly . . . it stank of their feet and their breath and their horrible food. That was bad enough.'

'All right, all right, don't be thankful for small mercies – why should you, after all? You've got me and Adrienne to slave for you.'

Rochelle glared at him, then softened and went over to plonk a kiss on the dusty hand grasping the books. It was quite safe to do so for, somewhat to her disappointment, Laurie had his affectionate self well in hand and only offered her the most chaste salutes. She missed the warmth of his hugs and kisses but told herself that he was being sensible and she must be sensible too. Very soon now M. Laurient would be home and then she would be able to take her time with Laurie . . . she could not have her dear monsieur come back only to find her mooning over his son. It would be a dreadful thing to do to anyone.

But now Laurie grinned at her and blew her a kiss back, though with a look in his eye which she could not interpret. 'What was that for? Sorry you're so mean to me?'

'Well, you and Adrienne did get landed with cleaning out the study, and it was easily the worst room. And you're right – it can't have been the officers who did . . . that; it must have been other ranks.'

He laughed and turned towards the door which led into the hall.

'I imagine that the other ranks wanted to show their dislike of the officers and chose that particular way to do it. They never thought we'd reap the benefit instead of the Jerries.'

Someone had shovelled the contents of a lavatory into the study. Rochelle had cried so bitterly when she opened the door that Laurie had become a despot. He had taken her into the kitchen, sat her down at the table with a mountain of peas, and told her to hull them whilst he and Adrienne dealt with the study.

'That room meant a lot to you,' he said. 'You mustn't think of it as you just saw it, but as it will be when we've finished.'

He had worked on that room until it was as fresh as a rose, and Adrienne had worked every bit as hard, for the older woman had been a tower of strength.

This was undoubtedly partly due to the fact that her husband had been told by some interfering busybody, as Adrienne phrased it, that his wife had been having a gay old time whilst he fought the Boche. And, as she pointed out, he couldn't have been all that innocent himself, since he had written a very nasty letter, the substance of which was that he had met a 'pure and lovely lady' in England and intended to marry her as soon as he could divorce Adrienne herself.

'So I'll come to the manor, with you and Maman,' she had said, still a trifle tearful over what she plainly thought was her husband's cruel desertion. 'Not a word did he write about our poor little Livvy, and he didn't want to hear about Hans . . . he's changed, that's all I can say.'

Her decision to come to the manor had not been disinterested, of course. Not by a long chalk. It was true that she worked hard for Laurie and Rochelle, but it kept her out of the way. The Islanders, not unreasonably, had gone on a rampage against those of their number who had, they felt, fraternised with the enemy, sometimes greatly to the detriment of local people. Informers, Jerry-bags and those who had quite deliberately ranged themselves on the side of the enemy had been dug out of concealment, and tarring and feathering, shaving heads and generally doling out brisk, well deserved punishment had been the order of the day.

Rochelle did not think, because of Olivia's death, that Adrienne would have suffered, but she did not say so. Everyone knew that young Mme Buchet had been easy, giving her all for a pound of butter or a pair of silk stockings. She felt safer, as well as more useful, in Augeuil Manor than she would have felt in St Helier, and her husband's sister-in-law, a plump, maternal woman who had long bewailed her childless state, was in her element looking after Hans. Rochelle guessed that Marie and Paul Buchet would adopt the child and she thought it the best thing for him. No slur would attach to him because of his parentage, and the couple undoubtedly adored the little boy.

'That's the lot, except for the things by the sink,' Laurie said, coming back into the kitchen. 'I'll get them, and then that'll be it.'

'I'll go,' Rochelle said at once. 'I've got to check the place over, make sure nothing's left. You stay here and clean up.'

'We'll both go,' Laurie said easily. There had been rumours lately of British troops fraternising with local girls, to their intense pleasure, and he did not want Rochelle wandering the woods alone. Rochelle, well aware of his feelings, grinned at him.

'Do you really think some sex-starved soldier will pounce on me if I'm alone in the woods for five minutes?' she demanded.

'No, of course not. But a sex-starved airman might,' Laurie said, grabbing her neck and growling softly. 'Oh, Chelle, we've been happy in the dower house, but won't it be great to be back at the manor? When my father comes . . .'

413

'You make it sound as though you'd lived in the manor before,' Rochelle said. 'Now, we'll want it perfect for M. Laurient. We'll clean the piano, and . . .'

'Sure, message received and understood. As soon as everything's here we'll *really* start.'

They entered the dower house as they always did, straight into the kitchen. Rochelle swept the cleaning materials into the old cloth bag she had been using to carry stuff from one house to the other and turned triumphantly to Laurie.

'There, you see? There was no need for you to come at all, but since you are here you can carry the bag.'

Laurie took the bag and turned for the back door.

'Sure; it's light enough. All clear now?'

'Yes . . . no . . . what on earth is this?'

Rochelle had run her hand along the back of the dresser and was now contemplating a filthy, stained piece of paper, examining it with distaste.

'Just one of my love-letters that you've cast aside, I guess,' Laurie said, grinning. 'Chuck it away, honey, and let's get on.'

'It's one of the things that were in your pocket when you first came,' Rochelle said. 'This and a couple of coins and a stub of pencil.'

She made to throw the paper down, but Laurie took it from her, frowning.

'Hey, d'you know, an old boy gave it to me, with an apple. He was talking French, but I think he said something about justice after the war . . . let's see.'

He frowned over the paper for a moment, then straightened, brow clearing.

'Got it! It's pretty filthy, but just about readable. It says Augeuil, then something I think must be manor, and then Magog. That's all.'

'That's here! Why on earth should an old Frenchman write a message about this house?' Rochelle said, frowning down at the paper. 'I don't recognise the writing. It's very wobbly and poor, isn't it? Why Magog? What's he done?'

'Who is he?' Laurie asked. 'One of the farm hands?'

'No, silly. It's the big china dog we use to keep the kitchen door open so that the animals can go in and out. It's hollow. I wonder . . .'

They both rushed to the kitchen, then stopped, grinning sheepishly.

'It's already at the manor, of course,' Rochelle said. 'Race you!'

She won easily and had already got the china dog upside down when Laurie burst into the kitchen, panting.

'There *is* something there . . . not loose, taped to the china,' she said. 'Hang on, I've got it . . . here you are.'

'It's a roll of film,' Laurie said, taking the small object from her hand. 'Who put it there? What's it all about?'

'It must be the photographs M. Laurient took of the Russian prisoners,' Rochelle said slowly. 'M. Laurient sent us a message so we'd find the film, just in case. It must have been him who gave it to you!'

'No way! I can remember him; it was an old boy, white-haired. And French, I'm sure of it.'

'Then your father must have sent the old boy with the message,' Rochelle said excitedly. 'What an incredible bit of luck that it was you who got it and brought it back here. What luck that you didn't just chuck it away . . . what luck that I didn't do the same! Oh, I can't wait to see whether it really is that film . . . I'll take it into St Helier tomorrow. Mme Barfleur's brother Henri is a chemist. He'll develop it for us, I know. And then we'll see.'

'Sure. Whilst you do that I'll bring some of the furniture up from the cellar and start setting it out again. Tom can give me a hand if he can be spared from the garden, though I can't promise that we'll put the stuff in the right places.' They had taken on a lad to help with the outdoor jobs, and already they could not imagine how they would manage without him.

'You are kind, Laurie. I'll bicycle in first thing, then.'

'And now, petite, we float them in this solution and you'll see the pictures gradually appearing. The negatives were so small that it was difficult to get much of an idea, but the prints will make it all clear.'

The chemist and Rochelle hung over the tray of developer. They watched the magic moments when, slowly yet inexorably, the black and the white began to separate out, darken, turn to a variety of shades, and the pictures came into focus.

'Yes, it is the Russians,' Rochelle said, her nose only inches from the surface of the liquid, her voice squeaking. 'There's our dear Radek . . . there are the soldiers, watching. Oh, my God, I'd forgotten . . . how could I ever forget?'

All over again, in silence and stillness, the Todt men emptied the bath of steaming potatoes into the filthy mud and water of the fish-pond. Horrified, the chemist put more pieces of the light-sensitive paper into the developing liquid and fresh scenes came sharply into focus. Men jeering and laughing as the prisoners scrabbled helplessly for their food; other men in uniform kicking potatoes deep into the mud; and the brutal figures of the Todt, their broad shoulders and well-clad bodies contrasting cruelly with the skeletal frames and suffering faces of the prisoners.

'They are terrible pictures, but nevertheless I'm glad to have seen them,' the chemist said at last as the final photograph was hung on the line to dry out. 'And you say you found them in a china dog, as a result of a message brought by the young American?'

'Well . . . yes. Only of course when M. Laurient gets home he would have shown them to us.'

'If he gets home,' the chemist said sombrely. 'You've not heard from him?'

'Heard? Well, no, but everyone says they'll soon be released.'

'But surely my sister was saying that no letters had come through the Red Cross? Doesn't that worry you?'

'Well, the letters might have gone astray, or he may have escaped and not be able to write to us,' Rochelle said doubtfully. 'But he'll come back . . . I'm sure he'll come back.'

'Yes, of course. Do you know, Rochelle, you're my first post-war customer? Now, my dear, these photographs must go to the bailiff, who will want them as evidence when these Germans come to trial, as they assuredly will. I'll make two sets of prints, shall I? Just to be sure.'

'Oh, yes, please. Perhaps three, in case the others get lost,' Rochelle said. 'I couldn't face M. Laurient if I'd lost his pictures.'

'Our people have coped with five years of Nazi rule. They'll cope with the aftermath, too; they won't lose important evidence. But you're right to be cautious, and I will do another set.'

'Thank you, monsieur. I'll take the first set to the bailiff's, shall I? How much do I owe you?'

But the chemist would take no payment, saying it was his civic duty, no less, to see that the crimes of the Nazis were put before the authorities. Rochelle thanked him fervently and soon set off, first to hand over the prints to the bailiff and then, hot-foot, to get home with the other set as quickly as possible. The third set had been left in the chemist's safe.

Laurie, she knew, would be as intrigued by the photographs as the chemist had been – and as keen to see justice done as she was herself.

* * *

417

'Laurie, Laurie, leave that and come, oh do come! Tom's just got back from taking the butter to market and he says the ship's arriving in an hour! They'll all be on it – the prisoners released from the concentration camps! Laurie, M. Laurient will be there . . . your *father*, Laurie!'

Laurie had been placidly ploughing a thin and ragged piece of pasture so that it could be fertilised and planted later in the year, but with Rochelle's abrupt arrival at his side he shouted to the horse and drew to a halt, wiping at the stinging sweat which ran down into his eyes, for it was a hot and breathless day.

'Steady on, honey,' he remarked. 'Start again . . . and how can I leave a horse and a plough in mid-furrow?'

'Tom's coming . . . look, he's running so we can leave at once. Come *on*, Laurie, or the ship will be in and we won't be there!'

Laurie found himself affected by her excitement. He was in patched and faded clothing, and he was dirty and sweaty, but he found himself as reluctant to waste time as she and merely waited for Tom to take the plough from him before grabbing the bicycle Rochelle had brought and wheeling it over the lumpy, thistle-rich pasture and on to the lane.

'Don't try to hurry,' he adjured her, however, as she set off, legs fairly twinkling, towards St Helier. 'You know what it's like – folk say an hour and it's more like two, and then the passengers have to disembark . . . just take your time. You'll find we'll still be there before there's a sign of a ship.'

'I can't. I have to hurry, I'm so excited,' Rochelle exclaimed. 'Mme Barfleur's making a beef stew with dumplings because he loves it, and one of her special apple and vanilla tortes, because he loves those as well. And I told her to get that red wine out of the cellar – there are a couple of bottles left – because he likes that too, only it has

418

to be served at room temperature so she has to get it out and let it breathe, whatever that may mean.'

'And you've lost your ribbon,' Laurie said with some satisfaction. He was excited himself, of course, but it was almost hurtful to see her so lit up, so radiant, at the prospect of seeing his father again. Now she wailed and turned back to peer down the road in the vain hope of seeing the little tail of red ribbon which had, until five minutes or so ago, adorned the end of the long, fat black plait which fell down the middle of her back.

'Oh, Laurie, how maddening! Never mind – you can lend me a bit of string or something, can't you? Or I could let my hair loose, only I don't have a comb . . . oh, I'm so excited!'

'I expect he's pretty high as well,' Laurie said. 'You'll point him out, won't you, honey? I feel a fool not knowing my own father!'

'Oh, you'll know him, he's ever so like you,' Rochelle said impatiently. 'Not so tall, and darker, but like, even so. Anyway, you'll know him because he'll come straight to me and I'll go straight to him. Oh, there's so much to tell him, so much to show him!'

'PM23 won't bloom this year,' Laurie said. 'But she's looking fine, I grant you that. And the house is looking good, if a bit bare. Still, we've done pretty well.'

'How do I look?' Rochelle said, turning towards him and then turning back again rather quickly as her bicycle hit a stone and wobbled. 'This is an awfully old dress . . . I wish I'd had time to put a clean one on, and some good sandals . . . oh, I wish I had a comb!'

'It won't matter, and you look lovely, old dress or not,' Laurie said, softening at the look of sheer happiness on her small, pointed face. 'Blue is your colour. It makes your eyes look brilliant.'

'It's very nice of you to say so,' Rochelle said gratefully.

'You're a kind person, Laurie, just like your father. Oh, I'm so excited!'

She kept up a continual gabble all the way down to the harbour and all the time they waited for the ship, and Laurie soon realised that it was mainly because she was terribly nervous. She knew she had changed, grown up, become a woman instead of the child his father had left, and she must have realised that Charles Laurient, too, would have changed. Laurie had said nothing to her about the sufferings of some of those who had fallen into German hands, but he supposed she must have a fairly shrewd idea that her M. Laurient would be a different person from the man who had been deported all those years ago.

When the ship came in she fell silent, however. Her small hand crept out and grabbed Laurie's, and she clutched him so tightly that he felt afraid for her – she was so tense, so terrified, so over-excited. What would she do when his father actually came ashore, and she saw him at last, face to face?

But the question, it turned out, was academic. The people who came off the ship were terribly thin, like the Russian prisoners of war in the photographs she had shown Laurie days before. Some of them looked scarcely human, and had to be helped ashore; others wept, the tears running down their grey faces, their mouths moving convulsively.

Beside him, Laurie felt that Rochelle was actually shrinking, becoming smaller. Once she pulled his head down so that she could whisper into his ear.

'Laurie . . . I've recognised someone. See that man . . . it's Albert Rousillon, the baker. I know I'm right, because his daughter just went forward and took his arm . . . but Laurie, he was such a fat and jolly man, always full of jokes and chatter. He doesn't have any cheeks at all, now, they've just caved in, and though he can't be more than thirty-five or six he's walking as if he was seventy. And his hair's completely white.'

'I guess it changes you, imprisonment,' Laurie muttered. He found he was afraid himself, now – afraid for his father. To come in good faith and joy to meet beloved ones and to see them reduced to these pathetic wrecks . . . no wonder Rochelle was trembling against him, her fingers in his as cold as ice.

The last person came down the gangplank, sailors began to move about the decks, and the crowd on the quayside dispersed. Rochelle gave a huge sigh and rubbed her nose with the back of her hand.

'He wasn't there,' she said. 'After all that, he wasn't there. Oh well, I suppose there will be other ships, other camps.'

There were other camps, and other shipments to the island as well. Few of those who had gone to Germany came back, but some did.

But Charles Laurient was not amongst them.

18

The sun shone hotly down on Laurie's head as he drove the old tractor with the binder attachment carefully round the far end of the six-acre, leaving stubble and sheaves behind him and facing, once more, into the golden sea of wheat. This was their first harvest and it looked like being a good one, though the seed had been sown late and was being reaped late, too.

A movement by the gate caught his eye and he glanced across, but quickly. Tom was stacking sheaves so that Laurie could have a go with the tractor, but he had never before driven on such a slope and was being extra-careful; the tractor had been old in Charles Laurient's day, the binder about the same vintage. It would not do to put either under too much pressure.

Rochelle was just coming through the leaning gate, lifting it so that it did not drive itself into the ground. She waved, and then went into the shade of an ancient oak tree which he had not yet approached with the tractor. She sat herself down on the cool grass with a thump.

'Dinner, Laurie,' she shouted. 'Dinner, Tom!'

Tom, coming along the line Laurie had just reaped and standing the sheaves up in stooks, bawled back some acknowledgement of her words, and Laurie waved carefully and was rewarded by her gurgle of laughter. She was amused by his reaction to their small, sloping fields, and said that if he was really coming back when he'd been demobbed he might as well get used to them, for nothing on earth would make any Islander knock down his hedges and his ancient trees just to please a crazy Yank who thought everything should be big and easy.

That had made him laugh, too. He had said that he knew one part of Jersey which was neither big nor easy and looked pointedly at her, but she had not understood, laughing with him but with the wide-eyed ingenuousness which he had no desire to see her lose.

Their relationship had not changed, though he thought it was warmer and closer; they were still friends rather than lovers. Never, since that memorable day at the beach, had she allowed him any sort of intimacy save that of living in the same house and sharing her problems. She was charming and affectionate, she asked for his advice and occasionally took it, but she never left him in any doubt that she was waiting for Charles Laurient's return and anything else was in the nature of a stop-gap.

It would have hurt him deeply had he not understood her so well. She was fiercely faithful, would never let a friend down, and she knew she owed everything she valued to Charles Laurient. That his father would accept the fact that she could want a lover whilst still needing the father-figure he had become did not occur to her. She believed that it was a sort of infidelity to love two men, so she would not let herself fall for Laurie. But when the elder Laurient comes back, Laurie told himself now, it will all be so much easier. I can wait.

'I'll just finish the row,' he shouted as he passed her. She nodded, setting out the food on a cloth, pouring cider into glasses.

She grew lovelier with each passing day, Laurie thought. She would always be slim, but with better food and less anxiety she had a glow of health and a *rounding*, which suited her. Today her long hair was plaited and the faded cotton dress showed her lithe body tanned to a golden brown. She would have looked good in any society, at any time; a summer girl, healthy and content.

He finished the row, turned off the engine and climbed down. He was wearing an old shirt of M. Laurient's, open

423

down the front since he was a bigger man than his father, and told himself as he strolled across the stubble that he really should take time to buy himself some pants and shirts. When he went back Stateside he could scarcely go as a farmer's boy!

He reached Rochelle and slumped down beside her. It was good to be in the shade for a while, to hear the country silence broken only by the buzz of a passing bee, the lark's song rising into the blue above.

'Have a pasty,' Rochelle said, leaning nearer him with the luscious object in one hand. 'There's a big one each and some little ones for later.'

Laurie and Tom both reached forward, grinned, apologised and did it again. They all laughed, but Rochelle clapped a hand to her brow, saying, 'Oh, Tom, I've just remembered. Your mother asked me to get you to run home if you would, just for a few minutes. She's had a letter from London and isn't too good at reading English. Do you want to have your dinner first, or go now and eat later?'

'I'll go now,' Tom said, heaving himself to his feet. 'I'll just have a swig of cider, then eat my pasty on the hoof. I shan't be long.'

Rochelle handed him a glass and Tom drank, eyes closed, throat working industriously, then wiped his mouth with the back of his hand.

'Jeez, I needed that!'

'Tom, if you start using American slang I'll send Laurie right back where he came from,' Rochelle warned, giggling. 'What would your father say?'

'Does it himself,' Tom said laconically. 'Save me some of those cheese and onion things.'

'I'll put them back in the basket right now,' Rochelle promised. She picked up her own pasty and bit into it. 'Gosh, Mme Barfleur is still the best cook in the world,' she announced thickly.

424

'She sure is; and just why did you want to get rid of Tommy?' Laurie asked, sitting up and reaching for the beer bottle. 'Has his mother really had a letter from London?'

'Yes, really. So've we.'

She produced, from the pocket of her dress, a square white envelope. 'It's addressed to both of us; shall I open it now?'

'Woman, you must be devoid of all human curiosity,' Laurie said lazily. 'Addressed to us both? Yes, you open it.'

She slit the envelope and drew out several pages. He saw that her fingers were trembling, and moved nearer to her so that he could read over her shoulder. Together, they scanned the letter.

Dear Miss Dubois and Mr Laurient,
   As you know, your guardian and parent is a client of mine and, according to instructions given me before the war, when hostilities ceased I waited for him to contact me. When he failed to do so I opened a letter, addressed to myself, which he had written to accompany his Will. Though I helped him with his affairs he was, as you know, a lawyer himself and had drawn up his own Will some time before.
   M. Charles Laurient's letter informed me that should he fail to contact me after the cessation of hostilities it would almost certainly mean that he was dead. In the event of his death he wanted me to get in touch with you both and to implement at once the terms of his Will, including the handing over of various stocks and shares which I hold for him and the recovery of certain valuables stored, I understand, in a sea-cave, the whereabouts of which are known to Miss Rochelle Dubois and no one else.

Rochelle gave a muffled exclamation. 'I'd almost forgotten the sea-cave,' she said. 'But M. Laurient *isn't* dead. This fellow had no right . . .'

Laurie stroked her cheek and put a finger over her lips.

425

'Finish reading the letter and then we'll discuss it,' he advised.

Naturally, I was most unwilling to assume that my client was dead when I had made no proper enquiries [the letter went on]. So I at once put such enquiries in train. It was easy enough to discover that Charles Laurient was taken from Jersey and brought by ship and train and Army lorry right across Germany to a small camp near the town of Welmsdorf. This camp was heavily bombed by Allied aircraft in the early months of 1944 and many of the prisoners killed. Since Charles Laurient was not amongst those liberated in June 1945, we must, I fear, assume that he was killed in the course of one of our Allied raids.

Accordingly, I am now putting his instructions into effect and therefore enclose the Last Will and Testament of Charles Edward Laurient, along with details of properties held in this country by me in trust for Rochelle Dubois and Daniel Laurient, his joint heirs and successors.

Rochelle finished reading as Laurie did and sat back on her heels. Tears shone in her eyes but her cheeks were flushed with temper and she shouted at Laurie, as though he had denied it, 'He is *not* dead! This fellow has no right ... I don't want the money or the estate or the stocks and shares. I want M. Laurient!'

'All right, all right,' Laurie said soothingly. 'But honey, what else is the guy to think? People did get killed in bombing raids, and if he was alive he'd come forward, surely?'

'No, not necessarily. He's probably got a very good reason for not coming forward ... he's lost his memory or something, but it'll come back and then he'll come home, you'll see!'

'You may be right. But in the meantime, Rochelle, this guy's right too. We've got no claim on the estate, the money, anything, until my father's legally pronounced dead, and we can't run the place on air. Wouldn't he want us to go on running it?'

'Yes . . . but I can't say he's dead when I know very well he isn't, and I don't want the damned money or the manor . . . not without him.'

'I know how you feel. Look, let's leave it until I'm demobbed, shall we? I'll be leaving here in a few weeks; perhaps I can do some finding out on our own account. What do you say to that?'

Rochelle sighed and put her hand into the bowl of fruit. She drew out an apple and bit into it.

'All right, I suppose so. Unless I was to go . . . I'd know him at once, of course.'

'Don't be silly; who's going to run this place if you leave? Who's going to make sure that Pure Madonna blooms next season? Who's going to see that it *is* Pure Madonna, come to that? After all your work to keep the orchids alive . . .'

'All right, all right, I give in. I'll stay here and vegetate and you can go and have adventures. I tell you what, though, Laurie . . . when Pure Madonna does bloom and we put it on show he'll see it and remember and come back to us. It's been his life, creating that flower.'

There was no arguing with her. He found himself agreeing to write to the London solicitor, to start another search going, and not to do anything about proving the Will until they had concrete evidence of Charles Laurient's death.

'Or proof that he doesn't want to come back for some reason,' Laurie said, but this was judged too foolish even to be considered by his co-heir.

'Look around you, Laurie! Think of the manor, the orchids, this beautiful island,' Rochelle urged. 'Who wouldn't want to come back to all this more than anything in the world? Only a madman.'

And Laurie, looking at the waving golden wheat, at the wooded hills and the Jersey cows grazing nearby, could only agree with her. This was paradise – who could possibly want more?

* * *

427

Rochelle had never visited the airport before, she told Laurie, and she never wanted to come again. She had been dry-eyed over his leaving until they reached the airport, and then it was as though she had suddenly realised how much he meant to her and how much his going would mean, too. She cried silently, tears coursing down her cheeks and soaking into the neat grey wool dress she had bought from Olivia's small store of garments when Adrienne had decided to sell anything she could not wear herself.

'Don't cry, goose,' Laurie said bracingly. 'I'll be back one day.'

'But I thought you were just going home and coming straight back again,' Rochelle wailed, clutching his new tweed jacket as though she would have to be prised loose when the plane landed. 'Now, out of the blue, you say you could be months . . . years!'

'Rochelle, you must be fair . . . what is there here for me? You won't agree to proving the Will and of course whilst you think my father's still alive nor should you. But winter's over and spring's nearly over too and no one's seen hide nor hair of him. We've had reliable people searching and the only crumb of information they've come up with is that when the concentration camp was bombed as many as a hundred of the inmates were known to have died. They can't give them names, honey, because . . . oh, hell, because they couldn't sort out the bodies, but they put Charles Laurient down as missing, presumed dead. What more can they say?'

'He probably escaped,' Rochelle said wildly. 'He'll come back soon, I know it!'

'Sure, I hope he does, but in the meantime we can't live on air, hon! We've been scratching and scraping just to keep going, the estate desperately needs money spending on it, and all you'll say is that things will get done when M. Laurient comes back. The house is crumbling around

428

our ears, we can barely raise enough to pay Tom's wages and feed ourselves, yet you won't draw money from the stocks and shares even to keep the place going. At least with me gone you'll have one less to feed.'

'But we need every man we can get,' Rochelle mumbled, hiding her face in his sleeve. 'You know you do most of the work – I'm just not strong enough for lots of things. And I can't pay another man, so how shall we manage, Tom and I? And then there's the orchids . . .'

'The orchids are the main reason I'm going,' Laurie reminded her patiently. 'Your trouble, Rochelle, is that you're too damned pig-headed. You won't let us try to turn Augeuil Manor into an hotel because you say when Charles comes back he'll be upset. You won't let us draw money from the estate to get the farmland back into use and to employ help on the land. So I reckon we're going to have to use the orchids instead of just raising them, as my father did.'

'There aren't enough specimens for anyone to be interested in seeing them, not now,' Rochelle said, between gulps. 'You say people will pay a lot of money to be shown round the glasshouses once they're in full production again, and we'll raise cash by selling stud plants and cut flowers, but how can we? We've barely got a dozen different species and they're all hardy ones.'

'Precisely. So I'm going to get us hundreds of different species, mainly tropicals. And then we'll be able to make a good living without touching the house or the money in the bank. All right?'

'No. It could take years,' Rochelle objected, rubbing the tears from her eyes the better to glare at him. 'Why bother to come back at all, Laurie, if that's the way you feel? Why not just stay away?'

'Perhaps I will,' Laurie said gently. 'I'd come back for your sake, Chelle, not for my own. But if that's how you feel, perhaps I will.'

She stared at him; the big eyes grew bigger as more tears came and rolled unchecked down her pale cheeks.

'Wouldn't . . . wouldn't you miss it?' she whispered at last. 'Wouldn't you miss the island . . . the manor? Me?'

'Of course – especially at first. But honey, what you've got you don't value. Perhaps when you haven't got me you'll begin to value me a bit.'

He had not meant to tell her the real reason why he was going, but now it was out and she was considering it, a frown etched between her winged brows, white teeth chewing her lower lip.

'Value you? But I do . . . you're wonderful. I don't know how I shall manage without you. Only . . . I'm waiting, you see.'

'Yes, I do see. And you won't let me be anything but a friend and I can't stand it, honey; no red-blooded guy could. So I'm off. If you ever change your mind, decide you want me back . . .'

She scrubbed fiercely at her eyes again.

'I shan't need you or want you back once M. Laurient comes home,' she shouted. 'You go, Laurie, you go! I'll manage somehow.'

The plane was long in; now his flight was called. He tried to take her in his arms, to say at this last moment that he was sorry, that they must part friends, but she was halfway to the door, refusing to hear his shout, putting on a spurt of speed when she heard his footsteps behind her.

Laurie stopped and stood watching as she ran towards the door. He felt old, suddenly, and tired. She was only speaking the truth when she said she did not want him, so he had best forget her, and the island, as soon as he could.

On the other hand, he mused as he queued to board, he *was* his father's heir and he did love the island and the manor. Why should he give up everything just because a spoilt brat of a girl was fool enough not to fall in love with him? He would go home, collect his orchids, and then marry the prettiest, silliest girl he could find and take her back to Jersey with him. That would give Rochelle something to think about, when he turned up with a wife and demanded his share of the inheritance.

The thought was the only thing which gave him satisfaction on the long journey back to America.

Alone once more, this time in the manor house and not the cosier dower house, Rochelle set out to show Laurie that he was completely and utterly wrong. She could manage simply by farming the land, and rear the orchids for pleasure not profit. No one wanted orchids, so far as she knew – certainly no one had approached her for them – so she would soldier on somehow, and show him that it could be done.

She often wished she had not been so rude, so hurtful, though. She dreamed of writing to him, explaining that she had been tense and not herself when she had spurned his help, his ideas. Still, having done it, she should prove first of all that she did not need him. When she had done so, perhaps she might look a little deeper into her heart – which ached and ached in the long, lonely nights – and see that she had been foolish and impetuous to send him away, deny that she loved him.

Because with every aching, empty hour that passed, Rochelle knew that Laurie had been more than a strong arm, a willing back, more even than a partner and helpmate in farm and glasshouse. But she did not intend to tell him this, not until she could make him see how independent and self-reliant she was.

But the day she went out to the glasshouse and found the first bud on PM23 she very nearly did something desperate – what good is success if you have no one to share it with? – and cabled America. She was only prevented from doing so by the fact that she had no idea where Laurie had gone; she did not even know his mother's

431

address. He had said he would write when he was settled and he had not yet done so.

So she gloated over the orchid alone, and told herself that her pleasure was the purer for being unshared, her joy more unalloyed. And then, to prove it, she went into St Helier and told Mme Barfleur and Peter and his sister, his parents, as many of her schoolfriends as she could find, even her great-aunt, whose indifference to her grandniece was almost as deep as her indifference to orchids.

Only when she went out to the L'Oyette place did she get the sort of enthusiastic reaction she longed for, and that, she acknowledged to herself, was only because it gave Tante Denise hope that, when the orchid actually flowered, it would persuade Radek to get in touch.

Because there had been no word, no letter, nothing, and Tante Denise was seriously afraid for her boy. She had heard with horror of the terrible vengeance wreaked by the Russians on their returning prisoners of war, on the shifting and unreliable grounds that because they had been in capitalist enemy hands they could no longer be trusted as Communists.

But Radek would surely not have gone home to Russia, when he had been fighting with the Allies, speaking English, for so long? So she waited and hoped, and encouraged Rochelle to go down to speak to a reporter on the local paper so that when the plant flowered it would at least have local coverage.

And in the meantime, waiting, Rochelle sowed her seeds in a new way, in a test-tube of agar-jelly mixed with a salt solution, and waited for them to germinate, which would take at least a year. This was the way the big professional growers used, and since she intended to become a big grower she might as well start with the seeds. She knew that M. Laurient had preferred the more traditional approach, but she could only go so far in her efforts to please a man who was not on the spot to be consulted. So

432

she used her little wand to fertilise the flowers in order, she hoped, to start a new hybrid line, and she planted the resultant seeds in the agar-jelly and gave the orchids all her love because, just now, they were the only ones who seemed to want it.

She could not help getting excited as the summer advanced and the buds on PM23 got bigger and bigger and another specimen from the same hybridisation also budded. She saw a pale, creamy-gold lining on one of the buds and rushed to the house to look up the old sketches M. Laurient had done of his father's plants, but there were no pictures of buds and the full flower showed no sign of creamy-gold.

The man from the newspaper came to see her – he was young and keen, but he blotted his copy-book by suggesting that the manor might easily be turned into an hotel when Rochelle told him that the estate money was tied up.

And then, tragically, Senna died.

He had been playing with something he had found in the woods, Pod hanging about near him and drooling, but with typical labrador greed the moment Rochelle had demanded to be told what he had, sir, he swallowed it. Next day, when she went down to the kitchen, he was dead.

Pod had had none of it, whatever it was, or so Rochelle told the vet when she and Tom carried the body into St Helier. Yet Pod died twelve hours later, in the same way as Senna – quietly, in her sleep.

It was a mammoth task but Rochelle buried them both in the orchard, she and Tom digging the grave deep and broad to accommodate the huge dogs. Rochelle comforted herself and everyone else by reminding them how old Senna and Pod were – fourteen, she thought – and by telling herself that they had led happier and more eventful lives than many a human being.

But she missed them; missed them sorely.

19

In her small bedroom at Augeuil Manor, Rochelle was dressing. Alone. It was a week to the day since she and Tom had buried the dogs and it was high time, she knew, that she got herself a puppy and began to try to remember Senna and Pod with affection and not with tears.

Today she was going down to the sea-cave, because she had finally decided that over some things, at least, Laurie was right. It was July, Laurie had been gone four months, no word had come from the London solicitor about his continuing search for M. Laurient, and Rochelle needed money.

She had decided that, rather than go mad with loneliness and overwork, she would employ Mme Barfleur, Adrienne, young Tom and one more person to help on the farm, her old friend Peter de Causis from school.

Peter, working in a bank, had been far keener to change his job than she had dared hope. His father's smallholding was not sufficiently lucrative to keep all the de Causis boys employed, so Peter had entered banking as a teller, and very boring he found it. He was delighted to have the chance of working for the estate, especially with a view to one day becoming estate manager, for Tom, though a good lad, could never aspire to such heights.

But in order to pay fair wages and to buy all the seed, fertiliser and equipment she would need, Rochelle had to go to the sea-cave and bring back some of the goods she had helped M. Laurient to hide. She salved her uneasy conscience by telling herself that she would put half the money she received straight into the bank in Laurie's name, and remembered that M. Laurient had actually told her that if she ever needed money and he was not around she might sell some of the goods in the sea-cave.

She did wish, though, that she had visited the cave with Laurie. As it was, she had cruelly and selfishly refused to show him the way, so that if anything had happened to her he would simply have had to forget the treasures his father had hidden. At the time she had done it out of pique, because he had tried to persuade her to use some of the estate money, even though he agreed that his father might well still be alive somewhere, but now she regretted her pettiness.

And who should she take with her to M. Laurient's treasure trove? Tom was simple and honest, but she knew very well that he might tell someone without really meaning to do so. Peter was a grand chap and would keep the secret . . . but it was not her secret to share. She knew, of course, that she must go alone, but she was putting it off until the last possible moment.

And now the last possible moment had come. She remembered her own childish awe over what M. Laurient had said were 'negotiable assets', the gold and jewellery which he had bought so that they would have something of permanent value to sell when it was needed.

'A hedge against inflation,' the solicitor had called it, rather grandly, when Rochelle had gone to the enormous expense of phoning the mainland to ask for his advice. He had encouraged her to sell some of the jewellery, but he had worried her by begging her not to sell the family sapphires, nor such items as were old Laurient jewels.

'Look at the portraits,' he had advised, and Rochelle had rung off before remembering that the portraits, too, were down in the sea-cave, whence she could scarcely remove them by herself. Indeed, it was this which had largely persuaded her that, despite the solicitor's warnings, it would have to be the jewellery which was sold. She could fill her pockets with gold chains and ruby rings, but she would need both hands to climb back up the cliff and she could not see herself doing it with huge portraits of long-dead Laurients in her arms.

Now Rochelle put on an old grey shirt which had belonged to M. Laurient and had to be folded almost twice around her small person, and some faded grey trousers which she had acquired from a church jumble sale the previous winter. In these and with a rope around her waist, she hoped to get to and from the sea-cave safely – and unseen.

Downstairs, Mme Barfleur and her daughter squabbled over breakfast; Adrienne had a new gentleman friend, Mme Barfleur told Rochelle sourly, and he kept her out too late at night for a decent household. Adrienne said that provided she did her work and was always on time in the mornings it was no one's business how she spent her nights.

Rochelle kept quiet; she had sympathy with both parties but did not intend to get involved. Instead, she ate her cereal with creamy milk from their own cows, had a boiled egg which the hens had laid out in the henhouse only the previous day, and finished up with toast and butter – more home produce – and a cup of real coffee.

It was a good meal and she felt she needed it to get through the ordeal ahead. It was a cold day and a sea-mist hung about the coast; she had seen it, thick and white, from her bedroom window. She would have liked to add a stout jersey to the rest of her outfit, but was afraid she might find it too cumbersome and hot, so despite Mme Barfleur's automatic objection she set off just in the shirt and trousers and a pair of rope-soled yachting shoes which she would shed as soon as she got near enough to the cave to climb. She had far more faith in the soles of her own feet so far as clinging to a rock-face was concerned.

The road down to the cliffs was familiar and she enjoyed every foot of it. The beauty of woodland, pasture and heath always delighted her; a whole world in miniature, it

436

seemed. But today she knew she would be descending the cliffs, and it took some of the shine from the day. It was odd, she thought, because she had never feared heights, had always enjoyed scrambling about on the rocks. Perhaps it was because she still felt guilty about breaking into M. Laurient's treasure trove for her own use. Also, there were more people about in July than there would have been, for instance, in March. If she was seen – if someone followed her – then she would perforce lead them to the treasure-cave and the 'hedge against inflation' would be lost to Laurie as well as herself – and M. Laurient, of course.

It made her feel ill to contemplate such a thing, and once again she blamed herself bitterly for not letting Laurie help her empty the cave and bring the stuff to the bank for safe-keeping. And then it occurred to her that someone might already have discovered the cave, might have emptied it long since – a German officer, or a group of Todt men, or even local boys who needed money to get abroad and fight the enemy.

It was a horrid thought, but at least it galvanised her into action. She reached the cliffs, glanced round at the misty morning, looked down to check on the state of the tide and found that she could see nothing. It was like looking down into a swirling cup of milk.

But it made her feel safer, that mist. She lowered herself over the cliff, praying hard that she could still remember the route after so long, and found that her feet and fingers seemed to know the way even if her conscious mind had forgotten.

Rapidly, skilfully, she traversed the rock-face, then began to climb down, up again, sideways once more. It was not easy, it had never been easy, but it was, happily, perfectly possible provided you never looked down or considered defeat.

Presently, she knelt on the ledge outside the sea-cave. There was a bad moment when she found she was shaking and knew she could never go inside, into that place which she had last visited with M. Laurient, and then she controlled it, slid sideways into the narrow crevice, and was once again standing in the sizeable sea-cave. Ill-lit, rock-floored, but dry – and piled with the canvas bags and packages and boxes that she and M. Laurient had brought here over six years earlier.

A sigh escaped her. It was all here; she had not brought them to ruin with her horridness. In a moment she was ferreting through the bags, not bothering to open them, feeling and squeezing until her fingers found the canvas bag with the leather straps and the metal fastenings, heaved them apart somehow and slid inside.

In the semi-dark she would never have been able to see the contents properly, but her fingers recognised them at once. Chains . . . bangles . . . rings . . . this must be the bag she wanted. She had no desire to carry it, though; it was too different, too obvious, if she met someone. Instead she brought a couple of fat handfuls out of the bag and crammed them into her trouser pockets.

Only then, with the stuff safely stowed, did she turn round and try to check that all was well with the rest of M. Laurient's treasure. Everything appeared to be here . . . square shapes which were pictures, boxes holding family silver, a bag she remembered dragging through the crevice herself which M. Laurient had told her contained a silver jardinière of great value and surpassing ugliness which he hoped might lie here for many a year.

However, her pockets were full, and she must set out on the return journey. It was odd, though, how reluctant she was to leave now that she had gained the sea-cave. She longed to look into all the bags and boxes and packages, to see just what it was that had lain here throughout a world war, waiting to be brought out again to face the light of the sun.

But there was no point in hanging around here until the

sea-mist had cleared and everyone could see where she had been and what she was doing. Resolutely, Rochelle started off once more. This time the jewellery with which her pockets were laden made her ascent awkward, the weight at times swinging her rather dangerously sideways.

But she made it. She reached the lip of the cliff and swung herself on to firm ground, and then set off at once for the manor without so much as a glance behind her.

Dog-trotting along the dusty lane – for she had no wish to fall in with someone who might want to steal her recently acquired treasure – it occurred to Rochelle that this was the first time in heaven knew how many years that her day had not started with a visit to the orchids. Should she just pop in and take a look at them on her way back to the manor?

With a fortune in your pockets? she scoffed at herself as she climbed the stile into the home meadows. You couldn't be so silly! It won't take a moment to go back indoors and leave the jewellery there.

But she could not resist a quick peep in at the first glasshouse, the one which contained the plants of the PM23. And as she looked in, colour met her gaze . . . blue, white and pink!

Rochelle forgot the jewellery, forgot her recent fears, forgot how frightened she was over the responsibility of selling the stuff in St Helier later in the morning. She just gazed and gazed, and then tears began to fall and she wept . . . because it had happened. After all the years, it had happened.

They had made Pure Madonna, she and M. Laurient, and he was not here to see!

It was everything she had dreamed and more – a pastel flower, the colours merely tinting the purity of the white, sepals the palest of lavender blue, the petals small and flicked in to form what looked like gold curls, and the lip of

439

the flower just shaded with pink so that at first and indeed at second glance the whole formed a face, with golden hair and a blue virgin's veil surrounding it.

Even the features could be imagined . . . nay, could be *seen*, Rochelle realised with wonder. They were merely the faintest bruise of shading on the lip but because of the shape of it, because of the image in your mind already, you could see the lowered eyelids, the small, straight nose, and the mouth, pale-lipped, closed, prim. Secretive. Totally beautiful and totally different from any other orchid that Rochelle had either seen or imagined.

She stood in the glasshouse for a long time, just gazing. Only one bud was in flower, the topmost one. With her previous experience to go on, Rochelle guessed that the madonna image would be clearest on the first day, as the bud unfolded its petals. As it came to its fullest flowering it would look more commonplace, more ordinary – less, in fact, like the face of the Pure Madonna Charles Laurient's father had called it. Even so, it was a wonderful thing, which would intrigue orchid growers all over the world.

Presently, she remembered her duty; she turned and the jewellery in her pockets made little warm movements against her thigh and she knew she would have to work quickly now to ensure that the orchid was seen by everyone at this precise moment of its perfection. She had no idea how long the flowers bloomed, though she seemed to remember that M. Laurient had said they were not particularly long lived and would not outlast a week or two.

She ran to the house; Mme Barfleur and Adrienne were still in the kitchen, but they were no longer alone. Tom and Peter were having their elevenses at the big kitchen table: milky coffee and bread and cheese with pickled onions. Peter had an onion in one cheek and a big mug in his fist; he was trying to talk with his mouth full, with muffled results. Tom was interposing remarks here and

440

there; both young men looked happy, well fed and intent on each other. No one looked up as Rochelle burst in.

'It's flowered!' Rochelle shrieked. 'It's out . . . it's the one, the one we wanted, it's the Pure Madonna . . . come and see!'

They were as excited as she; to a man they rose and left the kitchen, running – or waddling, in Mme Barfleur's case – to the glasshouse, standing stunned in the doorway, then exclaiming, laughing, almost weeping, seeing as clearly as Rochelle herself that this was an extraordinary and wonderful thing, this creation of a new flower never before seen except by Edward Laurient and a handful of estate workers more than thirty years earlier.

'You've done wonders, girl,' Mme Barfleur said. She hugged Rochelle hard, then kissed her forehead, a benediction. 'You've worked like a slave, spent all your free time in here, and now you're rewarded. Eh, I never thought I'd live to see the day.'

But Rochelle could not allow this to go unchallenged.

'Oh no . . . not me, M. Laurient,' she reminded them. 'He did it all, the experimenting, the tries that nearly came off but didn't quite . . . he did this one, too, remember. It takes six years for some orchids to flower; M. Laurient set the seed for this one more than six years ago . . . more than seven, probably nearer eight . . . because of course we couldn't give it perfect conditions whilst the war was on. But now . . . oh, madame, do you think he'll come back to see it?'

Mme Barfleur looked startled, then sad . . . and then enveloped Rochelle in another warm and breathtaking hug.

'My dear child, haven't you realised? *You* were the little flower M. Laurient was most interested in – yours was the flowering he waited for most urgently. Had he been able to do so, he would have come home as soon as the war was over, to see how his particular *petite fleur* was blossoming.'

Rochelle stared at her for one long, aghast moment and

441

then buried her head in her hands, shutting out the kindly, interested faces, the concern on them, even shutting out the Pure Madonna.

'No . . . no, you've got it wrong,' she whispered. 'It was the orchid, it was always the orchid.'

But her heart was heavy; Mme Barfleur's words had the ring of truth, and it was a truth she dared not let herself face. Or what was the point of living?

Far away, in New York City, three old friends sat round a table with maps spread out in front of them and cups of coffee at their elbows. They had been out drinking earlier to celebrate their reunion: one of those odd coincidences which happen once in a lifetime.

Laurie, having made as many arrangements for his orchid-collecting expedition as he could — having obtained orders and promises of help, and engaged an experienced packer to join him — put an advertisement in the *New York Times* asking for anyone interested in an adventurous and financially exciting expedition to the Andes to contact him at a box number.

He had scores of replies, mostly from cranks or madmen, all of which he threw in the wastepaper bin. But two of the applicants interested him strangely. One, a certain José Santander, claimed to speak fluent Spanish of the type spoken in South America, and the other, one Solomon Cohen, announced he had money to sink into a lucrative venture and a great thirst for new places and new people.

He had arranged to meet these two at a well known drugstore just off Times Square, calling himself John Daniels. Their astonished delight on seeing each other paled into insignificance upon discovering the real identity of 'John Daniels', and when they heard that Laurie was set on hunting orchids their delight reached new heights. They admitted total ignorance but vowed that they would read books on orchids until they could recite the details in their sleep, and Solly's money, which Laurie had suspected to be fictitious, was in truth there and at his disposal.

'My grandpa died and left me his shekels because I fought in the war,' Solly said, grinning. 'Oh, boy, how bored I bin ever since we got demobbed! I ain't no tailor, to sit cross-legged in the city stitchin'. I got better things to do with my time.'

'Like hunting orchids, amigo?' José said slyly, and they all fell about laughing because it seemed such an unlikely way to earn a living.

'But there's a great deal of money in it,' Laurie said, and told them what he had already been promised for new stud plants, for a good many of the orchid growers, both in the States and in England, had lost plants through disease or ill luck and needed fresh, virgin stock from the jungles to revitalise their own strains.

'And what's the reason for you giving up the little girl in Jersey?' José asked at length, as they studied maps of the country they intended to visit. 'I thought you'd got it bad, Laurie.'

'I had; she hadn't,' Laurie admitted. 'It's partly for her sake that I want the orchids, actually.'

And he told them how the estate and the money had been left, and all about the Pure Madonna which might even now be flowering on Jersey.

'But it may never flower at all, or it may not be the bloom she wants,' he added. 'And she's very short of species, now, after the war. If she won't turn Augeuil Manor into an hotel and she won't take her inheritance and use it to get the farming land shipshape, then about all she can do is rear orchids, show them and sell them. And she can't even do that without new species to enrich her stock. Why, she hasn't got a decent exotic left, apart from the hybrids of the Pure Madonna.'

'Which may turn out nothing special,' Solly concluded

for him. 'Well, shall we do it? Shall we team up with this madman and take a chance with your neck and my money?'

'We sure will,' José shouted, making a number of heads crane in their direction, for they were still in the drugstore. 'We'll make our fortunes and startle the world . . . it's better than clerking or selling nails to fat real estate men.'

Laurie had no idea what he was talking about but he got the gist of it.

They were on!

The venture was real, and about to begin!

'He's coming right away! I wish I had banks of orchids in bloom. I wonder, should I take the pot out of the glasshouse and stand it in front of the manor? Or does it show best with a plain background? Yes, I suppose it does. I'll leave it where it is.'

'Any other girl would be wondering what to wear herself, instead of fussing about a flower,' Adrienne grumbled. 'Put on a bit of make-up, girl, in case he wants you in the picture as well. And change out of those dreadful trousers, do. You must have one decent dress . . . what about the ones I let you have?'

'He won't bother about me,' Rochelle said impatiently. The editor of the paper had been really interested and had very kindly offered to send not only a reporter but a photographer too. 'He'll just want to see Pure Madonna at her best . . . I wish newspapers did colour pictures. I wonder . . . do you remember that article in the magazine, Mme Barfleur? It had a lovely picture of the house, and another one of M. Laurient. I kept it – it's somewhere in my room upstairs. Do you suppose they might run a picture of the orchid?'

They were in the kitchen, whither they had repaired after seeing the orchid for themselves. The older women were sitting at the table regaling themselves with tea and Mme Barfleur's light and delicious scones, whilst Rochelle ranged the room, 'nervous as a virgin on her wedding night', as Adrienne had somewhat maliciously put it.

'He'll be here in an hour . . . I wonder will the light still be right? The noon sun can be very trying even to the most perfect specimen – too strong, you see, too much brightness and shadow. You can't see the soft shading of colour at all.'

'It's a newspaper picture, not a beauty contest,' Adrienne said. She cut herself a piece of carrot cake, a confection born during the war and since perfected by Mme Barfleur. 'You worry too much, Chelle. If the picture isn't perfect simply tell them not to publish.'

'Oh, I couldn't,' Rochelle said worriedly. 'I want them to publish it, because . . . well, I just do. But it's got to be right . . . do you think he'll understand the importance of the light? If the sun goes on shining . . .'

Adrienne was sitting facing the back door. She shook her head chidingly at Rochelle.

'He's here, so stop fussing and go and let him in. Oh dear, your hair's still in a plait . . . come here at once, you silly child.'

Rochelle, poised to rush to the door as soon as she heard a knock, went reluctantly over to the table. She tried to remember that Adrienne had lost her own daughter, so when Adrienne attempted to mother her in her easy-going, half-hearted fashion she usually let her, though it some- times went against the grain. Especially as she also thought quite often that she herself, and Mme Barfleur, mourned Olivia more truly and faithfully than ever her own mother did.

'Here you are,' Adrienne said. Quick, experienced fin- gers unbraided the long plait, riffled through the thickly shining strands, and wielded the comb to such good effect that by the time the knock sounded she was able to give Rochelle a little push in the back, flicking the long hair forward over the younger girl's shoulders.

445

'There, that looks very pretty. Off you go, then.'

Rochelle ran halfway to the door, then slowed down. She walked the rest of the way, her back very straight, her head held high. She was telling herself that for M. Laurient's sake she must impress the reporter and the photographer with the importance of this new hybrid, and she must make very sure that the photographs showed it at its best.

Only Rochelle could never think of PM23 as 'it'. Pure Madonna was a woman through and through, she was telling herself as she pulled open the heavy kitchen door.

'It's a remarkable story . . . touching,' the reporter said, when Rochelle had finished her tale. 'And Charles Laurient has never come home? But you're sure he's alive, somewhere?'

'Yes; certain,' Rochelle said eagerly. 'I think he may have lost his memory, or be staying away for some other reason, but I don't think he's dead.'

'It's a good story,' the reporter said. 'Alex . . . got some good pics?'

'I think so; it's a photogenic flower,' the photographer said, grinning at Rochelle. 'How about one more, though . . . with the young lady here holding it close to her face?'

'Might as well,' the reporter said. 'Human interest sells papers. 'Where do you want them?'

'Anywhere,' the photographer said promptly. 'The light's ideal . . . it's the blinds, of course. They keep it dimmer; just right for me.'

'OK. Over here, my dear,' the reporter said, rather annoying Rochelle, who thought he was not a lot older than she. 'Sit on the shelving, would you?'

'It's called staging,' Rochelle said, obediently sitting on it. 'Is this all right?'

The photographer squinted through his lens and then moved her a trifle to the right. Then he bade her, in quick succession, to smile, half close her eyes and lower her head

446

to look up at him, raise her chin and stop smiling but look down at him and, finally, to look at the flower as though she loved it.

'I do,' Rochelle said, complying.

'Good. That's great,' the photographer said, and the reporter, putting away his notebook, remarked rather acidly that he had not realised he was working with a budding *Daily Mirror* photographer.

'There's nothing wrong with wanting a decent pic of a pretty girl,' the photographer said defensively, and then the two newspapermen grumbled themselves off to their car.

'Fame at last,' Mme Barfleur said placidly, when Rochelle, having watered, misted and generally dealt with her daily tasks in the glasshouse, returned to the kitchen to tell everyone that she had been photographed with Pure Madonna. 'You'll be a film-star at this rate, you and that flower of yours.'

She was teasing, but Rochelle was delighted with the pictures in the paper when they arrived and announced that she was cutting one out and sending it to the horticultural journal which had previously published the article on Charles Laurient and Augeuil Manor.

She had not heard from the editor two days later, but when she came down to breakfast Mme Barfleur handed her a letter with an English stamp on it.

'For you . . . London,' she said briefly. 'Probably from that solicitor.'

It was not. Rochelle slit the envelope and pulled out the single typed sheet, then gave a squeak of excitement.

'It's from a London newspaper . . . one of the famous ones,' she said. 'They want to come over and take some pictures! Oh, Adrienne, Mme Barfleur, we really are going to be famous!'

* * *

'That one'll do!'

Laurie, José and Solly were buying their equipment for the expedition. They had taken advice from old hands and would wear floppy Mexican-style hats – bush-hats, Solly said. He had been stationed with Aussies at one time. They had also purchased baggy trousers, because an old hunter had told them that you could tighten baggy trousers by lacing them with string, pushing them into knee-boots or simply rolling them up, but there was nothing you could do with tight trousers except sweat in 'em. They bought long-sleeved shirts for the same reason, though Solly, who was rather a snappy dresser, thought that it was a shame to cover sinewy forearms tanned by the tropic sun.

'No, I know they ain't *yet*,' he said, when the other two stared pointedly at his rather stringy white arms, 'But they will be – right?'

'They better be, or we aren't gonna have much luck with the orchids,' José remarked rather gloomily. 'Jeez, Sol, you're in poor shape!'

'Yeah, well . . . what about this one?'

They were selecting machetes, the chopping implements with which they would fight through forest and vine to the orchids, and long, narrow knives which they would use to slice bread, cut chickens' throats and do anything else which needed a blade.

'It's a bit fancy,' Laurie said doubtfully. The blade was all right but the handle was richly gemmed with artificial stones. 'I'd go for something a bit more practical if I were you, Solly.'

'It'll look good on the photos,' Solly said wistfully, but José pointed out that the peons, simple souls, might well slit his throat to possess such a knife and Solly hastily chose a plainer and more practical version.

'We'll go and talk nicely to the airline people now,' Laurie said, when they had completed their purchases. 'I want to make sure we can air-freight the plants whenever we decide we've got enough to send a batch home, not when the airline people decide they've got a gap in their hold.'

It was all go. Laurie had never been so busy, and he should have been happy, too. He was, most of the time. When he was working, talking, making arrangements for the big adventure.

But at night, when it was chilly in his apartment and he could not sleep, misery haunted him. Why had he gone off on the dam' plane and left Rochelle cross and unhappy? She had not meant half the things she said and he knew it – he was years older than she, understood that she was just hitting out at him because he had said he would be gone a while. Why could he not have been big enough to make up with her and get another plane?

There had been a good reason, of course – the best. He was being flown home by the Eighth Army Air Force so that they could demob him; it was not just a pleasure trip. It might not have looked so good if he had had to admit to missing a plane just so that he could run after a spoilt little girl.

But she had not written. She could scarcely do so, he remembered, until she had his address. Every night he vowed to send it to her, and every morning, in the cold dawn light, he reminded himself that he was not going to think about her or worry about her until he had something to show her, namely the orchids. It was no use writing and apologising when it was her bad behaviour which had parted them, no use at all.

But perhaps he could just send her his address? With a note to say he was preparing to leave for the south any day and would write properly when he returned? Or was it better to leave it, now, until he had an address in Colombia? They had decided to start there and work further inland, if possible leaving the orchids of the high Andes until last.

449

Just before they left, he weakened. He bought a colourful postcard of the Statue of Liberty, addressed it to Rochelle at Augeuil Manor, and then put her firmly out of his mind.

Or tried to do so.

'They're sending a reporter and a photographer and they're putting up at the Pomme d'Or,' Rochelle said in tones of awe. 'Imagine . . . just to photograph Pure Madonna!'

'And you,' Peter reminded her as they sat in the kitchen and ate Mme Barfleur's steak pie with a mound of potatoes and a generous helping of string beans. 'They want your picture as well, the letter said so.'

'Well, yes . . . but they may change their minds,' Rochelle said rather hopefully. She had been pleased with the pictures in the local paper, but had felt bored and embarrassed posing for them. 'What about the French magazine . . . what was it called?'

'Paris-something-or-other,' Peter supplied, whilst Mme Barfleur and Adrienne laughed at his ignorance. 'You didn't approve of their picture, I take it?'

'It was stupid,' Rochelle scoffed. She put a large piece of potato into her mouth and spoke with some difficulty. 'You could hardly see Pure Madonna, it was all me!'

'What about the caption, eh, Chelle?' Adrienne asked. *'Girl with face of a flower and flower with face of a girl?'*

'Stupid . . . but it sells papers,' Rochelle said, with the superior knowledge she had so recently culled of the world of the press. 'Though I don't know how it can sell more copies than a really good picture of the orchid would . . . I mean, that flower is so beautiful, and it's a first. Blue orchids are rare enough, but blue and white ones, with the toning of ours . . . well, the orchid world is going mad about it.'

'And are you going to supply them with the secret? Are you going to tell them how to get Pure Madonnas of their own?'

Rochelle was well aware of the commercial value of a bit of secrecy; she twinkled at Peter but shook her head.

'No. It isn't my secret, anyway. And even if someone stole a plant, there's no guarantee that the seeds would be true. So we just smile when people ask and say we aren't at liberty to tell until M. Laurient comes home . . . that way at least everyone is guaranteed to try to spread the story around.'

'The growers won't like it,' Peter said, finishing off his plateful of food. 'When do these photographers arrive?'

'At two o'clock. I've bought a new dress, but they'll probably hate it,' Rochelle said sadly. 'Still, I like it and Adrienne said it suits me.'

'And you'll have to take that postcard out of your brassiere, if you're going to wear that low-necked dress,' Adrienne said, and Rochelle felt her cheeks grow warm with embarrassment.

'Oh, is that where I put it? Of course I'll take it out – I'll throw it away now I've read it.'

'Now you've learned it by heart,' Mme Barfleur corrected, with a throaty chuckle. 'He'll come back, petite, never doubt it.'

'I know he will . . . he said he would,' Rochelle said, halfway to the door but stopping for a moment to answer what she clearly felt was criticism. 'Only I can't write back, you see, because he doesn't have a permanent address.'

'He'll write again,' Mme Barfleur said gently. 'Never fear, he'll write again.'

Rochelle nodded, then slid out of the kitchen. She supposed she had better put the new dress on for the press men – it was rather a nice dress, dark blue because it would show up the orchid better. It was a happy coincidence, Rochelle told herself, that dark blue was a colour which also suited her.

She went straight to her room, a child's room still with her books and games, the photograph of M. Laurient, cut

451

from the magazine, in a silver frame she had found, empty and discarded, in the small parlour, and had taken for her own. The new dress hung in the built-in wardrobe, not quite alone but almost, for Rochelle had better things to spend her money on than dresses. She went along to the bathroom and washed luxuriously, splashing about, tempted to have a bath but not wanting to be caught in the tub by the press men, then put on the new dress and brushed out her hair. Should she leave it loose, or plait it?

After consideration she left it loose, tucking it behind her ears, then eyed herself in the mirror. She looked neat enough, clean enough, and the dress would show the delicate colours of the orchid off to its best advantage.

She lingered in her room, though. The dress did have rather a low neckline but she still had the postcard tucked inside her bra, pressing against her breasts. She liked to have it there, on her skin; it made her feel that she was in touch with Laurie, that the card he had chosen, looked at, written his brief message on, was now close to her heart.

She was still trying to arrange the card so that it did not show, even when she leaned forward, when she heard the low, demanding note of the front door bell. She waited until Adrienne's high heels had clicked across the black and white marble tiles and then she went downstairs. She had not intended to make an entrance but realised, guiltily, that she was doing so as she rounded the corner of the stairs and saw three men, all turning simultaneously to look at her, all gazing upwards, mouths a little open, eyes fixed.

Rochelle smiled and began talking as she descended, wanting to put her visitors at their ease but also wanting to appear self-confident, relaxed with them.

'Good afternoon,' she called. 'I'm sorry I wasn't downstairs. I was just changing out of my working clothes into a dress – in the mornings I have a good deal of work on the estate to deal with.'

The tallest of the men answered her easily, his voice as confident as she would have liked to be thought.

'It's good of you to see us, Miss Dubois. If we could just have a few words . . .'

Rochelle came lightly down the rest of the flight, enjoying the unaccustomed flare of the skirt as it belled out round her legs, even enjoying the admiration she could see on three of the four faces in the hall beneath her. Adrienne's face merely reflected satisfaction that she had been right about the dress.

'Of course,' she said. 'We'll go to the drawing-room.' She turned to Adrienne. 'Could we have a tray of tea there, do you think?'

It was an act for the press men's benefit, of course, rehearsed beforehand. Adrienne all but curtsied.

'Certainly, madame,' she said demurely. 'I'll bring it at once.'

Rochelle inclined her head graciously and led the way into the drawing-room.

20

It was dark in the hut and after a long, tiring day Laurie should have been sleeping like a log – certainly the others were. He could hear Solly's uninhibited snores reverberating round the confined space and José's heavy breathing, occasionally interrupted by a gurgle, as though he was being quietly but efficiently strangled.

They were in Colombia, and the search for orchids had begun. Well, Laurie thought, it had not actually *begun*, because they would not set out on the trail until dawn the following day, but they were poised in the last large village they would see for a long time, ready for the off.

Earlier in the day they had engaged peons, who would do a good deal of the actual collecting, and a pack-mule to carry the gear: loosely woven baskets in which to put the orchids, cottonwool to be soaked and placed around the air roots, and food and a change of clothing for each man.

José's Spanish had already proved invaluable; he could chatter away to the peons, certain of understanding and being understood, for even the most uncouth dialect was readily translated by one who had spoken Mexican Spanish since childhood.

The marked maps were in the baggage too, though few trails were shown on them. But they were invaluable in that they had belonged to an old orchid hunter and he had marked areas where, before the war, orchids had been pretty well collected clean away. This meant that they would not needlessly search areas which had already been over-attacked. According to the experts, it took thirty years at least for orchids to reassert themselves even in quite small numbers once collectors had stripped a region.

What else, what else? Laurie's mind nagged at him. He had done all the things he'd been advised to do. He'd chosen reliable-looking, athletic men to do the climbing and they had rented a hut – this one – so that when they brought their bounty back they would have somewhere to clean and pack the plants. Women, Laurie had decreed, would almost certainly pack better than men, but the briefest acquaintance with the local ladies had made him unsure on this point. You only had to see them doing their washing in the river which ran through the village to realise that brawn and not brains came first with them. They rolled the clothing into a tube, tied a knot in it, and then belaboured the rocks with the unfortunate garment until they thought it was clean. Packing the delicate plants, therefore, might fall to the lot of Solly, José and Laurie himself, much though he abhorred the thought of the time wasted when they might be out collecting. Anyway, he would try the local women first, see how they got on.

He had not realised when he set out, however, just what dangers he would be asking his pals to face. Oh, he had been told about the jaguars, the poisonous snakes, the insects, and he had believed what he had been told, but he had not, somehow, taken it seriously. He had assumed that these things would occur from time to time as great and glorious stumbling blocks to be overcome. He had not then been attacked by a million vigorous fleas, bitten by ants and stared at by a poisonous snake. Fortunately the snake had been as shattered by his presence up its own particular tree as he had been by its sudden appearance, and after a long, cold stare from eyes which had almost hypnotised Laurie with their green and gold beauty it had silently disappeared again, into the mass of parasitic plants which throng every tree in the jungle.

But the next one, Laurie thought, beating a strategic retreat with the small orchid he had climbed the tree to capture dropped down into the waiting hands of José, the next one might bite first and ask him what the hell he was doing up its tree afterwards. And he had seen a spider in the village which looked capable of killing all three of them ... Laurie had never been keen on spiders, not even the leggy but harmless ones you find in a Jersey cornfield, so he had no desire to further his acquaintance with the giant of the species in the chief man's hut. He had remarked on it, though ... his host had glanced up at it, made a menacing gesture which the spider had mimicked, it seemed to Laurie, and remarked that it did *caballeros* no harm but was useful against the flies.

His mind reverted to its more immediate problems at this point, not wanting even to think about the spider. He had climbed the tree to fetch down the little orchid just to show them it could be done, and to demonstrate to the peons what he was employing them to do once they reached specimens worth collecting. They had nodded wisely, but the looks they gave each other had seemed to indicate that here was a rare bird, a congenital idiot who would have to be watched lest he run amok with the shiny machete he carried.

And though this large village was a hive of industry and a centre of civilisation compared with others they would stop at in their quest, it still had no hospital, no doctor and remarkably few of the other amenities which Laurie and his crew had taken for granted.

Still, we've got medicines in the kit, Laurie reminded himself now, checking the contents over in his mind. They had all been taking anti-malarial drugs for weeks, and should be safe enough on that score. They had water purifying tablets, salt tablets, sulphonamides, aspirin and vitamins. The dangers of the local diet, which consisted largely of starchy stuff – yucca, bananas and rice – had been impressed upon them and they had a quantity of dried greenstuff which they would try to eat each day.

Yes, but what else haven't you thought of? Laurie's mind

456

demanded tetchily. When you need it badly, when it's a matter of life and death, that's when you'll need ... whatever it is you've forgotten. Think, brain, think!

But it was no use. What with the heat, the snores and the attentions of the fleas, Laurie knew he would never sleep. He would set off next morning already tired, he would make some fatal mistake ... and all his worries would be over, except the worry of how to get his badly injured body back to civilisation.

In his bed, Laurie shrugged. So he would fail – so what? He was too tired to care. He might as well give up courting slumber; he was clearly doomed to wakefulness.

Having decided this, he slept heavily until morning.

Rochelle had slept lightly and woke as the dawn came greyly in at her window. She immediately began to worry away at her own particular problem, as she had been doing before she fell asleep in the early hours.

Because of the photographs, and of course because of the orchid, she had become something of a celebrity. This was all to the good ... except that, despite all the publicity both for Augeuil Manor and for Pure Madonna, there had been no word of M. Laurient.

Why had he not returned? He must have seen the articles if he was still alive and interested in orchids, yet there had been nothing – no letter, no rumour, certainly not the sudden personal appearance on which Rochelle had set her heart.

And now she had had two really exciting invitations. One was from the British Orchid Society, who had asked her to go to London to exhibit Pure Madonna at their annual show next August. It was only May, so she need not make up her mind quite at once, she had thought, but it appeared she was wrong; the Society wanted to know right away since if she decided not to go they would have to ask someone else to give the prize for a certain class of orchid.

'It is a great honour,' local nurserymen told her when she talked about the invitation.

'You must go,' Mme Barfleur said, beaming. 'This is an honour not just for you, my child, but for M. Laurient and his work as well.'

The other invitation was extremely practical and fitted in well with the first. A large and apparently famous firm who made artificial pearls had written to her asking whether she would consent to take part in an advertising campaign for their products.

'If you are coming to London, we could combine your trip with our campaign,' the managing director had written. 'Naturally, we would be willing to use the orchid as well, since no doubt you will be marketing the flower during your stay in our capital city.'

They had mentioned a very large sum of money as casually as though Rochelle would only consider it as a sort of added attraction, but Rochelle, with the need to go to the sea-cave again very pressing, had seized upon the offer as a lifeline to keep her going until either M. Laurient or his son came back.

For she acknowledged, now, that Laurie had been right. Whether M. Laurient was alive or dead was no longer the question. If the estate was to be kept as it should be kept she must get some money from somewhere, and until she really could market the orchid it would have to come from selling what was in the sea-cave. And that was Laurie's property as well as her own . . . if it belonged to either of them, that was, if M. Laurient really was dead . . . which meant that she had no right, or felt she had no right, to sell it.

What was more, there had been a slight scene over the first lot of jewellery she had sold.

She had thought that M. Laurient had no living relatives

except Laurie, but this, it appeared, was not the case. A handsome, aggressive cousin had turned up all the way from Cornwall in England where he had a large estate, and he had come up to the manor specially to demand of Rochelle what she meant by selling a particularly ugly and ornate gold necklace which, he said, had been in the Laurient family for generations.

'Who told you I'd sold anything?' Rochelle had demanded angrily, and the man – Abel Pencarew – had said simply that he had come over to St Helier on business, seen the necklace on display in a jeweller's shop, and asked where they had got it.

'Well, I didn't know,' Rochelle had mumbled. 'I thought it was all part of the stuff M. Laurient bought when the Nazis came. He said to sell it if I needed money, and I do – I mean the estate does.'

Abel Pencarew had been quite nice about it, but he had gone with her to the shop and insisted that she buy the necklace back.

'Charles would turn in his grave if it ever graced any neck but a Laurient's,' he had said, and Rochelle had lost her temper and had shouted that since Charles was not dead the question did not arise, and she would thank him to remember that the only other Laurient was in the United States of America and might never set foot on the island again . . . might never marry, or have children to value the horrid, ugly necklace.

Abel had not taken offence but had nodded, smiled, and bidden her visit him next time she was in England. And Rochelle, trying to atone for her outburst, had nodded too, attempted to smile, said she would be delighted to see Cornwall – and vowed never to go near the place.

But the whole incident had worried Rochelle, who now felt that if she put a foot wrong the entire Laurient-by-marriage clan would descend on her and drag her through the courts, and might even succeed in having her kicked out of the manor altogether.

She had consulted a local solicitor, a kindly, sensible man called Bradley Sangen, who assured her that, if she would only accept M. Laurient's death and let them prove the Will, her troubles would be over. No one, after that had been done, would have a leg to stand on, even if she chose to sell all the heirlooms, paint the manor bright pink, and have a bonfire of the orchids.

'I can't, not yet,' Rochelle had explained, quite meekly for her. 'You see, I'm only joint heir and the other one – Daniel Laurient – is in South America somewhere collecting orchids. Until he comes home I can't do anything.'

She had grown diffident about mentioning that she was sure Charles Laurient was still alive; it was painful to see intelligent expressions change to pitying solicitude. They thought she was mad, she supposed, so started, for the first time, to keep her hopes to herself, especially as they were beginning, even to her, to seem less and less likely.

So now, as the dawn light grew, she considered her dilemma. To leave or not to leave. Once there would have been no question; she would not have budged whilst there was the slimmest chance of M. Laurient's returning. But now everything had changed. There was Laurie, off enjoying himself on the adventure of a lifetime, hoping to make a fortune and bring back enough orchids to start a whole new collection on Jersey. And here was she, stuck, like a country yokel, slaving away on the estate with no thanks, at work which was too physically hard for her and which, half the time, could have been done as well if not better by most labourers.

And her old loves, the orchids, did not need her any more. PM23 had bloomed and proved herself to be the Pure Madonna they had waited so long to see, and the others, poor dears, were only special because they had managed to survive the war despite the lack of heat and

460

feeding, to say nothing of the spider infestation, the over-richness of the compost and the other ills which had come about because she could only do her best and that, sometimes, had not been enough.

She did not long for personal fame, nor particularly for fortune, though it would be nice to have more money to spend on all the things the estate needed . . . and she would have liked some pretty clothes, a modern bicycle, perhaps even a car of some description one day. If she went to London . . . and then she knew very well that Laurie would not be back for absolutely ages; it clearly took a lot longer to get an expedition to South America than he had imagined. She had received another card only a couple of days ago, telling her that they had arrived in a Colombian town of reasonable size and would soon be moving into the interior. It had shattered her, that he had not yet even begun to collect plants, but it had made it a far easier thing to leave the island.

I'll go, she decided now, as the sky began to streak with palest gold. I'll go and see this chap, this Angus Brookes, who writes nice, complimentary letters which are balm to my pride, and perhaps they'll take my photograph with the pearls around my neck and Pure Madonna near my face and perhaps . . . who knows . . . someone who loves me will see it and come to me.

On a practical note, she must first make sure that Pure Madonna would be in bloom. This would be its second year, and during the course of that first amazing season they had discovered that the flowers lasted as long as three months on the plant. Rochelle had not been able to bring herself to cut one, so she had no idea how long such a one would live, but she was hopeful that it might be for a month, at least. She had read her orchid books and knew from personal experience before the war that the blooms of Cypripediums, for instance, which can last for three

461

months on the plant, generally keep for three to four weeks when cut.

To tell the truth, she was almost more nervous about this year's flowering than she had been about last year's. For more than three months then her fame and the orchid's had gone hand in hand, but it had been a nine-days' wonder. The orchid's beautiful blossoms had faded and died, and the newspapers in which she had appeared had no doubt been used to wrap fish and chips or light fires.

This year, however, more of the specimens would be in bloom because she had been able to heat the houses all through the winter. She would be able to try out the sale of cut flowers if she wanted to, and she had collected seed last year – having performed the fertilisation rite herself – which had already produced several minute seedlings, each pushing its four tiny green leaves up out of the agar-jelly.

Growers had already intimated their willingness to take the risk that the orchid did not breed true, and wanted to buy her seedlings as soon as it was possible to transplant them into individual pots. She was playing her cards close to her chest still, but she thought she would probably sell some in a year or two, when she had plenty of her own blooming well. It seemed mean, small-minded, not to do so.

So she would go to London and see Angus Brookes about his pearls, and she would take the original Pure Madonna and half-a-dozen more. She would show them at the Horticultural Show, and at the Orchid Show, and she would make enquiries about the sort of prices she ought to ask.

And I'll damned well enjoy myself, she found herself thinking, as she got out of bed and padded round the room collecting her working clothes for the day. I'll dance and sing and eat beautiful meals and flirt with handsome young men and behave like all the other girls . . . and if Laurie doesn't like it he can do the other thing!

She was in the bathroom and lighting the geyser – a dangerous and chancy business – when two things occurred to her. One was that Laurie would probably be totally indifferent as to whether she went to England or stayed in Jersey after her treatment of him. The other was that the bathroom floor was flooding.

After a moment's investigation Rochelle discovered that an underfloor pipe had burst, and realised that the room beneath – which she thought was the morning room – was probably flooded too. She turned off the tap, the geyser blew flame into the room before the gas flow stopped, and then she padded back to her bedroom unwashed and cross.

That settled it! The whole damned house would fall down around her ears if she did not do something fast, and then Laurie would really be entitled to feel irate with her. She would *definitely* go to London and earn some money and have much-needed repairs done on the house.

'A bit more to the left, José . . . keep clear of the trunk . . . now put your right arm up . . .'

Laurie's voice, which had begun as a happy bellow, grew anxious and small as José climbed higher and higher, straining every nerve and muscle to reach the *parasitos* whose delicate but brilliant yellow had caught his eye even from the forest floor far below.

'Got it? Good man!'

The peons were supposed to do the climbing, but it did not always work out like that. Tomas was an excellent climber, a fat youth of about sixteen who seemed to have sticky pads on his hands and feet, like flies, judging by the way he swarmed up the forest giants.

Pedro was a thin and gangling man with a droopy moustache and a tendency to giggle when nervous, but he was a good collector, more careful of the plants than Tomas, who tended to cut first and find out later that he had mortally wounded his 'find'.

Gomez was the leader of the three, a well-set-up young man in his middle twenties who also acted as guide in this particular region. He had a wife and two children at home, which meant that when a tree looked particularly difficult, as this one had, he announced portentously that it was 'for single men' and sent either Tomas or Pedro aloft.

But Tomas and Pedro had their sticking point, and a very small orchid at the top of a very tall tree was apparently it. They had both declared themselves unable to see the flowers, for a start, and had then both remembered that this particular tree belonged to a species beloved of poisonous snakes and biting ants.

'It's too durn high,' Solly muttered, as the six of them stared, heads dangerously far back, eyes watering from the unnatural position. 'I doubt I'd make it . . . how about you, Laurie?'

'I could, I think. Jo?'

José not only declared he could but said he would, and had started the climb at once. He had reached the *parasito*, as the peons called all orchids, and Laurie saw his machete flash as he detached the lovely thing from its resting place in the tree. Despite the name, orchids are not parasitic and do not take nourishment from the host tree, but merely use it as a resting place whilst their air-roots reach out and absorb moisture from the air around them. But they cling very tightly to their tree with these roots, and each one has to be carefully detached. If you just chop, as the peons had been inclined to do at first, your plant is unlikely to live long.

As a rule, the climber gently dropped the orchid to those waiting below, but it soon became clear that in this instance José could do no such thing. So high up was he, and so profuse and tangled the vegetation below him, that had he done so the orchid would simply have roosted further down the tree, perhaps in a position from which he could not take it again. So the watchers saw, with watering eyes, José

464

drop the plant into the bosom of his shirt and begin the long descent.

Laurie never took his eyes off the climber and his lips moved as José's small figure began to grow larger. These two men were his pals. He had brought them here, and it was up to him to get them back in one piece. When he was the climber he knew real fear – the sort that twists your guts and turns them to water – as well as various sources of pain: the bite of passing insects, the agony of skin scraped off knees and elbows, the cramp which attacked his hands and feet from fingers and toes held too long in one position. But never the terrible anxiety that comes from being responsible for another man's life. Only when Solly or José was high in a tree or slung over a rushing torrent or deep in a cave did he feel almost crushed by his conscience, for it had been his idea in the first place, all of it. And although Solly and José would be handsomely rewarded for their efforts, the only member of their group who actually needed the orchids was himself.

Lower came José now, and lower. He was a beautiful, economical climber, Laurie thought admiringly. Not so tall as himself, José could get from branch to branch as well as Laurie could just by using his muscle-power to spring, balance and reach out. Now he was poetry in motion, descending the tree rapidly and without wasting an ounce of energy.

He dropped on to the ground beside Laurie, snatched the orchid from his shirt-front, and proceeded to tear off his shirt and roll around on the ground at their feet, swearing softly beneath his breath.

'Ants?' Solly asked solicitously, but with a trace of laughter in his voice.

'Ants,' José confirmed, rubbing his chest with both hands and killing ants by the score as he did so. 'In the damned plant, I suppose.'

'That's right. Odd that they seem to live in it without

actually harming it. Sorry, José, but you've done superbly well. Unless I'm much mistaken this is a member of the Vandeae tribe, a tufted orchid called Cyrtopodieae. Well, we've found one, so the chances are we'll find more.'

'Not so high, I hope,' José groaned, shaking his shirt vigorously. 'I wouldn't wanna do that climb every day of the week.'

'Nor you shall,' Laurie said bracingly. 'It's Solly's turn next.'

Solly's smile was uncertain. He was quite a good climber, and getting better, but he had no head for heights.

'Me? Aw, gee, Laurie . . .'

'I'm kiddin',' Laurie said. 'Next one's the peons. I don't care how difficult they find it to see a flower, they're well paid to see 'em.'

The newly collected orchid was shown to the peons so that they would alert the party if they spotted another of the same species, and then put carefully into the wicker collecting basket. There was little competition over who would carry the basket, since, although the basket-carrier did not climb, he did not get a bonus for the plants brought down either, besides having to stand the weight as the basket grew heavier. But this was just a recce, really, to find a good species for collection, and to find it in quantity. One orchid was beautiful and interesting, but it would not make them much money in the orchid-hungry world outside this particular little patch of jungle.

'Right, are we ready? Off we go, then. We'll stop in an hour and have a beer, then we'll move on again. And if we make our find today, we'll bring the mules and their *costales* and take all the plants we collect back to the village at the same time.'

Laurie, with all his friends at ground level once more, no longer minded being the boss, taking command. Already, after only a few weeks, they were beginning to realise that the plants were there, in the forests and beside the mighty

466

rivers; it was just a question of finding them, getting them down from the trees or rocks in one piece, and keeping them alive back in the village until they had sufficient specimens – they reckoned three thousand – to make it worthwhile air-freighting them back to the States.

'One more good strike this week, a bit of a rest, and then we'll go after the more popular forms . . . the ones that'll really bring in the money.'

'Sure,' Solly said appreciatively. 'What are those scented ones called? I think they're real lovely.'

'Oh, Cattleya schroderae. Yes, it's a gorgeous thing. The smell must attract insects for miles around, I should think – it's one we should be able to sniff out, and of course it's extremely popular – women love 'em. If we can find them in quantity we'll be on to a very good thing; we've thousands ordered.'

'Does it grow at enormous heights?' José asked, rubbing his bruised elbows as they walked along. 'Durned if I know why they flourish up there . . . seems against nature.'

'I don't think the Cattleyas will be all that high off the ground; they're pretty large specimens on the whole, and the flowers themselves are very big. I hope we'll find them in the first or second crotch of the trees instead of at the very top like the smaller orchids.'

'Good thing you're an expert, Laurie,' Solly remarked as they swung their machetes automatically. No one could merely walk through this tropical rain forest; they had to chop and slash and fight their way through thick, lush undergrowth. 'Guess one way and another we're not such a bad team, eh? For collecting as well as flying, I mean.'

Laurie chuckled, then slapped at his arm as an insect landed, bit, and was slain on the wing.

'And when I think how sick-scared I was flying missions over Germany,' he said pensively. 'I used to think of a dozen bad ways I might end up, but not one of 'em compared to this!'

467

'Poor old Laurie,' said Solly, 'first you was responsible for us as our pilot; now you're the same because you're leadin' the expedition. No peace for the wicked, eh?'

And Laurie, raising his machete and bringing it down on a liana which proved to be harbouring a huge spider and a couple of small but spiteful snakes, could only grin and salute Solly's perspicacity.

London!

Rochelle had never dreamed of it, but if she had it would have lived up to her highest expectations. Mme Barfleur had warned her that it would be noisy, dirty, as different from St Helier as a nettle from a rose. But Rochelle, against all her own expectations and certainly against those of Mme Barfleur, loved it.

It was so different! People said that London before the war had been exciting, colourful, cosmopolitan; but to Rochelle it was all those things now, in 1947. The height of the buildings amazed her, for a start, and the Cockney accents, the hustle and bustle, the traffic . . . even a certain griminess, the tired air of some of the streets, seemed foreign and exotic to Rochelle.

Then, of course, there was the history. It seemed to Rochelle, wandering round the streets, squares and parks, that she had heard of even the tiniest alleyway in her reading – and she was an omnivorous reader. Hyde Park, Speakers' Corner, The Strand, Piccadilly, Fleet Street . . . she greeted them all as old friends and derived great pleasure simply from the fact that she, Rochelle Dubois, was here, in the very spot where once momentous things had happened.

She was enormously impressed by the Tower, too. And the Thames – now that was enough to impress anyone, a river as huge as that, so wide that proper ships came up it, making the bridges raise their arms in amazement – or that was how it looked to Rochelle, watching open-mouthed from the bank.

She was not staying in an hotel, having discussed the matter exhaustively with everyone who would listen to her. Her solicitor friend, M. Sangen, had visited London many times and told her that if she did not intend to draw on the estate for her expenses it might be better to stay in a little guest house rather than a grand hotel. Since Rochelle had already decided that a grand hotel would scare her half to death, she was glad to take his advice and had booked into a quiet little place in Marchmont Crescent which was homely and close to the British Museum, another of the many places Rochelle intended to visit before she went home again.

On her second day in London, she telephoned Angus Brookes and told him she had arrived, was living in Marchmont Crescent and had already delivered two of the four orchids she had brought with her to the home of the secretary of the Orchid Society, who had promised to look after the Madonnas as though they were his own.

'The other two are both in flower,' she informed Mr Brookes, 'and they'll stay in flower for ten or twelve weeks . . . I just thought I should let you know.'

Mr Brookes promptly invited her to dinner and Rochelle, after some initial dithering, accepted. He said he would pick her up and introduce her to his wife. This last was a relief, since Rochelle had no desire to have to fight off the attentions of a rich but elderly man; she had never met Mr Brookes, but she imagined that the managing director of a firm like Gempearls would probably be both.

So seven o'clock on the appointed day found Rochelle, in a dusky pink dress and high-heeled black court shoes – her first – and with her hair plaited, waiting on the steps of the guest house in Marchmont Crescent.

A long black car drew up beside her and a man stepped out. He was of medium height, inclined to swarthiness, and must have been in his late fifties, but he came up the steps to Rochelle like a boy, one hand extended.

'Miss Dubois . . . Angus Brookes, at your service. And that's my wife, Gemma, in the back of the car. Shall we go?'

Rochelle nodded shyly; she liked him at once and presently, when she got into the car and was introduced to Gemma Brookes, she liked her as well. Gemma was smaller than Rochelle, compactly built and probably in her fifties, but her red hair showed only the slightest trace of grey at the temples and her beautiful, humorous face was unlined, the skin smooth and pale except for a band of golden freckles across a small nose.

'Hello, Miss Dubois. I've heard so much about you from Angus already that I've been quite nervous of meeting such a paragon, but I see you don't consider yourself a paragon at all, which is reassuring!'

'Well, I'm not,' Rochelle said frankly. 'And my name's Rochelle . . . I shan't know who you mean if you keep calling me Miss Dubois – no one else does! And all I've done is manage not to kill M. Laurient's orchid, you know.'

'Apart from surviving the Nazi occupation of your home, and seeing friends killed and your guardian taken from you,' Gemma said gently. 'You must call us Gemma and Angus, of course, and we'll be delighted to call you Rochelle. What a pretty name it is . . . as pretty as its owner.'

Rochelle blinked. Compliments usually embarrassed her; she was never sure why one person should want to tell another she was pretty – surely actions and character were what mattered? But Mrs Brookes – Gemma – had spoken so gently and sincerely that she could only smilingly change the subject.

'Well, everyone on Jersey had similar experiences, and many much worse,' she explained. 'But we're a tough breed – a bit like the orchid, PM23.'

'A Royal breed,' Gemma said. 'You see, I'm learning about your precious plants. My husband has filled the house with books about them, so I shall end up an expert.'

'I can be very boring on the subject of orchids,' Rochelle warned her. 'Where are we going to have dinner? Oh, I find London so exciting, so full of life!'

'You like it here? I'm glad, because Angus and I have become very fond of the city. I'm from Edinburgh, as I expect you can tell by my accent. We Scots don't seem to lose it the way southerners can.'

Angus, sitting in the front seat beside the driver, turned at this point and smiled at Rochelle.

'My wife is a terrible chatterer,' he said. 'She's forgotten to say that we were going to dine at the Savoy – unless you would rather eat more simply at home, with us?'

'Och, Angus, how can the child do anything but agree, when you put it like that?' Gemma cried. 'Besides, we're going to see a lot of this young lady, I hope; she can dine with us at home tomorrow evening. She mustn't miss the Savoy.'

Angus shook his head gently at his wife, then patted Rochelle's shoulder.

'Gemma's right; she nearly always is. We'll take you home another evening; right now we'll take up our booking at the Savoy.'

The Brookes' car dropped Rochelle off at her guest house as midnight was striking. Rochelle used her key – for the landlady had to be up early and warned her guests that if they arrived any later than eleven they would have to fend for themselves – and went straight to her room. It was lovely to be able to switch on the light first and pull the curtains afterwards . . . only then of course she saw London, or some of it, stretched out beneath her, and could not bring herself to shut out even such quiet nightlife as

471

existed in Bloomsbury until she had perched on the wide windowsill for a few moments and feasted her eyes.

A couple passed below her window, arms entwined. A cat slid neatly through the railings of the garden in the square – it was a round garden, but Rochelle had already learned that any piece of green in London was referred to as a square – and a policeman and policewoman turned the corner, strolling quietly, their heads close as they exchanged a remark.

Rochelle sighed blissfully and drew her curtains across. The city slept – but some were wakeful still, as she was. She began to undress, hurling her pink dress across the room to ornament the dressing-table, kicking off her shoes – which hurt – and dropping underwear on to the floor. She was tired, but probably too excited to sleep . . . what an evening she had had! She thought the Brookes were quite the nicest people she had ever met. Gemma was a warm-hearted, affectionate woman and Mr Brookes – Angus – reminded her more and more of M. Laurient. No higher praise could possibly have come into Rochelle's mind than that. He had laughed at her, teased her, brought her out, killed any lingering trace of shyness stone dead . . . and had asked her if she would like to move into their home instead of staying in the guest house in the Crescent.

'After all, you're employed by my company now,' Angus had said. 'We would be paying for your accommodation . . . no, my dear, don't shake your head. We could scarcely have asked you to come to London and not pay your expenses . . . so it would be cheaper for us to have you to stay!'

Rochelle had laughed but she had not been fooled for one moment. They had asked her to stay because they liked her, enjoyed her company and thought she would be more comfortable with them than in a guest house, no matter how good. And they were right. Seeing London by herself had been joy unalloyed, but seeing London with

Gemma and Angus would be sheer bliss. And of course there was the added bonus that when they started work on the advertisements for their product she would be on the spot, able to fit in with whatever schedule Angus wanted her to follow.

Already they had made plans. Gemma would go with her to the horticultural shows, Angus would turn up when and if his business permitted, and, the next day, she and Gemma were going shopping at the big Knightsbridge and West End stores.

'I shall get clothing coupons from people who would rather have money,' Gemma had said authoritatively when Rochelle had pointed out that she doubted whether her own coupons would be valid here in London. Even if they were, she did not have very many left, having bought the dusky pink dress, the shoes and a certain little cream-coloured jacket and skirt which was at the moment the delight of her heart. 'There are always coupons available on the black market and I think, in the interests of our advertising campaign, that you must be adequately dressed.'

'I do have a suit,' Rochelle murmured, but Gemma said kindly that she doubted whether a suit purchased in St Helier would have quite the éclat which was necessary for modelling.

But the suit should not be wasted, Rochelle vowed, and planned, as she jumped into bed, to wear it next day so that the big London stores should not think her a country bumpkin who could only buy overalls in her small-town shops.

Morning found her awake bright and early but with no chance, this time, of going out on to the streets before breakfast to surprise Londoners at their shop-opening, street-tidying tasks. Instead, she had to pack, which did not take long, eat her breakfast, and pay her bill with the money Angus had insisted on giving her the evening before. Then she waited, on the steps in the sunshine, for that long black car.

When it came, and Angus himself with it, she hopped aboard as blithe as a blackbird in spring, eager to start this new chapter in her suddenly full and exciting life.

'I don't know when I've taken such a liking to a girl,' Gemma had said to her husband as they sat in the sunshine, eating breakfast. 'And I could tell you were very smitten, my dear.'

'She's charming; she's got a great deal of quiet determination but she's as innocent as a new-born lamb,' Angus had replied. 'And no one of her own – not a single blood relation, so far as I can tell, save for that crotchety old aunt who refused to take her in when her parents died.'

Rochelle had poured her heart out the previous evening, but with never a grumble or a moan. She had merely told them how she had come to find herself in charge of the estate and the orchids.

'I'm determined to take her in hand,' Gemma said. 'But you can help her, Angus, in ways that I can't. I'm going to have the dressing of her, though . . . that dreadful pink dress she was wearing . . . does she have absolutely no clothes-sense, do you suppose? It's far too short, it makes her look gawky which she most certainly is not, and the colour does nothing for her lovely clear skin.'

'You'll know best, of course, but I should say she's fairly indifferent to her appearance,' Angus remarked, and was frowned at, but persisted doggedly. 'She's had so little opportunity, you know, and no one at all who could point her in the right direction. From what she told us last night, I should say the last thing the Islanders thought of was fashion.'

'You're right, of course. Very well, then – I shall take her in hand with even more enthusiasm. I'll teach her how

474

to judge what looks good and what doesn't, and before you know it you'll have a beauty advertising your pearls, not just a little *gamine* with big eyes and an appealing smile.'

'It's the *gamine* with the big eyes and appealing smile I want, don't forget,' Angus reminded her. 'I could have all the polished young ladies I desired – if that was what I wanted. Don't you go and add a hard gloss to our little Rochelle.'

They were a childless couple who would have made marvellous parents had things been different. They had had a daughter once, Angus's child though not Gemma's. They had adored her, called her Louisa after Angus's mother, brought her up as their own ... and she had died of meningitis before her third birthday. They had never wanted another child, but now Gemma could see in his eyes that Angus had fallen for this one ... for although Rochelle claimed to be nineteen she seemed very much younger in her quick enthusiasms, her shyness and the friendliness which was held out so hopefully to every acquaintance.

'I won't sophisticate her, if that's what you mean by hard gloss,' Gemma said, laughing at him. 'But for her own sake she's got to learn that the whole world isn't peopled by well-wishers. You do realise that she's going to have young men after her in droves, once she's dressed properly? And not all of them will be selfless heroes who want nothing but to give her a good time in exchange for a few kisses.'

'I didn't know dressing properly was so important to young men,' Angus said, very tongue-in-cheek. 'Odd, because I remember the first time I saw you you were simply but unappealingly clad in a very large sweater and a tweed skirt so old and baggy that I thought it was plus-fours!'

'Och, you know right well what I mean, you old fool,' Gemma said, bristling and giggling at the same time. 'Men aren't attracted by the simple look, not these days. They want a girl to have style.'

'All right, I give in. I'm a mere male and don't understand my own sex at all,' Angus said. 'Here, if you don't want that last slice of toast I might as well eat it . . . waste is abhorrent to me.'

'Yes . . . we'll have to be careful about that as well,' Gemma said thoughtfully. 'Did you notice the chocolate gâteau?'

Angus chuckled. 'I thought she'd have the pattern off the plate – I'm sure she'd have licked it if she had been alone.'

'Yes . . . and the mints!'

There had been chocolate mints, one with each cup of coffee. Rochelle had picked hers up, placed it upon half a bread roll which had been left beside Gemma's plate, and eaten it, apparently oblivious of the moment's stunned silence her frugal action had brought about.

'When you've eaten dead seabirds and raw swede, I suppose you get cross about wasting anything,' Angus said now. 'I nearly laughed when she put the salt off her plate back into the salt-cellar, but I don't think the waiter did. His eyes bulged.'

'She'll learn,' Gemma said comfortably. 'She's bright as a button; you've only got to look at her to see that. And now if you've eaten all the toast we'd better get moving. I've a feeling that Rochelle will be ready spot on time.'

Rochelle was enormously impressed by the Brookes' house – she was beginning to feel quite ashamed of her own round-eyed wonder at the marvels about her – and with good reason. It was a Georgian manor of moderate size with a garden running down to the river, and it proved to be in Chelsea, some way out of the actual city . . . though with a good bus route just down the road and taxis everywhere this, Gemma assured her guest, was no problem.

'This is your room,' Gemma said, accompanying Rochelle up a curving staircase and on to a white-carpeted landing. She threw open a panelled door and there was the room of most young girls' dreams – a positive bower, with a tiny balcony furnished with white wrought-iron chairs and table, a quantity of flowering plants and a gaily striped garden umbrella which could be angled according to the whereabouts of the sun.

The room itself was attractively decorated. The wallpaper was probably rather old-fashioned, Rochelle thought, seeing the bunches of roses, the lovers' knots and the tiny lilies of the valley depicted on it, but, old-fashioned or not, it exactly suited the room with its long, narrow windows opening on to the balcony, the pink handbasin in one corner and the floor-length curtains in deep rose-velvet.

'The bed's comfortable,' Gemma said, throwing back the white silky counterpane to reveal a fat pink eiderdown and pink blankets. 'And there's a bell on the wall; if you ring it someone will come up from the kitchen to see if they can help you. We mean to get telephones installed, but it's difficult to get work of that nature done at the moment since no one could pretend it was essential – there's a phone in our room and two extensions downstairs.'

'It's beautiful,' Rochelle said, rather feebly, she felt. 'I've never seen a nicer room. Shall I unpack? It won't take me long. I don't have many clothes,' she added, a little conscious, amongst all this comfortable splendour, of her own lack.

'Yes, you settle in, and then we'll have some coffee and biscuits and order the car to take us up west,' Gemma said. 'Do you know, Rochelle, I haven't felt so excited about a shopping expedition since I was a girl myself.'

'I'm pretty excited too,' Rochelle admitted. 'Imagine,

being told to choose clothes and not having to pay for them!'

They laughed together over this feminine dream, then Gemma headed for the door.

'Right. I'll give you half an hour . . . can you find your way down to the terrace? It's through the living-room, which is the third door on your right as you come down the stairs. But it isn't a large house; I don't think you can get lost.'

'If I do I'll stand still and shout,' Rochelle said. 'Shall I wear my new shoes or can I go out in sandals?'

'Wear whichever is most comfortable,' Gemma advised. 'We've got a long day ahead of us!'

It was a long day, but a memorable one. From the moment Rochelle came on to the terrace in her cream-coloured suit, she and Gemma thought only of clothes.

'That suit is really pretty, and stylish, what's more,' Gemma said as soon as Rochelle appeared. 'Do you like milk and sugar in your coffee?'

'Oh . . . yes, I think I do, please.' Rochelle sat down on the little chair with the green silk cushion opposite her hostess. 'I'm glad you like the suit. It's easily the prettiest thing I've ever owned.'

'It's definitely good,' Gemma confirmed. 'But sweetheart, it's a bit on the short side. Do you like your skirts above the knee?'

'No,' Rochelle said. A deep blush suffused her face but her eyes met Gemma's squarely. 'It isn't that I like it, it's that I'm a bit taller, perhaps, than the person this suit was made for. I do have difficulty in getting things to fit, because I've got longer legs than I should have.'

'Nonsense. Your legs suit the rest of your figure perfectly. Let me look at that skirt.'

She turned the hem backwards and smiled triumphantly.

'Thought so. See – the hem's at least five inches deep, which means you could let it down a good four inches, and that would make it a perfect fit for you. Let's do it right away. It won't take a moment.'

'Oh . . . but I can't sew,' Rochelle said at once. 'I wouldn't know how to start!'

'I'll do it this once,' Gemma said, tugging at the hem and finding that it was far too well made for such cavalier treatment. 'Oh, dear. Just ring that bell, would you, love?'

There was a handbell on the wrought-iron table. Rochelle picked it up and rang it and after a short pause a woman appeared, a tray in her hands. She looked at the table, came towards them, and stopped short.

'Sorry, madam. I thought you'd rung for me to clear the coffee, but I see you haven't quite finished. Was there something else?'

'Yes, Joan . . . Rochelle, this is Joan, who runs the house for me and cooks exquisite food, as you'll soon discover. Joan, this young lady is going to be staying here whilst she's in London; she's going to do some modelling work for Mr Brookes.'

'How d'you do,' Joan said, smiling at Rochelle. She was in her forties with wild salt and pepper hair and a broad grin which revealed a missing front tooth. 'You'll do well with Mr Brookes, miss . . . he's a hard worker and expects the same from his staff, but no one minds that when it's one rule for all.'

'That's true. Joan, I want some scissors and my sewing box; would you be so kind as to fetch them for me?'

''Course I will,' Joan said robustly. 'I'll be back in a brace of shakes.'

She disappeared and Rochelle said uncertainly, 'What should I do? Take the skirt off?'

'Do you have a petticoat underneath? Then it would be quicker, probably. Nip into the living-room, my dear, and I'll follow in a moment. We'll have that skirt the right length in no time.'

* * *

479

It was typical of Gemma, Rochelle thought later, that she had wanted as near perfection as she could get for her protégée, even when the skirt concerned had not been of her choosing.

And when they got to the shops, Rochelle realised that Gemma knew just what she was talking about and was highly regarded both as a customer and for her natural good taste.

'We don't want gaudy colours, because they tie you so,' she explained as Rochelle went through the racks of mouthwateringly pretty dresses, skirts and tops. 'We want good basics, to start with.'

'Good basics' proved to be beautifully cut, simple garments with labels in the necks or waists which seemed, to Gemma, almost as important as the garment itself. She would not let Rochelle even try on certain things because she said they were for older women, or for what she termed 'difficult' figures.

'Don't I have a difficult figure?' Rochelle asked at one point, remembering how hard she had to search for a skirt which covered her knees.

'No,' Gemma said shortly. 'The better manufacturers, the good names, make clothes for figures like yours – young figures. It's the older women who have to search for what's right with such attention to detail and cut. You would look good in most of this stuff.' Her gesture encompassed the entire department.

But despite her words, she made Rochelle try on clothes until even that young person's interest began to wane. 'You must choose *carefully*,' Gemma impressed on her. 'You need a few very good clothes and a lot of bright, easily changed accessories. I can provide most of the accessories, or we'll see what friends of mine can spare, so we're free to spend our coupons on the things that matter.'

At the end of the day the 'things that matter' comprised a deep brown skirt of some fine woollen material which

Gemma teamed with a blouse of flame-coloured wild silk, a lovely, full-skirted dress in deep blue which she said exactly matched Rochelle's eyes, and a green skirt with thousands of tiny pleats, to be worn with a blouse and jacket which, Gemma explained, she had bought when she was rather slimmer than she was today.

'The blouse is cream silk . . . I'll show you when we get home,' she said. 'And the jacket is dark green velvet . . . it'll make your skin look like the petals of a rose.'

'A red rose?' Rochelle said, wistfully stroking a poppy-coloured cotton skirt and top. She would have loved them, but realised that with coupons in short supply it would be foolish to choose an outfit which once seen would not easily be forgotten.

'No, silly, a white rose. Now we must get you some shoes, though the black ones you brought with you are very smart, and quite high-heeled enough for someone of your age.'

Shoes, however, proved more of a problem than either of them had anticipated.

'Slim fitting,' the assistant groaned, taking Rochelle's foot in his hand. 'I'm sorry, madam, but we're chronically short of both slim and broad fittings. We seem to get more standard widths in for some reason.'

'We'll try sandals, then,' Gemma said, and after a little searching they found a pair of cream leather ones which might have to be dyed if they were to complement some outfit such as the blue dress. Rochelle, who had never dreamed of matching shoes to a dress, swallowed and said of course she would happily dye the sandals, and then, since she was as worn out as if she had been ploughing the six-acre unaided all day, she agreed to have tea in Swan & Edgar's . . . the cakes might only have been mock-cream, but they were marvellously good . . . and then sank into the back of a taxi and stared admiringly at Gemma.

'I think if you'd been on Jersey you'd have chased the

481

Jerries out without any help from anyone!' she exclaimed. 'You really enjoyed that, didn't you? And you aren't a bit tired!'

Gemma laughed and patted her neat, head-hugging red hair self-consciously.

'I love shopping,' she admitted. 'But I didn't have to keep struggling in and out of clothes today. That is tiring, especially if you aren't used to it. But you'll be glad you did it tomorrow, when Angus wants to take some shots of you and your orchid . . . and his pearls.'

'Is that why most of the things we bought had low necks?' Rochelle asked, suddenly putting two and two together. 'I wondered, because you said you liked the ash-grey dress, but the neck was wrong.'

'Yes, it was. And remember that Londoners have had their fill of utility colours and utility cuts and want a bit of glamour now the war's over, so I don't know that I'd have been very keen on the ash-grey anyway . . . not but what we could have made it look pretty impressive with a bright scarf at the waist and the pearls. Only the pearls would have argued with the embroidered neckline, and that would never do.'

'I'm learning an awful lot,' Rochelle said contentedly, leaning back in her seat. 'Do you know, I've never worn a pearl necklace in my life, and now I'm going to wear several!'

'Yes, but not all at once! In fact, Angus will want to give you one, I'm sure, so that you can wear it and advertise us at the same time.'

'And are all your pearls artificial? Don't you use any real ones?'

'Yes, indeed. We've sold cultured pearls and real oyster pearls for years, but this artificial pearl is a new venture for us. We don't do a lot of advertising for the real thing, you see, because if people want that they'll go to a jeweller's and choose the necklace they prefer. But with the new line, the Gempearls, we want customers to ask for them. They'll be different customers, too,' she added. 'People with good taste, we hope, but not a great deal of money to spend. And since they're very good artificial pearls not many people will be able to tell the difference.'

'Pearls and orchids,' Rochelle said, as the taxi turned into the drive and stopped in front of the main door with a great scattering of gravel. 'I don't suppose people have had many of either with the war on – it'll be a wonderful way to show you love someone, to give them pearls and orchids!'

'And a good many pearls and orchids will probably come your way over the next few weeks,' Gemma said, half laughing but half serious too, Rochelle could tell. 'So don't let it go to your head! If in doubt, ask me – or Angus – whether the young man's respectable.'

'Young men?' Rochelle gave a gurgle of amusement. 'Oh, Gemma, you needn't worry. I'm not nearly pretty enough for young men to take an interest. They like golden girls with really good figures – lots of bust and hips and things.'

The taxi driver grinned from ear to ear and turned round in his seat.

'Some does, but some goes for style,' he announced. 'I goes for style, meself!' He turned to Gemma. 'Your little lady's got style, I'd say, missus. Ho, they'll go for 'er, the lads, like bees go for honey.'

Gemma smiled at him and climbed out of the taxi, paid him and then turned towards the house.

'Out of the mouths of babes and taxi drivers,' she remarked sagely. 'Don't you underestimate yourself, Rochelle. You're going to have a big surprise, one of these days.'

21

Despite Laurie's fears, the women, once they got the idea, proved very good at packing. When they were shown how to handle the plants – cleaning the air-roots, cosseting the leaves and flowers, packing them tenderly in the big, airy boxes which the men of the village made at Solly's instruction – they did it as near perfectly as possible and never lost their tempers, slung plants about, crammed them in or did any of the things which the men had done right from the start.

Being freed from the responsibility of doing anything bar actually collecting the plants meant a great deal to Laurie and his friends; they could collect almost continuously, and when they needed a break they could take a proper one, doing what they wanted instead of spending what should have been spare time in preparing the plants for shipment.

The men had returned to their village headquarters with a good collection of Masdevallia, particularly ordered by a breeder who had specialised in them but had lost most of his plants during the war. They had collected more than they needed, sure that once the striking and unusual dwarf orchid was seen it would speedily be bought, especially the floribunda variety, which seemed to flower under any conditions and produced a mass of blossoms even whilst merely tucked into the packing shed at headquarters.

'With this little lot off our hands we're free to go a bit further afield and search for other species,' Laurie said, as they dumped the Masdevallia in the packing shed and advised the women that they would be loading this particular batch quite soon. 'We should hear any day now how the first lot travelled.'

'Until we do, I think we should have ourselves a break,' José said decidedly. 'If we go to all this trouble and the plants arrive in a bad state the other end, we might as well give up. No one'll buy from us. So let's wait a day or so.'

'We-ell, shall we make our way into town when the packing cases go?' Laurie suggested. 'We could just mosey around until then. Or how about hunting for that lost city the German told us about?'

'He kept saying he was Austrian, not German,' Solly objected, but Laurie shrugged.

'What does it matter? The Austrians fought against us; they could have stayed neutral, I suppose. They're all Huns . . . all right, all right, what about the lost city the *Austrian* told us about?'

'What about it?'

'Well, maybe it's hung with orchids . . . or we might find Inca treasure,' Laurie said hopefully. He could not stand inaction and was always eager to move on, try something fresh. 'I wouldn't mind finding a gold ring for my love.'

'Which love? C'mon, man, you said you didn't have a girl,' José reminded him. 'You said you were going to find one soon's you got back to civilisation.'

'Hmm. Your memory's too good. But what better way to get a girl than by giving her a gold ring from an Inca city?'

'What about the pretty piece on Jersey?' Solly said lazily. They had abandoned the packing shed, where the women were busily cleaning, and had made their way back to the living-room of their small, thatched house. Now, Solly lay on his back on one of the long cane loungers, José occupied another and Laurie paced restlessly up and down like a tiger in a too-small cage.

'What about her?' Laurie's tone was belligerent. 'She was just a girl. My father was her guardian so we're joint heirs to the estate . . . but you know all this. Damn it, Sol, I'm collecting orchids so that we can build up my father's

485

collection again, show it to the public, make some money for the estate.'

'Yeah. I often wondered why she didn't come with you,' Solly said, still gazing up at the ceiling.

'Why . . . words fail me! What good could a dame do, here?'

'Oh, I dunno. But if she's nothing to you, why did you come orchid hunting? Just for your own sake? If the two of you are to share the estate . . .'

'I reckon she'll try to buy me out,' Laurie said bitterly. 'Just like a woman, to . . . but we'll see, when I take her the orchids.'

'Wonder what happened to that orchid she was so keen on . . . PM something or other? Wonder if it ever flowered?'

'PM23,' Laurie supplied. 'Dunno . . . but if it did it should make her some money, because it's quite different from any hybrid which has been bred before. My father claimed it looked like a woman's head – that's why he called it Pure Madonna.'

'I knew it had a weird name,' Solly said, snapping his fingers. 'Pure Madonna . . . that's it. Did you see those *New York Times* we gave the women to use for packing?'

'Can't say I did. Why?'

'Well, I saw something about it in the paper . . . they're all old copies, but it's worth having a look.'

Laurie said not a word but made for the packing shed; the other two, lying on their loungers, could hear him cross-questioning the women in his limping Spanish. Presently, Solly craned his neck and then chuckled.

'What's he doin'?' José said softly.

'He's goin' through them newspapers like a whirlwind,' Solly said equally quietly. 'Don't do to say so, José old feller, but Laurie's crazy 'bout that gal. Yeah, crazy about her.'

'Guess you're right,' José said, after some thought. 'Can't see any sane guy comin' out here unless he was desperate strapped for cash, and Laurie's got his demob money and all.'

'Yeah. But she's a . . .'

Solly stopped short as Laurie rushed through the doorway, waving a newspaper.

'Got it! Gee, wait'll you see! She's done it! It's an oldish paper, but the plant bloomed last summer . . . Pure Madonna! And there's Rochelle, right slap-bang in the middle of the picture. See?'

He held the paper out. There was the orchid with its mysterious, madonna-like blossoms and there were the dark eyes and the pale, triangular face of the girl they had last seen dancing and singing on Liberation day.

'My God . . . the *Times* – she's famous!' Solly said, sitting upright and taking the wildly waving paper from Laurie's hand. 'Yeah, she sure did do it. This here paper calls her a modern Jersey Lily, whatever that may mean . . . she sure is a fine little lady, your Rochelle.'

He looked sharply up at Laurie, at the fatuous smile on his pal's bronzed face. This time there was no denial that the girl was his Rochelle. Laurie was too busy staring at her photograph, with his heart in his eyes.

'Got it bad,' Solly muttered to José as Laurie turned to leave the room, his gaze still on the photograph.

'Careful,' José muttered, but he need not have bothered. Clearly Laurie could think of nothing, just then, but Rochelle.

Three days later, the rains started. It was odd, Laurie thought, lying on his cot and staring up at the ceiling, which had an ominous damp mark spreading slowly across it, how he had longed for the rain to cool him off a bit but now it had come he longed for its cessation. It did cool the atmosphere down a little, but on the other hand being constantly soaked to the skin did little for anyone's temper.

'We can't stop collecting just for a bit of rain, though,'

Laurie pointed out, and was immensely cheered to be told that here, even in the rainy season, one quite often had several days together when not a drop of rain fell and the sun shone with warmth and brilliance.

'This time we want Cattleyas; the scented ones, schroderae,' Laurie instructed them. 'I've asked around and most people say we'll find them – if we find them – near rivers. They're arboreal, of course, but we'll hope they don't grow too high – Cattleyas are all big plants and so far the bigger plants do seem to have been growing lower down the trunk. So are we off?'

'We're off,' assented Solly, though José looked rather doubtful. He had recently been troubled by a festering sore on his right leg just behind the knee, and despite sulphonamides and disinfectant and the most rigorous attention to diet the sore would not heal.

'We want the grasslands this time, according to rumour,' Laurie said briskly. 'What the natives call the Llanos . . . that's where they say Cattleya schroderae grow. Perhaps it'll be easier to spot them in grasslands . . . I mean, the trees will only be growing alongside rivers, for a start. It won't be like cutting our way into the rain forests.'

'And where will we sleep at nights?' José demanded. 'No chance of getting back here, is there? I've looked at the map and it's several days' hard slog just to reach the Llanos.'

'Yes . . . but we're hiring a jeep,' Laurie explained. 'We can take turns to drive, and we'll be there in under a day. We'll use a small town as our headquarters – Pueblocito will be fine – and any orchids we collect can be left there until we've got enough to bring back here.'

'A small town? Oh, that isn't so bad, then,' José said, perking up. It was clear that he had expected something far more hit and miss than Pueblocito. 'Well, when do we actually go?'

'Tomorrow. I've hired the jeep, spoken to the staff here,

and all that remains to be done is to get ourselves some food for the journey, pack a couple of decent *costales* in case the mules on the Llanos don't have the right sort of containers for carrying orchids, and . . . well, and shift our butts.'

'After a good night's sleep,' José said. He sighed deeply and stroked a hand gingerly down the back of his injured leg. 'Perhaps the grasslands are good for sores and this'll clear,' he added hopefully.

'Perhaps. Well, lads . . . I'll wake you at dawn. Best to get an early start.'

Dawn was still only greying the eastern sky when Laurie shook the other two, pummelling Solly, a slug-a-bed, with more enthusiasm than kindness.

'Come on, Sol . . . we're all set for the start.'

It was raining, but not as heavily as it had been over the past few days, and the three of them donned their black rubber *encouchados*, their trusty sombreros and the knee-boots which they relied on to keep them relatively safe from snake, scorpion and the worst of the water. Then they went out to the jeep where Tomas, Pedro and Gomez already sat, looking half asleep still and more than a little depressed.

'Is no good, lookin' for plants in this downpour,' Gomez muttered, but it was a token grumble and they all knew it. Life continued despite the weather – it had to, because in Colombia the rainy season came twice a year instead of just once, which meant that no one could simply curl up and do nothing when the thunder clouds rolled over the peaks of the Andes and the rain fell in slanting silver sheets.

'Where are we going?' Pedro demanded. 'Far from here, Gomez says.'

'Well, I did tell you . . . to the Llanos.'

'The Voragine – the Vortex,' José said, his voice low. 'They say it's an enchanted place; once seen never forgotten.

489

They say you'll hunger for the sight of the grasslands for the rest of your life if once you go there.'

'Superstition,' Laurie said drily. 'Still, it's bound to be a change from the rain forests. I'll drive, shall I?'

There was not much competition. José's leg made driving impossible and Solly was a wild and unreliable driver whose skills were not often called upon.

'Right,' Laurie said when no one answered. He got behind the wheel and the other two crowded into the cab with him, whilst behind, beneath the canvas shelter, the peons muttered, occasionally laughed and played a game with dice and matches.

The road was spine-chilling. It looped and switchbacked high into the mountains, often a single track upon which two vehicles could not pass. Nose to nose, the drivers would argue it out until one or other backed, usually incredibly fast, down the road to a passing place.

Laurie drove on, hour after hour, and it was natural that his thoughts should switchback, like the road, from his present surroundings to Jersey, and Rochelle. Was she missing him? Did she set great store by his postcards or did she merely glance at them and then throw them into a drawer or into the fire? But he knew her better than that; he was sure she was genuinely fond of him, even though they had parted in high dudgeon. And anyway, soon . . . in another three or four months . . . he would be back in the United States with a permanent address and he would write to her and wait for a letter back. A letter saying 'Come!'

He was collecting the orchids for her, of course. He was delighted that Pure Madonna had come into flower at last and brought her a measure of success, perhaps even a moment or two of heady fame. But it would be a nine-days' wonder, not something which could make her independent of the vagaries of the farming world as a full collection, properly marketed, would.

490

The windscreen wiper clicked back and forth, swished to and fro, and the rain beat down on the canvas roof over the travellers' heads. The clouds parted now and then, and once Laurie announced that there was a patch of clear sky ahead, but still it seemed they were destined to drive for ever in the rain. Once they were held up by a landslide, a great pile of mud and rocks which had descended from the cliff above on to the road. It often happened, one of the men working to clear it told Laurie laconically, in the rainy season. And he directed them to drive along a little side path, slippery with mud, which was normally used by cattle drovers taking their herds to market.

It seemed to Laurie that they were never going to gain the plains, that they would continue to drive for ever along the narrow, looping road with an immense drop on one side and a tall rock face on the other. And then they rounded a curve . . . and Laurie jammed on his brakes with a gasp which was echoed by both the front seat passengers.

Below them, at long last, was the plain, the Llanos: a great ocean of softly waving, greeny-gold grass, bisected by the meandering waters of a great river, so large that in places it split into a dozen or more streams, divided by great golden sandbanks.

And the scene was sunlit! The sun, which had remained hidden all day, was shining now, and as it burned on the grasslands steam rose like a wavering mist and blurred the landscape, making it appear even more dreamlike and unreal.

'Where are the trees?' José murmured at last, as Laurie started the engine and began, almost reluctantly, to drive down into the enchanted plain. 'Where's Pueblocito?'

'There,' Solly said, pointing to a huddle of whitewashed mud houses with corrugated iron roofs. 'See, there's the church . . . a little hospital . . . a few shops . . . that's Pueblocito.'

'And the trees are still a bit of a journey away,' Laurie

admitted. 'They surround the river as it nears the foothills of the Andes. I believe they're all very tall and the vegetation is quite different from what we've seen in the rain forests. That's why I think we may well find the orchids we want here . . . plus the fact that it's very underpopulated and other collectors don't seem to have been.'

'We won't go today, will we?' José said anxiously. He was very pale and it was clear that his leg was giving him quite a lot of pain as he tried to hold it still against the constant swaying of the vehicle. 'I couldn't face a long trek.'

'Of course not,' Laurie comforted him. 'We'll leave at dawn tomorrow, if we can find a native to point us in the right direction.'

At dawn next day, however, only two of the travellers were fit to set off in search of the scented orchid. José's leg had been giving him such pain that when they arrived in Pueblocito Solly and Laurie took him straight to the hospital. They saw an American doctor, the first fellow-countryman they had set eyes on for many weeks. He had taken one look and advised them that José could travel no further until the infection had cleared up.

'It's ulcerating; he needs complete rest and plenty of green food and salt-water baths each day,' the doctor said authoritatively. 'If you're set on leaving tomorrow, this young man may stay with me. By the time you get back he'll probably be well on the road to recovery.'

There was no option and the small group realised it. José was left in the hospital with a pretty young nurse to look after him and the American doctor to oversee his treatment. Solly and Laurie set off back to the rooms they had rented, half envious of their companion but mainly anxious for him. Suppose the doctor could not stop the infection? José, they guessed, could lose his leg. But with luck they had caught it in time and José would soon be well enough to come out with them once more. Neither Solly nor Laurie was sufficiently optimistic to believe that they would find the scented orchids at the first or even the second try. Past experience told them that it might be weeks before they found one Cattleya schroderae, let alone hundreds.

'I'll wake you early,' Laurie said to Solly as they collapsed into their cots. 'We won't go to the hospital before we leave, but we'll go as soon as we get back.'

'Sure,' murmured Solly sleepily. 'G'night, Laurie.'

'Goodnight,' Laurie said. And then added, more to himself than to Solly, 'And then there were two.'

It was a sobering thought to go to bed on.

'Can we take the mule through?'

The great river, the Rio Quanquat, must have been almost a mile wide at this point. Laurie, Solly and the three peons stood on the bank, narrowing their eyes against the brilliance of the sun and wondering whether the water was full of crocodiles, or piranhas, or was simply flowing too fast and too deep for safety.

Laurie had found a ferryman with a big, leaky, flat-bottomed boat in which he intimated he would take passengers for a small sum . . . about ten cents a head in real money, Laurie thought. But it was clear that the mule would barely fit into the boat even if they could have persuaded it to try, and no one looked too willing.

'The mule can swim behind,' the ferryman said in Spanish. 'Mules swim quite well, the water is deep, and if one of you holds the creature's halter he should come ashore safe.'

The peons said they would willingly hold the halter provided they might ride in the boat and were not expected to swim with the mule, so Laurie paid the ferryman and they all crowded aboard. The mule showed a distressing tendency to try to join them, and hooked its forefeet appealingly over the flattened stern. Although the ferryman first tried to evict it and then charged Laurie extra, they decided it was a better way to travel in dangerous waters than swimming, so the boat made even heavier weather of the crossing than it usually did. Nevertheless, it gained the further bank with the mule and all their company safe.

'Off we go,' Laurie cried heartily as they assembled. 'This is very different country from what we're used to, but that doesn't make it more difficult. I have a hunch we shan't have to work too hard to find our quarry this time.'

It was true that the trees frequently gave way to grass, huge areas of which could be scanned at one time, but as they neared the mountains the trees began to cluster more thickly.

'What exactly are we looking for?' Solly asked, as they started to peer upwards in the way they both knew only too well. 'I know about the scent . . . but what do they *look* like?'

Laurie was beginning to tell him when one of the peons, wandering ahead with the mule, gave a shout and came back towards them, his sombrero waving in one hand.

'*Parasitos!*' he exclaimed. 'A hundred, many hundred, maybe a t'ousand!'

'It can't be Cattleya schroderae,' Laurie muttered. 'You know what these men are like. Any flower that grows in a tree is an orchid, and ten look like a hundred.'

Nevertheless, he followed the peon, now hurrying back into the trees.

'There! I, alone, have found it!' Pedro declared, straightening his stringy figure to its full height and beaming proudly around him.

Solly stared upwards and around, then looked at Laurie. 'Well? What is it?'

But Laurie's face was one huge, beatific beam.

'What a sight,' he murmured. 'What an unforgettable sight!'

494

Orchids crowded the branches of the trees, their flowers white, blush-pink, rose, and red deepening to purple. The beauty of them was startling, and the number gave the first impression that the trees were suddenly blessed with coloured boughs, or that someone had emptied tins and tins of paint in glorious profusion into the branches.

'Cattleya trianae,' Laurie said, on a gasp. 'Oh, Solly, stare! There ain't many men who can say they've seen a sight like that!'

'They sure are pretty,' Solly said. 'But are they what we want? Are they valuable?'

'Valuable! Well, yes . . . though we only have a few orders. But I'm sure if we take these back we'll find a ready sale for them. Have you ever seen anything lovelier, Solly?'

'I guess not,' said the unromantic Solomon stolidly. 'I guess they're lovely, all right. Particularly if they're valuable.'

'I will mount the first tree,' Pedro said, all but beating his skinny chest. 'I have found a fortune in *parasitos*. I should climb the first tree.'

'Very well, but treat them carefully,' Laurie implored. 'We can't take many now, but we'll come back tomorrow.'

'With more mules?' Solly said. 'In that boat?'

Clearly, it was not a prospect that filled him with enthusiasm.

'Guess so – unless you'd like to spend the night here with this mule and I'll bring the rest over in the morning?' Laurie said.

'Guess not,' Solly sighed. 'I'll go up after some of these . . . there are so many I reckon I can't make a mistake.'

The mistake he meant had been a common one, since he had ascended a tree in pursuit of a fairly abundant orchid, Restrepia sanguinea, and had come down with an Odontoglossom crispum, which was far rarer and more valuable. But, as Solly had explained when he reached ground level once more, the 'little red one' had been halfway along a thin and rotten-looking branch, whereas the 'big white one' had been comfortably clinging to the sturdy crotch formed by a big, reliable branch and the main trunk of the tree.

'You did well,' Laurie had praised him. 'But we might have been kicking your ass down every trail in the forest if it had been the other way round . . . think about it, Sol old pardner.'

Now, however, Solly went up the tree like a monkey, using a thick liana, and was soon cautiously astride a big branch taking the orchids neatly off it, to cast them gently down into Laurie's glad embrace.

'I wish Rochelle could see this,' Laurie found himself thinking, as the pinks and roses and reds and purples multiplied around him. 'Oh, how I wish Rochelle could see this!'

José recovered from his malady but, with the rains, various ills befell them. Solly slipped when climbing a tree and a number of thorns embedded themselves in his person. Two of the wounds went septic, and though they managed to clear the infection after a few days it meant that they were a man short whilst he was recovering.

One of the peons chopped his own leg whilst clearing a thicket and had to be carried many miles to hospital. He was replaced by a fourteen-year-old boy named Peder, and scarcely had the 'new boy' got into his stride when Tomas was back with them, his leg stitched and healing well, and very insistent that Peder's services should be dispensed with in favour of his own.

Since the stitches meant that though he could climb trees he was rather slower than before, Laurie decided to keep both men on, Tomas to deal with the mules and the other three to climb, but this of course added to the expense of the trip. And though they had collected several hundred of the Cattleya trianae, they still had not had a sniff – literally – of Cattleya schroderae.

'And I've got a filthy cold; I wouldn't smell one if it was right under my nose,' Laurie grumbled, as the little gang set off once more into virgin territory. 'Let's hope we strike soon, or their flowering season will be over and they really will be hard to spot.'

'When do we have to give up?' José asked practically. The three of them were on muleback since they had decided, in view of the increasing urgency of their search, to take the full complement of mules and peons on every foray. Should they happen upon the orchid they wanted, they would thus be able to start collecting immediately and not lose a day.

It also meant that they got along more quickly, for the peons jog-trotted and the mules did likewise. Once they left the main trail, however, the mules were nothing but a nuisance, and this was where Tomas came in useful. The rest of them made their way into the jungle whilst Tomas – and the mules – remained on the path.

Of course when a strike was made they would need both Tomas and the mules, but while more searching than striking was the order of the day it was far easier for each man to machete himself a path than to clear a big enough gap for mules and men to pass.

'You mean give up hunting Cattleya schroderae?' Laurie said. 'We can't. It's the biggest firm order we've got. And the grower who ordered them is a big man in the business, so we absolutely *must* find them. We know they're here . . . somewhere.'

'That's done it; any god listening will make damned sure we never see the little beauties,' groaned Solly. 'You shouldn't tempt fate by saying we must find anything, you bum.'

And indeed it seemed as if Solly was right. Laurie slogged along, his machete swinging rhythmically, the rain sluicing across the brim of his sombrero and straight down his neck despite the collar of his *encouchado*'s being turned up as high as it would go. The cold made his head feel as if it was stuffed with cottonwool, and he ached as the damp seemed to penetrate to the very marrow of his bones. The catarrh was making him deaf, too, so that he could not hear the others above the croaking of the frogs and the dripping and chuckling of the raindrops.

In a moment I'll stop and shout, he kept telling himself. But somehow it seemed simpler to keep going, to slash and chop with the machete to win another few feet, to find a clearing, check that there were no scented orchids on the boughs of the trees, and slog on.

In a way he rather enjoyed the solitary work. The chorus of the frogs was rather attractive, the little, emerald green ones with the big black eyes chirruping on a high note, the big flat-headed ones with the golden eyes bassing away like gongs. And there were other noises he could hear if he stopped chopping for a moment and listened. Bird-calls sometimes, though not often; the creak and squeak of insect-life; and the roar of water, coming strongly now from his right.

A river? It was a fact that they often found orchids on trees which overhung a river, especially a fast-flowing one. The flowers seemed to flourish better than in the warmer, more humid jungle.

But perhaps it was about time he got in touch with the others again. He was always warning them to stick together, never go far from the track without checking that they knew its whereabouts . . . and he had changed direction so many times, following his hunches, that he could not have found it unaided for a fortune.

Shaking his head at his own stupidity, Laurie turned back, away from the roar of water, and began to follow his own erratic trail.

He followed it doggedly, thinking he could not go far wrong, for where he had chopped a path the broken wood and vegetation was clear to see. He smiled to himself, remembering the first time he had chopped a low bough off one particular tree – and the wound had filled up with what looked just like blood. He had felt a superstitious thrill at the sight, though seasoned peons assured him that it was merely scarlet, sticky sap which was used as toothpaste by the Indians.

A monkey, chattering overhead, caught his attention and he tilted his head up to look. The tree was shaggy with tree-pineapple, and some orchids bloomed there, nodding their frail pink heads as though greeting him, but none was the scented Cattleya. The monkey which had first caught his attention was gibbering down at him, and then it leapt from one bough to the next, still looking at Laurie. It had rather a pretty little face with full creamy sidewhiskers, and Laurie laughed up at it, almost forgetting his head-cold and the rain.

'How about giving me a clue, old pardner?' he said. 'Bet you know where every durn orchid in this jungle hangs out!'

The monkey leapt once more and Laurie, for something to do, followed it. And presently, there was the track, right in front of him.

'Mighty good of you, little feller,' Laurie said as the monkey disappeared into the trees once more. 'Mind you, I'd have found the trail without your help, but . . .'

He stopped short. The path was empty. No mules, no Tomas, and no other member of their expedition either. It was clearly the wrong track.

I'm lost, Laurie thought. But he did not believe it, not really. He would shout . . . walk up and down the path a while. It had to be the right one; it was just that he had struck it too far east or west because of following the monkey instead of keeping to his own machete trail.

Three hours later he knew he was well and truly lost. He had shouted until he was hoarse, his head ached, his joints hurt . . . and he was lost.

It was getting duskier, too. The rain had stopped a while back, so at least he was beginning to dry out, but the sun which had followed the rain was sinking rapidly in the sky, the rays penetrating the trees red now, not gold. When it got dark the jaguars would come out to hunt, Laurie reminded himself. When it got dark the only safe place would be up a tree . . . but jaguars climbed trees, and so did snakes . . . and scorpions. And poisonous spiders.

He could not just stand still and wait to be eaten, strangled or stung to death, however, so he kept moving. Even now, when despair was near, he kept calling out as well, just in case. But his voice was thin and cracked . . . and he was thirsty! And pretty damned hungry too, when he thought about it, only the fever made a drink much more important . . . if only he could hear that river again! He wished now that he had stayed on the trail, instead of imagining he heard voices and plunging back into the jungle. He had tried hard enough, God knew, to get back on the path, but with no luck. It was just trees, trees, trees, and some of them he was pretty sure he had seen a dozen or more times in the past few hours. One particular bunch of orchids, dwarf Masdevallia chimaera, he believed, almost waved at him as he passed beneath it . . . I'm hallucinating, he thought drearily, when I think orchids recognise me . . . and then, into the deepening gloom, came a sharp memory of those same orchids and a monkey, chattering at him, leading him on . . .

Laurie stood stock still. And listened with all the power of his stuffy head and bunged-up ears. And heard the roar of water from his right.

He *had* recognised those orchids . . . he was near the very spot where, earlier in the day, he had realised he was lost!

He looked around him. There were machete marks all right . . . but since he had been blazing trails for hours now, it would be madness to try to pick out one and follow it. In fact it might be a good deal more sensible to choose

500

the one part of the clearing which had not been minced by the lost Laurient – the side from which the roar of water came strongest.

If I don't get a drink soon I'm a dead man, Laurie told himself, so I might as well find that river. And he raised his machete and struck at the vines nearest the sound.

The river was probably not more than quarter of a mile from where Laurie had got lost, but it took him the best part of two hours to reach it, the undergrowth being particularly lush and well grown, the trees crowding close to be near the water. When Laurie at last burst out on to the bank he was so exhausted that he nearly fell to his knees, but instead he stared, stunned.

The river, at this point, fell away in a swooping, gleaming waterfall, down down down into the depths of the forest below. He had reached a mountain peak, even if the mountain was covered in tropical jungle and was more like a mighty plain . . . and from the top of a mountain, Laurie reasoned groggily, a man might see for miles and miles . . . he might see a village, or a town, or even a little, winding trail with four mules waiting patiently on it.

But he had not got the strength to climb a tree, even quite a small tree. All he felt capable of doing was kneeling on the river bank, very carefully, and dipping his cupped hands into the water.

He drank and it was sweet and cool, better than a pint of beer or a hot cup of coffee, the best drink in the world. Laurie buried his nose in his hands and drank more, until his stomach felt pleasantly distended and his hunger had disappeared along with his thirst. When at last he straightened, darkness had come with the suddenness and totality which shocks the unwary at first. But full to the gills with water Laurie felt almost brave. He had found the river . . . admittedly at this point it was completely unnavigable because of the waterfall, but people had been using rivers

501

for all the ages of man, and this particular *torrente* could be no exception. Sooner or later, if he walked along the bank, he would come upon a human settlement, or a hut, or . . . well, or something. And if he could just survive for long enough his friends would get a search party together and find him. There was no need to despair.

But where to spend the night? Laurie looked round and decided to try a fat, squat tree which looked as though he could almost have walked up it. He was still weak, but not as weak as he had been, so he tried the tree and found, as he had hoped, that he was capable of getting into the lower branches.

They were not comfortable, but he did his best. He rattled and shook all the foliage hopefully to rid it of snakes, scorpions and any other creepy-crawlies which might have thought of sharing it with him, and then looked apprehensively upwards, to where the branch above, sadly shaggy still, overhung him.

But there was little he could do about it, so he did nothing. He wedged himself into the fork of the tree, drew his legs up on to the branch so they would not dangle like a tempting snack for any passing jaguar, and tried to make himself very, very small.

And then he put his head down on his knees, his arms around them and let his mind drift pleasantly off to dreams of rescue, thoughts of a triumphant return to their thatched headquarters and the money he would be paid by grateful growers when he had fulfilled all his orders.

Then, quite naturally, he let his thoughts dwell on Rochelle's amazement when he turned up on Jersey with his specimen orchids for her collection. He had got to a most satisfactory part in this particular daydream – where Rochelle, her face streaked with tears and softened by love, fell on to his chest, warm and willing, and promised to marry him tomorrow – when he most unexpectedly fell asleep.

* * *

502

Back at their rented rooms, acrimonious apportioning of blame had long ago ceased. They had searched for Laurie until the light had gone and darkness mocked their efforts; they had shouted for him until they could scarcely croak. They had roamed the paths, seen what they took to be his machete-marks on various trails, yet apparently never come within half a mile of him.

'And he wasn't well,' moaned Solly now, lying sleepless on his cot and glaring up at a lizard which lived somewhere amongst the rafters. 'That cold . . . it was probably influenza . . . he won't last the night. The old hunters told us when we were starting out that a man won't last a night in the rain forest. Not alone. Well, not even with a tent and camping equipment.'

'It ain't just the jaguars,' José agreed. 'There's all sorts out there at night. Some of the snakes . . .'

'Yeah, yeah. Do you reckon some of the Indians might have taken him in, though? He might get bitten – they have fleas and bed-bugs like no one else – but in a hut he could survive, right?'

'Oh, sure . . . if they take him in. Them and their poisonous blowpipes,' José said. 'Nasty, real nasty, some of 'em. That flat-eyed look . . . and they're all unhealthy themselves; they could do him more harm than good.'

'In a night? Oh, God, let him find shelter,' Solly said, his monkey-face grimacing with the intensity of his prayer. 'Let him be all right, let him come through . . . if You let him come through tonight I'll . . . I'll climb the next real big tree that comes up and never a word of complaint.'

'You never do complain,' José said gently, quite touched by Solly's concern for their friend. 'Never heard you moan yet, Sol.'

'You may not have, but the feller upstairs hears a grumble or two,' Solly said, jerking his head at the rafters. 'Never again . . . just let the guy get through the night, Lord.'

'Sure. I second that,' José said gruffly. 'Now we gotta try for some sleep. We'll search the better for it tomorrow.'

'Sleep?' Solly laughed hollowly. 'I'll never sleep, not with Laurie out there somewhere with jaguars, and poisonous snakes, and . . .'

'Sure, I know, with a whole zooful of danger. Just hit the hay, will you?'

'Yeah. You're right, Jo. Sorry.' Solly rolled over and buried his head in his pillow. José did likewise.

Their worry was real, and their grief for their friend's plight, but they had had a long and exhausting day.

Presently, they slept.

Laurie was woken by a noise, or perhaps by the first glimmerings of light in the east, he could not tell. He started to stretch, to roll over . . . and realised, with horror, that he was not in his nice safe cot but on the branch of a tree with God knew what lurking all around and a hell of a drop should he move unwisely.

For a moment he froze, then forced himself to relax and put his hand out to pat the branch. It was wide and strong and it had supported him throughout the darkest hours, and now, with greyness glimmering through the leaves, it would support him still, provided he stayed just where he was.

He snuggled back into his comfortable, almost pre-natal, position and tried to go back to sleep, but whatever had woken him would not let him rest. He concentrated on his surroundings. Had something moved nearby? His nose was blocked, his head felt like lead, his hearing and sense of smell were impaired and even his night-eyes were gummy with sleep and misty from fever.

He closed them, and immediately knew why he had woken. Someone was breathing heavily nearby – snoring, almost. And human beings snore, Laurie said joyously to himself. There must be an Indian encampment quite near, or, at least, one Indian hunter, snoozing happily.

He listened harder; it was actually in the tree, he was sure of it. It sounded as though it came from the branch above, and as the light increased even his streaming eyes could make out a hump in a fork almost directly over his head, where the man had obviously curled up to sleep in safety.

Laurie was about to call out when it occurred to him that most of the Indian hunters carried blowpipes through which they blew poisoned darts at their prey – or at their enemies. What was more, if Laurie woke the man suddenly he could easily do what Laurie himself had almost done: roll over and plunge to his death twenty or thirty feet below.

The best and safest thing was simply to lie quietly until the man woke of his own accord and then address him in Spanish, which he would almost certainly know.

As the light strengthened, therefore, Laurie practised a few welcoming words. Good morning, and how are you? might not be the most scintillating conversation, but it seemed, by and large, the safest opening gambit. Then he could get to the nitty-gritty of where are we, how far from your village, can you take me there, I am very hungry and similar useful phrases which he knew by heart.

In the meantime, day was gradually arriving and Laurie, in his perch far above the ground, found time, now he knew that help was near, to appreciate the dawning beauty of the scene. Birds sang, birds he had never heard before and certainly had not realised made their home in the jungle. Insects clicked and whirred and mumbled and started their day-long breakfast on the leaves about him, and the frogs renewed their eternal chorus – not that it had stopped when darkness fell, but merely slowed and softened.

Presently, however, Laurie decided he would simply have to try to blow his nose. God knew whether it would respond to such treatment, but it was messily running and he felt so rotten that only a good blow would help. It might wake the man on the branch above, but that might be no bad thing. The sound of a nose being blown is not, after all, a particularly menacing one. The Indian hunter would wake, look below to see who was wielding a handkerchief . . . except that all the Indians Laurie had met so far had blown their noses straight into their fingers. And then, Laurie recalled, the Indians offered these odd strangers their locally brewed fire-water or freshly baked unleavened bread. Perhaps, Laurie thought as he got his handkerchief out of his pocket, I won't tell the chap I'm hungry. Perhaps I could wait for a meal until I get back to the guys.

He tried very hard to blow his nose, but it was simply too solidly blocked. Despite himself, Laurie gave a groan, and then tried again. And the sleeper above awoke and looked down.

A black head, spade-shaped. Long, bristling white whiskers. Two huge eyes which burned amber.

Laurie's nose cleared instantly as his feverish cold fled. It, if nothing else, would not remain at such close quarters with a jaguar! Laurie shrank closer to the tree-trunk as the great beast growled menacingly under its breath and dropped, light as a domestic tabby, on to the branch which held his cringing form. The big cat took two steps along it. Laurie had time to admire its huge, softly spreading paws with their remarkably well-sharpened claws, the length of its tail, and the fact that, as it turned towards him, it gave a definite, interrogatory mew.

'Bugger off,' Laurie said, now pressed flat as any pancake to the tree-trunk. 'Go on, bugger off!'

Perhaps it was a young jaguar, or perhaps it simply wanted to oblige, but as he spoke the great eyes widened, the lips curled back and the whiskers bristled whitely . . . and it jumped down, to the branch beneath the one Laurie was standing on.

Laurie grabbed the trunk and peered downwards. The huge cat was making its way down the tree from branch to branch with all the savoir-faire of a commuter descending into the subway. Once on the ground it did not look back, but slipped, wraithlike, into the surrounding tangle of undergrowth.

Trembling with recent fear, Laurie crouched on his branch for about five minutes, staring at the ground. Would the jaguar do a double-take, realise it had just passed up a perfectly good breakfast, and return for him? Or did it have business of its own to see to? It had certainly behaved like a cat with a mission in life. And when five minutes had passed and it had not reappeared, he began to wonder whether he had dreamed the whole episode. Jaguars were not commonly black, were they? And they were supposed to be fiendishly clever and extremely ferocious, particularly when startled. *Had* he dreamed it? A part of him knew it had been real, but another part, he realised, would be far happier, when trekking through the jungle below, to tell itself that the jaguar had been a figment of his cold-soaked brain. It had been bad enough facing it along the suddenly too-short branch, but having an eye to eye encounter on the ground would be infinitely worse.

Though I've got my machete, Laurie reminded himself, fishing the gleaming blade out from its resting-place close at hand. He could shout, make at the jaguar with machete whirling – perhaps the combination would send it off before it did any mortal damage.

Laurie decided he would descend the tree and circle the clearing cautiously, ready to take to the branches should anything larger than a rabbit stir. For the first time, he looked around him in full daylight, simultaneously registering that there was a really beautiful scent up here, as though he had shared the tree last night not with a jaguar but with a bevy of beautiful girls.

And his eyes told his unbelieving brain that he had – he had indeed. As far as the eye could see, on his own particular tree and on many others surrounding the clearing, Cattleya schroderae spilled its delicious fragrance and pale rosy petals prodigally across the branches. Laurie had slept in a bower of the orchids he was searching for, and because of his cold he had been entirely unaware of the fact.

'Never say I'm all nose, because this schnozzle led me to you,' Solly declared exuberantly later, as the three of them stood in the clearing where Laurie had spent such an eventful night. 'Find that orchid and we'll find the guy,' I said, so we searched and sniffed and followed our conks . . . and there were the orchids with you amongst 'em, like an earwig in a rose.'

'And you spent the night in that tree?' José said, staring admiringly at Laurie. 'Gee, feller, I'd have died!'

'No you wouldn't, you'd have hung on and prayed, same as I did,' Laurie replied promptly. 'I slept too, believe it or not.'

'Gee, that uneventful a night, eh? No bogeymen? No slithering snakes or Indians with blowpipes trained on you or big cats casting greedy glances at your hams?'

Laurie hesitated. He ought to tell them; it was true, after all. But they would never believe it, not in a thousand years; they'd think he was shooting a line. And besides, with his rescuers' arrival he was growing feverish once more and starting to wonder again whether he had dreamed it. A *black* jaguar? Anyway, what mattered now was not his night on the tiles but the speedy collecting of the masses and masses of scented orchids by which they were surrounded.

He said as much, brushing his adventure aside, and José and Solly were glad to agree. They insisted, though, that he sat on one of the mules and had a good breakfast first, and stayed in the saddle until he felt strong enough to take a hand with the work.

Hours later, with the *costales* tightly packed and the scent of the orchids pervading everything, Laurie nearly did tell them. One of the peons, fourteen-year-old Peder, remarked casually as he pressed another handful of plants into the nearest *costale*, 'There was a jaguar here last night; his spoor goes across the clearing and down to the river, where he drank. It was lucky the boss was aloft in his tree before the big cat came by.'

Six pairs of eyes were fixed on Laurie's face; should he tell them? But the moment passed. Solly went to the head of his mule and said he would lead off, adding that when they got back to the village he thought their first stop should be at the *posada*, where they could get something decent to drink.

'It'll help get rid of that cold,' he said to Laurie.

'Aw, it's on the mend already,' Laurie said easily. It was true. The cold had fled when the jaguar appeared and had not yet returned.

'Yeah? First time I ever heard a night in a tree was good for a cold in the head.'

'Maybe it was the scent of the flowers,' Laurie said, grinning at their patent disbelief. 'We'll sell any unordered plants on medicinal grounds – *Spend a night inhaling the fragrance of the rare and lovely Cattleya schroderae and you'll find your head-cold has quite disappeared.*'

'It might even work,' grinned José. And Laurie, getting a firm grip on the saddle of his mule, let the matter drop, but could not help reflecting that selling the cold-sufferers orchids to sniff would be a very much easier task than providing the black jaguar.

22

'Ooh look, Mum, it's the pearl-girl!'

The first time it happened, when she was riding on a number 72 bus, Rochelle was thrilled and could not wait to get home and tell Angus and Gemma. The second time, she merely wished they had not chosen to spot her as she sat in the hairdresser's, having her hair cut just a little and expertly waved.

After that it was commonplace, for there was no doubt about it: the advertising campaign which was meant to focus attention first on the new artificial pearls and second on the orchid was making her famous. Of course it promoted the pearls as well, but they did not have faces which could be spotted on a bus or in a department store, paddling in the Serpentine or buying oranges.

For Rochelle had taken to London like a duck to water, and Londoners had taken to her. She was, as Gemma had predicted, showered with invitations. When she went dancing her photograph appeared in society magazines as well as the popular press; well-wishers surrounded her modelling sessions in Hyde Park; and she need never have paid a bus fare or for a meal, because there was always someone willing to treat her.

Then some bright young reporter pointed out that Rochelle Dubois meant Rochelle of the wood, and the nickname pearl-girl was superseded, for a while, by such phrases as 'our own woodland nymph' and 'the forest-flame from Jersey', and all these captions were underlined by Rochelle's pale, mischievous face and large wondering eyes, by her slim, graceful body and by her appealing, three-cornered smile.

'It's partly your own particular brand of charm and partly the war,' Angus told her, squiring her to a party one night when Gemma was too tired to accompany them. 'London's been drab for so long that the sight of you, young and pretty and full of life, is enough to bring a smile to the most jaundiced face. And you're different, and you've got a heroic story.'

'Me? Heroic?' Rochelle laughed. 'What about Londoners, then? All that bombing, the terrible things they suffered . . . at least on Jersey we weren't in fear of our lives every night for weeks and weeks.'

'Perhaps not, but you actually lived under German rule. What's more, you managed to fool them by continuing to grow your orchid despite all their rules and regulations. And Londoners never starved.'

'Nor did we . . . quite,' Rochelle reminded him. 'Who told them about M. Laurient and me hiding the Russian prisoner of war, though?'

'I did,' Angus said, looking guilty. 'It's all true, my dear, and it's such a marvellous, heart-warming story. They love you for that, too. You risked your life for that young man, and your guardian probably lost his life. You mustn't mind if people love you for it!'

'It's very nice . . . but I don't think Simon loves me for what I did for Radek,' Rochelle said, dimpling up at Angus as they danced sedately round the highly polished ballroom floor. 'You like him, don't you?'

'Who? Simon?' Angus was a good dancer; now his arm tightened just a little around Rochelle's narrow waist and she nestled closer to him, happy to have his affection. 'He's not a bad young man and he's certainly got the means to keep you, if that's what you want. But . . . he doesn't have half your guts and get-up-and-go, Rochelle.'

'No; he's a bit feeble, really,' Rochelle admitted. 'Don't worry. I don't take Simon seriously, but he's fun to be with

511

and I don't think he'd ever try to . . . to do anything I didn't like.'

'What a twerp he must be,' Angus said gravely. He rested his chin on the top of her smooth head. 'If I were twenty years younger I'd do all sorts of things – and you'd like 'em all!'

'That sounds more like Mark du Sattay,' Rochelle observed. 'He's not rich or particularly handsome but he's full of ambition and drive and he likes me a lot. Only I'm not looking for a boyfriend, far less a husband. I'm too busy having fun.'

'That's right, the fun you missed because the war came along,' Angus agreed. 'I shouldn't tease you about your young men, my dear. It makes me sound like a jealous old fool.'

'Ha . . . as if you needed to be jealous when I love you and Gemma so much,' Rochelle said, twirling lightly in his arms. 'You've both been kinder to me than almost anyone else in the world. Whatever becomes of me, I'll never, never forget you!'

'*Almost* anyone else? Who are you thinking of?'

'Why, M. Laurient, of course. If he hadn't taken me on when my parents were killed . . . well, I'd have been stuck in some orphanage and I'd never have amounted to a row of beans. I – I need love ever so badly, Angus, and I always have.'

'Yes,' Angus said musingly. 'If I was jealous of anyone, my dear, it would be of your M. Laurient, but one can't be jealous of a dead man.'

'Jealous of M. Laurient? Why should you say that?'

'Because you loved him as a parent, and that's the way Gemma and I want you to love us. Haven't you guessed how very motherly Gemma feels towards you? And I think of you, often, as being like the little daughter we lost. Had she lived she would have been your age, you know. And she was like me, dark-haired. Oh, right from the start you

512

made me think of Louisa. Or perhaps that's the wrong way round. You are how we would have liked Louisa to be – honest, generous, outspoken, but above all, loving. Can you understand that, dear Chelle, and accept it without resentment?'

'It's a great compliment,' Rochelle said quietly. 'You know how fond I am of you both . . . I love you as I love M. Laurient, who is the only father I've really ever known. But . . . there is another sort of love, isn't there? The sort of love one might feel for, say, Mark du Sattay?'

'Yes, of course, but . . .'

The music ended and the couples on the dance floor stood for a moment, the men applauding, whilst the orchestra waited to strike up the new tune. Rochelle caught Angus's hand and pulled him towards their table.

'Let's sit down and talk, just for a moment.'

'If we sit down you'll be besieged,' Angus pointed out. 'Let's walk on the terrace.'

They crossed the wide ballroom and made their way out on to the terrace through the french windows. Other couples were strolling there, and the lights had attracted a variety of moths which whirled above their heads. Angus led his partner to some steps leading down into the shadowed garden.

'Come on, let's have a romantic moonlit walk, and I'll try to forget my arthritic knees and the weight of my years.'

Rochelle tucked her hand into his elbow and together they made their way along the gravel path. Long lawns bisected by yew trees clipped into exotic shapes gave way to beautiful rose gardens, an ornamental lake. It was as they stood beside the water that Angus finally answered Rochelle's question.

'Mark du Sattay . . . yes, my dear, there is another sort of love indeed. You've felt that to love any man except M. Laurient was disloyal, but indeed that isn't so. Had Louisa lived I might have felt a little initial resentment when I found she loved another man, but it would have been no more than a pang because my girl was becoming a woman. M. Laurient must have seemed to you the perfect knight of legend, who came cantering up on his great charger to change the overlooked, unwanted child of a hardworking peasant couple into the much-loved foster-daughter of a rich and successful man. But that doesn't mean he wouldn't understand when the time came for you to love another as well, though differently.'

'I do understand,' Rochelle said. 'If only M. Laurient wasn't so far away ... if only I could talk to him, explain ...'

'You won't have to explain. He's got a son, you said? Then your M. Laurient loved a woman once, probably very much. He'll know that no matter how much you love him, that love must give way to a greater love.'

'A *greater* love? Oh, but Angus ...'

'Yes, Chelle, a greater love. Or perhaps that isn't quite what I mean. You see, I not only love Gemma, I'm in love with her. Perhaps that's the difference you were finding it so difficult to grasp, that loving and being in love are two quite separate emotions. Both are strong, both are beautiful, but they must not be confused or you'll make some young man very unhappy.'

'I ... I think I may have done just that,' Rochelle said, her voice low. 'Then you wouldn't think I was being disloyal if I did love someone ... say someone like Mark du Sattay?'

Angus grinned and squeezed the hand tucked in his elbow.

'What a serious child you can be, Rochelle! When you fall in love you must grasp it with both hands, not hold back for fear of hurting your M. Laurient! And now we'll go back indoors and I shall buy myself a whisky and you a lemonade!'

* * *

514

'Gemma dear, I knew you'd tell her to go ahead but Rochelle insisted you be asked. She's been invited to New York next spring to show the orchid . . . they clearly hope that by then she'll be ready to part with the secret of its parentage . . . and to do an advertising campaign for Gempearls on the other side of the Atlantic.'

Angus and Gemma were preparing for bed, Gemma sitting in front of her dressing-table brushing out her hair and Angus cutting his nails into neat half-moons. Now, Gemma swung round from the mirror to gaze, open-mouthed, at her husband.

'New York? For Gempearls? But I didn't know they were going to be exported to the States. I thought it was too soon, the competition too great . . .'

'That's precisely why we're going now: striking whilst the iron's hot. I'll be honest with you – she doesn't really want to go, it's too far, and she's happy in London, but I believe it's in her own interest as well as ours. The States will want that orchid once they've seen it, and she can make enough money to do whatever she wants to her stately home on the island as soon as she's got enough hybrids to sell to everyone who orders them. But it takes time – five to seven years, she tells me. The money she'll get for modelling the pearls is money *now*, and she can't afford to sneeze at it.'

'I see,' Gemma said slowly. She lowered the brush and turned to face him, her hair crackling out round her head from her recent attack. 'But it's such a long way, Angus. I'll miss her terribly, you know.'

'If Louisa had been her age, she would have been wanting to leave home about now, wanting to spread her wings,' Angus reminded her. 'The girl's young and full of life; she needs to see other countries, meet other people. And she'll always come back, you know. She's the faithful kind, is Rochelle.'

'Yes . . . yes, I understand all that. But losing Louisa

515

would have been different, because we'd have had her for so much longer . . . all her life, in fact. Losing Rochelle is harder because we've had her for such a short time . . . months rather than years. Couldn't we go as well? Just for a few weeks?'

'I wish I could say yes,' Angus groaned. 'But I simply can't, my love. Don't you see how it would look – as though we were so possessive we couldn't even let go of her for her own good? I want her to go away happily and come back even more happily, and that's what will happen if you don't make her feel . . . oh, as though she owes us something. Let her go now and you'll have her for ever; go with her or try to hold her back and you'll lose her. Believe me, I know.'

'I see,' Gemma said slowly. She stood up and walked over to where Angus sat at the foot of the bed, then bent and kissed his nose. 'Poor darling – it's got nothing to do with the talk, has it?'

Rochelle had turned down Simon's proposal of marriage and Simon's fond mother – not a nice woman, Gemma said decidedly – had promptly put about a rumour that Angus was in love with his protégée and planning to leave his wife and whisk her off somewhere. It was just nastiness because her beloved son had been turned down, Gemma knew, but she did wish that Angus had not given fuel to such rumours by dancing with Rochelle half the night at that party and walking in the gardens with her the other half. It was her own fault, of course . . . Rochelle had had plenty of partners wanting to take her to that particular ball, but she, Gemma, had thought how nice it would be for Angus to take her . . . hence the talk.

'The rumours, you mean?' Angus smiled, his eyes glittering wickedly at her. 'Well, if she goes off to New York and we follow, it won't exactly damp down the flames, will it?'

'No, of course not. You're right, as usual. Then I'll tell her to go and enjoy herself, and to come back when she's tired of New York . . . or I suppose we could go over there if she wants to stay very badly, couldn't we? In a few months?'

Angus got up and put his arm around his wife's bare shoulders. He gave her a squeeze and kissed the side of her neck.

'Of course we could . . . perhaps she'll be married by then!'

'Another cup of tea, dear?'

Gemma took Rochelle's cup and filled it, then turned to her husband. 'Angus? More tea?'

'I'm having coffee,' Angus said patiently. 'But I'd like another cup. Well, Rochelle, what have you got planned for today?'

It was a beautiful spring day, with birds on the lawn outside singing loudly and the soft scent of viburnum coming in through the open french windows. Rochelle was wearing a wrap-around silk dressing-gown and old slippers. She had her hair in a long plait and her face was devoid of make-up; she looked, Gemma thought fondly, like a sparklingly clean child, almost ready for school. She had been reading the paper whilst absently eating toast, but at Angus's words she looked up.

'Today? Oh, I'm doing that river-trip advert, then I'm having lunch with Frank, and then Gemma and I are going down to Kew. I've been promising myself a trip for ages . . .' she smiled affectionately at Gemma '. . . and today's the day. Why? Want to come?'

'I'd love to, but I'm going to Manchester on business. And I don't want to hurry you, but I must have a reply on the trip to New York today, Rochelle. If you aren't going to go then we'll need to get someone else.'

'I don't think I can tear myself away,' Rochelle said reluctantly. 'I'd love to go, but it's so far from Jersey! I'm hoping that a friend may get in touch with me there quite

517

soon . . . that's why I spend so much money on telephoning Mme Barfleur.'

'Why now?' Angus asked. 'Why couldn't the friend contact you before?'

'Because he's been away,' Rochelle said. 'He's been abroad for ages and ages, but I've had a strong feeling lately that he'll be back soon, and I don't want to miss him.'

'Why? Is this the mysterious lover I've always thought was somewhere in your past?' Gemma enquired, and was disconcerted to receive one of Rochelle's most intense stares.

'Perhaps. I'm not sure. A friend, anyway.'

'Oh!' Gemma said feebly. 'Well, then, I suppose you can't leave.'

The door opening saved her from any further foolishness, for she was uneasily aware that Rochelle had not appreciated being teased about a mysterious lover. She was a strange girl in some ways, but now her bright, sweet smile appeared and she leaned over and stroked Gemma's hand.

'Sorry . . . but I had this friend and we quarrelled. He went away. I don't talk about him, ever, but that doesn't mean I don't think about him, because I do. All the time, on and off. So you see, I can't very well just leave for New York, can I?'

Behind Gemma's head, the young girl who helped the housekeeper cleared her throat.

'Post, m'm,' she said gruffly.

'Oh? Thank you, Susan,' Gemma said, taking the letters. 'One for me, six for you, Angus, and two for you, dear.'

Rochelle took her letters and glanced at the envelopes, and then went very still. It was such a profound stillness that both Gemma and Angus stared at her, then at each other.

'Who's it from, pet?' Angus said at last, as Rochelle showed no desire to open either envelope but merely continued to stare at one of them as though at a deadly viper. 'What's the postmark?'

'One's Jersey . . . it's from Peter,' Rochelle said. 'The other . . . it's a New York postmark.'

'Oh, it'll be from Richard Carewe, our New York agent,' Angus said at once. 'Trying to persuade you to give the campaign a boost, I dare say.'

The tension drained out of Rochelle. She smiled and opened the envelope . . . then tensed up all over again, her eyes darkening as they lifted from the letter to meet Angus's enquiring gaze.

'It's . . . it's from that man, your agent,' she said. 'But there's a message from . . . well, read it.' She passed it across to Angus, who read it aloud.

'*It would give us great pleasure if you could come over to see us in about a fortnight,*' Richard had written. '*The weather here won't be too hot by then, but you will have plenty of sunshine for photocalls. Also, a friend of yours has been in touch with us with a cryptic message for you. He didn't give his name, but said you were close friends from a long while back – he mentioned Jersey. He said to tell you that he was sorry he hadn't been in touch before, but wanted to do so as a success this time and not just as a penniless admirer. He read about you in the press and saw an item saying you would be in the States in the spring, so he contacted us. He said he's got an orchid which will make you open your eyes, and then he just said you'd know who he was and rang off.*'

'That's nice, an old friend,' Gemma said placidly when Angus finished reading. 'Who will it be, Rochelle? Anyone special?'

Rochelle's face was blazing with excitement, her eyes dark with it.

'It – it could be someone rather special,' she said, her voice trembling a little. 'It – it could be . . . someone very special. Yes, I shall go to New York.'

* * *

519

For a girl who had spent the first nineteen years of her life on a small island in the English Channel, Rochelle was certainly going places. First it was London, and now here she was sitting in a luxurious first-class cabin drinking champagne and eating oysters and talking to the sophisticated and beautiful woman in the seat beside her as though they had known one another for ever.

In fact, Rochelle and Lynda Banks had only met when Rochelle started working for Gempearls, but they had hit it off from the start, each finding something both likeable and admirable in the other. Lynda liked Rochelle's willingness to do what was required of her whilst clinging stubbornly to her own particular standards, and Rochelle liked Lynda's no-nonsense approach and the fact that the older girl would stand by her models even when her clients, who were paying vast sums, clearly felt they had bought more than her advertising technique.

What was more, Rochelle had been aware for some time that she badly needed a friend to fill the gap in her life left by Olivia's death. Gemma mothered her, as Mme Barfleur and Adrienne did, but Lynda treated her as an equal, regarding the ten years which separated them as beside the point, and never letting Rochelle feel inferior because of her limited education and rather narrower outlook on life.

We are quite alike in a number of ways, Rochelle thought now, as the pair of them drank champagne and gazed round the cabin at the other first-class passengers. We both come from working-class stock and we've both risen by our own efforts – and, of course, on my side, by a good deal of luck. But then Lynda had been blessed with a face whose beauty still turned heads wherever they went, which was as lucky, perhaps, as being chosen first by M. Laurient and then by Angus and Gemma. Rochelle thought her own black hair, blue eyes and white face an odd sort of combination, but accepted the fact that for some reason she took people's fancy. She knew she was not beautiful . . .

she only had to look at Lynda to realise the truth of that, for Lynda had hair of that lovely shade between red and gold, a retroussé nose and full, sweetly curving lips. She was also what an appreciative American two seats in front of them had called 'well stacked', a phrase which suited Lynda's full breasts and curvy hips. She was wearing a pale green suit, a dark yellow blouse and pale green shoes with heels so high that when they stood up she dwarfed Rochelle. She looked lovely, Rochelle thought, and was proud to be travelling with her.

'When we get to Idlewild – that's the airport – we go through Immigration and Customs first and then we'll see either Richard himself or someone come on his behalf to meet us. If it's Dick I'll recognise him at once, of course, but if it's someone else we must keep our eyes peeled for a notice with either your name or mine on it. It's an easy method of identification . . . you'll see lots of white cards with names written up, so just look out for Banks or Dubois, because it'll be one or t'other.'

'And then . . .?' Rochelle breathed, entranced by the prospect awaiting her. 'What next?'

'Oh, well, then we'll be taken to our hotel, which is called Hammonds. It's quiet because you said that was what you wanted, but central, because that's what Gempearls will want. We'll have a shower and a nap, I think, and then I'll ring through to your room . . .'

'Telephones? In our rooms? Gosh!'

'They have telephones in hotel rooms in London, Chelle,' Lynda assured her. 'Surely you must have seen them?'

'No. I stayed in a guest house until Gemma and Angus moved me in with them. What happens next?'

'Dinner. Then a quick look round the sights, and then bed. If you try doing too much on your first day you'll flake out before the end of the week. Trust me; I know what I'm doing.'

'I'm glad someone does, because I don't,' Rochelle said.

She had a packet of salted peanuts by her glass and began to nibble them, turning to glance behind her down the aisle. 'When's lunch? You said we'd eat on the flight.'

'So we will, but they've only just served the champagne and the oysters; surely you can't be hungry already?'

'Yes, I can. Excitement makes me ravenous, and anyway they only gave us a couple of measly little tinned oysters each,' Rochelle observed. 'Oh, Lyn, I can't wait to get there!'

'Yes, that reminds me; what's this about a mysterious admirer? I had Dick on the phone yesterday with some story about a bloke who keeps ringing up to see if you've arrived yet.'

'Well, I don't know . . . not exactly,' Rochelle said. She took a big mouthful of peanuts and munched hard, not speaking again until she had swallowed them. 'There's a man I know . . . I like him very much, but we quarrelled . . . he's in America somewhere, I believe.'

'And you think it's him? Now that I call romantic!'

'It might be him. Or . . .' Rochelle hesitated, glancing sideways at Lynda out of suddenly wary eyes. 'Or I suppose it's just possible that it could be . . . someone else.'

'Well, yes, that makes sense,' Lynda said, grinning at her. 'In fact if it isn't your mysterious friend it's just about certain to be someone else, I'd have thought. Say what you mean, girl!'

'I mean I suppose . . . perhaps . . . it could be M. Laurient himself!'

Even saying the words made her go hot, then cold. Could it possibly be he after all this time? The war in Europe had ended nearly three years ago – why should he suddenly get in touch with her now, and in America of all places? But of course there could be a thousand reasons – memory loss, illness, a desire to let her have all the glory for Pure Madonna . . . she could find any number of excuses for him, all of them good enough for her.

'Your guardian, you mean? The man who was sent to Germany and never came back when the war ended?' Lynda shook her head, then patted Rochelle's hand. 'It isn't even on the cards, love, and the sooner you face it the better. Haven't you seen the physical wrecks who came out of those death-camps? I read in a magazine before I even met you that your guardian was in one of the really bad camps which was bombed in '44 by the Americans. Believe me, sweetie, if he was killed he probably thanked the Yanks from the bottom of his heart. But dead he must be; men don't go through that and live to have the strength to go into hiding and become someone different.'

'Yes. I suppose you're right. But I've always had the feeling that I'd have known, Lynda, if he'd died. And I'm convinced he's still alive, somewhere, and one day he'll come back to me. Though the feeling was getting weaker and weaker until the phone call in America, and somehow that started it all up again.'

'Then the sooner Mr Mysterious comes clean the happier I'll be for you,' Lynda said. 'He shouldn't raise hopes he can't satisfy.'

'But if it's M. Laurient . . . oh, all right, all right, don't shake your head at me. If it's my other friend, it would never occur to him that I could still be hoping, after all this time. He'd just assume I'd guess it was him . . . which I have done, except for this hopeful little niggle at the back of my mind.'

'Right. And who's the friend?'

'Oh, someone important. Look, if it is him you'll meet him, I promise. And if it's . . .'

'Don't say it!' Lynda said warningly. 'You're building up for a big fall, sweetie. Expect nothing and then whatever you get's a lovely surprise.'

The truth of this statement was so self-evident that Rochelle nodded, then smiled broadly at her friend.

'I wish someone had said that to me years ago,' she

observed. 'It might even have made me act more sensibly, not to mention think more sensibly. I mean, the time you waste hoping . . . expecting . . . and then being cast down.'

'That's youth for you . . . a time for vain hopes,' Lynda said, laughing. 'Just remember you're not yet twenty years old, you're heading for the most exciting country in the world, and you're going to make a big impression on everyone you meet because you're British, you're from the Channel Islands and lived under German rule, and you're an orchid breeder. What more could you ask?'

'Nothing. Because if I expect nothing then whatever I get will be a lovely surprise,' Rochelle said smugly.

Lynda leaned back in her seat and laughed again.

'Serves me right! And now I'm going to have a snooze until lunchtime.'

If London had impressed Rochelle, New York dazzled her. The height of the buildings, the number of people in the streets and the thousands and thousands of cars were marvellous enough, but the colour! Times Square, which she saw the first evening, with all its flashing lights and moving cartoons, was quite literally an eye-opener. And the cars – which they called automobiles – were coloured too, not just black, like British cars. And the clothes! Women in brilliant garments, some of them wearing trousers not to work in but to play in. And the shop windows! Food piled high, tottering masses of it; little cafes which were called drugstores with colourful drinks the like of which she had never seen; fascinating bread in all sorts of shapes and sizes; cakes and biscuits with odd names – pretzels, bagels, blintzes!

'I thought you were tired, love,' Lynda protested, but Rochelle felt she could never be tired in such a lively, throbbing city. She hauled Lynda out of the hotel foyer – lobby – and on to the pavement – sidewalk – and danced beside her as Lynda patiently, or fairly patiently, pointed out some of the sights.

'That's the Empire State Building – the tallest building in the world,' she said at one point, and regretted it when her companion demanded to be put into a taxi – cab – and taken there at once.

'It won't be open; you won't be able to go up, and it's the view from the top that's so spectacular,' she assured the pink-cheeked Rochelle. 'There's plenty of time to see everything. You don't start work on the Gempearls stuff until next week, so you can roam the streets tomorrow until your feet fall off and I'll go with you . . . but tonight let me sleep!'

'I'm a selfish pig,' Rochelle said remorsefully, taking Lynda's arm. 'I'm tired too, but I'm so excited that it doesn't seem to matter. Look, we'll go back to the hotel now . . . but I'll hold you to your promise to take me sightseeing tomorrow.'

'Perhaps your friend will do it for me,' Lynda said hopefully. 'Maybe the phone'll ring in the morning and he'll say, "It's me, honey!" and you'll go off with him instead.'

'And you'd give a sigh of relief and totter quietly round the shops,' Rochelle said. 'Oh, Lynda, I'm sorry to be a nuisance, but it is exciting, isn't it? No rationing, all the clothes you want and all the food you can eat . . . all you need is heaps and heaps of dollars!'

'Right. And you'll soon discover that everyone's friendly and helpful, except the cops. They're pretty hard-boiled – I think the crime rate here's higher than at home. Want to use the lift?'

Rochelle was not wild about the lift, which left her stomach in the lobby whilst whisking the rest of her up to the seventh floor, but she got into it with Lynda, bade her goodnight outside her room, and opened her own door.

The room was what they called 'en suite' which meant,

apparently, that it had a dear little bathroom and lavatory all to itself, except that the bath did not exist and there was a marvellous shower in a little glass cubicle in its place. Rochelle was actually rather tired, but she was still too excited to think about climbing into the bed with its pink and white floral counterpane and frilly pillowcase. Instead, she stripped and got into the shower, and found out how to freeze oneself and then burn to a lobster brightness before finally getting the setting just right. After that she enjoyed the shower so much that she nearly fell asleep in it, rousing herself just in time with the recollection that if she rang down to reception on the sweet little white telephone (white!) by her bed she had it on good authority that someone would obligingly bring her some supper.

Food seemed like a good idea, so she got out of the shower, wrapped herself in two of the enormous fluffy white towels provided by the hotel and picked up the phone.

After a moment a voice answered brightly: 'Reception; can I be of assistance?'

'Oh . . . yes, please. May I have some supper?'

'Supper?'

'Yes. Well, something to eat.'

The voice changed subtly. It said in a bright, pleased sort of way, 'You're English!'

'Yes, that's right,' Rochelle said politely. 'Well, British, anyway. May I have something to eat, do you think?'

'Sure, honey,' the voice said. 'Pardon me, can I have your room number?'

'Oh . . . hold on.' Rochelle rushed to the door, opened it, and found she was room 7003. She gave the number, awed to think of the other 7002 rooms in what had appeared from the outside to be quite a small hotel by New York standards.

'Right; now what would you like to eat? Shall I send a menu up?'

'No, I don't want a meal,' Rochelle said virtuously,

526

although in fact she found she could have eaten ten courses without undue fuss. 'Just a snack.'

'How about sandwiches?' the voice suggested brightly. 'And a cup of coffee?'

'Yes, sandwiches would be lovely,' Rochelle said gratefully. 'What sort?'

'Gee, most anything,' was the mysterious reply. 'Ham on rye? Cheese on rye? Pickle and liverwurst on poppy-seed?'

'Yes . . . the last one,' Rochelle said at random. What was the point of being in America if you did not try their extraordinary food? 'And may I have sugar in my coffee, please? Just one spoonful.'

'Sure,' the voice said, sounding startled. 'I'll charge it.'

Rochelle was still trying to work that one out ten minutes later when there was a knock on the door. Cautiously, for she was still towel-clad, she padded across the room and opened it. A boy in uniform stood there, a tray in his hands.

'Pickle and liverwurst on poppy,' he said in a sing-song voice. 'Charged to 7003.'

'Oh . . . thank you very much,' Rochelle said. She took the tray from him and he stood still, staring at her. He did not look more than about twelve, so she wondered why he did not trot off, and then remembered what Lynda had said about tipping. It was important over here, apparently, so she told him to wait and went back into the room for her purse.

She found an American coin and gave it to him. He grinned at her, pocketed it and said, 'Thanks, sister,' which she guessed was cheeky of him, but she could not mind because he was such a little boy.

As soon as he was gone she examined the food. It was quite disappointing, really; just thick, brownish bread with dots in it filled with pink meat and pickle. But the coffee was in a little jug with its own tiny pitcher of cream and a small basin full of sugar lumps. Rochelle had not seen sugar lumps since the war and promptly tucked one into her cheek; then she felt guilty and sucked some coffee through it, which seemed fairer, somehow.

Still in a mood to be easily pleased, she decided to get into bed and eat her sandwich there. Food in bed seemed faintly wicked, a sign of decadence, so she would enjoy it all the more.

The sandwich was nice despite its appearance, but the bread was definitely odd. The little black dots crunched down all right, though, and the coffee was delicious, quite the nicest Rochelle had ever tasted.

When she had finished her repast she switched on the little wireless set by the bed. There seemed to be hundreds of stations instead of just one and foreigners, but she tried to get something which sounded familiar. After a short burst of excitable American voices advising her to buy this and do that she realised that this was commercial radio, the sort she had heard about but had not previously experienced. She listened for a while, and then, really very tired by now, switched off.

The bed was comfortable, the sheets clean and laundry-smelling. She had already drawn the curtains – drapes – across the window, but even so she could see the dim reflection of the street lights far below dancing on the ceiling.

Tomorrow, she promised herself, she would do all sorts of things. See what New York had to offer, talk to people, ask a policeman – cop – the way just to hear his voice. And tomorrow she might well get that phone call from her 'old friend'.

She fell asleep quite quickly despite the traffic noise, which continued to roar, she thought, throughout the night. And dreamed of aircraft, exotic food, buildings tall as canyons and canyons deep as coal mines. And of Laurie, wearing a bell-hop's uniform and trying to persuade her to spend a fortune on liverwurst sandwiches. She wanted to buy them to please him but, unaccountably, her money was missing. It was whilst she was searching for it in the most ridiculous places that she saw, in the hotel lobby, the figure she had not seen in reality for five years. Charles Laurient stood there in her dream . . . but he was going, leaving the hotel, walking out of her life, and she had not spoken to him, he had not seen her.

She ran across the lobby, but the thick carpet had got thicker, softer, spongier . . . she sank in it up to her ankles, up to her knees, and she tried to cry out, only to find that her voice had sunk to the tiniest of whispers.

'Have a good day, now,' the girl on the reception desk called out, her voice as shrill and harsh as a parrot's, and Charles Laurient turned and said something to her, then raised a hand and was gone, passing out through the revolving doors into the street where, Rochelle knew, he would be immediately swallowed up by the anonymous crowd.

Despair gripped her. He had been here, and she had missed him. She wept, crying bitterly for her one chance, lost . . . and woke in the dark with the tears still wet on her cheeks, alone in the grand bedroom with the coloured lights flashing on the ceiling and Jersey a thousand miles away.

23

The ringing of the telephone bell woke her; it was insistent, shrill, and foreign. It also sounded impatient, so that she sat up in a panic, fumbling for the receiver, dropping it on to the bed at the first attempt and only getting it to her ear, in the end, by luck.

'H-hello?'

She was afraid she would hear the voice on the reception desk chiding her for some unimaginable misdemeanour, but instead it was Lynda.

'Hello, love,' her friend said gaily. 'Don't say you were actually asleep! I thought you'd have been up for hours, going round the zoo in Central Park or making yourself sick on off-ration candy – chocolate to us.'

'Aren't sweets rationed? Goody! But actually I overslept. I had a nightmare in the middle of the night and it woke me up and I took a while to get back to sleep. Well, what shall we do? It's a nice day, isn't it? I mean, I can see sunshine round the edges of the curtains, I think.'

'You can. How about joining me for breakfast? We can have all sorts, but I've ordered orange juice, waffles with maple syrup and coffee. Will that suit you?'

'That'll be lovely. I'll be round in ... oh, say ten minutes?'

'Don't you intend to wash? Oh, I suppose a shower's quicker ... what'll you wear? It's pretty warm already.'

'Something easy – my blue cotton frock?'

'Fine. We'll just relax and enjoy the day. See you in ten or fifteen minutes, then.'

A quarter of an hour later, Rochelle, in a thin blue cotton frock and open white sandals, her hair tied back with a white ribbon, walked the short distance between her room and Lynda's. But before she could knock the bell-hop came along the corridor, saw her, and came over.

'Excuse me, ma'am . . . you number 7003?'

'Umm . . . yes, that's me,' Rochelle admitted, having glanced at the door of Lynda's room, which was 7005. 'I didn't ring for anything, though.'

'No, ma'am. Delivery.'

He was holding something lightly wrapped in cream and gold paper with a tiny note and a bunch of ribbons at the top.

'For me? Oh . . . can I take it here?'

'Sure you can, but you'll want to get back in your room, I reckon; got your key?'

'Yes, here.' Rochelle brandished the large, gold key with its tag exhorting hotel guests to leave their keys in the lobby or to post them back to the hotel – free – when they found they had taken them home.

'There, then, ma'am.'

The boy placed the light, oddly shaped package in her eager hands.

'Thanks,' Rochelle said. 'Oh . . . can you wait whilst I go back to my room? I don't have my purse with me.'

'Sure,' the boy said, undoubtedly realising that his tip would repose within the purse.

Rochelle returned to her room, grabbed her little suede handbag and tipped some loose change into his small paw, then, still clutching her gift, returned to room 7005. She knocked on the door and it was answered at once by a Lynda very glamorous in a frilly housecoat and pink furry mules.

'Good morning, Chelle,' she said cheerfully. 'I thought you'd have been round ten minutes ago, but even so I daren't leave the door on the latch – you hear such funny stories. What's that you've got there?'

'I don't know. The bell-hop brought it just as I was

531

coming round to your room,' Rochelle explained. She stood the light little thing on a side table and began to attack the paper carefully, peeling it back a bit at a time. 'Oh!'

It was a tiny gilt basket with cherubs round the handle and a flying ribbon. Inside the basket was an orchid.

'There must be some clue as to who sent it,' Lynda said for the hundredth time as the two of them sat on her balcony, sipping their orange juice and trying to eat waffles without dribbling syrup – an almost impossible task. 'You wouldn't recognise the writing . . . it's the florist who writes on the label . . . but can't you recognise the style, the way it's worded?'

Rochelle picked up the tiny card and read it aloud once more, frowning.

'*To a beautiful woman who was once a charming child,*' she said slowly. '*From her most devoted admirer.* That could mean anyone . . . it needn't be either M. Laurient or my friend Laurie.'

'Then perhaps it isn't. Let's not think about it, and then when you've really forgotten all about it the truth will pop into your head. Or if it doesn't, the chap's bound to want to meet you properly so he'll either come round to the hotel or write again.'

'Isn't it pretty?' Rochelle said, picking up the little gilt basket once more. 'I've never seen such a thing in a flower shop in Britain.'

'I rather suspect that the basket was bought in a jeweller's . . . yes, I think it's not simply a bauble,' Lynda said, examining the tiny thing. 'Perhaps I was wrong when I said the florist had written the note. Probably it was written by the jeweller when the fellow – if it was a fellow – took the orchid in and asked him to send it to you in the basket.'

'It's a Masdevallia caudata,' Rochelle said wistfully. 'They need heat . . . I lost all ours. Isn't it beautiful . . . so small and dainty. It's a favourite of mine, but not many people know that – probably only M. Laurient, in fact, because by the time Laurie came to the island all our tropical orchids were either dead or hibernating.'

'Forget it,' Lynda said, but kindly. 'You'll find out soon enough.'

They shopped entrancingly, and very soon Rochelle's arms were full of small presents for the Barfleurs, for Peter and his sister, for just about every worker on the estate. She had also eaten rather a lot of chocolates and felt ever so slightly sick. The shops were so big, the goods on display so tempting! Bloomingdale's on 59th Street seemed vast until she entered Macy's on Broadway. Wide-eyed, she wandered round the main floor, where she saw everything from people selling nuts and roasting them before her eyes to demonstrators of vegetable slicers and egg mashers. 'Thrift tables' sold goods cheap, while slick gentlemen barked the delights of an absolutely automatic, fully electric floor-cleaner, a machine which would wash your dishes so clean that they were as sterile as the instruments in a hospital, and a butter knife which was heated so that even on the coldest day you could curl butter without effort.

'If I had the money I'd buy them all,' Rochelle confessed to Lynda as they made their way out through the crowded entrance. 'I suppose it's being without gadgets and things for so long, but I just love the thought of machines trotting round the kitchen doing things for me.'

'Do you hate housework so much?' Lynda asked lazily. 'No, don't tell me, because I loathe it too, so I engage someone to do it for me.'

'What about something to eat now?' Rochelle said brightly. She did not like to confess that at home in Jersey she let Mme Barfleur and Adrienne tackle most of the housework whilst she worked outside or in the glasshouses.

'Definitely. I thought we'd try an ice cream parlour.

There's a really good one on Seventh Avenue; I thought we'd go down there.'

Presently, perched on a high stool with a vast concoction before her consisting of ice cream, cream, fruit, jelly, chocolate and nuts, and aptly named the Kitchen Sink, Rochelle had time to ask a few questions about the next week's work.

'It's an advert for telly . . . ever seen telly?' Lynda asked, eating her own humbler concoction, a Bird of Paradise Sundae with what looked like half the bird's plumage sticking out of the top of it. 'It's very popular over here; most folk have got a set.'

'I saw one or two in London, but it was rather dull and flickery,' Rochelle said, through a mouthful of cherries. 'Still, Angus said they'd pay me awfully well. Do we do the filming outdoors or in a studio?'

'Both, I think,' Lynda said. She swore softly as a drop of jelly fell on the white perfection of her crisp linen suit. 'Damn. I should have known better than to wear this thing in a city . . . it's strictly indoor wear, really.'

'What'll I wear for the filming, do you think?'

'Don't know. You've not met Richard yet, have you? He'll tell you to pick something out from Wardrobe . . . or perhaps they'll choose something for you. Wait and see. D'you want to see the zoo this afternoon, or would you rather do the botanical gardens? They're bound to have some of your precious orchids, I should think.'

'I've never been to a zoo . . . I think I'll go there first.'

'Right. We'll have lunch at a little place I know just a few blocks from here where the cooking's French and out of this world, and then you can gaze your fill at okapis and zebras and God knows what besides.'

'Tigers? Crocodiles?' asked the literal Rochelle eagerly. 'I always meant to go to London zoo, but then people said it wasn't what it had been in peacetime because of so many of the animals being put down and so on in case of air-raids. We'll do the gardens another day.'

'Lovely. By the time you're ready to walk your feet down to the ankles slogging round looking for orchids, that fellow of yours is bound to have turned up,' Lynda said. 'I wouldn't want to take the treat away from him, whoever he is.'

Filming was fun, exhausting and all-consuming. An excitable little man in a black sweater and tight black trousers dressed Rochelle in a clinging lemon-yellow gown which he assured her would look white on the television screen, and then placed pearls reverently round her neck and an orchid – Pure Madonna, of course – close at hand.

'We haf an artificial flower made,' he explained, 'for the plant is not blooming so early, no?'

'No,' agreed Rochelle, rather bemused. 'It's awfully good.'

'On the screen one will no difference see,' he assured her. 'All the real thing will believe it is.'

'Yes, I'm sure,' Rochelle murmured, and did whatever was asked of her with enthusiasm, for this was not just a 'still' but an 'action' shot, and she had to walk across the set from one side to the other, with the artificial orchid on one shoulder and the pearls gleaming at her throat.

She had to speak, too, and her voice drew admiring remarks from one and all. They admired her accent, they assured her, and Rochelle, who knew she had a slight island burr, smiled at everyone and told them that she loved their accents too.

'The American accent is so warm and friendly,' she said. 'You're all so kind, so generous!'

But, really, American accents made her think of Laurie.

When she had finally finished on the set and been told that the shots were perfect she and Lynda left, so tired that they did not even consider eating out or doing some more

535

sightseeing. Richard, who had come to the filming and been absolutely delightful to them both – though it was clear, to Rochelle at least, that he had designs on her friend – tried to suggest taking them for a meal, but Lynda was firm.

'Not after a day which started at 6 A.M. and finished at 8 P.M.,' she assured him. 'Tomorrow, perhaps. Today, not a chance!'

They arrived back at the hotel and went to their respective rooms with a promise to meet for dinner in an hour, but scarcely had Lynda run herself a hot and scented bath when there was a tap on the door. She opened it and Rochelle stood there.

'Look!' she said.

It was another orchid, clear, sparkling white with a creamy gold lip and green and white striped petals, and this time it was in a tiny gilded cage which it shared with a thin gold bracelet.

'That is just beautiful,' gasped Lynda. 'Do you know what it is?'

'Cypripedium "Clair de Lune",' Rochelle told her. 'It's what they call a robust hybrid, which means it's capable of withstanding much lower winter temperatures than most orchids, and it isn't so likely to die if you over-water it . . . or under-water, for that matter. It's a popular sort to start on – and isn't it striking?'

'Yes, awfully. What does the card say? Oh come in, do; I've just remembered I've got a bath running.'

Rochelle walked into the older girl's room, undoing the miniature envelope and drawing out the tiny, primrose-yellow card which was inside it. She opened it and read aloud: '*Another little gift for my darling girl from her old friend: enjoy.*'

'Well?' Lynda said eagerly. 'Has anyone ever called you his darling girl?'

Rochelle shrugged helplessly.

536

'I don't know . . . I don't think so! Isn't the bracelet lovely, though, Lyn? Look at it – it's got tiny flowers instead of links.'

'So it has; this thing's been custom-made,' Lynda said, clearly impressed. 'I wonder what it'll be tomorrow?'

'I don't know. I . . . I hope there's nothing more,' Rochelle said. She gave a little shiver. 'I'm not sure that I like it. It's as though . . . as though someone was trying to frighten me. I wish he wouldn't, whoever he is.'

'Your guardian? Or Laurie?'

'Neither,' Rochelle said definitely. 'A cage . . . that's a frightening thing.'

'Ye-es . . . unless it means he was caged. Rochelle, I'm sure that's what he means by it . . . Who was caged?'

Rochelle stared back at her, huge-eyed.

'M. Laurient,' she said. 'M. Laurient! Oh, Lyn, can it . . . could it really be he?'

Rochelle put the orchid in a crystal vase and slid the bracelet on to one slim, golden-tanned wrist. Then she went to bed and lay and tried to contact the sender of these pretty presents. Who would send her a little cage . . . even the bracelet could be interpreted as meaning a chain . . . save for her dear, dear M. Laurient? She could think of no one. Certainly such a thing would never occur to Laurie, who was very sensitive to her feelings in that direction. It seemed as though it absolutely must be M. Laurient . . . could it be? And if it was, when would he come forward and show himself so that she could hug him tight and know that all her worries were at an end?

And yet all the while, through all the hope, all the childish crossings of fingers, telling herself to believe because by believing she might actually make it happen, there was a small, steady voice saying that surely this was not M. Laurient's style, not his way of doing things? He was straightforward, honest, uncomplicated – unless he had changed? But in that at least he and Laurie were very alike. Neither would want to make a song and dance over something that could be done more simply.

But this sending of small but precious presents, all of which meant a lot to her because of the inclusion, each time, of an orchid, this surely was a genuine wooing? A romantic wooing. Was M. Laurient trying to make up for his former lack of outward affection? If so . . . she curled up in bed and hugged herself, arms going tightly round her narrow shoulders. If so, then it must surely mean that M. Laurient was alive and well and would presently come to her, in New York, and share the triumph over Pure Madonna.

But still, as she drifted off to sleep, she knew that she did not believe it. Whoever was sending her the presents and for whatever reason, something which knew M. Laurient a good deal better than her conscious mind did was telling her she was wrong; it was not the way he would do things.

That left Laurie, and at the thought that it really might be Laurie her heart began to bumpety-bump, very fast, very irregularly. Oh, but she was sorry she had been so horrible to Laurie, she had missed him so much, she would so love him to share her delight over Pure Madonna. And this was his country, his wonderful land flowing with milk and honey, with warmth and kindness and honesty. To have him here, beside her, would mean more than almost anything.

More presents followed. For the next three days, Rochelle filmed at the television studio and did stills for magazines, all of them featuring Gempearls. However, with Lynda acting as her agent, other things came in. She was interviewed at least a dozen times by different radio stations, and she also had a couple of television interviews with people keen to know all about Pure Madonna and what it had been like living under enemy occupation.

538

Each evening, when she got back to the hotel, the orchid would be waiting, in its beautiful or elaborate gift wrapping. The third orchid arrived in a tiny gilded carriage with the message that her most ardent admirer would be riding beside her in a few days. Then came an orchid with a pearl necklace wound round its stem . . . the message was that she was the pearl-girl and these were the only pearls she should ever wear.

'They're genuine wild pearls,' Lynda said, with awe. 'A beautiful set, and they fit your throat exactly – not one too many or too few.'

But the fifth orchid was the best . . . it was the one which made Rochelle cry out and hold it, for one ecstatic moment, to her breast, then to her lips.

'It's Cattleya schroderae, the scented orchid,' she breathed to Lynda. 'It's my very, very favourite – the colours are so wonderful, that glorious rose fading to snowy-white, and the scent . . . oh smell it, Lyn!'

'What's the message?' Lynda said, reaching for the small envelope. 'Open it, do. And what other present came with it?'

'A golden locket shaped like a heart,' Rochelle breathed. She knew her cheeks were flushed and her eyes bright with excitement and hope, for when Laurie had left the island it was with the expressed intention of finding Cattleya schroderae to bring back for her, so that she might breed hybrids from it and raise specimen plants, in Jersey. He had known it was the orchid she had pined for most during the war . . . she had said so often enough . . . and the message with the locket seemed, suddenly, to be just the sort of thing Laurie would have said.

'*My happiness is in your hands*,' Lynda read out. '*Do you care?* My word, Rochelle, this guy's got it bad. *Do* you care?'

'Oh, I do,' Rochelle breathed, starry-eyed. 'More than I thought I did, Lyn . . . I've been so lonely for Laurie, particularly here, with every second man sounding just like him. Michael Duvantos even called me honey the other night . . . I *longed* for Laurie then.'

'Let's have a look inside the locket,' Lynda said, but Rochelle, suddenly excited, warded her off.

'No . . . let me look first!'

She wrenched the little gold catch open and then held out the locket with the small piece of paper it contained. It just said 'Tomorrow', and was unsigned.

'Well, that's to the point,' Lynda said. 'Tomorrow's Sunday, too, so he must guess you won't be working. Excited?'

'Yes, yes! I'm so excited I can hardly breathe! It must be Laurie . . . and don't think I've forgotten dear M. Laurient because I never, never could. But Angus made me see . . . there's a difference between the way I love him and the way I love Laurie, and it's right that there should be. Angus says that M. Laurient would expect me to love a younger man, wouldn't feel at all hurt or betrayed by such feelings. So you see . . .'

'I see you've got yourself sorted out at last,' Lynda said approvingly. 'Are you fit to come to the theatre, then? Richard got us seats for *Carousel*. It's had rave reviews in all the papers, so I think we should enjoy it.'

'I doubt if I shall understand a word, but I wouldn't miss it for anything,' Rochelle said, taking the locket, the orchid and the little note and going to the door. 'I'll wear that glorious white broderie anglaise dress, I think, with the orchid pinned to the strap – and the locket, of course.'

'Of course,' Lynda said, smiling at her. 'And I'll wear the midnight blue; that way we'll draw every eye in the house. By the way, did I tell you who Dick's invited to make up a fourth? We're having supper afterwards at Rumpelmayer's.'

'Who?' Rochelle said politely, but her supreme indifference would have made the inclusion of Attila the Hun perfectly acceptable.

'Frederick Forster.'

'Lovely,' Rochelle said, and, in the doorway, did a double-take. '*The* Frederick Forster?'

'The very same. He's an old friend of Dick's and apparently suggested that he'd like to meet you . . . aren't you honoured? That a Broadway star should have heard of you, I mean?'

'Oh, I'm just a nine-days' wonder; he's probably after you,' Rochelle said blithely. She left the room and hurried down the corridor with Lynda's scornful snort still in her ears. Frederick Forster! What did he matter compared with seeing Laurie – it had to be Laurie – the following day?

Rochelle had expected to be able to dream quietly all through *Carousel*, but in fact the poignancy of the story reached out to her, reminding her, at the climax, where Billy Bigelow dies, of how M. Laurient had been snatched from her. She wept, not even discreetly, when Billy was allowed back to earth to see his daughter, and positively howled when the star Billy had stolen from heaven was found by his wife as her first intimation that he really had been with them once more.

If she expected this uninhibited behaviour to put Frederick Forster off her once and for all, however, she was doomed to disappointment. He was fascinated, showed it, and said so. He proved to be quite a lot older than he had appeared on stage, but he had a great deal of quiet charm and humour and fitted in nicely with the general mood of the evening. Whether he was aware that Rochelle scarcely noticed him, save as a member of the same small group, she neither knew nor cared. She ate the delicious meal set out before her with a good appetite, though afterwards she would not have been able to say precisely what she had eaten, admired the Rumpelmayer decor, the mirrored walls and columns inlaid with mosaics, and said very little. She explained this, when teased, by saying that her mind was still with the cast of *Carousel*, but in fact, although the music was running through her head, she was imagining the moment, tomorrow, when she would see Laurie face to face for the first time for more than two years. How she would run to his arms! How she would hug him, kiss him, tell him he had been right and she wrong the last time they had met! She would have loved to buy him a present, but there was nothing she could think of which would give him the pleasure his gifts had given her.

'If I loved you . . .' Rochelle hummed beneath her breath as they left the restaurant at last and headed for their hotel. Fortunately, the cab driver immediately engaged Frederick Forster in conversation, thus saving Rochelle the trouble of even pretending to listen, since the Brooklyn accent with which he spoke was more than she could possibly cope with in her present exalted state. 'If I loved you . . . if I loved you!'

No more ifs, she told herself as she made her way to her room, having bidden the others goodnight and left Lynda to make any further excuses for her disappearance which she thought necessary. She had been so lucky! She had found love, failed to recognise it, lost it . . . and now she had found it again!

Tomorrow, tomorrow, she dreamed as she cuddled down in bed. Oh, tomorrow, come soon!

The next morning Rochelle and Lynda were up very early indeed . . . Lynda because a bright-eyed Rochelle had rung her room and ordered breakfast since she couldn't sleep and apparently intended to see that no one else did either.

'How can you moan, when the sun's shining and the air's still quite fresh?' Rochelle demanded, entering the room with the boy delivering freshly squeezed orange juice, croissants with butter and black cherry jam and a tall jug

542

of coffee. 'Of course if you don't want to get up I'll eat both breakfasts . . . I don't mind.'

'You can bring mine over to the bed,' Lynda said crossly, sitting up all rumpled from sleep, her white lawn nightie rucked up to show one creamy shoulder. 'How can you do this to me after last night?'

'Last night? What about last night?'

'You ran off, didn't you? And quite soon after that Frederick left, but Dick stayed on and on . . . I darned nearly invited him to stay for breakfast, except I knew very well he'd accept!'

'He likes you,' Rochelle said, stating the obvious.

'Oh, sure. He's liked me for ten years, but that still doesn't give him the right to keep me out of bed till all hours.'

'Better than keeping you in it,' Rochelle said calmly, pouring orange juice into a glass clinking with ice cubes. 'Don't you like him?'

'Sure. But not like that.'

'Now, I know what you mean,' Rochelle said. She carried one of the glasses of orange juice over to the bedside table. 'Here, drink that whilst I butter you a croissant.'

'Oh, all right,' Lynda said, admitting defeat. She sat up and reached for the juice. 'Why are you wearing your old blue cotton dress? No, don't tell me . . . this bloke once admired you in it. Am I right?'

'More or less. I was tempted to glamorise but then I thought better of it. I shall probably plait my hair later, too.'

'Don't you dare . . . not if you're going out of the hotel, anyway,' Lynda said at once. Rochelle laughed and brought her a croissant and she bit into it, then smiled beatifically as she ate. 'They really do melt in the mouth, these things . . . any more?'

'A pile. I thought we'd have a change from waffles. Lynda, when do you suppose . . .'

The telephone rang.

Both girls stared at it as though it was going to bite them and then Rochelle said, sounding oddly relieved, 'Oh, it'll be for you, of course. No one knows I'm here. Shall I answer it?'

'Please,' Lynda said through croissant.

Rochelle picked up the receiver and held it to her ear with one hand; the other held her glass of juice.

'Yes?'

She listened, and then said hollowly, 'Yes, she's here. Can you ask . . . oh!'

'What was it?' Lynda said, dusting her hands and picking up her own glass. 'Go on, don't just stand there staring, tell me!'

Rochelle came abruptly to life.

'He's on his way up!' she squeaked. 'They tried to stop him at the desk, and the girl was in the middle of telling me when she suddenly said he'd made for the stairs. Oh damn, oh, damn! I'm not ready, I haven't got shoes on . . .'

'I'm still in bed,' Lynda moaned. 'Go and meet him. Go on; you can't bring the fellow in here . . . go *on*, Rochelle. Get out at once and . . . and take him to your own room!'

'Yes . . . oh, but suppose I miss him? Look, I'll take him away as soon as he rings. We'll go – oh!'

Someone knocked impatiently on the door, with little, staccato raps.

'Answer it!' Lynda hissed, shrinking further down the bed. 'Go on, answer it!'

Rochelle felt the warmth rise up in her cheeks until she must, she thought, be red as a peony. She crossed the room, hesitated, opened the door . . . then relaxed.

'Oh, I'm sorry. I was expecting . . .'

'My very dear one . . . look again! It is I!'

Rochelle frowned, stared, and then began to smile.

'My goodness . . . it isn't . . . it can't be! Radek, is it really you? This is so strange, for I was expecting . . .'

544

She stopped short. She tried to keep her expression warm and pleased, not to show the sudden, heart-stopping disappointment. Could she possibly have been mistaken? Could it have been Radek all the time?

24

Radek Pokovski!

Rochelle had not thought of him for years, but here he
was, and now she acknowledged what she should have
known all along . . . that there were others who knew her
well enough to send the orchids, write the notes.

Radek had heard her talking about her plants a thousand
times, and knew how she loved the scented Cattleya. He
had told her he loved her, lightly, laughingly, long long
ago. But he had never once got in touch with her since the
war, and though she knew he had joined the Allies and
fought with them she had had no idea what had happened
to him afterwards, how he had prospered. Indeed, she had
been afraid that he might have been one of the many
Russians to be repatriated, only to find himself imprisoned,
treated as a criminal, perhaps even killed.

Now, she stared at him; at the square jaw, handsome,
laughing face, light blue eyes. By the time he left Jersey he
had been strong, but he had had a spareness about him
which, she supposed now, was the result of the long years
of deprivation prior to his escape. His hair, as she recalled
it, had been light and curly, but now it was one of the first
things you noticed: the thick crop of golden curls, the tan,
and the gleaming white teeth.

But as she stared she saw a flush creep up into his
cheeks, the light eyes veiled, for a moment, by golden
lashes. He was not quite as self-assured as he seemed, then.

'Radek . . . I'm overcome. Look, should we go down to
the lobby, find somewhere where we can talk?'

He recovered his composure at once, his face eager.

'What's wrong with your room? Did you like the orchids

546

'. . . the little gifts? You aren't wearing the locket; didn't you like it?'

'This isn't my room,' Rochelle said. She closed Lynda's door gently behind her. 'I'm just up the corridor, though, and I'm sure it will be fine to talk in there for a bit. As for the lovely gifts, who could fail to be pleased and . . . and touched? I loved them all, Radek, only why the secrecy? Why didn't you sign the cards?'

'I thought it would be more romantic, and I thought you were bound to guess,' Radek admitted, following her meekly along the corridor like an enormous tame lion. 'Oh, Rochelle, you don't know how I've missed the island . . . and missed you most of all.'

'Why didn't you write, then?' Rochelle demanded, ushering him into her room and wishing devoutly that she had tidied it up a bit before hurrying off to have breakfast with Lynda. But how could she possibly have guessed that anyone would come so early, and actually march up to her bedroom. He had a nerve – but then, had he really been Laurie, she would have been delighted that he wanted to see her so badly.

'Me? Write? In *English*?' Radek's voice rose several decibels and Rochelle crushed a strong urge to tell him to pipe down. She did not want it known all over the hotel that she was entertaining a man in her room at such a very early hour!

'If you'd written in Russian I doubt that any of us could have understood it,' she said patiently, instead. 'You're a very clever person, Radek; don't tell me you can't write!'

'Not in English, I couldn't . . . not until fairly recently,' Radek admitted. 'Besides, I didn't want to get in touch with anyone until I was a success . . . what would have been the use? My dear maman, your Tante Denise, wanted her adopted son to do well, you may be sure.'

'She wanted you to be alive and happy, Radek, that's what she wanted most,' Rochelle said gently. 'If you knew

547

how she has worried these past couple of years . . . and you never went back . . . why not?'

'I am going to send for her,' Radek said rather defiantly. 'What else should I do? There is no place for me on the island, not now. I've outgrown it, my sweet Rochelle, as you have.'

'Me? Outgrown Jersey? Don't be so stupid,' Rochelle said sharply. 'I'm only here to do a job; when it's over I'll go straight back home. Oh, New York's wonderful, I expect the whole of America is wonderful, but it isn't my country; my country's Jersey, my home's there, and that's where I'll spend the rest of my life.'

'You will vegetate on that tiny island, with no one to appreciate your delightful looks and personality? Oh, Rochelle, I've so longed for this moment, and now we're nearly quarrelling. Aren't you going to give your old friend a big hug? And for old times' sake you'll let me take you out for the day?'

'Well, of course,' Rochelle said rather dully. She went to him and he scooped her up in his arms, holding her gently at first, touching her face with his lips and then kissing her mouth.

It was an exciting kiss; Radek's mouth moved on hers, whilst his hands smoothed her back, holding her so close that his warmth seemed to become almost a part of her. He eased her down on to the bed and the kissing continued, but presently Rochelle pushed him gently away and sat up, smoothing her long hair back behind her ears and smiling at him.

'Dear Radek, I'm so fond of you, though I'm still rather cross. I don't understand why you didn't get in touch with us before, and I can't imagine you think I'll just rush into your arms now simply because of some expensive and imaginative gifts. So suppose you tell me exactly what it is you want?'

'You, as I have always wanted you,' Radek said ardently,

548

and looked hurt and even rather annoyed when Rochelle gave an involuntary snort of laughter.

'Oh, Radek, honestly! I've been living on Jersey for three *years* and you didn't even send a telegram! Clearly you're after something, and I want to know what it is!'

'I want you to marry me,' Radek said sulkily. They were sitting side by side on the bed and he took her hand, carrying it to his lips and planting an ardent kiss on the palm. 'I loved you when you were just a child, but now . . . ah, how beautifully you've grown up, and how much more I love you!'

'What's this successful business of yours, then, if you won't give me a straight answer?' Rochelle said, taking her hand back rather more suddenly than politeness demanded. 'It was sweet of you to send me pretty gifts and flowers, but it's all too sudden, Radek. You'll have to tell me in the end, so why not now?'

'Oh, yes, I suppose . . . but you do believe me when I say I want you? You always were a lovely girl, Chelle, but now you're a beautiful and desirable woman and I want you more than ever!'

'I believe you. Now tell me about your business.'

'I am a goldsmith,' Radek said proudly. 'In my own country I worked with metals – gold, silver and platinum – and here I answered an advertisement, showed them my work, and got a job.'

'Oh, yes? And how can I help you?'

'Well, now I have my own firm – New World Gold, I call it – and it is doing very well; original designs, some gilt work which sells well, such trinkets as women like . . . we are going places, the business and I.'

'Oh . . . the lovely presents . . . did you make them all, Radek? I never knew you were so artistic,' Rochelle said sincerely, remembering the workmanship on some of the tiny gilded toys he had sent her. 'Everyone who's seen them has admired them.'

549

'Thank you, dear Chelle. What a team we would make – how well we could go on together, you and I! You could have a dozen glasshouses if that would make you happy, and a big staff to do the work, and we could put your marvellous orchids with my marvellous jewellery and become rich and famous.'

'I thought you were rich already,' Rochelle said. 'Do you know I'm starving hungry? Shall I ring down for some breakfast?'

'No, I'll take you out right away,' Radek said, jumping to his feet. 'We'll have a huge breakfast at Zoe's and then go to the botanic gardens in Brooklyn. We'll have a lovely day and I'll outline my plans for my future – our future.'

'Radek, I'll help you in any way I can but I won't marry you and I won't stay in New York once my work here is over,' Rochelle said frankly. 'It's very flattering of you to say you love me, but even if you do it just isn't my kind of love. And anyway, I'm in love with someone else.'

'Ah yes, the so charming M. Laurient. But, my dear love, I have read your interviews, and there is no chance that he has come through the war and not got in touch with you. You are angry with me for not writing, but how much angrier should you be with M. Laurient, if you believed for one moment, in your heart, that he is alive and able to write!' Radek took Rochelle's hands and patted them gently, fixing her with his frankest and most noble look. 'One day, dear Chelle, you will know who is your true love.'

'I know now,' Rochelle said, gently extricating her hands. 'And you're right, of course. It isn't M. Laurient; that was just a child's day-dreaming. I've met someone else, Radek.'

It was a shock to him, Rochelle saw with some irritation. What conceit, to think that she would have gone through life not falling in love so that when he saw fit he could come forward! But she had wronged him in one sense.

'Someone else? Oh, what a fool I was not to get in touch before! But I wanted to be able to tell you that I owned my own place, was independent, thriving . . . I left it too long, too long!'

'Yes, you did,' Rochelle admitted, secretly rather amused, now, by Radek's dramatic tone. 'Look, are you going to take me out or shall I telephone down for some breakfast?'

He sighed rather theatrically but took her hand and led her to the door, then disarmed her by looking down at her with the old wicked, boyish grin she remembered so well from those far-off wartime days.

'Oh, well . . . you've broken my heart, Chelle, but I dare say I'll recover. I should have guessed you'd meet someone else, so bright and pretty you are, and so different. An American?'

'Yes,' Rochelle said, not wanting to give him chapter and verse. 'But honestly, Radek, there must be other girls.'

'None so beautiful as you . . . and none who could better show off my jewellery,' Radek said as they got into the elevator and were whisked down to the lobby. 'I am doing *very* well, but so are you, ma petite. And I thought if you would just give me a helping hand with an advertisement for my gold . . . I had such plans!'

'I'll model for you without marrying you,' Rochelle said with a giggle. 'I'll do it free as well, for old times' sake. Would that mend your broken heart?'

'It would help,' Radek said, giving her that old familiar grin. 'But I still love you, Rochelle, and want to marry you . . . are you sure you won't change your mind?'

'We'll talk about it later,' Rochelle said tactfully. 'Today let's enjoy ourselves!'

'What a day!' Rochelle flung herself down on Lynda's bed and brushed the hair back from her forehead. 'First I rang Angus in London and asked him if it was all right to do an

551

advertisement for Radek. Angus said go ahead as far as he was concerned. So then I went back and gave Radek the go-ahead and he didn't waste a moment. We spent the rest of the day in the botanic gardens, me posing and Radek and his friend Clem clicking away. Stills, all of them, but in colour and some pretty good, I think.'

'And tomorrow?' Lynda sat in her chair in front of the dressing-table, combed, powdered and beautiful, waiting for the telephone to ring to announce her date. 'Are you coming shopping with me?'

'Mm . . . perhaps. But I think it's likelier that I'll book my seat home. You're here for another fortnight, aren't you?'

'Yes, and so are you,' Lynda said, rather startled. 'There's another batch of filming to do, and . . .'

'I asked Angus and he said I could go home. You stay, Lynda, but I *have* to go home. Just seeing Radek made me realise how much I'm missing it – the glasshouses, the garden, the sea . . . oh, you don't know!'

'Angus told you to leave before you finish the work? Love, you aren't being fair to him – you're taking advantage. Just two more weeks . . .'

'Oh, all right,' Rochelle said, with a deep sigh. 'I did wonder . . . but let's get on with the work as soon as we can, so I can go home!'

Lynda agreed and later Rochelle went to her room and lay on her own bed, thinking.

She had never loved Radek, though she had liked him very much. Seeing him here, in this new setting, as a successful young businessman, she found she still liked him very much and, in different circumstances, might well have succumbed to his suggestion that at least they should spend time together, get to know each other all over again. But the crushing blow – that he was not Laurie – had left an aching void around her heart that nothing but her own home would fill. If I'm back on Jersey at least he'll know

552

where to find me, she told herself now, watching as the room gradually filled up with dusk and the coloured lights began to flash, reflecting on walls and ceiling.

Home, too, meant M. Laurient. He might never come back, but in a sense he would always be there, at Augeuil Manor. When she was in a glasshouse tending the orchids it was as if he was just around the corner, watering, spraying, potting up, separating. And in the house, too – a dim figure in the study, someone sorting books in the library. Always there, always comforting by his unseen but accepted presence.

Then there was Laurie. She loved him, needed him with an urgency which had surprised even herself when she had finally taken it out and looked at it. She had been a fool to send him away, and she had been punished for it, but unless he was dead he would come back, because she was sure, now, that he had understood her love, even understood that the foolishness was a part of it.

He would not look for her here, though, in New York. He would ring, or write, or come himself to Augeuil Manor, and it was there that she should be as soon as she possibly could.

Angus, of course, thought that when she said 'come home' she had meant London. Well, he was a dear and so was Gemma, and she loved them both, but they were not what she wanted and needed now. As soon as she was able, as soon as all the filming was over, she would go home.

The fortnight dragged, but it passed. On the last day, Rochelle and Lynda went out for a meal with Radek and they talked about old times and Radek promised to come to Jersey to see them all and Rochelle knew he meant it – and would probably never come. Life was too exciting here, too full, and his new world meant more to him now than her tiny island could ever do. Perhaps you've got to

553

be born and bred there to love it the way I do, with pain and joy, Rochelle thought as she kissed Radek goodbye.

'What'll you *do* there?' Gemma asked tearfully, when Rochelle had stopped off in London to say goodbye and Gemma had insisted on accompanying her to the airport.

'Do? Why, everything! I shall begin to buy in stud plants for my orchid centre; I shall start to get the house properly straight so that I can run a hotel there, if that's what my partner and I decide would be best. And . . . and I shall run on the long beaches, right down into the cold blue sea that isn't soft and warm, like the Med, or chlorinated and healthy, like an American pool, but makes you tingle all over and want to shout. And I'll search out my old friends, and tell them what I've been doing and show them my photographs. And Peter and I will talk about the estate and what crops do best where, and I'll get my old rubber boots out for when winter comes, and my disgusting old anorak . . . and I'll be happy.'

'But . . . you'll come back? To see us, from time to time? Or does your island have everything you need?'

Gemma looked so woebegone that suddenly Rochelle felt the older one of the two. She put her arm round her friend's shoulders and hugged her tight.

'Gemma, dear Gemma, of course I'll come back! And you must come to Jersey . . . why don't you and Angus come and live there? The climate's wonderful, the people are the friendliest in the whole world, and I don't believe you'd have any trouble finding craftsmen for Gempearls. You said you wanted bigger premises, that you didn't want to stay in London . . . why not try Jersey?'

'Angus did hint that he'd like to go over, take a look round,' Gemma said. She suddenly smiled through her tears, her small face rosy. She dabbed resolutely at her eyes, then blew her nose resoundingly. 'Could we do it? Would we be welcomed?'

'Oh, yes . . . you'd be bringing employment to the island,

554

and apart from farm produce and holidaymakers we don't
have a lot of industry or anything like that to keep young
people on Jersey when they grow up. Honestly, Gemma
. . . do make Angus think about it and then come over and
see us.'

'Well, I will.'

The anonymous voice from on high reminded passengers
for St Helier, Jersey, that they should be boarding from
Gate 2. Rochelle took her hand-luggage, which Gemma
had been carrying, kissed her friend's cheek, and ran. She
could not bear to miss this plane, even though there would
probably be another before evening . . . she could not bear
it!

'Peter, it's good to see you! How are things?'

Peter and Rochelle were sitting in an old Ford, Peter at
the wheel with the back and boot crammed with Rochelle's
luggage. Now, he turned and grinned at her, but he did not
look happy. She had noticed right across the terminal how
pale and worried he looked.

'Well, Chelle, not too good. Mme Barfleur wouldn't let
us get in touch and worry you, but she's pretty ill. Dr de
Chabbre thinks she's not got long.'

'Dying? Mme Barfleur? Oh, Peter, no!'

'She's at the manor, and Adrienne's with her,' Peter said
hastily. 'You know my wife, of course, though you haven't
met her for a few years . . . Josie Tarraut that was . . . she's
helped to nurse the old lady. She's begun to fret for you a
bit – Mme Barfleur, I mean – and she'll be very glad to see
you. I think she felt the responsibility.'

'Oh, dear. It hasn't made her worse, has it?'

'No, of course not. She's awfully old, Rochelle; I hadn't
realised, but the doctor says she's over eighty, and the war
was pretty hard on the old people. Perhaps losing Olivia
was worst of all . . . she talks about her a lot now, as though
she were still alive. Sometimes she goes back to when the

555

pair of you were kids and M. Laurient was still around. It's queer to hear her. Josie's cried a couple of times – she said it was so sad to think that those days were all gone.'

'Yes,' Rochelle said thoughtfully. 'Poor Mme Barfleur. She's always been a tower of strength to the Laurient family; I wonder how we'll get on without her?'

'The house is in a state,' Peter warned, swinging out of the main road and on to the familiar side one which led to the manor. 'And the garden's not too good. I told you some months ago that Tom couldn't manage so I employed a girl? Suzanne Beaumont. Well, I'm afraid she really isn't up to it, but with you home and helping you'll probably get it straight in no time. Suzanne's been worried that she might spoil things by changing them.'

'We'll be all right,' Rochelle said absently. She was peering ahead. The road was the same – had she really expected change, here? – and the gateposts had not altered, nor the drive as the car swung into it. But presently it stopped on the gravel sweep, and Rochelle saw the change she had dreaded. Weeds everywhere, paint peeling, the door swinging open, a hinge broken . . . how could she have left it for so long, almost forgetting it in the pleasure of her lovely new life? But now she was back things would begin to return to normal, and she no longer minded robbing the sea-cave and taking the money M. Laurient had left so that the estate might be made good again after the war.

Josie stood in the doorway, smiling. A pretty, dark girl with olive skin and a slender figure, she gave Rochelle a quick kiss on the cheek, a friendly classmate's greeting.

'Rochelle, it's lovely to see you,' she said eagerly. 'Do come up to madame, now . . . she's very poorly.'

'Right away,' Rochelle said. 'Is she in her old room?'

'Yes. Her daughter's with her; they're talking about you, and about old times. I'll help Peter to get your stuff out of the car, and there's a hot meal ready in the kitchen when you've seen the old lady.'

Rochelle made for the stairs, calling her thanks over her shoulder. The banister was dusty, the landing showing signs of hasty and incomplete cleaning. The door to Mme Barfleur's room stood open, however, so she went straight in.

'Madame?'

Mme Barfleur was lying propped up in the big bed. She was so changed that for a moment Rochelle could only stare, and fight back tears. She had been such a large woman, such a presence, but now she was small, almost tiny, like a little thread against the mounded white pillows. Even her face was smaller, the full flesh fallen away.

But the eyes were the same: shrewd, very dark eyes, bright and full of purpose once, faded now yet still beautiful, still shrewd, and somehow a sign that Mme Barfleur had changed externally only.

'Ah, Rochelle!'

The old woman smiled, and Rochelle forgot the wasting, the changes, and saw her good friend as she was and had always been. She fell to her knees by the bed, clutching the clawlike hand, stroking the thin cheek.

'Oh, madame, how bad of you not to let me know you were ill! I would have come before . . . long before. How are you today?'

'All the better for seeing you,' Mme Barfleur said, her voice as tiny and thin as the rest of her. 'Now where's that bad girl of mine gone, that Olivia? Always after the men, always will be . . . but she's your pal, eh, Chelle?'

'Oh yes, always my pal,' Rochelle murmured. 'Do you want to see her for something particular, madame?'

'No, no. Let her have her tea. I dare say the pair of you have been in the sea all afternoon, sand in your clothes, salt-stains on the only decent shoes you've got left to you . . . but that's youth for you. Not a thought for us old 'uns,

557

trying to keep all tidy, but off to please yourselves all the day long – and why not, eh? Why not?'

'Why not indeed?' Adrienne said. She came in, a tray in her hands. 'I've brought you some hot tea, Maman, and a little cake. Can you eat it now?'

The old head turned restlessly on the pillow, the thin hair, which Rochelle had never seen out of place, loose and tangled.

'Just the tea,' she murmured. 'Just the tea, my dear. And then I'll have a little sleep. Send Olivia up to me when she's eaten.'

'She'll have forgotten by the time she's drunk her tea,' Adrienne said consolingly, accompanying Rochelle to the head of the stairs. 'She's worn out and running down, Chelle, but comfortably, in her own bed amongst people who love her. There are worse ways to go.'

Rochelle nodded and went down to the kitchen, where she rallied Peter and his wife with promises of extra help and more money. She had a good meal, enjoyed much promising gossip, and went to bed feeling that she would get the place right in a few months with the help of her friends and the money in the sea-cave.

But she cried in her sleep and woke to find her cheeks still wet with tears, and when she slipped out of bed and went along the landing to where Mme Barfleur lay she met Adrienne in an old brown dressing-gown and her hair tied up in curlers.

'What's the matter?' Rochelle whispered. 'Is she . . .?'

'She's all but gone; I've just rung for Dr de Chabbre and he'll come as soon as he can, but I think he'll be too late.'

'I'll sit with her – or would you rather I went down and waited for the doctor?'

'I'm not going to wait. I told him I'd leave the front door ajar and he could come straight up,' Adrienne said. 'You go through; I shan't be a minute.'

Rochelle went into the quiet room where the old woman

558

lay dying. The bedside lamp cast a pink shade on to Mme Barfleur's face, making her look rosy and healthy, but her breathing was slow, with long pauses between each breath when Rochelle thought she had breathed her last.

She sat down in the chair which Adrienne had obviously just vacated. As she looked, Mme Barfleur's eyes opened, wandered vaguely around the room and then fastened on Rochelle's face.

'Chelle? You here, then?'

'Yes, I'm here, madame. Is there anything I can get you?'

Mme Barfleur ignored this as clearly irrelevant. 'Are you well?'

'Yes, thank you, madame, I'm in good health.'

'That's right, that's right. A good little thing you were, a nice-spoken little thing. M. Laurient was so fond of you . . . oh, he doted on you! Thought a good deal more of you than those young parents of yours . . . oh, I cried when they were killed, but I'm thinking it was best for you, and best for M. Laurient, too.'

'I'm sure it was,' Rochelle said, through shaking lips. 'I'm glad to know these things, madame.'

'You changed him from a sour old bugger back to his old self,' Mme Barfleur muttered. Thin fingers plucked at the sheets. 'What's that? I can't feel it properly.'

'It's the sheet,' Rochelle said gently. 'Adrienne will be back soon; she'll make you comfortable.'

'Yes, a sour old bugger,' Mme Barfleur said faintly. Then she put her thin and wrinkled cheek against her hand and closed her eyes.

'She stopped breathing about two minutes ago, and I think she's gone,' Rochelle said to Adrienne as the older woman came back into the room. 'I'm sorry I didn't call you, but there really wasn't time.'

'She went gentle,' Adrienne said, kissing her mother's

already cooling-brow and folding the quiet and unresisting hands on the flat breast. 'Did she say anything?'

'Ye-es. She said M. Laurient used to be a sour old bugger,' Rochelle said.

'She didn't!' Adrienne said. A smile tugged at her lips. 'Oh, she was ever so fond of him . . . ever so fond.'

'I know; and she said it ever so nicely,' Rochelle said. They both began to laugh, and neither could have said when the laughter turned to tears.

It was different at Augeüil Manor without Mme Barfleur. Oddly enough, Rochelle seemed to miss not only the old woman, but Olivia too. It was as though, with her grandmother's passing, the old Olivia came back to haunt the house and grounds as she had once done.

There are more ghosts here than people, Rochelle said to herself, after a week of intensive work during the course of which she had been aware of Mme Barfleur waddling about her kitchen, M. Laurient browsing in the greenhouse and Olivia tap-tappeting across the garden with her baby in her arms. She consciously tried never to find Laurie in the gardens or the greenhouse, but he was there too, of course. Potting the tiny plantlets out in their first pots, separating the clumps of orchids which needed more space, shouting to two phantom labradors who came clumsily across the orchard towards her, tails wagging, bright eyes eager.

'I'd like to run away,' Rochelle told Adrienne one evening as the two of them sat in the kitchen and mended linen. 'There are too many memories, too many ghosts.'

'Ghosts have a habit of following you,' Adrienne said, biting off her cotton and rethreading her needle. 'Why d'you think I've never remarried?'

'I don't know. But I'm going to put another advertisement in the paper, for a housekeeper and a couple of girls to help in the house and gardens. And I'll get more orchids from the States. I don't know what happened to Laurie, but neither he nor his orchids seem to have put in an appearance and I can't wait for ever.'

That evening, she rang Angus and arranged for him and Gemma to stay in an hotel in town whilst they had a look round the island.

'I'm so lonely, I think I'll go crazy if you don't come,' she said, her first admission that she couldn't cope perfectly well by herself. 'Tell Gemma I'm going to buy a puppy when she comes. She can help me choose it.'

And then, that night, she dreamed.

She went upstairs late, tired out, and climbed into her bed by moonlight, not bothering with curtains or a good wash. For a while she lay in that odd state between sleeping and waking, watching the moonlight spill over the window-sill and splash across the opposite wall. If she half-closed her eyes she could make pictures of the light and shadow . . . she could see all sorts of things in it, beautiful things, ugly things, happy or frightening things . . .

And then she was dreaming.

The manor was perfect, as it had been when she had first come to live here, every piece of furniture in its place, polished and dusted, the floors gleaming, the flowers in the vases standing straight and tall.

But it was night, and moonlight flooded in through the open front door.

She went to the kitchen first. The fire glowed red in the grate, banked down for the night. A dog slept before it, paws twitching as it ran forbidden races, chased long-dead rabbits. Another dog raised a sleepy head and showed its teeth in a grin before collapsing back into boneless slumber once more.

Rochelle walked across the kitchen, searching for some-one, but apart from the dogs the place was deserted. She went into the hall, touched the tallest vase of flowers, felt the blooms cool against her fingers. She opened the living-room door and there was a jigsaw set out on a low table and the french windows were open. The jigsaw was an old favourite and it was almost complete – only a couple of pieces were lacking – so Rochelle leaned over to pick the bits up and finish it off.

It took her a moment or two, but she found the right pieces, put them in and completed the picture, then turned away. She was still searching for someone.

Halfway across the room she glanced back and the jigsaw was incomplete once more, the bits she had put in back beside it, so that it waited again for fingers more skilled than hers to finish it off.

She did not worry, though, for in her dream she knew that the puzzle would not be done until she found whoever – or whatever – she was looking for.

The library next. Books filled the shelves, and without running her finger along the wood she knew it was dust-free, beautifully clean and polished. Emilie would have done it only the previous day, or perhaps Mme Barfleur herself had run a duster round. No one here either, though. The room was warm, the fire only recently out, and it had that air of comfortable homeliness which means that it has only just been vacated.

The study then. Rochelle swung the door open . . . and her joy was so overpowering that she cried out.

'You're back . . . oh, you've come back!'

It was he, sitting behind the desk, his dark head bent over the books, his pen running neatly along a line, ruler held steady with the other hand.

He looked up – she got a quick, confused impression of dark eyes, a mouth that was beginning to smile . . . and then she saw his hands.

'Oh, my God . . . what have they done to you?'

She started forward, pity, love, indignation all surging in her like the spring tides running.

And woke.

She was alone in her moonlit bedroom and the dream was already fading so fast that in seconds all she could remember was the tilt of that dark head, the glow of those dark eyes.

And the mutilated hands.

25

Trembling, sick with excitement and a sort of dread, Rochelle got out of bed. She glanced at the little clock by her bedside and saw that she had barely been asleep more than ten minutes. Something was calling her, telling her that she must get up, she was needed. Something left undone? Something still to do? She had no idea; she simply knew that she must go downstairs.

She did not bother to dress. She was wearing a white cotton nightie which she had bought in New York; it was as beautiful as any ball-gown and floated ethereally around her as she moved. It was a warm night, and anyway she did not know whether she could lay hands on her dressing-gown in the big built-in cupboard. Better just go downstairs and see what had disturbed her. She was not alone in the house; Adrienne slept just along the hallway, but she did not even consider waking her. Whatever it was that called her, it was her business and hers alone. Adrienne worked hard and must be allowed to sleep until morning.

Down the stairs Rochelle went, quieter than a whisper. She gained the hall and for some reason saw a mental picture of two old labradors, both sleeping soundly. If they had been here in truth, Pod and Senna, no one would have been allowed to descend those stairs without their immediate and probably noisy presence. This was no house to be without a dog in – she really would buy a puppy or two when Gemma and Angus arrived.

She turned at the foot of the stairs – and froze. The front door was open. Not much, just a crack, but enough to make her realise what must have woken her.

Burglars! She must have heard the door opening. The

burglar wouldn't have liked to close it and risk the snick of the latch, and anyway the old door always stuck. Now he was somewhere in the house, rifling the place, and she would have to find him. She would never get up the stairs without disturbing him; there was a creak in every tread, just about. Heaven knew how she had got down without making enough noise to wake the dead, let alone a man alive to the slightest sound! She wondered whether she could get to the telephone . . . but it would make a noise when she picked it up and though the staff on the exchange were very good it would be a moment or two, at this time of night, before they spoke to her. And if it was old Mrs Mouley, who was a bit deaf, Rochelle would have to shout . . . no, she must tackle this person alone.

She went towards the study first, because she saw that the door was very slightly ajar, which meant that she could peep inside without actually turning the handle. She pushed, ever so gently, and the door whispered wide.

There was a man in there! Sitting behind the desk, where M. Laurient had sat so many, many times, his dark head bent, his hands spread out on the blotter in front of him. He did not look up as she softly entered; his eyes were fixed on something before him.

She knew him, knew that dark head, the angle of his cheek, even the way he sat. She said, very softly, 'You've come back . . .' and his head jerked up and she saw his face.

She was so frightened that she felt all the blood rush from her cheeks, leaving her cold and faint. Her hand flew to her throat . . . and she knew, at that moment, that her belief in M. Laurient's survival had long fled, and that she feared a ghost.

Then she saw his hands, and he smiled sleepily . . . and it was Laurie!

* * *

565

'How in God's name did you get here? Oh, Laurie, Laurie, Laurie!'

They were cuddled in each other's arms, Rochelle still shaking with reaction, pushing close to his all-too-human warmth, wanting the security of his hands on her, his body near hers.

'I came on the boat . . . missed the one I meant to catch and got a later one . . . arrived after dark and walked up . . . the front door wasn't locked so I slipped in . . . couldn't risk waking you, so sat down in the study and must have snoozed off . . .'

He spoke in snatches, between kisses. She was curled up on his lap, the pair of them squeezed on to the big sofa in the drawing-room with the moonlight painting big white squares on the carpet and dust thick on the mantelpiece.

'And where've you come from?'

'South America, then New York . . . saw your pictures, tried to find you . . . got chucked out of your hotel . . . went and telephoned the bailiff, who said you were back . . . got on a plane . . . then 'nother . . . then the boat . . . bingo.'

'Gosh . . . oh, Laurie, it's like a dream to have you here . . . the best, dearest dream in the world.'

'It's no dream,' Laurie said. He demonstrated the truth of this statement, and Rochelle enjoyed every minute of it. 'Hey, is this thing a nightdress?'

'Mm hmm, and you'll tear it.'

'Sure I will. Honey, have I ever mentioned I love you?'

'Ye-es, I think so. I love you too, Laurie.'

'Prove it.'

There was a long, dreamy silence whilst they both proved it. The moonlight illumined his dark, spare figure, tanned to a rich brown by day. It played on Rochelle's waist-length black hair and on her white and muffling nightgown. And presently the white and muffling nightgown went sailing through the square patches of moonlight and the long bars of shadow and lay innocent and empty on the dusty parquet flooring.

And Rochelle and Laurie learned to love one another.

'I dreamed a very odd dream,' Rochelle said to Laurie next morning, when they had eaten their breakfast, explained themselves, more or less, to Adrienne, and gone off into the garden to enjoy the sunshine. They lay on the lawn and basked, and every time they caught each other's eye they smiled with a smugness which would have done credit to a cat in a creamery.

'No doubt. Before or after?'

'Oh, before. It was why I came downstairs. I had the oddest feeling that someone was calling me . . . it was you, I suppose.'

'Sure. You mean you dreamed someone was calling you?'

Rochelle frowned. In the bright light of day, with the sun shining and millions of daisies turning the lawn white, the dream seemed a long way off. All that was still clear was a pair of hands, the wrists purpled with scars, the fingers turned inwards.

'Well, I can't remember much. But what frightened me . . .' His arm tightened round her, the fingers caressing her cheek. Rochelle pushed her head into the hollow of his neck and purred like a kitten.

'Yeah? What frightened you . . .? Go on.'

'There was a man . . . oh, I don't know, it's all very confused, but I thought . . . but it was you, I suppose. Except that the wrists were scarred and the hands were held oddly. Oh, Laurie, it scared me . . . I woke up very quickly and my heart was beating so hard it felt as if it would hop out of my chest.'

'The wrists were scarred,' Laurie repeated thoughtfully. Long ago, a very long time ago, during the war, he had come across a man somewhere, sometime, who had scarring like

567

that. 'I wonder . . . d'you reckon people can get inside other people's dreams, Chelle?'

'I don't know. I shouldn't think so, though I don't know why not. What makes you ask?'

'I met a guy with scars like that, a long time ago. He gave me an apple.'

'Really? That's odd. Was he anyone you knew?'

'Nope. Just a guy. When can we get married?'

'Why? Does it make a difference?'

'It sure will to our kids. Suppose we get ourselves into St Helier right now and make some arrangements?'

She loved him! Endlessly, helplessly, for always. She knew it now, had known it for ages, but last night had confirmed it once and for all. Laurie was her man and she was his woman. They were meant for each other and would be an unbeatable team. Apart, she decided, they wouldn't amount to much. He had come to her last night with no pretty presents, no poetry or romance. No orchids, either, though they would be arriving by ship in a week or two. But there was no room for doubt; she was choc-a-bloc with love, certain of her own feelings and his.

They had not slept much last night, save for a brief hour, decorously, she in her own bed and he in the spare room, before they came down for breakfast. Now they were dozing off in the sunshine, too full of love and happiness to stay awake.

Rochelle made one last effort.

'Laurie . . . there was a jigsaw in my dream; it wouldn't let me finish it.'

'That's real hard luck, honey.'

He was mumbling, half asleep already, but she could not let him rest. There was something else she must ask him, if only she could think of it.

'I didn't mind . . . but what does a jigsaw mean, when it won't let you fit the last few pieces in?'

568

'Guess it's Freudian somehow. Let's lie here a bit longer, then go into town later. How's that sound?'

But she was already asleep, close to his chest, warm in his arms.

Laurie lay for a little on the delicious borderline between sleeping and waking. Scarred wrists, bent fingers . . . and an apple. A note wrapped round an apple slipped into his hand . . . gee, he'd not remembered that in years . . . and because of the note they'd found the film showing the guys in rags, thin as skeletons, fishing potatoes out of filth. And then, just for a moment, Laurie understood it all; he put one piece with another and the entire jigsaw was plain before him, the whole picture. He *had* met his father. It was Charles Laurient who had slipped the apple and the note into Laurie's hand, because he had been desperate to get the information back to Jersey. He must have known then that he wouldn't be returning himself, and that if he didn't send word the only bit of hard and fast evidence of that shocking affair would be lost.

And then, without warning, Laurie fell into deep and satisfying sleep like a man diving into a warm pool.

When he woke he had forgotten everything, except that he and Rochelle were going into St Helier to arrange their wedding.

Epilogue
1955

They had been together all day, touring the beautiful countryside, and now they were exploring the little market town.

Maman had baby Charlotte in her arms, though he knew that baby Charlotte was very heavy and Maman ought really to let her walk. He was walking, but then he was a big boy; past five years old and a great help to both his parents as well as the best big brother that baby Charlotte could possibly want – Maman and Papa told him this often, so it must be true.

They had come to this particular part of France – the Moselle valley – because of the wine. Their beautiful home was not an hotel, much to young Edward's pleasure and relief, but the Orchid Centre, which was just at the bottom of their garden and separated from them by a thick belt of cordon apple trees, was opening a restaurant and Papa thought they ought to know a bit about the wine they were going to serve. Hence a whole beautiful two-week holiday, with Maman free to play with them and swim in the sea and the river, instead of having to spend ages and ages every day tending the orchids in the glasshouses and being nice to the visitors.

She was the best person in the world, his maman! But his papa ran her a pretty close second, for all he didn't speak *patois* very well and used some funny words now and then. Papa had put his arms round them all, this very morning, and said, 'We're the four luckiest, happiest people in the world', and Maman had said that it was true, but it didn't mean Papa could relax and think he was going to laze on the beach, because she wanted to visit a famous rose nursery near here.

They had all complained – well, not baby Charlotte, but the men, he and Papa – but Maman had been adamant. It was only when someone told her that the town had a market today and many marvellous roses would be on show that she had said all right, they would pass the nursery up and go to the market instead.

And Edward had had a *great* time! He had played on a swing for ages, and visited a little fair and thrown pingpong balls into empty goldfish bowls and won himself a goldfish. He had whirled on the roundabout, which Papa called a carousel, and eaten toffee apples and candyfloss and a big bag of coloured puffed-wheat which Papa called popcorn. And now he had got away from the grown-ups and the baby – though he could see them all right; he didn't want to lose them – and was exploring by himself.

One stall particularly fascinated him. It was a rose stall, selling hundreds and hundreds of really beautiful roses of every colour you could imagine. The scent was super; you could smell it three stalls away and the third stall sold onions, which just went to show.

But it was the man behind the stall who caught Edward's attention. He was so *nice* looking. He had a very brown face and very black eyes, and the brown face was all seamed and a bit baggy, but it was seamed, you could tell, with laughing and joking, not with crossness. He had white hair, too, very thick, with the tiniest bit of a curl to the ends. He was a nice man, Edward was sure of it. He smiled at Edward twice, and the third time he called Edward over to him and gave him a rose, for the 'woman in your life', as he put it.

'There's baby Charlotte . . . is she a woman?' Edward said in French, because naturally one spoke French whilst in France, and the man smiled at him again and gave him a second rose, a little white bud of a rose with petals just

571

touched with pink. 'A baby, eh, mon brave?' he said, and then he leaned forward and whispered in Edward's ear, in English this time. Then he stood back and patted Edward's shoulder, and smiled again, but seriously now, and there was sadness in the back of his dark eyes. 'Tell your mother that when you get home,' he said. 'You won't forget? Good man!'

Edward went back to Maman and Papa, who were hugging and being very silly, as they sometimes were, and Papa picked him up and hugged him too and said, 'Gee, these stupid women . . . what we guys have to put up with, eh, Ted?' and carried him all the way back to the car, whilst Maman lugged baby Charlotte who was beginning to whine a bit and make hungry baby noises.

They motored back to the coast then, and there was a nice high tea and then bed, and the following day they went home properly, to Augeuil Manor, on Jersey.

That night, as Maman was putting him to bed, Edward saw the rose in her blouse, looking very sweet but a little faded now, and touched its petals and reminded her who had given it to her, so that she kissed him again.

'It was me, but the man on the stall let me have it free,' Edward said, not for the first time. 'He told me a secret, too . . . he said I was to tell my maman when we got home, which is now, isn't it?'

Maman smiled with her beautiful, curly mouth and with her big blue eyes as well and said yes, just before bed was about as home as you could get.

'What did he tell you?' she teased, tucking him in.

'Well, I told him about baby Charlotte and he gave me another rose, for her. And then he whispered a whisper in my ear. He said, *Ask your maman who used the wand*. So now I've asked you, Maman.'

She stood by his bed, staring down at him. Her beautiful face went very white indeed, and her eyes were blue and still. And then he saw colour creep up her face as the sea creeps over the sand when the tide comes in, and he thought it's all right, I didn't say anything I shouldn't.

'Maman? Is it a good secret?'

She sat down on his bed with a thump, missing his toes by inches, and grabbed his hands, holding them tight.

'Sweetheart, dearest Ned, what did the man look like?'

There was such urgent entreaty in her voice that he grew frightened, sure that this mattered, was important. He tried very hard to think, but only white hair and dark eyes rewarded him ... and there was no way, was there, of saying that he looked nice?

'White hair,' he muttered. 'White hair and brown eyes.'

'And did he say anything else? Did he speak in French, or English? Did he look happy, my little love?'

'He was kind,' Edward whispered. 'That's all I 'member. He was kind.'

'Yes. He always was kind,' Maman agreed, and tears were running down her face, but she was smiling gently, as though she was thinking something beautiful. 'Especially to children.'

Just as she reached the door, calling over her shoulder that she must just have a word with Papa and then she would come back and tuck him in and mind he was asleep by then, he remembered something else.

'He had poorly hands,' he whispered, remembering the cruel, withered, purple scars. 'He *did* have poorly hands.'

But he did not think she heard.